THE GODLY SERIES
The Girl with the Sword

DISVON RAYFORD

Copyright © 2024 by Disvon Rayford

Paperback: 978-1-964744-95-7
eBook: 978-1-964744-96-4
Library of Congress Control Number: 2024917679

All rights reserved. No part of this publication may be reproduced, distributed, or transmitted in any form or by any electronic or mechanical means, without the prior written permission of the publisher, except in the case of brief quotations embodied in critical reviews and certain other noncommercial uses permitted by copyright law.

This Book is a work of fiction. Names, characters, places, and incidents either are the product of the author's imagination or are used fictitiously. Any resemblance to actual persons, living or dead, events, or locales is entirely coincidental.

Ordering Information:

Prime Seven Media
518 Landmann St.
Tomah City, WI 54660

Printed in the United States of America

BOOK SERIES READING ORDER:

GODLY BEGINNING: SEBASTIAN'S STORY
TRINITY
GIRL WITH THE SWORD
QUEST FOR VENGEANCE

Table of Contents

Chapter 1: What's The Deal With Emillie? 1

Chapter 2: Premeditated Murder 22

Chapter 3: The Sad Story Of Awalli Dat 48

Chapter 4: The Strange Possession Of Sandin Tillo 84

Chapter 5: You're A Goddess, Emillie 113

Chapter 6: The Should-Be Queen 142

Chapter 7: The Truth About Slayn Tillo 165

Chapter 8: Mean Grandma 186

Chapter 9: Besties 208

Chapter 10: Time To Wake Up 237

Chapter 11: The Girl With The Sword 259

Chapter 12: Enter Lona: Emillie's New Lesson 286

Chapter 13: Who Is Septima? 304

Chapter 14: War In The Streets 324

Chapter 15: Amana's Biggest Secret: The Return 338

Chapter 16: Enter Layna Lon 362

Chapter 17: Growing Up With A Goddess 392

Chapter 18: Emillie Meets Brixin 441

CHAPTER 1

What's The Deal With Emillie?

*L*ODY: I have seen a great many things in my years as a guard force officer. I've seen murders, kidnappings that end in murder, torture that usually turns into a murder, and gang murders. All this time, the one thing I've never seen is a child get murdered. I like to think nobody would harm a child. They haven't had the time to do anything to anybody that would cause them to be on some kind of hit list. Plinth is the planet I live on, and North Edge is my current city. I resided in South Edge, but unfortunately, after what I can only describe as getting on the wrong side of the wrong gangster, I was relocated to North Edge, where I've joined their seventh precinct. There are nine in total. The first, second, third, fourth, and fifth precincts are all within close proximity of each other and often get into turf battles, while the other four are separated throughout the downtown area. While a lot of my colleagues have boasted about really big arrests, the truth is not much happens in North Edge. It's extremely quiet most days and you don't have a whole lot that is happening. When I first moved here, all the quiet drove me insane. And having close to no cases to work was the absolute worst. I had gone from busting drug dealers and catching killers, to passing out citations for not having dogs on the leash, or even leaving flars(Floating.

Location. Acceleration. Rovers) parked in the wrong place. I was so tired of dealing with these stupid kinds of things and I missed the thrill of the chase that you get with the dangerous elements I usually chased after. I needed more danger. I know that it seems like suicide, but in truth, that was the reason I became a guard. The guard force is separated into three groups. There are the grunts, which are just the normal foot guys. Then there are the workers, which is what I am. I'm an investigator, and I look into crimes that need solving. Back in South Edge, it was easy to know the bad guy from the good guy. This made my cases easy. But the last group are the captains, who are in charge of the grunts and us workers. All they do is provide obstacles to make it tougher for us to solve crimes. In South Edge, it was no secret that the guard force was dirty. Most of the politicians pay to get away with whatever they want and even worse, is that some of those politicians are actually in charge of the whole damn guard force in Edge. Now while North Edge doesn't see much crime, it doesn't mean that it is without it. Every once in a while, I'll get some file on my computer of a dead vic that just arrived. The hard part about this part of town is that people conceal their crimes really well. Often, I say to myself, what kind of Sebastian-created-asshole could do some of the shit I see? We had found a woman in a dumpster. She had been mutilated beyond recognition. In my computer file, I had her identity. Looking at her picture, and looking at what was left of her, you wouldn't think that was the same person. The woman was quite beautiful. Young too, only eighteen. The autopsy reported she had been abused sexually, and then tortured. Then the sick son-of-a-smich actually cut off all of her parts, one by one. I had seen a lot of sick shit in my time, but this was disgusting. "Hey, Red, you got someone here to see, ya.", said Tillo, another worker like myself. Often, Tillo and I would work together, so I guess you could call him my partner. Tillo was annoying sometimes but he was definitely someone that you wanted to have your back. "Alright, who is it?", I asked, not looking at him, but still reading the report on the young girl. "I don't know who she is, but she is a pretty one.", Tillo said, winking at me as I finally looked in his direction. "Okay, I'll go talk to her.". I stood up, and Tillo wore a soft grin. I didn't say this before, but I was a ladies' man. I often would end up sleeping with suspects, or women that were just too close to the case I was working. I made my way down the stairs, passing a young man delivering a pasta pie. I grabbed a slice and the boy looked at me, "What? I'm sure that whoever paid for this would have given me a slice anyway. Tell them Red took a slice.". Red is my last name. It wasn't really funny being named after a color, but I got by and dealt with the jokes. When I saw the woman, she was indeed beautiful. In fact, she was so gorgeous I almost choked on my pie. She had black hair and her eyes were magenta. She was wearing a blue business suit. Others were walking by and turning their heads. She pretended not to notice and was looking at something on her cell. When she noticed me watching, she quickly approached me, "GO Lody Red? I'm glad to finally meet you. I'm Senator Raby. Can we talk somewhere private?", she said, putting her cell away and shaking my hand. I nodded and led her to an interrogation room. When she sat down, she took her cell back out and checked it again, then put it away. "So, what is it you want, Ms. Raby?", I asked, also sitting down and finishing my pie. "Mrs. Raby actually, and, well, there is no easy way to brief you on this, so I'm just going to do it. I understand that you were the one working the Mccloud case ten years ago, correct?". I remembered that quite well. Bill Mccloud was a huge business tycoon who was shot right in the heart. His wife, prior to that, was taken in by some government officials. Nobody knows the real story there. But the sad part of this is that ten years ago, their only child, Adem, was left with no parents at the age of ten and shortly disappeared after his father's murder. I tried locating the smich who did it, but he was a hired cannon and, well, they are quite good at not being found by the GF. It was this case that drove me to my spirit consumption. I couldn't focus on the other cases that I had mostly due to the fact that just the thought of poor Adem, losing so much, and now being out there alone and scared, made me feel like the worst kind of failure. But that was ten years ago, and if Adem is dead, then I'm going home to drink. I nodded to answer Raby's question. "Well, I felt that since you were the GO in charge, you should be the first to know that Adem has suddenly reappeared.". When she said this, I was stunned. It must have shown on my face because she smiled some, "You were quite worried for him, weren't you?", she asked. "Well, he just disappeared. What do you think? So, is that all? You just wanted to let me know that Adem has returned? Good. Anything else?", I asked, wanting to get back to my computer now. I didn't like thinking about the Mccloud case and was upset that this lady showed up dragging it along with her. But Mrs. Raby didn't stand up. She continued to sit in the chair and watch me for a minute. I thought she was checking me out, until the door opened, and another woman stepped in. This woman was off the scale beautiful, even though she had a scar on the right side of her face that looked ancient. "Oh, you're here? I was beginning to think you had forgotten.", Raby said to the woman, who just ignored her. "Lody Red. Interesting finally meeting you.", she said, as she, too, pulled up a chair and sat next to Raby. "What the hell is this? Can I go now or what?", I asked, becoming more frustrated by the second. "No. You can't go. There are some things I need to tell you. Things that are going to start happening soon here in North Edge. It's the reason I had you moved here.", the strange woman said. "NOW HOLD ON A MINUTE! I wasn't placed here by YOU! I don't even know who you are!", I yelled, standing up now. Raby looked somewhat unnerved, while the other woman looked bored, "Are you done? Because we have a lot to discuss, and I am a very busy person, so please, sit down, Mr. Red.", she finished saying, taking something out and placing it on the table. There suddenly was a faint hissing noise and I knew she had done something. I had heard of gadgets like this only in films. I sat back down, interested now in what this lady had to say. "So, as I'm sure Gail has informed you of Adem Mccloud's return, you must see the immediate issue.", the strange lady said, crossing her hands and placing them on the table. "Well, I'm just glad he is alive after what happened.", I said, not really taking my eyes off of the woman. She had flaming red hair and was wearing what appeared to be some kind of leather military garb. As I tried to think or even guess what exactly she was doing here, she grew tired of waiting for my questions on Adem, "So, anyway…there is a woman who lives in this city, and she is…different.". I didn't understand what that meant. "May I ask you for your name?", I said, feeling I should know. "No. You may not. Now listen, you need to be on the lookout for anything out of the ordinary. I mean, if you see someone doing something un-Plinthinian like, don't hesitate to call this number.", she said, handing me a card with just a bird symbol and a number. She then took the device off the table and began pocketing it. "That's it?", Raby asked, looking surprised. "Well, what did you expect?", the red-headed lady replied, standing up, and already walking towards the door. "Now wait a minute! What exactly am I looking for? I don't understand!", I yelled, standing up myself. "Sir, if you see something that doesn't seem normal, call that number on that card. I really don't see what you are confused about.", "Well, for starters, what un-Plinthinian things am I looking for?", I said. The woman looked at me like she was looking through me, then said, "If you see someone use strength that isn't normal, or perhaps you see somebody flying, or maybe somebody summons an object from out of thin air, those are all reasons to call.", she said mockingly, already turning the knob. Mrs. Raby was now standing up as well. "Now wait!", I said, but the woman now turned angry. "I DO NOT HAVE TIME FOR THIS! I HAVE TO LEAVE!", she yelled, then left. I looked at the woman named Gail, who was standing near, looking as confused as me. "I'm quite sorry about that, Mr. Red. She isn't having a good week.", "Who the hell was that woman?", I asked. "I'm sorry, Mr. Red, but I'm not allowed to give out that information. It's classified at the highest level.", she said, looking sincere, "Do try and keep an eye out though for what she has mentioned. It's very important that we get this figured out.". Gail now turned to leave and took a step out, then turned to me and whispered, "She is in charge of the secret military unit known as P.E.D. She is older than she looks, and I'm not sure she can be trusted.". With that, she left. I returned to my desk and began to pick up where I left off on that file. The girl that had been mutilated was still visible on my screen. Carla Nos. That was her name. Poor girl, I thought. She was important in the royal city. "So, what happened with that skeeter?", asked Tillo, as he, too, returned to his desk. A skeeter is what we Plinthinian men call beautiful women. "Nothing. Just a small warning.", I said, hoping he'd drop it. But of course, knowing Tillo, he didn't. "What small warning? About what?", he said, now coming to stand over me. "It's classified, alright? So drop it and leave me the hell alone.", I said gruffly. "RED!", came a loud shout from the other side of the office. Then I looked up, and a silver-hair colored male was approaching me, holding the pasta pie box I had taken a slice from, "I AM NOT OKAY WITH YOU TAKING A SLICE OF MY PIE WITHOUT PERMISSION!", "Sorry, Yellfy, I didn't think you'd mind at all.", "You do this all the time! I'm getting tired of your attitude. If you steal from me again, I'll be reporting you to Captain Walsh!", Yellfy finished, and then turned, and went back to his desk. "Pissy prick, eh?", Tillo said, laughing a bit. I smiled and then got back on with my file.

Later that night, as I was leaving, I was approached once again by the beautiful woman who refused to give her name. "Hello again,

Mr. Red. I just thought I'd remind you of the importance of being on the lookout for those things I mentioned.". This woman was annoying me. "I already said okay. What more do you want to hear?", I asked her, annoyed by her smug attitude, and the fact she would approach me again so soon. "I don't think you quite understand, Mr. Red, so I'll need you to follow me.". She led me to a room that I didn't really notice before. I'd seen the door but never thought about what was on the other side. Once inside the room, I realized it was just another interrogation room, but with a t.v. "So, what is this all about, then?", I asked. "Have a seat, Mr. Red.", the lady said, taking out a small device and attaching it to the t.v. "Pay close attention to the monitor.", she said, turning the t.v on, and then folding her arms. On the screen was a man I recognized as one of the Royal Family members. He was just standing in one place. As I began to think, what am I waiting for, the most unexplainable thing occurred. A woman materialized out of nowhere and was talking to the man. For a minute they spoke, and me and the red-headed lady were just watching quietly. Soon, the woman on the screen lifted her hand and I watched, as a light started to glow from her hand, and then she punched the man, and her fist went straight through his chest. The man fell to the floor in a heap, and the woman looked at the camera, and then vanished just as she had appeared. "What the hell was that?", I asked, in a confused tone. "You just watched the murder of Reginald Tib. One of the members of the Royal Family of Plinth. I'm quite sure that you have now gained a better understanding of what you are looking for, correct, Mr. Red?", the lady said, in a bored tone. I on the other hand was shocked by what I had just witnessed and still didn't understand. "So, what was that woman?", I asked. "She, too, is a member of the RF, but unfortunately has been removed from the immediate family members. She has recently learned of her relations and has discovered a great secret about herself. Now this secret she has discovered has led her to an artifact that is very dangerous, and with it, she poses a great threat, not just to her family, but to others as well. The Carla Nos girl. She was the one who did that to her. She took Carla as a sign. A warning really. So, as you can see, there are some frightening things coming to North Edge, and I need you to be vigilant.", "But Carla Nos was raped and mutilated!", I shouted. "Yes, and our lady friend has built herself quite the army. You see, Ms. Nos was the stepdaughter to Tek Tib, Reginald's brother. She was taken, and raped, and tortured, and then she was cut into pieces. So, as you can see, this woman is very dangerous.". I was indeed getting a clearer picture, but I still didn't understand how this woman was this strong. "What is this secret that she has learned?", I asked, hoping the woman would answer. "Are you that daft, Mr. Red? I thought you were smart. The Royal Family are descendants of the noble House of Tig and Tisiphone. The King and Queen of ancient Nasher. Their family goes back generations. But the secret you speak of isn't just about Tig and Tisiphone, but rather the wife of their son Nigel. Mileeda. She was different. She contained blood tainted with a certain bloodline. This allows her descendants to use these ancient artifacts we call godly items. So, in other words, Mr. Red, the myths are real.", she finished saying, now once again starting to gather her things and be on her way. "Now wait! You're telling me all the fairy tale bullshit is real? The whole, Princess Amana and Calypsa shit? Give me a break!", I said. When I was a kid, my mother used to tell me stories about the old kingdoms; Nasher, Kindy, and Dasha. Alexandria was supposedly the kingdom of the gods. It was just a story though and had no reality to it. Yet, how do I explain what I just saw? And this woman standing in the room with me, was, as Mrs. Raby put it, older than she looks. But seeing the look on the woman's face, told me she wasn't joking, and I quickly started to feel smaller. "So…you expect me to believe this, then?", I said slowly. "Personally, I don't care if you believe or not, Mr. Red. But I have given you a fair warning. Now I won't be returning to North Edge for a long time, so I will give you something that will make this easier. The woman in the video feed is named Awalli. And she is looking for a girl that lives here in North Edge, so in other words, she is coming here.". At this point, I began to feel myself shake with fear. I had never dealt with anything like this before. "Who is the girl she is looking for?", I asked, trying to keep the fear out of my voice. "The girl's name is Emillie, and she is the one I warned you about earlier. You'll know when you meet her, Mr. Red. Now I must be going. Do you think you have enough information?", "Lady, there isn't enough information in the world that could help me with this.", I said, breathlessly. "Well, just remember, this is a need to know basis. You don't reveal what I've told you. This conversation does not leave this room. Even when you're speaking to Emillie. She is not to know you were warned about her.". The woman left, and I didn't stop her. I had some thinking to do. So, the fairy tales were real? That can't be. Because if it is, then I'm pissing myself right now. How can a normal man like me, fight a goddess? There were heroes in those stories, but most of the heroes died. Was that going to be me? I didn't know, but I didn't want it to be.

DALIA: I have lived for many, many, many, many years. In all those years, I've seen and experienced very sad things. I've always lived to help people, though. My first career was in medicine. Next, I was heavily involved with science and chemical mixing. This is the reason for my longevity of life. From there, I had become best friends with a goddess, who trained me to fight and be strong. But that was short-lived, because of my ex-lover, who warned that I should refrain from doing anything dangerous anymore. I did, and quickly learned why she had told me to stop. All the things that have happened since then have soon become reason enough for all of us to never show our faces. I soon took over a new role in life. Taking care of children who have been sadly abandoned. Looking at their sad little faces, and listening to them question why or what happened? Why are they forced to live like this? I quickly built up my orphanage and have been running it for the last seventy years. Of course, people who have worked with me note that I don't seem to age, but most don't really go into it too much. Twenty years ago, I had the saddest child brought to me.

It was a rainy night and I was completely exhausted. I had spent most of the day playing with the children and holding adoption interviews. Most of the children I bring in usually get adopted if they are under the age of six. Six-year old's usually end up growing up in the orphanage, sadly. But this child was brought to me at the tinder age of two days. As I rushed all the children to bed and started to have the matrons clean up and make sure everything was clean before morning, the bell of the manor rang. One of the other matrons went to answer the door and then came looking for me, "Madam, there is a soldier here, and they have a babe with them.", she said, looking frightened. We both knew it was late, and it was very strange that someone would be bringing a babe at this time. "Okay, I'll see to it. You finish putting everything in order here, okay?", I said, going towards the front. As I arrived, there was indeed a soldier standing there, with a babe in a babe carrier. "Excuse me, but do you realize the time? The hours for bringing…", the soldier held up a note. I took the note and began to read it. As I finished, I felt nothing but anger. "Does she seriously think she can just do this? Where the hell does she get off? This is unacceptable! You tell…", "Mam! I'm terribly sorry, but I am just following orders, and my orders are to drop off this babe here to your orphanage.", the soldier said. He handed me the carrier, and then turned to leave. He opened the door and then looked back, then left. I looked at the letter again and crumpled it and threw it away. I sat down in a chair and placed my face in my hands. I looked at the babe and she was sleeping peacefully. I picked up her carrier and took her with me to my chambers. "Excuse me, mam, would you prefer I ready her a bed?", one of my matrons asked. "No, that won't be necessary. I'll be keeping her with me tonight. Perhaps tomorrow.". The matron nodded and stepped out. I looked at the babe again who awoke with a quick start. Her eyes were a sharp gray with a faint golden glow, and I knew right away that this wasn't going to be easy in the slightest.

Five years later, Emillie grew into a beautiful young girl. And very smart, just like her mother. I was very proud to be the one raising her, while at the same time, saddened by the fact that I played a part in her misery. Emillie was like most orphaned children, and often questioned where her parents were, and if they were dead or alive, or if they just didn't want her. I knew the truth, and was forbidden from telling her. But worse than that, Emillie wasn't allowed to be adopted. Now this was for obvious reasons. She isn't a Plinthinian, but a goddess. So of course, she can't just go live with some random people. It was already complicated enough hiding this fact from everyone here in the manor. This was made worse, though, by Emillie watching a good majority of her friends be taken to new homes, while she was constantly passed up. She would always cry when these situations occurred, and I hated myself. "Mother Dalia…why…why…why do they…always ignore me?!", she yelled and cried at me one evening after watching her friend, Celda, go with her new parents. Celda had tried to convince them to adopt Emillie as well. It was a very horrible exchange, which ended with Celda being dragged apart from Emillie and their other friend, Vaness. But what Celda, Vaness, and Emillie couldn't know, is that I tell every couple and person that comes here looking to adopt, that the girl with the red hair and gray eyes is not available.

Years passed by, and Emillie was soon a beautiful teenage girl. She spent most of her time telling stories to the other children or studying in the library. She was very fascinated with the fairy tale stories. I knew that was a bad sign. Unlike most children or people who grew up reading these stories, Emillie saw some connection to herself and these stories. How she could possibly do that was beyond me but didn't surprise me. Most children who have been left here often do these things. Emillie liked to pretend she was the daughter of Ko-e. She felt she was the most honest and innocent princess in the story and related herself to her. I felt it was wrong in every way, since I knew that Ko-e was definitely not her mother. Emillie was also very fond of candy. I found it hard to keep her from the stuff. Vaness hadn't been adopted either by this time, so her and Emillie were like sisters. Vaness was a tough girl, though, and often, I had to pull her off of the boys who would have a go at Emillie. After all, those poor boys couldn't know what was truly affecting them. Vaness and Emillie had no time for boys, though, because the both of them had a mission. This mission was to prove the fairy tales weren't fairy tales. Of course, Emillie had put pieces together I couldn't have imagined. She used references like the Royal Family lineage, and the fact that Sebastian was tied to the story. Sebastian was very interesting to Emillie. He was a major factor in the stories, and she found it odd that in the church, Sebastian has no children. She started to realize the church was wrong. Of course, once you're seventeen, you are an adult and Emillie and Vaness were two gorgeous women. Vaness had joined the GF and became quite busy. Celda, who had been adopted, still came to visit Emillie, who was still staying at the orphanage. She was helping me out and I knew mainly because she loved it here. While it saddened her growing up how no one had adopted her, she soon moved past it and became a huge figure within the manor. She aided the kids with their studies, helped the matrons keep the manor clean, helped keep the children fed and clean, and most importantly, kept them entertained by telling stories. Emillie was an excellent storyteller. While this was all great, it didn't stop her obsession with fairy tales. When she was a little girl, she told me her view of the stories, "I believe Amana and Calypsa are the true villains in the story.", she said. "And why is that?", I asked curiously. "Well, Amana starts off as a hero and someone you can admire, but later she becomes obsessed with undoing the murder of her sister. She leaves everyone behind and just disappears. It makes sense that she is the true villain.". I always thought it was kind of a cosmic joke that Emillie hated Amana but loved Ko-e, and she didn't actually know either one of them. She had only ever read the half-truth, half-lies of the tales written about them.

When a few more years had passed, Celda was on holiday with her family. And I mean her family. She had gotten married and had a little boy, and they had decided to go see the Royal City, Nocton. While Emillie was glad for her friend, she deeply missed Vaness, who had been moved to South Edge and was in one of their GF precincts. Emillie worried about Vaness all the time, considering that she was doing a very dangerous job in a very dangerous part of Edge. I tried taking her mind off it and so did the children, "Come on, Emillie…", Bart, one of the children, was pleading with her one day, "…you said you would show me!", he was saying. "Alright, I'll come.", Emillie said, smiling, and standing up. I decided I'd follow and see what Bart was referring to. It was an old necklace I had given Emillie that Bart was excited to see. It was an interesting object but nothing special. Of course, leave it to Emillie to create a special function for it. "This necklace was worn by my mother, Ko-e. In this necklace is the power of a goddess.", Emillie said, as Bart's eyes grew wider than a plate. "But it just looks ordinary.", he said, starting to lose his excitement. I decided to oblige and took a red liquid out of my pocket, along with my flamer and sprinkled some of the red stuff on parchment, then set it ablaze, "Whoa! Look what Emillie did, Bart!", I said, as the boy looked on in amazement. Emillie turned and smiled at me. "That's enough magic for today, Bart. Don't tell the others, okay?", Emillie asked, as Bart nodded and hugged her, then me, then ran off. "I know I shouldn't do stuff like that, but I just love the look on his face.", Emillie said, with a smile that quickly turned into a frown as she put the necklace away. "Say, why don't we do something today? Why don't we get out? Go do anything, but stay here?", I said. "Really? You never really want to do anything outside of here. Shouldn't you stay here just in case?", she said with surprise. "Well, I know it's hard just sitting here, so yes, I think some fresh air will do us both good.", I said, trying my best to not mention Vaness.

As we had got dressed and stepped out of the manor, I still hadn't figured out what we were going to do. "So, what do you think we should do, Emillie?", I asked. "Let's go to church.", she replied. I felt my stomach lurch. "Isn't there anything else?", I asked with a hopeful tone. "Nah, I just want to hear a good story.", "Well let's go to the film house. Surely there is something better there than just stories of Sebastian.", "No. I want to go to church.", Emillie said. I decided there was no changing her mind. Once in church, we found ourselves a seat. The pastor was already in full sermon, "...we live like this? Sebastian taught us many years ago that living in this sinful way, will only result in a life of damnation. How do we stop living in sin? Well you must first turn away from all those things that Sebastian would say, "No, means no."". Coming to church was annoying. Sebastian never taught any of these lessons. I knew Emillie didn't fully understand that, but I couldn't hold it against her for wanting to be here. We sat and listened to the rest of the sermon, which ended with the pastor explaining how we will all perish one day by a mighty hand.

By the time we had left the church, Emillie had that thinking face she always made on. It reminded me heavily of her mother. "What are you thinking about?", I asked her. "Well, it just always fascinates me how some churches talk about Sebastian like he is the only creator, and others will speak of Trinity as well, or only Trinity. Isn't that interesting?", she said, with that curious voice accustomed to her. "I suppose so, Emillie. It is definitely a bit strange. But that is just how church is.", "I know you have never really believed in it, so thank you for coming with me.", she said, stopping to hug me. "It was my pleasure. I just didn't want you staying cooped up in the manor all day.". We made our way back to the manor and discovered a military flar outside of the manor. Military flars had certain colors to them to let you know they were military. This one was an Edgian colored flar which was black and green. We proceeded into the manor and discovered Vaness with the children. When Emillie saw Vaness, she ran to her and threw her arms around her, "I was so worried about you!", she said, crying into Vaness' shoulder. "I'm fine!", Vaness said, in that raspy voice she has. Vaness looked like she had seen some action. She didn't have any scars, but just looked tougher than before. She had cut her brown hair to where it was short but in waves, and wore a black and green uniform, which meant she was no longer GF, but had joined the army. "Vaness, when did this happen?", I asked, surprised by this sudden career change. "It happened last week. I'm here in town for a few days before I leave for training. I thought we could do something fun! I heard Celda is in Nocton with that 'prat husband of her's and her son.", Vaness said, hugging me now. "Well, yes, she is. So sad, she would have wanted to be here.", I said, with a sad tone to my voice. "Well, let's not waste time, let's do something!", Emillie said, immediately heading back out the door.

I hadn't joined Emillie and Vaness. I let them go out on their own. While they were gone, there was a knock at the manor front. One of the matrons went to open the door. Soon there was a knock on my office door. "Yes.", I answered. "Mam, there is a Mr. GO Red here to see you.". GO was an abbreviation for Guard Officer. "Yes, let him in.". The door opened, and a very handsome man walked in. He had faded blue hair, showing he was aging, and extremely chiseled features. He stepped into my office and I noticed he had very friendly eyes, but when he spoke there was a roughness to his voice, "Hello. Ms. Dalia, correct?", he said, extending his hand for me to shake it. I shook his hand and he sat down. "How can I help you, Mr. Red?", I asked. "Please, call me Lody.", he replied, with a slight smile. "So, what brings you here, Lody?", I asked. "Well, I just have a few questions for you.", he said, getting more serious now, "I understand you have been running this place for a while. Almost seventy years. Which is surprising, since you don't look anywhere near as old as I am.", he said, looking hard at my face. "Rumors, Mr. Lody, that is all that is. I can't have been running this place that long. It's physically impossible.". Lody looked at me as if he was determining if I was lying to him. "Okay, well then my next question is, have you ever heard of anybody with the name Awalli?", "No, can't say that I have.", I said. I was confused as to why he would be here asking me these questions. "How long have you been in charge of this place, Ms. Dalia?", he then asked, standing up, and walking around my office. "I've been here only twenty-three years, and can you please sit back down? You standing up and walking like that is making me nervous.", "That is something that guilty people say. Do you mind?", he said, now taking a file off the top of one of my cabinets. "Actually yes, I do.". He slowly lowered the file again and then sat back down. "Listen, I know it seems a bit strange...", "Mr. Red, can you please get to the point of why you are here?", I said, irritated. My use of his last name brought him to his senses, "Alright, then. I understand you have a girl here named Emillie Panahelios. Is this true?", he asked. "Why does that matter? Is she in some kind of trouble?", I asked, now becoming extremely worried. "I'm really not sure yet. I'm just trying to fit the pieces together, if you know what I mean.". I had no idea what he meant. "Sir, what is your business with Emillie?", "I understand she came here when she was only two days old. I also understand that you've been telling people she wasn't up for adoption. Now why would you do a thing like that?", he asked me, now crossing his arms and watching my face closely. "You've been quite busy, Mr. Red. To come here with all these accusations. You must have talked to almost every parent that has adopted from here in the last fifteen years.", I said, now starting to get an understanding. I was still confused as to why he would be investigating Emillie. "Well, believe me when I say it wasn't something I enjoyed. But the whole thing is becoming quite interesting. Now, please answer my question. Why was Emillie never allowed to be adopted?", "Because, she is a special case.", "Why? What is special about her?", he asked, still watching my face. Just then, there was a noise from downstairs, symbolizing the return of Emillie and Vaness. "Look, I won't take up any more of your time, but I will be back. So, I suggest you prepare to answer these questions.", he said, standing up, and walking towards the door. As he opened it, Emillie and Vaness were already outside of it. I watched as Lody's eyes lingered on Emillie, before, "GO Red, sir! I wasn't expecting YOU to be here! Are you adopting?", Vaness asked. "No, I just had some questions for your den-mother here. But I was just leaving.", he said, never taking his eyes off Emillie. I watched as he walked past her and still continued to stare. Emillie stared back, then waved him off.

LODY: I knew it the moment I had laid eyes on her. I stepped out of the manor and went straight to my flar. Her eyes were different, but the red hair and that face told me everything I needed to know. Emillie was the red-headed woman's daughter. But if that is the case, then what is the special case surrounding Emillie? So, Emillie was dropped off at the orphanage twenty years ago. From there, the den-mother, Dalia, refused to allow her to be adopted. But why would she do that? Unless the red-headed lady ordered it. I was tired, and sleepy, and had barely been able to sleep since seeing that video of the woman who punched a hole into Reginald Tib's chest. I kept running it over in my head. Writing down what I felt was important to remember and trying to understand why Awalli would be looking for an innocent girl that was raised in an orphanage. I had checked the system and could confirm that Emillie had no record. She had never been in any trouble. She was a grade-E student, which meant she was a genius. After a few more days of watching her, I noticed she had a very friendly and open personality. She waved and smiled at everyone, even though she was upset by the departure of GO Tes. Vaness Tes had grown up in this orphanage and hadn't really spoken about it too much in all the time I've known her. I may have heard her mention Celda or Emillie once or twice, but she never spoke too much about her childhood. Most orphans weren't happy about their childhoods, so it made a lot of sense. But Emillie was different. She seemed to be thriving in the orphanage.

One day, while sitting in my flar, I had fallen asleep, and was sitting there with pasta pie on my face. There was a knock on my window, and it was Dalia. "Mr. Red, why are you outside of my orphanage?", she asked in an irritated tone. "I told you to call me Lody.", I replied, straightening myself out, and wiping my face. I felt embarrassed. "Mr. Red, let me make something clear for you. I don't like you hanging around my place like this. I'm going to ask you to leave now.", she said in more of a commanding tone. "What's the problem with me hanging out? I'm with the guard force. So, I'm only looking out for your protection.", "No, you are looking out for Emillie, which you still haven't told me why.". I thought about the answer to that and realized I couldn't tell her. I wanted to be honest with her, but knew that it might come back on me badly. "Listen, I have orders to investigate, and so all I'm doing is following those orders.", I said. Dalia's face made a recognizable face and then she became angry, "And the one who gave you this order, was she more beautiful than anything you've ever seen? The kind of woman a man would worship rather than boss around?", she asked me. "Well, yes.", I said surprised. "Well listen to me, if you continue this course, you are going to die, Mr. Red.", she said, now straightening up, and walking back towards her manor. I got out of the flar and followed her, "HEY, WHAT DO YOU MEAN?! HEY!", I yelled at her. She turned on me quickly, "Lody, if you value your life, you will not do a thing that woman tells you. Quit the guard force if it's the only way. But you don't want to be involved in this.", she said, turning away again. "Now I have just about had it with all this secrecy! Tell me, what is the deal?! What is the situation with Emillie?!", I yelled, forgetting I wasn't supposed to be discussing this loudly. Emillie was walking out of the manor with a young boy. She stopped and looked at me. "Uh, I mean to say…", I tried to think on the spot, but the damage was done. Emillie continued to watch me and Dalia. Dalia looked scared out of her mind, but Emillie just walked off with the boy and ignored me. "I think it is seriously time for you to leave.", Dalia said through gritted teeth. I decided to listen to her.

    I had returned to the precinct. I was going over whatever I could find on Carla Nos' family and trying to understand the full connection. I remembered I was told by The Commander, this was the nickname I had given the red-headed woman, that Carla Nos was Reginald's niece. This made sense. But what didn't, is that if Awalli was only after Reginald, why kill his niece and then him? Or was it Reginald first? I couldn't know, considering that it was in South Edge this happened, and I would have to request the information from the corresponding precinct. As

I was gearing myself to request the paperwork from the clerk's office, Tillo came running to my desk, "There is a foxy one coming. A skeeter the likes of which I've definitely never seen! You have to let me in on this one!", Tillo said. I thought perhaps The Commander was coming. Almost seemed like it when I saw the red hair, but it was Emillie. It was late and I knew she must have snuck away. Tillo was looking excited. "Hello, Mr. Red? I have some questions.", she said, a bit nervously. I wondered if Dalia had spoken with her. I looked at Tillo, who was all ready to hear what she had to say. "Tillo, sorry, mate, but can you give me and this young lady some privacy?", I asked Tillo. Looking disappointed, Tillo went back to his desk but I could tell he was listening. "I overheard you talking to Mother Dalia.", Emillie said. I was thinking more yelling at her than talking, but I nodded to see what else Emillie was going to say, "So, I just wanted to know, why were you even at the orphanage? And what is it that concerns me?", she said, now sitting in a nearby chair. "Listen, Emillie, I can't talk about my cases with people off the street.", "But I'm not off the street, I'm from the orphanage and you said my name. So, don't you think if I'm in some kind of danger, I should know?", she asked, putting simplicity to the subject. "Have you discussed this with Dalia?", I asked her. "She became angry and told me to drop it. That was the first time I've ever seen her act that way towards me. So, I want to know what's happening.", "I'm sorry, Emillie, but I don't have anything better to tell you.", I said, hoping she would drop it at this point. "Listen, I know that I am different. I can't put my finger on it, but I know that I am different. Do you believe in the fairy tales, Mr. Red?", she asked me, now sitting back in the chair, and folding her arms. She reminded me heavily of The Commander. "I don't know what you expect me to tell you, I mean why the hell would I believe in that rubbish?", I said. "Because we both know that it isn't rubbish. You've been watching me for days and when I first saw you, you looked like you recognized me from somewhere, but I had never seen you before. So, please? Mr. Red, can I just know the truth? The one that I think you now know, and that Mother Dalia has hidden from me?", she said, now giving me a reprimanding look. I felt guilty, but none the less, remembered what The Commander said, "Emillie, listen to me, there are sometimes things it's best not to worry about. This is one of those things. So, please…". Before I could finish, Emillie was standing up, "Okay. I get it. You won't tell me.". She smiled at me and walked away. "Geez, Red, what the hell is going on with you lately?", Tillo asked, watching Emillie go down the stairs. "Follow me.". I led him to an interrogation room, where I told him what was happening. I needed to tell somebody, because I was going crazy not being able to tell anyone. "WHAT?!", Tillo exclaimed. "Yes, I know, it's all insane. I don't know what to think. I'm scared out of my mind and at this point, I'm afraid I can literally feel something on the horizon.", I said, giving Tillo a tired look. "Drinks. On me.", Tillo managed to say.

We were sitting in Laddies, a bar on the outskirts of North Edge. We weren't saying much because it was still fresh on our minds what we had just discussed. "Say, mate, do you think that Emillie is a goddess? How else can you explain her good looks?", Tillo asked. I could tell he was definitely feeling his spirits. I on the other hand wasn't questioning anything like that, but rather was worried about The Commander and what she would do if she learned I told Tillo what she said not to say. "Or, do you think she is just a gorgeous girl? What is the connection with her and this Awalli person? There must be something…", Tillo was thinking hard on this now and so was I. "We shouldn't do this here.", a voice at the back of the bar was saying. "If not here, then where? We need to send the message like the boss said.". I turned to look at what the hell was going on but before I could make a move, there was an explosion, and everything went black.

CHAPTER 2

Premeditated Murder

EMILLIE: I saw it on the news the very next morning. Laddies had been bombed. Nobody knew who did it yet. On the t.v, GO Red was in the explosion, but luckily, he and his partner survived, "…and whoever did this will be apprehended, you can bet on that!", a man with a big, bushy mustache was saying to the camera. "Thank you, Captain Walsh!". Walsh nodded confidently, and then returned to the scene. "Well, you heard it here, people. Captain Walsh and his men are on the case.". I could see Red, and the man that was with him last night, getting patched up. Red looked really angry. "Emillie, what is that on the news?", Dalia was asking. "There was an explosion at that bar by the edge of town. GO Red was there.", I said. Dalia rushed and looked at the television, but by the time she had gotten in front of it, they were discussing a new subject. "He looked fine, just beat up some.", I said. Something told me Dalia liked Mr. Red, and I didn't want her to worry. "That's…good I suppose. How are you doing?", she asked. I hadn't spoken to her since our argument about what Mr. Red was actually doing here. "I'm fine now. I'm not really worried about that anymore.", I said in what I hoped was a convincing tone. The truth was, I was doing my own investigation now. I was tired of being lied to by Dalia and everyone else. Dalia didn't look like she believed me but decided she didn't want to argue with me. "Emillie, I was wondering if you could help with the laundry?", she asked me. "Sure, I'll get started now.".

As soon as I was done with the laundry, I made my way out of the orphanage, and all the way down to the bar that had been bombed. There were still workers and grunts surrounding the situation. One of them, a silver-haired man, came up to me, "Excuse me, mam, but you are not supposed to be here. This is a dangerous area and the Guard Force has closed it off.", he said, pointing me away. "I just have a few questions.", I said, trying to look past him. Red wasn't anywhere in sight. "NO! YOU NEED TO LEAVE!", he yelled, now turning red and getting angry. I quickly walked away. As I did, I heard him say, "Watch that one. I have a feeling she is a danger groupie.". I walked to an area where the guards weren't all over the place and saw two people also checking out the scene. One was a man with a huge black coat on and green hair that formed into a mohawk. The other was a woman. She looked like she could have something to do with the bombing. She had dark-green hair that came down to her mid-back and she was wearing unmistakable mobster clothing, which were gray dress pants, and a gray shirt with a striped jacket. The man, now that I was looking at him, seemed to be a bodyguard. "Look at what I was forced to do, Li. They didn't care what I had to say, and now look at what they made me do.", "Shouldn't we split, boss? I mean the GF is right on the other side.", "True, that they are. Let us leave, then.", the woman said, turning, and walking away. I followed her. They headed to a flar that was parked not too far around the corner. There were people now starting to gather around the site. I had to push people out of my way to keep the man and woman in sight. They got into the flar and rode off. I had lost them.

Later that evening, I had returned to the orphanage, and waiting for me outside of the building was Red's partner, Tillo. "Hello, Em, got a sec?", he asked me. I could tell something about him was unnerved. I nodded and we stepped to the side of the manor. "Listen, I shouldn't even be here right now, but there is something I need to ask you.", he said nervously. "Okay, what is it?", "Do you believe in the fairy tales? You know, the princesses and the kingdoms and all that.". I nodded but was confused by this question. "Well, you see…the reason I ask is because when I was a boy, my mother used to tell me the stories. She said to me one day, though, that they are more than stories, they were real. She said that the government has been covering up the truth of the past for years.". When he said this, it made me remember the days of me and Vaness attempting to unravel this mystery. We put a lot of effort into proving the fairy tales were real, but in the end, Vaness accepted that they were just stories after all, and I was forced to continue on my own. I always believed that there had to be some proof out there, but it wouldn't be easy to find. The thought, though, that the government would go as far as to hide things that had to do with the past was infuriating. We all deserved the right to know what really happened. "Well, what is your point?", I asked, feeling like I knew that stuff already. "Well, you see, my mother and father were what you would know as diggers. They traveled a lot, and I used to go with them. But there was one time I remember, that we weren't allowed in a certain area.". I started to consider what he was saying, "Tillo, are you saying that your parents discovered some proof?", I asked, starting to feel excitement. I had waited so long for this kind of news. "Sadly, no. I'm here to tell you that you should back off the subject.". I was surprised by his change of tone. "What?", I asked, still not fully understanding why he was telling me to back off. "My father got involved with some things that to this day, I've never forgiven him. He's gone, Em, and do you want to know why?", he asked me, getting worked up. I shook my head. "Because he wouldn't let it go. He wanted that site so badly, that he snuck on and was shot for doing it. There was no warning of death, Emillie.", he finished, and I was horrified. "Who would do something like that to anyone?", I asked, almost wanting to cry. I felt horrible for Tillo, and wondered if Mr. Red knew this story. "A woman. With red hair, and a nasty looking scar on a very beautiful face. She ordered the site be guarded by men with cannons. It was…it wasn't right. We found out in the morning, and then…", Tillo was having a hard time getting to the next part, "…the woman came to me and my mom and told us. When my mom asked her why she would do this to us? She replied that he did this to us and left.". A woman with red hair? I was now thinking hard on this. "So, what I'm trying to say is, I heard you stopped by Laddies this afternoon. Please don't do anything like that again.", he said politely. "Okay. I won't.", I lied. I was curious about what Mr. Red was hiding, and now, Tillo shows up trying to prevent me from doing anything now? Something wasn't right. But I planned on figuring it out.

Tillo had left, and I could tell when he did, that he didn't believe I'd stay away. I spent the rest of the evening at the manor, nonetheless. I kept running it through my mind like a snake in water. How was I connected to this woman? I had a feeling she was the one that was controlling Red, and even possibly, Mother Dalia. I knew better than to ask, though. I kept thinking about the reason for the government cover up of the fairy tales as well. Sebastian was a huge part of the stories. Maybe they didn't want his image tainted? Or maybe they just didn't want to let people know that the possibility of people doing impossible things was possible. I looked in my old book of fairy tales, and was looking at the story of Ko-e. Ko-e ran away from the kingdom of Alexandria because she was saddened by the lies of her family. In different versions of the story, she fled to meet Amana and Calypsa because they are her sisters. But in the main story, she isn't related to them. She falls in love with Prince Scion of Caprica, and they end up living happily ever after. The main issue with this part of the story is that there really is a royal family, and the rumor is they date back to King Amacus. King Amacus was known for being a descendent of Tig. Tig was in the fairy tales. Mentioned as Sebastian's trusted liaison. So, if Tig was in the fairy tales, then doesn't this mean that there was some truth in there somewhere? It only made sense if you really stopped and thought about it. But this is why most people consider the fairy tales a work of fiction. The original writer died over five-hundred years ago, and all the other iterations were all things added by other people later. I now had a better understanding than I did when I was a child, so I understood there was a good chance that this red-headed woman that Tillo mentioned is connected to the stories as well. I thought about how far fetched it was, but kept coming back to the same conclusion. Then, something unnerved me. Vaness, a while back, had given me a different book of fairy tales. I didn't like these versions, though, because it depicted Ko-e, my favorite character, in a way I couldn't get behind. She was highly suicidal. In this version, Amana and Calypsa were her sisters, and Ko-e was heavily involved with Calypsa's death. She blamed herself for it and demanded that Amana kill her as well. Amana had to kill Calypsa because she had become dangerous. She was evil like her mother. But this part always saddened me, for Amana and Calypsa were best friends. I started to realize I was just telling myself the same things I already knew.

I had decided to take a walk in the manor garden. Some of the kids were playing there. A few of them rushed past me yelling, "Hi!", as they did. I sat down in the flower patch on a bench. I was just sitting, and pondering on everything I had figured out so far, when a strange voice sounded off in my head, "Find me, find yourself.", it said. I jumped up from the bench, hair on end, and looked around. There was no one. Perhaps one of the children had played a trick on me, I thought. I looked some more, but since I didn't see anybody, I left the garden. I made my way into the city. It was late now, and I didn't usually go out at night. I was near downtown NE, and decided I'd go to a bar. The bar I entered was called, The Wasted Dattur. I thought about the humor in the name. I was, after all, reading fairy tales all day. I sat down, and the bartender didn't come right away. She was a surly-looking girl and her face wasn't much to look at. She ended up walking towards me, and I noticed the vibrant color of her hair, which was magenta. "What you drinking tonight, dear?", she asked me in a kind tone. "Just water please. And maybe a shot of ticenta.", I said. Ticenta wasn't a tough spirit to drink, but it did give you a head buzz that I sorely felt I needed. As the bartender handed me a glass of water and the shot of ticenta, I took the shot and let the hot taste go down my throat, where it sizzled and burned. "Don't get a lot of pretty women in here, what brought you here tonight, darling?", a man was saying next to me. "I'm just trying to think.", I replied. "What are you thinking about?", he asked me. I turned and looked at him, and was shocked for a second. It was the big man with the mohawk. "Just about what happened at Laddies.". The bartender seized up at the mention of it, and walked quickly away. "What about what happened at Laddies?", the big man asked. "Well, it was bombed, so I'm interested to know what happened.", I said. The man looked me up and down, then said, "I could tell you, but what are you doing when you leave here?", he asked me. I knew what he intended. I'd only done that once and had no intention of doing it with him. But I could tell he was willing to give me some info. "I don't know yet.", I said, smiling at him and giving him a small but obvious wink. The man blushed and ordered another shot of whatever he was drinking. I started taking out my money to pay. "What's the rush, darling? Stay a while.", he said, watching me. "Why don't we hurry and get out of here?", I said. The man looked positively excited at the fact, and quickly finished his drink, stood up, wrapped his arm around me, and walked me out. As we were walking out, I noticed Tillo across the street, but he was locked in conversation with a woman, and didn't notice me. The man walked me to his flar, which I realized was one of the old models that still had wheels. I got in, not feeling afraid at all. Some part of me told myself that I shouldn't be going with this man, but everything else in me said that I was about to get answers.

Before we even got out of the flar, he was trying to kiss me. I put my hand between my mouth and his, "Hold it. I want to hear what you have to say first.", I said. He backed down, disappointed, but allowed me out of the flar, and led me into a nice-looking warehouse. It was almost like a house inside. The furniture in here suggested that people were living here, but it also seemed to suggest that it was a place of opportunity. There were other men in here, all looking at me. I was used to how men drooled over me, but this was ridiculous. I started to feel nothing but regret in coming. I didn't even know why I came. At first, I felt like it was leading me to some great thing, but now, with all the guys around, and of course, mohawk guy, I was getting nervous. "This way, sugar.", Mohawk said. He pointed in the direction of a room, and I walked in. I looked around and realized it wasn't a bedroom, but a sort of display room. It was luxurious. It was like the warehouse itself, not what it seemed. Mohawk was watching me look at all the stuff in the room. I felt a certain energy flowing through my body and thought I was crazy, until I heard, "EMILLIE, YOU ARE CLOSE. BEWARE YOUR SURROUNDINGS. FIND ME!". I stumbled back, unable to grasp what I had just heard. "What's wrong with you?", Mohawk asked. Just then, a woman burst into the room, "YOU IDIOT! DON'T LET HER GET THE RING!", the woman yelled at Mohawk, but I suddenly found myself holding a ring. Before I knew what happened, there was a blinding light. It was so bright, I couldn't see anything at first, then, for a few seconds, I saw a woman. With hair that seemed to be a strange mix of pink, purple, and red. She pointed to me and then I lost all train of thought.

SANDIN: "JUST TELL ME THAT YOU KNOW WHERE SHE IS, DAMN IT!", Ms. Dalia was yelling at Red, and pounding on his chest. Four days ago, there was another explosion, but this time at a warehouse. And this one was different, there were more dead. Twelve people to be exact. All of them mobsters. It seemed almost like some crazy mobster-war attack like back in the days. But upon investigation, and seeing the site myself, I've concluded, I was very wrong. It was like nothing I'd ever seen before. The dead bodies were hardly recognizable, like some form of radiation had burned off their skin. There were signs that they were making drugs here as well. But the part that hit me was what Red was standing over. It was a necklace. A nice one at that. Like something you'd see a queen or princess wear. At first, we didn't know who it belonged to. After putting it in the DNA tracer, it came back with results we didn't recognize, and none of the eggheads could figure out what it meant. But after running the code numbers, and calling the shop it came from, and making that poor person who answered the phone search through years of old purchase records, we found out it was Dalia who had purchased this necklace. Upon seeing the necklace in Red's hand, Dalia knew something must have happened to Emillie. She led us into the manor and straight to her office, where she asked to not be disturbed. She then closed the door, turned away from us, and started to cry as if she had just lost everything there was to lose. Red consoled her, "We didn't find a body, so Emillie could still be alive. Plus, there were signs that there was somebody else.", said Red. This was true. We were following Awalli. We had got a tip from a girl I knew back in the day. She had connections to some of the inside mob info, and we figured that this was the best way to get ahead of Awalli or just the whole situation entirely. She told us about the warehouse and said that a lot of the women that she knows go there to score lilac and other drugs. By the time we were approaching the warehouse, a bright light came from inside, and then suddenly, the warehouse looked rundown and destroyed. We called a clean crew to come and look for forensic clues, and Red and I checked. Awalli definitely ran out of there right at the moment of whatever the hell happened. "I told her not to get involved with any of this! I begged her!", Dalia was yelling into Red's chest. "Please, Dalia, calm yourself. You don't want the children to overhear you.", I said. She then took some deep breaths, "We have to find Emillie. I'm going to go fetch my coat.", she said, going to her closet. "Now hold on, Dalia, let me and Tillo worry about this. You don't get involved, okay?", Red said in a commanding tone. "But you don't understand! She could be hurt or dead out there! She needs me! She needs her mother!", Dalia yelled, pointing at herself. I hadn't thought about it, but Dalia was basically her mother because she took care of her for her whole life. Dalia began to cry again. "Listen, we are going to put our feet out there now and do everything we can to find her!", Red said, now grabbing Dalia and pulling her to him. She cried into his chest for some time, and it took us a while to calm her down. Finally, she calmed down enough to nod us out the door.

"Poor woman. I didn't know she felt that strongly about Emillie.", I said, as Red drove our flar. "Well, the girl grew up in her place. She has been with her since she was two-days old, so yes, it makes perfect sense. Do you think we can get another run on Awalli?", Red asked. I could tell after watching Dalia break down for several minutes, he was determined to find Emillie. I was, too. After all, she had been missing for four days, but I didn't have any more connections and was afraid that this was just going to become one of those headaches. We drove around for hours, hoping that we would find some kind of clue. We needed to recharge the flar eventually, and so we returned to the precinct and started to get ready to call it a night. "There isn't anything we can do right now, Tillo, so let's just head home and get some rest. See you tomorrow.", Red said, grabbing his briefcase and coat and heading downstairs. I, on the other hand, stayed. I hopped on my monitor and started to look through old mobster files, until I found the one that stuck out the most. It was an old file discussing a particularly nasty publicized hit. One of the Royal Family members named Tiggy Dat, had been arrested for not only producing and selling lilac, but also for kidnapping children and molesting them. He had been caught with pictures of himself and the children in various positions. The case was very high profile, considering everything. There were old clippings of Tiggy in the courthouse, and of course, there were some RF people who had stood up and testified against their cousin. But once Tiggy was being led to the jail, he was shot from miles away. The person who got the blame was Eddie Folto. A man who at the time was at war with Tiggy over turf rights. There was never any real proof that Folto was guilty. There was only one piece of evidence that I was surprised held up in the court. It was a long-range cannon with his prints on it. But Eddie claimed he had not only never held this cannon, but he never attempted to kill Tiggy since his arrest. This made sense, because after Tiggy was arrested, it was obvious that business started booming for Eddie. So, someone framed him. That much was clear. Somebody wanted Tiggy dead for what he did. It was obviously a hired cannon. My guess is that it was someone from within the RF. This made even more sense, as they would see Tiggy's arrest as an embarrassment. This all happened seventy years ago.

After looking through my files some more, I decided that I was also going home now. It had been a couple hours since Red had left, and I started to pack my things. Then I noticed I wasn't the only one here this late. Captain Walsh was approaching me. He stepped up towards my desk and gave me a look of what looked like anger, "Hello, Tillo. And might I ask why, YOU, of all people, are still here?", he asked me. I knew it was weird. I never stayed this late, and as far as I knew, I wasn't supposed to talk about what me and Red were working on. "I just wanted to go over some old files for a case that me and Red are on.", I said. "Yeah, about that case, what the hell? That thing at that warehouse on Ned St. What the hell is that all about, Tillo?", Walsh asked me, folding his arms. "Don't know, sir. It's what we are looking into.", "Not anymore. I'm putting Yellfy on it. I believe it is connected to what happened at Laddies.". I thought for a minute. "Sir, it was different. This was more of a chemical-based attack.", I said. "I believe both attacks were done by a woman named Awalli. She is a new element in the city. She is originally from South Edge. Now my question is, what is it that you and Red know, that you aren't supposed to share with your captain?", Walsh said in a tone that quite clearly suggested that I needed to come clean. "Sir, I'm afraid that I'm not at liberty to discuss that with you. Please try and understand, sir, that this is coming from high-up.", "Oh, I know where it is coming from, but I don't think the two of you do. But, we will discuss this tomorrow. For now, head home, Tillo, and try not to think about Awalli.". It was weird. I didn't know if he was trying to get an answer from me or if he was subtly letting me know that he knew already. I grabbed my stuff and rushed away.

Once in my flar, I kept thinking about Emillie. She had been missing four days, going on five now. Dalia was going crazy with worry, and Red has to prove that he can find her. I didn't want to believe she evaporated when that light went off, but there was no sign of her, except for the necklace. So once again, I found myself asking the same question again, and again. What really happened to Emillie Panahelios? I got home, and walked into my apartment. It was a nice, little, cozy home, and I quickly sat in my armchair, and had fallen asleep. When I woke up, my t.v was on, and I looked around, but felt hazy. I could make out a strange silhouette sitting on my big couch. It wasn't a person but just light. "You are looking for her? Stop.", the light said. I sat up and rubbed my eyes and the light was gone. I checked the time and saw that all the clocks in my house had stopped at three-forty. I jumped up and went into my bedroom, and then the light reappeared, "Help me...", it said this time. It started to move towards me, and I backed away into my wall. I put my hands above my head and the light stopped coming towards me. It looked at itself, and then screamed. I awoke and my first thought was of Emillie. Could that had been just a dream? I asked myself. My clocks were moving again, so now I was feeling more confident that I was truly awake. But what was that? My receiver started to ring, and I quickly answered, "Hello?", I asked. "Tillo, you need to meet me! Let's meet at the Dattur.", Red said. He seemed excited and I wondered what was going on.

As I arrived inside of the Dattur, Red was sitting at the back and was waving me over once he saw me. "Tillo, I may have news on Awalli and where she is!", he said, definitely more excited. "Well, what's the news?", I asked, hoping that Emillie would somehow fit in as well. "Well, after the explosion or whatever that was, she went back to South Edge to heal up. Emillie isn't with her.", he said, seeing that I was about to ask. Now I was feeling horrible. "Where do you think she is, Red? We can't let Dalia stay how she is.", I said. "I know that, Tillo, but you of all people understand it takes steps. At least we are somewhere with Awalli.". Even though Red was happy, I was finding it extremely hard to be happy. Emillie was nowhere to be found. Not a single trace of her. No DNA to work off of, nothing except that necklace that we already returned to Dalia. "But I do have some other good news as well. This does concern Emillie. We may have a lead on her whereabouts, but you aren't going to believe this. She was last spotted in Nocton.". Nocton was miles, and miles away from here. In a flar, you would get there in a few weeks. But I couldn't imagine how Emillie got there. Unless she took a birdie. "How do you suppose she got there?", "Well, that's the thing. This was seven days ago. Which is before this whole situation. Now I asked myself, did she take a trip or something? I never saw her leave town. So, that's when I realized I would have to contact the Royal Guard.", Red said, irritated. The Royal Guard is the Guard Force in Nocton. They are the most uptight bastards that ever walked this planet. "How did you find out she was spotted there?", I asked curiously. It isn't like Red had someone in the Royal City that could have spotted her and told him. "Watch this.", he replied gruffly, handing me his cell. I watched the screen and it was a news report following the indoctrination of the new Head of Family. This was a huge deal because the Head of the Royal Family made really important decisions regarding not just Nocton, but a lot of the contracted cities. The contracted cities were cities that had an alliance with Nocton and the Royal Family. Edge was not one of those cities. As I continued to watch the screen, that's when I saw her. She looked confused, but nonetheless was there. She was watching the whole scene, as Princess Layna took the crown and placed it on her head. Then she just disappeared, and nobody seemed to notice. Red took back his cell and looked at me, waiting for a reaction. I didn't have one. This was too much. "How could she had been there? She was at the orphanage!", I yelled, forgetting myself. "Now calm down, mate. This is what The Commander was talking about.". From the way Red had described The Commander to me, I knew right away that she was the woman responsible for my father's death. I didn't mention this to Red. "So, what you are saying, is what? She said to look out for Emillie appearing miles away from us? That is ridiculous. How did she get there?", I asked again. "Well, I saw Awalli do something very similar. She just appeared, and killed Reginald Tib, then disappeared again. I believe that Emillie may have teleported herself there in her sleep. Judging from the time the indoctrination was taking place, it would be night time here. Precisely one in the morning. So, with that being said, Emillie must have traveled there in her sleep. That would explain the look on her face. Plus, seven days ago, Emillie argued with Dalia over something that had to do with Sebastian. And she has that obsession with the fairy tales…", Red said, thinking hard on that part. I felt embarrassed, because I remembered discussing the fairy tales with Emillie, but didn't know she had an obsession. I started to secretly blame myself. "What obsession?", I asked. "Well, the girl believes she is the daughter of one of the princesses. She truly thinks that she is different. But we know she is, of course.". I couldn't stand it anymore. This mystery was killing me. "We need to go find her, Red. We need to find her now.".

Red had gone to visit Dalia, while I was hitting the pavement. I had returned to the scene where the strange light, that somehow burned everything, had first appeared. I entered the warehouse, and was looking around for anything we may have missed. I bent down and was squatting over a strange ring. I picked it up and for a split second felt it burn hot in my hand. I examined it and noticed that there was writing on the inside. It was circles. Just circles within each other. "It reads; Life is made to be protected.", said a voice. I looked around and saw nobody and felt fear. I pocketed the ring and ran out of the warehouse. I turned and looked back at it and saw that no one was there. I left. Soon, I found myself at the mercy of Captain Walsh. He had also been scouting the warehouse and came towards me as soon as he saw me. "Well, well, well. Tillo. Here again, are we? And what is it that you're looking for here?", he asked me.

As he asked this, a woman was stepping out of the same flar. She looked very important and was very good looking. I realized she was the same woman who first spoke to Red, "Mr. Sandin Tillo? It's good to meet you. We must discuss this situation immediately. Please accompany me and Captain Walsh here back to the precinct.".

Before we reached the precinct, the woman turned to me and began to introduce herself, "I am Senator Raby. I'm going to go ahead and guess that GO Red has already briefed you about me.", she said, smiling at me. I didn't respond. My first thought was that this woman works closely with the woman who killed my father. I slowly nodded, feeling my temple throb. "I know what you are feeling, Mr. Tillo, but I'd advise against these kinds of feelings.". I thought about what that meant, and realized that perhaps she was trying to tell me that she had knowledge of my father, and that I shouldn't hold a grudge about it. She obviously didn't understand. "So, you were looking for Emillie, right?", she asked me, still wearing that nice smile she had. Once again, I only nodded. "Well, Mr. Tillo, if I may suggest you stop searching for her, I will gladly do so. Unfortunately, I do not have that power, and I have instead been asked to tell you the opposite.", she said, now starting to remove the smile from her face. "So, I'm going to keep looking for Emillie? No problem there. But I do have some questions. Is Emillie capable of teleportation? Does she have abilities?", I asked, hoping to get a straight answer. "I'm afraid I don't know, Mr. Tillo. I'm going to go out on a limb here, and basically tell you that she is capable of anything, and don't let anything surprise you.", she said, now returning the smile to her face. "So, you see, Tillo, there are a lot of questions and we all want answers.", said Captain Walsh, who had been sitting and listening quietly. "Do you work for The Commander?", I asked. "The Commander?", Raby questioned, "Oh, yes. The Commander. She is a General, you know?", she said, smiling at me and Walsh. Walsh was looking impatient, "Can you get on with what you're doing here, Gail?", he said, almost too disrespectfully. Gail shot him an angry look, "You're lucky you've even been briefed at all. Originally, she was going to leave you out. Plus, I already said; WHEN WE REACH THE PRECINCT!", she told Walsh, who got quiet again and said nothing. I was surprised that Walsh was on a first name basis with Senator Raby and wondered where they may have met before.

We reached the precinct and went inside. Red was already there, looking extremely troubled, "When I went to see Dalia, the first thing she did was ask if I've found Emillie yet. I felt horrible telling her no.", he said, looking sad. Raby stood there and watched him for a split second. "Okay, follow me. All of you. You too, Mr. Yellfy.", she said, pointing at Yellfy, who looked shocked, but stopped what he was doing. She led all of us to a meeting room, where she sat down at the end of the table that was in here, and directed that we do the same. We all sat down, Walsh actually taking a chair and placing it at the other end, and then sitting down with a cocky smile, "So, now can we know?", he asked. Raby looked livid, but nonetheless, pressed on, "Some of you in here have been wondering about what happened at the warehouse on Ned Street. Well it wasn't an explosion. It was a godly presence.". Yellfy sniggered. "I'm glad you think that this is a joke, Yencid, but I promise you, it isn't a joke.", Raby said, and Yellfy removed the smile from his face. "Let me get this straight...you mean metaphorically? Right?", Yellfy asked. Yellfy was trying not to laugh but I could tell he was ready to burst. "No. I mean it really was. Let me put it in terms you do understand. A being, of immense power, descended upon that place in a raw form. This caused a reaction that caused damage that seems similar to radiation. But I promise you, once you get those reports back...", she paused, looking hard in Walsh's eyes, "...you will see what I mean.". I had started to think about that. Usually we get the reports the next day. I figured this one only was taking a long time because there were twelve dead. But I know the guys at the house of the dead, and those guys were pretty quick with those autopsies. "Have you been interfering with the autopsy reports?!", Yellfy yelled, "Do you know what you have done? It's been taking us longer than it takes just to figure out how…", "MR. YELLFY, I HAVE ALREADY TOLD YOU WHAT HAPPENED!". Red was looking shocked. I was, too. The kindly woman who continued to stare at me with nothing but a smile, disappeared in an instant. "I'm not going to buy that bullshit.", "Well, Mr. Yellfy, you will see the reports, and change your mind.", Raby said, reaching into her bag, pulling out some files, and throwing them at Yellfy, who snatched them up hungrily. He looked at it with eagerness, and we all watched him read. Then he slowly lowered the report, and looked confused. "Let me see that!", yelled Walsh. Yellfy was still too shocked, so Red walked over and picked it up and read it as he took it to Walsh. Walsh reached for it and took it out of Red's hands and looked at it. "What did it say, Red?", I asked him. "It says that…Emillie is dead. There was nothing left of her.", Red said, covering his face.

"Mr. Tillo, can I talk to you? I think it is quite important.". Red had left to go tell Dalia. I couldn't face her, so I didn't go with him. The kids, too, I thought. They were going to be broken. "Look, I don't know if I can handle anymore bad…", "Emillie is not dead, and it is now important that you tell Mr. Red, and nobody else.", "Where is she?", I asked, now becoming alert. "We don't know. We are looking for her.", "Who's we?". She didn't answer my question. "How can you be sure she is alive?", "We just know, Mr. Tillo.", "If you don't know where she is, then how do you know she is alive?!", I yelled. "Keep your voice down, please. Now let me say this to you, Sandin, if I truly didn't know what I was talking about, I wouldn't tell you these things. I have credible intel on this. But it can't be put on paper or even loaded onto a computer. It has to be word of mouth. I had to give that info to Yellfy and Walsh. But I didn't tell them everything.". Now, I was feeling a little shocked, "Wait, what do you know?", I asked, now starting to feel somewhat relieved. "We will wait for Mr. Red.", "But wait! Aren't we going to tell Ms. Dalia?", I asked, feeling it was totally wrong to leave her in the dark, when she was the one hurting the most. And Red had already gone to tell her that Emillie was dead, and there wasn't a body to bury. "No. She will learn when the time is right. I know. I want to tell her, too. I don't like to hurt her. I grew up in her orphanage.", "Wait, you? You grew up there? But, how?", "What do you mean, how? I was an orphan.", "But you were adopted?", I asked. "No. I left when I was seventeen and got involved with the City Council. I had a mind for it. But I'll tell you the rest when Mr. Red gets here.".

LODY: As I pulled up to the manor, the kids were outside playing, and I saw Dalia among them. She was holding a little girl's hand, and leading a group of children in a song. By the time I got out and approached her, they were done singing and one of the older kids approached her as well, "Mother Dalia, when is Emillie getting back? She SAID she would help me with my numbers work!", the girl yelled. "I don't know, Cynda. Now please, I have to speak with this gentleman.", "IS IT ABOUT EMILLIE?! IS SHE IN TROUBLE?!", the young girl said so loud, that some of the other children started to gather around. "Please, we need privacy. Cynda, see what you've done?", "We all want her back here, Dalia!", Cynda yelled, with tears coming to her eyes. I didn't want to tell them what I was here to say. I couldn't. I started to feel tears coming to my eyes. I've only cried on this job twice in my whole career. This was a new kind of sad story. I saw Emillie. Spoke with her. Could have even warned her about Awalli and kept her safe. This was worse than the Mccloud case, and I was now secretly cursing The Commander for doing this to me. The look on my face showed, and Dalia turned away from the children, and Cynda, and led me into the manor. We walked into her office and then she looked at me and asked, "What happened?". I told her about the warehouse and how we were briefed about some being coming down and causing burns around the warehouse, and now the thirteen dead, with the inclusion of Emillie. "A being of immense power…", she repeated, "Emillie isn't dead. I believe…", she paused before she said, "…Emillie was that being.". I ran that through my head and couldn't understand. "Please, say that again.", I demanded. "Okay. Emillie must have been that being. She is the only thing that could have caused something like that. You see, there are only two beings in existence that could and since I know they wouldn't be here, Emillie would make sense.". I still didn't understand what she was talking about. How could it have been Emillie? Sure, there was no trace of her left to determine anything. The only proof we had was her necklace, that after running it through the processor, we had determined it did indeed have faint traces of DNA. But that DNA was different from Plinthinian, so we figured it must have been some animal, and didn't try and confirm which. This is why we ended up running the code numbers on the necklace to see who bought it. Dalia was watching me to see how I was going to react once I fully processed what she was telling me, "I'm sorry, Dalia, but I think that is just what you want to believe.", I told her. She bit her bottom lip with her top teeth, then said, "There is something I need to tell you…", she said, and then my cell rang. "Red.", I said, answering. "It's Tillo, mate. You might want to hurry back here. Before you tell Dalia anything.", Tillo said, hanging up. I looked at Dalia, who now looked like she was sure this being was Emillie, but was still sad for some reason. "I have to go.", I said. She nodded and walked to her office door, opened it, and directed me out. "Don't mention this, please? You know, what I just told you. About those two beings.". I wanted to ask how she knows this, but then I thought about it. I wanted to just get away.

On my way back to the precinct, I kept thinking about Emillie. She was so kind and friendly. She was the daughter of The Commander, though, and this made me question some things. Like who exactly is The Commander, and why give her daughter away? Why is Emillie different? Why isn't The Commander around right now, considering that her daughter is possibly dead? I was angry about everything now. I wanted nothing more than to go home and crack open a bottle of spirits. I looked into my mid-compartment of my flar while I was waiting at a traffic stop, and pulled out my secret bottle of spirits I kept in there. I took a quick swig and then continued on my drive. As I reached the precinct, Yellfy was standing outside. "Got a minute, Red?", he asked me nervously. "No. I don't.", I said flatly, pushing past him. I proceeded towards my desk and Tillo was waiting there with Gail. Gail was wearing her smile again. "Mr. Red, we need to talk. Follow me, please.", she said, already leading us away and into a different room. I watched as Walsh watched us angrily. "He's been hovering around, wondering why Raby is still here.", Tillo said to answer the look I was wearing upon seeing Walsh. Once we were in the room where Raby and I first spoke, she sat down and so did we. "So, the first thing I'll say is that Emillie is not dead. She has ascended, apparently. Now I'm sure she will return, but we don't know the full situation with Emillie. You see, the full truth is that her mother is a goddess, but she is what you would consider to be a soft-goddess. She wasn't born of the cosmos, but rather was born through the power of the cosmos. But, Emillie's father...", she said, looking at us now more seriously, "...he is a god born of ancient power. In other words, the reason Emillie isn't like her mother is because she is filled with something known as old essence. Old essence is different from a soul or the regular essence that a god or goddess has. It's something that if extinguished in one vessel, it can be transported to another. If there isn't a vessel to return to, it will linger like a soul unable to move on. Regular essence can do this as well, but it is unpredictable.". I looked at Tillo, who looked just as confused, but at the same time looked happy with something, "I THINK SHE HAS BEEN TRYING TO TALK TO ME!", he said excitedly. "What do you mean, Mr. Tillo?", Gail asked him, now looking as if she had won something. "Well, when I was at the warehouse, I found this ring, and when I picked it up, something spoke to me.", Tillo said, placing a ring on the table. Gail looked at it with clear excitement. "I knew it. Listen, I'm about to send some men to the area to see what they can find.". Tillo and I both looked at each other confused. "Some men? What do you mean?", I asked. "Well, based on what you just told me, Emillie needs a vessel, and also based on what you just said, her essence is stuck in the warehouse. She is probably having a hard time processing what happened. We have men who have been training for something like this for a long time.", she said, taking out her cell, dialing some numbers, and then placing it to her ear, "Yes, it's me. I believe we've found her. No. There is still no sign of that, but I can confirm Awalli's location, and I can also confirm that Emillie is indeed what you thought.". Tillo and I sat and listened to her speak on the cell with who I could only imagine was The Commander. Tillo looked angry for some reason, but then his angry face passed and turned passive. "Well, I'd say lets get to work, but I think you boys are good for right now. Just focus on Awalli and let P.E.D deal with Emillie for now.", Gail said, now getting ready to leave the room. "I'm sure it goes without saying, but allow me to say that this conversation is not to be repeated outside of this room to anyone else. Especially Captain Walsh. We believe he is working against us.", Gail said with a smile, and then turned the knob to leave. I looked at Tillo, who was standing as well but looking angry again. "What's wrong with you?", I asked him. I had only seen Tillo get angry three times in my life. Once, when Yellfy had messed up his report, Tillo was forced to take over his case. The second time was when we were interrogating a nasty murderer who had obviously committed the crime, but was playing stupid with us. I had to stop Tillo from beating the smich. Then, there was the time when Laddies was bombed. He was angry we didn't notice anything and continued to be angry the entire night leading into morning. I couldn't understand what he was angry about now, considering we just learned Emillie was alive. "Nothing to worry about, Red.", he said, leaving the room. I didn't have time to ponder on Tillo, because I was more worried about what Gail said. So, Emillie is a powerful goddess. Her father is an ancient god. Sebastian? That was my first thought, but would Gail say that Sebastian is her father? Did The Commander have a relationship with him? What the hell is the truth? Sebastian wasn't real to me. I never believed in him. I never was forced to go to church when I was younger. I was never much of a fairy tale man, but The Commander said the fairy tales were real. She said that everything that happened in those stories were true. But there were different versions, so which one was the real one. I kept pondering what the hell was the truth. I sat at my computer for hours. Going over old case files. Wondering if there was ever a case I worked where The Commander's hand was involved. I soon found one, and had forgotten with everything that happened that I had heard about P.E.D before. Ten years ago, when Adem Mccloud went missing. Somehow, Adem was gone from the precinct where he was being kept for questions. I remembered leaving him for only a short time, but as soon as I came back, he was gone. I searched the whole station and had five other's helping me, and we still couldn't find him. After checking the cameras, we discovered he had been led out. But on the camera, there was nobody, and Adem just stood up, and then he was gone. To this day, we've never figured out this mystery and it was a huge embarrassment for my precinct. When I made the report, much to my embarrassment, I received a strange message when I tried to file it. The report was being uploaded to a different server. I tried to intercept, but it wouldn't allow me to. Then I got an email from someone calling themselves GENERAL A. It read;

Dear Mr. Red,

I'm writing to inform you that you needn't worry about the report you just uploaded. It is being handled by the proper people. Adem Mccloud will be found. Rest assured.

SINCERELY,
GENERAL A.

As I looked through my files, I came across this email and found myself angry. This was from The Commander. She had been controlling my situation even ten years ago. Thinking back to her, though, how was she telling me these things ten years ago, when she looks like she is in her early twenties? Sure, she looked tough, and definitely didn't seem like someone to piss off. But how was she so young? I remembered something similar with Dalia. All the info I had gathered on her, suggested that she was a lot older than she tried to pass off. I decided to go see her.

When I had arrived back at the orphanage, there was a part of me that wanted to tell her she was right. Emillie WAS that being that caused the warehouse incident. When I knocked on the door, a young matron opened it, "Oh, you must be here for Ms. Dalia. I'll take you to her.", the girl said, allowing me inside and then leading the way to Dalia's office. It was slightly late, so the kids were getting ready for bed. I saw Cynda, who noticed me and quickly approached me, "Hey! You're that GO! Where is Emillie? Is she...dead?", the girl asked. She looked at me with big green eyes that suggested that if I said yes, she would begin to cry. "No. Emillie is not dead. She is alive and well.", "Then why hasn't she been home?", the girl asked me more violently. "Because she is doing something very nice for you children and she wants it to be a surprise.", I said, hoping that she will accept this answer and leave me be. "Cynda, Mr. Red is here to see Mother Dalia. Now, move along, child, and get ready for bed.", the young matron said. Cynda obviously didn't like being told what to do, but she, nonetheless, went back to what she was doing. We reached Dalia's office and the matron knocked. Dalia opened the door, saw me, and then let me in and waved the young woman off. "So, more bad news?", she asked. She had been crying again from the look on her face. I saw ticenta sitting on her desk and was surprised that she didn't seem that drunk, but I could smell the spirit on her breath. "Not exactly. I have some questions. About you.", I said, a bit nervous. I knew she was still hurting. "Okay. What are your questions? I'll answer them honestly.", she said somewhat boredly, and sat down behind her desk, taking a swig of ticenta straight from the bottle. "Well, I once asked you how it is that you have been running this place for seventy years, when you barely look twenty-five, and your response was that this is only a rumor.". Dalia nodded, "I lied to you. I HAVE been running this place for seventy years. I'm a lot older than I seem, Mr. Red. I'm over three-thousand years old...", she said, laughing now. The spirit was affecting her after all. "I thought you said you would be honest?", I asked. "I am. I just told you the truth, I'm over three-thousand. I know. It's hard to believe. Can you believe in all that time, I've never had my own children? Didn't help that I fell in love with a goddess, though, did it?", she said, looking like she was thinking, and taking another swig of ticenta, "I have no descendants. My family all died out and I'm the only one living, while Nigel's family is constantly slapping me in my face. I dated him before I met Amana.", she said, losing herself in her story. I didn't want to interrupt, but it was the fact she mentioned Princess Amana that drove me to, "WHAT?!", I exclaimed, "You were with Princess Amana?

But that's...", "Just a story? Believe me when I say, it is not, just a story. Amana was my hero. Until she went mad. She spent hundreds of years trying to bring back her sister, Calypsa, unsuccessfully. The two of them had a bond I still don't quite understand. It's much different from her sister, and my best friend, Ko-e.". I started to assume she was mad. She was talking utter nonsense. "Perhaps you've had enough to drink?", I said, now standing up, and reaching out to grab the bottle from her hand. As I did, she held it very tightly and I was surprised with her strength. "You don't believe me? After everything that has happened?", she said, as I placed the bottle on one of her drawers and attempted to help her stand. She allowed me. "Where are your quarters? I'll take you.", I said. She led me out of her office and I took her to a nice room that wasn't too far from her office, only three doors down. As we reached her quarters she quickly fell from me and fell onto her bed. "Right, so you're good? I'm going to go home.", I said, turning to leave. "Wait. I'm not lying to you. I was with Amana. She was my lover. I...miss her. Tell her I miss her, next time you talk to her.". Next time? I was pondering on that, "What do you mean, next time?", I felt compelled to ask. "Isn't it obvious who the woman with the red hair is? She has a scar on her face from Queen Micka. I always thought that made her seriously attractive.". I backed away, unable to contain what she was saying. She started to breathe slowly, which suggested she was falling asleep. I sat in a chair not far from her bed and considered what she was saying. Three-thousand years old. The woman who refused to give her name had a scar on her face that looked ancient. She looked so much like Emillie, it was obvious that she is her mother. But now the questions that I had in my head were slowly starting to become answered. Who is The Commander? Why, she is Princess Amana. And who is Dalia? Well, she is a bit harder to explain, considering she was never a part of the fairy tales, unless she had a different name. Then she mentioned Ko-e, and Nigel, and how Nigel's family is slapping her in the face. I realized this was a jab at the RF and it's almost never ending list of family members. Then I lingered back on Ko-e. Then on the fact The Commander would trust Dalia to raise her daughter. I suddenly realized, it all fit. Emillie was a goddess. She was powerful and she isn't dead. Her essence is still in the warehouse, trapped, because it doesn't have a vessel it can flee to. So how do I help her? Gail said P.E.D would take care of it, but I'd only heard of them once. A secret military unit, and Gail is involved. Is Gail a goddess as well? Perhaps another child of Amana? No, that didn't make sense. Emillie isn't her sister, and she doesn't look anything like either of them. Then I remembered Tillo being upset when Amana was mentioned. So, since there wasn't much I could do about Emillie or Awalli, I decided that I was going to focus on what Tillo was upset about. I got up to leave, and then Dalia said something, "Don't go...Amana...please...?", she said in her sleep. I looked at her for a minute, still processing everything Dalia must have been through in all those years. I couldn't conceive of it.

CHAPTER 3

The Sad Story Of Awalli Dat

AWALLI: So much made sense in my life, now that I had finally found one of the objects of Sebastian. For a long time, I had no idea who I was, or where I was really from. For so long I hated myself and my life. At the age of three, I was forced to go live with a woman who isn't even my blood. She is someone that was once married to somebody with my blood. Nonetheless, she adopted me, and treated me like shit. She never raised a hand against me, no, she chose to abuse me with her words, "You'll never be shit, just like your shit-father. You're always going to be just a waste of space.", she would often tell me when she was forcing me to clean her filthy house, or do her disgusting laundry. I was never allowed to have friends. I was never allowed to do anything outside of the house. I was homeschooled. She was such a horrible person to me. When she was supposed to be teaching me, she spent a lot of her time telling me how stupid I was, and how I would never be anything in this world besides that. The first time I tried dating, I was fifteen years old, and that turned into a nightmare. I lost my virginity at this time and ended up carrying. Of course, my evil stepmother forced me to kill my child. Then berated me the rest of the day and night with how right she was about me, and calling me a little whore. "And to think, you actually believed I was going to raise another waste of space.". I grew into her evil ways and learned to stay on her good side, which really, she didn't have one. As life went on for me, I saw an opportunity to change my life.

It all started with Layna. I had always been interested in the RF. Even wished I was one of them. Who wouldn't wish to be rich and to be far away from a woman who does nothing but talk down to you? If I was with the RF, I would make HER clean everything, and also, lick the bottom of my shoes. Lida was my stepmother, and all she ever did with her life was drink. I never knew what her story was, only that she was with my father, and he was some kind of big deal. When people who knew my father talk to me, they treat me like I've got some disease that they don't want to catch. I didn't understand any of it, until I met Layna. I was only eighteen, and Layna was five years older. I had got a pretty decent job and was enjoying my life. I had grown up in Nocton and was very satisfied with the way things were. I no longer was living with Lida, and had moved in with my boyfriend of the time. He was a jerk, but I was just fine with him. He was mostly rude, and didn't always see eye to eye with me, but other than that, I didn't live with Lida anymore, and hadn't spoken to her in a year. I had brought my own flar, and even had found myself a nice little dog. Something about being a pet owner made me feel really good. My dog's name was Sparkz. I loved calling him to me because he would run towards me in a very humorous way. He had the littlest legs, and was covered in white fur, and black spots. He had a very soft and cute bark, and I just adored him. My boyfriend, who also liked dogs, often took him for rides in his flar while I was at work. It was one of the major things I loved about Tic. Tic was a simple guy. He worked in a diner not far from our home, and I worked in a manufacturing plant that produced components for pretty much everything. I was one of the engineers. Even though I was homeschooled, it was obvious that I was very smart. When I first looked into engineering, it wasn't something I really saw myself doing, but it grew on me quickly, and I often welded things for fun. Layna was actually the boss of this place. She was hardly seen on site, but when she was, it usually was because we were seriously behind. I was one of the reasons we always were able to catch up and hit our deadlines. Most of the time when Layna showed up, I would never meet her face to face. It was usually this big meeting where the whole damn plant turns up to listen to Layna threaten us if we didn't hit our marks. But since we usually did and I was usually the reason, the one little nudge we needed, it was only a matter of time before Layna came and met with me.

One day, as I was going for lunch and pondering on going home to see Sparkz, one of my coworkers came up to me, "Layna is here.", they said. "But, she was just here last week, and we already caught up! What is she doing here again?", I asked surprised. "I don't know, Awalli, but if I were you, I'd start getting ready for that promotion.". I knew it would happen sooner or later. I was doing really well with the company, which is called Rain's Tech, and I figured I'd be getting a promotion soon. Rain's Tech was a global company and was spread throughout even some of the non-contracted cities. It originally started in South Edge and even though the RF have business ties, it was owned by a man named Jonathan Raine. I smiled and Tedi walked away. Tedi was a good guy. He was into men, though, so I never worried about him hitting on me. The same couldn't be said for the other men, who I constantly had to remind that I had a boyfriend. Layna was walking towards me, and I looked around at everyone else who was watching her. Layna hadn't been crowned Head of the Family yet, she was still just a normal princess. As normal as a princess can be I suppose. There was always a part of me that worshipped her, considering she was rich, had a great life, and more than that, she was loved and adored by not just Nocton, but all the other contracted cities. "Awalli Dat? We need to talk.", she said, not even shaking my hand or anything. She led me to an office, and before I walked in after her, I looked back, and Tedi was giving me a thumbs up. "Please, close the door.", Layna said. I did. "Have a seat, please?", she asked me. I was wondering why she was acting so glum. The likelihood that I would be terminated was very low, yet, Layna was talking to me like somebody died. "So, do you have any idea at all why I've called you in here?", she asked. I shook my head. "Well, I'll be straight with you. Some of my family that is involved with this company know all about you, and how you have done a really good job keeping this place going.". Since she was being so glum, I gave her a small smile, which she did not return. "Awalli, I'm sorry to say that we are letting you go.", she said without emotion. I was stunned and didn't say anything right away. "But...I don't understand, I've always been good here! Why are you doing this to me?!", I asked in shock. "It's not really your fault. It's something out of your or my power. If it were up to me, I'd keep you. Obviously you have done really good here like you say but...", she paused, "...there are some things it is just best to walk away from. This way, you avoid the trouble that follows.", she said in a wisdomly sort of way. "I DON'T CARE ABOUT ANY OF THAT! WHY ARE YOU FIRING ME?!", I demanded. I felt my blood rising. "I'm not allowed to say.", Layna said, now sitting back in the chair with her arms crossed. "THIS ISN'T RIGHT! IT'S NOT FAIR!", I continued yelling. I imagined my coworkers probably heard me and were listening hard now. "Please don't make this any harder. If I had the permission to tell you why my family has chosen to let you go, then I would tell you. But from what I understand, it is a very sensitive matter within the family, and I'm not supposed to tell you the reasons. Now this can go two ways. The first, I will help you find another job. The second, you walk out of here and probably end up blacklisted. It's up to you.", "Why would they blacklist me?", I asked, no longer caring about how I sounded. "Again, I don't know. I was asked to come here and terminate you immediately. So what is it going to be?", she said, now looking me in my eyes more intensely. "It must be so easy for you. To be the PRINCESS. You don't have to worry about being fired, or blacklisted!", I yelled at her. "Actually, I deal with worse. Now, option one, or two?", she said. I didn't even answer, I just turned and walked out of the office. I went to my desk and started to grab things. I got a box that was next to my desk and started to pack. Tedi walked up looking excited, "So...what did she say? Are you the new...?", he stopped talking when he noticed I was crying. "Oh...", he said with a confused look, "But, you're the best engineer here! Why would they do this to you?", he asked, also becoming angry. "Just forget it, Tedi.", I said, unable to look at him. A lot of my coworkers didn't like me very much and saw me being fired as a great thing. I couldn't even face them on my way out of the building.

I got home and Sparkz ran up to me. I quickly picked him up, and he was licking my face, which still had tears. "Hey, babe, that you? I'm in the living room.", Tic said, as I made my way into the apartment. Tic seen I was crying, "What's happened?", he asked, looking concerned. "I was fired today.", "WHAT?! But why? That doesn't make any sense! You told me you were up for a promotion soon!", Tic said, looking just as shocked as Tedi. "Princess Layna spoke to me directly. She told me it had something to do with the family.", "The Royal Family? They requested your termination? But I don't understand. What the hell do they have against you?", "I don't know.", I said, placing Sparkz down, falling onto the couch, and covering my face. Sparkz jumped onto my lap and whined into my stomach. "Babe, there has to be more to this. Why would they just fire you? You were the one that kept that place going. Let's see how long they last without you.". I looked up and smiled at Tic. "I love you.", I said. Tic responded by kneeling and taking my hand and kissing it, "I'm sorry this happened to you, babe. I'm so sorry.". Tic and I had fallen into bed and I had forgotten about my troubles for a bit. But they came back in horrible fashion.

I had gotten out of bed. It wasn't exactly late, but it was getting there. Sparkz was asleep in the corner. I covered myself and went into the kitchen. I got out my PC(portable computer) and started to look for a new job. I realized I really had no choice now. As I was looking, an email appeared from an address I didn't recognize. The address said SECRETSOLDIER@L.COM. I had never seen this address and was curious what it was. I opened it, and it said;

Dear Awalli Dat,

I know that you are angry about the unfairness the RF have thrown at you and are probably confused as to why they would do this. Well, what if I told you that you are a part of the royal bloodline? Please respond quickly if you want justice.

Secretsoldier

I looked at the email again and again. I couldn't understand. How was I even remotely connected to the RF, besides the unlawful firing, which I did intend to sue over. There were GP's(guard protectors) that handled situations exactly like this. I looked it over some more before finally deciding to ignore it. It was probably a false email and I didn't want to get too into it. I continued looking for a job, then, there was a knock at the door. I looked at the time and it was nine-thirty. I went to look and see who was here and was surprised to find Layna outside my home. She was wearing a cloak and was obviously trying to conceal herself. Even though I was still angry, I let her inside, and she quickly pushed me back, and closed the door, "Okay, listen, I don't have much time, but I've come to tell you the truth.", she said sort of fast. "I don't care. I'm already looking…", she held her hand up for me to stop talking. "We are cousins. We are related. Okay? But your grandfather was removed from the family after being caught up in a scandal. I sent you that email. Okay?". Now I was even more confused, "My grandfather? Who was my grandfather?", I asked, realizing I had never heard of him, ever. My father, Gerard Dat, was someone who was both respected and hated. So I knew a little about him, but he died in an accident with my biological mother, with whom he was having an affair. This much I knew. But what I didn't know is where I was born or anything like that because Lida chose not to tell me. Lida was my father's wife and obviously didn't like me at all because I was the daughter of her husband's mistress. Layna looked like she was hurting over the situation. "Your grandfather was Tiggy Dat. A man who not only shamed our family by preparing and distributing drugs, but also was a child molestor. Once all this got out, he was taken to trial and was found guilty. This wasn't enough, so his brother, Lo Dat, hired an assassin and had him killed. He was written out of the family and anyone sharing his lineage. Meaning your father and yourself. When my family saw your name and looked into your past, they discovered you were Tiggy's granddaughter, and for that reason, and that reason alone, they fired you from Rain's Tech.". I didn't know what to think. A minute ago, I thought someone was just messing with me. Now all of a sudden, I was lost. I looked back on my PC to check and see if the email was still there and was surprised to find it was gone. I looked back at Layna, who was looking antsy now. I couldn't help but take in her beauty. She had gorgeous bone structure, and long flowing blonde hair that she let fall when she came in. But mostly, I noticed her eyes. All the RF have certain eyeliner they wear around their eyes. Layna's color was white on top and pink on bottom. Her eyes were a lovely light purple color that matched her eyeliner. Now that I thought about it, it made sense why she was antsy. Her whole get-up was extremely obvious. "Okay...let's say, I believe you. What now? I just become a princess? Like you?", I asked her. "This is not a game. Do you honestly think I enjoyed walking into that damn office, and FIRING my own DAMN COUSIN?! Because I can tell you, no I didn't. It pissed me off. More than you can imagine.". I didn't know what to say. I was touched, but remembered, Tic was sleeping. Just then, Sparkz came out barking. Layna looked at Sparkz and for the smallest second made a face. But then she looked back at me seriously again. "You are on the board now. They will do everything to bring you down. They will come after you. I've come here to take you out of this house before they come here.". I was panicking. None of this was making any sense. Just a few hours ago, I was having grief sex with my boyfriend, now I'm being told I'm a princess, and that I have to leave my home. "No. I live here. I'll call the Royal Force! They can't just come in here and kill me!", I yelled, beginning to lose all train of thought. At this point, Tic walked into the room, scratching his head, "Babe, who are you...?", he stopped speaking when he saw Princess Layna in our home, "Princess? What are you doing here? Come to apologize to my girlfriend I hope.", "I've come to save your damn lives! Listen to me. The family is filled with snakes. They will come at you hard. They don't want this Tiggy shit dragged back up, and are willing to do whatever it takes to make sure it doesn't come back.". I looked at Tic, who looked like he swallowed a bone. "Let me get...", "We have wasted enough time, get your...", she stopped talking because we all heard it. The first round hit Tic. He fell hard to the floor, like a marionette whose strings were cut. I watched him, unable to believe what I just saw. Then, Layna forced me down. "We need to get out. Is there another exit?", she asked me, but I was still too in shock, then I looked and saw Sparkz going to Tic's body, and I just stopped thinking, and rushed to him, yelling his name as I did, "SPARKZ, COME!", I yelled, and right when I did, another round went off, and Layna somehow moved me out of the way, instinctively, and then the round narrowly missed my leg but hit Sparkz, who made a sad squeal. "NO! No…", I couldn't think, but Layna somehow was able to get us out the door and down the stairs of the apartment Tic and I lived in. She shoved me into a nearby vehicle and then jumped in and started driving. "There is a place you'll be safe. I'll have to take you all the way there. Now. There's no coming back to Nocton. Do you understand? It's not safe for you here!", she yelled at me. I managed to say, "What about you?", "I'm the PRINCESS. I'm too high profile, and way too connected for them to kill me. They shouldn't be coming after us now. I'm sorry. I'm so sorry about your boyfriend. And especially, your cute dog.", she said, with all the sadness she was able to put into her words. I was lost. I didn't know when I passed out, but that's when the dream came.

"All seems bad, Awalli Dat, but trust me. You are destined for greatness. Your father almost made it. But where Gerard failed, you will succeed. You will succeed. YOU WILL SUCCEED!". I woke up with a pain in my chest I couldn't explain. I looked around, and there was nothing around me but what seemed to be metal walls. Then I realized I was in the flar that Princess Layna shoved me in. Princess Layna. Princess Layna saved my life last night. And told me that we are related. It would almost be a dream come true, if I didn't lose Tic, and my little Sparkz. I began to cry, and Layna looked back, "You're awake? Good morning.", she said brightly. "What's good about it?", I asked grumpily. "Listen, I know how you feel. I've lost people, too. Loved ones that should be here right now. Sparkz and Tic should be here. But THIS is what the RF is. This is what I'm trying to stop.". I suddenly realized that one thing they say is true; Be careful what you wish for. As the drive continued in long moments of silence, excluding the times when Layna would whistle a tune, I just continued to think about Tic and Sparkz. Poor Sparkz. He didn't even know what the hell was going on. I began crying again. I felt the flar stop. Layna was looking at me, "Get out of the flar.", she said. I listened to her. And she walked around and hugged me. "This is what we should have been doing when we met. It's okay. Cry. Cry on me.", she said. And I did. I cried for a long time. That's when a woman approached us. "Thanks for meeting us, Amana. I know this is really out of line, but they killed her dog. It was so cute.", Layna said to the woman. "Who is this, Layna?", I asked. The woman looked completely menacing, and definitely like somebody who could care less that they killed my dog. Yet she didn't look angry with Layna, more just amused, "Layna, I always told you that this was going to be hard, but you handled it well. And you've driven her far enough that if the family set foot here, they'd be starting a war. Good girl. But you still got a long drive to get to South Edge.", "South Edge? There? Why there? That's where Tiggy was from.", Layna said, becoming angry with the woman. "Well, how about we explain in full what's going on, Layna?", she then turned to me, "I am General Amana Tia. It's nice to meet you, Awalli. I've had my eyes on you for a long, long time. And the one thing I'm interested in knowing right now, is have you felt different since coming into contact with your cousin here?", Amana asked me, looking at me hard. "I don't know what you mean.", "Layna, tell her about yourself. Your true self.", she added, as Layna looked confused. "Please, don't make me show her this.", Layna said desperately. Amana just gave her a hard look, and then before my very eyes, Layna started to turn blue. "Layna, how...?", I said, stunned by what I was seeing. I didn't know Layna could do something like this. "Listen to me. I hate this. But this is something that runs in our family. You, all of us, are descendants of Nigel and Mileeda. Mileeda was different. She was experimented on, and transformed into a synthetic goddess. She is still alive. But she is hidden well. Whatever the case, it runs in your blood, too. And Amana, is curious to know if you are like me, because if you are, it means that you will have a seat at the RT(Royal Table).", Layna finished saying and I couldn't think of what to say. I looked at the woman calling herself Amana. Then I thought about it some more, then came to the realization that she was THE Amana. "How am I supposed to just handle all of this? Do you two understand what I've lost?", I asked them both. "Yes, I know for a fact. You know what I've lost.", said Amana. "You killed your sister in the story. You didn't lose her.", I said. She became angry, "I'm going to ignore that little sleight, because I know you are grieving, but I would advise you not to disrespect me like that again. I'm not someone to play with, Awalli. Layna here learned from a very young age the depths her family will go to bury secrets. So when I tell you that you will be watching your back the rest of your life, I'm not kidding you.". I swallowed. "Now listen, you're going to South Edge because you will be safe there. It is indeed the place I busted your grandfather, but it is also a place of great opportunity for one such as yourself. You're a smart girl, and I know a place you can work that the RF isn't connected and you'll make more. Will it bring back what you've lost? No. But, what is the other option? Think about that.", Amana finished saying. I had to admit. She was right. There was no going back to Nocton, and there was literally nothing else I could do but take her offer. I looked at Layna, who smiled and nodded. "Okay. Let's go.".

As me and Layna were leaving, Amana came up to my window, "Listen to me, Awalli, if you ever start to feel different in any way, you call me.", she said, handing me a card. I nodded and she turned and went back to her flar, which was strange indeed. As soon as she entered it, it disappeared. I remember thinking then, Amana was so cool. I just wanted to be like her and Layna. On the drive, Layna explained to me how she saved me. She is quite skilled at depth perception. She can predict where cannon fire might hit, or even predict your next move, or what you might do in a situation based on your motives in the past. "I'm usually about ninety-eight percent correct. Been doing it since I was five. When the family discovered I inherited the gift, they quickly turned into wolves.", she explained. "When is the last time that someone else had the gift?", I asked. "That was some time ago. Amana raised me a good majority of my life. I came back into the fold...", "I KNOW THAT PART! I uh... mean to say, six years ago, right?", I felt embarrassed. "People think the RF are about luxury and fame. Thrones and crowns. No. All I've ever done is try and survive in the city. You didn't deserve this.", Layna said, becoming angry again. Her cell rang and she answered, "Yes. Tor, slow down! What do you mean, when am I coming back?! You know where I've...oh, right. I didn't tell you what she said.". I wondered who she was talking to. She just quickly explained that we were headed to South Edge, then got off the cell, "Sorry about that. He's a friend.". I got the feeling he may be more, and this made me think of Tic. I began crying. Again.

The next few weeks passed by quickly. It seemed almost like a blur now. I slowly started to enjoy my happy little road trip with the Princess, now turned my cousin, Layna. It was interesting learning about the family and how Tiggy left Nocton to pursue his perversions. This way, he could hide it from the family. I was disgusted. But even more, I felt the same as the people trying to kill me. But, Layna explained that there was more to it than that. They feared I'd learn who I really was one day. Feared that I would come for a seat at the table. They had seen my bloodwork, and they knew I was like Layna. But I didn't feel any different. I kept trying to see if I could turn blue, but no. Nothing. I tried to see if maybe I had psychic powers. But I didn't. The only thing that did seem to be happening was that I was having strange dreams. Sometimes, they were dreams of Tic and Sparkz. We'd all be watching a film together. Or be at the park playing. Or just riding in the flar, while Sparkz sat on my lap, and put his head out the window. They were all happy moments and I usually woke up crying from these dreams. But then, there were the other dreams. The ones where it was nothing but darkness. And a voice just kept chanting the words, "You will succeed.", over, and over, and over again. I hated these dreams because I would have chest pains. We were passing through Bronxton, and Layna decided we should stop for breakfast. I just had another of those dark nothingness dreams and my chest was on fire. Then I thought I was going crazy, because I could hear faint whispers all around me. "I said, do you want to eat here?", Layna asked me, putting on a Tulsa and wiping her face with some kind of skin modifier. "Yeah, sure.", I managed to say. "Are you okay? You've been acting strange.", she said with concern. "I haven't been okay since we left Nocton. Let's just go eat.", I said, and tried to put a smile on my face. She got out of the flar, and we went into the eating establishment called Tollo's. I sat down quickly in a booth. My chest pain was dying down now and I was starting to feel better. "What can I get, you two? Would you like to start with some water?", the waitress asked, looking at me. "Water sounds good. For both of us, please. And does this place have stone cakes?", Layna asked. "Yes, mam, we do.", "Then we will take two orders of… How many do you want?", Layna asked me. "Ten.", "I'll take four, she'll take ten.", said Layna, and the waitress nodded. "I'll be back with those waters.". We sat in the booth for a while, then, Layna asked me, "Tell me the truth, Awalli. What's wrong with you?", she said politely, "I know you have been hurting, anyone would. But you've had plenty of grieving time. This is different. You've been clutching your chest. As if you're experiencing pain. What is going on?". I explained about my dreams. "We have another ancestor we don't speak of. But I suppose I should tell you. Mileeda had a younger sister. She, too, became something else. She is beyond us, that's what I was taught.

But at the same time, I don't know, I just used to think it was a way to scare us. Tell us she could hurt us, or kill us, and yes, we were terrified. But then I heard the truth when I was twelve. She will kill everyone. So, she is locked away. Sealed in something called The Void. And hopefully, she can never escape.", "Yes, but what is her name?", I asked. "I don't dare speak it, Cousin. It's too dangerous. Too risky.", "But you said it's just a child's scare tactic.", I said mockingly. "Once again, you're thinking I'm kidding. I'm not. When I was a little girl, I, too, had nightmares. You have to ignore them. Ah, foods here.", she said, now happily taking her stone cakes and putting butter and syrup on them. I decided to drop it and grieve-eat.

"Wake up, Awalli.", a voice was saying. It didn't sound at all like Layna. I opened my eyes, and Tic was sitting before me. I looked around and we were at Rain's Tech, in the office Layna had fired me in. "Why are we here, Tic?", I asked, confused by this whole scene. "Because we need to discuss HOW you will succeed.", "No, I want to wake up. Leave me alone!", I yelled. "Awalli, you don't get it, you are the pinnacle of modern science. A goddess. Born of the ancient line of Falsa. Yes, Mileeda was a creation of Trinity, just like the other goddesses. Now you have inherited this through genetics! Do you not see the wonder?", asked Tic. In a voice so unlike his, I felt compelled to ask, "Who are you, really?", "I am the one who will help you get your vengeance. Not just for the things you've lost recently, but for everything you've suffered. Even Lida.", said Tic, with a nasty smile. "You're that ancestor! The one Layna was warning me about! Show yourself!", I yelled. Then, Tic disappeared, and was now replaced by a woman with red hair, and a face so beautiful, she put Layna to shame. "You must find this girl. This girl will end you. She will stop you. You must kill her. KILL EMILLIE!", the girl yelled, and I woke up.

When I awoke, I could tell we were coming up on South Edge. The city was huge. It was one of the non-contracted cities, and that meant it was a bit lawless, but had its own army, and according to Layna, that meant I was safe. As we started to drive through the city, she took me to a warehouse. The warehouse looked sort of run down. I looked to see where we were and we were on Ned St., and for some reason, I felt this energy flowing through me. As if this spot was the center for something powerful. "Well, this is it. Your home-sweet-home.", Layna said, turning the knob on the door and allowing me in. I looked around and was shocked to find it didn't look anything like what it looked like outside. There was furniture, nice furniture at that. Antique tables and multiple televisions. I looked around even more, and noticed there was an upstairs, but when we were outside, it didn't look like it. The science was off here. Layna noticed my confused face and explained to me what was happening, "It's magic. I know, it's hard to accept at first, but you get used to it.", she said, amused by my confusion. "Magic?", I questioned. "Amana taught it to me. I made this place. It's sort of a getaway spot if needed, which, well, is needed.". I walked throughout the house trying to get used to everything. The upstairs was definitely the most confusing part. It was huge, and yet from the outside, none of this would appear to be here. "It's magnificent.", I said, finally coming back to Layna, who smiled. "So, I have to go. But I'll be sending you the info about your new job. In the meantime, I'll make sure you have shills to get around.", she said, holding out her hand. I gave her my electronic shill collector and she went ahead and put a whole lot of shills in there. Enough that if I had this many shills a few weeks ago, I would have quit Rain's Tech before I was fired. I looked at Layna, who wore a smile, "Chin up, Cousin, things are going to get better from here. Better, but remember to be very watchful.", she said, then hugged me again. Then she turned to leave. Leaving me with a lot of money, and a whole lot of sorrow.

A few weeks later, I was working at a new company, Taser, which did the same thing that Rain's Tech did, except it had more contracts, which meant more work. Amana was true to her word; There was no connection to the RF here and even better, in my interview, it was determined I should have a higher position here. I was made into Chief Engineer of Logistics. I enjoyed this job even more than my last. I wasn't allowed to have contact with anybody in Nocton, so I didn't brag to anybody. I focused so much on my new job, that nothing else seemed to bother me at all. I wasn't over what happened to Tic and Sparkz, but I had found it easier to move on. Layna never calls to check up on me, and neither does Amana, which meant that I was totally on my own now. I kept thinking about the fact that I was part of the RF, and that I shouldn't be forced to live like I wasn't. But I remembered they were trying to kill me, and I slowly started to think that I would very much like to kill them.

Two and a half years later, and I was still in the same position, but was highly respected in the company. I had even met a new man, Li, and had been casually dating him. We hadn't done anything yet, due to the fact I wasn't over what happened to Tic, but Li was patient. Too patient, I sometimes thought. I remembered Amana telling me I'd be watching my back my whole life, but it didn't feel like it. Two years ago, I was forced to leave Nocton, and since then, I haven't heard anything from anybody. I was starting to get back to normal, or as normal as I could get. But then I learned the truth about Li. Li wasn't just some guy I met by chance. He was the grandson of the man who my grandfather was at war with, Eddie Folto. Li knew who I was, and had sought me out for multiple reasons. How did he know I was in the city? The warehouse I'd been staying in belonged to my grandfather, and hadn't been used in over fifty years. It was apparently his hidey hole from his family. But Li had been watching the place for years and saw me and Layna heading in. He continued to watch for a couple of years before he decided to approach me. Now he wanted revenge, but not against me. He figured that I could help him get to the RF. "Li, I'm sorry, but I can't help you. I'm hiding from them myself. They want to kill me.", I told him. "But it said you would help me. It told me to find you.", Li said, confused. "What the hell are you talking about?", I asked. "I've been having weird dreams. Something in my dream told me to find you. It said you would help me discover my purpose. I didn't even know what that meant. Then I saw you!", he said. I looked at him, then remembered my dreams. The voice that had spoken to me. The one that had taken the form of Tic, and then that strange girl. "Listen, forget that voice. I don't listen to it, and neither should you.", I said, now waving him away. He grabbed me, and when he did, I yanked my arm away, and he flipped, and fell onto his back. I hadn't even been trying to do that. How did I? Li looked just as confused. "Now I understand. You're different.", he said. "Go away. Never come back here!", I yelled, getting worked up. Li stood up and turned to leave, then turned back, "You can't ignore what is right in front of you.". He left and closed the door. I sat for some time, trying to figure out how the voice would be talking to him. He wasn't like me or Layna, so why and how was it talking to him?

One day, while I was out doing my shopping, I came across a trio of girls. One had brown hair that touched her shoulders and had a loud but raspy voice. The other one had light yellow hair and was smiling between the other two. I lingered on the other one who was with them. She had red hair, and looked vaguely familiar. "Hello, excuse us!", the red-headed girl yelled at me. "Emillie…", I said under my breath, still watching her walk away. She looked back at me as well and I quickly turned away. That was Emillie, I said to myself. That was the girl the voice told me to kill. I went home that night, pondering everything. I had even done some research. Emillie grew up in an orphanage on the other side of town, in North Edge.

It was a very nice orphanage, run by a woman named Dalia. Dalia was very young looking. We looked like we could be the same age, yet the people who I spoke with about her, claimed she had been running that orphanage for a long time. Almost longer than twenty years, which I found impossible. Then I remembered what I had learned. I'm a princess. I'm someone who, if I so wanted, could request a seat at the Royal Table, and make big decisions, and be rich, and drive a nicer flar, and live in something nicer. Of course there was nothing wrong with the warehouse, aside from the fact that my grandfather used to operate out of here. I kept trying to understand how Emillie could possibly be connected to me. The voice said she would end me. What did that even mean? It wasn't like I was going after her.

That night, I had another one of those dreams. It had been two years since I'd had one, but this dream was different. I was wearing a suit with stripes, and Li was here, with a mohawk. I saw a ring that was sitting on a table. Almost like it was some kind of trophy. Then I saw a light so bright, I thought I was dead, but when the light faded, it was Emillie. She picked up the ring and put it on. She started to walk towards me, and Li was frozen. Not moving at all. Not blinking, or breathing. He was just there. "I'm going to kill you, Awalli. I will stop you.", said Emillie. "But, why? What have I done to you?!", I yelled back at her. "It isn't what you have done, but what you will do.", she said, pointing her finger in the corner. I saw a man with faded tan hair and he was signing off on something. He handed the paper to a man, who I noticed had glowing red eyes. "That man...killed Gerard Dat and his mistress.", Emillie said. I looked at the man again. This time, I was in a flar in the backseat. Emillie was with me. She pointed and I could literally see a cannon shell coming. It hit the flar, and caught my father in his neck. The flar spun out and I panicked. But then I was alive and my father was dying. I went to place my hand on his face and my mother grabbed me. I tried to scream, but couldn't, "AVENGE ME!", she yelled.

I woke up with a pounding headache and my chest on fire. I rushed to my kitchen and poured some water. I quickly downed it, but my chest was still on fire. I started to pour more, when my chest began to burn more intensely. I fell to the floor of the kitchen, clutching my chest. I wanted to call for help, but was in too much pain. I rolled around on the floor, spazzing out, all the way until morning. I was still on the kitchen floor when I woke up. I slowly got up, holding onto the counter. I was so angry with the events of last night, I decided to call Amana, who didn't even answer. I called again, and there was no answer, just a ringing tone for a long time. I threw the receiver, angrily. Then, there was a knock on the door. I went to open it and found a strange woman there. She had black hair that was down past her shoulders, and she wore a kind smile, "Ms. Dat, it's nice to meet you. My name is Gail Raby. I'm here to ensure that everything is okay. Amana has sent me.", she added, looking at my confusion. "Why didn't Amana come herself?", I asked irritatedly. "She is quite busy at the moment dealing with another situation and asked me to check on you. Is everything okay?", she asked me, looking very concerned. "I don't know.", I answered. "Well, do you feel different? You've been living here for two… Oh, do you mind if I step inside?", she asked me in a friendly tone. "Sure.", I said, stepping aside, and allowing her in. She looked around, "Layna is very talented. It's hard to believe she designed this place. It really is a good and interesting bit of magic.", Raby said, making her way around. "Um, have you forgotten me?", I asked. She looked back at me, "Oh, I'm so sorry. Magic just always amazes me. So, what has happened?". I didn't know if I should tell her, so I just started from the beginning. Telling her about my dreams. "Okay. Now, how do you feel? Is your chest hurting?", she asked, and I nodded, "A lot. It burned all night.", "Oh dear…", she said in an almost frightened manner. She took out a pad and started to write on it. "And how often have you felt these chest pains and is it only in your chest?", she asked me, almost like a nurse analyzing a patient. "I haven't felt this pain in two years.", I replied, wondering how this is helping me. She looked up, "You mean you felt this pain when you came into contact with Layna?", she asked me. I hadn't thought about it, but now that she mentioned it... "Yes, actually. That is when it started.", "Have you had any strange dreams? Voices speaking to you that shouldn't be?", she now asked me in a serious tone. "Yes.", I said. "Then I'm afraid you will need to come with me. It's too dangerous to leave you on your own now.", she said and I agreed. "Where are you going to take me?", I asked her, not wanting to leave my new job. "I'll be taking you to a different safe house. Just for a few days while we sort out your issues.", "And how will YOU sort out MY issues?", I asked, becoming angry, but I didn't know why. "Well not me directly, but we have people who are trained for this.", she said. I didn't know how I felt going to a bunch of strangers and letting them check me out. "Are you sure this is necessary? Can't I just stay here and they can come check me out?", I asked in a hopeful tone. "No. You will need to come to the site. You see, let me try and explain; You are being contacted by a very dangerous entity that is trying to use you for its own purposes. You must come with me to detox or else it will start to consume your mind to the point where you believe it is right.". I stood shocked. "Is it my ancestor?", I asked, now getting a better understanding, and remembering Layna's words in Tollo's almost three years ago. Raby said nothing, but nodded and directed me to go outside. "Shouldn't I pack or something?", I asked, shocked at how crazy this all sounded. "No. That won't be necessary. We have clothing for you. Just, please come with me.", she said, with that same smile on her face. "Okay.".

We had arrived at a location not too far from Dalia's orphanage. Even before we set foot out of the flar, I felt the pain rising in my chest. Something immediately told me, it had something to do with Emillie being nearby. If this was the case, then this place couldn't possibly help me. Raby led me inside of a building that seemed to be three stories high, and almost looked similar to a hospital. But once we were inside, it wasn't a hospital, but some kind of military operation. There were contracts that Taser had with the Edgian Military and I often would visit those sites to show what we were offering or trying to sell. But this was one I'd never been to, or even heard of. I looked all around me, and there were men and women either training, working out, or just plain old looking over paperwork. There were men and women sitting at computers, and there was some kind of service going on because they seemed to be responding to calls. As we reached a door, with a nice knob that had been welded into the shape of a letter P, Raby opened the door and led me inside. Inside, I was shocked to find Li in here. "What is he doing here?", I asked. "He is here because he, too, has been experiencing bad dreams. Just please, can the two of you wait here?". Raby smiled at us, then left the room. I looked nervously at Li, who just smiled, and waved his fingers at me. "How did you get here?", I asked him, thinking about how the hell he got involved with this place, and Raby. "I was at home one night and that woman showed up at my house. Told me she knew all about me and what I was experiencing. Then she brought me here. I've been here for two days.", he said, almost too happily for my liking. "Why are you so jolly?", I asked him. "Don't you get it? This is where we are supposed to be. As soon as I saw you walk through that door, I knew it was right about us. We are going to get revenge.". I backed into a corner, "I don't want to hear anything else. I'm here to get rid of the dreams. To get rid of IT.", I said schathingly. "You think you just can? You don't know what you're talking about. It's been guiding you this whole time. How do you think you got here? You seriously think that?", he asked me, now standing up. "Sit down.", I said, and he did. Just then, the door opened and it wasn't Raby that entered, but a rather fierce looking man. "Okay,

I'm Captain Brom. It's time we discussed what is going to happen to you two.", he said in a very mean tone. "Where is Raby? Where is Am…", "We don't say The General's name, unless we have to.", he said, giving a nod towards Li. "The two of you are being moved to one of our holding facilities. There you will be cleansed.", he said, looking at the both of us. "Wait, what does that mean? How are we going to be cleansed? I want to see Ama…", "WHAT DID I JUST SAY?!", he yelled at me. Li looked like he wanted to stand up and defend me, but didn't. "I'm sorry. I just don't understand what that means.", I said, trying to sound like I didn't mean anything. "There is no other way to put this, so I'll let you know. Cleansed, means you will be terminated. Sorry to have to tell you this, but you're both too dangerous. It's better to sacrifice yourselves.", he said, now turning to walk out the door. "WAIT! I HAVE A JOB! AND I HAVE…", "I'm sorry…", he said, cutting me off, "…but this is how it must be. It must be like this. You have to understand. You're putting the whole planet in danger just by being alive.", he said, and then left the room. My head was spinning, but Li looked like he didn't care. "They are going to kill us…", I said under my breath. "They won't get the chance to.", Li said, still in that jolly tone. "YOU HEARD WHAT HE SAID!", I yelled. "Yes, I heard, but I have faith in you. The voice told me to, and it hasn't been wrong yet.". I was seriously beginning to feel angry. I didn't realize, but I was digging my fingers into the wall and it was actually crumbling in my fingers. I looked at the wall, and suddenly realized what I had to do. I walked to where Li was sitting, and began punching the wall. It cracked, and my fist print was on the wall. I looked shocked at my fist, and then began to punch like crazy. As I did, Li just stood by with a big, happy, smile on his face. Finally, there was a hole. We were on the second floor, but it wasn't much of a jump down. I jumped first and landed cat-like. Li landed hard and on his side. "Come, on, get up.", I said, helping him up. "We have to get out of here! Quick!", I yelled, looking around. "Follow me, boss!", Li said, and he led me to an old model flar that just happened to be nearby. "Left this here before they arrested me and brought me here! Doesn't need a key.", he said, directing me to get in. As I did, he started the flar and we took off. I could see in the rearview, people starting to look out of the hole I made. "So, where are we headed, boss?", asked Li, once we had been riding for a few minutes. I didn't even answer. I was too busy thinking about the betrayal. Raby just left me at the mercy of Captain Brom, who told me I had to die. Where was Layna or Amana? Why weren't they there to tell him how much I already lost? Why did they just leave me? I began to cry in front of Li, who looked embarrassed. "You shouldn't be crying, boss. You just beat them!", he told me. "You don't understand, Li. I was doing really good. I had a good job I can probably never go back to. I had a nice home. Two years later, I'm told I have to die.", I said, now feeling the tears even more. Li just kept driving.

We arrived on the other side of Edge, which is the south. South Edge. Where I had been living. We drove past my warehouse, and there were soldiers outside of it and inside of it. "Don't worry, boss, you can come to my place. My place is your place.", Li said. "Stop calling me 'boss.'", I retorted. "But, you are the boss. Look, you'll see what I mean when we get to my place.", he said, now turning down a strange road, with nothing but buildings on either side, and people who looked lac'd out. Lac'd out being a term to describe people on lilac. Li finally stopped the flar and got out and ran to hurry and open my door. I got out and he led me into a filthy run down mansion. As I stepped in, there was a lot of ancient looking furniture, but finely decorated. It was still dusty, though. I looked around and saw a huge picture. "Is that your grandfather?", I asked Li. "My great-grandfather. But anyway, let me introduce you to the guys.", he said, leading me to another room, where three guys were sitting around a table discussing. "Guys. She's here. Tiggy's granddaughter.".

The three men looked up at me. "This is Tiggy's granddaughter? So now what? We're supposed to just listen to her? Li, this is ridiculous. You said that this was going to be some big thing. She just looks regular. Nothing special about her. She is a skeeter, though.", said one of the men. He was wearing a strange blue and faded red hat that looped around, and the point faced his forehead. It had little silver balls around the side and it didn't seem like it had been washed in a while. Then, on top of that, the other men sitting next to him were wearing the same, but different colored suits. One was black, the other was gray. The one in the gray had long, red hair. "Boss, meet Tom, Slith, and Cu-o. They are the street captains of South Edge. We got other people up in the north, but those are my guys.", Li said, pointing first at the man in the black suit, then the man in the gray one, then the man with the funny hat. "Okay... so what do you expect from me?", I asked, confused now. Earlier, Li kept calling me boss, I was getting annoyed. Now these men were sizing me up to see if I was good enough. "I'm not your boss. I just want to survive.", I said, looking at them all. "Listen, sweetie-pie, the thing is, we need somebody with blood like yours running this place.", said Cu-o. He got up and took something from out of his inside pocket. It was a rolled up file. "This here says that your blood is like that bitch princess'. You have something special in you.", he said, now handing me the papers. I read and was surprised with what I was reading;

TO WHOM IT MAY CONCERN,

Amalli Dot is to be monitored. She is believed to possess the gift, and if so, is a credible threat to the throne against Layna. This must not happen as Layna is receiving the proper training and SHALL be appointed HEAD OF FAMILY. Please consider her a threat until proven otherwise. Watch for the family and ensure they never find out about her. Layna has been briefed.

After reading the file, I was convinced that this is why they wanted me dead. I looked back up at the men, who were now watching me anxiously. "So, according to this, I can be the head of the family. I CAN BE HEAD OF THE RF?!", I yelled, looking at them. They seemed afraid for some reason. "The head is usually elected, but in this case it's more complicated. If you have that thing that Layna has, then you're just as powerful a figure as any of the royal shitheads.", Cu-o said. "We need someone of your status. She is perfect, Li.", said Tom, and he strode over and held out his hand to shake mine. "You want me to be...a mob boss?!", I suddenly realized what they wanted. They all wore looks of happiness now, Tom still holding out his hand. "Listen, thank you, but no. I have no interest in this business of yours.", I said, looking for the exit, and thinking how far of a walk I had to my warehouse. Then I remembered, I couldn't go back to my warehouse. "What else will you do?", asked Slith, speaking for the first time. He stood up, and walking towards me, continued to speak, "You are like Princess Layna. The RF would see you dead. Layna doesn't want you to challenge for the throne, so what other options do you have? You can challenge for the throne, but if you do, you won't win. Layna is too connected. But here, you will have power that will rival Layna. Edge isn't contracted, so what you need to understand is that us 'Mobsters', as you call us, are a controlling force in this city. And you? You taking charge of us, means that YOU will be powerful. You'll have my people, Tom's, Cu-o's...", "That is still up for debate.", interjected Cu-o. But Slith continued, "...and Li's, which means, you will be above the GF, and nobody can touch you.", "What you're saying is I'll be some kind of queenpin?", I said, not liking how this sounded at all, "I DON'T WANT TO FOLLOW IN TIGGY'S FOOTSTEPS!", I yelled at them. Tom now lowered his hand. "Listen, Princess...", began Slith, "...you have no idea what you're saying right now. Those military people want to kill you. The RF wants you dead. But WE want to protect you. Keep you alive.", "As long as I'm your boss.", I said angrily. But once again, Slith said, "What else will you do?". I knew he was right. Of course he was. Just like Li said, the voice led me here. Emillie is in North Edge. I'm close to her. The voice wants me to kill her. Emillie will kill me if I don't. As I pondered, Cu-o took out his cannon and pointed it at me, "If she isn't going to play ball, then fuck this.", he said. I quickly reacted, grabbed it, and crushed it in my hand. Cu-o stepped back looking at it, "Amazing!", he exclaimed. "Do you see now?", asked Li excitedly. It was obvious he never had an experience like this before and was getting off on it. I was looking between the four of them, wondering what they could possibly be hoping for now. "Look, I just need rest right now. Is that fine with you guys?", I asked. They all looked at each other, then nodded. "I'll show you to your room, boss.", Li said, leading me away from the other three. "Li, what is going on? Why do they think I should be in charge? I don't fully understand.", "Well you see, me and my step-sister have been the big bosses. The gangs used to be separated. Selling drugs on each other's turf and getting everyone all riled up. Now it's a totally different story. You see, I told them that Tiggy's ancestor would come, and that this person would be the boss. They didn't believe me, but now...they do.", "But what is so special about me?", "Are you seriously still doubting the voice?", Li said. "Li, the voice isn't good. It wants me to kill somebody. I'm not doing it.". Li stopped to look at me. Then without saying another word, opened up a door to a very nice room. It had a very luxurious bed in the center, with two dressers on either side of the room. The room was decorated black, and unlike the rest of the manor, seemed to actually fit. Li left, closing the door, still not saying anything. I couldn't focus on anything else, so I fell onto the bed, and fell asleep.

When I awoke, it was to find I wasn't alone. I quickly sat up and realized it was Emillie sitting on the end of my bed. "We are so close, yet so far. What do we do?", she asked me, looking at me confused. "What do you want from me?! You've already ruined my life!", I yelled, getting out of bed now. "I want you to succeed. It's what I always wanted.", "I'm not killing anybody.", I said flatly. "Ah, you don't want to yet…", said Emillie, now changing into Amana, "…but why hasn't Amana spoken to you? Or even your precious cousin, Layna? Amana raised Layna. Taught her to lie, just like she does.", said Amana, as she came closer to me, "Why didn't they tell you two years ago that they would kill you? Even without me, you read that note Amana wrote. Yes, those were Amana's words.". I thought about this. Layna saved my life. She didn't try to kill me. And Amana, too. None of this made sense. "You're the one that is lying.". Amana started to laugh, then once again, turned into someone else; Tic. "Listen to me, if you do not take control of this situation, they will kill you. Remember, you are never safe, as long as you contain royal blood.", "Please, just stop this!", I said, now starting to cry. "THEN KILL EMILLIE!", the voice yelled at me. I cried into my knees and then found I was barely waking up and was crying into my pillow. I was still in the room with the black decorations, and seemed to have a small but definitely there, chest pain. I sat up and there was a knock at the door. "Receiver, boss!", someone who wasn't Li or the other three said outside of my door. I went to open it, and it was someone I hadn't seen yet. I took the receiver from him, and he turned, and went back downstairs, from where I could hear lots of voices. "Hello?", I said. "Don't do this, Awalli.", a voice on the other end said. After thinking about it, I realized it was Gail Raby. "Don't do what, exactly?", I asked. "You need to get away from those people, immediately.", "These people saved my life!", I yelled through the receiver. "You were never in any danger! Brom was out of line! He shouldn't have approached you. There is more going on here than…", "JUST STOP! I'm sick of this shit. First my boyfriend and dog got killed two years ago, now you're telling me what, exactly?", I asked, starting to become frustrated with everything. "I'm telling you that you are being manipulated. Please, Awalli? Just let me come and get you. I can get you out before you get too deep.", Raby said desperately. "No. I think I'm fine where I am.", "Awalli, listen to me. If you join these men, Amana's protection goes away. Layna has no power over here. Amana is the one who has been keeping you safe. Please. Just come with me.", "Who the hell is Emillie? Tell me that, and I'll consider coming with you.", I said. "Emillie? I'm sorry, but I don't know anything about…", "YOU'RE LYING!", I yelled. Something inside of me told me she wasn't being honest. She knew exactly who Emillie was. "So, are you making your choice? You're going to stay with those mobsters, then?", said Raby in a final tone. "Yes. I'm staying here.", I said. Raby hung up.

I got into some different clothes. I looked at myself. I had put on a suit, with an overcoat. I liked how I looked. I made my way down the stairs and saw that there were a lot of men sitting around. Cu-o had a group of men surrounding him, and Tom was sitting with his own group, and Slith was waiting for me to come down the stairs. "Good morning, boss. How are you feeling now?", asked Li, entering the room from the kitchen. "Better. Listen, about yesterday…I was confused. But you're right, Slith. I must move on with my life. I'm royal blood. I need to have my own army. The RF can't touch me. They'd start a war. Neither can Amana.", I said, looking around at everyone now. Some of the men looked at me funny when I mentioned Amana. "So, you're a nutter?", one of the men sitting in Cu-o's circle asked. I walked up to the man and looked at him. "What is your name?", "Bimson.", the man said. "Bimson…", I repeated. I looked at Cu-o, who wasn't gonna do anything. "Well, sorry, Bimson, but you brought this on yourself.". Before Bimson could make a move, I smacked him, and he fell out of his seat, and onto the floor, passed out. The rest of the men now looked at me with interest, "I know, that I'm new here. But apparently, I'm in charge. So disrespect like that from now on, will be met with my wrath. Are we clear on that?", I asked, looking around. Everyone nodded. I noticed there was a woman in the corner. She was wearing a strange hyena mask and only her mouth was visible. She came out of the corner, "Finally. Someone with some spine. Like me.", she said, in a very nasty tone, "We've got some issues. The GF is all up in our business. And worse, now there was some attack recently on one of our North Edge locations.". North Edge and South Edge were different but similar. Each had certain areas that were mirror images of each other. For example, I lived on Ned Street in a warehouse, and there just so happens to be another warehouse on Ned Street in North Edge. The woman explained that we owned this warehouse but at the same time, there had been raids. "I'll take care of it. What else is there?". This time, Cu-o spoke up, "Well there are those insufferable Tibs! They have no jurisdiction here, yet they are trying to muscle me out of my turf.", Cu-o said. The Tibs. I knew that name. "They are royal blood, aren't they? What are they doing here in Edge?", I asked, surprised by this info. "Well they think that they can somehow abolish the mob. It's their thing. They are working with the GF and getting us out of neighborhoods. At least that annoying GO Tes is gone. She was the worst.". I was thinking about something else. "But doesn't the family care that Reginald and his brother are here stirring trouble?", I asked, feeling like I knew the real reason they were here. "Where are they hiding? Do any of you know?", I asked, looking around. The woman in the hyena mask answered me, "Oh, I know where they are, boss. Can I please be the one to take you?", she asked in an admiring tone. "Sure, why not?". She quickly pointed out that she would wait outside. Li, Cu-o, Tom, and Slith all approached me, "Good job.", Tom said, once again holding out his hand. This time, I shook it. "I was surprised, but I like how you handled that. This may work out after all.", said Cu-o, with a smile. The truth was I didn't know what had come over me, and why I was suddenly okay with being a mobster, but I needed this. This was how. This was how I was going to kill Emillie.

We had driven to downtown SE. This was the difference between NE and SE. While the rest of it were mirror images, the downtown areas were different. NE had corporate buildings and restaurants, but SE was nothing but corporate buildings. There were also hovels. These were basically where people who were just here on business could stay until they left. Some were very fancy, but there were rundown ones that you see throughout Plinth. As we pulled up on the hovel titled, The Run, Hyena pointed out of the flar. I looked, and saw a man who was obviously Reginald Tib. I then saw his older brother, Tek and the both of them were walking out, Tek with his wife and stepdaughter. We watched them walk out and down the street. I needed to know the real reason they were here. I felt like I knew already, but still needed to confirm. "The girl. We need the girl. We get her, then we find out why they are really here.", I said. "Yes, mam.", said Hyena.

For the next few days, we were following them. Taking turns. There was other business I had to attend to, concerning the mob, but I assured them that I had to deal with these Tibs. They were indeed working with the GF. They seemed to be legally doing whatever they were doing. Reginald would leave to go off on his own and watch some of Cu-o's locations. Tek watched after Tom's. They didn't actually go after them physically, but when they would catch a deal going down, they used Royal Tech to keep the perps there until the GF arrived. It was horrible for business. Because of this method, most of Cu-o's dealers had been put away. We had people in the GF, but only the grunts, and they can only do so much. I quickly realized we needed a worker who could get our boys off, or better yet, a captain. I started to study how the precincts worked. It was quite simple. The precincts here in SE were mostly willing to look the other way for some shills. But unfortunately, it was a lot more complicated than that. The GF here wanted dominance over the gangs. Telling them where they can sell and can't. What the Tibs have brought down upon us has got the GF working overtime. I decided I'd meet with the corresponding captain of the precinct for the downtown area. Some of the GF didn't like what the Tibs were doing, and pointed out that the Tibs were working with the goody-goodies, and that's why they are getting away with this shit.

One day when Ethel, Hyena's real name, returned to our hovel, she quickly told me what she learned on this mission, "Cu-o is getting restless. He's starting to doubt you again. He wants to know when you will make your move.", "And what do you think?", I asked her. "I see your design. I think it is flawless. Li is right about you. You're gonna make us powerful.", "Did you get the name of the person I need to speak with?", "I did. Percy Holld. Or should I refer to him as Captain Holld? Whatever the case, he is the one. Captain of Precinct seven here in SE. The other captain in NE is Captain Walsh. Or Leonard Walsh. Whichever you prefer, boss. But both are captains for their respective downtown areas.", "Okay. And what of Carla Nos? Have you narrowed down her schedule?", I asked, taking notes. "Yes, I believe so.", said Ethel, handing me a pad that she had scribbled times and locations on. "Ethel, I need you to head back to the manor, and from there, send out an order. I want everyone operating out of SE to be present in the next ten hours. I'm making my moves now. But you need to know, once I do, there is no going back, Ethel. The might of Edge, and maybe worse, is going to come down on us.". Ethel nodded that she understood and departed.

First I was going to have to deal with Reginald. The kidnapping of Carla was vital only to throw people off my real purpose. Which was to kill Emillie.

I decided to drive by the orphanage in NE. It was going out of the way but I felt compelled to come here. That's when she approached me, "After all this time, now you come.", I said to Amana, as she walked up to my flar. "You shouldn't be here, Awalli. It's dangerous to be here.", "Why? Is it because you know the girl here? Of course you do. You know everything. Just like how you knew you were going to kill me in the end.", I said haughtily. "Awalli, I was never going to have you killed. I told you to watch your back, three years ago, now, you're under target again. But now, it's because you're sailing in the wrong crowd.". I stared hard at Amana, who now made a face of realization, "Awalli, Layna told you to ignore the voice, but it seems you have already accepted what it's telling you. Is that correct?", she asked me. "I haven't heard from the voice in months!", I said, realizing this fact myself. But now I was doing what it said. I was trying to kill Emillie because she was going to kill me. "Who is Emillie, Amana?", I asked her. "That is classified info.", she replied, already putting her hand on her cannon. I noticed, then she noticed I noticed, and pulled it out, and pointed it at my face, "Rather it starts a street war or not, I will shoot you if you don't drive away from this orphanage, and never come back here.", she said threateningly, "Not even Layna knows Emillie. What makes you think you have the right?", "Because the voice wants her dead.", I said, and Amana flushed. She reached into my flar and quickly put two in my gut. I coughed up blood. "I warned you, Awalli, but you didn't listen, now you leave me no choice.", she said, putting two more in my gut. She then pocketed her cannon, walked away, and disappeared. I was still alive somehow and managed to get out of my flar, but fell on the ground.

When I awoke, I was in a med house. I looked around and I was connected to machines. "How…?". I began to say, when the most unlikely voice spoke to me, "I saw you bleeding in the street! They said you were shot. You are very lucky to be alive!". It was Emillie. "I stayed here until you woke up. How are you feeling? Are you in pain?", she asked me, as I continued to stare at her. The pain in my chest rose out of nowhere, and I screamed. "DO YOU NEED HELP?! I'LL FETCH A MED PERSON!", yelled Emillie, and she ran out of the room. I decided to get out of here before she came back. I was indeed weak. It was sloppy for Amana to shoot me outside the orphanage like that. As I began to ponder why she would do it that way, it dawned on me why. She was protecting Emillie. I didn't know why I didn't see it before. Maybe I was thinking that Amana is extremely old, so it wouldn't make sense, but now I realized that Emillie was Amana's daughter. I smiled as I snuck out of the med house, and made my way to the warehouse on Ned Street in NE. Ethel was there with a clutch of men. "What the hell?!", she exclaimed, as soon as she saw me. She had some men rush me to a bed, where I fell out. When I came to, Tom and Ethel were standing over me. Before I could say anything, "We've rescheduled. Don't worry, the Tibs don't suspect a thing. We've just been waiting for you to tell us how you got four in the gut and lived.", said Ethel admiringly. I realized how they must see me now. A hero to them. Someone they can truly rally around. It all fits. I sat up. "Don't worry about that, it's personal. Just tell everyone, I move tomorrow, so get ready.", I said. Tom nodded and left the room, but Ethel stayed, "It's strange. I've been the only woman, now you're here, and you can survive being shot so easily…", she said in a thinking tone. "I'm different. That's why.", "I know, but to see it… It's truly strange is all I'm saying. No disrespect, boss.", she added, when she saw that I was giving her a reprimanding look. I got out of the bed and stretched, and felt like I never was shot.

I knew Amana was on high alert now, and I couldn't go back to the orphanage, so instead I decided to be on top of the Tibs. I finally saw my chance to deal with Carla, who had something that would change this whole thing. An item of Sebastian. Carla wore a strange necklace that Tek had given her, but she didn't know that it had abilities. Carla was leaving her usual gym at the time that Ethel recorded she would. I quickly walked up behind her while nobody else was around her, and tapped her on the head, and forced her into her own flar. I got in and started it and drove her to my manor. Once inside, I brought her upstairs into my room. I waited for her to wake up, which was about one hour of waiting. "Where...where am I?", she asked, looking around. "That doesn't matter. What does matter is that you are going to answer some questions. I need to know why your stepfather is here in Edge.". She looked confused, like she didn't know. "Well, they want to stop the mob operations. That's all I know.", she added. "Just you saying that is all you know, tells me you know more. They've never discussed looking for another family member who was hidden in the city?", I asked her, now moving towards her. "I've only heard whispers. That is some secret mission!", she yelled frantically, "Please, let me go! I don't know anything else! My father will find out who you are and have you killed!", she yelled at me, as I stood over her now. "I don't think so, darling. As a matter of fact, the RF have been trying to kill me for years, and they haven't succeeded yet, so what makes you think they will now?". She looked more nervous now. "So then, what are you going to do with me? I've told you all I know!", "Have they ever mentioned Awalli?", I asked her. "NO! I've never even heard of that person! PLEASE?!", she yelled, now struggling against her restraints. "I'm sorry, Carla, I am, but I need the Tibs to know that I'm off limits. Finding you dead, will give that message.", I said, with almost no emotion. "PLEASE! DON'T!", she yelled, but it was too late. I allowed Ethel to deal with her, because I truly did not have the stomach. I could hear her screaming.

The necklace that she wore was given to me after Ethel finished. She had done too much to the girl, and it would give the GF a headache for a while. Once I put it on, I felt the power immediately. I wanted to be at Ethel's warehouse in NE, and suddenly, I was there. I needed more objects like this. Carla's necklace seemed to also want to lead me to more objects. I started searching for them. Some of them were in obvious places, and weren't so easy to take. Like in churches or museums. But others were just in random discarded places, or owned by people who didn't understand what they had. I started to go after the easy ones. Some I could only feel the power but they didn't work for me. Others I couldn't feel anything but the necklace reacted to them. Then I found the ring. As soon as I found it, I knew Emillie couldn't have this. I found it in a church and this was the one time I took one of the items from the church. It was a weird ring, with circles on the inside of it that supposedly was some kind of language. I couldn't understand it, so I stopped trying. Next, I had to go after Reginald. In the days that had passed since I kidnapped Carla and had her killed, there was a shake-up alright. Reginald was on the hunt for the bastards that did it and Tek was comforting her mother. I had made sure that Reginald would allow his emotions to control him so it would be easier to capture him. Not only that, but another thing I quickly realized was how Amana had found me that one day. There are literally cameras that she had access to. She probably saw me take Carla, but didn't send anyone after me, because she knows, just like I do, I'm too powerful.

With my new necklace, catching Reginald was easy. I just appeared before him. "Witch!", he yelled as soon as I did. "Poor Carla didn't know the real reason you're here. It's me. Isn't it?", I asked. "You? You kidnapped Carla? But...I didn't know you had...wait...you're controlling the mob now?!", Reginald yelled, taking out whatever he had been using on my men. I quickly punched him in his chest, leaving a gaping hole. He fell down in a heap and I left the spot. I returned to my manor, where the men all gasped at my sudden appearance. "The Tibs won't be bothering us anymore. As for the GF, I'm gonna get on that now. Trust me, men, and women…", I added, looking at Hyena, "…business is about to be good. I'm good at business. You see, Tek isn't stupid. His stepdaughter, dead, his brother, dead. He knows better now. He is going to leave, because if he doesn't, well, he'll end up like his brother.". Everyone cheered and shouted my name. I was revelling in it. Hyena nodded at me to symbolize what I knew she would. "Is it ready?", I asked her. "Yes, boss. My warehouse is all nice and ready for you to do whatever you want there.", she said happily. "Good. I'm headed there now. And I need privacy for a few days, so don't let anybody near. NOBODY. Okay?", I said, giving her a serious look that I knew she took as, do not fail. I headed to the warehouse immediately. They took my other one, but this one would be my new one. Unlike the one they took, it didn't have Layna's magic, so I was sort of on my own with that. I didn't know where I could learn that kind of magic, but I did have some idea how to use one of the items in my possession that might allow me to perform such magic. The ring. I put it on and thought about what I wanted the warehouse to look like inside, and sure enough, it worked. It was just like the one I'd been living in for the past two and a half years. Now I had it back. I turned one of the rooms into a small display room. This would be my room. I walked throughout my new home like I did when I first got to Edge. I looked all around me, and was excited that life was so much better now. I had power. I was the boss. Why couldn't I see this before? This is where I was meant to be. Of course it is. Now I just had to kill Emillie. Once she is dead, I can finally be happy, right? Once she is dead…I can be happy.

CHAPTER 4

The Strange Possession Of Sandin Tillo

SANDIN: It had been a long month. Red was acting strange all of a sudden. Yellfy was even weirder. And then there was Walsh, who was hovering around me and Red more than often. The word on the streets was that there was some kind of inner struggle going on with the gangs now, and that it had something to do with Awalli. I didn't know where she was hiding but I kept cursing her. I was having a hard time dealing with anything because I kept thinking about Emillie, and how they hadn't exactly found her yet. Red hadn't been to see Dalia in a while and I was wondering why. He never told me what happened, but he had gone to see her after Raby told us Emillie could still be alive. I wondered what rattled him. But I stopped bothering him about it once he started to question me about my past with The Commander, "JUST DROP IT!", I yelled one day in the break area. "Look, I'm not dropping it. Maybe if you tell me, I'll tell you what I've found out.". I looked at him in surprise, "What you've found out? You mean to tell me you're keeping things from me now?", I asked incredulously. "Well, you've been keeping things from me.", "But this is personal. And it doesn't concern you at all.". I started walking back to my desk, and Red followed me quickly. I was eating the seventh candy bar today, and the truth was, I didn't eat candy this much, and couldn't explain my sudden desire for it. "Listen to me, Sandin, I know something that would probably make this case a lot easier. I want to be straight with you, but you gotta tell me what your past is with The Commander.". I thought about it, "Alright. The Dattur. After we're finished here.", I said, and finally walked away, and he didn't follow. As soon as I got to my desk, I wanted another candy bar. Why the hell was I eating so much candy? And then the dreams. I kept having strange dreams. I didn't know what was happening most of the time. I just felt like I was waking up, but always with my clock at three-forty, and this strange being sitting nearby. I couldn't understand because it was made of light and strange colors. It kept trying to talk to me. I knew it was Emillie somehow, but I couldn't understand what the hell was going on. It was like the kind of thing I read about as a kid, except ACTUALLY happening.

By the time I had finished up, me and Red once again were approached by Yellfy, who hadn't been the same since he read that report, "You, two. We need to talk. Right now! I'm not taking no for a…", "Yellfy, do you want to just come with us? We're going to The Dattur for a drink and a conversation.", Red said. I felt a bit frustrated, because I didn't like Yellfy too much. I definitely didn't trust him, yet I allowed Red to allow him to accompany us. By the time we reached The Dattur, I felt the itch for some candy, so I ran into the store across the street, and brought a bunch. "Dude, is there something wrong with you?", asked Yellfy, as I vehemently opened two candy bars at a time and started to scarf them down. I looked up embarrassingly, and lowered the bars, "Look, I'm just a little hot at what I got to say right now.", "And what is that, exactly?", Yellfy replied. "The story of him and The Commander.", Red said. "Alright, she killed my father. End of story.", I said, resuming the consumption of only one of my candy bars. "She…how?", Red stammered.

"He trespassed.", I replied. "No way. And she shot him?", Red asked. "Wait, who is this...Commander?", Yellfy asked, looking confused. "Alright, guess it's my turn. Tillo, I don't think I've told you this, but Emillie was the daughter of The Commander.", Red said, and I felt butterflies I couldn't explain. "The Commander is Emillie's mother?", "But it's more than that. I know who The Commander really is. Dalia let it slip. And before I approached you with my theory of what I think I know is going on, I wanted to be sure. Damn sure.", Red added, looking at Yellfy, who looked like he would accept anything at this point. "What do you know, Red?", he asked, leaning closer in. "First, none of this can get back to Walsh. There are some things I've recently learned, and I think I'm getting a clearer picture. But I need you two to bear with me. Got it?". We both nodded. "Okay. The Commander is a three-thousand year old goddess all of us are familiar with. Amana Tia. The princess from the fairy tales.". I looked at Yellfy to see if he would laugh, but he didn't. "Now, Dalia told me, she and her were...lovers.", "The woman from the orphanage? Yes. I suspected her.", Yellfy said, "I've been doing some research, too. Especially on Emillie, who for some reason was never allowed to be adopted. I tried to look for birth records, or well, just about anything prior to her arrival at that orphanage, but I couldn't find shit.", Yellfy said, looking hard at Red. "I know, Yencid, I did the same research. Now listen, Dalia is also three-thousand years old. Now the stories are a jumbled mess of the truth, but from what I can understand, based on those stories, a god or goddess is always drawn to something that awakens his or her power. So, Emillie's powers haven't woken up. But what we confirmed is that her body, or vessel, was disintegrated at the time. But there is an old story. A really old one, and this one was my favorite. But it was burned. You can't find it anywhere anymore. The Sebastian story. The one where he died, and came back.", Red said, looking at us. My mother told me that story. It was made illegal through the Church Act.

Basically, it was the opening tale to the fairy tales. So I assumed it made sense that it would fit into what we're dealing with. "So what's your point, Red? We don't know when she is coming back. So all we can do is wait.", I said. "Yeah, but it's Awalli that I'm concerned about right now. There are things Amana and Raby aren't telling us about her. I looked into her past. She isn't from SE. She's from Nocton. The royal fucking city. She was fired from Rain's Tech. RAIN'S TECH!", Red said, tapping his finger on the table and giving us a certain look, "I looked into the woman's history and found a girl almost as squeaky clean as Emillie. Yet this girl, just three years later from the woman I just described, mind you, is now THE QUEENPIN OF EDGE.", Red said, looking at the both of us like we should already be catching on. In a way, I was, but I was still confused. "So what are you saying, Red? Out with it already!", I said. "What I'm saying is that Awalli is a goddess as well. I saw her punch a hole into somebody's chest. It only fits. Don't you two clowns get it? This is something like two goddesses fighting each other.", "Red, how did you find info on Awalli like that?", I asked, surprised by this info. Some of what he was saying made perfect sense. But I couldn't find anything on Awalli. Only that she is running all the gangs in both NE and SE. "Well, it wasn't easy. I got it the old fashioned way. Paper trails and whatnot. You see, first I learned where Awalli was born. Which wasn't easy because somebody deleted that file from the computer. So I took a secret trip to Nocton. You see, if she is of royal blood, which Amana told me she is, then there would be some file of it at the med house over there. So that's when I found out, she wasn't even born in the nice one.", Red said, now looking quite somber. "Wait, you flew to Nocton?", Yellfy asked. "Yes. I had to get away for a spell after what Dalia told me. But while I was there, I learned some very interesting things. Layna, three years ago, disappeared for almost two months. And so did Awalli.", Red said darkly. "Are you saying she has some ties to PRINCESS Layna? The fucking Head of the

Royal Family? No…", Yellfy said. "Look, what I can confirm is that Layna brought her here. But it isn't what you think. She brought her here to save her life. The Royal Family is trying to kill her. She most likely joined up with the gangs to gain some kind of power, but that's where I get confused. You see, she was an employee at Taser for two and a half years, then BOOM, mob boss.". I was finally starting to understand what Red was talking about. It didn't fit who she was. She seemed like a nice girl before all of this. "But why is the Royal Family trying to kill her?", I asked. "Something to do with…", Red took a swig of his drink, let out a breath, then said, "…challenging Layna for the I lead Seat.". Both me and Yellfy were silent. We sat for a minute drinking. And then I said, "Imagine that. A criminal queenpin being Head of the Royal Family. Ha ha ha…". I couldn't stop laughing. But at the same time, I kept thinking, she worked for Rain's Tech, and here Taser. Both are big major manufacturing companies with major contracts with the military and other major companies. So, this girl is smart. She's no idiot. And where does Emillie fit into her agenda? "Red, where does Emillie come into this?", I asked. "Well, here's what you're gonna find strange. So, after all that stuff I just told you, the first sign of something wrong in this girl's life was in NE. Far from where she was living, yet, guess where she was found with four slugs in her gut.". I felt like this was an easy answer, "Outside Dalia's orphanage.", Yellfy said, before I could answer, "I found this out as well. As well as the fact that it was Emillie who rushed her to the med house, because she didn't think the med flar would make it in time.", Yellfy said, in a scared tone. "Yellfy, you see what I'm talking about, don't you?", Red asked. And Yellfy nodded, followed by, "They're being drawn to one another.". I was completely shocked. It made sense now why Emillie was so attached to Laddies after the bombing, and why she was found dead in a warehouse that belongs to Awalli. "Red, what the fuck?", I asked. "Yes. Believe me. That's exactly what I thought. But you remember the Amana and Calypsa story in the dark tales? This was the exact same thing.", Red said, looking at us now with a mixture of concern and fear. "So, what are we supposed to do, then? Awalli has killed people, Red. We can't just ignore that. And if she has an obsession with Emillie, why? It doesn't make sense. And who put four slugs in her? What the hell?", I said, now getting angry. "Raby would know. But she hasn't been returning my calls. The last one I got from her, was her telling me that going to Nocton is ill advised. They aren't telling us everything they know. They probably know exactly what's going on with Awalli, and they are only telling us what they think we need to know. The only reason they involved us at all is because Awalli has people in the GF. Not just in SE, but here, too. Captain Walsh has definitely been bought.", Red said. This I was convinced of. He had been giving me weird vibes for the last two months. "Why hasn't Raby found Emillie yet?", I asked. "Because maybe she was wrong. Maybe we were. Maybe Awalli got to her after all.". I felt like this was wrong. Emillie was alive.

We finally split up, and Yellfy caught up with me, "Hey listen, I got something I need to show you. Come check this out.", Yellfy said, leading me to his flar. "My girlfriend gave me this two days after our discussion. I've been trying to show it to you.". Yellfy pulled out a file. I opened it and was completely mortified. "Yellfy, what the fuck is this?", I asked. It was pictures of men burned to a crisp. I recognized, in the background, a lab. It was a drug lab. "Somebody did that to them. This is happening in South Edge. Cu-o is dead. He was among those bodies.". Cu-o was a nasty son-of-a-smich. I couldn't believe someone killed him. "But…?", "Nobody knows. All anyone knows is it was someone…get this, doing magic and kung-fu.". I stared at Yellfy. "What the hell is happening, man?", I asked, lost for words. "Well, the sooner I find out more, I'll let you know.". He took the file, got in his flar, and left. Now I understood why he was acting weird. He'd heard this story and has probably been picking up anything weird he can. I decided to head home. It was late. But I noticed I was being followed all of a sudden. I tried to pick up the pace but whoever was behind me was quick. I suddenly walked into some kind of barrier I couldn't see, and then I was knocked out.

GAIL: I hated doing this to Sandin, but after searching the warehouse for any kind of god energy, all we had were remnants. Amana believed Sandin was different and it had something to do with his father. Whatever the case, after careful testing, we were right. Emillie's essence was inside of Sandin Tillo. Tillo had been knocked out for the last three days, while P.E.D scientists ran tests on him. We got confirmation two days in, but additional tests were run on orders from Amana, who said that Sandin possessed something called the god gene, and that this had to be removed from him, or else it could mean trouble. But the scientists on site were finding this extremely difficult to remove. One man had been fried once he even came close to it. "ENOUGH! We'll end up damaging his brain if we continue. Let's just get him to the recovery room. I have to speak with him.", I said, after the incident. Once he was moved to the recovery room, we put him on machines that would make him weak, but able to speak. Sandin awoke. He opened his eyes and looked around. "Raby? Where am I?", he asked, fixing his gaze upon me. "You are in a med house, Sandin. Do you remember anything?", I asked him. He tried to sit up, but couldn't, "I don't understand… How did I get here?", Tillo asked, now taking in all his surroundings. "Listen, Tillo, this might be hard to understand, but we believe, Emillie's essence is with you. We've tried removing it, but there have been complications. We will need to wait for Amana at this point.". I said. The conversation between Tillo, Red, and Yellfy was monitored. It was reckless to even have that conversation in such an open place. There was a possibility that

Awalli's people overheard. "What?", Tillo asked, looking at me extremely confused, "But…", Tillo began, but I cut across him. "We've been watching you, Sandin and your behavior has been strange. I have to ask you; Are you still dreaming about Emillie?", I asked, and he nodded his head, now leaning back, and closing his eyes. "So, when do you usually have the dream? Is it every night?", I asked him. He nodded again. A soldier came in and handed me a receiver. "The General, mam.", he said, and then walked out. "Hello?", I said, fearing what she would say. Especially because it took so long to realize that Emillie was inside of Tillo. "Well, I'm letting you know that I'm sending a new vessel, but it will take two weeks, so you will need to keep Sandin. Have a doctor send a note to his job. As for Red, you can brief him. Yellfy, too, I guess. Red has been looking into Awalli's past, so it's time to tell him the truth.", "Yes, mam. I'll get on it. Is there anything else?", I asked fearfully. "Yes, actually. Next time, don't take so long to realize the obvious. Tillo literally told you.", she said. "Yes, mam. It won't happen again. I promise.". I hung up and looked at Tillo. "You're gonna be here for a while. Don't worry, we'll take care of everything else.", I said, and he looked at me confused. "Where am I? What the hell is happening, Raby?", he asked, and I turned the knob on the machine to up the dosage. He fell back asleep.

LODY: It had been a few days since our meeting, and Tillo was out sick. It didn't make sense, so I went to his house to check on him, and then found Raby with a clutch of men in his house, "What the hell is going on?", I asked, walking in. "Red, I'm glad that you're here. It's time to tell you the truth about Awalli.", she said, directing me to Tillo's bedroom, where some men were running strange machines and detectors over Tillo's bed. "Out.", Raby said, and the men started to clear out. I noticed a Mamal symbol on the shoulders of their uniform. "The truth? And what is that, Raby?", I asked her, sort of angry, "Where the hell is

Tillo?", "Tillo has been taken to Base to be dealt with. Emillie has fled to Tillo. Her essence is inside of him.". I couldn't process this. Everytime I think I've heard everything, something new comes out. "So, what you are telling me...is that Emillie's soul...is inside of Tillo? How does that even happen?", I asked. "Well, you see, Tillo is a special individual. He has what's called the god gene. It is something in his brain. It attracted Emillie to him, and now she is living inside of him. She may not realize it, but it does explain Tillo's weird behavior.". This was true. Tillo had been acting weird ever since Emillie disappeared. Now it was making some kind of sense. "Yeah, but what are you doing here? And what are you doing to him?", "Nothing, we are only holding him until a new vessel is made.", she said quickly. "But what about...?", "Mr. Red, please, you have to understand, Tillo is sick. We are helping him and Emillie. You have to see that.", she said, giving me raised eyebrows. I did slightly see it, but still couldn't process it. "Well, what is this truth you want to tell me?", I asked, now starting to feel worried about Tillo. "Well, you see, Awalli is more than we've been telling you. You've figured this much out already. But what you haven't figured out, is why she would join the mob, or even become in charge. It's because she is following the directions of an entity. Something ancient. We tried to keep her from falling into its clutches, but we failed. Now we believe it has been commanding her to kill Emillie. This is the reason why she is after her. It's something she can't control. Emillie was mysteriously drawn to her. Something even The General isn't too sure she understands. But at this point, it's important to note that Emillie is still being drawn to her. If we didn't have Tillo, I fully believe he would try to find Awalli. Awalli at the moment is off the grid completely. We don't know where she is, and right now, we're hoping she can stay away longer until we get Emillie another vessel.", "And how are you GETTING Emillie another vessel?", I asked, feeling like that was impossible. "The General has tech that will make one.", "You mean to tell me she can make a whole person?", I asked, perplexed. "You shouldn't sound so surprised. The General keeps most of the dangerous tech for herself.", "Okay. Now I got a question; If Emillie is her daughter, why isn't she looking for her herself?", I asked. "Well, she is extremely busy. She doesn't have the time, that's why I'm here, Mr. Red.", she replied, now reaching into her bag and pulling out a file. It was just talking about Awalli's trip from Nocton with Layna. It also provided me with the info of her quick ascension into the queenpin. "So, she is Tiggy Dat's granddaughter? And she was immediately made the boss of all the gangs?", I asked, looking at Gail, who was sitting quietly while I read the file. "Not exactly. They made her the boss because Li Folto and his step-sister, who were already somewhat in charge, had recommended it. Li Folto was the Kingpin. He was running all the gangs but giving the impression they were still separate. What Awalli has done is brought them together in a way that you can easily see that they are all together.". This was the obvious point. I continued to read, and found that she had been experiencing chest pains for the last three years. She had a particularly nasty attack, and this led to her not returning to Taser. I also saw that Gail wrote up the report. "So, you've met with her before all this?", I said. Gail just nodded. There was obviously something in this file she wanted me to hurry up and read. I scrolled down until I found that one thing. "Aman…", "Don't say her name, Mr. Red. But yes. She shot her outside the orphanage. She thought she would die, but Emillie conveniently saved her. Which is what told The General then, that something was amiss. She realized that without trying, she inadvertently put Emillie in danger.", "But why shoot her? What made her do that?", I asked, now thinking back on Tillo's father. "Because she threatened to kill Emillie straight to her face. You see, that's how we knew she was lost. Awalli wasn't a killer. But slowly she has become one. And it isn't her fault. The General believes we may have been able to save her, but that it might be too late. She fears she has already fed the beast, so to say.", "You mean by shooting her and trying to kill her?", I asked, disgusted, "What made her think to do that? Why not just arrest her?", "And start a war? Mr. Red, why do you think we briefed you?", "Because, Awalli has people in the GF?", I asked. "That, and because it would start an international war just making a move on her. Had she died outside of Dalia's orphanage that day, it would have been mayhem. The General at the time didn't realize how connected Awalli had already become. She underestimated her prowess, and now we are gravely paying for this. With the death of Emillie.", "But you said she is still alive.", "Yes. Her essence can be put into another vessel, but we don't know what will happen when we do.", "So, why not leave her dead?", I said, starting to feel like this was the right action. "Because, Mr. Red, Emillie might be the only chance we have against Awalli. You don't understand how powerful she is. Awalli isn't just acting on her own strengths.", "What happened to Slayn Tillo?", I asked, hoping to get a straighter answer than the one that Tillo had given me. "That...is classified. But if it makes you feel at ease, he had to die, because he was ill.". I wanted to say something else, but thought against it. "Will you come with me, Mr. Red?", Raby asked, standing up. I nodded and followed her out of Tillo's home.

We proceeded down the street. "Do you recall when I told you that I don't trust The General?", Raby asked me. I nodded. "Well, this is why. Look at everything that has happened. She acts like we have some grip on things, but we don't. She didn't know Awalli would kill Emillie. She didn't realize she would actually succeed. And even now, we don't know where she is. And don't get me started on Mccloud.", "WHAT DOES THAT MEAN?!", I yelled. "Mccloud is somehow connected to her. But she refuses to brief me on it. She is handling that situation personally. I've worked with her for a long time, Mr. Red, and I've never seen her this frightened before.".. Amana was scared? I wondered what she was scared of. "But, I don't get it. What does this have to do with Mccloud?", I asked. "Forget about Mccloud. He's alive and he's in SE. But what you need to be focusing on, is Tillo and why Emillie chose to go to him. Did you notice anything odd between them? Before Emillie's death.", "No. There was nothing. He had only seen her once.", "And you're sure that he didn't have some...attraction to her?". I thought this was a silly question. Emillie was gorgeous. Any man would have an attraction to her. This answer must have shown on my face, because she rephrased her question, "Did they have an extreme passion towards each other?", she said. "No. They never even really saw each other.", "So, Tillo didn't tell you he went to speak with her after the Laddies incident?", she said more seriously. I didn't know. "No. He never mentioned that.", "Well, he told her about his father. What does that tell you? Or how about the fact that she has been communicating with him in his dreams? That didn't concern you the first time you heard this?", she asked me. "Shouldn't it have concerned you?", I replied. She looked slightly angry at this question and changed the subject, "Do you know what kind of stuff I deal with, Mr. Red? You wouldn't believe the stuff I've seen. I've been with P.E.D for thirteen years. In all that time, I've only ever seen crazy shit. But this is a new level. It's the kind of stuff I was trained for, but never actually experienced. When The General recruited me, it was specifically to help protect...", she stopped talking when she noticed someone was watching us. Actually, there were a lot of someone's. I looked to my left, and there was a man holding a cannon so large, I knew it would tear right through me. I grabbed Raby, who I was surprised to see already had two cannons pointed in both directions. "Where'd you get that heat?", I asked surprised, quickly pulling out mine, and looking at the guy closest to me, straight in the eyes. As we were squaring off, I looked up really quick and saw a sniper on the roof. It was a female. She had a mask on. I knew who she was, but I'd only heard of her. Before I could do anything, Raby was hit, and she fell to the ground. Her shoulder had been hit. I quickly shot the guy closest to me in the face and his head exploded. I moved out of the way and got behind the flar Raby was leaning on. She was already trying to patch herself up, "There is…", "I know… I see her.", Raby said, looking through some device. "What the hell are they playing at? Are they insane?", "They want me, Mr. Red. They are trying to kidnap me.". What the fuck? I thought. "Okay, so…", "GOT HER!", Raby yelled, and I heard a small scream. "Go, Mr. Red, I got this. Take them out.", Raby said, now laying down and firing. I quickly shot the next nearest gangster, who was walking up on us. I then jumped over the flar and started shooting like crazy at any target I saw. I felt a shell narrowly miss my ear. I shot off at a guy right in front of me, and shot him in the chest, then the heart. He keeled over. Raby was pretty good. She was covering me nicely. Once I made it to my flar, I opened the door and Raby yelled, "RED, THERE'S A BOMB!", and sure enough there was. I backed away, looking for another way. "There's nothing you can do, GO Red. I'll let you live, if you give up Gailly.", Awalli said, walking out of the cuts, followed by the injured Hyena. "Give up, who? I don't know anybody named Gailly.", "Okay, RABY, then. Bring her out here. She has much to answer for. STOP HIDING, GAILLY! COME OUT AND PAY FOR WHAT YOU'VE DONE!", Awalli yelled. She had no fear. She was completely off her meds. "Awalli, listen to me. This isn't you. I read up on you. You're smart. You're being used by something you don't…", I didn't get to finish what I was saying because all she did was look at me, and I felt the most terrible fear that I'd ever felt at any point in my life. She walked up to me, "Don't…ever…talk…about…my…life…before…this…city.". I couldn't move, I was paralyzed with too much fear. I think I actually peed on myself. "Leave him, Ms. Dat. I'll come with you. Just leave him.", Raby said, coming from behind the flar with her arm in a sling. I suddenly found my voice, "SCREW THAT!", I yelled, pointing my cannon at Awalli now. She turned, and looked straight down the barrel, then said, "Okay, Mr. Red. Go ahead and shoot. Shoot me straight in the face. Go for it. I want you to.". I was happy to oblige. "Red. Don't. Just, let this go. I know what this is about. I'll go.", "No. What is this about?", I asked, still pointing my cannon straight at Awalli's face, and she was still staring it down, then her eyes slowly moved up to me. In her eyes, I saw nothing. Just complete nothing. "What happened to you, Awalli?", I felt so compelled to ask. "Life. And the unfairness. Grab Raby.", Awalli told the Hyena, who snatched her quickly, and took her next to Awalli, who took a step back now, but didn't take her eyes off me. "You know what? I didn't want to keep you alive at first. I was going to just kill you. But, I think I see your purpose. Raby here is going to answer for her crimes, but you get to go free.", Awalli said. I looked at Raby, who didn't look the least bit scared. If she had some exit strategy, she wasn't sharing. "Raby, be reasonable…", I said, stepping closer to the trio, "…they are going to kill you, damn it!", I yelled. "I have to go. See you later, Mr. Red.", "Wait!", I yelled. But it was too late. Awalli teleported away. I hit the ground. I kicked. I screamed. I did everything imaginable. I knew there was nothing I could do. I went to the precinct to report the whole thing, and Walsh was there. Sitting in the back. On my computer. "Walsh. This is a very serious breach, even for a captain.", "I just need to confirm that this, Emillie girl, is really dead.", he said in a nervous tone. "What the hell does Awalli have on you, Leonard, for you to be like this?", I asked. He stood up straight now and looked me in my eye. "You were attacked? You and that little witch, Gail? I was told to keep the area closed off by Tillo's house. He hasn't been in. I went to see him, and found black-op military scientists all in and out of his house. What the hell is happening, Red?", "You first, Walsh! When did you start working for Awalli?!", I questioned him again. "You want to know what she has on me? I'll tell you. But you won't like it. She has everything, Red. Every dirty deed that's run through here. If she were to present that to the right people, this whole precinct is going down. Even you.", "What the hell does that mean? I've never done anything!", I said. "You think that will matter once the captain is defined as dirty? It won't matter. You, Yellfy, Bonnly, and the rest, are all going down.". He backed away from my computer. "What dirt, Captain? Tell me what the hell you're talking about.", "We've been looking the other way for years, while Folto and Brookemere were putting everyone together. It was less street battles. Less people dead. But more dope on the streets. We had to make a decision, and this was the smart one. We got some of his boys off. This came all the way down from the top. So it isn't just me. But when Awalli got involved, she changed the rules. She is threatening to destroy us all. She is physically, talking about destroying. She called us all together, and asked who was the head of all the captains. Then she killed Lox, then said she was in charge from here on out. This whole time, every order I give, I got to go through her, damn it!", Walsh yelled, now throwing something across the room. "What the hell is happening, Red? What the HELL is she?", he said, and started to break down. I suddenly realized why Amana was trying to hush all this up. It made sense just like that. The Captain was scared out of his mind. And so was I.

AWALLI: All I could think about was Emillie. I even started having the dreams again. But now, it brought a smile to my face, because in the dream, I always kill Emillie. When someone told me that Li had some beautiful girl with him, I knew it was her. I could feel her. I knew it might kill some of my men, but I couldn't let her get away. This was my chance. But Li had her in MY room. Where I kept my Items of Sebastian. I rushed there and yelled for Li. But then I saw she was moving towards my favorite object. The ring. I quickly let off a small bomb I had crafted, and the next thing

I knew, as I watched Emillie blow away into nothing, there was a bright light that filled the whole damn warehouse. Then just like that, I found myself waking up in the manor in SE. "BOSS! YOU'RE ALIVE!", yelled Li, hugging me. "Get off.", I said, pushing him away. "Boss, why did you do that? Why'd you kill that girl?", Slith asked, also standing in the room. "Fuck that, she killed my men!", Cu-o yelled. "Listen, that girl…would have stopped everything that we are building. She had to go.", I replied. "And as for your men, that wasn't the boss. What the hell was that?", Li asked. "I think we just killed a goddess. I did it. I killed Emillie!", I yelled happily, but suddenly, I felt the chest pains and let out a moan. "What's wrong?", Li asked. I thought about what I was feeling. "Get Walsh on the line. NOW!", I yelled, and Slith left to get the receiver. Cu-o was still looking angry. "Cu-o, I killed the bitch that killed your men. Now stop fucking pouting, and make yourself useful. I need you to go and see if we can get Holld on the same page as Walsh.". Cu-o looked back at me and didn't move. "Cu-o, don't make me repeat myself. You better move, now.". It was obvious Cu-o thought I was weak in my position. Since he was one of my captains, I decided I wouldn't kill him, but just teach him a lesson. All I had to do was point at him, and he couldn't breathe. Slith came back with the receiver, "Walsh, how are you today?", I said. "What do you want?", Walsh asked grimly. "I need you to confirm a death for me. A girl. Named Emillie Panahelios. I need to know she is dead.". I heard Walsh sigh, "Okay.". He hung up. Then I looked back at Cu-o, and allowed him to breathe, "Cu-o, go make sure Holld is on the same page.", I repeated. This time he got up, straightened his stupid hat, and walked out without looking at me. I thought about the fact he might cry, and laughed a bit. "Boss, why would you think that skeeter isn't dead?", Li asked. "The voice never told you of her?", I asked, and Li shook his head. Well, this doesn't surprise me, I thought. After all, Li isn't a god or anything. Just a normal Plinthinian, who has no idea how big this game really is.

A few hours after I had tortured Cu-o, he was killed, along with a group of his men. "How did this happen?", I asked a man who had been let free. "Mam, I don't know how to explain it! He just busted into our pad, started kicking our asses, and shooting red shit from his hands. And before we knew what was going on, he already had Cu-o, and was burning him in his bare hands. Then the smich turned to us and said to tell our real boss he's coming.". This was too much. I already had Emillie to contend with, because every part of me believed that she wasn't dead. The receiver went off and I answered quickly, "Walsh?", "Yes. She is dead. I saw the report. But why does that matter to you? She wasn't anybody.", Walsh said confused. "Don't worry about that!", I said and hung up. I threw the receiver. "Boss? What the fuck?", said Hyena. "We need to find two women. One is named Gail Raby. The other, Amana Tia. YES, like the princess from the story. We need to find them, and we need to kill them. They are trying to bring her back.", "Bring who back?", Hyena asked, in a sort of questioning tone. "EMILLIE, DAMN IT!", I shouted, not meaning to. I caught myself. "Boss, can you please explain who this girl is?", Li asked me. I did. "So, Walsh says she's dead, then she must be.", "You don't understand, Li. Goddesses don't work like that. She could easily still be alive. That blast may have only seemingly destroyed her.", "So, we find Gail and Amana and stop this.", said Ethel, removing her mask for the first time. "WHAT?!", I exclaimed, unable to believe who was under the mask. It was a woman who was quite famous around SE. Ethel Brookemere. "You're the Hyena?", I asked. "Well, since you're being honest. This Emillie girl, is really what you say? A goddess? And she has abilities like yours?", asked Ethel, walking up to me, and placing her hands on my shoulders, "Why not get her to join us? Or even better, make the ultimate play?". Ethel was getting excited. The ultimate play? I thought. What the hell is that supposed to mean? Then it hit me. "You're talking about global distribution.", I said. Ethel beamed with glee, "YES! Imagine it. We become so powerful, that we even have ties all the way to Nocton.". Something about when she said Nocton, gave me a small feeling in my stomach. "I'll consider this.", I said smiling. She put her mask back on and left. "Li, stay.", I said, and he turned around. I walked up to him and started to kiss him but he stopped me, "Boss, there is something else I haven't told you. We're kind of, sort of related.". I dropped what I was about to do immediately.

Li explained to me that his mother is actually Tiggy's daughter, so she's my aunt. I felt so embarrassed. I was about to make out with my cousin and do more than that. "Why did you wait till now to tell me this?", I asked. "I don't know. I couldn't think clearly before. I was so focused on making you the new head of the mobs, that I didn't know when I should tell you.". I thought about this, then said, "So what do you think, Li? Do you think we should go global?", I asked. "Yes. You're powerful enough, and with that girl, E…", "She is not a part of this. Ignore what Ethel said. We don't have time for that. Emillie is the enemy.", "But Walsh says she's dead.", "Consider her alive until she shows up.", I said. Li walked out of the room and left me by myself. I was putting things together in my head now. Emillie is believed to be dead. Amana would have come at me with everything if she was. But who was this guy who killed Cu-o? Once again, I knew Amana would know. I knew she would have the answers. I needed to talk to her. I closed my eyes, hoping something would happen. Before I knew it, I was somewhere else, but I didn't know where. It was a house, but there was nothing in here except a receiver. It started to ring, I answered, "Did you really think it would be that easy, Awalli?", Raby said on the other end. "Where is Amana?", I asked, growing angry. "She is unavailable for you. She definitely will not be coming to you. And you won't be able to teleport to her.". I threw the receiver and it hit the wall. I went and picked it up. "Hello? Raby?", I asked. "Yes…", she responded.

"I'm coming for you, bitch!", I screamed into the receiver, and was about to walk out, when the house exploded.

I woke up, suddenly frightened for my life. I was surrounded by my men, again. This time, minus Cu-o. Tom was the first to speak, "Boss, this obsession you have. With this Emillie girl. We've already got confirmation she is dead. But you keep chasing after her?", he asked me. I looked at Ethel, who was wearing her mask, but even through that, I could see how she felt. "All of you don't understand. That girl will finish us. You'll see. We have to make sure she is dead.", "Boss, if you keep this up, you'll be dead right along with her.", said Ethel, then she continued, "If Li hadn't been there, you would have died. What was so important in that building? As far as we knew, there was nothing there. Literally.". I couldn't explain to them that I teleported there looking for Amana. But I decided to go after the bitch I could catch. "Have you got any information on Raby?", I asked Ethel. "Yes. I've seen her at the warehouse. But recently she left. You've been out for a spell. While you were out, my sources tell me that GO Tillo is sick. He's been out. But my other sources say he had an interesting conversation in The Dattur. They mentioned your name, but nobody could really make out what they were talking about.", "Thank you, Ethel. Listen, Li brought me to you. I'm meant to BE here. Trust me. Just listen to me. I know Cu-o is dead, and we will deal with that guy. Have we seen him since he killed Cu-o?", I asked sympathetically. "No. He hasn't shown his...whatever that thing he was wearing was.", said Ethel. I had them explain the mystery guy. "Ethel, how is it you can be a mobster? Why even be one? You're rich enough you don't have to be here. You have a controlling stake in a company. Take it and go.", "No way. I'm the one who proposed to Li that we unionize the gangs. You know what I make.", Hyena replied to me. Since discovering her amongst my ranks, I did some background checking on her. She was traumatized as a child because she witnessed a murder. Then she went through some kind of therapy. The Hyena is the result of that therapy. She is cunning, smart, and fast with weapons. She also happens to make the best batch of Lilac in Edge. I looked into the others as well. Especially Li. My aunt had a strong affair with Eddie Folto's grandson. This is how Li was born. It was understandable now how the voice was communicating with Li. He is family. But he doesn't have the gift. The voice needed me. She needed me. Corsa needed me.

"BOSS! WE GOT RABY CORNERED!", someone yelled. I turned away from the map of the city I was studying, and turned my attention now to this golden moment, "PERFECT. And where is Ethel?", "She is on the scene, but I got word she is injured or something.". I knew where to go. I appeared right on the spot. I saw GO Red, a man who I tried to kill once I knew Amana was meeting with him. But all of a sudden, he was like a machine out there, mowing down my men. Then I noticed, Gail was covering him. "Boss…", said Ethel, walking up from behind me. "Don't worry. We're about to get, Raby.", "But, my men, we lost…", "THIS IS A WAR!", I said coldly, "I told you, there was no going back.". She nodded and then we proceeded out of the cuts. Red pointed his cannon at me, but I knew it couldn't hurt me. Then, Raby gave herself up. I didn't expect this of her. As soon as I got her back to the manor, I bound her the same way I had bound Carla, "Not so tough and happy now, are you?", I asked her. "Well, I don't know what you expect me to be, but I'm not frightened of you, Ms. Dat. Do your worst.", "I'm going to kill you, Raby. And be done with you. I'm sick of the lies.", "The only one lying is yourself. We tried to help you, Ms. Dat.", "STOP IT! STOP TALKING LIKE YOU'RE NOT AFRAID!", I yelled. She didn't smile that smile she usually wore, but rather looked at me very seriously. "The General thinks you can be saved. But looking at you, I don't see how.

You're crazy. You've completely lost your mind.". I ignored her, "How is Amana bringing Emillie back?", I asked. "You're even more crazy if you think I'm telling you THAT.", "Ethel, make her talk.", I said. Ethel moved forward, "Touching me is ill advised, Ms. Brookemere. Yes, we know who you are.", "All the more reason to off you.", said Ethel, reaching for her. The moment she did, a light erupted into the room, and we were blown back. I got to my feet and Raby was still bound on the bed. "I warned you not to touch me.", "Is this why you're not frightened?", I asked. "Maybe.", Raby replied mockingly. "I'll figure out whatever tech you're using, and find a way around it.", I said. "I'll tell you what I'm using. It's a hyper shield. And only people like me and above can have em'. So, do your worst. You'll never get past my shield. Even more...", she sat up as much as she could, "...you'll never get that info out of me.".

Raby had become annoying. I couldn't do anything to her. She would sing in the morning, "GOOD MORNING, OH PLINTH, TO ANOTHER...", "SHUT UP!", I banged on the door. I was entirely sick of having her here and came up with the greatest idea. "Tom, pack up Mrs. Raby.", "But, boss, you said no one can touch her.", "There is a way. She let us take her for a reason. We were able to touch her then...and Hyena shot her. There is a way.". I opened the door, and Raby looked at me with that smile, "Hello, Ms. Dat. Oh, and you've brought Mr. To. This is just great. So are you going to kill me today, or just continue to starve me?", she asked. "Ready to die now?", I asked. "No. Just hoping I could get you alone. Just for a minute.". I looked at Tom, who nodded, and walked out. "What do you want?", I asked her. "I want you to listen to me; Awalli Dat. You are not what you have become, and on behalf of P.E.D, THIS is your last chance, to turn yourself in, and seek help.". I looked at her in shock. I couldn't believe she just said all that. "Raby, I will get past your tech.", I said. "I don't think you understand. I'm only still here because I want back the old Awalli. Do you even remember her? She had a boyfriend, named Tic. And a cute little…", "Shut. up.", I said menacingly, "Who the fuck do you think you are to talk about them? You just shut the fuck up!", I went to her and grabbed her face. "I'm touching you…", "Yes…", she said through my clenched hand, "…but for how long?". Suddenly, she was behind me. But still restrained. "You're not the only one who can teleport. I can leave at any time. So my offer, or do you seriously want to challenge the most powerful woman on the planet?", Raby asked. "You are going to die, Raby.". Raby sighed , "I'm sorry it's come to this.", Raby said, teleporting out of the restraints, somehow restraining me, and then knocking me out. She took out her cell, "I got her. Best to take us now before her men catch on.". Next thing I knew, I was being taken somewhere. Then I was completely out.

DALIA: Red hadn't been to see me in a month. I figured I scared him off with my talk of being Amana's lover, and Ko-e's best friend. I hadn't spoken to either one of them in a long time, and I missed them both. Even more now that Emillie was dead. I had come to accept that she was dead. There was no other way of looking at it. Even if she came back, would she be the same girl I raised? I had barely shown my face to the children. I couldn't face them. This was the hardest thing I have ever experienced, and I hated Amana for this. She let this happen. She knows everything that happens here on this planet, and I don't doubt for a minute she didn't know this, Awalli person, was after Emillie, or that both were being pulled towards each other. I was terribly afraid to even look anyone in the eye, knowing that physically, Emillie was gone. There was a knock on my door. It opened and Cynda entered. Cynda had started trying to be more brave in front of the other children, especially Bart, but she knew that she could never take Emillie's place. Cynda was thirteen and was three and a half years away from being an adult. "Dalia, can we talk?", she asked, closing the door behind her. I knew she was worried about me, just like the others. "I don't wish to talk, Cynda.", I said without looking at her. "Dalia, you've been locked in your room for weeks! We need you out here!", Cynda yelled. I knew she was right. She was a smart girl. Then again, she grew up around Emillie. Cynda was like her shadow. She worshipped Emillie. I knew Emillie being gone was hard on her, but I was her mother. I felt like a part of me died. "WE all miss Emillie, Dalia, please?", she said, now starting to tear up. "Cynda, I can't. Just let the other matrons know…", I reached into my drawer, "…this is what I need done today.", I said, handing her a list. She took the list. "But, these are your responsibilities!", she yelled, looking back up at me. "Cynda…", "NO! You need to come out of this room. You act like you are the only one hurting. None of us know where Emillie is or what happened to her. You've been staying in this room for too long and refusing to speak to us! What the hell is going on?", Cynda asked me, coming closer to my desk. "Cynda, Emillie is never coming back. But I need you to not bring this up to anyone. She is…she is…dead.", I said, now putting my face in my hands, and crying even harder than I had yet. This is why I couldn't face the kids. I couldn't lie to them. They all adored Emillie like she was a big sister to all of them. I secretly cursed Emillie for doing this to us. I remembered our argument, "Emillie, you don't need to know why Red was here. It's better if you don't and just stay out of trouble.", "But, what trouble am I in?", Emillie had asked. "EMILLIE, JUST DROP IT!", I yelled. I felt horrible now, and wished that I did tell her what was happening. Cynda broke down, and fell on the floor crying, "Why didn't you just tell me?!", she yelled. Cynda had been checking every night and morning to see if Emillie had returned. She had her hopes up that she was coming back. She would often sleep by the door and wait. Once, I was walking back in, and Cynda thought I was Emillie. She was so excited that she jumped up and hugged me without looking to see who I was. When she saw it was only me, she sadly carried her blanket back upstairs. I got up to console her and she got up and threw my arms away from her, "You should've just told me!", she yelled and then ran out of my office, "CYNDA! WAIT!", I yelled, chasing her, but she was fast. She had run out the front and was gone. "CYNDA!", I yelled, looking up and down the street. She was nowhere to be found.

The matrons and I spent all day and evening searching for Cynda. I had tried calling Red, but he wasn't answering. He had given me Tillo's number just in case I couldn't get a hold of him, but Tillo wasn't answering either. I returned to my office, where I completely broke down and cried. I was devastated. I fell onto my chair behind my desk, and continued crying. "I didn't expect you to be this broken.". I looked up, and knew before I saw her, it was Amana. She was sitting in the corner like she always does when she wants to surprise people. "YOU!", I bellowed at her, rushing from behind my desk, and grabbing her by her arms. "You knew this would happen! You knew!", I yelled, half cried into her chest. "Dalia, Emillie is coming back. She is almost ready. But I think you know why I'm here.". I backed away from her, "I'm not doing this with you.", I said, thinking she just wanted sex. "That's not why I'm here. I'm here because Emillie is going to be very confused. I don't think she will realize she was dead. I need you to keep her from finding out.". As much as I was happy at the idea of Emillie being alive again and just holding her, I didn't trust what Amana was saying, and didn't like the sound of it, "And what about the children?", I asked her. "I can modify their memories so they never knew she was miss…", "NO! I'm not letting you do that to these kids!", I yelled at her. "Dalia, if I don't take the memory away…", "I'd rather Emillie never come back, if that is the cost. She would feel the same.", "She is my daughter.", said Amana, looking at me with something close to anger. "No… She is my daughter. I raised her! You did nothing but abandon her at my doorstep!", I replied. I could see her mind trying to work out ways to convince me. "Dalia, I know how you are feeling, but let's not forget what we are dealing with.", "When were you going to tell me about Awalli? When were you going to tell me how much danger she was really in? When you first had her brought to me, it was because you couldn't raise her. You were too busy raising a girl that wasn't your daughter!". Amana looked livid, "YOU KNOW WHY I HAD TO RAISE LAYNA! HER FAMILY WOULD HAVE KILLED HER!", she yelled. "And her family succeeded with Emillie. You think I haven't looked more closely at Awalli since she murdered Emillie?! I've been looking into her. It's where I've been going at night. You brought her here!", I yelled. "Because the RF wants her dead. I thought I could protect her. But somehow, that thing that is inside her head, had me beat. I didn't know it was leading her to Emillie. How the hell could I? I didn't know that until she told me. Right outside this house.". I suddenly remembered almost a few months ago, when Emillie drove a woman, who disappeared at the med house, and left no name or anything that would have helped to identify her. I knew now it was Awalli. "Amana, what have you brought down upon us?", I asked her. "I don't know. I haven't seen this since I had to kill...Calypsa.", she said sort of oddly, "I don't understand why it would go after Emillie. It knows she can stop her. But I don't understand why it used Awalli. I don't know, Dalia. I'm afraid. I really am. Everything is like how it used to be. Pretty soon, I won't be able to keep everything a secret anymore. I already got people in P.E.D trying to out me. I can't have you and Ko-e working against me. Where is she?", Amana suddenly asked. "I don't know.", "Now is not the time for false loyalty. You need to tell me where my sister is...now.". I had quickly forgotten how cold Amana is. "I told you, I don't know and I'm telling the truth.", "I know she is here in Edge. She has to be. She was living here. In the future. But I don't know where that was. I couldn't find her. And I've never seen Scion or Alexa.

Dalia, things aren't what happened before. I don't understand it. And the people who could explain it are too busy or not talking to me.". Now I had a better understanding. She was confused. "Amana, why not just bring Emillie back, end this whole thing, and never let her come here?", I said gravely. "I thought about that...but, the kids. They want her back. They deserve her back.". I didn't think she cared. "She is almost ready, but if you insist on the kids remembering she has been gone, that is your choice. Hopefully you'll have her by tonight.". This sounded too good to be true.

SANDIN: I woke up feeling completely like a flar hit me at full speed. I couldn't make out what was happening around me. There were men in hazmat suits and they were pricking me almost every chance they got. I looked around, and Raby was standing to my right, "...mmmmmhhmmh...", I couldn't speak. "Sorry, Sandin but you have to be awake for this part. I'm truly sorry. But it's almost over.", "Whtsalmovr?", I managed to garble through the thing in my mouth, which I realized was a teeth protector. "Remember our last conversation? Maybe, you don't, I suppose, you have been extremely drugged up. Well, I told you that Emillie is inside of you. Today we are extracting her soul from you and putting it in a new vessel.". I shook my head, then I saw a tube. They lifted me into the tube and I was concealed. I was scared. Then opposite me, I saw a beautiful woman also in a tube. She had gorgeous red hair and her face was very similar to...Emillie. Oh my god, I thought. Suddenly there was a bright light that filled the entire place, and I realized it was flowing out of my tube and into the other one. I started to have certain feelings leave my body. It was a strange sensation, then I passed out. When I awoke, I wasn't in the machine, but rather, I was standing on a nice plain. I looked around and there was nothing but green and purple blades of grass. "Tillo?", I heard a voice and turned. It was Emillie. "Emillie? Where are we?", I asked her. "I don't know. I've been here for a long time. How did you get here?", she asked me. "I don't know. I was in a...", bits and pieces started to collide in my mind. Suddenly I was back in that tube. "WHERE DID SHE GO?!", someone yelled. I realized it was Raby. "Get a fix on her. Now! We do not want her doing anything reckless. Find her! And someone start de-prepping Mr. Tillo.". I felt myself fall from the tank, but was too weak to move. I was then moved to what resembled a med house room, but it was surrounded by military people. One military man walked in. "How do you feel?", he asked me. "I don't know. Hungry.", I replied. "I'll see what the cooks can whip up. Now tell me, are you now just, you? Do you feel anyone else?". What the hell kind of questions are these? "Where am I?", I asked. "Classified. I just need the questions answered please.", "Not until you tell me where the hell I am!", I yelled, trying to move but was still too weak. "I'll come back when you're ready to answer.", the man said and walked out. I yelled in frustration, trying to break whatever spell was over me, but couldn't. About an hour later, they actually came back with some food. I was given a shot of something that helped me move so I could eat, but then later after I ate, I was my weak self again.

After it had been a few days of me being here, I started acting more cooperative, so they let me move around. I started to explore what I quickly realized was a military base. But it was P.E.D. Everywhere I looked, the Mamal symbol could be seen. I realized the Mamal was a Phoenix and it had flames trailing behind it. I thought it was pretty interesting, but who had actually ever seen a Phoenix? As I continued moving around this place I found that I was in a part that was specifically for people like me. I was considered a non-lone. Which is, I can't see what else they have here. Non-lones were people that P.E.D had to bring on Base for whatever situation befell them. But most people had gone through a detox(Mind Wipe), and didn't remember why they were brought here in the first place. One of those people I met was named Shinh. He had some run in with an alien species or something like that, and that is how he ended up here. He was waiting for detox, and the poor bastard didn't know what that meant. Another one I met was Wallo. He had a similar situation to Shinh, but claimed that an alien forced him into the future. I laughed slightly at this one. I figured the detox fucked up his brain. As I continued to try and explore the P.E.D base, it was at this time that Raby came and found me, "Mr. Tillo, can you come with me, please?", she asked me. I nodded and followed her. I wasn't too sure how I felt about Raby now. She kidnapped me, then basically had me experimented on. "There is someone I'd like to show you.", she said, opening up a door that led to cells. I noticed these cells had certain writing on it. "What is this place, Raby?", I asked. "These are our holding cells for people with other than normal abilities. Perhaps you would like to meet Awalli Dat?", she said, stopping, and pointing at a cell. Awalli was sitting inside and was looking brain dead. "What the hell has happened to her?", I asked. "The thing that is in her head, it is confused. While we have her like this it can't act, so, Awalli here is coming to terms with the choices she made.". I looked at the girl, who looked like she couldn't even think for herself enough to feed herself. "Have you drugged her?", I asked. "No. This is the magic of this cell area. It will keep her from being able to do anything.", Raby replied, looking at Awalli with sadness. "Let's leave her.", Raby said, and she led me out. "So, now what?", I asked. "Well, Mr. Tillo, I would love to tell you that it's over, but I can't. The General believes that Awalli WILL get out of this cell and still continue to go after Emillie.", "But how? You have her all doped up!", I said. "She is not... Mr. Tillo, listen, after everything you have experienced, you still are confused as to the impossible. You need to start thinking outside the box. It's one of the first things we are trained on here. The impossible is possible.". I thought about this and started to think about everything that had happened, then suddenly realized, "Where is Emillie?", I asked. I hadn't been thinking about her like I was, and a lot of the strange urges that I had were gone. "She took off the moment her essence entered her new vessel. We have been trying to locate her for three days, Mr. Tillo. There isn't a sign of her, but we know she is alive now. But with Awalli here, we don't have to worry about her being in danger right now. But it is very important that we find her.", said Raby seriously. "Well, I don't understand how she is going to get out of that…", right when I said that, there was a scream so terrible that I thought someone was dying. When we went to investigate, Awalli was screaming her head off, and clutching her sides. "MS. DAT, CONTROL YOURSELF!", Raby yelled, while I just stood by looking horrified. "Where is she…? Where is Emillie? I can feel her!", Awalli said, as everything started shaking. "Oh my!", Raby yelled, as she quickly took out a cannon and pointed it at Awalli and began shooting, but there was some invisible field that the shells couldn't pass through. "Raby, I'm still going to kill you!". Raby took out her cell, "General, you should hurry back here. Now, please.", she said, hanging the cell up, grabbing me, and leading me away from the prison. "What the hell is happening?", I asked. "It appears we may have underestimated Ms. Dat.".

CHAPTER 5

You're A Goddess, Emillie

CYNDA: I cried all the way down the street. I had been hiding out at a friend's house for the last three days. Her parents liked me, and once I told them, Emillie, my big sister, was dead, they allowed me to stay. They called Mother Dalia and told her I was with them. I couldn't believe that Mother Dalia hid this from all of us. Emillie was special to me. She always made me smile when I was sad and made me happy when I would often think of my parents. I was very sad after they died. They died in a flar accident when I was only four that resulted in a few deaths. My parents weren't rich people but rather were just hard workers. I can't remember what my father did, but my mother worked in a flower shop. I often wore a necklace with a pendant attached that had my mother's picture on it. Whenever I would look at her picture, it always reminded me of how kind she was. It always made me cry. Emillie used to check on me personally. She would hold me until I fell asleep. She would tell me stories to help take my mind off things. She was really good with storytelling. I wished she was here to tell me one now, but it was to take my mind off the fact that Emillie will never hold me again. She'll never hug me and tell me it's okay. She'll never sneak me candy and eat it with me anymore. I couldn't stop crying. I couldn't go back to the orphanage right now. I couldn't face everyone knowing Emillie was dead, like my parents. "Why did Emillie have to die?", I said out loud to myself. I was sitting in my friend's backyard because I wanted to be alone. I continued to feel this way, and then, there was a light. I looked up and Emillie was standing over me. "Cynda...", she said, confused. "EMILLIE!", I shouted, and I jumped up, and hugged her tightly. She confusedly hugged me back. "Where are we?", she asked. "We're not far from the orphanage. Did you want to go home?", I asked her. "No... I need... I need to know what happened to me.". I looked at her and she was truly confused. "Emillie, Dalia said you died.", I said, looking at her now, confused myself. If she died, then how was she here? "I...died?", she asked me, "No, that's impossible, I'm here. I would know. I would... know.", she said, almost trying to convince herself. "Emillie, let's just go home.", I said, grabbing her hand, but then before I knew it, we were somewhere else. I looked around and it looked like where we just were, but the street sign read SE Tol Street instead of NE Tol Street. "Um, Emillie, how did we get here?", I asked. "I don't know.", she replied. We watched, as a woman was leaving what appeared to be a warehouse across the street from where we were. "Emillie, this place looks dangerous.", I said, but Emillie was watching across the street. Then suddenly, we were in front of the orphanage. "Emillie...", "Go inside. I'm going to find out what happened to me.", Emillie said. "But, I don't want you to go.", I said, hugging her, and crying. "I'll be back. Just... Something isn't right.". She let me go inside, and then I watched, as she disappeared.

EMILLIE: That feeling that you have when you first wake up in the morning, and for that first split second, you think you are still asleep. That is what I was feeling, except it wouldn't just disappear. I continued to feel this. I had this strange feeling that I needed to talk to Tillo, but I didn't know where he was. Then on top of that, Dalia said I was dead, but I'm alive. The last thing I remembered was being in the warehouse on Ned Street and somehow I was somewhere else. Thinking about this other place gave me a headache. I needed the truth. I felt some kind of vibe. I looked up and could tell it was coming from above me. I closed my eyes and then found myself in some kind of prison. As I walked, I noticed some of the cells were open, and on the inside was blood. Blood seemed to cover everywhere and I could hear shouts and screams. I looked ahead of me, and that's when I saw her. The last thing I remembered seeing before the light. My head started pounding. I was grabbing my head before I realized that the woman was now six feet away from me, "Emillie. You came. I summoned you, and you came.", she said, walking up to me. I didn't know what she wanted from me, but my head was killing me too much to say anything. "So, I have to kill you, or you have to kill me.", she said. "But, why?", I managed to finally say. "Because, that is our destiny. I won't try today. No, I see you have awoken. But one day soon. For now, I leave you with the same words your mother left me with; Watch your back.", she said, then she lifted her arm and I flew back and fell onto the floor. "GET AWAY FROM HER!", somebody yelled from behind me, and I realized it was Tillo, followed by Gail. "Gail! What is…?", before I could ask her what was going on, she and Tillo began shooting at the strange girl, who just smiled, and disappeared. "Who was that? Why does she want to kill me?", I asked Gail, who quickly threw her arms around me. "I thought you were gone!", she said. I was looking at Tillo, who was also looking at me strangely. "Can someone please tell me what is going on?", I said.

"You see, Emillie, you are a goddess. Like you always believed. But you're much different from The General. You're more of a…well we don't really know. We are very surprised that you returned the way that you have.", Gail was explaining to me. Gail was thirteen years old when I first came to the orphanage. Much like how I am with Cynda, Gail was the same way with me. She often would sleep with me when I wouldn't get adopted, or when I would watch my friends go. It was hard to believe that Gail had also gotten involved with the military, but then again, it answered why we haven't seen her in a long time. I couldn't believe what she was saying to me. "So, I'm a…goddess?", I asked, looking at her and Tillo. "Don't look at me, Emillie, I couldn't even begin to tell you anything.", said Tillo, still looking at me. I couldn't stop feeling like him and I had some connection I couldn't explain. "So, if I was dead, then how am I alive again?", I asked. "Your mother made you a vessel.", "And who is that?", I asked. "Someone I thought would be here by now. I know she is on Base, but she isn't answering my calls.", said Gail. "So, you know who my mother is?", I asked, becoming somewhat upset that she didn't tell me she knew my mother. She looked at me and realized I was thinking this, "Emillie, I wasn't allowed to say. I'm still not. Your mother is a very difficult person, but…", she stopped talking because her cell rang, "Yes… she is here. But she is… General, I think that is ill-advised. But…okay.", she said, finally putting the cell down and looking at me sadly. "Tillo, escort Emillie back to the orphanage. And that is all.", she added, giving him a stern look, "And, Emillie, just stay at the orphanage until further notice.", "But what about my mother?!", I yelled. "She isn't ready to meet you yet.", she replied, looking angry. "But…I want to…", "Emillie, I know. But your mother has a purpose for everything she does.", "What is her name?", I asked. Gail ignored me, "Take her, Tillo.", she said, standing up, and walking out of the room. I looked at Tillo, who pointed me towards what appeared to be some kind of POD area. We both fit into one and some men and women who were working around the area, made sure we were secure. I felt the pod fall, and then suddenly, we were standing in a field that was also surrounded by men. I looked around, wondering how the hell we got out of the pod. Tillo was looking confused as well. "Well, thank you, you two, now if you follow Hephzibah, she will lead you off this base and back to Edge.", a man with a clipboard came up and told us. Hephzibah led us to a flar that she said would deliver us to Edge, and then from there, we were on our own.

As we were riding in the flar, my head was buzzing with so many questions about the woman that is supposedly my mother. The woman that just left me. Gail Raby was a woman I've known most of my life. She works for the military. But it wasn't any kind of military I ever saw. Then there was the man sitting across from me. I looked at Tillo, who was purposefully avoiding my gaze. "Tillo.", I said. He turned in my direction, "Where were we just now?", I asked. Tillo explained that it was a secret military base. The military unit known as P.E.D, is some kind of secret force that specializes in strange things. My mother is in charge. Tillo tried to tell me my mother's name, but his tongue got all tied up. It was actually funny at first but became infuriating later. "Why doesn't she want me to know? I don't understand.", "Maybe she's ashamed of the fact that she abandoned you.", Tillo said in an angry tone. I remembered he told me about his father. "Wait, did my mother…?", I started to ask, but the answer was on Tillo's face, "My mother killed your father? That woman, too afraid of meeting me, killed your father?", I asked. I didn't want to meet her. I felt like I already hated her. What's funny is I kind of always have. I didn't know if she was dead before or what may have happened to her, but to learn she is alive and thriving, and is some kind of big individual, was enough to make me never talk to her either. I continued to stare at Tillo, who quickly turned away from me once he answered my question. "Who was that woman? Why does she want to kill me?", I asked him next. "Awalli. She is a mobster, and she is obsessed with killing you. You two have some kind of connection.". I thought about this. The first time I had ever seen her was months ago. She was casually shopping. Then again, when I found her bleeding outside of her flar. I noticed then that I had seen her before. Then I saw her again at the warehouse that night. It seemed like the both of us couldn't stay away from each other. "Tillo, why are you so nervous?", I asked him. "Well, I don't know how else to say this, but you and I were together.". I kind of knew what he was talking about. I remembered having strange dreams about him and being in his house. "I kind of remember.", I said. He turned to me now. "I kept eating candy. Is that something you do?", he asked. "You wouldn't happen to have some on you? I'd kill for a chocolate bar.", I said, and he shook his head. I realized it was a poor choice of words. "What do you mean we were...together, though?", I asked him. "Well, your essence, or soul, or whatever, was inside...me.". I thought again what the hell that meant. I continued to stare at him. "Emillie, can you please stop staring?", he asked me finally. "No. I can't stop thinking about you. Why?", I asked him, now moving sort of closer. "I don't know, either. But, I just want you to be safe. Awalli is out there and she is trying to kill you.", he said, desperately trying to move away from me, but I kept getting closer. "I know she is out there.", I said, now close to his face. I was about to kiss him, when the flar stopped, and we were outside of Dalia's orphanage. I moved away from him, not knowing what the hell was even coming over me. "You're home.", he said nervously. "I'm sorry.", I said embarrassingly and got out. Tillo looked like he wanted to follow me, but didn't. As soon as the flar drove off, I continued to think about him.

I went inside and all of the children were waiting for me to come in. They rushed me, and hugged me, and then I saw Dalia, who turned and walked away. "SEE, I TOLD YOU!", Cynda yelled. I knew that I needed to speak with Dalia. I tried to get away from the children, but they were all too excited. "CYNDA FOUND EMILLIE!", they were all chanting. "Please, children, I must speak with Mother Dalia. I'm not going anywhere.", I said, and they finally started to clear a path for me, "I'm home now. Okay? I'm home.", I said, tears coming to my eyes. I was so confused with everything, and didn't remember anything, except seeing Awalli before I died, and Tillo. I was right outside of Dalia's door, and I was about to turn the knob, when a voice I hadn't heard in months spoke to me, "You don't look dead. You look very much alive. Flin owes me seventy-shills.". I turned to my left, and was so shocked to see Celda, I forgot what I was doing and charged at her. I don't know how long I was crying with her, but she finally got us into Dalia's office. "Celda, I'd like to speak with Emillie, alone. Just for a minute. Please?". Celda obliged and walked out, closing the door. I immediately had so many questions and wondered if Dalia knew my mother's name. "Your mother was here. She told me you would come back. How do you feel, Emillie?", Dalia asked, looking at me as if I was a monster. "I feel fine. I guess. Just confused more than anything.". Dalia continued to look at me like I was something different. Then she stood up and walked up to me. "What's the last thing you remember?", "I remember a bright light. That's all. Then I was with Cynda. She told me that I was...dead.", I said dreadfully. "You were. And it was your mother's fault.". Everyone seemed to know my mother but me. "Dalia, what is her name?", I asked pleadingly. "I can't say it. She's put some curse out to where you can't say her name. But...let me try something.", Dalia said, taking out a piece of paper and simply writing on it. When she handed it to me, there was nothing there. I looked up at her. "Let me see it. Fucking... She made it to where you can't even see it.". Dalia said, throwing the paper away. "Who the hell is this woman? How is she my mother?", I asked. This was ridiculous. This is not what I thought of when I thought of my mom. I imagined a woman who wouldn't give me up unless she really had to. But what was this woman's deal? I couldn't even know her name?! "Dalia, please? There has to be a way to say her name.", "I know your mother. But forget about her. The truth is, you need to worry about Awalli.", "Everyone keeps telling me that, but I'm sick of it. I don't want to kill her.". I truly didn't.

Even though I know she killed me. "Emillie. Back in my day, I saw things that would scare the shit out of people today. That is what you and Awalli are. Hell, you two aren't the only ones. Your mother has been hushing everything for years.", "How many years?", I had to ask. "Thousands.", Dalia said, now giving me the most serious look she can muster, "This isn't something you can just wait around for, Emillie. You need training.", "I don't understand why my mother won't just train me.", "Your mother is scared of facing you. Scared of how you'll react to how she really is.", "How is my mother?", "A cold, heartless, bitch. I lived for thousands of years. Pining after her. Feeling connected to her. Do you know what it's like, for a normal girl like me, to turn yourself into something else?", Dalia asked me. I shook my head. "Well, it's like waking up one day and realizing you've won forty-million-shills. It's a dream. That's all it is. I wish I had died with my family. But I just had to be with… She messed up my entire life. I can't blame her, though. Part of it is my fault.", "Dalia, how am I supposed to be trained to fight something like Awalli? I've seen what she is now. She can summon me to her at any time! What am I supposed to do?!", I said desperately. "There is only one other person that can help you, but she is being a bitch like your mom. No, I don't mean that. She isn't like your mother. She told me that I would have to separate from her in order to ensure our victory.". I had no idea what Dalia was talking about. "Ensure our victory?", I asked. "Emillie, I barely know what that means, and the only person that would know, has also forbidden me from telling you her name.", "Do they hate me?", I asked sadly. I couldn't understand why people were choosing to hide things from me. I couldn't see the point. I just wanted the truth. Why was that a bad thing to have? "No. As a matter of fact, strangely, they love you but in their own ways. They have lived for a long time, Emillie. This is how people like them show their love.", "And what about you, Dalia? I've known nothing but love from you. So what makes them different?", I asked. Dalia looked like she was trying to tell me what was wrong but, like Tillo, she was unable to tell me anything that might help me figure out the identity of my mother.

SANDIN: I kept thinking about Emillie now. But it wasn't like before. I couldn't believe we almost kissed. As soon as the flar stopped and I was outside my home, I noticed my flar was parked in its usual spot and I wondered who drove it here. I walked into my home and everything was all clean. Too clean. I looked around my home, feeling like I was going to find something left behind. There was a knock on my door. I went to open it, and it was Red, "Tillo, mate. I've been checking your house everyday. She took Raby.", "More like Raby took her. Lody, I just had the craziest adventure of my life.", I said. I then explained to him how Emillie was extracted from me. How Raby showed me Awalli, who shortly after was able to get out of her cell. Raby and I were forced to have to fight a bunch of the other prisoners, who were mostly people suffering from some kind of mental disease. I told him about P.E.D, and how they specialize in these situations, and that Raby grew up in Dalia's orphanage and knew Emillie. When I finished telling Red everything, he looked at me cross. "So, you and Emillie have some connection?", he asked me, raising an eyebrow, "And you say she is alive now? And she knows that she is a goddess?", Red said, pacing back and forth, "Tillo, Raby told me that you would have gone after Awalli if she didn't take you like she did. She believed you were channeling Emillie's emotions. But I have a more serious worry.". Red told me of Captain Walsh and his fear of Awalli. Ever since Red and him had it out, Walsh has locked himself in his office everyday. Yellfy on the other hand was the more surprising factor, "HE DROPPED OFF THE FORCE?!", I asked Red, after he explained to me how Yellfy told Walsh he isn't going down with him. "Yeah, and I think we should follow suit. Awalli has taken control of all the GF precincts. She is threatening all the captains with exposure and death. So, I say we get away from that until this whole thing is clear. And it will be.", "What do you mean, Red?", I asked. "Emillie. Emillie has awoken. Now is the time for us to stay clear, Sandin. If we get anymore involved than we already are, we are going to die, mate.". I knew he was right. This was way beyond anything we have dealt with. I thought of Raby, though. "But, Red, Raby deals with this kind of shit. Or at least she is trained for it. Why can't we be?". There was another knock at my door. This time, it was Yellfy. "You're finally home.", he said, entering my apartment. "Listen, guys. I've met him. I've met the kung-fu guy. But more than that, you won't believe this. Take a look at what Awalli has been doing.", Yellfy said, as he handed us a list of certain accounts that have been opened, and purchases made, and calls. I realized right away what I was looking at. "She is trying to take over globally!", I yelled, unable to believe what I was looking at. I quickly showed Red. "This is what I was afraid of. Awalli is something different. The mob has never had someone like her leading it. Now this is the result. So here is the question. How do we stop her?", said Red, now getting new vigor since learning this new info. "Oh, I have some ideas.", said Yellfy, who was taking out some more paperwork, "Tillo. I've recently learned something. About your father. It was covered up for sure, but I found out the REAL reason this, Commander, killed your father.". I thought about it. Did I really want to know? I was more comfortable with the anger. I slowly nodded my head to symbolize I'll listen. "This is going to be hard to take in, though, Tillo, so brace yourself. Your father had some kind of disease he contracted before you were born. Something that started to eat at his mind. This had something to do with something he found on one of those digs he used to take you on. Not even your mother would have known.", "How did you find all this out, Yellfy?", I asked him, growing angry. "Well, that's just it. I found this out once I started investigating this Commander. I figured there was more to her than what you've told me. I wasn't looking into your past on purpose, mate. It just popped up in my investigation. She was very skilled at hiding herself. And now that I've been learning that magic and all that crap is real, I've discovered she is very adept at it. She hides herself well. But whatever the case, from what I've found of your father, he was killed, because if he wasn't, he would have killed you, and your mother.".

I kept running Yellfy's words in my head. He would have killed us? But how? What disease? And it was before I was born, so how come I never noticed? Then, Red said something, "Awalli used to be a nice girl, then something changed her. What if it was the same thing?", "What?", I asked. "What if the same thing that is in Awalli, was also somehow in your father?", said Red, thinking. "I doubt it. We aren't RF.", "What if you don't have to be?", replied Yellfy, "Look, everything that I've learned suggests that this epidemic is what The Commander was trying to prevent. But whatever it is, she isn't exactly sure herself. So far, it has outsmarted her. Emillie's death was plotted out, but why? Because she can probably stop this thing.", "Yellfy, Emillie is alive. She is back at the orphanage.", I said. "Then I will have to question her.", "No, leave her alone for a while. Those kids are probably really happy she is home.", I said. "And you think that's safe? Think about it. She has a homicidal goddess after her. She will probably see those kids as collateral. And you know I'm right.". He was. "Look, let me tell her. It will seem rude coming from you, Yencid. I'll handle Emillie.", I said. Red hadn't been to see Dalia in a while, so he was happy to tag along.

When we arrived outside of Dalia's orphanage, I felt a chill run through my whole body. As we exited the flar, Emillie came out and we locked eyes. She smiled and waved for us to come in. "It's good to see you, Mr. Red.", said Emillie, hugging Red as he walked in but still keeping her eyes on me. She then looked at Yencid, who was watching her curiously. "So, Emillie, it's nice to finally meet you.", said Yellfy, holding out his hand. Emillie shook his hand and Yencid looked like he would never wash that hand again. "Look, I know why you're all here. And, I think you are right. So I'll be getting my own apartment.", "How did you know why we are here?", asked Yencid, surprised. "Because I thought about it myself the moment I got back. Plus, I just discussed it with Mother Dalia.", "Where is she?", asked Red. "She is in her office if you'd like to go see her.", said Emillie, pointing up the stairs. "I think I'll join you.", said Yellfy, and they both proceeded up the stairs. "So...", Emillie said, turning back to me, "...let's take a walk.".

We proceeded into the garden. It was getting late now and I was feeling embarrassed. Emillie was holding my hand. "So, are you okay, Sandin?", she asked me. "Emillie, please, you need to stop.", I said, taking my hand from her. She took it back and stopped walking. She then grabbed my other hand. Holding both hands now, she looked up into my eyes, "I can't stop. I want you. I don't even know why. Everytime I'm apart from you, you stay with me.", she said, getting closer now. "I...can't stop thinking about you, either. But it has something to do with before, so maybe we shouldn't be...", before I could finish, she was kissing me. She dropped my hands, and wrapped her arms around me. I never felt so good in my life. I felt a shock going through my body and I didn't want to let her go. "Ooo.", said a girlish voice from behind one of the tall bushes. "CYNDA!", yelled Emillie, "Cynda! You're supposed to be in bed! Get inside!", "But, Emillie, you said you were leaving and...", "We'll discuss it later. Right now, I need to talk to GO Tillo.", "More like, make out with GO Tillo.", said Cynda, laughing. "Get inside.", said Emillie, with a smile on her face. Cynda listened and ran back up, taking the time to turn around, and stick her tongue out. "Sorry about that. Well, when I have my own place, we will have more privacy.", said Emillie, taking her arms off me, resuming holding my hand, and leading me around the garden. "Emillie, I found something out about my father.", "What is it?". I told her what Yencid told me. "So, my mother was saving your life? Interesting.", she said. "But what gets me, is why not tell me and my mother the truth?", "Where is your mother, Sandin?", asked Emillie, once again stopping our walk. "She is living on the outskirts of Bronxton. She hasn't been the same since my father really. She's sick.", I said. But now, I was thinking about it in a way I never had. Suddenly, I felt like I needed to see her. "I'll go with you.", said Emillie, even though I didn't voice my thoughts out loud. "Emillie, can you read my mind?", I had to ask. "No, but I can feel your feelings. Like I'm sure you can feel mine.". I did before, but now it was different. "I think I want to stay with you tonight. Is that okay?", asked Emillie. I wanted to say hell yeah, but I knew that this wasn't the time. "No. I think you should focus on getting yourself situated into your new situation.", "Then I want you to come. Sandin, don't be an idiot.", she said, giving me a strange look. I knew what she meant. "Alright. We can stay together. Tonight. But you have a lot going on and I don't want to be a distraction to you.", I said, giving her a reprimanding look. She smiled and nodded.

LODY: As Yencid and I entered Dalia's office, she was sitting behind her desk scribbling on some papers. She looked up, saw me, and made to get up, but stopped when she saw Yencid. "What is this, Red?", she asked, while watching Yencid. "Hello, Dalia. It's good to see you. Yencid just has some questions. He isn't with the GF anymore and I'm thinking of following suit.". Dalia looked at the both of us, then started to laugh. "Dalia, we want to know how Emillie is coping.", said Yencid. "Well, she has only been back a couple of hours, and I imagine since you left her with Tillo, she must be kissing all over him by now.". I thought about this and looked out the window. Sure enough, I saw Tillo and Emillie holding hands. "Would you look at that?", I said, unable to believe it. Raby was right. They were attracted to each other. I looked back at Dalia, who was once again, drinking. "Dalia, are you feeling alright?", I asked her. "No. I'm not. That thing out there is not MY Emillie.", she said darkly. "What do you mean?", asked Yencid, sitting down, and gazing at Dalia. "She is something her mother created. Something that isn't normal. I...sound silly in a way. But the truth is, I can't have her here. I told her she would have to leave. She agreed. But she doesn't know the real reason. Her mother has made it to where you can't tell her anything. The poor girl has no idea what is coming for her. And I want to help. But I can't. I can't. It isn't my place. Now, my daughter is dead. That thing out there is some kind of...monster. She just can't see it herself. If I were you, Lody, I'd tell Tillo to stay far away.", said Dalia, taking a swig of ticenta. "Dalia, what do you mean, though? Are you talking about Awalli?", asked Yencid, taking out a notepad. "No. Awalli is just the tip of the iceberg. She is the beginning. But definitely not the end. What I'm trying to say is...Emillie isn't the only thing in this city right now that poses a great threat to your life and the balance of it. Emillie is more of an entity than a person. Just like me. Just like her mother. Just like her aunt. There are others. Others that are different, Mr. Red. People you wouldn't believe have been alive as long as me.", "And you have been alive for three-thousand years. This is correct?", asked Yellfy. Dalia nodded, and Yellfy scribbled on his pad. "And what was it like exactly? Three-thousand years ago?", asked Yellfy, now sitting back in the chair, waiting to write on his pad. "Well, it was similar to this. The truth was, back then, things like this were considered almost normal. For a long time, the gods and goddesses fought each other. It's the reason why the RF have been killin em' off.", said Dalia, taking another swig of ticenta. She looked directly at Yencid and said, "This is all happening, because Amana spared Layna the same fate as her ancestors.", "What does that mean?", asked Yencid. "It means that because of Amana, we now have more gods and goddesses running around. It means they will fight one another. It means chaos in your city. What more do I need to say?", Dalia said, putting her head down now. "But aren't YOU a goddess?", Yellfy now asked, looking at me, and then back at Dalia. "Not the kind that Emillie is. I made myself this way. Just like Mileeda. She was… Is a synthetic goddess. But her descendants have inherited her genetics. Hence the RF being as powerful as they are. But only certain ones are born with the gift. Layna was born with it. So was Awalli. Awalli is going to challenge Layna. It will start a war the likes of which this whole planet hasn't SEEN in…I'd say about two and a half thousand years.". Yencid looked shocked. I knew how he felt. It all made some kind of sense. "And the kung-fu guy? He, too, is a god?", Yencid asked now. "I don't know anything about a kung-fu guy. The thing that you have to understand is that this is all Amana's doing. She had Emillie, and of course she saved Layna, and Awalli. Then I don't know who this kung-fu guy is, but I know for a fact, he is connected to…', Dalia's tongue got all tied up. She started laughing, "The other one. That's all I can manage to say. Amana's curse is only around Emillie. She is so scared of what her daughter will say about her.", "But who is Emillie's father, Dalia?", I asked. "Someone who isn't even from this planet. All I know is, Amana sought him out and made some sort of deal. This is how Emillie was born. And I don't know who he is. I couldn't begin to say. But I was told that Emillie was too much for Amana, and she trusted me to raise her. That's all.", "But what do you mean by, spared Layna from the same fate as her ancestors? Can you be more specific on that part, please?", Yencid asked, once again leaning forward. "Why do you think there has been peace? It's because of the fact that the RF, for generations, has been killing anybody born with the gift. They ensure that there will be no more gods or goddesses. This started after the last war. I can't say that I wholeheartedly agreed, but it did stop the violence. Then the gangs started to spring up, and that was a whole new kind of violence. Something that Amana ensured she had control of. Now, I'm confused. Because she is causing a lot to happen. A lot that she has been trying to keep from happening.". Now I was thinking. She warned me about Awalli, then someone blew up Laddie's while I'm in it. Tillo was there. Maybe Tillo was the reason I survived. Tillo, who has some connection to Emillie. Sandin Tillo. "Why are Sandin and Emillie so attracted to each other? Tillo is a good looking guy and all, but what does she see in him?", I asked, looking back out the window, as Emillie and Tillo were kissing. "She doesn't realize it, but I did the moment I met Tillo. I just couldn't tell you then, Red. Tillo is different. He has been touched by god energy. This means that his physiology has been altered in a way that makes him almost godlike.", "What, the, fuck, are you saying, Dalia?", I asked, unable to buy this. "I'm saying that Tillo has been made whole by merging with Emillie. But he is still just a guy. I knew another just like him. My king. Tig.". Yencid dropped his notepad. "Tig? THE Tig? Sebastian's best friend in the fairy tales?", Yencid asked unnerved. "Oh yes. He was a very happy-go-lucky chap. Then he ended up involved with a god. He was found with circles carved into his body. His own son had to kill him.", "When you say...circles?", Yencid asked. Dalia got up and went to one of her cabinets. She took out a really old scroll and unbound it, rolled it out, and handed it to Yencid. I looked at it. "What the hell is that supposed to be?", I asked. "This is the language of the gods, Lody. I know it has been a long time, but I can promise you, I never learned how to read it. To me it just looks like circles. But this is what was carved into Tig's body. His own son had to kill him.", Dalia said sadly. "Nigel killed Tig? Is it silly to ask if Nigel was also different?", Yellfy asked, now writing vigorously on his notepad. "Nigel was just a normal man, who got old and died. While his wife, she remained young looking. Never aging. She went mad. Wanted vengeance for everything that happened in her life. But now she is hiding from her crazy ass family while we have to deal with everything.". Tillo walked in the office, "Emillie is going to pack. What did I miss?".

After we quickly explained to Sandin what Dalia told us, Sandin took a deep breath, "There is something I should share with you two. Something I never told anybody. About my father. I barely remember, because I was so young, but he found something that he gave to me. I've never been sick. I've always healed fast. And most importantly, I've always survived in the most questionable situations. Like at the bar.", Tillo said, nodding to me, "I seem almost invincible. But I don't have powers. Or super strength. I don't know what I am.". Tillo looked up and put his hands in his pockets, "This is why I'm going to see my mother. I'm going to get some straight answers about me, and my place in this crazy shit.". Tillo understood perfectly. What he was experiencing with Emillie was all the proof he needed. A goddess pining after a regular-joe like him. Tillo wasn't much older than Emillie. So it wasn't strange. But her beauty far surpassed what someone like him would be seen with. We made our way out. Emillie taking things to her own flar. "Sandin, aren't you going to help your girlfriend carry those things?", Yellfy asked jokingly. "Haha. She said she doesn't need me to help her. She feels stronger.". The kids were all in bed, so they wouldn't see Emillie leave. "Sandin, aren't you coming with me?", she asked, looking hopeful. Tillo looked at me and Yellfy. "Guess I'm going with her.", "Tillo, look, mate, you need to be careful. I think you're forgetting what Emillie is.", I said. "No. I know what she is. But you don't get it. I have to BE with her. I can't explain it. But that's why I'm going to see my mother.". Sandin walked over to Emillie's flar, got in, and they drove off. Me and Yellfy got back into his flar. "So, he is going to screw her. He is very lucky, Lody.", "I guess. I don't know. Dalia says she is a monster.", "I don't think so. The way she smells. The way she talks. Her voice. It's all so heavenly. I don't know how to explain it, but tell me you felt that as well.", Yellfy said unnerved. "I did feel something different. Maybe, Dalia is right, and Emillie is now something she doesn't fully understand.", "Should we try and stop Sandin?", Yellfy asked. "No. We should proceed with what's next. That means we need to learn as much about how to stop a mad goddess as possible.".

EMILLIE: My new apartment wasn't far from the orphanage, so I could still visit. As Tillo and I arrived, I looked at him, "My mother is the one who gave me this apartment.", I said, staring at him. "Well, do you trust her?", he asked. "Not, for, one, second. If she won't even let me know her name, then what is the point? Besides, I'm just going to have to wait it out if nobody is going to train me.", "Train you to be a goddess?", Tillo asked, "Emillie, maybe you just need to learn how to fight. I could teach you that.". We got out of the flar and walked into my apartment, which was on the second floor of a four-plex. I was surprised to see there was furniture already. I looked around and went into the kitchen and found all my favorite types of candy. In the fridge, there was food as well. I looked at Sandin, who was also surprised by this. "So, not bad. Now if she just wasn't so afraid to meet me.", "I think there might be more to it, Emillie. Now about what I said. Teaching you to fight. I'm a pretty good fighter. I used to compete in fights when I was eighteen. So, I could teach you.". I looked at him, then I walked up to him, "There is nobody to distract us, Sandin.", I whispered in his ear. He wrapped his arms around me and I kissed him. We quickly fell onto the kitchen floor and basically tore our clothes off. Then we were in the living room. Then we somehow found the shower. Then we were back in the living room.

Finally, we were in the bedroom. I felt like I hadn't had sex before. There was a boy I liked a long time ago, and I tried it with him. It was only a quick session, though, that didn't last more than four minutes. But with Tillo, I was like a mad beast. I needed more, and more. I kissed him, as he continued thrusting inside of me. Finally, we were done. I didn't know how long we were going. But at some point, we fell asleep.

"Emillie. I see you. I see you, Emillie. I'm coming for YOU!". I woke up in a pool of sweat. Sandin wasn't in the bed, but he came into the room when he heard me scream. "What's the matter?", he asked. "I had a dream about Awalli. She says she is coming for me.". Sandin came and put his hand on my shoulder. "Listen, you are going to beat her.", "But, she killed me already!", I yelled and cried. "And you're here. She is trying to scare you. You need to show her that you aren't afraid of her. Try and get some rest, okay?", he said, kissing me on my forehead. I layed back down. I tried to think, then I had another dream. "Emillie, you can win. I believe in you.", "Who are you?". A woman so beautiful, that she was glowing brightly, was standing before me. "I am not too far from you. But you can beat the false goddess. You have help. You are not alone, Emillie. Your mother may have you thinking that, but I assure you, that YOU ARE NOT ALONE.". I woke up, and this time, I felt completely relieved. I realized that Sandin had left, but there was a note;

```
Dear Emillie,

    I have gone to meet with Red and Yellfy. I
will return for our trip to see my mother. Just
try and be patient.
```

As I re-read the note to make sure I understood, I decided to sit down and relax. I took a shower, then got dressed, then ate a shit ton of that candy, then I found there were films here. So I watched them. I quickly grew bored and missed Sandin. The receiver rang, and I didn't even realize there was one. I went to answer it, "Yes?", "Hello, Ms. Panahelios. How is your new apartment?", Gail asked. "It's nice. I'm just enjoying it now, but I have a question. What the hell am I supposed to do about Awalli?", I asked. "Well that's why I'm calling. I need you to meet with me. Have you ever been to Linix?", "No. I haven't.", "Well, I'll send you the address. It's important that we meet there. I'll be on my way there shortly.". Gail hung up. Then my cell notification alert went off. I looked and it was an address. I decided to head to that address. Once there, I saw Gail, who gave me a hug, then led me inside. "What is this place?", "It's a restaurant. That's all. Sorry for the strange theatrics. But it is one of the safe havens for P.E.D.", "Yeah, about P.E.D, can you please tell me, fully, what it is? And how is my mother in charge? And somehow can you manage to tell me WHO SHE IS?", I said. Gail just watched me for a split second. "Emillie, I need to know where you were for those three days you were missing.", "Three days? What are you talking about?", I asked her. The only thing I remembered was waking up to Cynda. "Emillie, listen to me. I don't think you understand what you are. There is another force inside of you. When your essence returned to it's vessel, something ELSE returned with it. It's hiding inside of you now. But we can't figure out what it is. I've told The General that meeting you at this point is essential, but she...", I felt a weird feeling in my stomach. My chest started to burn, I looked at Gail, who was getting up, "OUT, EVERYONE, OUT, NOW!", she ran out with everyone else. There was a bright light that filled everything. Then when the light was gone, I was standing in the restaurant, holding something. Gail walked back in. "Oh my...", she said. I looked at what I was holding, it was a sword. A fancy-ass sword. The blade was red and black on each side, and the hilt had black wings coming out. And along with that, I had armor. It was black with red rubies across my stomach and shoulders. I looked at Gail, who looked positively frightened. Then, I passed out.

SANDIN: When I left Emillie in the morning, it was the hardest thing I'd done in a while. I was going to see my mother without her. I knew she would be upset. Especially after that crazy night we just had. We spent the entire night having sex. I kept running it over in my head. Every stroke. Her perfect lips on mine. Her body. Everything seemed too good to be true. And yet, something told me, Emillie wasn't ready to be out in public yet, no matter how she tried to pass it off. While she was asleep, she kept talking in her sleep. And at one point, she started to glow. I got out of bed at this point. I was afraid of having sex with her ever again, in case she started to glow again. But something told me, I'd do it again in a heartbeat. I proceeded to The Dattur, which was our new meeting spot. Red arrived with Yellfy in his flar. They both signaled for me to get in. "Morning. And how was YOUR night, Tillo?", Yellfy asked, as soon as I put my safety strap on. "It was interesting.", "Want to share details?", Yellfy asked with a smile. "Not really. But, what I will say is, Emillie is definitely something different.". I told them about how Emillie started glowing, and how she was muttering in her sleep, and having dreams about Awalli. "I read something similar in Raby's report on Awalli. It said something about Awalli experiencing bad dreams and chest pains. You might want to ask her if she is going through anything like that.". I thought about it and realized she probably did have chest pains. She kept clutching her chest the whole night. Not to mention how long we were having sex for. I'd never had sex that good in my life. I couldn't explain it to Red and Yellfy, though. "So, we're going to Bronxton? That could be a while if we drive. Maybe we should fly?", Yellfy suggested. "I agree.", I said. I only agreed because I couldn't stay away from Emillie for that long.

When we reached the birdport, we immediately purchased tickets and waited for an hour. Finally, we boarded the flight and made our way to Bronxton. "We should get a hovel. That way, we don't have to leave until morning.", Red said, looking at me. I knew why. "I'll let Emillie know.". I knew she would be angry with me for going without her, but I felt like I had made the right choice. I went to the receiver and called her cell. "Yes, Mr. Tillo?", answered Raby. "Why do you have Emillie's cell? Where is she?", I asked, starting to panic. "Emillie has had...let's say an accident. But she is in good hands, Mr. Tillo. You just focus on whatever it is you're doing.", "No. I want to talk to her.", "That is quite impossible. Like I said, she had an accident.", Raby said in a sort of scared tone. "What accident? What happened?", I asked. "Are you near a t.v? Turn to the news.". Raby hung up. I quickly rushed into the room we had rented and turned on the t.v. It was indeed a news report in Edge. A restaurant named Linix was now the latest place to be attacked. "...woman, who warned everyone to exit the building, leaving one lone person inside. Others are saying that the person left inside began to glow and that it was really strange.", the reporter finished saying. I listened to the report again. I called Emillie's cell again, but Raby didn't answer this time. I was becoming worried. "What's wrong?", Red asked me. "It's Emillie. I think she is in trouble. I need to...", "Do what? You're too far away to worry about that. You need to focus on why you're here.", "That's easy for you to say, Red. You didn't just spend a night with her.", I replied, once again calling her cell. There was still no answer. I threw the cell right when Yellfy walked in. It hit him in the face. For a second, we just all stood there. Then we started laughing. We laughed for about five minutes. Finally, "So, are you ready to go see your mother?", asked Yellfy. "Yes. I guess so. I kind of wish I didn't lie to Emillie, though.", I said, thinking about her. I could see her face in my mind. She was so beautiful. I wanted her.

"Let's get some rest. Try and get ready for tomorrow.", Red said, as he stretched out on his bed and turned over.

I awoke in the middle of the night and found Emillie in my room. "What...?", I began, but she quickly covered my mouth. "I'm okay. I'm back on the P.E.D base. Something happened to me. I don't know how to explain it. But I came, because...", she looked nervous to say what she wanted to say. "You want more.", I said. She quickly kissed me. "Wait, is this real?", I asked. "Yes. It's real.", she said, taking her shirt off and kissing me. Once again we were having sex. But this time, I found myself waking up embarrassingly the next morning. "Tillo, I had no idea it was THAT good for you.", Yellfy said, laughing. I looked at my surroundings and realized what was different in the dream. Yellfy wasn't there and neither was Red. Both were somehow not there. But both woke up when I started making strange noises and moving strangely. "I think it was just a dream.", I said, after I explained Emillie being in our room. "She wasn't here last night. I think she pulled a dreamscape on you.", Red said, smiling a bit. I didn't know what to think. I called her cell again, to which there still was no answer. "You need to not think about her right now, Sandin. That's probably what gave you the dream.", Yellfy said. "I don't think so. It felt real. Like she was here. Sitting on my bed. Plus, how do you explain her telling me where she is?", I said. I knew it couldn't have been a dream. We all got ready, and got into the rental flar we had, and drove to the place my mom was staying. It was a nice complex for people that had been through certain ordeals. As soon as we arrived, I recognized the lady who I met with when I brought my mother here. "Mr. Tillo? Good to see you. And who are these men?", Ladis asked. Ladis was the woman who owned this place. She was a very short blonde lady, who had black eyes and a friendly face. "These are some partners of mine. This is Lody

Red, and this is Yencid Yellfy. We just need to see my mother.", I said. "I'm glad you came. She has been acting very strange lately.", Ladis said, directing us inside. I knew that was a bad sign right away. My mother 'acting strangely' when all this goddess stuff is taking place. As soon as we were near her room, I could hear her muttering, "...Sandin needs guidance, Slayn, he needs to know... Wait, our son is coming.". As we entered the room, I looked at her. Her hair was askew, and she had the look of a lady who's lost all her cats and can't find them. "Hello, Mother.", I said. Red looked shocked, and Yellfy looked at her and me with pity. "Sandin, you need to speak with your father.", she said, grabbing my hands. "I can't, remember? He is dead.". She shook her head, "No. He is just sleeping.", "Tillo, why didn't you tell us how she is?", Red asked in my ear. I ignored him. "Mom, I need to know about what is happening to me. I recently had a very strange experience, and I think it has to do with Father. What did my father do to me?", I asked her. "Your father, blessed you. We found something special. It still had power in it. Your father says you were already special, but this made you more special. This made you invincible.", she said with great vigor. I looked at the other two, who looked at me like I was insane for even listening to her. "Mom, I need to know what you two found.", "We found that.", she said, pointing at my finger. I looked, and realized what she was pointing at was the ring that I had found in Awalli's warehouse. I had been wearing it and didn't really stop to think why. "What do you mean you found this?", I asked. "It's the ring. It belongs to her. To the one you are destined to meet. The one your father was warned about.". Now I looked at the other two, who were surprised by this as well. "Who was my father warned about?", "The daughter of the woman that killed him. Emillie, is her name.". We were all shocked to find out my mother, who had never met Emillie, or should have any knowledge of her, had knowledge of her. "What does that mean?", asked Red, now dropping his disbelief. "It means that she is the one who holds my son's heart. Tell me, have you met her? You have… I can feel her emanating off you. You've been sleeping with her already. This is how it starts. She is going to save us all. Emillie will save us. We've been promised.", "By whom?", Yellfy now spoke. "Ko-e.". We looked at each other again. "Ko-e? Like the girl from the fairy tales?", Yellfy said, taking his notepad back out. "That must be the other one!", Red said, looking at Yellfy. "I think you're right, Red. But what does that mean? What does that mean for us? Where is Ko-e?", Yellfy asked. "She is hidden from her sister.". My mother was like an information well. How she knew all this stuff, I didn't understand. Then my mother got faint, "She is coming. She is COMING!", she yelled and started to panic. "Who is coming?", I asked. "Awalli!", she replied. We looked at one another, then were surprised when Awalli was standing in the doorway. We all pulled our cannons out, "Now hold on. I'm only here to speak with Mrs. Tillo.", "YOU STAY THE HELL AWAY FROM HER!", I yelled, moving closer. "Red, good to see you again.", Awalli said, walking in, and closing the door. My mother looked like death just arrived. "Get out!", I said. "Not until I get what I came for. I've come for two things. I need to know where the other goddess is hiding. Ko-e. Amana's sister. And I need…", she looked at the ring on my finger, "…my property back.", she said menacingly. "It's not yours. It's mine.", I said. "Tillo, you have no idea how badly I want to kill you. But I think I have a better idea. You're Emillie's new boytoy. So why don't I make sure you're good enough for her?", she said, reaching her hands towards my face. Red shot her and that's when all hell broke loose. Me, Yellfy, and Red, flew in different directions. "Big mistake.", she said. She walked up to my mother and placed her hand on her shoulder, "No! Don't touch her!", I yelled. "Hopefully, next time we meet, Sandin, we can do more than just tease each other.", she said, then disappeared, with my mother.

EMILLIE: I woke up feeling like shit. I looked around and found Gail sitting next to me. "What happened?", I asked. "The other entity showed itself, then disappeared.", Gail said gravely. There was some kind of dark-green glass that I couldn't see through, but something told me that there was someone on the other side. "Gail, what's happening?", I asked. "Emillie, I'm very sorry for everything that is about to happen.", she said, then stood up and walked away. I looked up at the glass, "WHO'S THERE?!", I shouted. No reply. "PLEASE?!". Still no reply. Then I felt something enter from the top of my skull, and I screamed. I heard the sound of the drill on my skull. Then it stopped. I laid back and felt the blood pouring down my face. Then there was something else. Something was messing around in my head. It felt like little hands. It felt like hours. I had no idea what the hell was happening to me. Then, suddenly, "STOP!". The little hands went away. I was surprised I didn't really feel the pain anymore. Then someone came into the room and stood over me. "There is something inside of you. Something that isn't supposed to be there. But trying to extract it will kill you. I have no choice but to leave it. But understand this, Ms. Panahelios. I will be watching you. And the moment you do anything that threatens innocent people, I'm going to take you again, and this time, I'll let that drill run. You are dangerous. You're not what you were and you had better learn that fast.".

I didn't know where I was. Sandin was here. "Sandin!", I yelled, extremely happy to see him. "Emillie, where the hell are we? It looks like that place we were before.". There were blades of green and purple grass, I looked around, and saw nothing but the two of us. I ran to him and kissed him. We were about to satisfy my need for extensive sex when, "Emille, no. Its weird. Red and Yellfy are with me, and if we start having sex... It was weird last time.". I looked at Tillo half amused, "Okay. Where are you?", I asked him. "We...went to see my mother. But it's good you didn't come! Awalli was there, Em! She took my mom!", Sandin said, almost on the verge of tears, but he held it in. "Sandin, I'm going to save your mom. As soon as I get out of here.". I woke up, with Gail sitting next to me in tears. "Emillie, are you okay? Please tell me you're okay!", Gail said, desperately crying at my side. "Gail, what happened to me? What the hell was happening?", I asked, confused, with tears in my eyes. "You… were under surgery.", she said. "Gail, I didn't consent to any surgery.", I said, now crying with her, "Gail, tell me what happened! The truth!", I shouted. Gail looked at me, lost, then said, "Your mother…", "That is enough, Mrs. Raby. I'll take it from here.", said a voice I recognized. It was the voice of the woman that just tortured me. She walked into the room with a cocky look on her face. I knew right away. "No. Why would YOU do this to me? WHY?!", I yelled, and the lights flickered some. "That's why.", said my mother, "You don't know what you are, hell, I don't know. You are unique, yet dangerous. And out there, it's getting more and more dangerous. I can't have you running around screwing Sandin Tillo every chance you get, destroying restaurants when you feel like it, or possibly, destroying buildings and murdering small, innocent, orphans.". I thought about what she was saying. Gail came up to me and showed me video footage. I looked and I saw myself light up. The building I was in looked like something terrible happened there afterwards. Then I saw myself glowing, holding a sword, and wearing armor. Gail stepped back. "That's what's inside of you. I tried removing it…", "WITHOUT MY CONSENT!", I shouted. "I don't need your fucking consent, Emillie.", my mother replied. "Who are you? What's your name?", I asked her, hoping to finally get an answer. "Amana.", Gail said, glaring at her. "No. You're, Amana? You're my mother? Amana.". I couldn't believe it. I hated her. I hate her now more than ever before. "I want to leave.", "You can't. I have more tests to run.", "No. I am not your pet. I want to leave.", I said, and I tried to teleport, but couldn't. "Emillie, this room is shielded from that kind of magic. No one can teleport in or out.", Gail said. "Gail, get out.", Amana said. Gail did, hesitantly. "Close the door.", Amana commanded, and Gail did. "So, you think that you're a badass now? Is that it?", Amana asked me. "No. I just don't want to be HERE with YOU! I HATE YOU!", I shouted at her. "You, stupid, little... Do you have any idea how much I sacrificed, just so you could exist?!", she replied back. "I don't care what you sacrificed! I never asked to be abandoned!", "I left you with someone I trust and love very much. You have no idea how much it pained me to even give you to her. You are my only child. I never wanted to abandon you like...", she stopped, "Listen, I just wanted you to grow up happy. But then, Awalli happened. Now it is different.", "Why is it different now?", I asked, glaring at her. She wasn't fooling me. I could tell what she was. Calculating. Trying to manipulate me for her own gains. But nothing can make me forget that she tortured her own daughter. "BECAUSE SHE KILLED YOU!", she replied, "I didn't know if the vessel would work or if it would be okay for your particular brand of essence. You don't understand how different you are. But, I can't ignore what is right in front of me. Awalli and you. You two are drawn to each other. At this point, I'm certain that you are the only one that can kill her. Believe me, I tried to kill her myself. I heard you don't want to kill her.", she said. Then I remembered, she has my boyfriend's mother. "No, just stop her.", "What if I said, the only way is to kill her?", Amana asked. "Then I will find another way.". Amana smiled, "Awalli is passed saving. I'm sure you will feel different. But I can't let you leave. I need to know what is living inside of you. I need to know, Emillie. Because what manifested inside of Linix, was something reminiscent of my father.", "Sebastian?", I asked in awe. "Emillie, you are his direct grandchild.", "Are you lying to me?", I asked. I couldn't believe her. I didn't know if I could trust her. She was skilled at lying. "Emillie, you are my daughter, and I am Amana Tia. Daughter of Alisa Tia and Sebastian.", "I thought you were the child of Trin…", "DON'T SAY THAT NAME!", Amana yelled. I shivered some. "I am not the child of that…thing.", she said unnerved. "Okay. I'm sorry. I didn't know.", "It's a lot more interesting learning the truth, isn't it?", she asked me, now smiling as if she wasn't angry less than three seconds ago, "Emillie, I will train you. I'll teach you to do what you have to do. But I need you to understand that there is no room for mistakes. This thing that you are entering into is a war, being fought on multiple fronts. Once you journey down this road, it's all in, or nothing.". I gulped, but knew I had no choice. I nodded. "This doesn't change things between us.", I said. "Oh my god. Okay, how about this? Do I have your permission to run more tests on you to fully understand what has melded with YOUR essence?", she asked me. "FINE!", I said. "Great. Nice finally meeting you.", she said, opening the door, and walking out. Gail stood in the doorway, "Emillie…", "Get out.", I said, without even looking at her. All my life, I wanted to meet my mom. And well, what a hell of a meeting. She tortures me, then asks me to get ready to kill someone, and to fight in a war. All I wanted more than anything in the world was Sandin, and some candy.

CHAPTER 6

The Should-Be Queen

WALLI: Once I arrived back at the manor in SE with Mrs. Tillo, I made sure to secure her in a room with no entrance. This was a bit of magic I had picked up on since meeting Emillie on the P.E.D base. To my men, it looked like I just walked out of the wall, but to me, I just came from my hidden room. "Boss, I need to ask you a question.", Li said one day, as I was exiting the room. I had been questioning Mrs. Tillo for the past three days on where Ko-e might be hiding. The energy she put off told me that she was exposed to raw cosmic energy. It is the reason she has seemingly lost her marbles. But she hasn't lost her marbles. She has gained a connection to Heaven. She can sense heavenly beings that are here on Plinth and I knew she could tell me where Ko-e is hiding. But she was very resilient and wasn't saying. Even when I threatened to bring Tillo here and torture him in front of her, it wasn't enough. She was too sickly for me to torture and I needed some incentive. "What is your question, Li?", I asked impatiently, after another tiring round of questioning Mrs. Tillo. "Well, some of us were wondering what is the deal with the old lady you brought here. And some of us are also wondering what you intend to do about Sylvia.". Sylvia Lon was another member of the RF. After what happened to Reginald, I allowed Tek to return home. Dear Cousin Sylvia complained to Layna about the lack of attention she was giving me. I didn't hear what Layna said, but it was enough to make Sylvia come here. Sylvia didn't have the gift, but from my understanding, she was a bit tougher than the two brothers. "I'll deal with her. But I've already told you all to not meddle in my affairs.", "Your affairs?", Li repeated, "Listen, when I brought you here, it was…", "At the behest of Corsa. She had you put me here. So don't try and say it was your decision. I told you that Emillie must die.", "Yeah, you keep saying that, but she is…", "Alive. She is with her mother right now. I've seen her. So what else are you going to say?", I asked him irritatedly. I knew that he didn't understand why I was so eager to make sure she was dead. I also had been slightly avoiding him since we almost kissed, and well…he IS my cousin. "Well, why? This girl can't be that dangerous!", Li said. "Li, the girl died, now she is alive again. What more proof do you need? I know what I am talking about. And the old lady I brought here is to take care of our other friend.", I said. Li realized what I was talking about. "That kung-fu guy? Okay. I see.", he said, now scratching his chin. "How does she help with that?", he asked now. "Look, tell the guys that EVERYTHING that I am doing, is for the betterment of all of us. I'm ensuring that we do not fail. Why can't you be more like Ethel? She is fully accepting this new change.", I said. This was true. Although she lost a good amount of her men when we were bringing in Raby, she now had a better understanding. All my men wondered where Raby had taken me, but were shocked when I returned once again. Ethel didn't question me anymore after this. She fully understood that Emillie was the only one who could kill me. Li looked like he had more to say, but dropped it. "So, what do you want us to do in the meantime?", Li asked. "Just focus on business. Keep the streets hot. Trust me, right now, nobody can touch us. Not even Sylvia. I'll find her right now.".

I teleported to her location but found myself in a strange building. Then something hit my shoulder and I was almost knocked off my feet.

I looked around and saw a brown-haired lady, with some kind of huge cannon that hung off her shoulder. "What the hell do you think you are...?", before I finished my sentence, she shot me again. "Get up!", she yelled at me. I tried to stand but found myself weakened. I looked and realized I was covered in gold dust. "Having a hard time aren't you? Yeah, I bet you are.", Sylvia said, coming up to me, and kicking me in my face. I felt my nose crack under her foot. "I TOLD Layna not to leave you on your own three years ago! I told her, now look what has happened. You've lost your damn mind! Teaming up with the MOB! Killing Reginald! And my personal favorite, trying to start a war with Layna.". Sylvia picked me up by the sleeves of my shoulders and then headbutted me. There was blood on my face and I couldn't do anything. No matter how I tried to move, I couldn't. "Listen, let's talk plainly. You have the gift, but you don't fully understand it. You didn't know you could be weakened. I bet you thought nobody could hurt you.". At this, it was obvious that she didn't know about Emillie. Amana had told me that Emillie was secret even to Layna, whom she raised almost like her daughter. I tried to teleport but couldn't. "I'm going to kill you. As soon as I can move again.", I said. "That's nice. But I'm not going to give you the chance. I've rigged this place with explosives. Explosives designed to kill someone of your particular nature. I'll be walking out of here and YOU will be buried.", "YOU CAN'T! YOU CAN'T JUST DESTROY PROPERTY!", I yelled. "I can if I own the building.", she said, now kicking me again in the face, and walking out, "Goodbye, Awalli.", she said. Then there was a huge explosion. I was buried under the rubble.

SYLVIA: I knew I would end up having to do this in the end. It was obvious to me. Ever since we learned of Awalli's existence and how Amana tried to hide her from us, I knew I would be the one to kill her. Why did I know that? Because I was going to be Head of the Family.

Layna stole my position with her GIFT. Now I have to try and make a difference with my actions. Awalli should have never been allowed to live. Or at least we should have kept her in our sights. Amana had already proven to us that she wasn't capable of making sound decisions. She was always against killing those born with the gift. She felt she could just hide Layna away. When Layna came out of hiding, she announced herself as a member of the RF and immediately became the darling of Nocton. She established relationships with all the contracted cities. Where was I while she was doing this? Honestly, being a spoiled brat and enjoying the rich life. It wasn't until the family wanted me to try and take the reins to ensure that Layna can't, that I began to see things more clearly. But we failed. She had already gained too much notoriety. Plus, she was good at hiding and not being found until she held a public event, at which we knew better than to attack her. Attacking her meant war with P.E.D, and we could not let that happen again. So when I heard that Amana had tried to kill Awalli herself, I knew it was time to strike. As I looked back at the building, I was completely satisfied. I took out my cell, "Layna, it's me. She is dead.", I said. "I told you not to go.", Layna replied in an angry tone. "Well one of us had to! She was going to start a war with you!", I yelled back. "And I told you that I would deal with that when the time came. But now, you just violated a treaty. You need to get back here, now, before you do anymore damage.", Layna said, then hung up. I was pissed, but then I heard a noise. I looked up, unable to believe what I was seeing. "I TOLD YOU, I'D KILL YOU!", Awalli was saying as she came out of the ruins. She was covered in dust and blood. I tried to shoot at her, but as soon as I did, she put her hand up and I couldn't move, or breathe. Somehow, she pulled me to her with her mind. I thought to myself that not even Layna is THIS strong, or if she is, she has given no hint of it. Luckily I had gold powder in my pocket, and I quickly found my strength and reached for it. I then slapped it into Awalli, who dropped me and was weakened again. I knew that I couldn't just attack her like I did before, so I took off, quickly. "SYLVIA!", Awalli yelled, and I kept running.

Two days later, I was in a hovel. I had taken out some shills to actually use, so Awalli couldn't trace my shill collector. I was scared, and I am not afraid to admit that. Awalli wasn't at all like I thought and now I was thinking maybe, Layna knows that. My receiver in my room rang and I didn't know who it could be. I answered, but didn't say anything. "Ms. Lon. This is Gail Raby with P.E.D. I believe we should speak.", "If you are going to arrest me, for performing an op on non-contracted soil…", "No. Nothing like that at all. We would like to bring you to Base. But not to arrest you, but more in an assisting capacity.", Raby said. I'd heard of her. She was considered a badass by a lot of Royal Soldiers. She was from NE but had proven herself during one of Amana's black-op missions. I'd only heard nothing but tales of her and was excited at the prospect of meeting her. "Okay…so when did you want to meet?", I asked. "I can come to you, right now.". Suddenly, a woman materialized in my room. "Hello, Ms. Lon. I'm very pleased to meet you. You can belay what Layna told you. P.E.D has a need for you.", "And what does P.E.D want with me?", I had to ask. "Well, you are royal blood and have been taught how to face those with the gift. We would have you train one of our new subordinates. Is that okay with you?", asked Raby, with a nice friendly smile. "Sure. I guess that can't be that difficult. So, who am I working with?", "Someone we believe is capable of ACTUALLY killing Awalli.". I felt my heart leap. "Someone strong enough? But that would mean they have the gift! Another family member Amana has hidden?", I asked. "Not at all. She isn't royal blood. At least not to you anyway. Just trust me when I say, she can use your expertise.". I didn't know if I fully trusted Raby, but I decided I'd go with her to the P.E.D base anyway.

When we arrived, it was very busy. "What's going on?", I asked. "We have got a lot happening right now. Thanks to Awalli, and your little op, we have been working overtime to cover up what you did down there, and also, we have scouts trying to locate Awalli. She hasn't returned to the manor in SE, so we are very worried right now.", Raby said, leading me to a building with a huge Phoenix on top. I admired it. Then I saw a gorgeous red-headed girl, with her arms folded, and looking very unhappy waiting inside. "This is Emillie. Emillie, this is…", "I'll hear it from her. Thank you, Gail.", Emillie said. She was obviously upset with Raby. Raby turned slowly and walked away but looked back once. "I'm Sylv…", "I know who you are. I've seen you on t.v.", Emillie said, still angry. "Well, they want me to train you.", "I know. Because I won't work with my mother.", she replied. "Your mother?", I felt compelled to ask. "Yes. Amana.", she said. I couldn't believe it. None of us knew Amana had a hidden child. But then, if she IS Amana's child, then that means she isn't just gifted, she is a full on goddess. Even more dangerous than Awalli. "Let me get this straight; You're the daughter of Amana?", "Yes. Like the Amana from the fairy tales.", "I know. But you are her daughter? Who is your father?", I asked. "I don't know. She won't tell me.". I didn't fully understand, but figured that maybe I should just focus on her defeating Awalli and deal with the fact that she is a goddess later.

I started to understand only after a few hours why they wanted me to train Emillie. She was completely not happy about this situation. She continued to treat the whole thing as a joke. When she wasn't being sarcastic with me, she was just out right not listening, "Emillie, listen, I have faced Awalli. If you come at her like this, she will kill you. There is no doubt in my mind.". I had been briefed on their situation. Apparently, Awalli was dreaming about Emillie and this is what led to her stalking her and eventually killing her. Amana had brought Emillie back, and when she did, something else returned with her. "I doubt she'll have it that easy.", Emillie replied, sitting down, and ignoring the chart I placed before her. "Listen, these are basic techniques used in martial arts. These three in the corner are… Emillie, please pay attention.", I said, because she had closed her eyes, and was acting like she wanted to sleep. I hadn't even been with her for that long and she was infuriating. I decided not to say another word, and went straight to Raby. "I can't do this. She doesn't want to learn.", "Sylvia, please, you have to. She won't listen to me or Amana. And if Amana goes back at her, I'm afraid she'll end up strangling her. She already tortured her upon her arrival, so please, I'm counting on you.", Raby said pleadingly. She didn't want Amana to hurt her? "But isn't she Amana's daughter? Why would she torture her, or even…?", "I can't answer these questions.", "Then I want to talk to Amana.", I said. "No need. I'll go and deal with her right now.", Amana said, walking past me. I followed her back to the building, Raby rushing at Amana's side, "Please, General, just…", "NO! I've had it with her! She thinks that none of this matters! But I'm going to show her. The two of you, leave me alone.", Amana said, as she went towards the barracks. She walked in, and Raby and I looked at each other, and knew she was about to fuck Emillie up.

EMILLIE: I didn't care what any of them had to say. I couldn't look past what my so-called mother had done to me. I couldn't forgive Dalia for keeping her a secret, and I couldn't forgive Gail for never telling me that she was working with my mother. I sat down on my bed and didn't know what to do. Sylvia wasn't very nice, either, and it almost seemed like the only nice person on Base was Gail. I tried to teleport to Sandin, but no matter how hard I tried, I couldn't pull it off. "You won't be teleporting out of here. I told you that before.", Amana said, as she entered my room. "I told you, I don't want to see you.", "And I told you, I don't give a shit."

You think that I'm playing around here, but I'm not.", Amana said, taking something out of her pocket and throwing it at me. She then rushed me and started literally pounding my face in. She then picked me up, tossed me to the wall, and then stuck her knee in my gut. I fell to the floor on my stomach. "Now you listen to me. Nothing about your situation is a game. You have an extremely homicidal goddess after you, and on top of that, you also have abilities that you don't understand!", she said, kicking me in my face. I screamed in pain, "STOP!", I yelled. "No.", Amana said simply, and continued to kick me in my gut, "I need you to understand the severity of your situation. If Awalli was here right now, what do you think she would be doing? If you yelled stop at her, do you think that she would? I'm trying to make you understand that you are not normal. I'm sure there is a part of you that understands that at least.", Amana said, walking back and forth now. I couldn't even look up, all I could see was her feet rising and landing upon the floor. I felt blood pouring from my nose and mouth. Then a file landed on the floor with pictures that had fallen out. Amana forced me to sit up by turning me over and pushing me up from my back. "Look at these. Look.", she said, brandishing the memory sheets under my eyes. "This right here is Awalli's work. Look at this girl! You can't even recognize her! And I bet you recognize this person?", Amana said. I did. Reginald Tib. He was a part of the RF. More than that, he had a hole in his chest. "Or how about this person?", Amana said, showing me another sheet. This was different. I hadn't ever seen this woman before. "This was her stepmother. She traveled to Nocton and killed her. Now she is on a quest, not just to kill you, but to also kill Queen Layna. She wants to start a war, Emillie. You are the one chance we have at stopping this madness. So, I will beat you everyday until you understand this.", she said, planting her foot on my side. I coughed up blood. I was able to move somewhat now and I sat up. "Oh stop crying, you'll heal fast. But you had better get used to this. We don't get what we want in life, Emillie. We can only deal with what gets thrown at us.", Amana said, now leaving me. "Gail, don't you go in that room. Leave Emillie alone.", she commanded when Gail was about to rush in. I was left by myself. My mother just kicked my ass. I noticed that she left the memory sheets. I pushed them away from me. I put my face in my hands and cried. I cried for a long time. Then, just when I decided to fall asleep, there was a voice that spoke to me, "Do not worry, Emillie. Soon you will leave that place, and you will face Awalli when YOU are ready. I'll help you.", "Who are you?", I asked. "Someone who will be with you until the end, Emillie.", said the voice. I woke up and found that I was still in my room. I went to open the door and was surprised it was actually open. I went out for a walk and found myself in a strange room. It didn't have any doors, and the door I just entered disappeared. I started to get worried, then, I felt something on my leg. I looked down and it was a furry little creature. I'd never seen anything like it before. It looked like a dog, but was just a bit bigger than a squirrel. I picked it up and it nestled itself in my hand. "She's cute, huh?", said a voice behind me. I turned, and there was Dalia. I ran to her and hugged her. She placed my face in her hands, "What has that woman done to you?", she asked. "Dalia, where are we?", I asked. "I used to be Queen here, so I know places that have different magics. I created this room a long time ago. Casian, here, sometimes comes in here just for some space.", Dalia said, looking at the cute creature. "Casian? Like…?", "Yes, Emillie. That Casian.". I looked at the creature who was all settled on my shoulder now and resting. "Amana has given you quite the beating.", Dalia said, clearly angry. "It's my fault. I saw what Awalli did to Carla Nos and Reginald Tib. I just can't process how I'm the only one who can defeat her.", "Ko-e, a long time ago, told me that certain things are destined to happen. Gods and goddesses are affected differently by fate. It has a stronger pull on us. We somehow live outside of the realm of reality that normal people live in. For example, I'm here, but I'm really not here. This is the kind of magic that you experience once you've studied the art of it. Emillie, whatever Amana is telling you, please, just do what she is saying. She isn't wrong about Awalli. She killed you once already.", "But she is a bitch!", I yelled at Dalia, who I was just now remembering, knew my mother for thousands of years. "Yes, she is. No disagreement there. But what you have to understand about your mother is she has always put everyone's well being before her own. When she was forced to kill Calypsa, a part of your mother died that day. You have no idea how close those two really were.", "Well, then if that's the case, why is she so damn evil?", I asked. Dalia laughed. "Evil? Your mother is just on a different level of understanding, Emillie. She needs you to understand that as well. I can see what's inside of you. It's powerful and it wants to be set free, but it's dangerous. You must learn to control it, Emillie, or else I can't let you back around the kids.". I thought about this and knew she was right. "Dalia, what is Trinity to my mother?", I asked. "That is something you should ask her.", she replied. "But she won't tell me. She calls her a thing. What is Trinity?", "I don't know, Emillie. There was a lot happening back then that I wasn't privy to. And in all these years, neither Amana, nor Ko-e have told me what Trinity was. They both seem to want to forget about Trinity.", Dalia said, thinking, "I must get going, Emillie. But I'll let the kids know I've spoken to you. I do hope you can learn to control what is inside of you.".

When I awoke, I was back in my room. There was no Casian or Dalia and I knew that I was in for another hard day. My mother was right. I had healed quickly, so when I got up, I quickly wanted candy and I knew where to get it. I made my way to the food center and ran into Sylvia. "Emillie.", she said, not looking in my direction. I saw my reflection in a nearby window and realized, although I healed, my face still sported a black eye and bruises. "Sylvia. I'm sorry about yesterday.", I said. "I bet you are. Amana taught you good, huh?", she said, now turning to me and taking in my face. "Yes. Whatever. But I'm willing to listen.". Sylvia thought for a minute, "Okay. But I had better get more respect out of you. I almost died a few days ago trying to take down Awalli on my own, so I know for a fact she has gotten too powerful.", said Sylvia, now taking a piece of stony out of a pot. "Okay, I'll do whatever you say.".

SANDIN: I couldn't believe it. On the day Awalli took my mother, I was going nuts. I made us all rush to the birdport. I demanded a falcon since someone's life was in danger, but that was too costly, and between the three of us, we didn't have enough. We got on the first bird headed towards Edge. As soon as we arrived, I rushed us to South Edge and checked every gangster spot that I knew. Finally, I came to Tom's hideout and nothing was stopping me. I barged in and punched the first two men that came at me. Red and Yellfy were right behind me with their cannons already out. "WHERE IS MY MOTHER?!", I yelled, as I found Tom and grabbed him. "I don't know anything about your mother, Tillo!", he yelled back at me. I punched him and he tried to grab me but I kept punching him. "WHERE IS SHE?!", I yelled, as I continued punching him. Red finally grabbed me, "Tillo, he probably doesn't know.", Red said, as he tried to grab me, and Yellfy tried to separate Tom from me. "He's lying! He knows where she is! He's one of Awalli's captains, he has to know!", I yelled, trying to break from Red's grip. "I swear to you, I don't know. She isn't anywhere in the manor! That's the only place Awalli would have taken her!", he yelled. I finally broke free from Red's grasp and took out my cannon and pointed it at Tom, "I swear you had better tell me…", "Look, Awalli brought some old lady to the manor yesterday, but none of us have seen her since!", Tom said. "No…", I said, backing away. "Now that doesn't mean she's dead, Sandin, it just means he doesn't know what Awalli has done.", said Yellfy. "I say we kill every bastard here and send a message.", I said, looking hard at Tom. "No. That would give every captain in every precinct a reason to pursue us. We have to just leave. But we aren't quitting the search, Tillo.", Red added, when he saw I was gonna say something.

We left Tom's hideout and proceeded towards the manor that Tom mentioned. We sat outside, waiting to see if we'd spot Awalli leaving, and sure enough we did. She walked out of the front, barked some orders at some men standing around, then she disappeared on the spot. "Damn.", said Yellfy, "How the hell are we supposed to compete with that? She can be anywhere she wants.", he said, shaking his head. "This is why we need Emillie.", I said. "No. You saw her. She destroyed Linix. I'm sure she wasn't trying, but she is lucky nobody was hurt. She needs to learn to control herself.", Red said. I agreed, but I was so angry and I was getting impatient. I wanted my mother safe. I knew she wasn't all the way there in the head, but there was something special about her. How could The Commander have missed something like this? My mother knew things. She knew about Emillie, but it isn't like Emillie had ever met her. And she wasn't a part of the fairy tale stories, so, how could my mom have known about her? How did she know that she was the daughter of The Commander? It didn't make any sense. She said that her and my father found the ring I'm wearing, yet Awalli had it before. So where did she find it if it was something my parents found? And then even more questions started to arise. Like, how did my father discover this ring and is this ring the reason he is dead? Awalli appeared back at the manor a few hours later with blood all down her shirt. From the looks of things, it wasn't her blood. I tried to get out of the flar but Red stopped me, "That can't possibly be your mother's blood.", he said. "How the hell do we know that?!", I replied. "Because I'm sure your mother is in that house, Tillo. Awalli has magic. She has probably used some to hide your mother.", Yellfy said, sure of himself. "Well at some point we are going to have to storm this place.", "I disagree. I think we need to get out of here. Especially you, Tillo. I believe that Awalli will try to use you.", Red said, starting the flar. "Now wait a minu…", "NO! YOU WAIT, TILLO! Look, I get it. Your mother is being held captive by a homicidal woman with other worldly abilities. So I get it, but we can't go rushing in without knowing the full picture. From watching this place all day, I've determined that this is the main meet up spot for all the mobs in Edge. So your mother is definitely here.", Red said, now driving us away.

Later that night, I had a strange dream. I was in a nice home, but it seemed uncared for. I heard voices behind a door, so I decided to see what was happening. I opened the door and Awalli was here, along with a woman whom I had never seen. "I'm going to ask this once…Mother… then I expect the correct answer.", Awalli said. I looked at the woman she referred to as Mother, and then realized that this must be Awalli's stepmother. I had no idea what was going on. "Awalli, I'm trying to explain to you, I can't just tell you!", the woman said, clearly frightened. I didn't blame her. "I want to know why Amana gave me to you. Why didn't she just kill me?", "Because she said she needed you alive! She paid me well to raise you!", the woman said. "Oh, Lida, if only it was that simple, but I know, Amana told you more. What else did she tell you about me?", Awalli said in a very scary tone. "She just said that you weren't allowed to be around anyone!", Lida said, tears in her eyes now, "Please, Awalli, please?!", Lida shouted. It was at this time that I noticed that she was being forced against the wall. "Not until I'm done asking you questions. What was it you used to tell me? Oh yeah. You can't leave this room, until we're finished.". Lida looked deathly and was breaking down. Awalli slapped her, "GET AHOLD OF YOURSELF!", she yelled at Lida. Lida tried to stop crying but was finding it difficult. "Now, let me ask you again. What else did Amana tell you about me?", "She said that you would one day become dangerous and that I was supposed to tell her! She never said anything else!", "She never mentioned that I could challenge Layna for the head seat? She never mentioned Emillie? She never mentioned that the RF was trying to kill me?", Awalli said, holding Lida's head with one of her hands. Lida shook her head, still crying. "Well then, I can tell you aren't lying. Now I have another question. Maybe this one will be easy to answer. Why did you treat me like shit all my childhood?", Awalli asked, removing her hand now. "Because of what you are!", Lida said, becoming brave. "And what am I?", "An abomination! You should never have been born! You were nothing but the child of a slut, and my good for nothing husband, who couldn't even find a way back into the good graces of his family!", Lida yelled. She immediately lost all her bravery once she saw the look Awalli's face wore. "You shouldn't have said that.", Awalli said. She took a knife off the counter while she still had Lida psychically pinned to the wall. She then stabbed Lida in the stomach. She let the knife stay in then took another knife. She cut her shirt off and started to carve into her. I was disgusted. I turned away but couldn't block out Lida's screaming. I woke up sweaty. I looked and saw someone else was in the room, "Emillie?", I questioned. "No.". I got up and turned on my light and realized it was Amana. "YOU?!", I said. I reached for my cannon. "Are you serious, Mr. Tillo?", she said, taking out a device that took my cannon right from my hand. "What are you doing here? Where is Emillie?", I asked. "Emillie is safe where she is and people are safe from her. I've come to give you info on your mother. She is alive and well. Now what I need for you to do, is stay away from that manor. If you go off in there trying to play hero, you are going to get yourself killed, and then I'll have a very disturbed Emillie, who will do nothing but cry.". I thought about what she was talking about. "But...", "She is alive, Mr. Tillo. Awalli isn't going to torture your mother. But she will take you and try to torture you in front of her. Your mother, as I'm sure you have noticed, is very connected to the other realm. She can sense and see things that others can't. Awalli is trying to use this to her advantage.", "How did she even know about my mother?", I needed to ask. "Well, she has people everywhere. She is beginning to gain power not just in Edge, but in Nocton, Bronxton, Sicilia, and Nash. Soon she will be able to declare war on Layna. We can't let that happen. So, what I need you and your two friends to focus on is keeping these drugs off the streets. I want you to slowly take down Awalli's drug spots. Once you start to slowly take her currency, she will start to become weak politically.", "But what about Emillie?", I asked. With my mother being held by Awalli, I had almost forgotten about Emillie. But my obsession and need for her was slowly coming on. "I told you, she is being taken care of. There is no reason to worry about her.", "I can't stop worrying about her!", I said. "Okay. I'll let her visit you on a weekly basis. But she is going through training. So you better keep an open mind.", Amana said. Then I woke up. Apparently, Amana could also visit my dreams. I didn't like that.

LODY: I hadn't seen Dalia on my own, so I went to the orphanage. Tillo was going insane with his mother being held captive, and Yellfy said he had to go see someone. So I decided to just take some time. When I arrived at the orphanage, I was accosted by Cynda, who walked up to me and gave me that attitude that seemed to fit her so well, "So, what have you done with Emillie, now?", she asked me. "Nothing, I haven't even seen her, Cynda. Maybe you should ask GO Tillo next time you see him.". Cynda looked positively angry but let me pass. I proceeded to Dalia's office, and when I opened the door, there was another woman in here. She was of a very different type of beauty and I had to do a double take. They didn't notice I had walked in and were deep in conversation,

"...Amana will know. Soon she will. But we have to keep up the charade.", "SHE IS BEATING HER!", Dalia yelled at the woman. "Yes, I know. I've seen her.". The woman turned around and noticed me, "Oh, well, it seems you have a visitor, Dalia. I'll visit again soon.", the mystery woman said, now walking past me. "Mr. Red.", she said, and walked out the door. "Who was that, Dalia?", "I guarantee, the moment she said your name, she put a jinx so I can't tell you. And has blocked your neural pathways so you can't put it together.". I realized Dalia was right. So I changed the subject, "What have you been up to?", I asked. "I went to see Emillie. I can't take it. I don't want this situation, Lody. Amana is treating her like shit and I can only imagine how she must feel. Did I tell you she has always disliked Amana? She hated her mother before she ever met her. Lody, I just want my daughter back.", Dalia said, breaking down. I went and patted her shoulder. "How is Tillo holding up?", she asked. It had been on the news what happened at the home where Tillo's mother was. She was on sheets all over Bronxton. Sheets that read; Please help find her. "He's not doing too well. He's going insane. Even more, he wants Emillie. Dalia, what is that about?", I needed to ask. It had been bothering me. When Sandin awoke me and Yellfy, it occured to me that he was probably experiencing an intense dream. "I told you, Sandin is special. He has the god gene. That means that he is being drawn to his destiny more intensely than a normal person. This is why he survives certain situations. Because he will die when it is his destiny.", Dalia said, taking out a bottle of ticenta from her desk, along with two glasses, "So, how has life without a job been for you?", she asked me, smiling. "Well, it has been tough.". That was an understatement. In truth, I had forgotten how we all quit the GF and were now doing our own thing. With Tillo's mother being taken, we had definitely gotten extremely busy. I told Dalia the whole story. "Sandin and Emillie were visiting each other in the dream realm? Hmm...", Dalia said, thinking. "The dream realm?",

I asked. "Yes. It's a place that gods and goddesses can visit quite easily. You would call it, astral projection.", "So, they can meet up in this other realm...and fuck?", I asked amusedly. "Yes. They can do anything. Have a picnic, fight a battle, make love, start a band, whatever they fancy. Amana and I used to do this when she was in hiding. We made love this way many times.", Dalia said reminiscently. "And then she abandoned you completely.", I said. Dalia looked angry.

After we had drank for some time, I had convinced Dalia to tell me the story of her and Amana. She had told the other matrons she wanted no visitors or appointments and sat behind her desk, "Amana and I met a few days after her sister died. At the time, I knew her only as Princess Amana. I didn't know anything else about her. I had no clue she was a goddess, or that Princess Calypsa was her sister. It was that day that I learned this. She liked me right away. I worshipped her, long before I even met her. She was the reason I got involved in medicine. When she told me she wanted to bring her sister back to life, it sounded cool. So I was immediately attracted to the whole idea. The first night we had left Nasher, Amana told me then, the full truth of her and Calypsa. She told me that they had met when they were children, and that together, they planned, and turned Plinth, and its kingdoms, into a paradise.", Dalia paused to take a sip of her ticenta. I had grown fond of listening to her stories. These weren't like reading the fairy tales, this is the actual stuff. "When we arrived in Kindy, she made me the queen in her place so she could spend all her time trying to bring back Calypsa. She never told me what happened to her mother. And everyone else acted sort of morbid about the subject. The only time I asked, Amana beat the hell outta me, and told me never to ask again.". I was surprised to hear this, "She...beat you?", I asked. "Oh yes. Before I made myself strong enough to fight back, Amana was quite abusive with me. She has a very bad temper, Lody. Why do you think I'm scared for Emillie? That woman used to beat me senseless. But I loved her. I couldn't explain it. Until I found out about the god gene. I had it in me. I started to learn the ways of magic and I experimented with something that Amana has made sure nobody can get their hands on. It's a flower that you will not find anywhere today. It extruded certain chemicals that, if put into the right person, can turn them into a cosmic being.", "And this is how you have been living for thousands of years?", I asked. "Yes, Lody. This is how I became a synthetic goddess. I had the god gene. My destiny was a great one. And here I am. Three-thousand years later. Sitting in an office. Some destiny.", she said, taking another swig of ticenta. I was thinking hard now. "So wait, what you're saying is that you haven't realized your destiny yet?", I asked her, staring at her, as if I could see the truth by doing so. "No, I have. My destiny is intertwined with Amana's. Just like Scion's was to Ko-e, and now, Tillo to Emillie.", "And where is this, Scion?", I asked. "He is beyond the both of us, Lody. He is gone. As far as I know, he only comes here to see Ko-e, and seeing as how I haven't seen her in a long time, that would mean that there isn't much I could tell you about Scion.". I thought about Scion, then about Ko-e, and then realized something, then forgot what I realized. "Lody, let me ask you a question. Why are you still pursuing Awalli? You don't have any reason to be after her. You'll die. Maybe.", Dalia said, looking at me sadly. "Well, it is because Tillo isn't going to stop, and I can't abandon him. And Yellfy has taken an interest. How can I walk away from them?", I said. "Well, convince them. Help them to see the risk. You know that it is dangerous to keep on chasing her.". Dalia was right. But I knew I couldn't walk away. Something told me that even if I wanted to, Amana isn't going to just let me. "What more can you tell me of the past, Dalia?", I asked her. "I can tell you that Amana and Ko-e aren't working together. But I can also tell you that Amana is scared. Someone within P.E.D is trying to out her as

The General. I'm afraid of what will take place if that happens.", "What would happen?", "Lody, Amana started P.E.D. She is the one who has made the most sacrifices to protect us all. I know that Emillie being with her is a good thing, but I can't help but worry about her.", Dalia said, taking another sip of ticenta. "Yes, but what happens if Amana loses her position?", I asked again. "Chaos, Lody. Just simply chaos.", she said, standing up, "I'll walk you out, Lody.", "I was thinking of hanging out for a bit.", I replied. "Lody, I can't. I can never. I'd feel like I'm betraying Amana.", "WHAT?!", I exclaimed. It didn't make any sense, "But you said that you haven't been with her for years!", I said. "I know, but it's more than that. She'd feel it. I can't.", "And what about Emillie? Was she some sort of accident? What is the reason she exists?", I said. "Get out.", Dalia said, simply in anger. I walked out, feeling embarrassed.

Once I had returned to my flar, I felt the urge to go back and apologize. I wondered what could make someone feel so strongly about someone who betrayed them. Sure, you see it all the time, but Dalia was different. Her and Amana had thousands of years between them. Thousands of years where they were off and on and probably declared hatred for one another. I thought about her telling me Amana used to abuse her. I thought about how she made herself strong enough to fight back. I imagined a girl who was so hung up over being with her idol, that she didn't care about the pain her idol was causing her. I thought about Emillie and how she was born, and who her father was. Amana obviously chose Emillie's father over Dalia, but the question was, who the hell is that? I felt like Amana was just a bitch. It was all I ever sensed from her. From our very first meeting. Dalia walked up to my flar. She knocked on my window. I rolled it down, and she quickly grabbed my face, and kissed me. "I'm sorry, Lody. I know I've been rather difficult, but I do still love Amana. I hope you understand.", she said, then walked away from my flar.

When I got home, I found Gail Raby waiting for me there. "Didn't think you'd survive Awalli and Hyena.", I said. "I told you I'd see you later.", she smiled and waited for me to open my door. "Why are you here?", I asked her. "I've come here to discuss Emillie. I need your help.", she said, now removing her smile and looking distraught. I waited for her to tell me the issue. "Emillie is suffering at the hands of her mother. I need… Want to sneak you on Base so you can free her.". I looked at her like she was crazy. "Raby, maybe I've been drinking too much today, but Dalia says that Emillie is where she needs to be.", "Dalia is wrong. She doesn't understand what The General has been doing to her.". At this point she took out her vid device and plugged it in. I watched as Amana beat the crap out of Emillie. She was ruthless. She didn't show her any emotion or any kind of restraint. I was horrified. I watched as she left Emillie alone, and she was crying by herself. I thought about what Sandin would do if he saw this. "This is only the first time. She has been visiting her everyday and beating the shit out of her. Emillie is barely recognizable. She isn't trying to teach her a lesson, Mr. Red. This is pure hatred. Please, you must help me!", she said, grabbing my shirt. I looked again at Emillie, who was crying but also staring at something on her floor. I zoomed the vid in and realized they were the same photos from my files. I looked at Gail, who was on the verge of tears, "Amana is teaching her, Gail. She needs to know what she is up against.", "DO YOU REALLY THINK THAT'S WHAT SHE'S DOING?!", Gail yelled, "I've known The General for a long time, Mr. Red. Amana is only taking her anger out on her. I love Emillie like a younger sister and I can't sit by and listen to her do this anymore.", Gail said. "But, isn't Emillie strong? She heals fast right? And also, can't she fight back against her mother?", I asked. "No. She can't. She isn't as strong as Amana. She could be, but she doesn't know how to control herself yet. She is learning. But with Amana and her fighting everyday like they are, it is only going to end badly.", I tried to think about what Dalia would want. "Dalia wants her to be there. She feels the same as you, but understands that Emillie needs it.", I said. Gail slapped me, and it hurt more than I thought it would. She then pulled her cannon out, "Listen to me. I want your help, and you are going to give it to me.", Raby said, striking me with her cannon.

EMILLIE: It was getting late. Sylvia and I had been training for two weeks now and I felt like I was getting better. But this didn't stop Amana from visiting me. She would come to my barracks and attack me almost every night. Finally, I tried to fight back, but still wasn't good enough to take her down, "Emillie, I told you that I will come here every night until you get it.", she said one night, after a particularly bad beating where I had successfully grabbed her hand. This was a mistake as she proceeded to pound in my face and kick me even though I was down. Gail had started trying to clean me up after every session, "I'm so sorry, Emillie.", Gail was saying, as she tried to hold in tears. "Why are you sorry? You're the one letting her come here and do this every night.", I said, still angry with Gail. I eventually threw her cleaning tools away from me, and Gail slouched out of my room. I went to bed and was surprised to wake up in a room familiar to me. It was Sandin's house. He was sitting in his room, "Sandin…", I said. He looked up at me and horror fell onto his face, "What the hell has happened to you?!", he yelled, rushing to me. He placed his hand on my face and I could still feel the marks left by my mother. "Who did this to you?", Sandin asked. I started to cry and couldn't even answer him. I cried for a long time. Then, almost as if I was being pulled away, Sandin was gone, and there was nothing but white all around me. "Emillie, I promise, soon. Okay? Soon.", said the voice that had been communicating with me. I realized this was the same voice I heard after my nightmare that first night in my apartment. I looked around, then I found myself somewhere else. It was an underground cavern. I looked around me, and all I saw were walls, with strange paint all over them. Upon looking closer, I soon saw that it was writing. It was nothing but circles. Then the circles started to glow. They glowed intensely to where I could feel the heat. I started to burn all over. Then I felt something inside of my head. I looked up, and saw a woman I'd never laid eyes on before. She had strange colored hair, and a face that glowed so brightly I couldn't see what she looked like, "The sword is yours. Use it well.", the woman said.

I woke up drenched in sweat and felt my chest beginning to burn. I rushed out of my bed and ran to the nearest water fountain. It was at this time that Casian found me. She jumped onto my shoulders and I felt relief instantly. I petted her and took her back to my room. She landed on my bed and settled in. When I was about to sit back on my bed, I noticed something had been left in my room. It was a file that had no label. When I opened it, it revealed info on Awalli I hadn't heard quite yet. I read the info. It spoke of her childhood, and how she was handed to a woman named, Lida, who was married to her father. I gathered as much that her father had been assassinated. As I continued reading, I found that Queen Layna brought her to SE and left her. I read how she worked for Taser. I had been offered a job there, but turned it down. Now, I was glad I did. As I continued reading, I saw that my mother had tried to kill her. Amana told me as much, but reading it in the file after everything else I read made it seem uncalled for. She was a nice girl. I kept thinking, what turned her evil? I looked through the file again and started to catch things that I missed. One of those things was the fact that her chest would burn after having nightmares. My chest burned, too. I looked into her past more and found she had gotten pregnant when she was fifteen. I started to gain an understanding of her that I didn't have. In the back of the file was another sheet that spoke of an entity;

The entity's age is unknown, but presented itself back in the days of the kingdoms. It is a credible threat that if left unchecked could destroy the whole planet. It is believed to be a familiar person that The General has encountered throughout this planet's history. It is imperative that you keep a close eye on this entity and watch for signs in those containing Mileeda's blood and or even The General's. If this entity returns, it can mean death to everyone on this planet. Please keep all eyes open and watch for this THREAT.

I re-read the letter again and again. I now started to understand. This entity was controlling Awalli. Or at least that's what it felt like I was reading. I went back and checked Awalli's file again. When I felt like there was nothing else, I decided to sleep. Casian had laid on my pillow and I decided to let her sleep there. I laid down, wondering, what really happened to Awalli? What really happened to that nice girl who didn't want to hurt anyone and just live her life?

CHAPTER 7

The Truth About Slayn Tillo

SYLVIA: Emillie was getting so much better. She had mastered martial-arts in three weeks. Now I was giving her sword training, which I didn't fully understand, but decided not to question, "Emillie, the motion is not back and forth, its side to back and forth to center. That is how you have the element of surprise.", I told her one day. Her face still sported bruises from her beating the night before. "When is Amana gonna go easy on you?", I asked her. "I don't know, and I don't care.", she said, as she continued to swing her sword in the motion I was teaching her. I watched her for a few minutes. She was graceful. Elegant. I was sort of jealous. She reminded me of Layna. "Okay, that's enough for now. Let's get some food.", I said, packing up the equipment. Emillie wiped herself and drank some water, then followed me. "I'm gonna tell Amana how well you did today. Maybe she won't have to pay you a visit tonight.", I said. "No. Let her.", Emillie said with a determined face. "But…", "I understand why she comes. I know what she is doing.", she said, wiping more sweat off her face. Raby was walking towards us, followed by some soldiers. "Emillie, Sylvia, I need to speak with you. You all, wait for me, then we'll depart.", Raby said, leading us away from the soldiers. "Listen, I'm going on a mission and probably won't be back for sometime, and I need to know that everything is going to be okay with you two.". Raby had been extremely worried about Emillie. Emillie, who wasn't talking to her or Amana, still showed no signs of letting up. Emillie just looked the other way as I nodded. Raby was watching her, "Emillie?", she said. "Fine. I'll be fine.", Emillie said, still not looking at her. "Emillie, please?", Raby said, now looking as if she might cry again. "Gail, I'll be fine.", Emillie said, now facing her. Raby held her arms open for Emillie to hug her. Emillie did. They hugged for some time before Raby broke from her, smiled, and then left with the soldiers. "So, have you gotten over it yet?", I asked. "Not by a longshot. I know she was only acting on orders, but still. She lied to me for a very long time.", Emillie said, as we entered the food hall. "But, Emillie, you have to understand, we aren't in a position to do what we want.", "Don't you think I've realized that by now? All I'm saying is that it isn't fair that for most of my life, Gail has been working with my mother and didn't tell me anything. And it would be one thing if my mother hadn't told her that I was her daughter, but Gail knew. She knew.", Emillie said, looking down at her bowl of oats and beginning to load it with a lot of sugar. "That's not good for you.", I said, watching her. "I need sugar.", she said, as she stirred it around. It took her a minute to stir because she put way too much sugar. I watched as she took a bite and looked like she had died and gone to Heaven. It was at this time that one of the many soldiers on Base, who had been watching Emillie, decided to walk over, "Oats for breakfast? I usually watch you eat the whole candy machine.", the man was saying. Emillie didn't even look at him as she said, "I have a boyfriend.". The man looked surprised for a minute, "I don't see him around.", he said, smiling. "Listen, I have no interest in you. I've seen you watching me. So you can go watch from over there.", Emillie said, pointing at a group of men and women sitting at a table, all eagerly watching the scene. "Some of us just want to know who you are, sweetie.", he said, looking back at his friends. "I'm not your sweetie, and if my boyfriend was here, he'd kick your ass.", "I doubt that, sweetie.". Emillie stood up now, "Walk back to your friends, now, or get embarrassed.". I was watching with a smile on my face. "Embarrassed?", the man asked, standing up to Emillie. Emillie quickly grabbed his hand, and twisted his arm behind his back, and slammed him down on our table, knocking down her oats as she did, "I told you, to return to your friends. What do you think now?", Emillie asked him. He wasn't screaming or making any hints that he was in pain. Just like a good P.E.D soldier. "I'll go back now.", he said. Emillie let him up and he looked like he wanted to hit her. Emillie stood her ground and waited to see what he would do, but he just turned around and went back to his table, where his friends roared with laughter.

Later that day, we were resting in the barracks. Emillie and I were in her room. She was showing me a file that she had been looking over. It was a file on Awalli. Most of everything in the file, I knew. But the thing that threw me off was the fact that I hadn't been briefed on Awalli's possession. Something inside of her was making her act how she was acting. I kept reading the note on the entity, because it was something Amana had never told us about. As I continued looking it over, I noted that it said; Those with Mileeda's blood. I had always thought that the only thing that could hurt someone gifted was pure gold. But now, looking at this, I wondered if this is why Grandmother has been rarely seen for all these years. Maybe she was hiding from this entity. Emillie also had the small Dattur, Casian, with her. I watched as the creature ate some of Emillie's candy and seemed to be looking over the both of us. "Wait, Emillie, I need to ask; Do you know anything else about this entity?", "I believe, Awalli may know. But I'll need to speak with her to be sure.", "Speak with her? Well I guess that ain't gonna happen.", "Why not?", Emillie asked me in a surprising tone, "She is dangerous, yes. But we know she can't just easily kill me. I want to get some answers from her.". I looked at the pictures that were in the file and found Lida

Dat. "I didn't know she killed Lida.", I said, shaking my head. She had carved into her. "She carved vengeance on her. That's what the circles say.", "This is a language?", I asked, shocked. "Yes. I don't exactly know how I understand it.", "Have you seen it before?", I asked her. I had no knowledge of this. "Well, I think so, but I'm not sure. When I try to remember, my head starts hurting.". I was looking at the pictures, and came across Carla. I couldn't look anymore. Carla was a good girl. I had befriended her when Tek first started dating her mother. Looking at that picture told me that Awalli needed to die. But what if all this wasn't really Awalli? What if all this is the work of this so-called entity? Amana and Raby were right. Emillie was the key. Even I could see that now. But the question was, when does Emillie realize this as well? There was a picture Emillie had of a man. I looked at it. He was slightly handsome, but not so much. "Who is this, Emillie?", I asked. "He is my boyfriend. Sandin.". I looked at her surprised. He looked tough, and like he could be military. "What's his occupation?", I asked her. "He WAS a guard force officer, but now he is doing his own thing.". Emillie looked sad all of a sudden. "What's wrong?", "I haven't seen him in weeks. I miss him.". I was even more angry with Amana. Despite what Emillie said, I decided I would speak with her.

"Amana, we need to talk.", I said, finally being allowed into her office. She was either commanding the people outside to tell me she was too busy or she just didn't want to see me. But now, after weeks of not letting up, she finally decided I could enter her sanctuary. "Well, talk.", she said without even looking at me. I noticed her desk was a computer screen, and it had labels for almost every location on Plinth. "Well, I want to talk to you about your constant beatings you've been bestowing upon…", "I don't need to speak with you about that. She is my daughter, and I will treat her how I see fit.", she said before I could finish what I was saying, "If that is all, Ms. Lon, I have a lot of work to do right here, so I'll need you to…", "NO! THAT IS NOT ALL!", I yelled. Amana was so infuriating. She had been this way ever since I was a little girl and we first met. "Amana, Emillie is doing really well and I don't think she requires that anymore.", "Starting to feel something for her, are you?", she asked me. "No. I just don't think she deserves it.", "And I wonder how Awalli feels.", Amana said, now looking at me for the first time. "I don't care how she feels!", I retorted. "You should.", Amana said, standing up, walking around her desk, and coming up to me, "Emillie is in grave danger. She has never been tough. Dalia babied her until she became just a spoiled little brat. She thinks the world revolves around…", "I'm sorry, Amana, but I disagree. Emillie is taking all of this very seriously.". Amana watched me for a quick second before she spoke, "Emillie may be taking things seriously now, but we both know she can't afford mistakes. So I will beat her every night until she understands that part.", "Some of the other people on Base are wondering who she is and why she is getting special treatment. Don't you think you should address that?", I asked her. "Not at all. Emillie handled herself well this morning. She was very quick. You've trained her well, Sylvia. But what I do with my daughter behind closed doors, is my business. You can see your way out now.", "But…", "You can see your way out now.", Amana repeated, pointing me towards the door. I didn't move right away, but decided I had better just leave. Amana was going to keep beating her. Emillie says she is okay with it, but I don't know. "Excuse me, but are you, Sylvia Lon?", asked a very gruff voice from behind me. I looked, and it was a man with faded blue hair. "Who wants to know?", "I'm Lody Red. Gail asked me to come here and check on Emillie.". I found it odd. "Gail sent you here? Why?", "Because he is here to take a job. Lody has recently left the GF and is in need of a great deal of shills. Correct?", Amana said, who now had come out of her office. Red looked surprised by this and just nodded.

"Great. Welcome to P.E.D. If you follow Ms. Lon, she will direct you to the briefing. You'll need this to get the exact briefing you need.", Amana said, handing Red a card. "Follow me.", I said, sort of in a grumpy tone.

"Sylvia Lon? As in the RF's Sylvia? What the hell are you doing here?", Red asked me as I led him to the briefing rooms. "I came here to kill Awalli. I ended up being recruited.". Red thought for a minute. "So is the whole RF trying to off her or was it just you?", "Layna, in her great wisdom, said we should leave it alone. I guess she believes Amana has it well-in-hand. That's Layna's problem. She is too trusting with Amana.", I said, still angry that Amana brushed off my attempt at getting her to stop beating Emillie. "Where's Emillie?", Red now asked. "She is in her barracks, waiting for her usual nightly abuse.", I said through gritted teeth. "Gail asked that I come here and stop that from happening.", "Fat chance.", I said, "Amana and I just settled that Emillie is her daughter to do with whatever she wants.", "Emillie doesn't feel that way?", "Oh, Emillie wants it. She told me so herself. Says that she UNDERSTANDS.", I said, looking at Red. "I need to speak with her.", "After your briefing.", I said. I pointed him to one of the briefing rooms. "Enter the card there and it should have all the info on it that you need.", I said, now turning and walking away. I was so upset with Amana. I knew she was headed to Emillie's room.

EMILLIE: As usual, my mother came into my room. I stood up, ready for her. Casian, whenever my mother would enter, would just hide until she was done with me. "So, let me ask you a question...", she said, not moving towards me yet, "...why is it that you think I'm entering your room every night?", she asked me. "Because you want me to be strong. You're showing me what to expect when I face Awalli or any other enemy.". My mother, for the first time, truly smiled, "Yes, Emillie. That is exactly why. You've put up quite the fight since we first started. You've made little improvement, though.", she said, now taking her hands from her sides. I could tell she was getting ready to attack me. I quickly responded and attacked her instead. She grabbed my head from the back and slammed it into my door. But I didn't let that phase me. I then quickly turned and placed my leg behind hers and took her down for the very first time. She stood up and was very happy with me. But the moment passed, as she rushed me again, and then started to pound on me anywhere she could land a fist. I tried punching her back. I tried using the techniques Sylvia had been teaching me, but nothing seemed to work. I grabbed her hair when I felt all else was failing, and then she punched me in the face, and then grabbed my head, kneed me in the face, and then took out her cannon and shot me in my gut. "Why did you use...your cannon?", I asked her, coughing up blood as I did. "Because you should expect everything, Emillie.". She turned and walked out of my room, leaving me once again defeated.

LODY: I had finished listening to the briefing, which turned out to just be a welcome video, explaining the importance of P.E.D, and how we are all sworn to secrecy. I left the room and couldn't find Sylvia. I finally spotted Amana, and was going to say something, when I noticed her putting her cannon in it's holster. I hid from her and watched her walk away. I went to the door she had just exited out of and knocked. The door opened to reveal a very beaten face, Emillie, "Oh my god…", I said, looking at her. "It's nothing, Mr. Red. Just a training session. Come in.", she said, allowing me inside of her room. It wasn't much. Just a bed, a dresser, and one picture of Tillo. "So, she really is giving it to you everyday.", I said. "It's not how it looks. Everyone thinks she is being cruel, but she is showing me what to expect.". I noticed the cannon shell remover kit she had out. "She shot you?!", I said, unable to believe this. "She did. First time. It's okay. Awalli would probably try something dirty like that.". It was shocking how accepting Emillie was of her abuse. "Listen, Dalia told me that Amana has an anger issue.", "She does. I've learned that.", "But what you need to understand is that she is hurting you, Emillie. Gail wants me to take you from here.", "Gail just feels guilty. She'll get over it. How is my Sandin? Is he okay? I know he must be all messed up because of his mom.", Emillie said, looking at me. I thought about how she had referred to Sandin as her's and smiled somewhat, "He isn't coping too well. Everyday he gets closer and closer to storming that manor in SE, and I'm afraid Yellfy might not be able to stop him.", I said. "I want to go to him, but in truth, I don't want him to see me...", she said. "I get it. But that's why you should let me take you.", "Take me where, Mr. Red? You do realize my mother knows you're in here by this point. She has made sure to keep me here. I've already tried to leave, that isn't happening.", "So, what are you going to do?", I asked. "I'm going to stay here and finish my training. I'm no good to any of you if I don't.". Emillie had accepted her situation after all. "If you are truly fine with staying here, fine. But just know, I'm not too far away if you need anything.", I said. She nodded, then went to her door to let me out. I looked at the creature who was on her bed and realized it was an animal I'd never seen before.

After leaving Emillie, I decided I should check on Sandin. I went to my new room, which wasn't too much better than Emillie's, and took out my cell and dialed Sandin's number, "Hey.", Sandin said, once he answered. "How are you, mate?", I asked. "I'm as good as a guy who's mother has been held captive for over a month could be.", he said in a depressed tone, "My mother is what we need, Lody. She had all the answers we needed and Awalli just...". I could tell how he was feeling, and I debated telling him that I had become a P.E.D agent, "Listen, I just want you to know that everything will work out, Sandin. Don't lose faith.", "Sure, Red. Whatever you say.", he said, now hanging up. I knew that was a bad sign and needed to get to him immediately. I went to Amana's office, which was all the way on the other side of Base. Base was interesting. It held mostly barracks and buildings that seemed to house projects. Some of the buildings were labeled with certain major manufacturing company names, and others were not labeled at all and the windows were tinted. By the time I made it to the main building where Amana's office is located, I noticed a statue that was sort of run down and a castle that looks like it was being torn down. But from what I could make of it, it was ancient and had been here for a long time. I wondered what it looked like when it was in full form. "Mr. Red. What do you want?", Amana asked, exiting out of the building. "I wanted to talk to you about Sandin.", "His mother? There is nothing I can do for her. She is hidden from me.", "WHAT?!", I exclaimed, "How can she be hidden from you?", "Well, Awalli does know how to perform magic. She is using certain magic that doesn't require a spell to cast. So, with that, she has hidden Mrs. Tillo really well, and there is nothing I can do about it.", "But, we know she is in that manor!", I said. "I believe you're right. But all the thermo scans show nothing. Except the usual traffic. So like I said, nothing I can do.", "What about teleportation? Can't you teleport?", I asked. "Yes. I have that ability, but I need to know exactly what I'm looking for. Awalli has magically hidden her and I can't sense her because she is outside of our realm. The only one who could possibly even find her isn't ready for that kind of mission.", "Emillie? You think she'd be able to find her?", I asked. "Of course. My daughter is much tougher than she seems, Mr. Red.", "Is that why you shot her tonight?", "All a part of her training. She understands. We've spent enough time together.", "Dalia told me that you used to hit her.". Amana stared at me, then responded, "That's none of your business, and literally, old news.", "Well how do I know you aren't just taking your anger out on Emillie?", "Mr. Red. Did Dalia tell you everything? Did she tell you how Nigel was her first time? Did she tell you that she hasn't been with anyone else since she's been with me? Did she tell you about the first time I fucked her?", Amana asked me, looking at me hard. I felt like she was staring through my soul. I didn't shake my head or answer. "When I first touched her, she melted in my hand. She didn't even ask if I wanted to, she just started to throw her clothes off at the…", "Stop.", I said. "Then don't try to come at me about Dalia. That is my personal business.", she said, "Now, as for Mrs. Tillo, I'll tell you what you need to do. Nothing. Awalli at this point has no intentions of hurting her, unless you give her one.". Amana walked away and I wondered where she was headed. I felt ashamed. I couldn't believe what Amana said to me. I thought of Dalia and how I was beginning to like her. It didn't bother me that she had been with Prince Nigel, seeing as he has been dead for thousands of years. But the worst of it is listening to Amana describe her as if she was some sort of whore. I thought about what Dalia had told me, that she would feel like she was betraying Amana to be with me. Now I realized that Amana was probably angry with me for even having feelings for her. This wasn't fair, considering that she had some secret lover she refused to speak of. I tried to put my feelings behind me but was finding it difficult. It was at this time that I called Yellfy to tell him to keep a close eye on Tillo. I then informed him that I was on the P.E.D base and didn't know when I'd be coming back down there.

I returned to my room where I was alone. I called Dalia now, "Yes, this is North Edge Orphanage. How can I help you?", she said. "Dalia, it's me.", "Red? What number is this?", she asked. "It's a new cell I was given now that I'm a P.E.D officer.", "You're with P.E.D now? Are you insane?

Everytime I think you can't get any crazier, you prove me completely wrong. Lody, you need to get out of there.", "Not until you tell me the full truth of you and Amana.", "Amana? What do you want to know?". I swallowed, then asked, "I want to know if you REALLY still have feelings for her.", "Red, I've told you already.", "And I know what she just said to me.". Dalia was silent. "Red, what did you say to her?", Dalia said in a scared tone. "Nothing. I just told her that you told me she is abusive.". Dalia hung up. I didn't know why. She didn't give any hint that she would. I wanted to rush down to her. I left my room and went to the pod area so I could depart. "Sorry, Mr. Red. But I have orders not to allow you off Base.". I didn't need to ask from whom. I knew already. I called Dalia again, but there was no answer this time.

DALIA: As soon as Red had told me what he'd done, I knew already that Amana was coming here. I quickly rushed to my room, and sure enough, she was sitting in there, "So, telling all our dirty little secrets, are we? I always knew it was too dangerous to just let you do what you want.", Amana said, standing up, and walking towards me. "I didn't tell him anything that would damage anything.", "You told him about US!", she said, clearly angry. "And so what? He knew we were lovers before!", I retorted. "No. Not like how he knows now. I'm not going to tell this to you again, keep our relationship, where it belongs!", "And where is that, Amana?", I asked her, now starting to become angry as well. I didn't want to fight her here because the kids were here, so I quickly grabbed her, and teleported her into a field. I threw her, "Really? Are we doing this?", she said, standing up. I just glared at her. She rushed at me and I punched her. She began to punch me back, and we were both just swinging at whatever we could touch on each other. Then at one point in our fight, she grabbed my head and kissed me. I pushed her away, but she quickly grabbed my whole body and threw me down. She started to kiss me all over my face. I tried pushing her away, but slowly started to succumb. She then started to remove my undergarments, "Amana, I don't want to!", I yelled at her. "Bullshit.", she said. I felt her tongue move across my clit, and that was the end of it. I moaned into the night, and then grabbed her, and kissed her. We made love in the field. By the time we were done, I felt disgusted with myself. I got up and started to dress quickly. "Been almost seventy years, hasn't it?", she asked me, also getting up, and getting dressed. I didn't say anything, and without looking at her, I teleported to my manor. I began to cry on my bed. I cried for hours. I realized what time it was when it hit four a.m, and I didn't get out of bed. Usually, I get up and make some coffee or something, but I can't. I was too ashamed of having allowed Amana to pull me in like she has done in the past. No matter what I told myself, I couldn't just ignore her.

LODY: I woke up in the morning, feeling like I had done something wrong last night. I came out of my room and was quickly greeted by Amana, "Good morning, Mr. Red. Follow me.", she said. We walked past Emillie's room and proceeded all the way to the other side of Base to her office. "I think I was a bit unfair with you last night. I get sort of angry when Dalia gets mentioned. But after a nice little TALK I had with her last night, I'm quite sure that we have an understanding on things now.". I had no idea what the hell that meant. "Anyway, I need you to go on a mission.", "A mission? For what?", I asked. "Well, usually my people don't ask me for what, but you are new. I need you to keep an eye on your friend. Tillo. He is going to get his mother killed and I need you to prevent that.", "You could have by bringing his mother here in the first place!", I yelled. "I could have done no such thing. I don't think you've gotten an understanding of how P.E.D works, Mr. Red. It isn't about just doing what I want. Plus, I didn't know Awalli would have gone after Mrs. Tillo. That didn't seem likely. Now things are changing, and there is nothing that I can do for that situation. But I can ensure she doesn't die.", "How do you even know she is still alive?", "On that note, I know she is still alive because, Emillie is here on Base, Ko-e hasn't revealed herself, and there are a lot of things that Awalli still needs answers for. So, like I said, Tillo is the only thing that can endanger his mother. Your job, as of now, is to ensure he understands that. I'm letting you go back to your home, Mr. Red. But I'm going to let you take some very interesting toys with you.", she said, now leading me to a wall. She touched it and the wall vanished to reveal a shit ton of weapons. There were cannons, small, big, and just straight up unbelievably nice looking. There was one that had a very nice fine point tip. "What the hell is this, Amana?", I said, picking it up. "You like that one? It is designed for silent kills. The only thing is, you have to be precise with it, and it's more of a close-range weapon.". I looked at all the nice cannons, but there were blades as well. Serrated, straight-edge, and one that was just a sharp long needle attached to the hilt. I picked this one up and examined it. I didn't need Amana to tell me what this was used for. It was a quick kill. Or even could be used as a torture device, "Amana…", I said, confused why suddenly she was being so nice. "It's General, Mr. Red. You are now a P.E.D soldier and will address me as such.". I nodded and then proceeded to the pod area. "I have orders to leave.", I said to the guy who had turned me away last night. He smiled. "Fine by me, sir.", he said, directing me to a pod. When I got in, it was a surprisingly quick trip. I was on the ground and hadn't even exited out of the pod. I looked and realized I was now in a receiving area. "I'm Hepzibah, nice to meet you. Red, isn't it?", she asked me. Just from how she was looking at me, I could tell she thought I was attractive. "Yeah. So how am I getting to Edge?", I asked. I looked around and saw a group of flars. Hepzibah pointed in their direction, "You'll be taking one of our self automated flars.". She walked me over to the flars and I got in one. She programmed it and then smiled, waved, then closed the door.

During the ride, I was reading a file that had been placed in the flar. It was on Sandin. It spoke of his childhood and the events surrounding his father's death. His mother and father had been digging for over thirteen years. During the first five of those years, Sandin was born. He was their miracle child from what it seemed, because in the file, it's mentioned that Mrs. Tillo was unable to have children. But the more I read into it, it seemed like whatever the object is mentioned in the report, had everything to do with it. Sandin displayed strange behavior from an early age. He was very wise but settled for less. I realized this was true. As long as I'd known him, he always seemed to be smart. Something about his way of handling things told me most of what I needed to know. He was meticulous, usually, despite what was going on with his mother. The only time I've ever seen him do anything out of the ordinary, was once he had met Emillie. Thinking about it now, why didn't I see it sooner? Dalia saw it right away. She said Tillo and Emillie were connected. He was onto her and she was onto him. But now I had an understanding of it that was completely different. Gods and goddesses exist in a different realm. They are attracted to their destinies differently than normal people. They have a stronger pull on them. Emillie was drawn to Awalli and Sandin. I started to think that maybe there was a connection, not just for Emillie and Sandin, but for Sandin and Awalli as well. Awalli knows about Emillie and Sandin, which means that she will eventually use him as leverage. But what was really throwing me off even more, was the fact that Emillie was so willing to take the beatings Amana was giving her. I thought about how Sandin would feel. He'd probably storm Base. Then I remembered what my mission was. To stop Sandin from getting his mother killed. But if Awalli needed her, would she kill her just so no one else can have her?

The flar finally stopped and I realized I was at Dalia's orphanage. I got out, and the Flar drove away. I wondered why it brought me here, but then realized right away when I saw Tillo here, "Tillo, what are you doing here?", I asked him, approaching the front yard beyond the gate. "I'm here to get some answers.", he said, turning, and knocking on the door. Cynda came to the door, "Oh, it's you. Where is Emillie?", she asked. "I don't know. Now please, I'm here to see Dalia.", "BUT, the other guy said YOU knew!", Cynda said, on the verge of tears, "What is going on? Is she dead again or not?!", Cynda yelled, beating into Sandin's abdomen. "I really don't know where she is, Cynda.", Tillo said, trying to get away from her. "You're lying! You're her boyfriend!", Cynda said. "Cynda, I've spoken to her, she's fine and she misses you. She promised me she'd be visiting soon.", I said, saving Tillo, and rushing him passed Cynda, who still looked like she didn't believe us. We walked into Dalia's office and just looking at her, I could tell something was wrong. She seemed sort of distracted and didn't want to face me, "Red, Tillo. Good to see you two.", she said strangely. "Dalia, I need some answers. What is this?", Tillo said, holding up his hand. I realized he was talking about the ring. "I can't say, Tillo. I've never seen it before.", "BULLSHIT!", Tillo yelled, pounding on Dalia's desk. "Tillo, just relax!", I yelled, trying to calm him down. "NO! I'M SICK OF THIS SHIT!", he yelled, now staring Dalia down, who was quickly gaining her anger. "First off, there are children here, so you need to stop shouting, and second, like I said, I don't know what that is. Yes, I can feel its energy, but I can't tell you what it is.", Dalia said, glaring at Tillo. I looked closer at her face and saw some bruising that seemed to be healing rather quickly, "Dalia, what happened?", I asked her. She looked at me, then sat down, "Nothing.", she said, trying to busy herself, "Look, if you two are finished, I've got two new children coming today and I need to…", "I'm not finished. I need to know what energy you feel.", Tillo said, calming down, and sitting down as well. Dalia looked at him, and saw how intent he was. "Dalia, I can see the marks on your face. Did Amana come here?", I asked. I was now afraid

I may have gotten her into some kind of trouble. "Tillo, do you mind if I talk to Red? I promise I'll tell you everything you want to know.". Tillo looked like there was no way he'd wait. He stood up slowly and looked at me. "It'll be short, mate.", I said. He walked out the door, and I could tell he was waiting right outside, "Dalia, I…", she held her hand up. "First off, I'd like to thank you.", "For what?", I asked. "For reminding me that I belong to Amana.", she said, looking at me sadly. "What the hell are you talking about?", "She was indeed here last night. And things didn't exactly go well. We…had sex last night.". I didn't say anything. I was sort of numb. Dalia could see my feelings. "I warned you, Lody. I told you not to get involved with me. I told you to walk away.", "You couldn't just say no?", I asked her, finally finding my voice. "I TRIED!", she yelled. "Then she raped you?", I asked. "No. She just made me… I don't know.", she said confusedly, "I told you, it's all mixed up, me and Amana. I can't explain to you why I feel for her like I do.". I felt like I didn't want to hear anymore, so I opened the door for Tillo. Tillo slowly came back in and returned to his chair. Dalia looked hurt, and stood up, and walked up to me, "Red…", "You'd best tell Tillo what he wants.", I said, barely looking at her. "Can you please tell me about the ring?", Tillo asked impatiently. "Like I said, Tillo, I can sense its power, but I can't exactly understand it. Amana would know better than me.", "What about that other woman I've been seeing here?", Tillo asked. Tillo must have been watching the orphanage. With no word from Emillie, and his mother being held against her will, I imagined this was the only safe thing that made sense to Tillo. Like I said before, he is meticulous and wouldn't just place himself in danger so easily. I wondered why Amana sent me here if she knew that, which I figured she must. "Tillo, I don't know what you're talking about. What other woman?", "Don't play dumb, Dalia! There has been another goddess that has been coming here! I've seen her! I know she's a goddess! Who is she?", Tillo asked. "She is someone that has ensured I can't tell you or Amana anything.". Tillo looked livid, "ALL I WANT IS TO SAVE MY MOM!", he yelled, now standing up and starting to get upset. "Tillo, I know how you feel, but we all know how dangerous Awalli is. She is also very well versed in magic. I'm sure you've come to understand. So trying to go for your mother in this way isn't going to help. As for that ring, you should let Emillie have it.", Dalia said. "Sure. When Amana lets us see one another.", "Emillie is choosing not to visit you, Sandin.", I said darkly. "Why not?!", he said, surprised. "Because she is training and doesn't want the distraction. She wants to save your mom, but she wants to do it right.", I said. This got Sandin to calm down somewhat. "Emillie… I miss her.", he said, sitting back down again. "You aren't the only one.", Dalia said. "Tillo, let's go, mate. Come on.", I said, pulling him out of the chair, and leading him out of Dalia's office. Dalia watched me go, sadly, and I looked back at her, and our eyes met. For a moment, I could tell she wanted me, but the moment quickly faded when I thought about the fact Amana came here and fucked her after our conversation.

"At least she didn't rub it in.", I said, once Tillo and I had gotten to his flar, and I had explained what was happening between Dalia and I. "So, Amana did that just to spite you? She is so messed up.", Tillo said, taking a swig from his flask. Tillo had grown a beard as well and was looking more depressed than anything. "So, Red, how is it you've spoken to Emillie?", he asked. I hesitated, "I've joined P.E.D.". I looked at him sideways. "So has Yellfy.", he said. "What? When?", I asked, shocked at this new bit of info. "Two weeks ago. He's already on a mission. Him and Raby. He was very hushed up about what it is, though.", "I'm gonna talk to Amana about making you an agent as well. You need to get paid.", "And laid.", he said, taking another swig. "We could both use that.", I said, holding my hand out. Tillo passed me the flask, "I think you just need to have another go at Dalia. She isn't with Amana. Amana is just trying to piss on your leg.", he said. "I know. But I don't think it's wise. It'll piss Amana off and give her a reason to hate me.", "Suit yourself, but I think you're missing out.". Part of me knew Tillo was right. I started the flar and we headed towards his apartment.

Halfway there, Tillo demanded that we go to Emillie's apartment. Once we got there, I saw why. He had been coming here three times a week and cleaning the house. I sat there and watched him clean. Then I showed him the file I was reading earlier. He read it with great vigor. I could tell he was taking in every single word. It occured to me that I could have shown him this when we were at Dalia's manor, but I had other things on my mind. "Can you believe what this says? It says that my father was infected with some kind of disease. Something that got into his system. But I don't understand. It doesn't clarify what that is, though.". He continued reading until he got to the part speaking of his mother;

> Ayrellia Tillo is to be constantly monitored. It is believed she is channeling the energies put off by the cosmos. If this is the case, she may be in danger from those that might try and take advantage of her knowledge. Be vigilant and keep eyes on at all times. As a side brief, also watch Sandin Tillo(her son), for he is also channeling energy from the cosmos but also possesses the god gene. He will be drawn to someone and it is imperative we find out who.

After Tillo showed me what he had just read, it opened more questions. "When I asked Amana why she didn't just bring your mother to Base, she said she couldn't just do that. But reading this, I have to be honest, I don't think Amana wrote this.", I said, thinking hard about the last sentence; He will be drawn to someone and it is imperative we find out who. "I kind of see what you mean. But how old is this letter?", Tillo asked. "The date is on the back.", Tillo turned the letter over. "This was twenty-three years ago. When I was born. But my mother wasn't sick when I was a child.", Tillo said, sitting down, and looking lost. Tillo never spoke much of his parents and I wondered if he was remembering something. "Red, my mother used to tell me that the fairy tales were real. She said they weren't just stories made up by some fool on lilac. What if my mother knew what she was talking about? What if she actually KNEW?", Tillo said, getting excited. He looked at the ring, "Oh. I can't believe this. Why didn't I remember this?", Tillo said, getting even more amped up. "Do you want to share with the class, mate? What have you figured out?", I asked, feeling highly confused. "Red, this file just told me that my mother was exposed to something cosmic. This ring. I remember it. I remember when my dad gave it to me. I was really young, but my mom said I would put it on the finger of a goddess. Somehow, I think my mother was told of Emillie. Her and my father. I don't know why Amana killed my father yet, but once I do find out…", he drifted off. He looked at the ring again. "Do you think this ring will help Emillie control her power? You know, so there isn't another accident like at Linix.", Tillo said, still looking sharply at the ring. "Maybe. It's hard to say, Tillo. I've got so much that I don't really know.", "Well, tell Amana, I'm in. Something tells me that THIS is where I'm supposed to be.", Tillo said, becoming sure of himself. "What about your mom?", I asked him. "She will be…okay.", he said, as if he wasn't really sure. I dialed Amana's number, "Yes, Mr. Red?", she asked, in that bored tone of hers. "I've spoken with Tillo and he wants to join P.E.D as well.", I said. "Well, that's nice. I'll send a PC with the briefing and start the funds immediately. Sounds nice?", she said. "Well, why can't he just…?", "I hope you weren't trying to find a way to bring him and Emillie together. Emillie doesn't want to see him yet.", "Why can't they just see each other once?", I asked quietly while Sandin was distracted. "I'm not keeping them apart. I told Sandin I'd let Emillie visit once a week. Every time I've let down the teleport dampeners, she doesn't go to him. That isn't my fault.". On that she was right. Amana hung up and I went back to Tillo. "You're in.", I said. "I know. My shill collector just started going crazy.", he said. "What the…? She didn't do that for me!", I said. "Well, maybe I have more to offer…", he said, not in an insulting way, but like he was thinking. "Listen, Amana needs to see this letter.", I said. "But what if she wrote it?", Tillo asked. "I don't think so. There's no doubt, this is indeed an official P.E.D statement, but I don't think Amana is the one who issued it. So that means there's someone else in P.E.D. Someone undermining Amana. She could be in some kind of danger and not know it.", "How could that woman be in danger and not know it?!", Tillo asked. "Tillo, whoever did this was smart enough to do it behind Amana's back. I think that Awalli's extra power and the reasoning behind her trying to kill Emillie, is because this person, who wrote this letter, is Awalli's puppet master.", I said. Tillo looked at me for a minute. I knew it sounded far fetched, but what if? "Red, I think you might be right.", Tillo said. I called Amana back, "Amana, sorry, but I think I have something you need to see.", "Okay, I'll come.". She teleported into the room, "What?", she said. I showed her the note. "I've seen this before, Mr. Red.", she said, handing it back. "AND?", I asked. "I know who wrote it.", "Who?", I asked. "Classified.", she said, "If that's all…", "NO. I think this person is behind Awalli.", "That's impossible, Mr. Red.", "Why?", "Because the person who wrote it is dead. It was Slayn Tillo.". I looked at Sandin, who flushed, "What the hell are you talking about? Why would my dad write a letter like this? You killed him.", he said in a silent, angry, kind of tone. "Well, usually, I don't tell people things unless I need to…", Amana said, rubbing her index and thumb finger on her chin. "Fine. I'll tell you the truth.". I was thinking about Dalia and what she told me, but decided this isn't the right time to say anything about it. "Your father was a P.E.D agent. I didn't recruit him.", "What do you mean, YOU didn't recruit him?", Sandin asked, growing angrier and impatient. "You two will soon learn that I may have started P.E.D, but that doesn't mean that I'm the only one who started P.E.D, nor am I the only one in charge.". Me and Sandin looked at each other and I started thinking about everything that has happened so far. It didn't make sense. She has a lot of power, that much I've confirmed. "So, who else has power in P.E.D?", I asked. "Her name is Mileeda and she is the origin of the RF.".

CHAPTER 8

Mean Grandma

SYLVIA: Emillie was doing amazing. She had cleared most of the blade training and was now doing exercises to perfect her art. She had her own way of using the blade and her own unique way of fighting. We were sparring, and that same guy that had been watching her before was standing nearby. "You've gotten pretty good.", he said, walking up. "Don't you have something else to do?", Emillie said, stopping our sparring session. "Not really.", he said, smiling at Emillie. Emillie was still not having it. "Listen, it's getting to a creepy factor. I don't have an interest in you. I am in a relationship. I'm happy with my current situation. So, can you leave me alone now, please?", Emillie said, looking at him intently. "You're The General's daughter, aren't you?", he asked. "That's enough. She said go away, now I'M telling you.", I said, stepping beside Emillie. "And?", he retorted. "Do I have to bring this to Amana?", I asked. "The General doesn't like for people to use her name. Perhaps I should tell her about you?", he replied. "Screw this.", Emillie said. She quickly punched him. He tried to fight back, but Emillie quickly subdued him. I noticed that Amana was standing nearby, watching. After Emillie finished beating the man's ass, she quickly picked him up, threw him into a nearby pillar, and then pinned him to it with a blade she summoned from out of nowhere. I had no idea she could do that. "EMILLIE!", Amana yelled, now moving towards her, "SYLVIA!

SHE WILL HURT HIM!", Amana said, pointing for me to get Emillie. I started to move towards her but was blasted back by some field I couldn't see, "EMILLIE!", I shouted, but she didn't seem to hear me. Then, Amana moved in and threw something, and Emillie was blasted away from the man. He fell down, gasping for breath. "Get out of my sight.", Amana said, and the man got up and slinked away. Emillie was getting to her feet. She rushed at her mother, who I was surprised had a hard time taking Emillie down. Emillie had swung her blade at her and Amana dodged and punched her in her gut, but this did nothing. Amana then got punched and she went down. I decided to step in, but Emillie only waved her sword and I couldn't get near. She started slowly approaching Amana, who I noticed was playing possum. As soon as Emillie was close, she sprung up and placed a device on Emillie's head that made Emillie stop and fall down to the ground. The sword disappeared. "I'll take Emillie. I'll let you know when she wakes up.", "What was THAT?!", I felt compelled to ask. "That's, what's hiding inside of her.", Amana said, staring down at her. I thought more about it later and realized that Emillie had lost control. I truly believed she would have killed that man. As I pondered on it, Red was arriving on Base with someone else. I recognized him as the guy Emillie had a picture of in her room. "Sylvia, where is Amana?", Red asked. "She took Emillie earlier. Something happened.". I quickly told them the story. "No.", said Tillo, after I finished, "I need to see her.", he said. "Tillo?", said a voice. We turned and were all surprised to find Emillie standing right next to us. The two eyed each other for a minute, then grabbed one another, and I lost track of their faces. They were practically glued.

Emillie and Tillo had disappeared, leaving me with Red. There wasn't a lot to do on Base most days, so I often passed the time reading, whenever I wasn't training Emillie. Red was telling me all about Tillo, and his parents. Tillo's father, Slayn Tillo, used to be a P.E.D agent. He was recruited by my ancestor, Mileeda. Mileeda had him searching for objects of Sebastian. Him and his wife found a few. But it's the ring on Tillo's finger that holds most of the importance. This object infected his parents with a toxin that connected them to the cosmos in different ways. Mrs. Tillo had gained knowledge of all the gods and goddesses present on the planet. She could sense them and tell you exactly where they are. As for Mr. Tillo, he had lost his mind and believed he had to kill his wife and son. The day he attempted this, Amana herself showed up and shot Mr. Tillo, killing him on the spot. Poor Sandin, I now thought. His mother slowly started to deteriorate. She wasn't all the way there in the head, and was slowly starting to lose her grip on reality. Tillo managed to grow up and take care of himself and his mother. I admired his tenacity. Red also told me how Tillo was connected to Emillie, and that when Emillie was dead, her essence fled to Sandin. Red seemed like he had some kind of grudge against Amana. "So, what did Amana do to you?", I asked him, after finally getting tired of his grunts every time he said her name. "Nothing to bring up.", he said, trying to move away from me now. "Oh, come off it. She has easily pissed off almost every single one of my family members. I can see what she did to Sandin, but what did she do to you?", "None of your business.", he said, now picking up the pace. It was getting late and I was hungry, so I decided to go to the food hall. Emillie was there with Sandin. They looked completely happy and didn't want to be bothered from the looks of things. I saw the man Emillie had accosted earlier, watching them with jealousy. "So, what happened after that beating?", I asked him. "I was written up. I didn't know it was that serious, but I should have known once I guessed who she was.", the man said, looking me up and down. I thought he was a good enough looking man, and considering I hadn't been laid since I set out to kill Awalli, it didn't take much for me to convince him to follow me.

We were in my barracks. I hadn't even asked him for his name. I was kissing him, and he went for my neck. "So, ah, I have a question.", I said, as he was gently stroking my flower. "What's...that?", he said between kissing my neck. I pushed him away, "I need to know who you're working for.". He looked at me confused. "Don't play dumb. You're no idiot. You're P.E.D. And if you knew she was the daughter of The General, then why even test her?", I asked. I watched him closely to see what he was going to say. "Well...I just thought she was a skeeter. What do you expect to hear?", he said, now also watching me closely. "Okay, I'm gonna ask again...", "Amana.". I thought about his answer and watched to see if he was lying. "Then why did you test Emillie?", "Because, Amana told me to. She said she wanted to see what's hiding in her.", "And did you understand what that means?", I asked. "No. She never gives straight answers. I knew it meant something to do with that crazy shit a couple months ago.". Now, I was even more intrigued. I pushed him up against the wall. "Listen to me. And listen closely. I came here to kill a woman named Awalli. She runs all the mobs in Edge. Now I'm here, training Emillie. But I think Emillie is ready to face her.", I released the man, "What's your name?", I asked him. "Tem. And I know who you are. You're, Sylvia Lon.", "I want to speak to...Mileeda.", I said, sort of nervously. I wasn't sure if asking for her was wise. Everyone knows that she is hidden and only comes out when she wants to. She isn't the nicest one, either. Requesting to meet her COULD be a mistake. But she is the beginning. The whole reason the RF are kin to giving birth to those who carry the gift. I was lucky. I didn't have it. But Layna, she did. Her father was killed. Layna was supposed to be with him but she was rescued by Amana. Only thing was, back then, we didn't know that Amana saved her. Then, when she was eight, she reappeared but under a different identity. I hated her then, even though I didn't realize she was my cousin. I was just a kid. But when she turned seventeen, she was appearing everywhere. Telling everyone she could, every single ally, that SHE was royal blood. She did favors. Sorted out issues. She gained more than allies, she gained FRIENDS. So we were unable to execute her. Doing so would bring down a wrath not worth facing. And thus, Layna wormed her way into what WOULD have been MINE! I stared at Tem, waiting for an answer still. "That is something, you have to ask Amana.". He quickly got away from me. Amana was going to tell me no. Mileeda gave Layna her blessing to make her the Head of Family. I needed to change Mileeda's mind. Mileeda hadn't given any kind of fucking blessing in eons. Suddenly, Layna was good enough? It didn't make sense, and had been plaguing me and the rest of the family. We kept wondering how the hell Mileeda saw fit to bless anyone, when SHE didn't want to be seen. The last time she was seen, I was a little girl, and we were at a Year End party. Mileeda had heard about Aunt Tena's debacle that resulted in the death of four children. Mileeda had taken her into a room. We all heard her screaming. Of course the party ended with Mileeda coming out of the room and telling us all to stand down, while good ol' Aunt Tena came out of that room, never the same. She was quiet, and never spoke much. And for Bastian's sake, don't say Mileeda around her. Sometimes we used to do it just to see her reaction. But that was the last time any of us had seen Mileeda. Tena was Head of the Family at that time. Then after that, it was my father, Solron Lon. That's why I was next up. But Layna stole that from me. She was there. At that Year End party. Nobody knew she was gifted. She was with Amana. Amana referred to her as her daughter, and nobody thought that strange.

I had resolved to abandon the situation for now. I was more intrigued about Emillie. What was that sword that appeared? I couldn't get it out of my mind. And how did she materialize it? First off, okay, of course this is something most gifted can do. Yes. I've seen Layna do it. But it is also a simple magic to perform. Even I can do it. But the RF has technology that does it for us. We manipulate the molecules in the air, and transform it into what our mind perceives. It wasn't easy tech to develop, but it is definitely possible. But, Emillie didn't have that tech on her. She also didn't mutter any incantation. Which means that she summoned that sword from somewhere. She summoned it, and it brought with it the energy from wherever it came. It's dark, that I could feel. Emillie lost control once it formed in her hand. She wasn't herself. And her power. It was incredible. Amana owed me some answers. I had been training Emillie for two months after all. I'm quite sure Emillie didn't think to summon that sword of her own accord, and I need to know what is happening. I approached her office, swallowed, then knocked. The door opened, and I went in. There were other people in here. They all turned at my entrance. Layna was amongst the people in the room. "Cousin Sylvia.", she said cordially. "Layna.", I replied. All the people disappeared. "Well, I hope you're happy. You just interrupted an important meeting.", Amana said, looking not too happy. "Screw this. I want to meet Mileeda.". If I thought Amana was angry a second ago, it was nothing to how angry she became at this request, "Are you out of your mind? Do you know what that woman will do if I tell you yes?". I thought about the answer, "I imagine she'll do something terrible. But why? I'm family. I want to see her.". I'd gone too far, "OUT!", Amana barked, also pulling out her cannon and pointing it at me. I hesitated. She never scared me. But at the moment, I didn't want her to throw me to Awalli, so I listened. I didn't understand what the deal was with Mileeda. Why was she so keen on keeping away from everyone? I needed the answers. Then I remembered I wanted to ask about Emillie, but knew it was too late. There was no going back into that office.

SANDIN: The moment that Emillie and I got away from Red and Sylvia, we began going at it. We didn't even make it to her room before we found the first door and pried it open. It was an empty room. We began undressing and I quickly put her on top of a table and began fucking her. I could feel the jolts going through my body with each thrust. Finally, she climbed off the table and pushed me onto the floor. She was on top of me. Grinding hard and thrusting. I needed this. I needed it badly. "We...ahhh, have to.....stop...uh, for a second.", I tried to say, as I started to fear someone might hear us and come in, "NO.", Emillie said, in a voice unlike her own. She put her arms out and the doors disappeared. "Emillie, how did you learn to...?", she grabbed my face, and began kissing me, and continued thrusting on me. Then she demanded I get on top of her. I kept fucking her, until I climaxed. She held me tight, then grabbed my face, "I missed you.", she said in her voice and kissed me. She was kissing my face and I was thinking, was it just me, or did something seem terribly different this time?

As we got all cleaned up, Emillie was showing me around Base. I had left Red and started to wonder where he was. I told Emillie about her mom and Dalia, and what her mom did after Red approached her, "My mother. I like her less and less.", she said. "She's the one putting the bruises on your face?", I asked her, examining her face for the first time. "Well, to be honest, I need that. It has made me stronger. Except, I don't know what happened earlier. One minute, I was just trying to teach a guy a lesson. Then, I'm waking up, and my mom is telling me I get a pass tonight on her usual ass whopping.", Emillie looked at me and smiled. She was so different from the nice girl out of the orphanage. "Cynda is worried sick about you.", "I'm going to visit tomorrow. I finally called, and spoke to her today.", Emillie said, looking even more cheerful. "Emillie, I don't want to sound mean, but do you think you're ready for public outings yet?". Emillie's smile faded, "Listen, learning martial-arts has taught me to harness my chi, and focus this energy I feel inside of me. I can't fully control it, but I can guarantee that there won't be another

Linix.", she smiled again now. She placed her hand on my face, "I'm starving. Let's go get something to eat.". She led me to the food hall. I noticed that there was a man who looked in our direction as soon as we entered. "I guess that's the guy I almost killed.", Emillie said. I looked again so he wouldn't notice me looking, but I saw he was jealous. "Did he try to hit on you?", I asked. "Yes. But don't worry, he learned his lesson, I'm sure.". We sat down and just stared at one another. She played with my hand and I just stared into her eyes. They were a dull gray, but somehow matched her beauty. "I learned about my father. I know why Amana killed him.". Emillie continued to smile at me, "Why?", she asked, as she rubbed her small finger down my middle finger closest to her. "Because he was trying to kill me and my mom.". She stopped playing with my hand now. "What?", she said, more serious now. "He was sick. This ring. It had some kind of power they couldn't handle. Dalia said I should give it to you.", I said, holding the ring out. She took it, and immediately, I felt an energy emanate off of her. She held it in her hand, then looked up at me, "Let's go back to my room.".

In her room, we had more sex. I lost track of how long. But we finally stopped and then I noticed something in the corner. It was breathing. "What the hell is that?", I asked, looking at it more closely. "It was the pet of Sebastian. A small but very powerful creature. It is wise not to underestimate it.". Emillie didn't sound like herself. She got out of bed, waved her hand, and made her panties and shirt appear upon her, and approached the creature. She held her hand out and it came to her. "Her name is Casian. She is very ancient. But my father has a pet similar to this. All the gods have something.", "Emillie, what are you talking about?". As I asked her this, she suddenly looked alert, "Well, anyway, Casian, do you want to meet Tillo?", she said, now coming towards me in her usual, friendly, manner. I was all sorts of confused.

After Emillie had fallen asleep, I snuck out. I had been here before, so I knew where to go if I wanted to find Amana's office. As I was approaching it, I overheard voices. I don't know why, but I hid, "So, what you are saying, Amana, is that you prefer, I deal with her myself.", "No. What I'm saying is that you have a responsibility TO deal with THEM yourself.". The voices got quiet for a minute. "Okay. I'll…approach both of them. Anything else after that, I can't be held accountable.", "DON'T HURT HER, MILEEDA!", Amana yelled, "Look, I need her to keep working with Emillie.", "Yeah, about that… She seems like she could be an issue. I heard she almost lost control and killed someone.", "Things like that can easily happen. You know why she is needed. Stop playing with me, Mileeda.". Mileeda didn't seem fazed in the slightest. I figured they were talking about Sylvia Lon. "If Emillie becomes too…dangerous, can I count on you to do the right thing?", Mileeda said. There was silence. "Are you seriously asking…?", "Oh don't even. I was there. I was with you when you killed Calypsa. So don't try to compare this to that. You know that Emillie is dangerous. You know she is, I know she is. So, if you have to, will you kill her?". I felt my heart drop. "If she becomes… too dangerous.", Amana said. "Fine. I can live with that. And I'll talk to my dear… Oh, I lost count. Descendants.". Mileeda departed. I waited for a while, before I came out of hiding and went to Amana's office. As I approached the door, I smelled flowers. I didn't know why, but it was really strong. I looked around but there weren't any flowers in sight. I decided to forget about it and knocked on Amana's door. The door opened and I entered. Amana was staring over a table that seemed to have a screen. When I got closer, I noticed it was a giant monitor. It seemed to be scanning areas. "Good evening, Sandin. Shouldn't you be in a broom closet screwing my daughter? That's all you two do, isn't it?", she asked me, as I approached the giant monitor. "I have a really important question. What happened to Emillie, earlier today?", I said, sitting down on one of the chairs nearby. "Emillie, is channeling energies connected to her father. She is gaining knowledge that isn't really hers.", Amana stood up straight and put her face in her hands, "I saw this coming. But WE NEED Emillie. She must exist. Listen to me, Sandin, Emillie is on the verge of learning to control this thing.". I thought about the ring. "And what about the ring?". As soon as I said this, confusion and fear at the same time crossed her face, "Ring?", she asked me. "Yes. The one Awalli had. The one I found. Didn't Raby bring it up?", "Raby, is a good soldier.", Amana said, taking out her cell and sending a message. Suddenly, a woman teleported into a chair next to mine. It was Mileeda. "Did you forbid Raby from telling me about a certain ring?", Amana asked. "Yes.", Mileeda said simply. "So. We are back at this again?", "Why is Sandin Tillo here?", Mileeda asked, looking at me. "Because he is Emillie's toy. And I need him to be in the know of what is going on. But I can't work, if you are working against me.". I thought about what was going on. Red told me that Raby doesn't trust Amana. But so far, she has been Amana's main woman. As of now, she was on a mission. So now I wondered if maybe she was on a mission for Mileeda, and not Amana. "I'm not working against you.", Mileeda said, simply looking at her hand. "Mileeda…I'm not playing.", "Neither am I.", "Where is Koe?", Amana asked, placing her hands on the table. "She is hiding from me as well. I've been telling you this for years.", Mileeda said. "And have you even been trying to find her?", Amana said, through gritted teeth. "Listen to me, Amana. You and I both know I have more important shit to deal with then looking for your sister, or having to worry about your damn daughter. So let's hurry and cut to the chase. I had Raby not tell you about the ring, because I've been searching for it. But not so Emillie could have it.", "You knew it was in that church. After what it did to the Tillos!", Amana shouted, "Then Awalli got her hands on it. It's funny the things your little DESCENDANT manages to get her hands on. She is like an evil version of Layna.", Amana said. Now I knew who they were talking about earlier. "I told you, I'll talk to her. And I'll talk to Sylvia. What more could you ask of me? And where is the ring?", Mileeda asked. "Tell me why you want it.", Amana said. Mileeda sighed, "Because it is obviously dangerous. It isn't an object of Sebastian. My sources said so ages ago.". I swallowed, "So, what you're saying...is that the reason my parents lost their minds, wasn't because of Sebastian?", I asked. "Sandin, whoever that ring did belong to, lets just say they are long gone. Without that ring, I imagine they can't control their power. We'd easily find them. Are we done, Amana? I was in the middle of something.", "You are lying about Ko-e. I can feel it. You know where she is, Mileeda.", "You know the game, Amana. I don't tell you all my secrets.", "He is killing everyone in his quest for vengeance, and I KNOW Ko-e is the one who put him up to it!", Amana shouted. "I don't know anything about what you're saying, Amana, but on that, I stand by what I said. Don't make a move.". Mileeda teleported out of the room, and Amana took out her cannon, and started screaming, and blasting it off. I looked in the direction she was firing and there was a firing range that had appeared. It disappeared as quickly as it had appeared, and Amana was clearly steaming. I knew I should leave but my questions hadn't really been answered. And now I had more. I looked up at Amana and thought the first thing, "Quest for vengeance?", I asked. I had heard about the kung-fu guy that Yellfy was talking about, also killing Tom, shortly after I paid him a visit. Awalli was losing her captains, and it was all thanks to this mystery guy. Amana knows who he is. "Out. Please. You've heard enough classified info. But now you understand.". I knew what she meant.

After I left, I thought more about what Amana was doing. Then suddenly it all made sense. She must have heard or seen me when her and Mileeda were speaking earlier. But she called her in later, so I could see what she was telling me and Red. She isn't in full control. She must have known about the ring, of course. But Raby didn't tell her. Or if she did, she also told her she wasn't supposed to. Or she didn't say anything, and Amana truly didn't know. When I returned to Emillie's room, she was gone. The ring was gone as well. Casian was on edge, though, "What's wrong, girl?", I asked, looking around the room. Then I picked up Casian, and heard something in my head, "Emillie is in danger. She summoned the sword while you were gone. You must warn Mileeda.". I didn't understand why I had to warn Mileeda, and didn't know where this voice had come from. Then I heard it again, "It is I, Casian.". I looked at the creature, as if I was going mad. "I can speak to you. You have the flow of the cosmos, but we don't have much time, Sandin. I can take you to her. You can save her.". Before I did anything else, Casian had teleported us somewhere. It was the manor in SE. The one where all the mobsters meet up. And things were already looking wrong. I saw a massive blood trail leading from the stairs to inside. There were two dead bodies already outside and I could hear screaming and cannon fire.

EMILLIE: When I awoke, Sandin was gone. I got up, got dressed, and was getting ready to go look for him, but then something happened. I felt my chest burn. I grabbed it, then the sword appeared. I looked at it and then I was somewhere else. I felt like I had been here before. There were a few men outside of a huge manor. One of them walked up to me. "What do you got there, sugar?", he asked, reaching for me. I quickly stuck the sword in his gut. Suddenly, I knew what I was looking for. I forced the man down to the ground, while the other men pulled out cannons and started firing at me. The shells couldn't penetrate my force field. I dragged the man on the end of my blade up to the manor. I then lifted him on the end of my blade with one arm, and threw him into the doors. He crashed through them, leaving blood all over the front of the manor. I rushed the other two and killed them quickly. There were other's now, coming outside, and I rushed in. Slashing anyone and everyone, I kept making my way through the manor. I saw a man with long, red, hair rushing towards me, shouting as he did, "IT'S HER! THE ONE THE BOSS HAS BEEN WARNING US ABOUT!". He pulled out his cannon and I hit him with the flat side of my blade and he flew into a large portrait of a man with a white suit on. The men were all shooting at me, but nothing could hurt me. I could sense Mrs. Tillo. She was here. That's when I finally found the blank wall. I closed my eyes and then a door appeared. I went in, and Mrs. Tillo was lying in bed. She seemed to be in good condition. Then, Awalli appeared in the room. "Emillie.", she said, snatching Mrs. Tillo out of the bed. Mrs. Tillo woke with a shock and looked in my direction, "So, it is now.", she said. At this time, Sandin came rushing into the room. Casian was on his shoulder. He looked at his mother, whom he had been worried sick about for over two months. Awalli looked at the both of us, took out her cannon, and shot Mrs. Tillo right in the heart, "NO!", Sandin yelled, and he rushed forward, while I attacked Awalli. She summoned a shield to protect herself from my blade, but that wasn't easy. She was having a hard time blocking every swing. Finally, I cut her face. She looked up at me and rushed me. She put her hands out in front of me and I was forced below the house. I was buried under rubble. By the time I had dug myself out, I found her quickly and rushed her. She grabbed my blade by its flat edges, and was trying to stop me from piercing her, when Sandin yelled for me, "EMILLIE!". I lost track of what I was doing, and Awalli caught me off guard. She shot me with her cannon and I was blasted back. She then started doing something. I could feel the molecules in the air reshaping. Then she was gone, and so was the rest of the manor. It was just me and Sandin, and his now dead mother.

"Sandin?", I said, walking towards him. It took a minute to realize we were transported out of the manor. Looking around, we were in a construction area. I looked around more, and saw signs that read; (Mccloud Industries, future location). "Sandin?". He wasn't answering me. He was holding his mother's body and tears were falling down his face. I went to him and kneeled next to him, "This is your fault.", he said. "No, Sandin, I…", "THIS IS YOUR FAULT, EMILLIE!", he shouted at me. My mother, and another woman I hadn't seen before, materialized in the area. My mother looked at Sandin, holding his mother, and then came for me. She relentlessly started attacking me. She kicked me in my face and then started to kick me in my sides. I felt my chest burn, and saw the sword start to materialize in my hand, but my mother placed something on my hand, and the sword disappeared. She then continued kicking me, "AMANA!", yelled the other woman. "NO! Look what she has done! You said yourself…", Amana said, taking out her cannon, "…to kill her if she became too dangerous.". I looked up at my mother, who was prepared to shoot me. "Amana, wait.", the other woman said, walking up. She had dark hair and was really pretty, but looked like she could be as important as my mother, "Let me take her.". Amana looked at the woman, then put her cannon away. "Sandin, you come with me.", my mother now said. Sandin didn't move right away. He was still holding his mother. I looked at them both and Sandin gave me a look of pure hatred. I was defeated. I started to cry. Then I felt a hand on me and I was back on Base, but didn't recognize this office, "Well, I tried to warn your mother, but she always thinks she knows everything.", the woman said, lifting me up, and helping me settle into a chair. She sat behind a desk, which I quickly realized was like my mother's. It was a huge monitor that showed what looked to be different parts of Plinth, "Emillie, how are you feeling right now?", the woman asked. I couldn't answer. I kept seeing Mrs. Tillo. "Emillie, I am Mileeda.". I looked up now. "Mileeda?

But that is impossible. You can't be.", "Why not?", she asked, now leaning forward. "Because she was Nigel's wife. In the fairy tales.", "And do you believe everything you read in those...fairy...? I can't even call them that.", she said, smiling somewhat, "Emillie, it is important that I take over and train you. Because your mother will kill you.", "Why?", I asked, shocked. I knew she was making me tougher by fighting me with no mercy, but would she go THAT far? "Because I asked her to.", Mileeda said, as if this wasn't that big a deal. "You...asked her?", I said. "Yes. It's my job to protect this planet from beings such as yourself. Beings like my sister. You're not a normal goddess, Emillie. Your father, who is to remain classified, so don't bother asking, is a very powerful god. He contained ancient DNA that Amana has passed onto you. I'm afraid that we don't know the full extent of your power. So the goal has been to help you control it. That ring that you're wearing, take it off.", she said, pointing at Sandin's ring. Looking at it made me think of Sandin and I felt tears coming from my eyes. I handed her the ring and then suddenly felt better. "This ring will make you more susceptible to whatever is inside of you. I believe that it IS you, but a different version of you. I've seen this once before.", she said, now putting the ring in a cabinet she unlocked. Once she placed it inside, she locked it back, and then placed her hand over it. "You can learn without the ring. It's the only option that you have.", "I want to see Sandin.", I said, still thinking about him and his mother. "No.", Mileeda said. "But...", "No.", she repeated. "LET ME SEE HIM!", I yelled. "Emillie, at this point, if you continue to ask, I won't let you see Dalia.", she said in a threatening tone. I wanted to see the children. I nodded. "Like your mother said, you're not normal.", "I KNOW I'M NOT NORMAL! BUT WHAT DO YOU WANT FROM ME?!", I yelled. I was frustrated. My mother was going to kill me. Now that I was thinking about it, I don't know why I went into that manor, or why I did any of that. I was confused. "I want you to be the best version of yourself. I know that you are dangerous, but that can be changed. I can train you.", Mileeda said, crossing her arms. "But what about Sylvia?", I asked. Mileeda made a face, then said, "Don't worry about her. Just focus on this.", Mileeda said, handing me a pamphlet. I opened it, and it was discussing different martial-art techniques from the one's Sylvia had taught me. "Take those back to your room. Tillo is most likely with your mother, but I don't think it's a good idea to go see him. Wait until this whole situation dies down. That is an order, Emillie.", she said, now walking to the wall. A door appeared. I exited the door, and once I did, it disappeared, as if it wasn't there. I realized where I was now and went for my barrack.

After I got back in my room, I started to cry. I sat on my bed and then I saw Casian, "What happened?", I asked her. "Something took over your mind, Emillie. Something was using you to quench its' thirst for murder.", Casian said in my mind. I continued crying, while Casian rubbed on my face from my shoulder. There was a knock on my door, and I opened it. Sylvia was standing there. "I heard what happened.", she said, entering, and closing the door, "Did you almost kill Awalli?", she asked. "Yes.", I said. Sylvia got excited, "And then she did, what? How did she get away?", she asked. "She teleported us away.", I said. Sylvia looked like she was thinking about this. Then she placed her hand on my shoulder, "How about we go finish the job? Let's avenge Mrs. Tillo.", she said confidently. "I can't. I need to wait until Mileeda tells me what to do.", "Mileeda?!", she exclaimed. Now she grabbed me and Casian fell off, "You've met Mileeda?! Why?!", she questioned. I realized why this affected her so much. It was because she is Mileeda's descendant. It made sense she would feel something, "Because it is my fault...that...Sandin's mother was killed.", I said, starting to cry again. "That wasn't your fault. You didn't have control of your actions. Trust me, Emillie, I know. I saw you earlier. You would have killed Tem. But you were so powerful. Where did this power come from?", Sylvia asked me, looking hard in my face. "I don't know, Sylvia!". My door opened, and Mileeda was standing in the doorway. Sylvia turned around and noticed, and grew as still as a statue, "Leave.", Mileeda said, not even acknowledging Sylvia. "Please… just…look at me…", Sylvia said, with a trembling tone. Mileeda froze. She turned slowly towards Sylvia. It seemed like it was taking all the energy she could muster, "I…said…LEAVE!", Mileeda said, grabbing Sylvia by her throat. "Mileeda, let her go!", I yelled, getting up, and trying to pry her off. Sylvia grabbed her throat after I got Mileeda off of her. She fell to the floor, and began to cry. "Leave.", Mileeda said again. Sylvia got up, opened the door, and left. "Now…", Mileeda said, brushing herself off, and calming down, "…where were we? Oh, yes. We need to talk about how you will be learning to control your ability.", "Why wouldn't you talk to her?", I asked, feeling extremely sorry for Sylvia. "I did. I told her to leave. She should feel honored.". Mileeda was cold. That much I calculated. But I couldn't understand how she rivaled my mother. Why was she just as powerful? "So, like I was saying, you will have to learn how to use your ability, without losing your mind. The only way to do that…", she walked up to me and stared hard into my eyes, "…is to lose your mind.".

SANDIN: I couldn't focus. I was just sitting there, staring at my mother's lifeless body. First my father, now my mother. Both were killed. Both were shot. I put my hands into a fist form and pounded them against my head. I couldn't stop thinking, Emillie got her killed. Red was with me. He wasn't saying anything. He was just sitting with me. When we arrived back with my mother's body, he had been exploring around. When he realized my mother was dead, he said he'd tell me later everything that he has been doing. As we sat with my mother for another ten minutes, a lady came, and started to have some people move her. I watched, as they lifted her into the sack and zipped it. I noticed the lady was crying, and thought it was strange. Looking at the sack, it was a clear sack, so I could see her. Her eyes were closed and she didn't look so crazy. I was now remembering my last moment with her. My last failing moment. When I arrived just in time to watch Awalli murder her. I walked away. All I could feel was anger. "Tillo, I know what you're thinking…", "Call Yellfy.", I said. "No. Plus, he's on a mission, remember?", "Call Walsh.", I now said, throwing caution to the wind. "Are you crazy?", Red asked. "My mother… my mother…", I kept repeating, as if this would make Red realize. I knew he already did. He wasn't gonna let me do anything drastic.

I waited until I had calmed down somewhat and told him the full story, "From the sounds of things, it wasn't entirely Emillie's…", "Don't, Red. Just don't. It was her. She went there knowing my mother was there. I told her she was. Sure, she could have killed Awalli. Sebastian knows she killed enough mobsters just on her way in. But I saw Awalli was frightened. And that's why she killed my mother. My mother knew something that Awalli didn't want Emillie to know. I just wonder what that is.", I said thinkingly. We were sitting in a bar. If you can believe it, Base has a bar. The bartender was a young woman and there were a couple of men standing guard with cannons. "Look, mate, don't you love Emillie?", Red asked me. "Dude, I seriously don't know. We just connected because of that whole, her soul fled to me thing.", "That's not true. Dalia said you two had a connection because of that god gene.", Red said, taking a shot. "Well I just don't want to think about her.", I said. But that was easier said than done. All I could do was think about her. Nothing I tried wiped her from my mind, and even worse, was that now all I could see was her hurt face, as I yelled at her, as my mother laid dead in my hands. She couldn't even say a last word.

I had greeted Red good night and decided to call it a night. I wondered where Emillie had gotten to. It was really late. All the events of the night seemed almost faraway. I had gotten into my bed and fallen asleep. At some point, I woke up, and saw my mother sitting in the chair in my room. I jumped up out of the bed, "Mom…", I said, crumbling at her feet. "It's okay, Sandin. I knew this was going to happen. Just like this isn't the last time I will speak to you, but it is the last time I'll speak to you on this plane.", she said, smiling at me. "Mom, I'm sorry. I'm so sorry. I did this to you.", I said. "No, Sandin. This was my destiny. This is when I tell you the greatest thing you'll ever hear.", she said, in an excited voice. Her voice echoed each time she spoke. "Listen to me, Sandin, Emillie is more than just a goddess. She is a cosmic being of ancient variety. She contains power to do things that you can't even imagine. She can make her own planet. She can phase in and out of existences. She is…oh, I can't tell you this part… I see. Well, my son, I love you. Please forgive Emillie, she was only following her destiny.", my mother said, fading away. "NO! MOM, COME BACK!", I shouted, but she was gone.

In the morning, I was hungry. I went to the food hall and ran into Red. He was eating a bowl of oats. As I sat with him, I watched Sylvia walk in. She had a bruise on her neck and seemed irritable. Next to walk in was a group of people, among them, the jealous guy. Then I saw Emillie. She walked in, saw me, and headed straight for me. I tried not to look at her. "Mr. Red. Good morning.", "Hello, Emillie.", Red said, looking at her grimly. Next, Emillie looked at me. "Go away.", I said, not looking at her. "Sandin, please? It wasn't me. I don't know what happened.", she said, already beginning to cry. I didn't want to embarrass her, so I got up and walked with her out of the food hall, and into the hallway nearby. "Sandin, I love you.", she said, immediately falling into my chest. "Emillie, I just can't look at you.", I said. "I CAN'T LOOK AT

MYSELF!", she yelled at me, defeating the purpose of me walking her out here. "Emillie, listen, okay, I can try and forgive this. I know it wasn't you, you.", "I'm going to visit the kids. Come with me. Please?", she said, looking up into my eyes. I did love her gray eyes. Her seemingly strange gray eyes that always seemed to make me want her. I kissed her without thinking. We started grabbing all over each other. "EMILLIE!", Amana shouted. We broke apart. I didn't even know why I started kissing her. I was still angry. "I believe you were ordered NOT to see Sandin.", "We ran into each other. I'm not angry.", I said. "Oh, I can see that.", Amana said, looking at the both of us. "Emillie, there is a pod ready whenever you're ready to go to Dalia. Sandin, I want to see you and Red in my office.", Amana said, turning, and walking away. I looked at Emillie. "I'll see you later, then?", she asked with a hopeful look. "Yes.", I said, and I pulled her to me and kissed her again. "I'm sorry I yelled at you. I wasn't thinking about…", "It's okay. Don't worry. It's okay.", she said, kissing me again. Now she let me go and walked away. I went back to the food hall and saw Sylvia had moved to me and Red's table. I sat down, and Sylvia was crying. "What happened?", I asked. Sylvia dried her tears quickly and then looked at me, "Mileeda. I met her.", she said, looking down. "So? What happened that's got you so upset?", I felt like I had to ask. "She wouldn't even look at me.", she said, depressed, "I'm her family. It isn't right.", she said, now getting a napkin and blowing into it. Suddenly, Mileeda walked into the room. She walked up to our table. Sylvia looked like a statue. She wasn't moving. "Up.", Mileeda said. Sylvia slowly stood up. "Come.", Mileeda said, already turning around, and Sylvia didn't follow right away. "Why?", Sylvia asked suspiciously. Mileeda turned towards her. She walked up to her, and whispered something to her. Sylvia swallowed and then followed Mileeda out of the hall immediately. "Amana wants to see us.", I told Red. He nodded, and finished his oats, and we both got up, and walked to her office.

As we approached the door, it opened by itself. Amana was here with Mileeda. Red looked shocked to see her again so soon after she took Sylvia. Then we both noticed Mileeda was wiping her hands. She was wiping blood. "Well, glad you two could make it. Just thought we'd have a little chat about last night.", Amana said. Mileeda was looking pissed, but seemed to be calming down. I was going to ask what happened, but thought better of it. "Okay, listen to me. You two guys are going down there, and you're going to meet with one of my people. They are going to escort you guys to a place in Sicilia.", Mileeda said, as she put her hands in ice water and continued cleaning them. She finally put down the rag. I was thinking, whose blood is that? Mileeda noticed I was watching her hands. So was Red. Amana chuckled, "I warned that silly girl.", she said, "Mileeda, please continue. Tell them what they are supposed to be doing.", Amana said, now getting impatient. "Yes, well...sorry you had to see me like this, but we just received this information. There is a special object that is very dangerous waiting in an underground cellar beneath a death yard. So, you two are to retrieve this object, before my grandchild.", Mileeda said. Me and Red looked at each other, confused as to whom she was speaking of. "Awalli.", Amana said, as if reading our minds. "We expect you two to perform perfectly well. As for you, Sandin...", Mileeda said, now coming closer to me, "...I expect even MORE out of you.", she said. Then she nodded at Amana and disappeared. As soon as she did, I quickly asked, "Who did she...?", "Not Emillie. So don't worry about it. Now, the pod leaves for you two in three hours.", "Why so late? What if Awalli gets to it by then?", Red asked. "We have eyes on as we speak. So like Mileeda said, all you two have to do is retrieve it.", Amana said, directing us to leave. It was at this point where we both acknowledged, "Sylvia.", we both said at the same time.

SYLVIA: I didn't know what to think. MILEEDA, finally giving me some kind of ATTENTION. I didn't want to ask for the Head Seat. I knew it would upset her. She was upset last night. I only wanted to be in her good graces. When I asked her, "Why?", she came up to me and whispered. "Child, now.", and I followed. We walked out of the food hall and down to one of the office buildings. Some of the people in there were trying to talk to Mileeda, but she ignored them. Then she touched a wall, "I'll be back, shortly.", she said to the young man holding a tablet, trying to direct something to her attention. We walked into a room. There wasn't anything in here. Just a desk and two chairs. Mileeda sat down, and I sat down. "Did I say, YOU, could sit?", she asked me. I felt it was ridiculous but I stood back up. "In all my years, and I have a lot, I have only had to walk into the room, to make my family shiver.", she said, looking at me straight in the face. Then she stood up, "But you... you think that you can disrespect me.", "GRANDMOTHER! PLEASE, I MEANT NO DISRESPECT!", I yelled. She looked at me, "I mean, please? I just always wanted to know you. Everyone does. I...", I didn't know what to say now. "What were you doing...in Emillie's room?", she asked me. "I was talking to her.", "About what?", she asked, watching me closely. "Just, asking about what happened. She was upset, and I was trying to cheer her up.". Mileeda looked me up and down, "Just like the rest of them. Do you see? How easy it was for you to LIE to ME?", she asked me. She punched me in my face and I hit the wall. I couldn't think or focus. She was really strong. She IS the first gifted, technically. Then she came to me, picked me up, and started to beat my face, "YOU, WILL, RESPECT, ME!", she yelled with each hit. Blood was dripping from almost every part of my face. Mileeda opened the door and took me out, "Someone, see to her.", she said, dropping me on the floor. I felt myself being lifted, and then I fainted.

CHAPTER 9

Besties

CELDA: Emillie was coming to visit, and me and Tin were really excited. Tin looked up to Emillie, as did most children. All we've heard was that she joined the military, like Vaness. I couldn't believe it. Not Emillie, I thought at first. It didn't make any sense. First we heard she was dead, then she is alive and well, then she joins the army? I couldn't make any sense of it, but grew tired of trying. All I cared about was my best friend coming to visit me and my son. My husband, at work of course, was also happy to hear Emillie was alive. Emillie meant a lot to me and my family. Emillie was there for us during my carrying period. She babysat Tin, when me and Flin were working overtime to save up for our trip to Nocton. Emillie was on her way, and I couldn't wait. "Dalia, what time did you say she'd be coming?", I asked. Dalia hadn't been the same since Emillie had left. Neither had the rest of the workers. Hell, the whole damn manor was offset. "She should be arriving any minute now, Celda, geez, be patient.", "But I haven't seen Auntie Emillie in a long time!", Tin yelled, pouting. "Don't worry, she's coming.", Dalia said, looking hopeful but worried at the same time. Finally, a flar appeared in front of us and I was excited as soon as I saw the red hair sticking out. But then I saw her face, and I felt my smile slowly disappear. "Emillie... what...?", I said, walking towards her. In all the time Vaness has been a GFO, she never came back with bruises like Emillie's. Her eyes were healing, but still were sort of purple, and her left cheek had a strange mark that looked horrible. It was purple and green. Despite this, she hugged me, and still smiled at me and Tin, "I'm so happy you're here, Celda!", she yelled, throwing her arms around me, and giving me the impression that nothing was wrong at all. Dalia looked pissed, "Emillie, your face…", Dalia said, placing her hand on it. "Dalia, I'm fine. Well, as fine as someone who got her boyfriend's mother killed last night could be.", she said, starting to break down. The kids, who were all waiting inside to surprise Emillie, didn't need to see her like this. So I handed her my handkerchief and then pulled her to the side. Dalia stayed with Tin, "What has been happening?", I asked. "I shouldn't have said anything. I'm not allowed to say. It's…classified.", she said, in a weird sort of way. "I've heard about Sandin. Vaness knows him. But you say you got his mother killed? How?", "Please, lets just forget it. I'm here to see the kids.". I looked at Emillie hard, and all she did was smile. "Okay.", I said. I walked her into the house and the kids all yelled, "SURPRISE!". Emillie was overwhelmed. She was hugging and kissing as many of them as she could, crying in between. I wondered if those were tears of joy, or tears of sadness.

After everything had calmed down and Cynda, Bart, and Tin had broken apart from us, me and Emillie were left to speak, "So, you really aren't going to tell me?", I asked. "How's Vaness? Have you heard from her?", she said, ignoring me. "Yes, I have. She is coming later. Emillie, where did you get those bruises?", I asked her again for the twentieth time tonight. She kept refusing to tell me. And the kids kept asking and she made up a story about fighting a terrorist, but I knew there was more. Dalia had been acting strange. Watching Emillie, and keeping a distance. Emillie noticed and then both seemed to grow angry at one another. "Emillie, do you remember when we used to watch Royal Nuts?", I asked. Royal Nuts was a reality show that followed a couple of the RF members. It would have various appearances from other members, and sometimes the more important ones, like Sylvia Lon or Layna Lon. "Yes, I do.", "Well, I feel like we are in an episode of Royal Nuts. So can you please tell me what is going on between you and Dalia?", I said, looking at her with all the irritation I could show in my face. "Mom, can I eat some more cake?", asked Tin, pulling on my hand. "Sure, son, sure.", I said to rush him away. Emillie tried to look tough, but then started crying, "Dalia knows. She knows what happened. I keep forgetting.", "Forgetting what?", I said. "That Dalia is one of THEM.", she said in a schathing tone. "One of whom?", I asked. Just as Emillie was about to say something, Vaness snuck up on the both of us. Along with Gail. "Gail?!", Emillie said, looking at her, surprised. "What? We were working together and Vaness said she was coming to see you here.", Gail said smiling. Emillie looked tense for a second and Gail's smile started to fade as she took in Emillie's face. "I give you permission to speak, Emillie. I have that authority. Let's go to Dalia's office.", Gail said, leading us up. I looked for Tin, and saw he was playing with Cynda, so I didn't need to worry. We went into Dalia's office and we all just stood there, looking at Emillie. "I don't know where to start.", Emillie said. "We heard about the manor.", Vaness said, looking at Emillie, almost like she'd never seen her before. "Is it true, Emillie? What Gail said about you. Are you a... goddess?", Vaness asked, walking closer to her. I couldn't believe what she just said. "You guys are playing a joke on me.", I said, looking at the three of them. "This is no game. Emillie is a powerful goddess. Her mother, has been training her.", Gail said, looking at Emillie sadly. "Now, Mileeda is training me.", Emillie said. "Mileeda? Who is Mileeda?", I asked. Vaness looked mortified, "No...it can't be...", she said, grabbing a chair. "I told you, Vaness. Just like Adem.", "Adem?", Emillie asked, looking up. "Yes. He is a god. I told Vaness, but she didn't believe me. That is the mission Mr. Yellfy and I have been on. We are going after Adem. It hasn't been easy. He is hard to catch. And it has to be P.E.D, because we are the only ones who know it's Adem Mccloud who is killing Awalli's captains.".

Gail had gone to meet up with some guy named Yellfy, while me, Vaness, and Emillie went to The Dattur. We sat down in a booth and Emillie told us the whole story of everything. Vaness didn't tell us too much about Adem and what he was doing. She just said they had to get him. "So, Edge has sent you in after him?", Emillie asked. "Well, kind of. He...killed someone close to me.", Vaness said. It was clear she didn't want to talk about it, and me and Emillie learned a long time ago not to press Vaness. "So, what are you going to do, Emillie?", I asked her. "Well, for one, I wish I could walk away from this, but I'm starting to learn that's impossible. My mother is a mean bitch, and Mileeda is worse.", "I can't believe your mother was going to kill you.", I said, shaking my head. "I can't believe your mother is AMANA.", Vaness said, smiling. "It's not funny. She is the one putting these bruises on me. She is the one who shot me. She is the one that...that warned me something like this could happen.", Emillie said thinkingly. "Look, you're not that sweet girl anymore, Em, and I like that. I think that it is about time. Now, we got to work on Celda.", Vaness said, obviously trying to lighten the mood. "Look, ladies, we should be celebrating. We're all here.", I said. Then, Vaness turned around. Standing there was Dalia. She looked at Emillie, and the two left out together. Vaness and I were left by ourselves. There were a couple of men that had been watching us the whole afternoon, and I was getting tired of it. "So, Flin says he is moving on from Dorrmer. Says that he got a better offer from Mccloud Industries. You heard he is opening a new site?", I asked, immediately forgetting that Adem Mccloud is a murderer. "I'm sorry.", I said quickly, "That is a bummer, though. That IS a lot of shills he is being offered.", I said, now playing at my own attempt of lightening the mood. Vaness smiled. "Listen, we need to focus on Em.", she said, taking a swig of her drink, and then, putting her cannon on the table. The men that were watching us turned away. "Like I was saying, we need to focus on Em. She is in huge trouble. This crazy chick is after her hard. I've been hearing about it for months. I thought it was a different Emillie, until Gail told me what's been happening. Things are crazy right now, Celda, and my advice…", she took another sip, "…is to stay away from all of it.", "What does that mean?", I asked her. "We need to keep a distance from Em. Gail told me that she lost control at that manor.", "Yeah, but they were criminals.", I said. "Cel, you didn't see it. I SAW it. I couldn't believe Gail when she said Emillie killed all those men. She killed several men. SEVERAL.", Vaness said. I thought about it, and then thought about her face. I didn't know what to think. Emillie was different.

EMILLIE: Dalia and I walked outside. We stared at one another. She wasn't looking at me like the woman who I considered my mother, but rather like something nasty she picked up off the streets. "Emillie, let me ask you something; At what point, were you going to tell me about your attacks?", she asked me. "My…attacks? What attacks?", I replied. "The ones that end up with you going on a killing spree. You killed more than those mobsters, Emillie. Amana hasn't told you what you've done, and WHY she has been forcefully keeping you on the Base.", Dalia said, looking at me now with pity, "I'm sorry, Emillie, I thought that I had been wrong, but I was right.". Dalia took out her cell. She went to the news site she always visited, and looked up an old story. I leaned in closer so I could hear what they were talking about, "…dead. I repeat, thirty-six men here were killed and lie dead. Some slashed, as if by a blade, and others…it is unspeakable. Some of the lucky survivors have claimed the strange woman was searching for a trinket. Something that Father

Lopim, protected with his life. It is my sad duty to tell you that Father Lopim, the man who was known for bringing peace at the time of the civil war within the cities, was killed by the strange girl wearing armor. It is also said that she appeared in a number of places over the course of a few days. If anyone has any news on this murderer, please alert the RF's hotline for RF most wanted fugitives.". Dalia took her cell away from my face and pocketed it. "I...no...I...that wasn't...", I stammered. I knew who Father Lopim was. He was HUGELY important. I couldn't have killed him. I wouldn't have. "Emillie, it was you. Amana told me. She said that you were on a spree for three days, then you appeared before Cynda, confused. Somehow, Cynda calling to you, awoke you. Mileeda will help you control this part of yourself.", "I DON'T UNDERSTAND!", I yelled and cried, grabbing my head, and running my hands through my hair. "I know, Emillie, I know.", said Dalia, pulling me to her as I cried. This part of me is the reason my love can barely look at me. This part of me killed a man I thought the world of. Most people did. He was a hero. And somehow, I killed him. "It's almost time for you to head back to Base.", said Dalia, giving me a kiss on my forehead, "I love you, Emillie.", she said, pulling me into a hug again. Vaness and Celda came out of the bar and also hugged me. "Actually, I'll give you a ride.", Vaness said. I nodded. Dalia and Celda left together and me and Vaness were in her flar, "Emillie, I need you to stay away from the orphanage.", Vaness said. I looked at her, "What are you talking about?", I asked her in an angry tone. "You know what I'm talking about! I saw what you did! I know about your three day killing spree. Gail told me everything.", she said, still not looking at me, and watching the road. I didn't know what to say. "I'm learning to control it.", I said. "That's nice. And what about in the meantime? Everyone is supposed to just be on edge? Dalia was watching you, just waiting for something to happen, and don't even get me started on how Gail was ready to pull her cannon out.", "Gail was only there to monitor me, wasn't she?", I asked darkly. Vaness got quiet. "I don't know, Emillie. Celda said that you were coming, and Gail had been telling me all the stuff that was going on, but I didn't believe her. Now looking at you, I don't know.", she said, "Maybe she was. Is that a bad thing? After all, technically you are wanted by the RF.". I didn't say anything else the rest of the ride. Once I had gotten out of the flar at the pod location, Vaness didn't say anything, either. She drove off. I didn't know what she was thinking, but a part of me knew what she was asking. I still didn't understand myself. I kept learning more things about me. And now, I've learned I've killed an important figure to the whole planet.

As I arrived back on Base, I tried looking for Sylvia. She was nowhere to be found. I ran into Tem and another girl, "Excuse me, have you seen Sylvia?", I asked. I knew it was awkward for him to be approached by me, but he didn't seem too fazed. The girl answered my question, "Oh, Ms. High Horse? She is in med house seven.", the girl said, laughing. Tem wasn't laughing. I went to the med house and asked around, until I found her. She was sitting up in bed, looking in a mirror. Her face had been beaten. It looked worse than mine. "Sylvia...who did this to you?", I asked. She didn't even answer or look at me. She just put the mirror down, turned over, and didn't say anything. "Sylvia...", I said, and she just covered her head with the blanket and began crying. I walked out and saw my mother walking towards me. "Best not to get involved with that, Emillie. You don't want to end up like her.", "Somehow, I doubt I'll end up like her. Did Mileeda do this?", I asked, feeling my anger rise. "Emillie, take my advice. You do not want to be on Mileeda's bad side. She is letting you live.", "Oh, I haven't forgotten. She told me she asked you to kill me. And you were very happily ready to oblige.", I said, stepping closer to her. "Yes. I was. So, you don't want to be on my bad side, either.", she said, staring straight into my face. "You are completely horrible. You and her.", I said, and walked away. "Mileeda is looking for you.", she said, also turning, and walking in the other direction.

Mileeda found me as I was returning to my room. Casian was on her shoulder, then she disappeared. "Emillie, it is about time. Let us proceed to my area.", she said, leading me. I followed, but was counting the seconds. We finally got to her area and we walked in. As usual with her, the door disappeared upon our entry. "So, do you get off on beating your family?", I asked her. Mileeda froze at this question. She was being quite friendly at first, but I wasn't afraid of her. I knew now that her and my mother were afraid of me. Mileeda looked at me for a few seconds before finally speaking, "Emillie, I would advise you to never question how I run my family.", she said. "Well, I find it hard, when you can ask my own mother to kill me.", I said. Mileeda smiled at me, "You know something, perhaps you think that because you are Amana's daughter, I can't hurt you. But what I need you to consider is that I am three-thousand years old. Amana is as well. But I know things that she doesn't, like how to do...this.", Mileeda said, as she reached deep into my chest. I looked down, unable to believe that her hand was inside of me. Then, she took her hand out and I felt completely different. I didn't feel like I had any kind of extra power in me. "How do you feel?", she asked me kindly. "Normal.", I said. "Exactly.", she replied, as she smacked me. Before I could hit the floor, she stopped me somehow with a wave of her hand, and then, she punched me repeatedly. I assumed this must have been how she beat Sylvia. I hit the floor, coughing, and crying. I was in so much pain. This was much worse than what my mother was doing to me. "You see, Emillie, I am never weak, so don't test me, ever again. And also, I'm your mother's boss.", she said, as I felt my energy return. I immediately felt my chest burning, "You feel the burn...don't you? Yes, we all feel it. The power coursing through us. That power that can make you invincible, can also make you vulnerable.", "I...wasn't...done...about Sylvia.", I said, grabbing her leg, as my strength was returning to me. Once again, Mileeda stopped talking and froze, "Do you want to know WHY I asked your mother to kill you, Emillie?", she asked now, "I asked her to kill you, because many years ago, your mother killed my son. So, I told her that if she ever has a child, and it becomes dangerous, she must kill it. Now I'm trying to prevent your death. But your intent to understand my cruelty towards my grandchildren is making me reconsider. It is not your business what I do with Sylvia. It is not your business what I do with ANY of those royal shitheads. Do you understand that, Emillie? Because if not...I'll kill you, right here, myself.", she said, now picking me up by my head. I realized she was still stronger than me. "Blink if you understand, darling.", she said coldly. I did. Then she dropped me, "Any more questions about my family, will result in me telling your mother I failed, and delivering your remains. If there is anything left after I'm done. Now, like I said, you don't want to be made vulnerable to your power. So, you must learn, when you feel this burn, to exercise it. If I might make a suggestion, you should piss yourself off at least three times a day.", Mileeda said, now pacing back and forth as I still laid on the floor, "I do hope you're not in too much pain, Emillie. Because we haven't even started the physical part of your training today.".

I had learned that Sandin left earlier on a mission to Sicilia. I knew it had to do with my killing spree. They were unraveling what I had done. I couldn't imagine what that was. Awalli had her hands full with Adem, apparently, and had almost forgotten about me until I had attacked the manor. I was already tired of Mileeda. I thought my mother was fucked up, but Mileeda was on another level. She was torturing me just to get me angry. Once I'd summon the sword, she would activate something that sapped all my strength, making me unable to do anything to her.

I was so tired of the constant torture. Then, Mileeda said, "All right. That's enough for today. Go. Rest.". I couldn't wait to get away. Once I was in my room, Casian appeared, "Why does it have to be her?", I asked. "Because, Amana failed.", Casian said. "How could she have failed? She didn't even try.", I said. "Just trust Mileeda, Emillie.", Casian said. "Only because you're asking.", I replied. She jumped onto my stomach and I felt myself fall asleep.

"Please? You must at least let the children live!", said a voice I didn't recognize. I tried looking at my surroundings, but couldn't make sense of it. "I will not harm the children, only the guilty ones. The ones that serve the dark one.", I said in a voice that wasn't mine, yet I'd heard it before, "You serve the dark one, and you would raise these babes to do the same.", I said. "SHE WILL END YOU!", said the woman I was threatening. I saw me raise the blade, and watched as the children disappeared, and I stabbed the woman through her stomach. I watched her flesh burn upon my blade exiting. She was still alive, "Tell me, where are the rest of the followers?", I asked. But the woman stuck her arm into the hole in her stomach and killed herself. It was at this time that I woke up. Casian had moved to my pillow and there was a knock at my door. I went to open it and was surprised to find Mileeda outside my door, "I thought I was done for the night?", I asked, for it wasn't no more than a few hours before I departed from her. "I just wanted to ask you, while you are in your right mind…", she said, now coming into my room and closing the door, "…if we are in agreement about my family.", she said. I couldn't believe her. I knew not to say anything else other than what she wanted to hear, so I nodded. "Good. Now, say it out loud.", she said. I watched her for a second, unable to determine what she was trying to pull. "We're in agreement.", I said. "Good. Because there are things you don't understand, Emillie. Like that dream you just had.". How did she know about my dream? "How…?", I began to ask. "Because, Emillie, I am linked to you. I am watching you, in every way. So, that dream you just had… What are the followers?", Mileeda asked me. "I don't know. I don't even know why I was looking for…followers.", "That woman killed herself. This paints you in a new light. Maybe you didn't kill that old git like you think.", "Don't call him that.", I said. "Are you commanding me?", Mileeda asked. "No…just… He was a hero…and he was…", "Did you know the man?", she asked me. "No.", I said through gritted teeth. "I did. He was no hero. He only was in the right place, at the right time. So, like I said, this may change things. Tomorrow, we will work on gaining your memories, and learning just who this Dark One is.".

SANDIN: Sicilia is one of the contracted cities. Red and I had been dropped off in the center. Sicilia was a nice place. The architecture here was fresh and innovative. Buildings were shaped into triangles and were at least fifty stories high. The businesses here were interesting, mainly because they focused on agriculture. Red and I spent a good amount of time just exploring, because both of us had never been here before. There were really beautiful women everywhere and they were eyeing me and Red. "You should go for it, mate.", I said, as one particular woman walked by and purposefully brushed her hand on Red's, giggling as she did. "No.", Red said, looking back at the girl and meeting her gaze. "Red, Dalia ain't gonna change.", I said. "I don't want to talk about that.", he said. "Okay, fine. Let's talk about this mission. Who is our contact?", I asked, wondering if we would be done in time for me to get back to Emillie. "Someone named Tor Sove. He is supposed to be here already, but Mileeda said he would reveal himself to us.", Red said, looking around. "Let's just go to the hovel where Mileeda has set us up.", I said. We looked for the hovel called Royal Lodge. It took an hour of asking and reviewing the map, but we finally found it. We walked in, and I was overwhelmed with the luxury. There was a giant green crystal chandelier hanging above us and artwork that depicted Sebastian and Trinity. It was glorious to behold. The stairs were all decorated with different colored crystals all wrapping around the railing, and the carpet was a vibrant pink and green. It was truly fancy. "Hi, how can I help you, gentlemen?", said a woman walking towards us in the same colors presented everywhere in the hovel. "We have a voucher.", Red said, showing her a card. She took the card, looked at it, then looked up at us, "Follow me, please?", she said, leading us to a desk and walking behind it, getting onto the computer, and setting up our account. Once she was done, she got our key, and handed it to us. And then handed us a map, "This is where you will find your room. It is the Royal Suite.", she said, smiling. Me and Red proceeded to look for the Royal Suite and quickly found it on the fourth floor. As soon as we entered, it was also nice, but the colors were blue and gold, which are the royal colors. We started to unpack and get ready for our stay, then we noticed another door. I opened the door and there was another room on the other side, but it wasn't as fancy. There were two beds in there and it looked like nobody had used the room in a minute. "I was wondering when you two would arrive.", said a voice from behind us. "HOLY SHIT!", I yelled, surprised by the sudden appearance of a young man. He wore a blue suit with a red tie. His hair was black, short, and put to the side. "Sorry, didn't mean to frighten you.", he said, holding his hand out, "Tor Sove, royal servant.", he said. Red and I looked at each other. "So, Mileeda sent YOU?", Red asked. "No, Layna...um...excuse me, Queen Layna.", he said, correcting himself. "I'm sorry, I'm confused...", Red said, "...but I thought we were meeting someone who works for Mileeda.", Red finished, looking at the funny young man. What exactly made him funny? Well he seemed to be looking at us as if we were children, but even more, he wore a certain pendant that suggested he was a fan of the sitcom, Rover, which was about a talking dog. "I work for and serve the RF. I mainly answer to Layna, who sent me here, on Mileeda's orders.", "But, I thought Layna was in charge?", I said. "She IS. She rules the family. But, Mileeda is the alpha. Whatever she says, goes. Mileeda hasn't really said much to anyone besides Layna, so I didn't know Mileeda was involved.", Tor said, now taking something out of his pocket. "So, what are we looking for?", Red asked, grabbing a seat. "Oh, I wouldn't sit down, sir, we are about to leave. But don't worry, the action won't start…yet.", Tor said, smiling.

We had left out of the hovel and made our way into the city. Sicilia was pretty. Everywhere I looked, I saw the most beautiful scenery. There was grass with the same kind of green and purple blades I saw in Emillie's death world. It was also noticeable that the leaves on the trees changed colors. They would shift from green, to blue, or purple. There wasn't much litter all over the place, it was very clean all over. Except for the leaves that had fallen from the trees. The people were all busy, but still waved and smiled. I hadn't been to Nocton before and I imagined that this must be what it is like. Even though I knew that there was shady stuff happening in the background. My cell went off and I checked it. It was a message from Emillie; (Love you.), it said. I didn't message back. I was still slightly upset with her. We made our way into a flar that was parked up the street. Tor looked around before he got in and unlocked the doors. We were sitting in the flar, when Tor swore, "SHIT!", he said. "What?", both me and Red asked. "Forgot my cannon. I gotta go back.", he said. "We'll wait.". I said, as Tor left to get his cannon. "Well, that was great.", Red said, chuckling. "Can you believe this guy?", I said. We waited for twenty minutes. "Sorry guys…", Tor said, as he got back in the flar, "…turns out I left my cannon all the way back in Nocton.", he said, looking at us like we were silly children. "Okay, well, we'll just cover you. Are we expecting Awalli to be here?", Red asked. "Well, no. I believe Ms. Dat is in Edge dealing with something entirely different. But we do need to be alert. Things look nice out there, but we are headed into dangerous territory, mates.", Tor said, taking out a strange rectangular device and activating it. "What did that just do?", I asked. "Oh, don't worry. I'm just making sure this thing is working. It was acting funny back in the room.", "Dude, are you sure you're up for anything like this?", I asked, starting to doubt Tor more and more. "Oh, I'm more ready than you think.", he said.

We drove around for half an hour, until we came upon a hill. We started to drive up. There were nothing but fields around us. As we made it to the top, I realized it turned into a more easier path that led to a death yard. "We'll be going into the mountain.", Tor said, looking around. All the way at the end of the death yard, was a small mausoleum. We walked through all the graves and finally made it there. Tor took out another device that he placed on the lock. Something inside made a noise and the door opened, "Well, after…", Tor began, but then he tripped on the step, not realizing it was so high. He fell practically on his face. Me and Red looked at each other, then went to help him up, "Thank you, gents. Very kind of you. Now, this way.", he said, leading us. I could tell Red was having doubts about this mission. I was wondering what Mileeda meant when she said she was expecting a lot from me. We walked down a very long flight of stairs until we reached the bottom. Tor reached into his jacket and took out what looked like a simple flamer. But when he sparked it, the flame was like a fireball that shot off and exploded, leaving the once dark tunnel illuminated. "What…?", "Classified royal tech, mate. Not allowed to tell you.", Tor said, pocketing the flamer, and leading us down the tunnel. The tunnel seemed to stretch for miles. At one point, I decided to ask, "How much longer?", "Oh, we are almost there. Just a bit farther. Tell me, I didn't ask, but which one of you is Mr. Tillo?", he said. "I am.", "Forgive me for not asking earlier, I was just sizing you two up. You're from P.E.D. Layna didn't tell me I'd be working with Amana's people.", he said, seizing up somewhat. "Well, Mileeda is the one who sent us on the mission. And we're sorry, too, but you surprised us.", Red said. "Mileeda…", Tor repeated, "She is such a mystery, and I do love a mysterious woman.", "Well trust us, you don't want to even talk to her.", I said, thinking about Sylvia and the blood Mileeda was wiping off her hands. "Well, I saw plenty of her when I was a child. She doesn't like to go around her family much, though. Last time wasn't a very happy occasion I'm afraid. Ms. Tena had sent some men on a mission to destroy one of Mr. Solron's properties, which resulted in the death of four children. It was a Year End soiree, and all was merry, until Mileeda arrived. She greeted everyone, but most of the family feared her, so they were all stone quiet. I remember she looked at me and my mother, and I felt nothing but shivers.", Tor said, shivering some. "Yeah, I get that she gives that energy off.", I said. "Well, I did feel quite sorry for Ms. Tena after what happened. The woman never was quite the same.", Tor said sadly. "What happened?", Red asked. "Nobody knows. Except, Ms. Mileeda and Ms. Tena, of course. Ah, it looks like this should be it.", Tor said, as we reached an old door. "Mr. Tillo, can you stand next to this door, please?", he asked. I approached it, and immediately, I felt something pressing me from the top of my head and all the way through my body. Then I felt a sinking feeling, and I backed away, "What…the… hell?", I said, breathing hard. Red put his hand on my shoulder, "What the hell happened?", he asked. "Ah, so, my wi… I mean, Queen Layna was right about you…", Tor said, thinking. He began to open the door, and Red grabbed him, "What the hell is on the other side of this door?", Red asked him. "It is a godly object I believe.", Tor replied. "Well, what just happened to Tillo?", Red asked him now. "Well, Mr. Red, he confirmed that there is indeed something on the other side of this door.", Tor said, yanking his arm away from Red. "Look, he was sent here to confirm.

You're here in case things go south. I'm here to retrieve this for Queen Layna.", Tor said, pointing at me, Red, then himself. Me and Red looked at each other and then I understood what Mileeda meant. As Tor turned back to the door and began to open it with the same device he used earlier, Red stepped back and took out his cannon. So did I. The door opened and then we walked in. I felt the feeling again, but not so intense this time. I looked around and the room had shelves of items. "Which one of these is the one we're looking for?", Red asked. "Mr. Tillo, can you start feeling objects?", Tor asked. I started to touch things. Nothing seemed to be what we were looking for. Red was just looking around the room, while Tor watched me anxiously. Finally, I touched an old cup, and the feeling came, followed by something else.

I was in a room. I didn't recognize it. "About time.", someone said, as I turned and noticed a woman. She had glowing black hair, and was honestly the most beautiful woman I'd ever seen besides Emillie. "Well, it took a while, but I got it.", I said. I wasn't me. And I sounded like a woman. I looked in a nearby mirror and realized I was Mileeda. As soon as I saw this, I was myself again. "Problems, mate. You can take point.", Tor said, putting the cup away. I was confused, until I heard the cannon fire. "Red.", I thought. I pulled my cannon out and ran towards the fire. There were strangely garbed men wearing masks making their way down the tunnel. "I can use some help over here!", Red yelled, blasting his cannon. The men also carried cannons and were firing back. "Close the door, Red!", Tor yelled, taking out that device from earlier in the flar. Red closed the door. "Come to me, gents.", Tor said, activating it. "Oh, shit.", he said. "What's, oh shit?", Red asked. "It isn't working…", Tor said, banging it with his fist. There was a banging on the door that said we didn't have much time until the men came in here. "Tor, whatever you are going to do, can you please put a move on it?", I said, pointing my cannon at the door. Then suddenly, the door burst open, but the men looked confused. They were looking around, but didn't seem to see us. "Find the cup, and find them.", said a deep voice, obviously muffled by the mask he was wearing. They started searching and Tor started to mouth, "To the door.". We made our way out and as soon as we got next to the door, Tor bumped into a table sitting next to it, and knocked something down that fell and broke. The men looked up and Tor's device had stopped working. They stared at us, confused for a minute, then started shooting. "Time to run!", Tor said, running down the tunnel, with us behind him. It was a deadly chase. The men were on our tails, and Red and I kept turning and firing every so often. Tor was ahead of us clearing the path. One man had managed to catch up with us, and I punched him, and shot him. Then another man caught up with us and I kicked him, and Red blasted him into the dirt. "They're still behind us, we need to hurry!", Red said, pointing his weapon down the tunnel.

We had finally reached the exit and made our way to the flar, only to discover it had been rendered useless. "Oh great.", I said. "Now, don't worry, we have more than one way to travel.", Tor said, taking out the same device and banging it again, then we found ourselves back in the Royal Suite. "How the hell did we get here?", Red said, looking around confused. "This thing. Classified guys. Well, it was nice working with you. But I suggest getting out of the city in a more...covert way.", Tor said. "Wait, that's it?", I asked. "Yes. Mission accomplished.", "But, who were those men?", I asked. "Don't know. Never seen them before. But there will be an investigation. I wish you two luck.", Tor said, as he left the room. Red and I decided to go get food. We went down into the lobby, where there was a restaurant. Our voucher allowed for two free dinners. As we took our food and found a table far in the corner, away from everyone, we looked at each other for a minute before one of us spoke, "So, what do you think?", I asked Red. "Well...I'm lost. So the mission was just to escort Tor to an object he has to give to Layna?", Red questioned, confused. "Look, Mileeda said we were meeting one of HER people, so I'm even more confused.", I said, cutting into my steak, and taking a bite. "Look, who were those men? That's the better question. And why didn't Mileeda tell us about them?", Red said, also eating and drinking his wine. "I don't know. So, do we call her and tell her mission accomplished?", I asked. "I messaged her, and she replied for us to stay here. She said that she wants US to investigate those strange men.", Red said grimly. "But...it's just US. Is she sending back up?", I asked, unable to believe that Mileeda had this much faith in us. "Well, I think they are either a new element, or something that both Amana and Mileeda don't know about.", Red said, eating his pasta. "Okay, I have an idea. Let's just run away.", I said jokingly. "Seriously, Tillo, we need to figure this out, because if the only thing we have right now is that small bit of info, they can easily find us.", Red said. "Well, it isn't like Amana has given us anything good to go by.", I said, thinking of Tor's device that somehow turned us invisible. "Yeah, I'm gonna request some equipment.", Red said, sending a message. There was an immediate response. "What's it say?", I asked. "Won't be necessary.", Red said in an angry tone. "Those men have weapons! Who did you ask?", "Mileeda. This is her op.", Red said angrily. "Do you think she wants us dead?", I asked. "No, I don't think so, Tillo. I think...Mileeda wants us to look into something to do with Emillie.", Red said, now thinking, "Raby told me something. She mentioned that Emillie disappeared for three days. And I remember a couple months back, before Emillie appeared, there was a series of attacks, here, Bronxton, and Nash. The reports all said it was a strange woman wearing armor.", Red said. "Yes, I was hoping we could discuss that.", said a hooded figure not too far from us. He removed his hood, and it was a scarred-face Father Lopim. He moved to our table. "You're supposed to be dead.", Red said. "Yes, I am. But I'm not. Now, you mentioned a strange girl, and the name, Emillie.", he said, looking at the both of us. I looked at Red and immediately started to pull my cannon out. "Oh, I wouldn't do that, Mr. Tillo. We need to discuss this topic, and my people have orders to kill that nice lady in the front if you don't talk with me, and let me leave once we're done.", he said, smiling at us. We looked at each other and put our cannons away. "Good, now about Emillie…", he said, looking hopeful towards me. "We aren't telling you shit.", I said. "Tell us how you're alive and why you're letting people think you're dead.", Red said. "Well, that is simple. Someone tried to kill me, and almost succeeded. Now, I'm only trying to understand.", he said. "The reason this person is trying to kill you?", Red asked. "Yes.", Lopim said. "And why do you think we'd know?", Red asked. "Because, you said something about the attacks being somehow related to a girl named Emillie.", he said, growing impatient. "Well, let me just say that Emillie has nothing to do with those attacks.", I said. "You are lying, Mr. Tillo. Mr. Sove came and took that cup and put it beyond our reach. But you two, you two have seen the alpha, the one that cup belonged to.", he said, now standing up. It belonged to Mileeda? What was so important about it? "Well, it has been nice, I suppose, but I see where your allegiances lie.", Lopim said, walking out. "Have a good night, gentlemen.", he said, and put his hood back on and left. As soon as he did, Red and I got up and ran to check on the lady in the front. She was still greeting people. Then we went outside and looked for Lopim, but he had disappeared.

After we had searched the nearby area, we returned to our room. We took turns using the restroom and then got into our beds. "Red, do you think that this is bad news?", I asked. "I think as soon as we wake up, we need to get to that birdport.", Red said, turning over. I laid awake, thinking about the whole thing. So, Emillie was the one who killed all those people over the course of the three days she was missing. Then she also was the one who attacked Father Lopim and supposedly killed him, but me and Red saw him tonight, alive. Then there were those men that came after that cup, and what is the deal with that cup? I kept running it over in my head, over, and over. Finally, I saw no point in stressing over it. Especially when I knew something was going to happen.

Red and I woke up early in the morning to try and get out of the hovel before Lopim's people discovered us. We made our way down to the first floor. Once we had arrived on the first floor, it was empty, except for a few people sitting in the lobby. It was obvious that they were drunk. We didn't see the greeting lady but rather a man. "Hope you enjoyed your stay.", the man said, as me and Red walked out. We had to order a flar to take us to the birdport. Once we got to the birdport, we were surprised that nothing had happened. Before we even made it into the building, there was cannon fire. I looked around and saw a man in a red mask walking forward. Then from the other side, there was another man in a mask firing his cannon. Red and I took our cannons out and started pointing. Then there were more men in masks, and women, too. All had cannons that I had to assume were loaded. We looked around, and it seemed like all the people that were around us were all Lopim's people. Me and Red were surrounded. Lopim walked from out of the crowd, still wearing his hood. "I'm hoping that you'll reconsider what we discussed.", "We still aren't telling you shit.", Red said, pointing his cannon at Lopim. Lopim just smiled, "Take them.", he said, walking away. Red shot him in the back. Lopim stood for a second, then fell down. Immediately, some men rushed to him and picked him up, while the others moved in on us. We tried shooting them but there were too many, and eventually, they got me, and then Red, who was now throwing punches. They loaded us into different vehicles and then drove.

I kept trying to unbind myself, but the bonds were too tight. I started to wonder where Red was and if he was okay. Finally, we arrived at a manor, not unlike the one in SE. They pulled me out, and carried me in. I tried fighting them off, but the men were tough. Then, Lopim came into the room they had thrown me in. "So, the only way your friend lives is if you tell me who Emillie is.", Lopim said simply. "Fuck you.", I replied, "How are you even walking?", I asked him, surprised that he wasn't in pain after being shot. "Oh, I learned magic a long time ago that helped me. You see, I am looking for certain objects that will help me get to my master.", Lopim said with a smile. "Who is that?", I asked. "Oh, we don't say names. We just refer to our master as the Dark One. And in truth, that is what my master is, dark. Now you will tell me who Emillie is, because my master wants to know.", Lopim said, coming towards me. "Your master...can kiss my ass.", I said. "Well, it is obvious you feel strongly about Emillie. I wonder why...", he said. "DON'T TOUCH ME!", I yelled, as he leaned over me and placed his hand over my eyes. "Ah, I see. She is your lover. This is why you are so protective.", he said, keeping his hand on my eyes. Then he took his hand from my eyes quickly, "No...she can't be...", he said. He left the room, leaving me bound and helpless. I tried again to unbind myself but found it impossible. About two hours later, a woman came in with food. She unbound me and I leapt up and then felt myself get thrown back, "You won't be able to attack me in this room. It's the room of peace.", said the woman. I tried moving, but couldn't. "The more you struggle to attack, the more strain is put on you. Best to relax if you want to eat.", she said, leaving the food on a table and walking back out. I wanted to shout, where was Red? But I couldn't talk, either. Once the woman had left, it was like a barrier was lifting off of me and suddenly I was able to move again. After I ate, and another hour passed, Lopim walked back into the room, bringing with him a very beaten Red. "What the hell have you done to him?", I asked.

"Nothing. He just preferred to keep getting hit, rather than tell me what I needed to know. You, Mr. Tillo, are something else entirely. You are like a well of information. The knowledge I gained from you, told me everything I needed to know about Emillie. Even the fact that my master has already had someone on her for years.", Lopim said. I tried to think about what he was talking about, but the only person that ever wanted to hurt Emillie in the past was Awalli. Suddenly, it all clicked. "Awalli…", I said. "Yes. The other descendant. The one who also possesses the gift. She has been working for my master. Emillie is dangerous to our cause and we need her gone.", Lopim said, looking down at me and Red. I looked at Red, who just nodded. I wondered what he was nodding about, I was lost. "Now, Mr. Tillo, I'm going to ask you one time, and lets see what you say. Where is Emillie? It's what I wasn't able to see and what Mr. Red refuses to say.", Lopim said, kneeling next to me. "Well, lets just say, she is out of your reach!", I yelled. Lopim smiled. "This room allows for no one to harm anyone. But remember this, the next time I take Red here, out of this room, he dies. Unless, you tell me what I want to know.". I looked at Red, who wasn't going to yield. If he isn't, then neither am I. I remained silent. "Well, this is just great. I need to know who you two serve. It is really frustrating fighting people all the time. Especially since everything was going so well for so long.", Lopim said, putting his face in one of his hands, "I'll leave you two to think over your situation.", Lopim said, leaving the room. As soon as he did, I turned to Red, who was still bound. I unbound him and helped him into a chair. "Why are they beating you, and not me?", I asked, feeling like this was important for some reason. "Because they can feel your connection to Emillie. These people…they know things, Tillo. Things about all that gods and goddess shit.", Red said, grabbing the trash nearby and spitting blood into it. "But, how can they?", I asked, confused by everything. Who the hell is Father Lopim really, and why is he after Emillie? Why did Emillie try to kill him? Now, I at least understood that it was indeed Emillie that killed some of these people, but who were they, and how many of them are there? "Tillo, no matter what, don't tell them who sent us. They don't know. And don't tell them who we work for. They also don't know that. All they know so far is that Emillie is the girl who has been hunting them, and that she is Amana's daughter.", "How can they know that Amana is her mother?", I asked surprised. "Because, Father Lopim knows her. Or knew her, whichever, I don't know. But what I do know, is that Amana has somehow managed to piss him off as well. So, another one of her issues.", Red said angrily. "Why not just give her up, then?", I asked. In truth, the only favor she'd done us was give us a job. Everything else was just waves of confusion and torture.

After two more hours had passed of me and Red sitting in this room, with no kind of info as to what was happening, Lopim walked back into the room. He came up to me and I tried to prevent him, but anything that seemed like an attack was prevented, and Lopim placed his hand on my eyes again. "Oh, I see. You're angry with her, but your obsession overpowers even this…", he said, removing his hand. "Why are you so keen to defend the woman that got your mother killed?", he asked. "YOU DON'T GET TO ASK ME THAT!", I managed to shout at him. He smiled at me, "But, it is an honest question, Sandin. Your mother is dead because of a woman you haven't been with for that long. Unless there is something I'm not seeing.", he said, placing his hand over my eyes again. I heard Red struggling against the curse in the room. "Hm…now this is interesting. You seem to be blocking me…ahh!", he screamed, backing away from me, "I should have known!", he said, now holding his hand, "Mileeda sent you.", he said. "No.", Red said. "No need to lie, Mr. Red. I know her magic. This is her doing. She let me take you. Damn it!", he yelled and left the room. We looked at each other and I could tell we were both thinking the same thing. Mileeda told us to stay. Then we get captured and tortured. From the sounds of things, Mileeda is using us. "As soon as I can, I'm calling Mileeda.", Red said. "No need.", Mileeda said, appearing in the room. She wasn't fully here because her form was transparent. "So, you sent us in blind. You knew about these people, and you let them capture us.", Red said in an accusatory tone. "Yes, and no, Mr. Red. I didn't know who these people were until Emillie revealed them to me. I didn't know they'd be after my goblet, but it's fine. Layna has it now. Now, they know that I'm the one that sent you, because I wanted that bastard Lopim to know. But he will never know where his most hated enemy is. Just know, this is all for Emillie.", Mileeda said, as she disappeared. Now Red and I looked at one another and I could tell he was thinking, how do we get out of this?

The girl who had brought me food earlier came into the room, and had two plates this time. Red didn't even try to fight. I jumped up and experienced the same getting thrown back situation, "I told you already, you can't do anything in this room.", she said, putting the food down. "I want to leave.", I said. "And I'm sure people in Hell want ice, but that ain't happening.", she said, turning to leave. Underneath her mask, her voice sounded familiar. Once she left, Red attacked his food. "Do you think it's wise to just eat what they give us?", I asked him. "Well, they said they can't harm people in this room, right?", he said with a mouth full of food. "That's not the point. What if there is something in there that gets us talking?", "Tillo, what more can we give to them? They obviously don't know anything about P.E.D, and they don't know anything about Mileeda and Amana working together. So, it seems to me like we're here to gather info on them.", Red said, now eating his food normally. "But, if we're here to gain info on them, what are we going to do when they get tired of us? We have absolutely no power here, mate.", I said, frustrated.

"Tillo, you're forgetting something. Didn't Mileeda just protect you?", Red asked. This was a true statement, but I had even more questions. Like, how? I felt like just because she is a goddess, shouldn't mean she can do stuff like that. Plus, not even physically being here, she somehow caused Lopim pain. I was running it through my head as to why. I remembered the feeling the goblet gave me when I was near it, and how when I touched it, I had become Mileeda. What the hell did that even mean? When I had fallen asleep, after Red and I sat up for a bit longer discussing our situation, I woke up in Mileeda's office. "What…?", I began to say, but then noticed Mileeda sitting across from me. "You're sleeping, Tillo.", she said. "How the hell are we talking?", I replied. "Emillie and you do this often, and you think it's weird that I have the same ability?", she said. "Well, I'm connected to Emillie.", "Amana has visited you as well, and you didn't think that was strange?", she asked. "I guess, I see your point.", I said, now settling down. "Now, lets talk about what you have learned.", she said, "Father Lopim is obviously using dark magic. He is no god. He is just a man who has learned magic. I didn't know anything about his secret following. Now, the other Emillie, she knows. But she is being rather difficult in giving answers. I don't know why.", she said, thinking. "What do you mean…other Emillie?", I asked. "I'll explain that later.", Mileeda replied. "Well, you know more than I do. They don't know about P.E.D.", I said. "Of course they don't. Amana and I have made sure that nobody really knows about P.E.D. But my biggest problem right now, Tillo, is that you and Red don't seem to understand the importance of stopping Father Lopim. The Dark One that he keeps referring to is finally known to me. They revealed themselves after I spoke with Emillie in her original form.", Mileeda said, standing up, and walking towards me, "The dark one, is my sister. Corsa. She is the one that Lopim and his people are trying to free. I thought my sister was only using Awalli, but it seems that she has found extra avenues to travel.", Mileeda said, going to her cabinet. She placed her hand on it and closed her eyes, then she opened it. I figured there must be some kind of magic to it. She took out a box that she carried to the desk and placed it in front of me. "Open it.", she commanded. I opened it, and was overwhelmed with images. In the images, I saw Mileeda and another girl. She had sort of red and orange hair and was very beautiful. She and Mileeda were singing together and enjoying each other's company. Mileeda closed the box. "That was your sister?", I asked. "Yes. My sister, like myself, became a goddess. She, too, possessed the god gene, allowing for this transformation.". I kept thinking about the images I saw, and thought about how happy Mileeda seemed. It was an old image, because they wore clothing that suggested that was years, and years, and years ago. "So, Lopim must be stopped.", Mileeda said, returning the box to the cabinet. "What is that?", I asked. "The last happy memories I have with Corsa.", Mileeda said, placing the box away, and closing the cabinet. "But, I'm somewhat confused. Why do you not want to save your sister?", I asked. "Because my sister isn't in danger, Sandin. She is the one trying to kill Emillie. She is the one doing a number of other things that will end very badly for every Plinthinian. So, I suggest that you take this mission seriously. Emillie is already fighting my sister, and I don't know why. It is infuriating.", Mileeda said. "Now, take all this info back with you and tell Mr. Red. And don't worry, I don't plan on keeping you guys in Sicilia that much longer.", Mileeda said. I woke up and it was the middle of the night. I thought about how silly it was, but I checked the door anyway, and it was locked. "You didn't think you'd be walking out of here that easily did you?", said the woman from earlier. She was sitting in the corner. "Why are you in here?", I asked her. "Well, I wanted to talk to you. You're the son of Ayrellia Tillo, aren't you?", she asked me. She stepped into the light, and I saw a familiar face, "Bonnly?", I asked. "I was quite surprised you didn't realize sooner.", she said, walking towards me.

"What the hell are you doing here?", I asked. Bonnly was a worker, like Red and I, but she was more than that, just a few months ago, at least to me. "When I heard that they had you in their sights, I decided to see what they wanted from you. You left the GF. Walsh has gone mad.", she said, watching me for an explanation. "What the hell are you doing here?", I asked her again. "I'm...one of them.", she said, looking down. "What?", I asked, surprised. I looked over at Red, who was sleeping, and didn't seem to hear us. "What do you mean...one of them?", I asked her. "Well, my parents were with this group. They were killed by that girl. The one that Lopim says you are protecting. Why? She got your mother killed. At least that's what I heard.", she said, looking at me sadly, "I'm sorry about your mother.". I didn't say anything. "Listen to me...were you with these people before, or after us?", I asked her. "It's hard to explain, Sandin.", "Make it easy.", I said, growing angry. "Okay. When I was a little girl, my mother and stepfather were always gone on the second day. I wondered where they went, but they would get me a babysitter and leave. I waited up once I got a bit older and asked. To this day, I regret asking.", she said, and looked at me hard. I had forgotten how pretty Bonnly was, because I'd been avoiding her since we split. She had gorgeous lilac colored eyes and her hair was a vibrant orange and blue. She was a dub. Dubs are people who are born with two different colors in their hair. I was always attracted to them. "Well...go on.", I said, waiting for her to keep talking, "Once I'd asked them about their outings on the second day, they told me that I was going with them to the next one. It was like a church, but strange. They kept talking about a dark one in a void, and how it is our duty, to free her.", Bonnly said, starting to cry, "My parents died for this, Sandin. They are gone, and I want to kill the bitch that killed them.", she said, looking at me harder now. "Jesy, I can't tell you about her. And you are in a cult, by the way.", I said. "You think I don't realize that? I haven't spoken to my parents since the day I turned seventeen and left. So, I know exactly what THIS is. But my parents weren't bad people.", "Yes, they were, if they were in the cult.", "THAT WOMAN MURDERED PEOPLE! GOOD PEOPLE, TILLO! WHY ARE YOU PROTECTING HER?!", Bonnly yelled, getting forced back once she tried to hit me. "Bonnly…?", Red said, waking up now, "What the fuck are you doing here?", he said, suddenly becoming alert. Jesy stood up and looked at Red. "She's with Lopim.", I said. Red just stared at her. "Okay. Look, I know about your parents, but you don't understand the situation, and you need to get out of here, now.", Red said. "Don't understand? She killed people, Red. Why did you two leave the GF? What the fuck have you been doing?", she asked, looking at the both of us. "Bonnly, did they send you in here?", Red asked. "No. I came in of my own accord. They know I want to help. But I'm confused here.", "They worship someone called the dark one, and you don't think that's strange?", I asked. "Well, she is the dark one, because she is in the dark. We must bring her to the light.", she said, as if this was a mantra. "Look, she is dangerous. You have to believe that this is why we left the force. What are the odds of them wanting to take us down? And what do you know about that goblet?", I asked. "Goblet? You mean one of the objects of Sebastian? Well, we need those, to bring the dark one out of the dark, and into the light.", Jesy said, confused. "I think I see what's going on.", Red said, standing, and walking towards Jesy, "You've been brainwashed.", he said. "You don't know what you're talking about. I just need to find this girl you're protecting.", "You won't. And we aren't going to say. We won't BE here much longer.", I said. Jesy looked at me hard. "You're making a mistake, Sandin. You should talk to me and tell me what they need to know. Please? I don't want my parents to have died for nothing.", she said sadly now. "JESY, wake the FUCK up! These people are trying to summon an evil goddess. Trust me, I know her sister. The dark one's sister. So, when I say, wake up, I mean it!", "Sandin, I don't really care about the dark one, I only want to kill the woman that killed my mother. I saw their bodies and I...", she couldn't say anymore. "This is getting us nowhere. Goodnight, Bonnly.", Red said, sitting back on his chair, and falling back asleep. Bonnly opened the door and walked out. I was left thinking about how she was obviously brainwashed somehow. But her vengeance against Emillie isn't right. I didn't know what Mileeda was going to do to get us out of here, but I was hoping it was soon.

CHAPTER 10

Time To Wake Up

EMILLIE: I decided to make another attempt at visiting Sylvia. It had been a couple days since my first visit. Mileeda was expecting me for her new torture in an hour and I decided to use this time to see Sylvia since Sandin wasn't answering my messages. As soon as I entered her room, she was standing in a corner looking at that same mirror she had before, "Hello, Sylvia.", I said. She turned to face me. Her face was still healing, but other than that, she seemed fine, "What do you want?", she asked me, in a bad-tempered tone. "I just wanted to check on you. What Mileeda did to you was horrible.", "No. It wasn't.", she said, putting the mirror down on her bed, and walking towards me, "I lied to her. I shouldn't have done that. I should have told the truth about why I was in your room. Then, Mileeda wouldn't hate me more then she did before.", she said, beginning to cry. "No, it's unacceptable.", I said. "You don't get it. She hates us all! And all I ever wanted was to be noticed by her. Receive her blessing!", Sylvia yelled, starting to lose her restraint. Mileeda entered the room, and Sylvia hadn't noticed, "She chose to bless Layna, and I want to know why!", she yelled, then turned around and saw Mileeda. She fell down onto her bed, "Grandmother...", she said, frightened. "Leave, Emillie.", Mileeda said darkly. "No. I'm not leaving Sylvia with you.", I said defiantly. Mileeda pulled out a cannon and pointed it in my face. "Emillie, just leave!", Sylvia shouted, now jumping up, standing on her grandmother's side, and trying to break up the situation. I eyed Mileeda, trying to be brave. "Emillie...have you already forgotten our deal?", Mileeda asked. "I...won't let you hit her.", I said. Mileeda lowered her weapon, then shot me in my leg. I felt the shell burn as it wormed its way through me and then out the other end. I fell to the floor, "Special shells. Designed just for you. Had these cooked up as soon as your mother created this vessel you're occupying.", Mileeda said, now punching me with her cannon, and then kicking me. "GRANDMOTHER! PLEASE STOP!", Sylvia yelled, trying to grab her. "Next time, Emillie, I won't be so nice. I said to stay OUT of my family affairs.", Mileeda said, throwing Sylvia off of her, picking me up by the back of my shirt, and throwing me out of Sylvia's room. I could hear Sylvia pleading with her grandmother for forgiveness.

Not too long later, I had healed up enough to walk, and I ran into Sylvia. "Are you...?". She interrupted me, "I'm okay. All she did was talk to me.", she said. "About what?", I asked her. "None of your business. Just don't worry about us, okay?", Sylvia said. It was obvious she didn't want Mileeda beating me the same way. Even though she was going to do it anyway. I went to Mileeda's office and knocked on the wall where there was no door. The door appeared and I entered. Mileeda was sitting on the other side of her desk, "Well, Emillie, thanks to your disobedience this morning, I now have to push MY SCHEDULE!", she yelled at me, "I'm going to be punishing you, of course.", she said. "But, you did.", I said. "No, that was just to get rid of you...", she said, now standing, and walking from around her desk, "...this is your punishment.", she said. I felt myself leave my body. I didn't know where I was. I looked around and saw Mileeda, but she didn't seem to be doing anything. She went back to her desk. I looked and realized my body was lying on the floor, with a hole in my head. Mileeda was doing whatever she does in her office, and I was helpless, just watching. I couldn't even hear anything. I was confused as to what was happening. Then, after what felt like hours, I felt myself waking up, "Welcome back to the world of the living. I suggest you go shower.", Mileeda said, seeing that I was waking up. "What did you do to me?", I said, feeling weak and sad. "I killed you. And I'll do it again if you don't listen to me. This time, it was only a few hours, but next time, I'll hold your essence for days. Maybe weeks if you piss me off enough. You need to stop testing me.", Mileeda said angrily. I thought about what she just said and became entirely afraid. I nodded. "That's all for now. Now, get out of my sight.", she said. I ran out of the door once it appeared, and ran all the way to my room. I threw off my clothes and placed them in the wash. I had soiled myself, and was embarrassed. I jumped into the shower and started to cry. I knew that I had died before, but somehow this was different. Somehow, Mileeda held my soul and wouldn't let me move on. My mother wasn't joking about not being on her bad side.

After I showered, Casian appeared in my room. I got dressed, laid on my bed, and continued to cry, "Emillie, you need to trust Mileeda.", Casian said. "How the hell can I trust her? She killed me!", I replied. "Yes...I don't agree with her methods, but I do agree with the results. You have to learn to trust her. She is only trying to help you.", Casian said, jumping onto my back. I laid down for some time, then finally decided to get up and go get some lunch. I hadn't eaten breakfast because I was worried about Sylvia, now I was worried for myself. I arrived in the food hall and found a table. I sat by myself and ate my pasta. Sylvia walked in not too long after and came to my table, "Are you okay?", she asked. "No.", I said. "What happened?", Sylvia said, looking at me sadly. I explained what Mileeda did. "She is the most vilest woman. I thought my mother was. Screw it. They both are the most vilest women I've ever met.", I said, looking at Sylvia, who laughed. "What is so funny?", I asked her. "All this time…I wanted to know things, and now…", she said, thinking about something. "What?", I asked. "Well…I think that your mother is more screwed up than Mileeda.", she said. "Your grandmother turned your face into a squashed tomato for lying to her.", I said angrily. "Yes, and I shouldn't have. But you haven't figured it out yet. Why they are, how they are, I mean.", Sylvia said, taking a bite of her apple. "And why is that?", I asked. "Well, they are angry, and old. But they don't look old. They look like they could be our age.", Sylvia said, "They have hang ups, and I personally understand why Mileeda hates her family. You on the other hand, can't see what they want from you, because they aren't telling you everything. There are things they are keeping to themselves. We need to find out what that is. Unfortunately, we can't just ask.", Sylvia finished, taking another bite of her apple. "So, what are you suggesting?", I asked her. "I'm suggesting we figure it out, without them. The answers are in you, Emillie. If we crack that before they do…maybe my grandmother might not hate me so much.", Sylvia said, now losing her positive attitude. "Okay, so what first?", I asked. "We get you to summon the sword. It's the only way to bring out this other version of yourself.", she said, throwing the apple core away. "I can't. Mileeda has been trying to do it.", I said. "Well, I know that you can, and I think I might know how to get it to happen.", Sylvia said, standing up, "Follow me.", she said.

We walked out of the food hall and went to her room. In her room, she took out a strange device, "I had this with me to face Awalli, but I think it should work for you.", she said. "What exactly does that thing do?", I asked. "It brings out your power in a way, or it can take your power. It's royal tech, so it's classified. So, you'll love it.", she said, turning it on. "Wait…shouldn't we…?", before I finished what I was saying, Sylvia stuck me with the device, and I found myself in my room in the orphanage. I didn't know what the hell I was doing here, then I saw another girl. She had black hair. She turned around, and it was me, "Hello.", she said. "What the hell is going on?", I asked. "We have to become one. It's the only way to defeat them.", said the other me. "What the hell are you talking about?", I asked. Then the other me walked towards me and grabbed my hand. It burned and then I woke up in Sylvia's room with the sword in my hand, "I KNEW IT!", Sylvia yelled happily. "Sylvia, what has happened?", I asked, surprised I was still holding the sword and thinking clearly. "It worked, Emillie! You've got control of the sword and the other you. Tell me, do you have the knowledge?", Sylvia asked. "What knowledge?", "The other you has certain knowledge of things. She knows things we don't. Mileeda asked me to test out my device on you. She thought it might work.", Sylvia said. "Mileeda asked you?", I said, still staring at the sword. "Yes. I thought she was angry with me, but she just told me to use my device on you and see what happens. I have to tell her now.", Sylvia said happily. I kept looking at the sword. It was black and red. I could feel the power emanating from it. "Yes, Grandmother, you were right. Wait, you want me to leave?", asked Sylvia, confused. She hung up, then looked at me, and walked out. Mileeda appeared in the room seconds later, "Good. Now, lets talk plain.", she said, activating a force sphere, "Now, lets talk about how you are trying to kill these followers. Why?", Mileeda asked. "Mileeda, I don't know.", I said. "No... this should have worked.", she said irritatedly, "You've got the sword, but why not the knowledge?", she said, taking Sylvia's device, and stabbing me with it again. This time, I wasn't in my room in the orphanage, but rather in the apartment my mother had given to me. "I told you, we need each other.", said the girl who resembled me, minus her hair color, sitting on my couch. "How?", I asked. "Accept it. Stop questioning. Clear your head, and allow the transition.", she said, grabbing my hand again. This time, I tolerated the burn. When I awoke this time, I felt different. "Why are you after the followers?", Mileeda asked again. "Because they serve my father's enemy. The Dark One.", I heard myself say, but didn't know why I said it. "So, even he is fighting my sister?", Mileeda asked. "No. But she poses a very dangerous threat. He is channeling his energy into me, so that I may deal with it.", I said. I couldn't focus or think about anything. "So, Corsa, IS the dark one?", Mileeda asked, looking at me hard. "Yes.", I said. Mileeda touched my forehead and I fainted.

When I awoke, we were in her office, and she was staring at me, "What happened?", I asked. "Me, and the other you, had a conversation.", she said. I remembered that. "Yeah, but what happened after that?", I asked. "Well, I sapped your energy so I could bring back the original you. And now, I'd say that I have all the info I need.", she said, now getting up, and coming to me, and kneeling, and placing her hand on my knee, "Emillie, you are going to help defeat my sister. Once and for all. But first, we need to deal with these followers. I believe they are looking for godly items that can help free my sister from her cosmic prison.", "I'm sorry, but, your sister?", I asked, unable to believe what I was hearing. "Yes. I have a sister. Or had.", she said darkly. "My sister died, technically, many decades ago. She was very pretty and happy. Until Trinity possessed her, then whatever took her over after that. We've still never found out. But we can't let her get free. These followers wouldn't really be a threat, but Lopim has certain knowledge.", "How?", I asked. "Well, he used to be one of my students.", "Students?", I repeated. "I once taught magic to those that were capable of learning. Lopim was one of those students. He has performed dark magic so he can live longer, and has taken the liberty to also summon my sister. This is how she was able to start using Awalli to further her goals.". Awalli was being used? None of this was making sense. And why hadn't Sandin returned? "Mileeda, where is Tillo?", I asked her. She didn't do that usual twitch she gets when you ask her something she doesn't like. But rather, she answered, "He is being seemingly held by a group of followers. Lopim is among them.", she said. "But...I thought he was dead?", I asked. "No. He is alive. I told you, he is using dark magic. It appears, Emillie, that it is time I let you know exactly what magic can do.", Mileeda said, standing, and stretching her hand towards me. I couldn't breathe. "Just simply thinking about it, MY connection to the cosmos allows me to do this. Others, such as your sweet Sandin, would have to murmer the incantation. They would have to do it correctly. It is very important, because one slip-up, and you could find yourself in another dimension with nowhere to go, except to the same place you were before.", Mileeda said darkly, then she let me breathe again. "Why...do...you...torture...me?!", I asked between breathing. "You think...I'm torturing you? Hahaha!", Mileeda began to laugh, "I want you to consider what I've shown you, and my grandchild, is not torture.", Mileeda said, calming down, and placing her hand on my face, "If only you truly understood the blood in your system. Why, you could be almost as powerful as your grandmother, if you let me train you, and stop complaining.", she said. "Grandmother?", I asked. Mileeda placed her face in her hands. Then she went to her desk, pulled out a bottle of ticenta and took out two glasses. She poured me some. I looked at it suspiciously, "Oh for Bastian's sake, it's just normal ticenta.", she said, drinking some of her own. I took a sip. Then another, then placed the glass down. "I'm going to tell you a story, Emillie, that will answer all your questions.", she said, "EXCEPT! Who your father is. That, I cannot disclaim. That right belongs to Amana alone.", Mileeda said, taking another sip of her drink. I took another as well. "I'm all ears.", I said. I was mostly glad to get out of her torture, despite what she thought it was.

"Well, I'll start at the beginning. I was about your age when I first met Ko-e. Oh my, was she beautiful. My sister and I worshipped her without question. We knew who she was, right away. She said that her father was Sebastian, and that our PRINCESS, and the Kindy Princess were his children as well. She said they were her sisters.", Mileeda took another sip. I was stone quiet. I was finally gonna hear it. The true story. Not the made up ones. The truth. The one I've been waiting to hear my whole life. "So, once we brought Ko-e back to our kingdom, Dasha, before it...oh, forget it. I'll just stick to the point. Calypsa, your dearly departed aunt, went mad. I wanted to kill her.", "Why?", I asked. "Because she, and your grandmother, mind you, killed my parents, and turned me...into this.", Mileeda said, turning blue. It was strange. Her beauty was still there and the blue somehow matched her. She was gorgeous in this form. Why she would go in her other form, I didn't know. "Obviously, today, I can't walk around like this. You forgot, we are connected. I knew what you were thinking.", she said. "Well? What happened after my aunt went crazy, and your parents died?", I asked. "Well, Amana and Ko-e were off somewhere together, and I thought I was on my own. Then, Ko-e turned up, after my parents had been mutilated by a beast your grandmother created.", "You keep saying my grandmother. Are you trying to tell me that Trinity did these things?", I asked. Mileeda smiled. A dark smile. Somehow, I could sense for a second why she was hesitant to tell me about Trinity. "Well, I'm getting to that part. You see, my queen was named Micka. She was an evil piece of work. She was also Calypsa's mother. Yes, Sebastian had his way with the Kindy queen, Alisa, my queen, Micka, and the other one, Alex.", "Queen Alex...was real?", I asked. I had always imagined her to be the most made up character. "Oh yes. All three sired a child.", "Then, her daughter was Ko-e?", I asked. Because my mother had already told me that her mother's name was Alisa. Once again, Mileeda smiled darkly, "No...actually, her mother was a goddess named Falta. She also went by Falsa.". Once Mileeda had said this, I felt nothing but dread. Falsa was the main villain in the fairy tales. She was the one they always had to stop. "So, Ko-e, is...evil?", I asked. "You know, at one time, that girl wouldn't even swat a fly away. But, she has changed over these past years. She is more focused and determined. She has hidden herself well. But to answer your question straight, no. Ko-e is far from evil. We may not all agree with the way we do it, but we are ALL just trying to do the same thing.", Mileeda said. I felt relieved, and couldn't believe that ko-e was actually my aunt. I imagined her being the cool auntie and giving me advice or something. "The only person who may know where Ko-e is hiding, has refused to say and remains neutral. That would be your stepmother.", she said. Dalia. "Dalia knows where my aunt is?", I asked. "We suspect, but her loyalty to her is strong. And, Ko-e is the most well versed in magic out of all of us.", she said. "Even you?", I asked. "She taught me.", she replied. I was stunned. "So, what's the rest of the story?", I asked. "Well, at a certain point, me and Ko-e were searching for Calypsa. We ran into Alexa, who was Ko-e's sister-in-law. Ko-e had a brother, who died a very mysterious death. A death that I think Amana may know more than she has told about.", she said thinkingly, "But, when we were searching for Calypsa, Ko-e found out that Calypsa had attacked Kindy, and that Scion had been taken by Calypsa, so of course, Ko-e rode off to save his sorry ass. Once she did, Ko-e ended up captured, while I had returned to see how my sister was doing. And...to kill the queen.", she added darkly. "For your parents...", I said. "Yes. But that's when we learned...that Queen Micka was a goddess. She fled. Then, Amana and Ko-e went off, while Scion disappeared. Then things were strange. A new king had taken over Dasha, then me and my sister escaped from there with Scion and my late husband, Nigel. That's when I first learned of Trinity. I didn't know what she was, or where she came from. But she used my sister's body to expel something from King Tig, then it took over my sister. We didn't notice back then. And then, Amana had to kill...she had to kill...", Mileeda suddenly stood and started breathing hard. "Mileeda, are you okay?!", I asked her. "Yes...it's just sometimes, I get sad, when I think about this. She was so beautiful. She was my princess, and I hated her, until I truly met her. Calypsa was a flower, stepped on by her mother. But what you have to know, Emillie, is that your mother and Calypsa...", "I know, they were close.", "Yes. Very close. They were, for whatever reason, drawn to each other since childhood. Your mother doesn't like to talk about this. At all. So I'd advise to never bring up Calypsa, unless you truly do want to die, and not come back. Your mother killed her, so that thing that was in my sister, couldn't hurt anyone. But in all these years, we've warred against one another, made mistakes. My family, being the biggest.", Mileeda said, closing her eyes, and slightly shaking her head, "Well, anyway, that's the story.", "But, you didn't tell me what Trinity is!", I said. "Actually...I told you exactly what she is. Now, enough of this. I have other things to attend to. You've just wasted a good moment of your training. But don't worry, I'll make sure that we make up for it in a few hours.", Mileeda said. Pointing for me to leave. I looked at her. Part of me felt sorry for her. But another part of me wanted her to clear up the mystery of my grandmother. How could she be three different people? That's ridiculous. Unless they are all married to Sebastian. But, Trinity has always been drawn as one being. So, what the hell is Mileeda telling me?

As I returned to my room, it was getting late, and I knew it was pointless to try and sleep, because as soon as I woke up, I was going to get a beating anyway, so I decided to pass the time by messaging Sandin. He still wasn't messaging back. I was growing frustrated. Then I remembered, Mileeda told me he was on a mission. I tried thinking about Corsa and how she was so powerful, but couldn't understand. How was she using Awalli? This is what kept bothering me. I fell asleep anyway and found myself in a hovel. Awalli was here. She was just sitting at a dresser, staring into the mirror. I could hear shouts, and what sounded like cannon fire. She turned and then stared straight at me, "What do you want?", she asked. "You can see me?", I asked, surprised. "Yes. Now, what do you want?", she asked again. "I want to know… about Corsa.", I said. Awalli looked at me like she had never seen me before, then she grabbed her head, and started to scream, "AWALLI!", I shouted, reaching for her, but I phased through her. "YOU WILL DIE, EMILLIE!", she yelled, somehow forcing me to wake up. When I did, I looked at the time, and realized I was running late for my session. I rushed to Mileeda's office. As I did, my mother was exiting. "You're coming with me.", she said, walking past me. I followed, looking back at Mileeda's door. "Why?", I asked, catching up to my mother. "Because, we need to talk.", she said, taking me all the way across Base to her office. Once we were inside, she told me, "Sit.". I listened. Then she also sat down. She stared at me, then said, "For a long time, I told myself, I would NEVER, become my mother. I told myself that my mother was a perfect woman. But I've been lying to myself. It's time I tell you… the FULL truth about Trinity.", she said. I perked up at the mention of Trinity. "Why now?", I asked. "Because, Mileeda has a big, fucking, mouth.", my mother said. For some reason, I pictured that Mileeda found it funny. "But, she didn't tell me anything about Trinity.", I said, remembering our conversation a few hours ago. "Oh, but she did. She told you exactly.", my mother said, with obvious anger. She started to get worked up, I noticed, and then she stood and took out her cannon. I flinched, but she turned and started firing down a range that appeared from almost out of nowhere. Then she pocketed her cannon, "Anger management.", she said. "Well, what did you want to tell me?", I asked, growing impatient myself. "Emillie…you don't understand…how hard this is.", she said, sitting back down, "I never saw my mother…my true mother, ever again!", she yelled at me. Then she stood back up. "SHIT!", she yelled, kicking her chair all of a sudden. "I can't do this. I'm not ready. Mileeda shouldn't have told you. I'm going back to her office.", she said, starting to leave. I stood up, "Wait! I deserve the right to know! Trinity, is my grandmother!", I yelled at her. She turned towards me, slowly, and as she did, she was taking her cannon out of its holster, "No...your grandmother...is...Alisa Tia. That was MY mother. Trinity...is nothing more than a thing. A thing, Emillie. That is all she is. My mother died, when Trinity came into existence.", Amana said, with an angry tone. "But, what does that mean? Mileeda told me that Sebastian had children with four women. Your mother, Micka, Falsa, and Alex. So what is the truth, Mother?", I asked her. She released her cannon and then looked at me for a minute. Then she closed her eyes and started to talk, "My mother, Micka, and Alex, were sisters. They didn't know. They, like me and my sisters, were lied to. They were seperated. But when they learned...they left to find their mother. Tila, my grandmother.", my mother said, opening her eyes, picking up her chair, and sitting back down. I sat back down as well. "Tila came to my kingdom, and told me that my mother had become Trinity...with her sisters. She told me, that is who they always were. The next time I saw my mother...my REAL mother, she was telling me that she wanted me and my sister to get close...just so when the time was...right...", my mother started to choke up. She, like Mileeda, suddenly had a hard time breathing. She looked up at me, then pointed to the door. "No! You need to tell me!", I said. She took out her cannon and pointed it at me, "Go. This...was a mistake.", she said. "I'm tired of this! If you're going to shoot me, then do it!", I yelled at her. She stood up straight and pointed her cannon at my face. Then she lowered it, "Please? Just leave.", she said, walking away from me and going to sit behind her desk. She then fell upon her desk. I watched her for a minute, then decided I'd leave. Before I left, I could tell she was crying.

JESY: When I woke up in the morning, I was thinking about what Sandin told me. I didn't fully accept that Father Lopim's people were trying to summon a goddess, but was confused as to why this Emillie girl was somehow strong enough to kill so many people with just a blade. I understood that people had shot at her with their cannons, and somehow, couldn't hit her. How was this possible? I kept asking myself the same questions again, and again. Sandin seemed convinced of this goddess, though, and I needed to know for myself. I was only here for my parents. But whenever I thought of the dark one, I kept telling myself, she needed to be brought into the light, and didn't even understand what the fuck that meant. Lopim had the answers, so I went to him. I walked into the living room of the house we were staying in. There were people in here, getting weapons ready. "Are we going to battle?", I asked Lopim, once I saw him. "Of course not, just being prepared. My former master is aware of us, so we need to be extremely careful.", he said. "Yeah...who is your former master?", I asked. It was mostly the worker in me that needed these answers. "It's too much to explain to you at the moment. Just know, we need to be ready.", Lopim said, placing a large cannon down, and picking up a smaller one. "Lopim, I'm sorry, but what is really going on?", I asked, now watching him load the smaller cannon with shells. "Jesy, what is happening here, is the beginning of something amazing. We are going to be the ones to witness our lord's coming.", Lopim said, directing me to help some other people with their weapons. "Look, I'm only here to get revenge for my parents, and I want to know what Red and Tillo have to do with this!", I yelled impatiently. "Mr. Tillo has info. I've already told you this. And I'm confused as to why you are asking me again.", he said. "I'm asking again, because it doesn't make sense.", I said sternly. "Allow me to show you something, my dear.", he said, leading me away. We walked into a room and he directed that I sit down. As I did, he opened a drawer and pulled out something golden.

He placed it on the table, and I realized it was a box. Just a little golden box. Gold was pretty hard to find, even for little objects like this one. He opened it and took out a small parchment. I opened it and read; (there is nothing more sacred, then the bond between a mother and daughter.). "I'm confused. What the hell is this supposed to mean?", I asked. "Our master had us find this box. The message contained inside was left by a goddess. A goddess who is familiar to me. Mileeda. She wrote this, pertaining to her own daughter. But, our master was going to use her child as a vessel, so Mileeda killed her own child.", Lopim said gravely. I was even more confused. "Who is Mileeda?", I asked. "She is my former master. She is a goddess…", "STOP!", I yelled, "There is no such thing as a goddess! So, we are holding two men against their will, for some fairy tale bullshit?", I asked, growing angry. Lopim just stared at me. "Well, it is obvious you don't share our beliefs, Ms. Bonnly. Which is a shame, because your parents believed with all their hearts. They died for this cause, and now you can't even find it in you to accept the truth. I'm sure Mr. Tillo told you his new girlfriend is a goddess. If he didn't, it would explain why she is capable of killing like she is.", Lopim said, now taking the note back and placing it back inside the golden box. "Why don't you go ask him to tell you the full story?", he said, getting up, and pointing for me to get out.

I had left the house. I was so angry with Lopim. I was angry with myself. I never bought into my parent's church, and now, they are dead. I kept trying to think what the situation was going to develop into. I couldn't understand what was even happening. I was drinking at The Shot, a bar in Sicilia known for its lagers. As I was sitting, a girl came up to me, "So, having a hard time believing?", she said, not even turning in my direction. I looked at her. She was gorgeous. Green hair, blue eyes, and she was wearing what appeared to be a business suit. I don't know why it took me so long to realize it was Awalli sitting with me, "What do you want?", I asked her, now losing my composure. "What I want...is the same thing you do.", she said, ordering a drink. "What exactly...do you think I want?", I asked angrily. "Oh, I imagine, revenge, for your parents. It just so happens, I want the same thing. Not the revenge part, but to kill the one who killed your parents. I want to kill Emillie.", she said, taking her shot, "Sadly, this is the only thing that can affect me.", she said, looking longingly at her empty glass, "I used to be different… Now, I'm special.", she said, smiling at me now. I turned from her. I slowly placed my hand on my cannon. "Don't.", she said. "I'll kill you before you can even make a move.", she said, grabbing my wrist. "I've heard of you, but I'm not scared.", "You should be. I'm that thing you don't want to believe in.", she said. "And what is that?", I asked. "A goddess.". I was quiet. I didn't believe her, but was too afraid to say, prove it. I drank the rest of my drink, while Awalli was still holding my wrist. Then I snatched my wrist from her, punched her, pulled out my cannon, and aimed it at her. People in the bar started to panic and run out. "I'm warning you, Jesy.", she said, pouring herself another shot. I shot her glass. She sat there for a second, "I see. You know, the only reason I've given you a chance, is because you have someone I want in your custody. Sandin Tillo. Bring him to me, and I'll forget about all of this.", she said, smiling at me. "Wipe that stupid smile, off your face.", I said, stepping closer with my cannon still pointed at her. She just sat there, staring at me. She made my cannon fly out of my hand. Then she took my head, and smashed it on the bar counter. Then, she threw me over the counter. She jumped on top of me, and started to beat me.

I woke up in a strange worn down building. Standing over me was Awalli. We were alone, as far as I could tell. "Waking up now?", she asked me. She then punched me. I spit blood. "So, let's try talking again.", she said. I realized, I wasn't even cuffed. I just couldn't move. I was sitting on a chair and just stuck. There was nothing holding me. No rope, no coil, no anything. What the fuck was happening? This had to be some kind of royal tech. I've heard rumors of the things they have, and can do. Maybe this is what this is. "I want you...to bring me, Sandin, Tillo.", she said. "For what?", I asked. "Because he is Emillie's lover. I need to take him from her, put him with his mother.", she said evilly. "You killed her.", I said. "Yes, I did.", she said darkly, "By now, Emillie has guessed... that she knew something. Something I know about her, that she doesn't know. Or at least, not the original Emillie anyway. There are two parts of her mind. One part is trying to kill me. The other is just a confused, scared, little girl.", Awalli said, not moving, but just standing over me. "Look, I'm not believing your crap. So I think that you need to stop with this fairy tale nonsense, and start talking plain. What do you really want? Are you really scared of this, Emillie girl?", I asked her. "Let me show you something.", she said with a grave tone. She grabbed my head, and suddenly images flashed before my eyes. I saw the first day I started school. I saw the first time my mother sold herself for shills because we were poor after my real father left us. I saw myself fighting in high school, because I was always called a slut. My mother was known. In the end, her and my stepfather became caught up with their church, so I was mostly on my own. I took care of myself. It was tough. I saw my worst, and best moment. The day a group of boys had cornered me. Last day of school, and they all had plans to do nasty things to me. Oh yes. I remember when they took off my shirt, and had me standing there in my holder. I remember growing so angry. I remember the boy who orchestrated it. I remember what I did. I kicked the shit out of all nine of those boys. And I walked out of that room, and I was declared a hero. A survivor. Everyone knew that I was going to have a job in law enforcement. Next thing you know, I'm working as a GO Grunt. It was hard back then, hitting the pavement, but… No…I can't let her see this! No! "GET OUT!", I yelled, finally gaining control of my thoughts. My head was hurting. I felt blood coming from my nose. I looked up and Awalli was smiling, "Do you understand now? Just a little more, and you would have shown me exactly what I wanted to see.", she said, "Now, you can do what I ask, or I can just take it the hard way, and MAKE you bring him.", she said. I felt myself begin to cry. I thought about everything I just saw, and then realized that she had seen it, too. But, those were my memories, and she couldn't have them. "So?", she asked. "Go to Hell.", I said. "You are tough. You will be a good little soldier.", she said.

SANDIN: It had been a long morning. Bonnly hadn't come back, and I didn't fully think she understood what was going on, and I wanted her to be safe. I started to realize there is a part of me that still cared about her. Not that long ago, she and I were like how Emillie and I are now. We were inseparable. We were partners. I remembered the first time it happened. We had been working together for two months. She was telling me that she wanted to take the Worker test. I remembered telling her, me, too. For some strange reason, that night, I noticed how beautiful she really was. Before then, you only really see a girl in uniform, but, that night…that was our night. And now she is getting mixed up in all of this. I didn't want her here. I didn't want her to get hurt. "Red, where do you think Jesy is?", I asked. "Probably somewhere in the house, now will you stop acting like a girl for a second? I think I know a way out of here.", Red said, thinkingly. "Well, how? I'm listening, and game for anything.", I said. "Well, Jesy says she doesn't believe in magic. She must think this room is using some kind of tech, but we know differently.", Red said, standing up. "Yeah, and how does that help?", I asked. Well…I know a trick to this room. There is a room like this on Base.", "How do you know about some room like this on Base?", I asked him, surprised.

"Well, let me tell you a little something interesting about Base. I think Base used to be Alexandria. The kingdom above Plinth. There are all sorts of magic corridors and things that are out of place. Almost like some kind of battle happened there. Now my thoughts are Amana and Mileeda. But, we'll discuss that another time. Let's just get out of here.", he said. "How?", I asked. "I can't harm you, you can't harm me. No one can harm anyone in this room, right?", Red said. I nodded. Well, when that door opens, and Lopim comes in here, there are two of us. One of us gets out, and the other one puts a bullet in him. Now, first off, there are a lot of men and women in the house, so if we are gonna cut through them, we might need something off set.", Red said, reaching into his pants and pulling out a small circular device. "What the hell is that?", I asked him. "Got it off Amana a few days ago. Anyway, this right here, is our ticket out. It's a molecule displacer. I've been working with it. It'll frighten whoever comes in here.", "Mileeda said she was getting us out soon, Red.", I said. "Yes, I remember you saying something about not being here much longer.", Red said slowly. Then, the door burst open, and it was Jesy. Her face was beat to shit, and she was looking dead at me. "Sandin...you...have to GO!", she yelled with great strain. I looked at Red, whose eyes grew wide, "AWALLI!", he yelled. She was stepping into the room. She knocked Jesy to the wall and she fell and was out. "JESY!", I yelled, and ran to her. I checked to see if there was a pulse. She was alive. I looked up at Awalli, "I've had ENOUGH of you!", I yelled, and ran at her without thinking. "SANDIN!", Red yelled, as Awalli grabbed me by my neck. Red ran to Jesy and picked up her cannon that fell and he started firing at Awalli. She dropped me, "I let you live once, Mr. Red. I'm beginning to think, that was a mistake.", Awalli said, now catching the bullets in the air and making them fly back at Red, who got hit. "RED!", I yelled. But then, I felt myself being pulled back towards Awalli. I fought against it. I had to check on Red. I had to. I tried to make it to him, then suddenly, the pull was gone, and I made it to Red, who was breathing, but barely. I turned, and a very pissed off Mileeda was standing in the room. Awalli stared at her, confused, "And, exactly, why are YOU here… Grandmother?", Awalli added mockingly. "You…are not yourself, child. But, I will make you see.", Mileeda said, as she reached out and touched Awalli, who I realized couldn't move. Then I watched, as Mileeda and Awalli disappeared. Suddenly, some men and women appeared in the room, and there was cannonfire. "Are you capable?", asked a gruff P.E.D soldier, handing me a cannon. I nodded and took it. The med people were already taking care of Jesy and Red. I watched Red especially, who was looking rather deathly. I ran out of the room with the cannon in my hand and started to blast these cult-ass-sons-of-smichs. Two of them had come out of the corner, and jealous guy was there to have my back after I shot those two, and one more tried to get the jump on me from a door I hadn't noticed. I looked at him and nodded. He nodded back and pointed down the hall. We both proceeded and quickly ran into Lopim, "Put it down, Lopim.", I said. Lopim was standing there with a shoulder cannon and definitely intended to fire at us. "This isn't how this goes, Mr. Tillo. I WILL summon my master!", Lopim yelled and started to fire. Jealous guy found cover faster than I did. I ended up jumping behind the same cover. "So, what do you think?", he asked. "I think we'll wait until he runs out of ammo.", I said. I saw a shell fly through our cover. "On second thought, if we wait, we'll end up being poked through. I think we should confuse him.", I said. I threw something in the air, and Lopim aimed for it, and then Jealous guy shot him. I stood up, and Lopim was down, with a shell straight through his dome.

AWALLI: We had arrived in my old house in Nocton. I fell onto the floor. I looked up at Mileeda. She was menacing. She approached me slowly. I waved my arm at her, and she just waved her arm back. I stood and aimed all the psychic force I could at her, and she just stood there in front of me, not moving or flinching, "Are you done?", she asked me, boredly. It reminded me of Amana. "Why are you here?", I asked her. "Well, you are my family, so it really shouldn't surprise you.", she said. She waved her hand, and I felt myself binded. Then I felt myself being forced into a chair, "Awalli. You poor child. Perhaps I was hasty in my decision, to ensure my family never births any more gods or goddesses.", she said, watching me with pity. "What the hell are you talking about?", I asked. "Well...Layna was supposed to be the last one, but then...you happened. I've watched you for a long time. Amana wanted you to be like Layna, but she wanted you stationed in the non-contracted cities. I, on the other hand, thought you needed to die.", Mileeda said, her tone changing, and her anger rising. "You want to kill me?", I asked. I felt sadness that I couldn't explain. "Yes. Because I knew that THIS was a possibility. You didn't get the same training that Layna received, and I knew Corsa could use you like she has been doing.". I thought about what she was saying. I didn't feel used. Mileeda placed her hands on my face. I couldn't move, but then, I felt something. An energy that left my body. I thought for a few seconds and realized that I wasn't angry. I didn't want to kill Emillie, and I was hurt. I kept seeing all the people I've hurt, "Make it stop.", I said. "No.", Mileeda replied, watching me. "I saw Mrs. Tillo die, then I heard Carla Nos screaming. I then saw myself, as I cut into Lida... "Please?!", I begged. "No.", Mileeda said, still standing over me. "Please, I can't watch anymore!", "So, you see what you have been doing? What you have allowed Corsa to do?", she asked me. I began to cry, and felt like I couldn't think straight. I looked up at Mileeda, who was still watching me with anger, "I'm sorry... I'm sorry.", I said, looking down. "I'm sorry doesn't make it go away.", she said, now grabbing my face by my chin, and forcing me to look up, "I'm so sorry that Amana did this to you, child. I told her to stay out of MY family affairs, and yet, now…she has ruined your life.", she said. "You would have just killed me.", I muttered. "Exactly. Would we be sitting here if I had? You'd never had existed. You'd be nothing. And me? Well, I'd be just a bit happier knowing that I didn't have to worry about my sister, taking control of any of my grandchildren.", she said, now releasing my face and pushing me back in the chair so I fell. She then stood on my chest, "Awalli, when I leave this room, you will lose your control, again. But, this time, it will be with clarity. I'll give you the choice. Leave, and disappear. Or, I send Emillie, and she kills you, your choice.", Mileeda said, taking her foot off my chest, stepping back, and standing over my face. "I'll leave.", I said. "Easy to say now, but once I'm gone…", she said, slowly. "Grandmother…please? Don't leave me! I don't want Corsa to take over again!", I yelled, starting to cry as well. "Don't leave?", she repeated. "I'm scared… Please?", I asked her, pleadingly. She bent down and brushed my hair with her hand. "I'm sorry, child, but it isn't my place to stay here with you. I have, OTHER, responsibilities. The only reason I'm here is because Amana asked me to be.", she said, now standing back up. I felt myself being able to move again. I jumped up, hugged her, and cried into her shoulder, "PLEASE?! DON'T GO!", I begged. She patted me on my head, pushed me away, and looked at me. "I know why she chose you… This is revenge…", she said, angrily, then disappeared. I fell to the floor, broken. I was crying and laid in a curled up position. I started to remember the day I killed Emillie. She was innocent, and had no idea I wanted her dead. Then I heard a voice speak to me, "Awalli…", it said. I knew who it was, "GO AWAY!", I yelled. It was Lida's spirit. She was looking at me with pity. "I'm sorry, Awalli. I should have been better to you. I should have been good to you.", she said. Then she disappeared, and was replaced by a woman with red and orange hair and dark eyes. She wore a red dress that came all the way down to her feet, and was lined with gold on both sides. Her face was lined with red that came down her face on both sides, "Awalli, come back. I told you...I'd always be here. I'm the one you should trust.", she said. "No! Please?!", I yelled, too frightened to move. "YOU BELONG TO ME!", she said. I kept crying and looking up at her with nothing but fear.

CHAPTER 11

The Girl With The Sword

SANDIN: P.E.D was going crazy. Something was happening in Sicilia that didn't seem to make any sense. There was a quake, as well as a beam of light that came from the sky. Amana was everywhere. She was yelling out orders and trying to keep everyone moving. As I stayed with Red and Jesy, I noticed Emillie and Sylvia watching the madness, "Sandin, what's going on?", Emillie asked, running to me. She then saw Red, "Oh my…", she said, coming to him, and placing her hand on his wrist. "They said he'll be fine. Awalli did this.", I said. Emillie noticed I was sitting next to Jesy's bed. She then noticed that I had been holding her hand. I quickly snatched it away. "She's a friend. She was hurt by Awalli.", I said, trying to explain. Emillie looked like she wanted to question, but Sylvia stopped her, "Where is my grandmother?", she asked, looking around. "Here.", Mileeda said, walking into the room. I stood up, "YOU! YOU WEREN'T SUPPOSED TO LET THIS HAPPEN!", I yelled at her. "Listen to me, Sandin. When it comes to magic, sometimes, I can't see certain things. Awalli appeared in that room, and I knew the magic Lopim had placed in the room was gone. That's why I knew to come. I didn't know Awalli was there. She isn't in control.", Mileeda said, walking up on Red, and looking down at him, "I'm sorry.", she said. "Does this have something to do with your sister?", I asked. "Everything.", she said, "Awalli, isn't the same. I've given her some of her own mind. She is now going mad with guilt. But...if she doesn't leave...if she continues to do what she has...then, Emillie, you must stop her.", Mileeda said, now turning to Emillie. "I won't kill her, if it really isn't her.", she said quickly. "You don't have a choice.", Mileeda replied. "Maybe, I do, and you don't realize that.", Emillie said mockingly. I could tell Emillie didn't care much for Mileeda. "Really?", Mileeda asked her, in what I assumed was a tone meant to make her frightened, "You're going to argue with me, right now?", she said. "I'm not trying to argue with you. I just don't see why I have to kill someone, if they aren't fully in control. What if I can make Corsa leave Awalli? Have you ever even considered it? Or do you just want her dead to get rid of another stain on your family?", Emillie asked. I was afraid now, "Look, she doesn't...". Mileeda stopped me by putting her hand up, "You just won't stop...will you?", Mileeda said, watching Emillie. Emillie stood her ground. Amana walked into the room, "What has she done now?", she said, looking at the scene. "Grandmother...", Sylvia said, trying to move closer to her. "Shut up.", Mileeda said to Sylvia, and she became deathly quiet, "She has disrespected me...again. This time, Amana...I leave you to deal with it, because I...don't have the patience.", she said, and teleported away. Amana turned to Emillie, who faced her mother, still unafraid. "I've had it with you.", she said. She grabbed Emillie, who I was surprised to see, actually tried to fight back. But Amana quickly subdued her, by punching her in her face, then grabbing her hair, and throwing her down. She then placed something on Emillie's back, and she was unable to move. Amana began kicking the shit out of her. "STOP!", I yelled, moving towards Amana. "Have you forgotten? She is the reason your mother is dead. And me, personally, I've had enough of her attitude.", Amana said, kicking her again, but not taking her eyes off of me, "If you don't want her to be beat, then convince her to listen, and learn some FUCKING respect!", Amana shouted, and then kicked Emillie again, looked at me, then walked out, and started to bark more orders.

After Amana had gone, Emillie was sitting up in a chair, while Sylvia cleaned her off. "Who is this girl, Sandin?", asked Emillie. I realized she must have been watching me check Jesy every five minutes. "I told you, she's a friend.", I said. "Sandin, don't insult my intelligence.", Emillie said, standing up, "You were involved with this woman.", she said. "Well, it was some time ago, so I hardly think it matters.", I replied. "But it does matter, because you still care about her.", "And how is that wrong? She is Plinthinian, isn't she? She deserves to have someone to care about her.", I said. "Why does that someone have to be you?", she asked. "Because...you killed her parents.", I said, before I could stop myself. "What?", Emillie said, losing her composure. "Emillie...I didn't...", I began, but she had already run out of the room. Sylvia glared at me, then followed. I felt like an ass. I didn't mean to tell Emillie that. She wasn't herself when she did it. I watched Jesy for a while longer, then she finally woke up. I knew I should have been trying to find Emillie, but there WAS a part of me still angry with her. And now she was acting jealous and bashful. I was starting to feel like I did rush things with her. "Sandin...where are we?", Jesy asked, as she tried to sit up. "Hold on, you're still sort of beat up.", I said, taking a wet towel, and wiping her forehead. "Where are we?", she asked more seriously now. "We are on the Base. P.E.D.", I said. "I've never heard of P.E.D. What is that?", she asked. I quickly explained. "So, what happened to Lopim? And Awalli?", she asked. "Mileeda says she did something to her, but Lopim was dead last time I saw him.", I said. I looked to check on Red, and he was breathing. Then I saw Emillie, and she was watching me with Jesy. I turned and ignored her. Jesy was looking in her direction. "Who is that?", she asked curiously. "Nobody.", I said. She knew that Emillie killed her parents, and the last thing I needed at the moment was an angry Jesy and a jealous Emillie. "Sandin…", Jesy said. She was giving me that look she gave me when she was feeling lied to. "It's better if you don't know.", I said. Jesy is a worker, she isn't an idiot, and knew how to put the pieces together. Something I had forgotten about her. Jesy became quiet, and didn't say anything else. She was refusing to talk to me now, so I decided to let her rest. I looked at Red one more time and walked out of the room.

"Sandin, I need to speak with you.", said Mileeda, as I was making my way to my room. "Okay.", I said. A door appeared, and I followed Mileeda inside. "Do you know what is going on down there?", she asked. "I heard about what happened as soon as we left.", I said. "So, let me be the first to say that Lopim only has to perform a few more tasks, then my sister is going to walk among us.", Mileeda said, now pacing behind her desk. "Well, Lopim is dead, so we don't need to worry about that.", I retorted. "That…is where you are wrong.", Mileeda said, taking out a device and pointing it at her wall. The wall was a giant monitor that showed some kind of footage in Sicilia. People were panicking and running. I watched as a father was running to his daughter, and something seemed to snatch him up. In all the chaos, I could see Lopim, standing next to a woman with faded green hair. She was wearing some kind of dark armor with bolts lined on it. "Who the hell is that with him?", I asked, perplexed by her. She had a certain beauty to her, but a very smug and over-confident face. "Lona…", Mileeda muttered. Amana entered the room and saw Lona and Lopim standing next to each other, causing mayhem. Amana literally growled, before she pulled her cannon out, checked it, and then disappeared. "NO! AMANA!", Mileeda yelled. "Sandin, I need you to go to Emillie, NOW!", she yelled, and also disappeared.

I ran looking for Emillie, and soon found her and Jesy, "YOU'RE HER!", Jesy was yelling, and brandishing a weapon she obviously just made at Emillie. "NO! You don't understand! It wasn't really me!", she yelled, half crying. Jesy went for her, and Emillie grabbed her by her throat, and slammed her against the wall. "EMILLIE!", I shouted, but she was already losing control. "I killed your sires, because they served The Dark One. I can tell, she has poisoned you.", Emillie said in that creepy voice. She held her other hand out and the sword started to appear. I ran to her, and punched her in the face. She stumbled for a second, then looked at me, then heartbreak fell on her face, "You love her.", she said, hurt. "Emillie, we don't have time for this! You need to get to your mother, now.", I said, sort of nervously. Jesy looked at me once Emillie dropped her. I could tell she wanted to do something. Emillie closed her eyes. Then teleported us to Sicilia. Me and Jesy looked at each other, then started to help whoever we could. I looked forward and saw Amana and Mileeda standing together. Mileeda was trying to convince Amana of something. I could tell by her body nature. Emillie was walking towards them. "See to as many as you can!", I yelled at Jesy. "Obviously!", she yelled back. I went to the trio. "Amana, you can't face her. We need more firepower. You're letting your anger best you.", Mileeda said. "Fuck you, Mileeda. She is standing right there! I'm not waiting another three-thousand years for her to come back!", Amana was yelling. "Mother. You should heed her.", Emillie said, still talking in that strange way. Amana looked at Emillie, then back at Lona, who noticed Amana now, and was quickly moving towards her. "Amana, look out!", I shouted. Amana turned and quickly fired her weapon. Lona did a quick dodge and kicked Amana in the chest. Amana flew some feet back and hit a building. She went through it. Mileeda grabbed Lona and threw her, and Lona flew through a building. Mileeda went after Amana. I looked at Emillie, who was watching the building with interest. Suddenly, Lona burst out of the building, and flew at Amana and Mileeda. Mileeda was helping Amana out of the building. Emillie summoned her sword and threw it at Lona. It hit her and she hit the ground. Emillie summoned the sword back to her, and it just appeared in her hand. "I didn't kill her. But, she is weak enough for my mother to leave. Go with her. It's too dangerous.", Emillie said. "But, what about you?", I demanded. "I'll see you shortly.", she said, waiting for Lona to get up. I ran to Jesy, "We have to leave.", I said. I felt a hand on my shoulder, and Mileeda had taken us back to her office. Amana was looking at the monitor. Emillie was there now, and Lona had gotten back up. "Well, this is it.", Mileeda said. Amana was paying full attention to the monitor. We all were. I looked at Jesy, who was also paying full attention. I wondered what she was feeling.

EMILLIE: I wasn't fully, not in control, but I wasn't all the way, either. I could feel my limbs and had the ability of moving myself, but the other me was in control. We were just standing by, just waiting to see what this woman was going to do. "You're supposed to be dead.", she said, approaching me. I felt my sword aim at her, then she summoned her own sword and swung at mine. We swung our blades at each other for a minute, until I had slashed her face. She stood back, grabbing her face, and I watched as she fell to one knee, "Damn it.", she said, then disappeared. I looked around and saw nothing but devastation. I flew around, trying to help the innocents. "Who are you?", a little girl asked, as I unraveled her father. "Emillie.", I said. The girl looked at me with nothing but admiration. The man was weak, but there were med people arriving and I left him in their care. I went all over the area, checking to see who else might need help and people started to point and cheer. Before I knew it, there was a crowd of people, and they were cheering at me. I felt the other me leave, as I felt complete control coming to my body. The little girl I had left earlier was standing nearby and she was yelling, "SHE IS EMILLIE! SHE SAVED MY FATHER!", she shouted to the crowd. The crowd all surrounded me, then I saw people with notepads in their hands. "Scuse' me? But what happened here? Can you give any comment?", one lady was asking. I was looking around and became overwhelmed. I thought immediately to teleport away.

When I arrived back at P.E.D, it was to tumultuous applause. "Wow!", Tem said, standing nearby with a few of his friends, who I still didn't know. I saw a bunch of other soldiers all yelling and cheering at me. Then, Sylvia came running up to me, "EMILLIE, THAT WAS AMAZING!", she shouted, throwing her arms around me. She led me to Mileeda's office. Mileeda was sitting in her chair, talking on her receiver, and my mother was surrounded by weapons she was loading and prepping. "Good job.", Amana grunted at me, once she noticed me. "Emillie, I can't believe you fought her…", Sandin said in shock. "Well, I don't know why or how.", I said, sort of angry. "Look at the monitor.", Mileeda said, smiling at me. "Well, I'm here standing in the center of Downtown Sicilia, where a strange number of events have been taking place.", said a reporter, "There was a woman and a man who looked like our departed, Father Lopim, and they seemed to be unleashing some kind of chemical on the city. There were quakes and strange lights from the sky. But EVERYONE is talking about the fight that took place here no less than half an hour ago. A girl, straight out of a film, came here. She had a sword and looked mysteriously like the girl wanted right now by the RF. She was fighting the woman, who seemed to be causing the city an immense amount of damage. The strange girl, almost like out of a fairy tale story, fought the woman to a stand still, and the woman just disappeared, leaving the girl standing victorious. I tried to get some answers from the strange girl, but she disappeared just like the woman. But sources at the moment are saying the girl's name is Emillie, and we all just want to know more about her.", said the reporter on the monitor, now switching the topic back to the events of the day. I was thunderstruck. "Congratulations. You're a celebrity.", my mother said, now checking and making sure her weapons were ready, "I'm going to look for Lona.", she said, picking up a particularly large cannon and placing the strap over her shoulder. She was loading all the other weapons onto her as well. My mother had all sorts of places to hide her cannons, apparently. "Amana, you and I can't just do stuff like that.", Mileeda said, frowning at her, "What you did was careless and risky.", she continued. Amana looked at her, and all I saw was the same pain I saw earlier, when she couldn't even finish telling me about Calypsa. "Mom...please?", I said, placing my hand on her shoulder. She disappeared. "Don't worry. She's gone to brood in her office.", Mileeda said, sighing. "Why does this woman make her so angry?", I asked. "Your mother taught her magic.", Mileeda said, pouring herself a glass of ticenta. "WHAT?!", I exclaimed. Jesy left the room, and Sandin quickly followed her. Part of me was interested in what Mileeda just said, but at the same time, I just remembered what happened before we left for Sicilia.

SANDIN: "Jesy!", I called to her. She had stopped and was breathing heavily, then she vomited into a nearby waste bin, "That, girl...", she said, now looking at me, "She is Emillie. She murdered my parents, but she saved those people...", she said in a confused sort of tone. "I told you, it's complicated.", I said. Emillie was approaching us, and Jesy quickly turned and walked away. "I don't know what to say to her.", Emillie sighed, watching her walk away. Jesy turned and looked at us, but then darted around a corner. "Well, neither do I.", I said. Emillie grabbed my hand, "I'm sorry I was acting all weird.", she said, with a sad look on her face. "Don't worry about it.", "Sandin, what am I supposed to do now?", Emillie asked me. "Well, it's like your mom said. You're a celebrity.".

Emillie pulled on me, and led me to Amana's office. We knocked, and there was no answer. Emillie entered anyway. As we walked in, Amana was sitting with a glass of ticenta in her hand, and the bottle not too far from her. She was looking down at something. "What's that?", Emillie asked curiously. "Get out.", Amana said, not even looking at us. "But... Mileeda told me, you taught that woman.", Emillie said. Amana looked up, stood up, then she took out her cannon, and rushed towards Emillie. She waved her hand, and I was stuck to the wall, "WHEN I SAY GET OUT, I MEAN IT!", she yelled, not only pointing the cannon at Emillie, but placing it on her head and pinning her to the wall, "I don't wish to talk about this. Not with you. Ever. Get out.", she said, releasing Emillie, who looked hurt, and left without taking me with her. I felt the force pinning me to the wall had left, and watched as Amana went back to her desk, placed the cannon down, and continued to look at something. "I don't understand you.", I said, feeling my anger rise. "You don't need to.", she said. "You're always treating her like shit. You didn't raise her, and now you won't even give her the respect you should.", I said, glaring at her. "What respect has she earned, Tillo? Have you forgotten that I had to beat her earlier today for disrespecting Mileeda? She needs to show respect, to earn it. She hasn't earned that right from me. Not at all. How long has she been here again?", Amana asked me. "Look, all I'm saying is that you treat her like she isn't anything to you, but she is your flesh. She is YOUR fucking daughter.", I said, then turned, and walked out.

Later, I found Emillie crying in one of the training rooms. She was working out, but also, wiping tears. "Hey, you alright?", I asked her. "I'm okay. Even though I hate her, I keep trying with my mother, and she doesn't even care.", Emillie said, punching a training bag. "I know.", I sighed. "Where is Jesy?", Emillie asked. "I don't know.", "You should go look for her.", Emillie said, now performing a combo and adding a kick.

"Why do you care now?", I asked, irritated. Emillie stopped. "Listen, I know what, other me, did. She killed her parents. But they were bad people.", "How do you know that?", I felt compelled to ask. "When she took over last time, I could feel myself learning some of what she knew. She showed me Jesy's parents. They were going to sacrifice kids. Kids that were living on the streets.", Emillie said, growing angry, and turning back towards her bag. "Do you have proof of that? She isn't going to just believe that, Emillie.", I said. "I know she won't. That's why I have to show her. I'm learning new things about my magic. Sylvia has been showing me.", "I didn't know Sylvia knew magic.", "She is royalty, of course she knows.", Emillie said, looking at me shocked, "Royal tech is mostly based on magic. Magic is technology that's misunderstood.", Emillie said. I didn't know shit about magic, but was very surprised to see Emillie performing magic before my eyes. She not only summoned her sword in front of me, but then pointed it at the bag, which turned into sand and fell onto the floor, "Unfortunately, I don't know how to return it to its original form yet, but I'm learning.", she said, smiling at me now. I looked into her eyes, and then knew what was gonna happen before it did.

When I woke up in Emillie's room, I decided to take a quick walk. I realized, unlike everyone else here on Base, I didn't have a training session to report to, or any other responsibility besides waiting for Mileeda or Amana to tell me what they needed. I walked for what felt like a long time. I eventually got to a part of Base where there were no personnel. As I looked around, I realized there were a lot of old buildings. I entered one of them, and was shocked. There were strange carvings all over the walls. Scars that suggested that there was some kind of great battle were also covering the walls, floors, and pillars. There were portraits that were askew, but one of them I recognized was Amana. Then I was surprised to see one of Dalia. There were others. There was a family. A woman with green hair, a man with hazel hair, and a little girl with… "What the…?", I said out loud, realizing the little girl in the portrait was the woman that Emillie fought. I could tell the portraits were ancient, but somehow, I could feel the energy coming from them. Something told me they were protected by some kind of magic. I kept looking around and wondered, what the fuck happened to this place?

As I had left that building and proceeded to another one, I passed through a bunch of rubble, but it was in this building that I found the most curious thing of all. I could tell that this was some kind of village, but at the back, there was a nice home. I entered the home, and saw things were just as damaged in here as the other building was. I looked around and then I saw what Red was telling me. Something in this house was out of place. I could feel it. I started to walk up the stairs, and as soon as I reached the top, I suddenly was back on the first step. "What the hell?", I said, starting to walk up again, only to have the same thing happen. I gave up on walking up those stairs and decided to check out the bottom part only. There were certain rooms that had the same effect. You enter, only to be back outside with the door closed, as if you had never opened it. I was very confused why this was happening. But then I realized that I could walk through the bottom part of the house without experiencing this weird situation. I only had to not enter any rooms. I looked into what appeared to be a kitchen and saw that things were tossed all over the place. I felt on the counter and could feel a great tragedy. I didn't know if I wasn't supposed to be this far on the base. "It's all weird.", Jesy said, coming from out of the living room, "I've been walking around this whole place. I'm confused but convinced.", she said. "Of?", I asked. "Well, goddesses.", she said, placing her hands on her hips and shaking her head. We both walked around the house and decided to sit down on the damaged furniture. "So…Emillie…what is the deal?", she asked me. I told her the full story of me and Emillie, including the part on why Red, Yellfy, and I, all left the GF. "Well, I'm not stupid. I had a feeling about Walsh being bought. But I didn't think it was anything like that. Awalli has to be stopped.", Jesy said. "Well, according to Mileeda, she isn't that Awalli anymore.", I replied, playing with the strange stuffing in the furniture. "Do you think Red will wake up tomorrow?", Jesy asked now. "Maybe. I honestly hope so.", I said, feeling bad that it wasn't me lying in the med bed. "So, are we really going to avoid the fact that you were fucking her earlier?", Jesy now said in a certain tone. "Look, she IS my girlfriend.", "She is something entirely different.", "Well, so am I.", "What the hell are you talking about, Sandin?", she said, now growing angry. I quickly told her about my parents. "So, you think…what exactly? You think you're a god? That is ridiculous, Sandin. Your parents weren't thousand's of years old.", she said. "Emillie and Awalli are both in their twenties. And also, I never said that I'm a god. What I'm telling you, is that there is something not normal about me. I don't know how to explain it. I have something called a god gene.", I said. Jesy looked like she was thinking about this now. She got up and started to walk into the other room. I just sat and waited. She then came back with some papers and brandished them upon the floor, "I found these. Some of them are written in a language I can't understand, but these ones over here translate this stuff. So according to the translations, it would appear that a god gene is something any Plinthinian can be born with. It gives the ability to access the cosmos and do things that would seem strange to most normal people. You can perform magic by saying the proper incantations, and you can also open up portals to…other dimensions?", she said, confused. She kept looking over the papers, then she sat down and looked at them again. "Other dimensions…", she repeated. "Let me see that!", I yelled. I looked at the translations and read the same thing. "How can I do something like that?", I questioned, so confused about what this meant. "Sandin, we should talk to Amana or Mileeda.", Jesy said. We got up and walked out of the building and overheard a loud commotion. Someone came flying past us. We looked back and saw it was Amana. "MOVE.", Amana said, pushing the both of us out of the way with a wave of her hand. I wondered who she was fighting, then saw Mileeda walking towards her, wearing the same kind of leather military suit Amana always wore. "I'm not going to let you go, Amana. You are going to jeopardize what we've built here. You need to THINK!", Mileeda said, taking out her own cannon and pointing it towards Amana. "Mileeda, what the hell is going on?", I asked. "Amana has lost her mind. She wants to go after Lona, and refuses to listen to reason.", Mileeda said, calmly, as if she has dealt with this before. "MOVE.", Amana said again, but this time to Mileeda. "Amana, I'll put you down, you know I will.", Mileeda said. "Then, fucking, do it.", Amana said, with each step towards Mileeda. Mileeda hit Amana with her cannon, then Amana dodged Mileeda's next move, and summoned her own cannon while she did, and also hit Mileeda. Then they were going at it, in a mish mash of hits. Amana getting her licks in on Mileeda, and Mileeda getting hers' on Amana. It got to a point where me and Jesy looked at each other. I'm sure she was thinking the same thing. Then, finally, the two sat down on the ground, "I want to kill her…", Amana said, calming down. "I…know.", Mileeda said, breathing hard, then waving for us to come over, "Jesy, you are to accompany Amana to her office and stay with her until I come for you. Mr. Tillo, we should talk.", Mileeda said, standing, and walking back towards the building that me and Jesy had just left. I followed her, looking back at Jesy, and watching as her and Amana disappeared.

"Amana and I weren't friends, for a long time, Sandin.", Mileeda was saying, as she walked around the large room we were standing in. She was looking around at the scenery. "But now, she is like my sister. I care about her. She is my family. But don't ever tell her I told you this.", she said, giving me a small smile. Mileeda was odd to me. Sometimes, she was cruel, then there are times like right now. "Why tell me, then?", I asked. "I remember when you were born. I knew your parents well, Sandin. It saddened me, what happened to them.", "Because it was your fault.", I said. "No. Your parents knew the risk. They were never expecting children. Yet, you stand before me. A miracle. I know you are very confused as to what you are.", she said, staring at me. "What am I? My mother said I'm invincible.", I said slowly. Mileeda took out her cannon and shot me. I looked at my gut and then passed out.

When I awoke, I was in a bed, next to Red, who was finally awake, and reading something, "Welcome back.", he said. "What? Mileeda... Where the hell is Mileeda?", I said, trying to sit up, and quickly realized, I wasn't as hurt as I thought I'd be. I had never really been shot before. I'd always gotten lucky. I was grazed once, but that healed quickly. "She brought you here. She said, she was showing you what you are.", Red said, looking shocked himself, "I watched her take that shell out of you. She cares about you. I'm surprised. Didn't think Mileeda gave a shit at all really.", Red said. "If she cared about me, I don't think she would have shot me. And why the hell would she...?", I suddenly remembered our conversation. She was close with my parents. I looked at Red, then proceeded out of the med area towards Mileeda's office. I knocked and went in. Emillie was standing in there, along with Jesy, "Look, all I'm saying...is if my mother was really involved with what you and Mileeda are telling me...then I guess I can't be angry. She did what she did, and she got what she got.", Jesy was saying, wiping tears. Mileeda looked towards me, "Emillie, can you take Jesy to the briefing area? I need to have a talk with Sandin.", Mileeda said. Emillie walked to me and kissed me, then led Jesy out. "Sandin, have a seat.", Mileeda said, pointing to a chair. "Now, do you have an understanding of what you are?", she asked. "No.", I said. She sighed, then placed her hands on her desk and faced me, "Sandin, you are not too far from a god. But you aren't completely a god. In truth, I'm the one that created you. I gave your mother something that might...aid in her endeavor to impregnate herself. And all her and your father had to do was find objects that gave off G-energy. When your mother was pregnant, I ran tests to see how you would come out, and I was right. You're different. You not only have the god gene, which connects you to the cosmos, but you also have a strange way of healing quickly and surviving. I've kept track of you your whole life, and always knew that you'd end up sitting across from me.", Mileeda finished saying. I didn't know what to say. "You...created me...by experimenting on my mother?", I asked. "Experimenting? That is a strong...and incorrect term. Your mother and father consented to testing. It wasn't expected to harm your mother, and it didn't. All it did was make you. It was the ring that I have locked away now, that hurt them. Why do you think I've been looking for it, Sandin? I was searching for it, because of what it did to your parents. Amana, blames me, too. You may have noticed, the first time we met.", Mileeda said, now actually wiping tears. I was remembering that night, and Amana did say something about Mileeda being aware of the ring. Plus, now I was thinking about how she commanded Raby not to say anything to her. It was personal. "But, I'm still confused… What did you have to do with my parents? Aside from the fact that they were recruited by you?", I asked. "Sandin, I knew your mother from the time she was six. She was a very smart little girl, and I knew right away that she possessed the gene.", Mileeda said. I was stunned, "I thought that she was just a normal person…", I said, even more confused. "No...she had the gene. The gene was passed onto you. But the ring… The ring altered her reality. And your father's. It showed them things, and they both accepted those things differently. Your mother...wasn't supposed to die how she did.", Mileeda now stood up and covered half her face and was breaking down, "Your mother was almost like a...like a daughter to me. I loved her. I told her the truth about me. About everything. She was the first one I'd opened up to after hundreds of years. When she met your father, I knew that her destiny was beginning. She was good enough to be P.E.D, and Amana wanted her. Amana wants all the smart, capable people. I argued...but Ayrellia wanted it. She looked forward to the adventure. So, I sent her on missions I didn't think would endanger her. But she proved herself. Her, and your father. They were partners. They married each other after three years of working together. They loved each other so much, and that's when Ayrellia learned she couldn't have children. She wanted to have a kid, but she didn't want to give up on being an agent for P.E.D. When she came to me for help, I knew ways...but I also knew that they were risky.", "What ways?", I asked. I couldn't believe what Mileeda was telling me. All this time, I assumed that Amana killed my father for no good reason. Now, I'm learning that my mother was connected to Mileeda. A woman who has hidden herself from her own family. "Well, me and Amana have come up with a lot of cures. Some of them, she came up with herself, but I found the cure for women who can't give birth. I tested it on your mother, which she was willing to do. I had already confirmed that she wouldn't be hurt. So, once she went through the treatment involved with administering the medicine, she came out of it perfect. Even better than perfect.", Mileeda said, now sitting back down. I was thinking hard on this now. "So, my mother was connected to the cosmos already?", I asked. "Yes. Exactly. And the ring only increased her connection. But being that she was only Plinthinian, she couldn't handle that much flow, and it started to cause her grip on reality to slip. Your father believed that you and her would stop something, so he tried to kill you. Amana, who had been keeping a close eye on the two of them, quickly acted, when I couldn't. I wanted to save your mother AND your father, but Amana said he was too far gone. She blamed me for what happened to them, because I never took the time to consider that one of the objects they were searching for, would do something like that. I always made sure they had the protection that they needed.", Mileeda said, sadly. I didn't know if I wanted to hear anymore. I'd heard enough. I understood why my father was dead. My mother, being recently killed by Awalli, made me feel even more angry. But, Mileeda keeping it a secret that she knew my mother well, was more of a blow. "Sandin...your parents made me your godmother, in case something happened to them. But you raised yourself well. You took care of Ayrellia, and I watched you succeed in school. You never needed me.", she said, smiling. Mileeda is my godmother. This was crazy. "Can I leave?", I asked. Mileeda looked slightly hurt, but nodded. I stood up, then thought of something, "Why is Amana so cruel to Emillie?", I asked. "That is because she is ashamed. She never wanted a child. Plus, there is more to Emillie's existence than you might think.", Mileeda said. "What does that mean? And what do you mean she never wanted a child?", I asked. "Amana is...well, she just never thought any man was good enough for her. She had very high standards. Emillie's father, of course, won out, but he didn't do it easily. And when Amana was pregnant, it was a nightmare. For me, her, and everyone on this Base. She made us all deal with it. As soon as Emillie was born, she dumped her on Dalia and moved on. Sure, she kept watch to make sure she wasn't losing control of herself, but she didn't want to be bothered playing mommy. If she had, we wouldn't be in the situation we are in, but Amana just has to be Amana.", Mileeda said, now sort of smiling. I didn't ask anything else and walked out. I couldn't wait to tell Red, Mileeda is my godmother, and that she knew my mom, and that my mom always had a connection to the cosmos. I was walking towards the med area where Red was, when something else occurred to me. Mileeda said she met my mother when she was six. So, how did she meet her?

Who were her parents? Why would a three-thousand year old woman befriend a six-year-old girl? This was the million-shills question.

JESY: After I had gotten Amana to her office, she pointed her cannon at me, and told me to leave. I didn't second guess. So, I made my way to the quarters I was given. It was small, but I didn't complain. I went to sleep. When I awoke, Emillie was waiting outside my room, "Can we talk?", she asked me. "Sure. I don't think I have a choice.", I said darkly. I didn't want to talk to her. She was the triple threat. She killed my stepfather, the one thing that changed me and my mother's life. She killed my mom, which, I don't have to explain how I obviously felt about that. Then, on top of all of that, she is fucking the man I love...which after last night, I was reminded why I loved him in the first place. He was different. I never realized how different. He saved me so many times, and the way he used to look at me...it just made me cringe. I was so happy to be with him, then we started to argue. It was really silly things at first, but then it grew to more serious stuff. Finally, we broke it off, and ignored each other for months. Then I hear he has dropped off the force, and then I find him being held by the cult my parents were involved in. "I'm really sorry that you had to learn I killed your parents.", she said. "What's done is done.", I said. There wasn't much else I could say. Mileeda was walking towards us, and she directed that we follow her. Once in her office, Mileeda directed me to sit down. "So...it's time we talk, Jesy. Your parents were trying to commit a great crime against the planet. And you were, too, by default. But, Amana has taken you on.", Mileeda said. I didn't say anything. Everyone had been saying my parents were evil. Mileeda looked at Emillie. "Listen, the other me...she showed me what your mother and stepfather were doing.", Emillie said, sadly. "What?", I asked, feeling like they couldn't have done anything that bad. "Well, they were...", "Killing children.", Mileeda finished Emillie's sentence. I looked at both of them like they were crazy, "WHY WOULD THEY DO THAT?!", I yelled. "To perform a curse, you must give sacrifices. Most of those sacrifices include the murder of innocents. You see…", Mileeda said, now standing up, and going to a cabinet, "…depending on the curse, you may have to kill thousands, or sometimes hundreds. In this case, Lopim has been making sacrifices for years. Sacrificing those nobody would think to look for. Now, he is closer than ever to freeing my sister from The Void. That's why Lona, or rather, Althea, is here. She is here to make sure he succeeds. We must focus mostly on two things. First, we must ensure that there are no more sacrifices. Next, we must find Lopim, and kill him, for good. Your parents were manipulated into thinking they were special, because Lopim comes across as a powerful man. But I taught him what he knows. So, in a way…it's truly my fault your parents are dead.", Mileeda said. I thought about what she was saying. "Listen, I know my parents were wrong. I was a GF officer, and I can admit that if someone did something they shouldn't have, then they have to pay. I'm not happy Emillie killed my parents, but she did what she had to do.", I said. Emillie looked at me, lost. "Look, all I'm saying…is if my mother was really involved with what you and Mileeda are telling me…then I guess I can't be angry. She did what she did, and she got what she got.". I noticed Sandin had entered the office, and Mileeda asked me and Emillie to leave. Emillie made sure to kiss Sandin before we walked out.

As we proceeded down the hall, Emillie was walking with me, nervously giving me side glances. I ignored them as long as I could, "What do you want?", I asked her, finally growing tired of her constant staring. "Well…", she said nervously, "…how do you feel about me and Sandin?", she asked me, in a scared tone. "Well, the truth is, I'm sort of confused. I don't understand how you two came together. Im trying to understand that.", I said. "We met at the number seven precinct.", she said. "Well, I'm still confused about how that happened.", I said. She looked like she was thinking hard about this, "Well, I just know him.", "That doesn't tell me anything.", I said. "I know him. I was a part...of him, for at least two months.", she said, still thinking. "You were a part of him?", I asked. I remembered Sandin telling me how she died, and her soul went to him. I still didn't believe she died and came back, but after everything else I've seen, I didn't know what to think anymore. "When we were joined, I didn't remember that I had died. I didn't know what was happening. But I kept dreaming I was at his house, and at the same time, I kept dreaming about this field of grass.". I was even more confused now. "I know, it's confusing. I'm still trying to understand myself. But, the main thing is that he and I have something that I can't explain.", she said. "Emillie, can you please leave me alone?", I asked her. She looked slightly hurt, but then decided to turn and walk away from me. I watched her walk away and she turned and looked back at me. Then she left officially and I was now left by myself.

    I wanted to explore the Base some more, but then decided that I'd go visit Red. When I arrived in his room, he was getting his wounds cleaned. I waited until the nurse was done. When she had left the room, I quickly found a seat next to Red, "So, what is going on?", I asked him. "Considering that I was knocked out due to bullets I shot, getting thrown back at me, I couldn't tell you. But from what I read in this paper, I see that Sicilia was strangely attacked after we left. I see that Emillie is known to almost all of Sicilia now. And I also see that there is a new goddess threat.", Red said, looking at a newspaper. "Well, I'm referring to what you think about Emillie.", I said. "She is a nice girl.", "A nice girl, who murdered my parents. A nice girl who killed mobsters and cult members. A nice girl.", I said sarcastically. "Look, you're new to this situation. From everything I've been through, I can tell you that poor Emillie isn't always in control of her actions. She IS a nice girl, but the thing is, she doesn't fully understand herself.", "Do you think that she should be with Tillo?", I asked. Now, Red gave me a certain look, "Bonnly, are you asking me this because you're jealous?", Red asked, in what seemed to be a reprimanding tone. "No...I'm asking this, because it seems strange. Sandin thinks he is a god, Lody.". Red didn't seem surprised. "You didn't see how Mileeda cared for him, after she shot him. There is a connection, and I'm waiting for Tillo to tell me what.", he said. "Well, she did take him, after she fought Amana.", "They fought?", Red said, surprised, and dropped his paper. I quickly told him the story of me and Sandin's rendezvous at the damaged area of Base. "Have you had the briefing?", he suddenly asked me. "Not yet. I guess Emillie was supposed to take me. But, I can't be around her. She is weird. Why can't Sandin see that?", I asked. I'd known Sandin Tillo for six years. It struck me as odd, that a guy as smart as him, was confused about having a girlfriend that was obviously dangerous in multiple ways. "He does.", Red said flatly, "But, you haven't been here from the beginning. I didn't catch on, either. But after she came back...", he said. "Came back? You mean from the dead?", I asked. "Well...it isn't how it sounds. Look, Amana used Emillie's DNA to make another her. Then, they figured out that her essence was inside Tillo. They extracted it from him, then put it in the new vessel.", Red said, looking surprised he even knew what he was talking about. I was taking in his words, shocked, of course. Emillie. The girl I was just walking with is only a few months old...technically. But her essence is the same twenty year old girl she was before. "What happened to her? How did she die? Exactly?", I asked. It was then that Red embarked on the full story of what had happened so far. During most of the story, I was lost. I had to ask several questions. But the part that stuck with me was that Emillie and Awalli were drawn to one another. From the very beginning of the story, it was Emillie and Awalli. Awalli approached me, saying she wanted to kill Emillie. Now she is doing what? "Red, have you heard anything about Awalli?", I asked him. He put his arms up in the air, in a questioning motion, and looked around sarcastically. "Okay. You could have just said no.", I said. "Bonnly, I'm trying to figure out something. Awalli, is at the back of my mind. I'm worried about this new goddess.", Red said, picking the paper back up. "Well, Emillie is gonna kill her.", I said. "Maybe not...", Red replied, "I saw her. Her portrait is in those ruins. Those portraits you can't mess with or damage. Amana is in there. So is...Dalia.", Red said, almost like it seemed hard to say. "What is your point?", I asked. "Well, think about it. Amana knows who she is.", Red said. "You're right. Maybe I can just ask her.", "Don't go to that office without that briefing. These women don't mess around, Bonnly. You've seen what they did to Emillie.", Red said. Her face looked pretty through all the scars, bruises, and fresh cuts. It looked like she was literally having the fight of her life every night. "They...did that? Amana and Mileeda? Good.", I said. I knew it was wrong, but a part of me enjoyed Emillie getting some kind of beating. "And Sylvia.", Red added. I thought about it. Sylvia Lon is the direct cousin to the Head of the Royal Family. So, with that said, I knew it was time for that briefing.

Red had told me where to go, from the med house he was in, to the briefing stations. There were a few of them, and he directed me to the nearest one. As I turned on the briefing, it first showed a Phoenix. Then it showed a random man, "Welcome to P.E.D. PLINTHS. EMERGENCY.DEFENSE. I know that you are new, and probably wondering exactly what you are being asked to do. Well, it isn't easy. So listen closely. Lesson number one, gods and goddesses exist. They live among you. Some of these people aren't gods, but will perform deeds almost similar to that of a god or goddess. Lesson number two. So, you are here to help us do anything in our power, to protect the masses and the rest of the planet from these individuals. Now I know the other question you got. Gods and goddesses being real? That is ridiculous. Next you'll be telling me that Princess Amana was a real person. Well... actually...that IS what I'm gonna tell you. And here to speak, and give you some words of encouragement on your journey with P.E.D, General Amana Tia.", the soldier said, and stood to the side. Then Amana walked up and started speaking, "I can't stress enough the seriousness of our existence. If you're watching this briefing, then I thought you had what it takes to handle the blackest, of the darkest ops, you will ever serve upon. So, take that...into high consideration.", Amana said, "But next, do understand that I am indeed over three-thousand years old. And I won't lie to you. I am a goddess. I am the direct child of Sebastian. My father has abandoned this planet. He's left me here to deal with all this bullshit, and I do. So now, you do, too. You will take this position seriously. Because the moment you started this video, it meant, your life is for me, to do with, whatever I please. And also, I am not the only one in command. There are others. But prove yourself more, and they will make themselves known to you. So, take great heed, soldier, for you now not only serve your city, but you now serve your planet.". The video clicked off. I sat for a second, thinking about what I just watched. I didn't know what to think. The daughter of Sebastian kept going off in my head like a firework. Not only that, but then there was the fact that I'd noticed that Amana is Emillie's mother. That was obvious, and I was sure I'd heard it before. Then there was another factor that made me even more concerned. There was that factor that Amana was three-thousand years old. Red and Tillo had this briefing, so they understood all of this. It made sense now why Tillo was so convinced. I wanted him. I saw him walking, confused. Not knowing what to think. I knew when he was making that face, that he needed an outlet. I went to him, "Sandin.", I said. He looked at me. "My mother...", he said, unsure of what to say next. "It's okay. Just tell me.", I said, moving closer to him. He quickly backed away, "Are you insane?", he asked in a hiss, "Emillie will annihilate you.", he said. "Sandin...I know you. Red even TOLD me that you are questioning things with this girl.", I said. "I...love her.", he said, sort of strained. I didn't know what to say. I was angry. I slapped him. He looked at me, then we started kissing. Then he backed off and quickly walked away from me. I knew he was right. I had to stay away. Emillie would kill me. And not metaphorically.

AWALLI: Everything was spinning out of control. I didn't know where to go. I could feel Corsa trying to re-sink her hooks in me, but I wasn't going to give her the chance. I figured I'd get as many shills as I can, and flee to Copania. It was the only place that was non-contracted that wouldn't care about where I was coming from, as long as I had shills. I made it back to the manor. Most of my stash was here. This was a mistake, because most of the men were here trying to clean up. Slith, who had been hurt by Emillie, was looking forward to killing her. He now fully understood what I was telling them from the start. But the only problem was...I wasn't that Awalli anymore. I tried to walk in all tough. I knew I'd have to play it right, if I wanted to walk out of here. "Boss, we were wondering what happened to you. We knew you were in Sicilia, and all that crazy shit happened!", Slith yelled, moving towards me. Li was silent. He wasn't saying anything at all. Just watching me. "Well, I tried to get Tillo, but I failed.", I said, "Look, I'm going upstairs, and I don't want to be disturbed.", I said, moving past Slith, and the rest. I didn't even look back at Li, who I could tell was watching my every move. As soon as I got in my room, I ran for my stash, and started to take as many shills as I could. Lucky for me, shills were light and easy to carry, so I took a good few thousands. As I stood up and thought of going out the window, Li was standing behind me, looking surprised. "Where are you going?", he asked. "Li...move, now.", I said. "You've met our grandmother.", he said. "How...?", I began. "I can feel it. I can't explain it, but I can feel it. What did she do to you?", he said, blocking my path. "MOVE!", I yelled. "What did she do?", he asked again. I held up my free hand and psychically pushed him up against the wall, "When I say move, move!", I yelled. I let him fall. I looked at him, then walked out. "Awalli, wait!", he yelled. He caught up to me. "Listen, you can't run away. We need you! The Hunter is killing off too many of us! You of all people can't abandon us! Not when my sister is already making all those sacrifices you told her to!", he said. I thought about Ethel, and how much she was putting on the line. She wasn't here, because of what I was ordering her to do. I looked at Li. "But...you don't understand.", I said. "No, I do. You're trying to ignore the voice, but I can't let you.", Li said, taking out something I hadn't seen before, and stabbing me with it.

I woke up. I was in my apartment in Nocton. Tic was asleep, and I looked in the corner and saw Sparkz. I got out of bed and went to him. I picked him up, and he woke up. "Sparkz...", I said, crying into his fur. He barked that cute bark he always had. Then, Tic was waking up. "Babe?", he asked, looking around, and realizing I wasn't in the bed. "I'm here. I'm here, Tic.", I said, getting back on the bed and piling myself on top of him. Sparkz jumped onto the bed and we both started to laugh. Then I noticed something. Blood. It was coming from Sparkz. Sparkz wasn't moving anymore. I screamed, and Tic's neck suddenly made a popping sound, and he was bleeding from out of his neck, but was already dead. "No...", I said, crying, and screwing up my face. I just laid there and held them, then, there was something else. A noise. A rattling noise. It was coming from under the bed. I slowly put my foot down and got on my knees and looked. There was nothing, and the noise stopped. Then I stood up, and Corsa was standing behind me. "Please? Just leave me alone...please?", I pleaded. "No. I need you. You have already accepted the meld. I just need you to make the final sacrifice. Then you're free to do whatever you want.", she said. "No. I don't want to...please?", I fell onto the floor in a heap and started to cry profusely. "Listen, child... do this, and you are free. You'll be free. I'll leave you.", she said. "What do you want me to do?", I asked. "Finish what you started. Kill Layna. Kill Emillie. Destroy them. They are Amana's daughters.", "I can't kill Emillie. She is too powerful. And Layna... I love her. She is my family. Please...I don't want to do this...", I said. "You are so pathetic. I've seen so many others with so much more backbone than you are showing me now. You are nothing but a sad, pathetic, little girl. Even Calypsa was braver than this, and she succumbed to my power the same way you have. If you don't play nice, Awalli, I will force you. Which do you prefer? Freedom... or slavery?", Corsa asked. I knew she was right. I was pathetic. Cowering before her. I stood up. I looked her in her eyes. "Screw you.", I said, trying to add bravado, but it faltered under my trembling tone. "Have it your way.", she said. I woke up again. Tic was asleep, and Sparkz was in the corner. I looked around and Corsa was gone. I got out of bed and went to Sparkz, who this time, was already dead. "You killed him.", Tic said, now already out of bed, and standing right next to me. "This isn't real. Stop it, Corsa. STOP IT!", I yelled. I woke up, and was standing inside of a totally different building from the manor. I recognized where I was. It was Ethel's estate. Ethel belonged to a very prominent rich family. I also knew why I was here. I knew that Ethel had the god gene, and I had been teaching her magic so we could fight The Hunter. "Okay, boss, I'm ready.", Ethel was saying. I realized we were right in the middle of a session. How long was Corsa controlling me? "Boss?", Ethel asked, looking at me worryingly. All I did was look at her. "I have to go.", I said. "But, we haven't done anything yet.", said Ethel, grabbing me, and kissing me. I forgot about this. I pushed her away. "I don't want that from you.",

I said. "But…the other night…", "Was a huge mistake. I need to leave.", I said, walking away. Then I felt my body seize up. "BOSS!", Ethel yelled, running to me. "What's the matter?", she asked, placing her hand on my shoulder. "Nnnhhh…Corsa!", I shouted. Then, I woke up in my apartment in Nocton again.

CHAPTER 12

Enter Lona: Emillie's New Lesson

CELDA: Flin and I were thinking of taking another vacation this year. It was something just to take my mind off of everything happening with Emillie and Vaness. I hadn't heard from either one of them since I last saw them, and Vaness didn't seem too happy with Emillie's discovery of herself. Then, Flin called me from work to tell me what was happening in Sicilia, and I couldn't believe what I was watching. Emillie was actually fighting some girl on the screen. They both had swords. Emillie looked incredible, and I wondered just what the hell she had been doing before all of that happened. I tried to call Vaness, but there was no answer, everytime. I was worried about both of them, and needed to see them. Emillie was becoming famous. Everywhere I went, people were talking about the girl with the sword. Emillie.

I had taken Tin to his regular martial-arts class. Flin was himself a Golden Strap, which meant he was a very skilled fighter. Watching my little boy become a fighter was cute at first, but then I started to think I didn't want it to give him the idea that he could go around beating people up whenever he wanted. He was only a Green Strap. Green Straps are the next level after the first, which is No Strap. "Come on, Tin.", I said, as I entered the building after running to the store. It had been two hours and we were now headed home. When we got home, Flin had made a toy replica of Emillie's sword for Tin. Tin was playing with it. I was watching him, while having flashbacks of Emillie on the news that day. There was a knock at my door, and I went to open it, "Hi. I was looking for Flin Nol. Is he in?", asked a handsome young man in a black and purple business suit. He looked like he was probably my age. His hair was a strange purple and black and was combed neatly to the left. "Um, no... he is at work right now.", "Oh...well, maybe I can talk to you. I'm Adem Mccloud. I just wanted to discuss a job opportunity for your husband.". I remembered what Gail said and knew that I wasn't supposed to know who he really is. "Oh...he's not interested.", I said, already closing the door. "Please, Mrs. Nol, you have to understand, I'm only trying to help your family. Your family is important to me.", "Why?", I asked, surprised by this bit of info. "Well, I know Mr. Nol. Flin's grandfather. I know something terrible happened to him. But, that's not why I'm here. I just want Flin to be treated with the respect he deserves.", Adem said, in a very respectable way. I couldn't believe, at all, what I was told about him. "I...guess you can come in.", I said, opening my door. He walked in, and I led him to our dining room, where he sat down, and I went and poured him some lemonade. I handed him the glass. "Mmm, just like my old maid used to make. Very good. This is...homemade?", he asked politely. "Yes, I have a tree out back.", "Very fascinating.", he said. Tin ran into the room with his sword and was slicing it everywhere and hit Mr. Mccloud by mistake, then froze, "Tin, go play in your room!", I yelled. "No. It's actually okay. So, you're, Tin. You are a very brave looking young man. My name is Adem. May I see your sword, sir?", Adem asked, playfully bowing before Tin. Tin brightly nodded and handed it to him. "Wow. This is a copy of the one that the woman on the news held. What do you think of her, Mrs. Nol?", he asked, handing the sword back to Tin, who had now left the room. "I don't know.", I replied. "Really? Well, I guess I'm not here to discuss that. Look, I want to offer your husband a really good position. I want him to be...my Vice President.". I accidentally spilled my lemonade. "I'll be right back.", I said, rushing to grab a towel. As I came back into the room, I just had to know, "Just wondering, are you still offering to pay him seventy-shills an hour?", I asked, wiping my mess. "Well, I was thinking more seventy-five now.", he said, with a smile. "Why?", I asked, "Don't you have a VP?", "Yes, but she hasn't been well lately, and I need someone who can also be a back-up.", he said, suddenly, in a very dark tone. But then he quickly smiled, "So, I'll just leave my card.", he said, putting it on the table. He then stood up, "That was very good lemonade, Mrs. Nol. And I do hope to hear from Flin soon. The board will try to appoint someone if I don't present someone right away.", he said with a smile, "Oh, do you mind if I say bye to your son?", he asked politely. Everything about him suggested, he was a very kind guy, despite his fucked up past. I wondered where he was for the last ten years and wanted to ask, but then thought better of it, "Sure. Tin, come say goodbye to Mr. Mccloud.", I said. Tin came out of his room, still holding the sword. "What do you think of the strange girl?", Adem asked Tin. "My Auntie Emillie? She's my auntie.", he said happily. Adem looked up at me, "Is this true? Are you related to that woman in some way?", he asked, looking at me indifferently. "Well, we grew up together. She is one of my best friends, but we aren't blood. She joined the military.", I said, trying to throw him off. "Is she with the city's military? Or...P.E.D?", Adem asked. I of course knew he knew about them, but didn't think he'd ask ME about that. "Look...I'm not supposed to...", "It's okay. You don't have to say anything. Good day, Mrs. Nol. Tin.", Adem said, walking out. "How about we go see Mother Dalia, Tin?", I asked my son.

We arrived at the manor, which was going crazy. Of course the kids had heard about Emillie, and were all excited. I went to speak with Dalia, who was, like always these days, brooding in her office, "Hello,

Celda.", she said when I entered. "Dalia, tell me what you think about what happened in Sicilia.", I said, sitting down. Tin was playing with the other kids, and showing off his sword. "Oh, what do I think? I think we are all fucked.", she said. "Who was that woman Emillie was fighting?", "She is like myself, three-thousand years old. Another relic, from another time. Her name is Althea. But she goes by Lona, named after her aunt. Her name also happens to mean vengeance.", Dalia said. Now, I was lost. "What was she doing here?", I asked. "What she has always wanted. To kill Amana, and free Corsa from her prison.", "Amana? Emillie's mother? Why does she want to kill her?", "Oh, Amana was being Amana and made a decision that has haunted her for a very long time. She also just so happens to be the one who taught Althea magic, and witnessed her use her teachings to kill her own mother.", Dalia stopped talking. She got up and looked out the window. Emillie was outside. She was walking in. Dalia looked back at me. I went to meet her quickly. The kids were already starting to swarm her. Emillie was smiling, like usual. "CAN WE SEE IT?!", an excited Cynda was yelling. "Yes, stand back.". Dalia was going to rush to her and stop her, but Emillie had already summoned it, "Now, don't touch it. Just look.", she said. They were all mesmerized. I was, too. I couldn't believe it just came from out of nowhere. Then as soon as it appeared, it disappeared. Emillie looked at me and Dalia. Then we all walked back up to her office. "ARE YOU MAD?!", Dalia rounded on Emillie, as soon as the door was closed. "No. I can control it now. I've gotten a lot better, Dalia. And…I needed to see you. Both of you. I had to get off of Base. Things are really stressful.", Emillie said, going to sit down.

We both sat down, listening to Emillie tell us what was going on, "…so now, Sandin and Jesy are acting strange, and I know SOMETHING is going on, but I'm too afraid of asking. I think in my anger, I'd hurt Jesy, and I don't want to do that. Then, my mother, no matter how hard I try to have a relationship with her, she won't talk to me, or even confide in me her full connection to Althea. It's too difficult for her. Then, Mileeda, and her new found love for my boyfriend is just as strange.", Emillie said. "What do you mean?", Dalia asked slowly. Emillie explained how Mileeda is apparently his godmother. "Oh my... Ayrellia... Why didn't I know this sooner? I should have known. But I never knew she was married... Oh my...", Dalia said, now starting to tear up. "Wait...you knew her, too?", Emillie asked. "Well...not really. She was someone that was connected to someone I know. I just...didn't know it was the same Ayrellia. Sandin's mother had the god gene. She was a smart girl. Too smart. So, naturally, she made it onto Amana's radar. But then, I didn't know she had a connection to Mileeda. That explains a lot actually. Well, that's besides the point. How is Lody Red?", Dalia asked. "He was hurt by Awalli, but he is fine now. He's awake anyway. I've gone to visit him everyday. He is really hurting over...", "YES...I understand that.", Dalia cut Emillie off. "How are you doing, Celda?", Emillie asked me. "Flin is taking that Mccloud job.", I said. "But, I thought you told him?", Emillie asked. "I did. But I've decided that I'm not going to allow him to not take it. He is offering way too much money, and he wants to make him his VP.", "Have you spoken to Gail about this?", Emillie asked me. "I don't need her permission. Look, I heard you all out. He's a murderer. But I've met him. He is seriously the kindest gentleman I've ever met. He was really friendly, and good with Tin.", I said. Emillie looked confused. "Of course he is polite. He was raised by Ko-e.", Dalia said, almost in a whisper. "KO-E?!", Emillie said, suddenly alert, "ADEM KNOWS KO-E?!". Emillie had always idolized Ko-e. So, it didn't shock me that she was super excited that Adem knew her. "Yes. But the Ko-e you think you know, Emillie, isn't the Ko-e that I know. She raised him to BE a killer. Polite when he needs to be, but fierce when he has to be. I know.

That's how she trained me, to fight back against your mother.", Dalia said, looking at Emillie. I felt like I should step out. "Red told me she used to...hit you.", Emillie said. I was even more shocked at this info, then all the info I had heard today. "Yes. It first started, when your mother thought she had found a way to bring back Calypsa. When she realized she failed, she was punching and shooting anything in her sight. I only tried to calm her down. But once I told her to give up...she lost it. Nearly killed me. This was when Ko-e and I first became close. She healed me. Then taught me how to protect myself. It was slow at first. I kept saying to myself to stop going back to her, but I couldn't. Everytime, I'd go back, thinking she would change, only to realize she'd gotten worse. Then, Mileeda was upset with her back then. She wanted Amana to pay for what she did to her first born, Vicdor. He was a bad one. He was Althea's lover.". Emillie had a look on her face that suggested that she was ready to leave all of a sudden. "Emillie?", Dalia asked. "Tell me more...of the one you refer to as...Vicdor. How were they lovers?", Emillie asked, in a different tone of voice. "First, tell me, are you Emillie?", Dalia replied. Emillie smiled. "We are one, she and I. My father...has made us so. I must defeat The Dark One. I must defeat Althea, and Lopim, and any who would see her freed from The Void.", Emillie said darkly. "What have you done with Emillie?", I asked. "Nothing.", Emillie said, normally. "We are one. Like she said. But...she is hiding things from me. Like who she really is, why she looks like me, and how she is even a part of me.", Emillie said angrily. "So...you've accepted this?", Dalia asked. "For now.", Emillie said again, in the dark tone. I was confused.

After I had left, Tin and I arrived home. Flin was just sitting in the living room with his head back. I walked up to him, and kissed him, "Sweetie, how was work?", I asked. "I quit. I saw the card on the table. I called Mr. Mccloud. I took the job. I'm sorry, honey. I know what you said about him and all, but…", "I was going to tell you to take it. He came here today. He was very nice.". I told him who raised him, and the things I learned today. "Can things get any crazier? I mean shit, first, Emillie is a goddess, Adem Mccloud is a god and murderer, and Emillie is as well. Now I'm supposed to believe that the man was raised by a fictional goddess?", Flin said. "Well, Amana, IS Emillie's mother. And Mother Dalia, IS over three-thousand years old.", I said. We just looked at each other. I knew what he was thinking. If all this is true, and the things we've been seeing on the news is proof of it, then it is like Dalia told me. We are fucked.

SANDIN: Emillie had left Base, and didn't come say bye to me. I knew she was going to Dalia's. Jesy hadn't come back around me, out of fear that Emillie would kill her. She was somewhere off on Base, training apparently. I went to see Mileeda, who these days, since telling me she is my godmother, had been a lot kinder towards me. As I stood outside of the wall to her office, I entered, and saw her looking at a hologram of someone. A man with short pink hair, and a rugged five o' clock shadow. She was admiring it, then looked up and noticed me. She quickly closed the hologram. "Sandin, how nice of you to visit.", she said, putting the hologram device away. "Who was that guy?", I asked. "An old friend, who is missing at the moment.", she said, sadly. "Listen, I need some more answers. I need to know what it is I can do.". Mileeda stood up, and went to her cabinet. She did whatever spell she had to do to open it, then she took out an old looking book. The cover was actually torn in certain places. "Take this. Read it, and the answers you seek will be provided.", she said, now sitting back behind her desk. "Why are you and Amana so secretive? Why can't I just know who that guy is?", I asked. Mileeda stared at me, then answered, "He is…Amana's brother.", she said. "She has a brother? I didn't know that. That's…really interesting.". No brother was ever mentioned in the fairy tales. "Yes, he wasn't from here. He was sent here because…", she stopped talking, "I'm sorry, Sandin. But THAT is between me, and him. I can't tell you that. What I will tell you…is that you will be meeting him. Now, take that book, and go. There are some things I have to do.", she said, with a kind smile. I got up and walked out. I was looking over the book, when I ran into Tem, "I see Mileeda has given you something special.", he said. "Not really. I barely understand this gibberish.", I replied. I stopped calling him, jealous guy. He was more friendly now since our little adventure. "Look, you need to be careful, man. Trusting Mileeda or Amana too much can have terrible consequences. Look what happened to me. Amana's daughter, your girlfriend, nearly killed me.", he said. "Yes, well she is learning to control all of that.", "And what about the other one. Bonnly? Is she free? I thought I had something with that Lon girl, but she just wanted to get close to her dear grammy.", Tem said. He was definitely trying to score. Jesy was on his radar, and I secretly wanted that to happen. It would put an end to the little triangle developing between myself, her, and Emillie. "Look, I'm going to my room to study this shit.", I said. When I got there, Jesy was waiting outside the door. "So, decided to show your face?", I asked. "Shut up. We need to talk. This is serious. In.", she said, opening my door, and pointing for me to enter. As I did, she followed and closed the door. "I've been hearing something about Captain Brom. Does he sound familiar to you?", she asked. "No. I haven't heard of him.". I felt like I had, but couldn't think where. "Well, I've been hearing talk of a coup. Against Mileeda and Amana. They are planning something. And from what I hear, it goes all the way through to the RF. I'm sure Layna isn't involved, but someone is definitely making something happen. And, I also heard some other whispers. Like, Lopim is also involved. This is all connected.", Jesy said. I thought about what she was saying. Usually, Amana and Mileeda were on top of things, so I didn't have to say anything. "But, Jesy, how are you getting all this info?", I asked. "Some of the soldiers. They are on board, and have slipped little hints. They don't like how Amana runs this place, and Brom is apparently an ex-Nocton soldier. He was in high-intelligence. Mileeda or Amana recruited him. So, now he wants to overthrow them...?", she questioned. I was confused, too. This didn't make sense. Well, some of it did, but there was a large factor that was really confusing. Like who is Brom, and how much power exactly does he have within P.E.D? Jesy opened my door. "Keep a lookout.", she said, and walked out.

Later, I was with Red. He was healing nicely, but was still bed ridden. "So, what has Mileeda told you now?", he asked me, as I was showing him the book. "Well, she wants me to read this. She said it will show me what I need to know.", I said. "Well, have you looked into it?", "I did...for a second. But, Red, I'm not a magic guy.", "According to a woman older than both of us, you are. Look, if she says read it, you should. She wouldn't do anything to hurt you, Sandin.", "Are you sure about that? I feel like she is trying to manipulate me.", "I don't think so. If she was, I'd know. I'm telling you, man, she loves you. She may have been absent in your life, but she definitely has been watching you.", Red said. He was learning a lot from his med room, apparently. "I don't know, mate...it all seems really strange. How could she have known my mother? I seriously am very confused about that part. She wasn't clear on how she knew my mother.". This was true in every way. She didn't say how exactly she knew her, but just that she knew her as a child, and watched her grow up. She had the god gene, so most likely, I inherited it from her. Then more than that, there was also the fact that she couldn't even have children, then I was born. "You're worried about the wrong stuff. Althea should be our main focus, and helping Emillie defeat her.". Emillie was avoiding me. Jesy and I had kissed, once, and never again since then. But Emillie was acting like I was meeting her and screwing her. I knew Emillie had gone to Dalia's, and I decided I was going down as well.

EMILLIE: Dalia and I were alone now. Celda had left after she felt she couldn't take anymore info. Dalia and I sat for a minute just staring at one another. "Vicdor was evil. Mainly because he was spoiled. He was half-Plinthinian, half-god. So, of course, he had women lined up outside the castle, and a whole lot of anger.", Dalia said. "Why was he angry?", "Well, because his mother was ashamed of what he had grown into. His father was too weak to do anything against him. Nigel, never prepared for such things. He thought he was on top of the world having a goddess as a queen.". For a minute, I had almost forgotten that she was speaking of Mileeda. "So, what happened to her other children? Didn't she have other children? Weren't they gods?", "Well, that is a bit harder to explain, Emillie. You see, Vicdor was Mileeda's first child. He carried most of her genes. Some of the Royal Family you see today are descendents of concubines and the like. Didn't you ever wonder WHY Mileeda loathes her family so much?", Dalia said, with a very dark tone, "All of the children that are left today, are the descendants of Vicdor. The other children…unfortunately all died. Very terrible deaths, I'm afraid.", Dalia now switched to a sad tone. "So, what you're saying…is that the entire Royal Family is made up of children that all originated from sluts three-thousand years ago?", other me asked. "I suppose that is the easiest way to put it.", Dalia said, chuckling somewhat. "No wonder… Sylvia…", I said. "Emillie, how are you able to cope with two personalities?", Dalia asked. "I…just do, I guess. But, I wish I could see who she really is.", "Do you know what happened between Vicdor and Althea, Emillie?", asked Dalia, suddenly. "No. I guess they were screwing each other?", "More than that. Althea saw herself in him. Someone who would do whatever it takes for ultimate power. And he saw the same in her. They were ruthless together. And almost nobody could stop them. Ko-e and I were fighting in this war together. We were trying our best to end it. Along with Mileeda's other children. But then...Vicdor was found dead. Then on top of that, Althea was missing. Nobody knew who it was. Until, Ko-e told me that Amana had visited her, with Althea all tied up. She told me what your mother did. She killed Althea's child. Her unborn child.". I stood up. I was taken aback by this info. I knew she killed Vicdor, but he sounded like an asshole who should die. But then, to hear my mother killed an innocent babe before it even entered the world, "How could she do that?", I said, already feeling my tears come. "I told you, she has lived with the regret of that decision for...", "Don't. Don't try to make her seem like the victim now.", "Emillie, that was three-thousand years ago! And your mother did that because Althea killed children! She didn't believe she deserved a child after everything she did. Althea killed her own mother for Bastian's sake, Emillie! Don't feel sorry for her.", Dalia said, giving me a very stern look. But I was already seeing how my mother chose that child's fate. "She couldn't have just taken the child from her? She had to kill it?", I asked. "Sure, she could have. Ko-e said the same thing. But what you don't understand is that Althea is the most evil thing to exist. Unlike Awalli, she isn't being controlled, and she was this way BEFORE your mother killed her child.". To this, I didn't know what I could say. "But...that child didn't do anything. She didn't have to kill that poor baby...", I said. "Emillie, Amana has always made the hard choices. It's the reason why she is where she is today. But, what I need you to get, is that Althea betrayed all of us. She killed her mother, Alexa, then she killed a lot of innocent people. Then she teamed up with Vicdor, and committed even more atrocities. So, yes, you can understand why your mother did what she did.". This was true. I did understand now. Didn't make what Amana did any better, though.

I had decided to leave Dalia's. As I was, Sandin was walking up. We looked at each other, then I walked up to him. "What are you doing here?", I asked him. "I came to see you.", "Why?", "I need you.", he replied. "Where is Jesy?", I asked. "Please, Emillie, there is nothing going on between us. We used to work together, and YES, we used to sleep together, but not now. You're the one I love.", Sandin said, holding out his hand. "Well...what about Mileeda?", I asked now. "What about Mileeda?", "Do you love her?", I asked. Sandin gave me a strange look. "Emillie, you are the only woman I've been with in months. Mileeda isn't even on my radar. Plus, she thinks of herself as my godmother. So, what are you talking about?", he asked me. "Sandin, right now, I'm not in the mood.". Sandin looked at me like I was a new person. "What's happened?", he asked me in a serious tone, "Let's go for a drink.".

We were sitting in The Dattur. I was looking into his eyes, and he was looking into mine. "Emillie, Jesy said that she has been hearing some strange talk.", he said, in a really low tone. "Like?", I asked. He leaned in closer and looked around to make sure that nobody was listening to us. "She says that someone is trying to get rid of your mom and Mileeda.", he said. I thought about this. While it did indeed seem probable, the likelihood that they would succeed was very low. My mother and Mileeda were way too smart. They would see through this right away. "I'm sure they are aware.", "No, I don't think that they are. I think that whoever this person is...has made sure it won't get back to them.", "Didn't you say Jesy has been hearing about this? If she has heard it, what makes you think that my mother and her friend don't know?". Sandin sat back. "I didn't ask them, either...", he said, thinkingly, "Actually...Raby did say something before...about not trusting Amana. But at the same time...she does take orders from Mileeda as well. The whole Base knows about Mileeda, but nobody down here knows Amana or Mileeda exist. The RF has some connections in P.E.D, that, I'm sure of. But where does that connection come from?", Sandin was saying all this, with a certain questioning tone with every word. He was trying to put the pieces together. I understood. He didn't want to approach my mother if she already knew about this and was doing something about it. "Is Gail still on her mission, Emillie? Have you heard from her?", he asked. "I don't think anyone has. But I also haven't tried to call her.", "Well, give her a ring.". I took out my cell and dialed Gail's sequence. The sound started off, and then, "Emillie?", "Yes. Gail, how are you?", "I'm good. How about you? I saw you, you know? You were incredible. Just wonderful.", Gail said. I could hear laughter in the background and the sounds of what sounded like a t.v, "Gail, where are you?", I asked. "Home. I'm vacationing. Didn't your mother tell you? Awalli is finished. And as for Adem…Mileeda said to do nothing. So, I'm home.". I thought about it, and felt relieved. I knew where she was. I nodded to Sandin to indicate she was okay. "What about Yencid?", asked Sandin. "Gail, what about Yellfy? Where is he?", I asked. "He is still on mission. It's classified. I can't share it with you. But you should stay focused on your mission.", Gail said, in a surprisingly urgent tone. "My mission?", I asked. "Yes. You need to stop that woman. Your mother has briefed me on her. She hasn't briefed too many about her. But she is trying to kill your mother.", "I know already. Dalia explained it.", "Well… did Dalia tell you everything?", she asked me. "Everything being what, exactly?", "I'm talking about the spell, Emillie. Did she tell you about the spell?". Gail grew silent. She was waiting for an answer. "No. There was no spell mentioned.". Gail didn't say anything at first, then said, "Emillie, there are places on this planet that have certain information. I think you should go to these coordinates I'm sending you.". Gail hung up, and suddenly I received a message. I opened it and it said; (21, 45, 98). I showed Tillo, and he examined it, then looked up, "You think they'd let us borrow one of those flyers they got on Base?", "Why?", "Because these coordinates indicate that we will be needing to fly.". I stared at him in disbelief. "Sandin...there is something I need to show you...lets go, where no one can see us.".

I led Sandin out back. We looked around to make sure nobody was around. Then I grabbed him and kissed him, "Do you trust me?", I asked him. "Always.", he answered. "Then hold onto me.", I said, as we began to lift off the ground. "Emillie, is it too late to take back what I just said?", he said, laughing. As we soared into the sky, I asked him to direct us to where we needed to go. Sandin used my cell. He was riding on my back and telling me which direction to fly. There were times where he would lean in, and kiss my neck, or nibble my ear, and finally, I decided to land us. "Emillie, we aren't there yet.", "I don't care. Come here.", I said, already throwing my clothes off. We made love on an island that I had landed us upon. Afterwards, I began to explore the island. There were some things I noticed right away. "Sandin! Come look at this!", I called. Sandin came. "What the hell? This is just like at Base. No wonder this island is located way out here. Nobody ever comes here.", "Nobody ever comes here, because they don't have the magic that we possess.", I said, feeling like I completely understood where we were. We were looking at the strange circle language, that for some reason, I could make out what it said. "There are only two...but only one, will bring death to all.", I read. "Emillie...you can read this?", "Yes...I don't know why. But what does that even mean?", I asked, confused. Looking at the message again, I realized that this was some sort of warning. "Let's get to the place we were headed.", Sandin said. He held onto my neck as we flew back into the air. We made our way to the coordinates that Gail had given us, and landed on an even more secluded island. This one had the unmistakable rubble of past buildings. Sandin suddenly had a fit. He fell onto the ground and started to convulse. "SANDIN!", I yelled. I tried to help him, but when

I did, a force threw me back. I looked up, and saw Althea. She was sitting on a rock, "This used to be an important place.", she said. I stood up and summoned my sword. She summoned her's as well. Lopim had come from around a large boulder, and Sandin, who was calming down, noticed him, and pulled out his cannon, "No use for that, Mr. Tillo. I've only come to talk.", Lopim said, smiling. Althea stepped closer, and I raised my sword. "Please? Ladies, lets just talk.", Lopim said. "Quiet.", Althea commanded, "Emillie… You're Amana's daughter… I don't want to have to kill you, but I'll do it if you don't step aside.", "What's here?", I asked. "Something important. Now, step aside.", she said, stepping closer to me. I rushed at her, and Sandin began firing at Lopim, who disappeared, then reappeared next to Sandin, and smacked him. He was incredibly strong. Sandin flew some feet and hit the ground. I didn't have time to worry about him and see if he was okay, because Althea was swinging her blade at me. I was deflecting her swings and blocking her attempts to run me through. She did a double turn that tricked me for a split second and she was able to kick me. I flew into a small hill made of stone. I pulled myself out of there and immediately looked for Sandin. He was fighting Lopim, who was also a skilled fighter. He was punching Sandin, while Sandin blocked his blows. He finally landed a blow of his own, and I was surprised to see that it actually affected Lopim. Sandin, too, looked surprised, and in that instant, Althea came at him. He shot at her, but she deflected his shells with her sword. I flew forward and hit her with my shoulder. She was knocked away, but was able to catch her footing. She quickly came back at me, and again, we were both swinging our swords. Sandin, who had finally got over the distraction, started looking for Lopim again, found him when he turned around, and Lopim had struck him. I could hear what Lopim was saying to him, "Mileeda has given you the book. I can feel its energy coming off of you. But you don't know what to do with something like that, do you, Mr. Tillo?", Lopim was saying. Sandin put his hand up, and I saw Lopim fly back. Althea caught me off guard and had actually managed to slash my side. I stepped back, holding my side, while blood flowed into my hand, and Althea was coming closer. Then, she was blown away by an invisible force. I looked up and Sandin was holding his hand out for me. I took it, and he led me deep into the wooded area of the island. "The coordinates are just a bit farther north. We have to get distance between us and them.", he said, pulling my hand in a panicked manner. I looked back, afraid of Althea catching up to us. "Wait, Sandin, what was that? How did you use your energy like that?", I asked. I had been studying energy waves and learning how to produce my energy into a weapon, but Sandin has already learned this. "First thing I read in that book.", he said, still pulling me, and rushing me away. My side was bleeding more and more and I felt my grip on Sandin's hand falter. I fell to the ground, Sandin still holding my hand. He turned and tried to pull me up, "Come on, Emillie! We can't stop here!", he said. Then, Lopim appeared and punched Sandin, who didn't fly back this time, but rather, started to exchange blows with the old man. Althea landed right next to me. She raised her sword and I quickly summoned mine and deflected her attack. "Give up.", she said. I tried to stand, but found it difficult at the moment. Just then, there was another strange energy. But this one, I felt upon me. I was able to stand. I summoned the black and red armor unto myself, and began to come at Althea with brand new vigor. She was having a hard time keeping up with me. Then, I sent the sword away and began to fight with my fists. I punched her with my right hand, and she stumbled some, and I advanced. I kept coming at her, with rights and lefts, then a spin kick to the face. She hit a tree and I summoned the sword and pointed it at her neck, "You give up.", I said. She smiled, then summoned a different weapon. She had summoned a cannon. She shot me in my gut and the shell bounced off of my armor. Now she looked scared. "I wasn't told of this… You're like a mini-Trinity. There are two of you…", she said, more to herself. She managed to kick me, and give herself enough space to start chanting a spell, "SLOVABENDA!", she shouted, and then I saw everything starting to burn. The trees were catching fire, and everything else around. But somehow, I knew what to do. I raised my sword, and a cold air filled the whole area. It was so cold, the fire started to falter. "No…", Althea said, looking at me truly for the first time. She stopped what she was doing, "Emillie…you are truly powerful. Your mother is a fool to underestimate you. Join me. We can kill her together, Emillie. She abandoned you just like she abandoned me. She taught me everything, then she tried to kill me. She succeeded in killing my child. She killed my lover. She doesn't deserve to live, Emillie.", "YOU KILLED INNOCENTS! DON'T TRY AND PLAY STUPID!", I yelled. Now I did understand what Dalia was telling me. Althea was an evil witch. She had no remorse for her crimes. "There are ways to depower you, Emillie, but I don't want to do that. I'd rather you join us. I can teach you what your mother is too afraid of teaching you. I know things about you, that, trust me, you want to learn about yourself. But if I'm forced to depower you, then you will be useless.", she said, now holding her hand out for me. I looked over at Sandin, but noticed him and Lopim weren't in sight. "Well? What is it going to be, Emillie?", "I'll never join you.", "Well, then I won't regret this too much, then.". Althea reached up into the air. I threw my sword at her, and she disappeared. Then, she appeared behind me. I turned and started to fight her, but she quickly subdued me. It became obvious at that moment, that she had been holding back the entire time. She was a lot like my mother. Fast, and almost impossible to land a hit on. She quickly took me down and then stuck me with a blade. It hurt going in, but when she removed it, it wasn't blood on the end of it, but rather a glowing black energy. I felt weaker, then she kicked me in my face. I stood up, and realized the armor was gone, and I was wearing my regular uniform again. I summoned the sword, but it was different. There was no black, only red. I tried coming at her, but my wound she had inflicted earlier was slowing me down. She was playing with me now. Hitting me, and watching me stumble. "You should have joined me. Now, you'll die, and I can rub it in Amana's face.". Sandin, at that moment, finally reappeared. He pointed his hand at Althea, but this did nothing. She continued to beat me, then waved her arm, and Sandin went flying into a tree. He was knocked out. "You want to know what's here? Let me show you.", Althea said, reaching deep into the dirt. She was using some sort of magic so her arm went through the dirt. When she reached up, she was holding a glowing orb. It was glowing silver and I could feel the energy coming from it. It was someone's essence. "This... belongs to someone who I've kept in good condition for a long time. And now, they shall have their essence back.", Althea said happily. I aimed my sword at the orb and suddenly heard a voice in my head, "It's pointless. Let her take it. She still won't win.". I looked up at Althea, then she planted her foot on my face, and I was out.

CHAPTER 13

Who Is Septima?

SANDIN: Lopim was too strong for his age. I could tell right away that this was obviously magic. Plus, I saw him die, and here he is again. I was shooting at him, but his ability to teleport made it easy for him to dodge my shells. I then went for him physically and was surprised to find that I could actually hurt him. Then I aimed my palm at him and my attempt at magic worked. I was shocked, and in that confusion, Althea had gotten the best of Emillie. I rushed in their direction. Emillie was on the ground while Althea punched the shit out of her. I tried using my magic on Althea, but with one wave of her hand, I was knocked out.

When I came to, Emillie was sitting against a tree, bleeding. She looked like she was holding on to life, barely. "Emillie…", I said, moving to her. I kneeled down beside her, and she was retching up blood, "The… wound…it…isn't normal.", she said. I looked at what she was talking about, and realized the cut on her side was swollen and bleeding profusely. "MILEEDA!", I shouted, hoping she'd hear me, and come fetch us. The whole situation was making it seem stupid that Emillie and I flew here on her own prowess, despite how impressive it was. Mileeda appeared next to me and Emillie. She looked down at Emillie, and shock crossed her face. She touched her, and then disappeared, leaving me behind on the island. Then, she reappeared. "What were you two doing here?", she asked. "Raby told us we'd find answers here.", "Answers?", Mileeda repeated, "That stupid woman. Well…I don't mean that. But I do blame Amana for this. Amana, and her constant heartache.", "What does that mean?", I asked. "The one who was buried here. The essence that was in the ground.". Mileeda looked mortified, and then started to become more aware of something. "Sandin, I need you to get back to Base, tell Amana The Willet has been breached.", Mileeda said, staring at a spot in the ground. She went to it, and her whole arm fit into it. Then, anger crossed her face, "Althea…", she said, "Sandin, why are you still here?", she asked. "Because, how do you expect me to leave?", I replied. "Have you been reading the book?", she asked. "I've barely read the front of it. I learned about energy waves, but what are you expecting from me?", I asked her. "Sandin, I don't have time to baby you. I'll take you to Base myself, but you need to study. IF you had been studying like I told you to, you could have healed Emillie. Now, I'm afraid, she is in more danger than she can know. The other part of herself is dead. Gone. She isn't two anymore.", Mileeda said. "Isn't that good?", "No, it isn't. Emillie is now what she was, prior to her death. She may still have some of her power, but without the other her, she isn't strong enough to face Althea.", Mileeda said, grabbing my arm. We were back on Base. We appeared right outside of Emillie's med room. There were nurses in there trying to patch up her wound, which was still bleeding. I looked at her life monitor, and realized she was fading. Jesy and Sylvia were also watching, "Come on, Emillie…", Slyvia was saying. Jesy was watching the scene with a mixture of pity and content, "Tillo, how did this happen?", Jesy asked. I looked, and Mileeda had taken off. I quickly told Sylvia and Jesy the story, "So, what are you waiting for, you fool? If my grandmother told you to do something, you should hurry and do it!", Sylvia yelled at me. I looked at Emillie one more time, then decided to rush off to my room. Once inside, I was finding it hard to focus. Emillie kept fading in and out of my mind. I kept seeing her coughing up blood, and looking into my eyes as if it were the last time she would. I thought about Althea, or Lona, or whatever she wanted to be called, and told myself, next time, I'll kill her.

I had been reading the book for a few hours. In my haste to read and forget about the situation, I had forgotten about Emillie. When I came to, I just finished reading the twentieth page, which spoke about dimensions. It didn't tell me how to open portals, but I could tell it was a serious subject, because it went on for at least thirty pages. The thirty pages were just info on the different dimensions and their importance to the balance of everything. I wondered how in the world I would be able to open doors to other worlds, when there was a knock on my door. I went to open it, and it was Tem, "Emillie is alright, man. She is just resting. It was some dark magic used on her. She is weak, but alive. She was asking for you earlier.", "I had to read this book.", I replied. "I get it. Mileeda gave that to you. She never gives anyone shit, except punishment. But why did she give that book to you?", Tem asked. "She says that it'll make me stronger.". Tem looked like he had to think about this, then decided to drop it. "Can we talk? It's pretty serious. It's about Red.", he said. "What about him?", "Well, he isn't laid up in the med house anymore, and nobody has really seen him. Is he the type that would be up to something?", "No. Red and I are new here and really have no idea what the hell is going on most of the time.". Tem leaned in close, "Yeah, I agree. But Bonnly...she is another story, though. What do you think?", he asked. "Dude, I told you, take your shot, I'm not going to care.", I said. "I'm not talking about hooking up with her. I'm referring to the fact she has been trying to enter Amana's secret room. Amana has a secret room where she keeps something hidden from everyone. Even Mileeda. Jesy has been desperately trying to enter into that room. Why? And how is it that she is doing so without fear of Amana?". Tem had a very good point. Although I had discovered her in the ruins looking around before, this was different. If it's a room Amana doesn't talk about, or tell anyone what she has in there, including Mileeda, then that means that Jesy is asking for it. "I don't know what to say to that. Maybe she doesn't know.", "Everyone knows that if a door is locked, or you're not supposed to be on a certain part of Base, they know that means severe punishment. But your old gal doesn't seem to care about that. Even worse…", Tem stepped even closer, "…is that she is being controlled. I'm telling you, because I was ordered to tell you, and no one else.", "Ordered by whom?", I asked. "Who else? Amana. She said that Jesy is being possessed by an entity from another dimension, and that to save her, it will require something out of that book. In other words, YOU have to do something.".

LODY: Emillie was stable, but she had fallen asleep. She was calling for Tillo, who had departed to go study that book he got from Mileeda. I saw Amana watching Emillie sleep. She was stroking her hair, and for the first time since I've been on Base, treating her like her daughter. She looked like she was pissed, but was holding in all her anger. I didn't want to enter the room, because I didn't want to disturb the moment. "Mr. Red, come in here, please?", Amana said. I walked into the room. "Say what you want to say.", she said. I didn't know where to start. "This could have been avoided, if you told your daughter the truth about herself, as soon as she was old enough. Awalli probably never would have killed her, if you had warned her and prepared her for the possibility.", I said in what I hoped was not a too reprimanding tone. "I agree, and disagree. Had I told my daughter the truth, she would have grown up with a high opinion of herself. Much like Mileeda's children, and her descendants.", Amana said, still stroking Emillie's hair, "I love my daughter, Lody. I know it seems like I've been nothing but cruel to her. Even abusive at times, but what she IS, Mr. Red. What she is…is incredible. I returned her from death, because I was granted one chance. But if she dies again, I can't bring her back. That will be the end of her. Im such a fucking idiot. Althea almost took her from me. She already has taken someone else special. Someone who was special to Emillie, too.", "Who?", I asked, thinking it must be her father. "Her sister, Mr. Red. Emillie's twin sister.". I was stunned. "Twin sister? But…how?", I asked. This didn't make sense. "When Emillie was born, her sister came right after her. But her sister was stolen from me. Later, I found out she was murdered by her kidnapper. That kidnapper… didn't realize I had TWO children, so that is why I gave Emillie up. I did it because I have many enemies, and they will use Emillie against me. Her sister, Septima, was already taken, but her father contained her essence. When I brought Emillie back in her new vessel, Septima entered into the vessel as well. She fused with her sister, much like how Trinity is made up of my mother and her sister's.". I was having a hard time taking it all in. Septima… Emillie's sister. "So, what you're telling me now, is that Septima was the other half of Emillie? She is the girl who went on the killing spree for three days? The one who has been overtaking Emillie's mind at certain times. That's Emillie's sister? How is something like that even possible, Amana?", I asked, soaking in my confusion and losing myself in the thoughts that followed. "Trinity is made up of my mother, Micka, and Alex. They were sisters. But, they were reborn as sisters. Originally, they were Trinity. Emillie and Septima were born separately, but some gods or goddesses are born with this ability to fuse with his or her siblings, becoming an ultra being.". I was speechless. "Septima comes from a realm where death works differently. This is the reason why she was able to hide her identity from her sister. Septima had to place her essence within Emillie, in order to live in our dimension, because where she comes from, her vessel cannot leave. Mr. Red, I once killed an innocent child, before it was even born. Septima, was my punishment from the cosmos. Emillie is my reminder of that. I couldn't lose her, the way I lost Septima. It hurt...worse than losing Calypsa.", Amana said, now starting to break down over her daughter. It was the first time I'd ever seen her act this way. "Is this why this Lona woman wants to kill you? You killed her child?", I asked. "Oh, it's a lot more than that, Mr. Red. You see, I'm the only one who knows her dirty secret. And through that alone, we were enemies. But worse is that she is actually done with the vengeance side of her quest to kill me. No. There is much more. But I can't tell you everything. Plus, that isn't the main concern at the moment. I need you to stay with Emillie, until she wakes up. When she does, give her this.", Amana was handing me the ring that Mileeda had taken from Tillo. "But I thought this thing had nothing to do with Emillie?", "It has everything to do with her. It belonged to her father. It was his ring. This ring... This cursed object, destroyed the Tillos, and imbued Sandin with the flow of the cosmos. Now it's all about what the ring will do for someone like Emillie.", Amana said, standing, and walking towards the door. She took another look at Emillie and walked out. I was left to ponder on what she had told me. Trinity was three separate people? But I didn't understand how that was possible, but then, Emillie was sharing a body with her sister. They were multiple people in one body. Both with separate thoughts from the other. Then I thought of Tillo and what that meant. So, was he fucking both Emillie and Septima? I was just too confused on this, but then, Emillie coughed and began to open her eyes. She looked around and then saw me, "Where...is Sandin?", she asked. Her voice was hoarse and she was obviously very weak. "He is studying that book he got from Mileeda.", "Oh...", Emillie said, now laying back, and allowing herself to relax, "She killed her. She killed Septima.", Emillie was saying. "So, you knew that the other you was your sister?", I asked. Emillie turned to me with surprise written all over her face. "No...I didn't. She told me her name, before she left me.", Emillie said, now starting to tear up, "She was my sister? Why didn't Amana tell me I have a sister?", Emillie was now growing angry. "Emillie, your mother didn't tell you, because Septima was killed by Lona.". Emillie now looked at me with so much anger in her face, that I couldn't even begin to describe her features. Emillie is always beautiful, but her face right now was contorted into ugly rage. She suddenly sat up, causing herself great pain in the process. She screamed, and some nurses came in, "You need to lay back down!", one nurse yelled, trying to force her back down. "NO!", Emillie yelled, and the nurses and myself were thrown back. Amana came into the room and stared at Emillie, then took out her cannon, "Emillie, calm down.", she said. "NO! THIS IS UNFORGIVABLE! I AM GOING TO KILL ALTHEA!", she was shouting, and then there was a large boom, and I felt myself pressed against the wall of the room. The nurses were all panicking, and Amana had been blasted out of the room. Emillie was floating above us, staring down at us with rage and determination on her face. She blasted through the ceiling and took off. Quickly, Amana activated something on her shoes and took off after her. I got up to help the nurses to their feet. I looked at the hole in the ceiling and was wondering where they were headed.

EMILLIE: I couldn't believe it. The girl who looked like me is my twin sister. Where I had inherited my mother's red hair, she took the color black. I was so angry that I couldn't focus on the entirety of the situation. I looked behind me, and Amana was catching up to me. I waved my arm at her, and watched her fall out of the sky. I continued to fly back towards the island. I landed hard on the spot where Althea had stabbed me, and killed Septima, again. I felt on the ground and realized that Septima's essence was still here somehow. "Emillie?", someone questioned. I turned, and Mileeda was standing nearby, with a clutch of scientist's scoping over the area with devices and meters. "Where is your mother?", she asked. I raised my hand and Mileeda deflected my attack and sent one of her own at me. She then rushed me, "DON'T STOP SEARCHING!", she yelled at the scientists, while she pounded me into the ground. Then she held her hand up in front of me, and I felt her energy waves weaken me completely, "Now...I'm guessing you learned about Septima, and I'm guessing you want to gain vengeance for your sister. Well, that's fine, but you aren't going to do it like this.", Mileeda said. She held her hand out for me to take it. I did, and she pulled me up. "Your sister's essence was here. Your mother buried it here. Well, some of it. Your sister's essence was split into three. Your father kept some, some was put into you, and some of it was buried here. The part that was buried here was taken by Althea. She killed the part of her living in you, which was mixed with the part that belonged to your father. So now, she is being held by Althea, and if she finds a way to destroy that essence she has taken, then your sister will be gone for good.". I didn't want that. I wanted Septima to live. I'd grown attached to her in the short time we've been together. But learning she is my sister, I couldn't allow her to fully die at the hands of her greatest enemy. "Mileeda, I have to save her...", I said, beginning to cry. "You will. I promise. We will.", she said, pulling me into a hug.

After I had sat with Mileeda for some time, Sylvia walked up, "We found this, Grandmother. I think it may have been connected to her.", she said, handing Mileeda a silver coin that was obviously buried in dirt. It was filthy. It was covered in what looked like dirt, but also rust, blood, and soot. "Emillie, do you feel anything?", Mileeda asked. I took the dirty coin into my hand and suddenly passed out. When I woke up, I was in my room in the orphanage. Septima was sitting down, looking out the window. "Septima!", I shouted, and ran to her. I threw my arms around her and she just sat there, "Emillie, hello.", she said awkwardly. "I'm so sorry, Sister! I'm going to save you! I promise.", I said. "All you need is Father's ring. Then you can summon my essence to you. Nothing can split us if you have that.", she said. "But, where is it?", "Back on Base. Mother gave it to Mr. Red. It's time, Sister. We are going to finish my murderer.", she said, now smiling slightly. It was insane. We were identical, except for our hair. But I couldn't help but also feel the darkness that was coming off of her. Something sinister was within my sister, but I didn't have time to ponder on that. I woke up, but this time in my reality. Mileeda had already brought me back to Base and was now discussing something with Sylvia, "...she is dangerous, but we need her. Her power to defeat Althea and possibly...Corsa, is sorely needed.", "But you never said it would take this! I can't let you!", Sylvia was shouting at her grandmother. She must be insane. I opened my eyes and looked around. I was in my room, but Mileeda and Sylvia were standing nearby. Amana was sitting in a corner, watching me. When she noticed I was awake, she held her hand up and pointed to me. All three looked in my direction. "I'm assuming you've spoken with Septima.", Amana said, now walking towards my bed. "I did. She told me I need the ring.". Amana looked at Mileeda, then Red walked into the room, followed by Sandin. "What the hell happened?", Sandin said, making his way to me, sitting next to me on my bed, and holding me. "Emillie finally learned of her twin, and how they've been connected. Now, what do you say, all of you get out? I need to speak with my daughter.", Amana said. Sandin looked up and was about to say something, when Red put his hand on his shoulder. Sandin kissed me, then got up and walked out of the room. Sylvia and Mileeda followed, Sylvia looking back, and Mileeda giving my mother a look of hurry. They all closed the door on their way out. "A very long time ago, I met a man. I knew right away that he wasn't just any man. I could sense his godliness. At first, I felt no different than how I always felt. Until I learned who he was, and what he could do. Emillie, you and your sister were born out of my weakness. I know that may be hard to understand, but one day, you will. Althea and I have been enemies for thousands of years. I taught her magic. I taught her our heritage. She used her knowledge to kill her father. He asked that I never tell the truth of his death. So, I didn't. But then, she also killed her mother. Her father was an accident, or at least that's what I used to think. Now, I know that he was just a test. She was testing herself. To see if she would really murder her parents. Emillie...I'm sorry I couldn't tell this to you before, but the pain is still too fresh.", Amana said, with a tear also coming from her eye. I didn't know what to think. This was the nicest she'd ever been towards me. I remained quiet, hoping she would say more. "My list of enemies doesn't just stop at Althea, Emillie. In truth, there are a lot of people that would use you against me, but only a few of them are actually powerful enough. I have no reason to fear those...but Althea, Duke, Abraxa...these are all people powerful enough to kill you.", "Who are Duke and Abraxa?", I asked. "A mother and son, hell bent on taking over the whole universe. There are things I can't share with you, Emillie. But you of all people should be told that Plinth is just one world of many created by Sebastian. My father doesn't have time for this planet. So, he had me sacrifice my sister, in order to create a magical barrier that protects Plinth from outside forces.". Now I fully understood. "That's why you hate them...", I said. I never felt more sorry for anyone than I did for my own mother at this moment. Losing Septima was hard enough to think about. But then, there is the constant reminder in the form of me. Then her own parents led her to kill her sister. Someone she loved more than life itself. Then I thought about Trinity. Suddenly, what Mileeda told me a month ago made sense. Trinity was made up of three different women. Just like me and Septima. Now that I was fully thinking about it, it felt like a part of myself was gone. "I hate my parents, yes. But I also understand them. They are old, tired, and many times have watched us screw up. I can't explain everything, but I will leave you with this...", Amana fixed herself and leaned in close to my face, "...I do love you. More than you can know. And the only reason I was ever tough on you or made you feel like I didn't care, is only because I needed you to become strong. Strong enough that you could protect yourself. You're meant to live for a long time, Emillie, and I don't want your life cut short like your sister's.", my mother said, now tearing up, and for the first time, kissing me on my forehead. I started to cry as well, then I grabbed my mother, and hugged her. We hugged, really hugged, for the first time. My door burst open, and then I saw Gail standing in my doorway. "Emillie!", she shouted. She ran to me, and pulled me into a tight hug. "I'll see you later.", my mother said, getting up, and walking out. I watched her walk out, and she looked back at me, and smiled.

Gail and I spoke for a long time, "...so, if it wasn't for that little vacation, I'd still be helping Yellfy. I'm glad I was told I could take off before it reached the point it's at now.", "Celda said she is still going to let Flin work for Mccloud.", "Oh, I suppose it's okay. Mileeda is treating the situation differently anyway. She seems to think that what Adem is doing is totally okay.", Gail said, looking at my face with worry, "Emillie, I'm sorry again about Septima. Your mother never told me she had another daughter. I've just always assumed you were her only child. I feel like it's my fault because I told you to go there.", Gail said, beginning to cry. "It isn't your fault. I just wonder why Septima kept herself a secret. Something isn't right with her, Gail, and I don't know what.", "She died when she was an infant, and your father, who I don't know anything about, did something to keep her alive in some way. That's all I know about the situation. Dalia would probably know more, but she has been a bit estranged lately.". I thought about what was probably wrong with Dalia, and decided I should visit her. I knew going to the orphanage was too dangerous now, and I had the ability of summoning her in the dream realm, so I decided I'd just do that. Gail and I went to get some food. We sat down in the break area. We were later joined by Sylvia, who had been spending a lot of time with Mileeda lately. "So, how is everything?", I asked her once she sat down. "Well, with worrying if you're gonna die, and all the other shit taking place, I'd say I'm doing pretty good.", "But what about Mileeda? Is she treating you okay?", I asked. "Incredibly. I can't believe it, but I think I'm finally on her good side! She has even been teaching me some of the forbidden magic.", Sylvia said excitedly. "Well, I'm happy to hear that, Ms. Lon.", Gail said, patting her on her shoulder. Sylvia smiled. "So, how are things for you, Emillie? How is Sandin? Are you still worried about him and Jesy?", Sylvia asked. "Not so much. I guess I was just acting jealous because I knew they were together before, but now, I'm more concerned with my sister.", I said indifferently. "You will save her, Emillie.", Gail said. "Will I? I'm just sitting here... I should be out there searching for her!", I yelled. I suddenly felt the urge to get up and leave. I jumped up and started to leave, and Gail and Sylvia followed me. "Emillie, where are you going?", Sylvia asked as I picked up the pace. I went to Red, who was usually these days, hanging out in the library. "Emillie, Gail, Sylvia.", he greeted us when we came in and surrounded him. I stepped closer, "I need the ring.", I said, holding my hand out. Mr. Red just looked at me, then reached into his shirt pocket and pulled it out. He handed it to me, and I felt an energy similar to when I touched the coin. I didn't feel this before when I had touched it, but then I suddenly wasn't on the P.E.D Base anymore. I looked around to see where I was, and strangely, it was a very nice house. I walked around for some time, examining strange artifacts that seemed to fill up the whole of the house. It was almost like a museum. I continued to walk around for what felt like twenty minutes. A few of the artifacts stuck out to me. One of the objects was a sword that was golden and white. I looked at it closer and realized I'd seen it before. "Interesting...isn't it?", said a voice from behind me. I turned, and the most beautiful woman I'd ever seen was standing before me.

I continued to stare at the strange lady, who just smiled in return. "Who are you?", I asked. "I told you…I'd be with you until the end.", she said. She walked up to me, and placed her hand on my face, "Oh, Emillie, you've been through a rough patch, but I will help you now. Because I knew this would happen to you. I knew you would lose your sister.". The woman removed her hand from my face, and we were suddenly sitting in her living room. I looked around again, confused when we entered and when I sat down. "How did we…?", "You are a very special woman, Emillie. You were able to contain another soul within yourself, and not just any soul, a goddess' soul. Your twin sister to be exact. But what you don't know…is that there is still a piece of her inside of you. If you truly wish for her to come back, then with the ring, just summon her. Althea took the essence your mother hid, but she doesn't realize what you really are, Emillie. Corsa only has an idea, but not the whole picture.". I was trying to take in all of her words, even though I was still confused as to who she was. Then, almost like I was shot again by my mother, I felt like an idiot for not realizing sooner, "Ko-e?", I asked. She smiled, "Yes, Emillie. I am Ko-e.". I didn't know what to think, or even what to say. I stared at my aunt, who was more beautiful than I could have imagined. She had an air about her that suggested she was nothing but kindness personified. I tried to tell her how much I've looked forward to meeting her, but the words wouldn't leave my mouth. "Emillie, I hate to be the one to tell this to you, but you are going to be very different from the rest of your family. You have no idea how big your family really is, and you will have a difficult journey. But most importantly, Awalli and you… You two are very special. It is the reason I've told Adem NOT to kill her.". In these words, I remembered what Adem Mccloud truly was and that Ko-e was the one who raised him this way, "Why did you make him into a killer?", I asked. I knew there had to be some good reason. "Adem is my pride. He is your family as well, but I'll leave your mother to explain that. Just ask her.", Ko-e said, as if that was easy. My mother was nice to me a few hours ago, but I was quite sure she would not tell me anything about Adem, if she really is connected to him. "Adem had anger. Anger that if left unchecked, he would have done evil things. I made it to where he channeled that anger into something of worth. I gave him a clearer purpose. To kill those that have killed others. Adem doesn't kill innocent people, Emillie.", "Yeah, but people should be given a chance! What if they can change?", I asked. Ko-e looked at me with pity, "You may have heard this from Mileeda or your mother, but we have been around for a LONG time, Emillie. There never is a time when people just change. I'm not saying it isn't possible, but the ones that Adem has killed, were never going to change, and stood to revel in their murders. I couldn't let that stand.", Ko-e said, with finalization added to her tone. Dalia had described Ko-e as kind, but also strict. The kind of person that would kill if she really had to. I had thought that maybe that wasn't really Ko-e, but now, I didn't know what to think. "Emillie, I don't kill people lightly, and neither does Adem. We both understand that line between murder and justice.", "But my friend Vaness said...", "I know what Ms. Tes believes, Emillie. She is hell bent on making Adem pay for who he took from her. But, even she will learn that sometimes it is better this way.". I wanted to ask who Adem killed that was close to Vaness, but then decided it was better to hear it from her. "Emillie, back to what I didn't want to tell you...", Ko-e began to say, but then stopped. She looked as if something was wrong, "I'm sorry, Emillie, but that is all the time we have for right now. I'll try and see you again, soon.", she said. She got up, walked over to me, and kissed me on my forehead, "I love you, Emillie.".

When I woke up, I was still in the library with Red, Sylvia and Gail. They were all looking at me, and then, Gail said, "Emillie, what just happened?". I quickly explained about Ko-e. As soon as I did, Amana appeared next to me, and grabbed me by my throat, "WHERE IS SHE?! WHERE WERE YOU?!", Amana yelled, as Red and Gail moved to pry her off me immediately. I grabbed my throat, coughing, "Why?", I asked, already starting to cry. "WHY?! I need to talk to her! Besides the fact she has been a fugitive for the last fifteen-hundred years, she knows what's happening and could tell us what we need to know! Emillie, anything you can remember...", Amana was now calming down and starting to talk to me softly. Red looked between the both of us and decided to block Amana from me, "General, maybe you should assume, Emillie can't tell you, because she doesn't know.". My mother looked like she was thinking this over. Then, Mileeda also came into the room, "We have a huge problem.". She led us all to her office, where she pulled up that giant screen on her wall and showed us the news. Edge city was now experiencing what Sicilia was a couple months ago. The news people, while trying to get as much footage as possible, were running around and trying to survive. I stepped closer to the screen, unable to believe what I was looking at. It was Althea, with Lopim, and one other woman. This woman had black and red hair, which made her a dub, and the sword she held was similar to mine. Then I looked closer and saw she... "THAT WOMAN LOOKS LIKE ME!", I yelled. I turned to my mother, who was also staring at the screen, but not as shocked as I was. "Shit!", she yelled. "Who is that, Amana?", Sylvia asked. "My first daughter. Alisa.".

SANDIN: When I had found Jesy, she was in the break room reading P.E.D policies. She saw me, and waved for me to join her. I walked over and sat down at her booth. "So, have you heard anything?", she asked me. I knew immediately to ask her about Amana's secret room, "Jesy, why are you trying to get past that door on the east side of the base? You do realize you're not supposed to be messing with that?", I said. She looked at me for a minute, then said, "Amana is hiding something in there. I've seen her go into that room for hours at a time. What is she doing in there?", "Maybe it's a secret lab.", "That's what I thought, too. But sometimes when she comes out of there, she's crying.", Jesy said, as if this should convince me to find out what's in there as well. "Jesy, Amana is going to obliterate you if you try prying into her personal business. She doesn't even share things with Emillie, and that's her daughter!", I said. "Yes, I get that, but I think you're ignoring something obvious, Tillo. You're ignoring the fact that she is over three-thousand years old. Whatever is in that room, is enough to make HER cry?", "Goddesses get emotional, too.", "Except that, Amana isn't like Mileeda. Did you know they run two separate divisions? Amana runs the dangerous technology side of things and Mileeda is in charge of magic.", Jesy said, pointing out these facts. I thought about it, and realized that this made a lot of sense. She had indeed touched on a good point. Amana was all about her weapons. I noticed this because on her uniform, she has several holsters to put different sized cannons all over her body. But Mileeda was all about spell casting. The book she gave me was definitive proof of that. I had looked into the book to try and determine if there was a way to find out if someone IS in fact being controlled. My conversation with Jesy wasn't revealing anything, but according to the book, possession doesn't work in the traditional way everyone thinks. An entity invades your consciousness, but they don't control you. They use your emotions to convince you that certain things are okay. After reading this passage in the book, I now had a better understanding of Awalli. She was possessed, but with everything she lost and some of the recent events that happened to her, she was easily manipulated into doing Corsa's bidding. A person can be set free, but if the entity had a sharp hold on the individual, it will still be there, and may even have the ability to perform actions, without the knowledge of the host. Some of the stuff I'd been hearing about Awalli, suggested she wasn't in control of herself in the slightest.

There was one word that I could say that would prove to me that Jesy is possessed, but I didn't know if I should say it now, because if I do, I may end up fighting something I can't handle, but then on the other hand, it couldn't be that bad. I decided to go for it, "Vendaveal.", I said. I watched Jesy for a second, then she suddenly started to have a fit. She got up, and ran out of the break room. I followed her. We ran all the way to the ruins of Alexandria. I had lost sight of her, but I was looking around. Then I heard cannon fire and felt myself get hit in my shoulder. I fell to the ground and clutched the spot that the shell had entered. I saw Jesy, aiming her cannon confusedly. I tried to rush at her, but she shot me again, this time, in the gut. I grabbed my gut, and tried to take the cannon from her. We were tussling with each other. Finally, I knocked the cannon out of her hand, and tried to perform the exorcism, but Jesy started to scream and punched me, and I fell back somewhat because of the pain in my gut and shoulder. "JESY!", I yelled, trying to get through to her, but to no avail. She jumped on top of me and started to pound on me. She hit my nose and busted it, and blood came flowing out. She was about to shoot me with my own cannon, when Red came running for me. He shot her in her shoulder, she grunted, and fell off of me. I quickly subdued her and placed her in binds. "We need to get her to Mileeda!", I shouted. "No. You need to come with me, Sandin, now.", Red said, leading me away. I was carrying Jesy on my shoulder when we made it to Mileeda's office. We entered and were all looking at the monitor on her wall. In the office stood Amana, Sylvia, Gail, Mileeda, and Emillie. On the screen was a woman who looked just like Emillie. She was swinging her sword and when she did, there seemed to be waves of energy that expelled itself, causing panic and destruction. I looked at Emillie, who was watching the screen with confusion and anger. Then she turned on Amana, "It never ends with you. Were you ever going to tell me about her?!", Emillie yelled at her mother. "Emillie…", before Amana could say another word,

Emillie attacked her mother. Everyone in the room tried to break this up. I was grabbing Emillie, but it seemed to be a waste of time. She hit me with her elbow and knocked me off of her. Sylvia was trying to get near her, but couldn't in all the commotion. Red was going for Amana, but Amana had put up some kind of field and nobody could get in. Gail was standing next to Mileeda, looking panicked, while Mileeda just watched, with something close to amusement on her face. "YOU KEEP HIDING THINGS! WHAT ELSE AREN'T YOU TELLING ME?!", Emillie shouted at her mother. Amana was grabbing her daughter's face and trying to keep her from being able to hit her. Emillie was grabbing her mother by her throat, "EMILLIE, I COULDN'T TELL YOU ABOUT HER! SHE IS MY FIRSTBORN AND SHE WAS DANGEROUS! I THOUGHT SHE WAS DEAD!". Mileeda, who had finally gotten bored with watching us all trying to break them apart, finally casted a barrier between them. Emillie was standing on one side, with hatred, anger, and pain, all etched into her features. Amana was standing on the other side looking angry, but hurt at the same time. "Alisa, was my first child. She was very powerful in a very major sense. But she wanted more power. She wanted to do something terrible, and in the end, I had to kill her. I HAD TO.", Amana said with emphasis. Emillie didn't look like she was easily forgiving. "What about Septima?", Emillie asked. "Septima was taken by Lona, I told you. But if your sister, Alisa, has her essence, she will try to use it to merge with her the same way you have. It looks like she has already.", Amana said. Emillie looked at the screen again, then looked at the rest of us, "For a long time, I thought I was an only child. I didn't know my parents, or where I came from. Then I learned...", she said, nodding towards Amana, "...but now, I see that things are never simple with family. No matter the fact you share blood, it is never a good enough reason. This is what happens to a family that doesn't care about what happens to their blood.", she said, pointing at the monitor, and gazing hard at her mother. She then looked at me, nodded, and disappeared. "Damn it! Find her!", Amana yelled at Mileeda, who just stood there. "I warned you, Amana. I told you that you need to keep her closer to you, but you didn't listen. I told you that after what happened to my precious, Salana, and my son, Tiber, that you wouldn't just be able to leave them unattended. Now your children are doing the same thing mine did. They are going to kill each other.", Mileeda said sternly. "Mileeda, just get her back here!", "No. It's time for you to learn from your mistakes, Amana.", Mileeda disappeared, and Amana disappeared as well. Me and Red looked at each other, while Gail and Sylvia started to exit the room. "We need to get everyone ready.", Gail said.

Red and I went to Tem, who we figured would know what to do with this situation. He quickly started to get a group mobilized. They were opening weapon caches, taking out mid-sized cannons, and cannons with straps to hang them off your shoulders. They had even taken out some of their other more classified tech, which was laser technology. Red was gearing up as well, and finally, after what felt like ages, Yellfy was making his way towards us, "So, big fight, huh?", he said, also grabbing some weapons and preparing. We quickly briefed him on the situation with Emillie's sisters. "Sisters? I can't believe it. All this time, she's had sisters? Wow, way to hold out, Sandin.", "Yencid, this is no game. Alisa is already fucking up Edge.", I said. "I know, I saw on the news. Adem is too occupied to help, and well, I came here to see what I could do.". We made our way to the pods, and found about four other squads also waiting to leave. A man was coming forward who had faded silver and black hair and looked like he was extremely militant, "OKAY, ASSHOLES, THIS IS IT! DOWN THERE, RIGHT NOW, THERE ARE NOT ONE, BUT TWO GODDESSES WRECKING HAVOC! WE ARE GOING TO GO DOWN THERE AND FACE THEM!

THEY HAVE BROUGHT AN ARMY WITH THEM, AND SO WE ARE GOING TO FIGHT IN THE FIRST WAR THAT'S HAPPENED IN OVER TWO-HUNDRED YEARS! GEAR UP!", the man finished, then he motioned for me, Red, and Yellfy. Yellfy looked like he didn't trust this man in the slightest, "Mr. Yellfy, and your friends.", he said, nodding at me and Red. "Captain Brom.", Yellfy said simply. I looked at the man, and remembered what Jesy said. Then I remembered Jesy, and the fact she was possessed. "You three are here on special technicalities. I don't think you're true P.E.D material, but I don't get that say. I wouldn't send you guys down there, but from what I understand, you've already been on missions for Mileeda, so I suppose that I'll just have to send you down there. But I need to at least ask…are you prepared?". We looked at each other. Personally, for me, there was Emillie, and I had to go for her. Red would want to have my back, and so would Yellfy. We all nodded in agreement. "Then, buckle up, you clowns. When you get down there, you are going to see some crazy shit.".

CHAPTER 14

War In The Streets

***E*MILLIE:** I had to find out where Ko-e lived. She had the answers and wouldn't hide things like my mother. As I was flying in the general direction of the energy I felt when I was near her, something hit me. I fell out of the sky and into a building. The people in the building all got up and started to run out. I started to get to my feet, and then took a quick blow to the face. I flew into a wall, hitting someone in the process. I quickly pulled myself out of the wall and saw the person was broken and hurt. I quickly and gently pulled them from the wall and started to fly them to aid. As I was, that same force that hit me before, knocked me down. The man I was helping fell from my arms, and my assailant walked up to him, and stabbed him, he died. I watched the light leave his eyes. I stood up in anger and summoned my sword. "You can't save them.", Alisa said. She looked just like me, but slightly different. Some of her features resembled our father. Her eyes were further apart, but that was it. She was beautiful. "YOU DIDN'T HAVE TO KILL THAT MAN!", I shouted. "You're right, but if I hadn't, you would have continued trying to save him, and we don't have time for stuff like that, Little Sister.", "You're going to pay for taking his life.". I lifted my hand with the ring on it, and aimed at her and summoned Septima. Immediately, she came to me. I felt her enter, and the armor came on, along with the proper colorization of my sword. I looked at my evil older sister, "Why? Why are you like this?", I asked. I had to ask. "You think I merged with Septima? I had no time for that, nor would I want to do that.", Alisa said, ignoring my question, "Where is our mother?", Alisa asked me. "I don't care where she is.", I said. Alisa smiled, "So...she's hid things from you as well... Typical. I bet she didn't tell you the reason I had Lona take your twin.", Alisa said. "But, she said...", "Lona killed her? Well, sort of. I asked her to take her. I intended to keep her from Amana, and our dear old dad. But Amana was smart, as always. She did something to her. So, I destroyed her vessel. But Father made her one that she can only contain within his realm. Once you crossed over, she was able to meld with you. Funny, you don't even fully know what you are. What WE are. But I don't care, because I'm going to kill you now, Sister. Nice, and slow.", Alisa said, rushing at me. I felt Septima take control, as she dodged and slashed at Alisa. Alisa was able to make Septima miss, and then retaliated by punching us. We stumbled some, but then she came at us and tackled us out of the building. We fell for twenty stories, then hit the ground. Alisa started to beat on us. I punched her, and I felt Septima getting ready to throw the sword at her. I let her, and she dodged, but got nicked on her shoulder. She smiled, then charged at us. I let Septima take full reign. She was giving it to Alisa. She punched her, then aimed the sword at her, and then stuck it in her shoulder. She then quickly removed the blade and stood back. Alisa stood up, waved her hand over her shoulder wound, and then stood before us as if she wasn't hurt at all. "I must say, Septima puts up a better fight than you, Emillie.", she said mockingly. I took control and rushed at Alisa, who summoned her blade and hit me over the head with it. I flew to the right and into another building. I noticed there were now P.E.D soldiers evacuating the people. I started to stand, then felt a hand on my shoulder. I looked and was surprised to find Awalli standing next to me. I turned from her and took out my blade, eyeing her. "Emillie...I'm not that Awalli anymore...", she said, pointing behind me. I turned just in time to see Alisa flying at me. She went to kick me, but Awalli grabbed her leg and tossed her out of the building. I looked at Awalli, who nodded. I nodded back, then we proceeded to see if Alisa was down. Of course, she wasn't. She jumped up immediately, "So, the traitor shows her face.", Alisa said to Awalli. "I can't betray you, if I was never on your side!", Awalli yelled back. "You were helping Corsa. You were doing everything she told you to do. Then one day, you decided not to. I call that betrayal.", Alisa said. I threw my sword at her and she flew out of the way, then rushed at me. Both Awalli and I grabbed her. Alisa really was powerful. She carried me and Awalli out of the building and threw the both of us into another one. This one was already empty. Then I saw Alisa get hit with a shell. She fell out of the sky. I went to see who fired the shell and saw my mother. She was pulling out one of her cannons and rushing forward. "About time.", Alisa said, with a nasty smile on her face. She slashed at Amana, and then, Amana barely dodged her and took out a knife she had. She sliced at Alisa, who stood back, "YOU BITCH!", she yelled, and flew away. My mother activated something on her boots, and she flew in the air after her. "We have to follow them!", Awalli said, quickly flying after my mother. I flew after her. We were flying back towards the island where Lona had almost killed me. When I landed, my mother and Alisa were throwing blows, "YOU JUST COULDN'T ACCEPT IT!", Alisa was yelling at Amana. "Accept what? That you were a murderous, little, cunt, who murdered her sister?", "Murdered my sister? Are you kidding? You and Father did something, way before I even touched her.", Alisa replied to my mother, jumping, and punching her in the face. This knocked Amana down. Awalli rushed forward, and started to fight Alisa. She grabbed the sword so Alisa couldn't swing it, then headbutted her. "Awalli, you are nothing.", Alisa said, as she broke free of Awalli's grasp. She went in for a kill slash, but I rushed forward now. I jumped and slashed at her face. I cut it, and that's when I saw what was inside of Alisa. Black ooze started to gush out of her face. She grabbed where I slashed her, "Emillie, you will pay for this.", she said, now flying away, back towards Edge. I went to help my mother up, who threw me off of her, "We don't have time! Go after her!", my mother yelled. I looked at Awalli, who nodded and flew after Alisa. I turned back to my mother, "Why didn't you just tell me the truth?", "Because it wasn't important. Alisa was dead. Lona stole her corpse from me, and preserved it. I'm sorry you had to learn this.", Amana said, now getting ready to fly after her, "Are you coming or what, Emillie?", she asked me. I shook my head, "I'm going to find Koe.". Amana looked angry, but didn't say anything else. She flew off after Awalli, and I decided to keep searching for my aunt.

LODY: When we had touched down in Edge, the first thing I saw was Walsh, leading some GF grunts into what I could only describe as Hell. I rushed forward, Sandin and Yencid right behind me, and quickly spoke with Walsh, "What the hell are you doing out here?", "What do you think? Look around you! Whoever these people are, even Awalli is fighting them.", Walsh said, as he was ordering a group of men to the west. I looked at what they were firing at, and saw strange creatures. They resembled dogs, but were a lot bigger than a dog. They were more the size of bears. They were mauling some of the grunts, and some grunts had turned to try and get away. I looked at Sandin and Yellfy. Yellfy cocked his cannon, "Let's do this.", he said, walking forward. We followed him. Yencid took out the first creature, and Sandin, using magic, took out the second. I started to fire, and I took out a good amount of the creatures, almost five of them, but they were still coming. Tem and a group of P.E.D men and women had come as well, and were firing their laser weapons on the creatures. I saw Sylvia also using magic. She had teamed up with Sandin, and they were working their way through the crowd of creatures together. I was making my way up the path that Sylvia and Sandin were clearing. As Yellfy and I found ourselves in an alley, we were quickly knocked down by something. "Mr. Red. If only you had seen the light during our small amount of time together.". Lopim was making his way towards us. Yellfy stood back up and started firing at him, but Lopim seemed to have a shield up, "Now, I'm forced to have to kill you. Corsa will be freed. Especially now that her favorite servant is awake.", Lopim said, punching Yencid, and kicking me while I was still down. "HEY!", I heard someone yell. Then I looked, and saw a man wearing a strange tan hunting outfit, with his face covered by some kind of black substance. "THIS DOESN'T CONCERN YOU!", Lopim yelled, as the man just pointed his hand at Lopim, and red energy was shot out of it. Lopim was knocked back, and I found myself getting up. I took out my hand cannon and fired seven shells into Lopim. "He won't die that way.", the strange man said. He kneeled and placed his hand over Lopim's chest. Lopim began to scream, and then, Lona appeared. "You're too late.", the man said. "You're going to die for this.", Lona said in an angry tone, flying at the mystery man, who grabbed her and was gone. I helped Yellfy up. "Looks like Adem was able to help after all. Let's go, Lody.", Yellfy said. I looked in the direction that Lona had flown off in. I was shocked to learn that the man was Adem but decided to hurry after Yellfy. We made our way into a building, where the fighting was intense due to the fact it was in such a small space. Laser beams were flying over our heads, while guts and blood were being sprayed everywhere. We finally made it through all of that, just to run into Lona again. "Well, this time, nobody will save you.", she said, pointing a finger at Yencid. I quickly jumped in front and pain like I'd never known was coursing through my body. Yencid began to fire at her, but she was whirling her blade too quickly and all the shells were being thrown elsewhere. It was then that I saw that beautiful woman I saw at Dalia's manor, appear behind Lona, "Hello, Niece.", she said. Lona turned and tried to do something, but the woman was very fast, "LANENDA.", she said, and Lona froze and fell. "I'll take her from here.", the woman said. Then she disappeared.

The fighting was getting much more intense, and it had felt like hours were passing us by. I was looking for Tillo, but couldn't find him anywhere. Then I saw Tem, who was nursing a girl. He was wrapping a bandage around her head, and ordering her to be taken to the med area, "Tem, have you seen Tillo?", "Yeah. Him and Lon are way over there. They were trying to help Amana.". Yencid looked at me, "I'm gonna see if I can find Adem.", he said, then ran off. I was on my own to go to the other side to look for Tillo. As I was making my way through the city, now turned into a battlefield, I noticed all around me that there were signs of grief. Citizens, who weren't evacuated in time were all over the place. Either they were hiding for dear life, or crying over dead bodies. Some were just looking for anywhere that was safe. "I told you, to walk away from all of this.". I looked at who was talking to me, and saw Dalia. I didn't know what to say to her, but she wrapped her arms around me, and kissed me. I kissed her for a long time. "See what happens when you get involved with goddesses?", she said jokingly. "Dalia, what are you doing here?", I asked, thinking she should be with the children. "I left the children with Celda. I had to come. I am a goddess, and you looked like you needed all the help you can get.", she said, with a cocky smile. I grabbed her and kissed her again. It was like Sandin had told me. Kissing a goddess, you can tell the difference. I followed Dalia towards where Amana and Sandin were supposed to be. Along the way, I filled her in on the situation, "I saw on the news. Alisa… I always had a feeling she would be back. I warned Amana that hiding her essence like that was reckless. Especially since Lona had stolen her vessel. Amana never listens. She always thinks she knows best.", "So, what do you think will happen after this?", "The same thing that happened last time. A goddess hunt.". We had found where Amana and Sandin were. Sylvia was wiping Sandin's face, which had blood on it, and Amana was loading her weapons. She looked up at me and Dalia, and then looked at our hands, which were clasped, "Where is Emillie?", was the first question out of Dalia's mouth. "I don't know.", Amana answered. "What the hell do you mean…?", "I DON'T KNOW!", Amana yelled at Dalia, "SHE ABANDONED US TO GO FIND KO-E!", "Amana, I think Ko-e was here. She took Lona, and left.", "WHAT?!", Amana yelled, then she disappeared. "Where the hell did she go?", I asked Dalia. "Most likely, she is following Lona's energy signature to see if it'll lead her to Ko-e.". I looked at Sylvia and Sandin. I didn't like the way Sylvia was carefully cleaning Sandin. It looked too obvious what she was feeling. "Can you blame her?", Sylvia said, "Emillie doesn't trust Amana in the slightest, and neither do I. She should have told her about Alisa.", Sylvia said, putting the rag down. "I agree. Now we have to find where Alisa ran off to. Amana almost killed her. Awalli took off to go search for Emillie as well. Awalli is apparently on our side.", Sandin said, confused. Yellfy came back, followed by Adem, who had removed the black substance from his face. "I don't know what more I could do. I've put up barriers around the city, and I've removed all the citizens to somewhere safe. Hopefully, it'll be enough. But you know what I have to do, Yencid, and this is perfect timing.", Adem was saying. "I agree, my friend. Good luck.", replied Yencid, then Adem disappeared.

AWALLI: I tried teleporting to Emillie, but somehow, she was blocking her signature. I continued flying through the city, and then finally, found a small but somewhat noticeable house. Emillie was standing in front of it. We were in South Edge, and the fighting was literally down the street. I landed next to Emillie, who looked at me, "We need you over there.", I said. "Ko-e knows things. I need to know what she knows.". Emillie knocked on the door. The door opened, and we proceeded inside. The first thing we saw was Lona, tied up in gold chains, and gagged. Ko-e was sitting across from her. She looked in our direction and stood up. "Awalli, Emillie, I have been waiting for this moment. She approached us and pulled us both into a hug. She grabbed Emillie's face, then mine, "Oh, Awalli, you look so much like Salana. Mileeda's daughter.". I understood now what my grandmother meant by, she understood why Corsa chose me. "And Emillie…", Ko-e said with a smile, "…I'm so sorry for everything you've been through.", "Why does my mother want to arrest you?", Emillie asked. "Because she is angry at me. Because I know something that she knows as well, but we have different views on it.", "And that is?", Emillie asked. "I'm sorry, Emillie. That is the one thing I can't tell you yet. But trust me, I will, when the time is right.", "NO! I WANT TO KNOW NOW!", Emillie yelled at Ko-e. Ko-e still smiled, and just pulled Emillie into another hug, "I know you want to know, and your mother has made you this way, with her constant secrets.", Ko-e said, pushing Emillie away from her, "We obviously don't have a lot of time, so I need you two to listen to me carefully. Alisa is indeed Amana's firstborn. She was an evil child. The moment she was old enough, she tried to kill her father. This is the reason she was banished. Through that banishment, Corsa found her. She joined Corsa for her own selfish gains. When she learned that Amana had twins, she took Septima, not realizing that your father and mother suspected she might. When she destroyed Septima's vessel, your father had already made her a new one. Your mother did indeed protect you, Emillie. She gave you to Dalia because Lona would have killed you to get vengeance for your sister. Alisa and Lona are best friends. A lot happened in those days of old. Alisa is over fifteen-hundred years old, so she has a lot more experience than the both of you, but it was twenty years ago that your mother had to put her down. It was the first time we agreed on something, but even then, I couldn't reveal myself to her.",

Ko-e said, with a sad tone. Lona was making some kind of movement, but Ko-e pointed her fist at her and opened it. Lona suddenly disappeared. "Where…?", I began to ask. "To another dimension for the time being, while I prepare some stuff.", "What stuff?", Emillie asked. "The stuff that will help you two win. Follow me.", Ko-e directed us to follow her deeper into her home. Looking around, I saw that Ko-e's home was a much larger version of my show room in my warehouse. She had all kinds of artifacts and things that I could feel all types of different energies from. Once she opened a door for us to enter, we noticed that the room didn't match the house. I was used to this sort of magic, Emillie wasn't. She was looking around in amazement. "You raised Adem here?", she asked Ko-e. "Yes. And also no. Adem had a hard time. I wasn't exactly easy on him, but you see how he turned out. Better than I expected.", Ko-e said happily, "Listen, Awalli, you are a great weapon. You are to face off against Alisa alongside Emillie. You two are going to win. But you must allow her to live. DO NOT kill her. Not yet anyway. We need her alive for much later.", "What's later?", I asked. "Corsa may not escape her void now, but she has done it before. It was the reason Amana had to kill my baby sister. Because Calypsa had been made into a tether. Something that will hold Corsa in this dimension. She has been making tethers for thousands of years now, but in my time, she had reincarnated herself, and this is who the Corsa I met was. Mileeda's sister. In truth, Mileeda didn't know this until I told her the truth. Until then, she had always assumed Corsa had been possessed. She never realized that Corsa was possessing herself. She spent over a thousand years trying to save her sister. When the Corsa from the void merged with the Corsa from our dimension, they accepted one another. She will escape, and when she does, that is when Alisa will come in handy.", Ko-e said. Then she reached into a bag and gave me a bracelet. She gave the same bracelet to Emillie, "You two aren't destined to kill each other. You're destined to be best friends. I've seen your futures. Corsa has been lying to you, Awalli.". I looked at Emillie and thought for the briefest of moments that this made sense. Emillie looked more confused than when we walked in. "So, I'm supposed to let my sister live? After what she has done?", "Yes. I know how hard that is, but really, is it?". Emillie thought about what Ko-e said. Then she nodded, and looked at me, "Awalli, let's go.", she said, walking back out. I looked back at Ko-e, who was nodding me forward.

Once Emillie and I were outside, Emillie closed her eyes, and then opened them, "I know where she is.", she said, then she flew up, and I followed her. We flew for five minutes, then we found Alisa, in the center of the city, between SE and NE. She was fighting my grandmother, who was easily subduing her, "You should have stayed dead, Alisa. Now I'm forced to kill you myself.", "It must be so easy to just kill me. After all, you give no shit's for your own family, and why is that? Is it because of…Vicdor?", Alisa said, and Mileeda froze, "We have his body, we just need his essence, Mileeda. You could have him back.", "Oh, and what about Salana? Can I have her back as well?", Mileeda said, now pointing a sword she summoned at Alisa. Alisa smiled and swung her blade at Mileeda, who did a quick dodge and aimed her sword at Alisa's head. But she missed. Then, Alisa noticed me and Emillie. She quickly flew at me, and then knocked Emillie out of the air. She grabbed me by my face and flew me into the ground head first. Then she lifted my head out of the dirt, "Salana is right here, Mileeda. She is the spitting image of her.", Alisa said. I saw her raise her blade, "No!", my grandmother yelled, as she rushed forward and started to attack relentlessly. Then, Emillie was also coming towards Alisa. She flew away with her. I rushed to my grandmother, who looked at me, and started to cry. She placed her hand on my face, and then pulled me into a hug. She cried into my shoulder. I had the feeling that I was the first family member in a long time that she had shown this kind of attention to. "Have you seen Amana?", I asked her. "No, she is looking for Ko-e somewhere. Listen, I need to get back to Base, but I need you to follow Emillie. Stay with her, protect her. She is more important than you can know, Awalli.", Mileeda said, standing, and dabbing her eyes. "Do I really look exactly like your daughter?", I asked. Mileeda looked me hard in the face. I could see the same sadness that she wore a few minutes ago. "I'll contact you.", she said, and disappeared.

I followed Emillie all the way to SE, where she threw her sister down into the large crowd of soldiers and beasts. I landed, and Alisa was running in between the beasts. Emillie was about to be attacked by one of the dog/bear looking creatures, but I came up and threw energy at it, and it exploded. Emillie turned to look at me, then smiled. We both made our way through the large crowd of people. Then we saw Red, Tillo, Sylvia, Gail, and Yellfy all bunched together. Tillo was helping a P.E.D agent take down a monstrous sized beast, bigger than the other ones. Tillo had jumped onto the creature's back, and was shooting into it's back, but the creature was really strong and wasn't going down. Emillie rushed forward and blasted it with an energy wave. The beast burned up, and Tillo jumped off its back. Him, and the agent shot it in the face, and it finally killed over. Tillo looked up at me, and then pointed his weapon at me, "Sandin, put your cannon down.", Emillie said, putting her hand on it, but he didn't lower it. "She killed my mother.", he said. I felt myself beginning to cry, "I didn't mean to.", I said. "HOW COULD YOU NOT MEAN TO?!", he yelled at me. Emillie stood between his cannon and me, "Sandin, Awalli is my friend. Please, she wasn't herself, she was being used. Please, put your cannon down.". Tillo slowly lowered his weapon, but still had that same look on his face, "So, your friend?", he said, still glaring at me. "Yes. Ko-e said...we are best friends.". Sandin looked at Emillie with horror on his face. "We don't have time for this.

Emillie, you need to go after your sister.", Red said, also looking at me confused. Then, another big creature was coming towards us, and Dalia landed hard on it, and blasted it until it was nothing. "Dalia!", Emillie yelled, throwing her arms around her. "Emillie, you have to go after Alisa!", she yelled, also hugging Emillie, but then pushing her away. I nodded at Emillie, and we both flew off.

SANDIN: I kept running it in my head. Awalli, the woman who killed my mother, is best friends with my girlfriend, who originally, was her greatest enemy? What the hell was happening? I kept thinking, this is really the end of times. Red and Dalia were working their way across the streets. I looked at Sylvia, who was getting ready for whatever was coming. Gail was arguing with Yellfy, "...I'm staying!", Gail was yelling at him. "Raby, as much as I would like to have you here, I think that your hu…", "LOOK!", Sylvia yelled, cutting Yellfy off. We all turned in the direction she was pointing, and there was a massive ship that had somehow entered our atmosphere. I couldn't believe what I was looking at. A beam came down, and I saw someone going up, then I saw two more people going up as well. I recognized them as Awalli and Emillie. "Emillie!", I yelled, making my way towards them. I felt Sylvia try to grab me, but I was already too far. I heard Red calling for me, but I wasn't about to let Emillie be on that thing with just Awalli as backup. I made it to the vessel, and found Amana also standing there, with the woman who I had seen going to Dalia's manor. "So…shall we go together, then?", the woman asked Amana. "Sure. But after…I'm taking you in, Ko-e. No more games.". Ko-e looked at Amana like she was joking. I could tell she wasn't. "WAIT!", I yelled, making myself known. "Mr. Tillo, you should go help your friends. This is too much for you.", Ko-e said. "No, Emillie is up there, I'm going up there.", "Emillie is with her best friend, she will be okay.", "Best friend? What the hell are you talking about?", I asked, but Amana was already flying up. Ko-e looked at me, then came to me, and placed her hands on my shoulders, "I know how you feel about my niece, but you don't understand the full severity of what she is. You can't stay with her, Sandin. I'm sorry to tell you that you and Emillie will not stay together. She is too important to the balance of everything. Now, go with Mr. Red, and the rest. You're needed there. I'll help rescue Emillie, and I will bring her back, but don't forget what I've told you.". Ko-e backed away from me, then flew up into the vessel herself. I didn't know what to do. I wanted to turn back and go help Red, but I also wanted to get onto that vessel. Then, I felt a hand on my shoulder. I turned around, and it was Adem Mccloud, "Trust Ko-e, Sandin. She wouldn't lie. I've known her for a really long time. She loves that girl. She really does. I didn't know who she was. But Ko-e has always watched over her. She isn't going to let her die up there. Come on, man. We'll go back.". I followed him back, and that's when Lona reappeared. She was angry. "We didn't finish, Adem.", she said, glaring at Adem. A black substance crawled up Adem's face, "Get outta here, Sandin.", he commanded. I looked at him, then decided that I wasn't leaving him. I threw a blast of energy at Lona. "Oh, you are dead.", she said, coming down, and striking at me and Adem. Adem was the most amazing thing I'd ever seen. He was fighting Lona and holding his own. Even more interesting was how he combined his magic and martial-arts. It was exactly like I had heard earlier, back when Yellfy first told me about the kung-fu guy. Adem was twisting and dodging all of Lona's attempts to hit him, while hitting her with magic. He eventually knocked her down, "Damn it!", she yelled. She looked up at the vessel, and was going to fly towards it. Adem made to grab her, but she slipped out of his grasp, and flew towards the vessel. I looked at Adem to see what he wanted to do, but then he looked at me with surprise on his face, "You know magic? I didn't know. Now I can feel it coming off of you.", he said, with curiosity in his tone, "After this is all over, come see me.", he said, then he disappeared.

I found my way back to the rest, and Sylvia was the first to check on me, "What happened? Are you okay? Where is Emillie? Where is my cousin?", she said. I had forgotten she was related to Awalli. "They are on the ship. Along with Amana and Ko-e. Lona just flew up there, too.". Gail looked at Yellfy, who gave her a certain nod. "I have to go.", she said suddenly and left. "Where…?", before I finished asking where she was headed, a bunch of Lopim's people came out of nowhere. They had cannons and were followed by the beasts. We all gave each other quick looks, then we charged after them. I basically dived into the crowd, blasting anyone with a mask, and anything with large teeth. Sylvia was watching my back, and Dalia and Red were doing the rest. Yellfy had taken his own group of P.E.D soldiers, Tem included, and was blasting cannon fire at the large beasts and mowing down Lopim's people. The battle was getting worse and worse, and eventually, I noticed a news bird hovering around filming everything. I grabbed Sylvia, and led us to a place where the battle was less intense, "What are we doing here?", she asked. "We're going to Mileeda. There has to be a way to end all of this quickly.", I said, already attempting, for the first time, to teleport. When I opened my eyes, I was standing directly in Mileeda's office. Mileeda was sitting, watching the whole thing on her screen, while there were people in her office moving around and doing whatever they were doing. Mileeda noticed me and Sylvia and motioned for us to come to her, "I know why you're here, Sandin, and I can tell you, there is a way, but you won't like it.".

CHAPTER 15

Amana's Biggest Secret: The Return

EMILLIE: Awalli and I arrived on the big vessel. We looked around and didn't see anyone out of the ordinary. We proceeded down a long corridor, where there was nothing but empty. "Where do you think this thing came from?", Awalli asked, looking around for any signs of life. "I don't know. But I was told that there is more than just one planet. There are other ones. Maybe this vessel came from one of those other planets.", I suggested. We proceeded further down, and then we both heard a noise. We looked around, and that's when shit hit the fan. The noise was getting louder. It sounded like a wounded beast. Almost at once, Awalli disappeared. "Awalli!", I yelled, but there was no answer. I looked around, and still saw nobody. Then I was hit. I flew into the wall, and then my sister landed on top of me. She began to pound on me. I eventually blocked her blows and started to throw some myself. My blows got to her, and then, she stood up straight and put her fists up. I did, too. We glared at each other. "Why did you kill Septima?", I asked her. "You wouldn't understand, Little Sister.", she said, stepping closer to me. I reached for her, and we began to tussle. She pushed me up against the wall behind me, and started to pound on me again, but this time, I blasted her with my energy. She flew back some, then got showered with cannon shells. The cannon fire made a hole in the floor and she fell in. I turned to see who had fired and, of course, my mother was landing next to me, followed by Ko-e, "Well, I'd say she might be down for a bit. Where is Awalli, Emillie?", "I don't know! She disappeared.", I said, starting to look for her frantically. "I tried to kill her.", Amana was saying under her breath. "That is the exact reason why you must listen to me.", Ko-e said. "I'm not having this argument with you.", Amana said, and she disappeared. "Does she know this ship?", I asked, wondering where she would teleport to. "Somewhat, it isn't the first time it's came here, it is the second time. Emillie, you must find, Awalli. You two have to end this conflict.", Ko-e said, then she ran off further into the ship. I started to call for Awalli, "Awalli! Awalli! AWALLI, WHERE ARE YOU?!". Almost as in answer to my question, a portal opened up, and Awalli stepped out of it. She was looking highly confused, but raised her hand at me, and blasted me. I hit the wall. "Awalli, snap out of it!", I yelled. Awalli came up and stood over me. Then she kneeled and started to blast me up close. I felt my skin sear. I pushed her away, got up, and charged at her. As I did, she suddenly was awake, "Emillie, wait!", she yelled. I stopped short of punching her, "I can't...", she was saying, grabbing her head. "YOU CAN FIGHT THIS, AWALLI! YOU CAN BEAT HER!", I said, finally catching onto what was happening. Awalli let out a scream, then I saw the spirit of a woman wearing a red dress. She was smiling and doing something with her hand that told me she was causing Awalli pain. "Stop it!", I yelled. The woman looked at me, surprised I could see her, "I knew it. Awalli, kill Emillie! Kill her, now!", the woman, I had to assume was Corsa, yelled at Awalli, who tensed up, and started to come towards me. "Awalli, please stop!", I shouted, summoning my sword. Awalli looked at it, then blood ran out of her eyes. She turned around and blasted at the lady's spirit form. Corsa was just amused, "You can't hurt me, Awalli, I'm not really here.", she said mockingly. "What about me?", I asked, as I moved in, and slashed my sword at her. Immediately, there was some kind of strange disturbance. She looked shocked, then slowly, she started to fade, "No…", she said, looking at me darkly. "You will die, Emillie. I'll see to it, one day.", she said as she faded. Awalli fell to the floor and was vomiting. I leaned down to rub her back. "NO!", I heard from ahead, and Lona came down and knocked me away, and picked up Awalli by her neck, "You think this is over, girl? This is just the beginning for you!", Lona yelled, as she opened up a portal and began to throw Awalli into it. "NO! Awalli!", I shouted, jumping up, and rushing for her, but before I could do anything, Lona had thrown her in. "NO…!", I tried to jump at the portal, but it was gone, "Bring her back! Bring her back!", I said, swinging my sword at Lona. "Oh, so now you care about her? What happened to wanting to kill her? She killed Ayrellia, or have you forgotten that? Emillie, you are such a gullible, little, fool.", Lona taunted me, as tears came down my face. "PLEASE! BRING HER BACK!", I said again, but Lona just kept deflecting my blade, and laughing at me. Then another voice rang in the area, "KILL HER, LONA!", something said. I looked around to see who was talking, but there wasn't anyone. Then, Lona came at me, but was thrown off by Ko-e. "Lona, stop.", she said. "Move!", Lona yelled at Ko-e. "I know the truth, Lona. You killed your father! You murdered my brother!", Ko-e said, moving her hands in front of her and causing blue energy to gather around her hands. "I…had to.", Lona said, in a strange tone. "Oh, and Alexa?", "They both had to die. It was the only way…to make Amana pay. She knew the truth about me! She knew who I'd be, and she didn't tell me! Nobody did. But that's old news, Auntie. Corsa has helped me, more than any of you ever have. Alisa has been a sister to me, and Amana killed her! Her own daughter! And you!", Lona yelled, pointing at me, "You don't even KNOW the things your mother has done! Or the woman standing next to you! Why don't you ask your mother…about who your father is? Because she won't tell you, I bet. Of course she won't. Because then, you'll be just like your big sister! A failure in her eyes. Worthy of beatings and torture. That is how Amana sees you.", Lona finished saying. I looked at Ko-e. I felt some truth to what Lona was saying. My mother had been abusive towards me. She told me she sees me as a failure, and she hasn't told me who my father is. "Emillie, certain things have been kept from you for your own safety. Lona has only ever known how to twist words and scenarios. It's the same thing Corsa does.". I looked back at Lona, who was looking murderous. She shot after Ko-e, who blasted her as soon as she was close. Lona shot her green energy out to defend herself. Both women were holding their place. I was just watching. Then, my mother came from out of nowhere and shot Lona with her cannon, distracting her enough to make her turn, and Ko-e's blast knocked her down. She didn't get back up. Ko-e went to check her pulse, and I saw relief on her face that she was still alive. But my mother stood over her, ready to kill her. "Amana…", "Ko-e, move.", "No, I told you before, you can't kill her.", "I told you, the next time you stand in my way…", my mother shot Ko-e. "NO!", I yelled. I rushed forward and started to fight my mother, "Emillie, no.", Ko-e said, trying to stop me, but I wasn't stopping. I hated her. All she does is lie and keep secrets. Then she tries to kill her own sister. My mother wasn't a pushover. She was able to dodge my slashes and counter with her cannon several times. Then she uppercutted me with her cannon butt and I fell to the floor. "I warned you, Ko-e. I told you…", my mother stopped talking. She looked around, and realized Ko-e and Althea were gone. "Damn it! Do you know what you've cost me?!", she yelled at me. "Everything that's happening around us, and you're more concerned with killing your sister?!", "It isn't like that, Emillie, I wasn't trying to kill her. Ko-e has been hiding things for centuries. You think I hide stuff? That woman is a library of information that she keeps hidden. Adem is the same, that is how she raised him. To keep secrets and hide things. I do it, for your safety. But the things that my sister knows... She knew this would happen. She warned me, and I thought I had it covered. But now...thanks to your stupidity, I've lost my chance to find out what she's hiding from me.", "SHE TOLD YOU TO LISTEN TO HER, AND YOU SHOT HER!", I yelled at my mother. She stared at me, then walked past me. "Where are you going?", "We have to finish this. This can't keep going. I've seen wars that lasted hundreds of years.", my mother said, cocking her weapon, and proceeding forward. I followed her.

We continued down the corridor. Every once in a while, I'd look at my mother, with nothing but anger. That noise that sounded before like a wounded beast started to come back. My mother put her hand out and stopped me. "What is that?", I asked. "It's a machine. It's in the center of the vessel. Maybe that's where Awalli is.", Amana said, moving forward cautiously. Then, the floor started to boil, and my mother jumped off the spot that was melting, and pushed me up against the wall, "Don't move.", she said, continuing to hold me against the wall. Suddenly, Alisa popped out of the floor, grabbed my mother, and threw her down the corridor. She came to me, and then tried to punch me, but I stopped the punch and punched her. We started to hit one another, until I grabbed her and flew her through the wall. I kept pushing her through until we reached that machine my mom was talking about. I couldn't believe what I was looking at. It was a gigantic creature, but attached to it were these gigantic pods that seemed to hold all these glowing lights inside. I noticed that the pods had wires that ran all the way down, and up, and connected to the vessel. I looked closer and realized that this giant creature was the same thing as those beasts that were in the city. I listened to it moan and cry. "What are you guys doing to this poor creature?", I asked, feeling sorry for it. "It powers the craft. And we use it's children as our soldier's.",

Alisa said. She summoned her sword. It was like mine. But different. The red and black were on opposite sides, instead of split down the middle on both sides. I summoned mine. "Alisa, please, we are sisters. We shouldn't be fighting like this. We should love each other.", "I...should love...you? Do you have any idea what is happening? Amana has kept you in the dark completely? Yes, I can see she has. My mother...did nothing but beat me. OUR mother...is a sadistic bitch. She plays the hero for a few hundred years, then she turns into a monster. I killed Septima, to spare her. I knew she wouldn't keep YOU, after THAT. That is the reason she returned to P.E.D in the first place. Because she couldn't face Father. She couldn't face the fact that I'm how I am, because of her. And you will join me. Because I can see it already. Do you think you're going to live for a hundred years, then one day...", Alisa stuck her tongue out and blew, "...no. You're going to live for thousands, and thousands of years. And in those years, you will join me, because Mother, and everything she loves, will belong to Corsa. And Corsa will make us queens. I'll rule Father's domain, and you can have whatever else you might want. Corsa is powerful enough to do that, Emillie. Join ME, Little Sister.", Alisa held her hand out for me to grab it. "Althea said that Mother used to beat you...why?", "Doesn't matter, it was hundreds of years ago.", "But if it doesn't matter, then what are you doing? Why join Corsa? Why kill your sister? You're lying to me.", I said. "Emillie, has there ever been a time when our mother showed you, ACTUAL, love? Tell the truth.". I thought about the time we were sitting in the med room, after Althea had almost killed me. I remembered my mother's sadness at the fact that I was almost lost. We hugged. She admired me. For a short amount of time, because then I learned about Alisa. Another secret she kept from me. Then there was the first day we met, when she experimented on me. How in the world can she be so cruel to her own child? The woman standing before me is my sister. She was beaten growing up. And for that, she joined Corsa? Would I join Corsa? Would I? I kept running it in my head now. I did hate Amana, and I didn't like Mileeda that much. Ko-e, I wasn't too sure about, but she did say the same thing about my mother. She said that she is only trying to protect me. Ko-e knows who my father is. Yet, she doesn't want to tell me, because she probably thinks my mother should. Alisa was watching me, waiting for an answer. I thought about the children, and I thought about Dalia, who I did love, and also Celda, and Vaness, and then, Sylvia, who I didn't like at first, but now, she was as close to me as Celda or Vaness. Then I thought of my Sandin, and how I loved him, and how Corsa hurt Awalli. Awalli, who I really was starting to like. "Bring back Awalli.", I said. Alisa looked at me confused, then she started to laugh, "She is far from your reach. You will never see her again.", Alisa said, sticking her tongue out at me, "Or, maybe, if you join Corsa, Corsa will return her to you.". I'd heard enough. I felt Septima taking control again, and then, suddenly, I held the sword up, and it disappeared. Then I felt Septima teleport us to Alisa's side, where my sword reappeared, and Septima grabbed it, and stabbed Alisa straight through her gut. Septima, twisted the blade, and Alisa just held onto it, while Septima walked us forward, backing Alisa into a wall, "Listen to me, Alisa. Father has a special place for you, when you get home.", Septima said through me, and then she ripped the sword out of her side, causing her essence to explode from her body. She screamed, and the whole room echoed with it. Then, an even more frightening thing began to occur. The blast hit one of the glowing pods, which exploded, and unleashed some kind of strange creature. It looked sort of like Casian, but bigger. Speaking of Casian, she arrived on my shoulder, "Amana has left the ship to search for Ko-e, but…", she stopped talking. Then I felt a hand on my other shoulder, "It's okay, Emillie, I'm here.", Ko-e said. She wasn't at all affected by the cannon shot, and was looking around at the creatures coming out of the pods. "We must free them, but not here on Plinth. I can call my husband.", Ko-e said, and disappeared. "She's married?", I asked, confused. "Yes, but that isn't the important part, the creatures will be taken care of. But you must go back to the city and help fight the Latturs.", Casian said. "Latturs?", "That is what this giant creature is. It is a queen. Its eggs were powering the vessel. Without them, the vessel shall fall out of the sky.".

SANDIN: "Mileeda, this is insane.", I said, as I continued to pack the giant shell into the bird. "I said you wouldn't like it, but at this point, the only way is a memory bomb. Our people will be protected, but everyone else will forget this happened. The creatures...we can destroy with a spell. I've already prepared it, but I'll need another goddess to help me. The energy required, it's too much. I need Amana, or Emillie, or my granddaughters, Awalli, or Layna.", "Well, call Layna. Last I saw Awalli, she was with Emillie on the ship.", "It's not that simple, Sandin. She is dealing with her own situation, and cannot just come here.", "Well, then what are we gonna do? Call Amana. Get her here.", "She won't answer me, Sandin. She is still mad at me for earlier.", Mileeda said, smiling. "You think this is funny? We need to hurry!", "DON'T, talk to me, like that.", Mileeda said, in a tone that definitely made me straighten up right away, "Listen to me...we've fought these creatures before. We've seen this ship. Twelve-hundred years ago. It's a long story, but today, we will make sure they don't return.". Emillie appeared in the room. She had Casian on her shoulder, and was covered in oil and blood, "Alisa is dead. Where is my mother?", she asked coldly. I figured it was Septima talking. "I don't know. She is hiding from me.", Mileeda replied, "Emillie, forget about her, I need your help.", she directed her to an area I didn't notice before. She had drawn circles on the floor. I recognized the circle symbols as the same ones from the ring on Emillie's finger. "I need you to stand in the circle.". Emillie stood in the circle, and the symbols began to glow.

Then they formed a wall around Emillie and Mileeda. They both stood there with their eyes closed. I wondered what was happening. Then I remembered the memory bomb. I didn't know what to think. It seemed wrong to do this.

LODY: Dalia and I had some extremely close calls. There was a beast that came at me, and I wasn't fast enough to turn and shoot it, and so it caught my arm. It hurt like a mother, but Dalia came out fast, and blasted it with some kind of orange energy. "Are you alright? I told you that you would die. Probably.", Dalia said. "I'm honestly surprised I'm still alive. These creatures seem to be coming hard. How can we deal with this? I think we're losing men.", I said, looking around at all the dead people. Sandin was nowhere around, and neither was Sylvia. I wondered where they were. Then, one of the creatures rushed at us, but stopped, and then keeled over. The other's started to do the same. I looked around at the surprised looks on everyone's faces. Then I looked up at the giant ship and saw that it was disappearing. Then, Ko-e was standing next to Dalia. I knew this woman was Ko-e. She looked slightly like Amana. "Dalia, the ship has been taken care of. There is nothing to fear. I see that Mileeda has performed the spell. Excellent.", "Okay, Ko-e, no more games.", Amana said, appearing next to her, and holding her cannon to her head. "Amana, I'd like you to know…I love you…Little Sister.", Ko-e said, then she quickly did some finger movement, and Amana was stuck. Ko-e stood in front of her, winked, and then disappeared. Once Amana was able to move, immediately, she fired her cannon into the air in frustration, "I WANT EVERYONE TO TRACE HER SIGNATURE, NOW!", Amana yelled. Everyone just stood there. A few people started to run their tracers. "Amana, you can't be serious. Ko-e saved us all.", I said. "Mr. Red, you don't understand, but I will brief you. Dalia, you should return to your orphanage. Yellfy, I'm glad you're still alive. We have a lot to talk about now that Brom is dead. Naser, I'm glad you're still alive as well. I need you to get the clean crew here and start getting rid of these carcasses. And I need someone to tell me they got a trace on my sister, and I need to hear that now!", Amana was giving orders to everyone, while I took Dalia's hand, and she teleported us to her orphanage. We went inside, and all of the kids were placed in the kitchen to keep them out of trouble and safe. "What's going to happen?", I asked. "Knowing Amana, she'll probably wipe everyone's memory of this. But I think it would be a waste of time. There is more coming. I can feel it, Lody. This is only the beginning.".

SYLVIA: It was hard to believe it was over. But now, my grandmother was getting ready to do something even I couldn't agree with. I was afraid to ask, but I knew I had to, "Grandmother…is this really necessary?", "Absolutely. People don't need to remember how close the world came to ending, and they definitely need to forget about these creatures and the Spaceship.", "But…isn't it better if people remember? I mean, this attack was so sudden, and nobody was really prepared. Next time, people could be.", I said. Grandmother stared at me for a minute, then waved her hand, and the man in the bird took off. "Nobody needs to remember.", Mileeda said. "You're wrong.", Emillie said, flying after the bird. "EMILLIE!", my grandmother yelled, but she was already almost upon the bird.

EMILLIE: I didn't care what they were sure of or what they've done before that worked for them, this was wrong. People deserved to know these kinds of things were out there. They needed to know that Awalli sacrificed herself for them. They needed to know how hard we fought. They needed to remember how they're loved ones died. They needed to remember all of it. I caught up to the bird, planted my hands into the side, and ripped a hole. Then I saw the bomb attached inside. I ripped all the riggings holding it in, and then flew the bomb away where there was nobody present for it to affect. It was then, I saw something I couldn't believe. Alisa was alive, but badly damaged. Septima flew us towards her. We landed and she looked up at us, "...so...you've come...to finish me?", she asked, coughing up blood. I felt Septima wanting to stick the blade in her, "How are you alive? I saw you die.", "I...have strengthened my essence. I can teach you things like that, Emillie. Just, help me… Help me, Sister…", Alisa said, holding her hand out. Her face and front were covered in blood, and the look on her face was one of failure. "Ko-e...she said NOT to kill you...but I don't know.". I kneeled next to her, dug deep inside, and I felt my essence, and I used it to heal her somewhat. She turned on her back, and breathed hard, "Thank...you.", she said. "Let's just remember this.", Septima said through me. "Sure, Little Sisters. I just need you to know…", Alisa got up, slowly, dusting herself off, "...Mother, is going to kill you for aiding me.", she said, then disappeared. I didn't know where she went, but then I thought about her condition. She was still weak and will need to heal. It will take time, and she can't attack. Ko-e has Althea/Lona. She should be secured, and I knew the Latturs were dead, so everything should be okay. As I turned to fly back, a portal opened up, and out stepped a very young boy. He looked like he could be Cynda's age. "Emillie...nice to meet you.", he said, walking up to me, and shaking my hand, "...Oh... and Septima as well. Nice to meet both of you. But, I think, Septima, it's time for you to go home.", the young boy said, and suddenly, I felt Septima leave. She was completely gone. I didn't even feel any extra energy, just… I don't know what I was feeling because it felt new. "So, like I was about to say… So...I'm Dooley, at least that's the name I choose to go by now. It's just easier.", the boy said, smiling at me. "So, um...Dooley, what are you doing here, and how do you know who I am?", "Well, I'm your grandfather. I know. It's strange, because…", he pointed up and down, indicating the fact he was a child. "You're...my grandfather? Like...my father's, father?", "No. I'm Amana's.", "But she is the daughter of Sebas…", "PLEASE...don't say that while I'm with you. My name is cursed. If you say it, someone who I don't want to find me, will find me.", Dooley said, looking around. "So, you're...him, but you don't want someone to find you? Who are YOU afraid of?", I asked. If he really is Sebastian, then what the hell is he doing here? Why is he just randomly appearing before me? "Good job. I'm glad you listened to Ko-e. She is right. Letting your sister live, will yield great rewards. As for your mother, well, she is becoming quite an issue. She refuses to listen to the warnings of Ko-e, so therefore, she is disobeying her mother, who has the highest authority, so, do you think you can do me a favor, and set up a meeting between us?", Sebastian said, looking embarrassed. This was just silly. "I'm sorry, but this is insane. If you're her father, why not just talk to her yourself?", "Because she isn't happy with me, or her mother. You see, Calypsa died, because me and your grandmother had no choice. She was the least prominent sacrifice.". I ran his words through my head, "What?", I asked. I felt like Amana's anger was justified. "Look, I get it, you're upset. Your mother has been extremely upset for thousands of years, but I need you to PLEASE, just get her to talk to me! You don't understand the seriousness of what Amana has done.", "What has she done?", "Something I can fix, but I need to speak with her about it. Please, Emillie...please.". Dooley knelt on one knee, holding my hand to his forehead. I didn't know what to think. "Why are you a kid?", I asked him. "Because, this is an easy form to hold for multiple years. An older form gets tiring. I'm a lot older than all of you. One day, you might do the same thing. But please, Emillie. Amana. I need to talk to her. I need YOU to tell her.". I decided to bring him to Base.

As we arrived, we were being stared at by everyone. Sylvia came up to me, and hugged me, "Emillie, you're filthy. You need to get cleaned right away.", she said, trying to direct me to my room. I looked at Dooley, trying to remember to call him that, and not Sebastian, "I have to take this kid to see my mother. Do you know where she is?", "She is extremely busy. She doesn't want anyone to bother her. Who is he?", Sylvia asked, looking at Dooley suspiciously. "I'm nobody, Sylvia.", Dooley said. Sylvia looked confused, but then walked on her way. "What did you do to her?", "I just put a thought in her head. I couldn't have her making a big deal.", "If you've hurt her…", "I know you don't fully trust me, Emillie, but I wouldn't hurt anybody with Tig's DNA.", Dooley said, with a serious look on his face. As I marched him to my mother's office, Dooley was looking around excitedly, "I am really impressed with what Amana has done here, though. I've always been impressed with her.", he said happily. Finally, we reached my mother's office. I opened the door, and there were holographic people inside, "This is it. We've allowed you to do what you want for too long. Now, you need to let, US, handle it for once.", a man with short black hair said, "Layna…how do you feel?", the man asked the blonde girl who was also standing in the room. I realized she was QUEEN Layna. "I trust Amana.", she said without hesitation. I saw my mother smile. "That is always your answer, Layna. This time…Amana has…", "Protected us, again. You always forget your place, Lyon. I think that she did a swell job.", "And the fact that she still failed to capture the fugitive, Ko-e? That is something you're okay with?". Layna bit her lip, but then answered, "Considering this is your mother we are talking about, perhaps YOU should spend time trying to capture her?". Amana stood up straight and stared at me and Dooley. Dooley smiled, but Amana grew angry. She looked back at the holographic people, "We will finish this later. Someone important just walked in.", she said, waving her hand, and making the people disappear. "Hello, Daughter.", Dooley said, walking forward. Amana summoned her cannon, "Don't get any closer to me than that.", she said, pointing it straight at his face. I didn't know if I should step in or not. "Amana...I've only come to talk.", "NO! What you've come to do is remind me of the importance of listening to that THING that took my mother.", "Considering she is a lot older than you, it would make sense for you to listen to her. You break our hearts everytime...", "YOU BROKE MINE! WHEN YOU TRICKED ME INTO KILLING MY SISTER!", my mother yelled, tears coming down her face, "And what did you tell Emillie? Did you fill her head with nothing but good thoughts of you? Did you make her think that bringing you here would be good?". I didn't know what to think. I knew she would be somewhat upset, but not to the degree she'd shoot her own father. Then I remembered, she shot her own sister, "How can you be mad at him, when I watched you put a shell in Ko-e?", "Emillie, stay the fuck out of this. You have no idea what this man has done to me.", "People say the same about you.", "Yeah, if you're talking about your sister, she is a liar and cannot be trusted. This man...or boy, or whatever, is nothing but a manipulator. Tell her how you manipulated me into killing my precious Calypsa. I miss her. Everyday, I think of her! I can't stop.", "I know, but I warned you NOT to bring her back, and you did anyway. She is getting worse and worse. Let me see her, and I can fix this.", "How?", my mother asked. "There is only one way, Amana. The same way I've been telling you for years.", "I will not, kill my sister, again.", Amana said, now moving directly in front of Dooley, and cocking her weapon. "Mother, no!", I shouted, but when she squeezed the trigger, nothing happened. She kept trying to shoot Dooley, but the weapon just kept making a clicking noise. "Amana, you know that won't work against me.", he said sadly. I could tell it was hurting him to watch my mother want him dead. "Mom, please, just stop. Hear him out.", I said. "Listen to Emillie, Amana. She is right. Just hear me out.", "Fuck you. Get out of my office, and never come back, or I will find a way to kill you...Father.", she said. She walked back behind her desk and sat down. When she saw that her father hadn't left yet, she stood back up, "Fine, what do you propose?", she asked now. "Let me take her with me. I can fix what you broke. I can make her better.". Amana looked like she was considering this, then took out a different weapon, a blade, and held it to Dooley's neck, "I'm warning you, this will kill you, now leave.", she said with finality. "Fine. I'll go. But remember, when all hell breaks loose, I warned you, again.", Dooley said, then he disappeared. My mother sat back down and once again, was crying. I went to console her, and she slapped my hand away, "How dare you bring that son-of-a-bitch here…? HOW DARE YOU?!", she said, now getting back to her feet, and pointing the blade at me now. "He said it was important that he speak with you. What else was I supposed to do?!", "It's all on me. I should have told you about him. I should have told you what he did to us.", "Us?", "Me and Calypsa.", my mother said. "You have told me. You said you had to kill her.", "The way I told you is the simple understanding. The truth is that my parents...created Calypsa, made sure me and her were close, lied to us for a long time, then, once we knew the truth, once we were finally able to be together, despite our mothers always keeping us apart, they made me kill her.", "I don't understand. What do you mean?", "Emillie, curses, spells, and sometimes jinxs, ALL require a sacrifice. Calypsa's sacrifice placed Corsa in The Void. Corsa had made Calypsa a part of her, so there was no other option.", "From the sounds of things, you did what you had to do.", I said, still confused how Sebastian and Trinity are at fault. "Emillie, Corsa was able to do that to Calypsa, because my parents ALLOWED it! They wanted so badly to destroy her, they sacrificed their own daughter, my sister, my… best friend.", my mother started to cry again. Now I really did feel sorry for her. "How could they…?", I asked. "Easy, they think themselves above everyone. Trinity, Sebastian, they are nothing but entities. They see us all as insects. Things to be controlled. When they bark, we jump, in their opinion. I don't give a shit about them, I hate them.", Amana said, now standing and firing her weapon down her interdimensional firing range. "Emillie, get out. Now. I have to finish talking to those people.".

I left my mother's office, saddened by what I learned, but also very curious. My mother brought her sister back, and she's here somewhere, and she is getting worse? Worse with what? I didn't understand what was happening. As I entered my room, Dooley was sitting on my bed, Casian in his lap, he was crying. "I'm sorry you had to see that.", he said, drying his eyes. "So, big, tough, you, crying?", "Emillie, I'm a child. Children cry when they get their feelings hurt.", "You're not a child. And is it true?", I asked. Dooley looked at me, with blurry red eyes. He reminded me so much of a child being dropped at the orphanage, that I forgot how angry I was with him. "Yes, and no. It wasn't mine or Trinity's idea to sacrifice Calypsa.". Now I was even more confused. "Then, who?", "It was Calypsa's idea. She knew your mother would never let her go through with it, so she went off on her own, knowing your mother would follow her, and knowing that she could set up the situation in which she needed to die. She understood the stakes.", Dooley said, placing his hands over his face. Casian was licking his tears. "So, you expect me to believe that Calypsa tricked my mother into killing her?", "Emillie, Calypsa saved everyone! Corsa was alive and well, and here! If Calypsa didn't do what she did, Corsa would have destroyed this whole planet!". I took in my grandfather's words, and realized they were true. I got the feeling that he wouldn't lie to me. "So...why haven't you told this to Amana?", "Because, she isn't going to believe me. She hates me.", Dooley started to cry again. I went to him and placed my arms around him, "Don't be sad. I don't think she likes me, either.", "Don't be ridiculous. Your mother loves you. She loves all of you girls. Even Alisa. She just… She is just hurt.", "Where is Trinity?", I asked Dooley. I was curious to know where she was in all of this. Why wasn't she here right next to him? "Well, she is somewhere, but I can't keep track of her all the time. She is like me, in child form. I believe she is somewhere in Space, looking for Abraxa and our grandson.", "Grandson?", "Yes, your cousin. Duke. He is the son of my son, Brixin, but Brixin was killed seventeen hundred years ago, so that is why Trinity, who by the way, if you do run into her, don't call her Trinity, call her Alex, her name is cursed as well, but that is why she is off the world.", Dooley said, smiling, and standing up. Casian jumped off his lap, and landed on mine. "Where are you going?", "I'm going to try to help my daughter. Calypsa.", "But, where is she?", I asked. "Ask your boyfriend. You'd be surprised what he knows.", Dooley said, then he hugged me. I hugged him back, "I love you very much, Emillie. You be good, okay?", he said, then he was gone.

I went to look for Sandin, assuming that he would know something about Calypsa, but I couldn't see how. His mother had that connection to the cosmos, but did that mean she may have mentioned Calypsa to Sandin? I couldn't find him anywhere at first. I looked in the break area, I checked up and down Base, and eventually went to his quarters, where he was still nowhere to be seen. I started to think something bad happened, then he found me, "Emillie, I was looking for you.", he said, wrapping his arms around me. I kissed him. "Sandin, I need to ask you a question.", "Sure.", "Do you know Calypsa?". Sandin looked at me with a puzzled face. He shook his head, "Isn't that your aunt? The one Amana is pissed she had to kill?", "Well, my grandfather told me that you would know where she is.", "Your grandfather?", "Sebastian was here. He was a kid...I guess, but he said you know where Calypsa is.", "Well, Emillie, I don't.". I kept running it in my head. Why would Dooley tell me this, if Sandin didn't really know? Then, another thought occurred to me. Mileeda. Her sister was Corsa, and Corsa was a reincarnation. Corsa's essence is the reason that Mileeda was transformed into a goddess. What if...?

"Sandin, did your mother...have a sister?", I asked. After careful thinking, this was the only thing that made sense. "Yes...she did. But, they stopped talking to one another, and I never really met her.", Sandin said, taking his wallet out, and showing me the picture of the woman who was supposedly Calypsa. I saw right away, she was different, but had similar features to my mother and myself. I took the picture out of Sandin's hand, who watched me suspiciously. "What was her name?", "Well...there is something I should have mentioned earlier, but I never even told this to Red, mainly because if you brought up the Mccloud case around him, he got all grouchy. Nora Mccloud was my aunt, which means, Adem, is my cousin.". I didn't know what to say. I dropped the picture. "Emillie, what's wrong?", "Nora Mccloud, is Calypsa's reincarnation.", I said, in almost a whisper. Sandin looked at me with amusement, "I doubt that. I think I would have known if my aunt was a three-thousand year old reincarnated goddess.", "Sandin, you didn't even know a three-thousand year old goddess is your godmother.", "But that's different! My aunt just disappeared, before her husband was...", Sandin stopped talking, and was now making a thinking face. "We need to go see Mileeda, now.", he said, grabbing my hand, and leading me to her office.

As we reached her office, the door opened on its own, and me and Sandin entered. Mileeda was sitting behind her desk, watching a monitor, and speaking with someone, "...we need you, it's time you come back. Please.", "No. I'm enjoying my peace and quiet. I'd rather not.", the voice said. Then Mileeda noticed us, "I'll call you back.", she said, closing the screen. "How can I help you two?", she asked. "Nora Mccloud, talk.", Sandin said. Mileeda looked irritated, but then changed her look, and answered in a friendly tone, "What about her?", "She's my aunt. And Emillie here says that Sebastian told her that...". Mileeda stood up, "THAT SON-OF-A-BITCH WAS HERE?! I felt a strange energy...", she said, now moving from around her desk and going to her cabinet, "I've always known Nora was Ayrellia's sister, Sandin, obviously.", Mileeda said with sarcasm in her tone. She took out a basin and placed it on her desk. She gazed into it, and then said, "Aha. So...that's how you've been hiding? Well, not anymore.", she said, then she started to perform a spell, the basin glowed green, as Mileeda waved her hands, murmuring to herself, but then the basin started to turn golden, and a voice came from it, "...no. You have to stop, Mileeda.". The basin flew off the desk and the whole room was alight with golden light. When the light faded, Mileeda was looking extremely irritable, and knocked all the stuff off her desk, "DAMN IT!", she shouted, "You should have brought him to me.", she said, looking at me with anger and frustration. I had no idea he would bring this much out of Mileeda, or the effect he had on my mother. "What do you want with Sebastian?", I asked. "I want him... That's none of your business. Anyway, what about Nora?", she said, now changing the subject and calming down. "She is Calypsa.", I said. Mileeda froze for a minute, not saying anything, then, "What...do you mean?", "I saw her picture. She looks sort of like my mom, and me. That has to be...", Mileeda held her hand up, then she summoned someone into the room. "What?", this mystery woman asked. "How is your patient?", "She's fine, as much as she could be, what is this about? Why are you bringing me here?", "Because, I think you and I both know something you've been keeping from me.", Mileeda said, brandishing her finger in this girl's face. As I got a closer look, I realized she was pretty, but also, I felt an energy from her. It wasn't like Mileeda's, or any powerful goddess, but I could tell, something was inside of her. "Well, I don't know what you mean, and I'd like to return to her.", "I always questioned why you settled for being a nurse, when you could have done so much more. Besides myself, or Dalia, you were, Ko-e's best student. You may play dumb, but we both know who your patient truly is.", "You're insane, Mileeda. I need to go.", the girl said, then disappeared. "Who was that?", Sandin asked. "She is the woman that watches over Nora Mccloud. As a matter of fact, she is another leader here. She runs the magical medical department. Her name is Clarise, and she is another three-thousand year old student of Ko-e.", Mileeda said, thinking. "So, you're saying I'm right?", "No, Emillie, there is a possibility, yes, but I would have known about this.", "Not if Amana didn't want you to know.", Sandin said darkly. Mileeda then summoned my mother, who actually appeared, and not in a good mood, "WHAT, MILEEDA?!", she yelled. Then she looked around at me and Sandin, "Oh, I know what this is about. Yes, I did it.", Amana said, staring hard at Mileeda. "Why didn't you tell me?", "One, I knew you'd stop me. Two, because I couldn't let her stay dead. She didn't deserve to die.", "You know, Amana, I never liked it, either, but Ko-e was very straight about the fact that if you brought back Calypsa, it would do something to Plinth. I'm not too sure, but I don't want to believe that what I've been monitoring these last forty something years...has something to do with that. Because if it does, and you are the cause, you know what that means...", "Cause of what?", Amana asked, now walking up to Mileeda, and getting in her face. Mileeda moved behind her desk and pulled up her giant wall monitor. We looked, and it was a geographical map of Plinth, "If you look around the southern region, you can tell that there is an energy that is being slowly depleted. I noticed it, around the time that Sana became pregnant with Ayrellia. Now, I chalked it up to just cosmic stuff, but now I'm starting to think there is a connection here.", Mileeda finished, looking at my mother with anticipation. Amana said nothing, but watched the screen with a mixture of fear and confusion. "Maybe you should ask my father.", "Oh, I'd love to...but he won't even see me. I tried to summon him, after he came and spoke to Emillie. Telling her that Nora is Calypsa. Now...tell me the truth, does Clarise know?". My mother's whole demeanor changed as she answered, "I couldn't hide it from her, as easily as I was able to hide it from you. Calypsa was her queen when she was a child, and she worshipped her. And, Ko-e taught her too well.", Amana said guiltily. Mileeda covered her face, and Amana moved quickly, she launched at Mileeda, punching her, but Mileeda quickly dodged her. Amana, realizing she didn't have the element of surprise anymore, disappeared. "Damn.", Mileeda said. "What the hell was that all about?", Sandin asked. I was trying to see if I could feel my mother's energy, but she was masking it well. "Amana has committed a very serious crime. Reincarnation is NOT to be performed. No matter who it was for. Amana will have to face justice for this.", Mileeda said, sinking into her seat. She put her hand in the air, and Clarise appeared again. This time, she had an angry look on her face, "I already told you, Mileeda…", "I know, Nora is Calypsa. Amana just confirmed.". Clarise looked around at me and Sandin, "Well, come on you two.", she said. We were suddenly in a totally different part of Base. It was a huge med area. We hadn't been here at all yet, and both of us had looks of shock and awe. "Follow me, Mr. Tillo, your aunt is this way.", she said, directing us into a room. We walked in, and there was a lady in a wheelchair. She was extremely young looking, just like my mother or Mileeda. Her hair was a strange mixture of black and purple like her son. She turned in Sandin's direction, and got out of the chair, "I've been asking when you'd come.", she said, pulling him into a hug, and then taking in his features. "The General told me that my sister was killed. I'm so sorry, Sandin. I wish I could have been there for you.". Nora didn't seem sick to me. She seemed perfectly normal. She turned towards me, and then something left her eyes. She stared at me with nothing but darkness, "Emillie…", she said, pushing Sandin aside, and coming up to me. She placed her hands on my face, and then she went into shock and started to shake uncontrollably, "WHAT'S WRONG WITH HER?!", I yelled, as Sandin knelt next to her. Clarise placed something on her forehead, and she started to calm down. She then lifted her and placed her in her bed. "Nora, can't handle what is inside of her. Her DNA is constantly rejecting the goddess essence that is within her. It started five years after she gave birth to Adem. Her essence was empowering her, but she couldn't understand what was happening to her. Now…she has some idea, but she still doesn't know who she is harboring.", Clarise said. She placed blankets over her and turned to us, "I'm sure you see why Amana is the only one who visits her. Because anyone else gets too near, and she freaks out.". I looked at Nora, who was now resting peacefully. "Sandin, lets go.".

"I just don't get it. Amana has done so much to my life…", Sandin was saying, as we were sitting in an ice cream parlor not too far from my apartment in NE. "I know. I don't know what to say. We should tell Adem.", "We can't, Emillie. We can't tell him about his mother. She'd freak out in front of him.", "We should at least tell him why.", I said, thinking about how I used to feel, before I knew my mother. Adem had been with his mother for five years, then she started to get sick. Dooley said that she is getting worse, and now, my mother has disappeared. I didn't know what to think, either. Everytime I think I have all the info I need, I find another one of my mother's skeletons. How was I supposed to live with this info? My aunt's essence is inside my boyfriend's aunt. I continued eating my chocolate ice cream covered in gummy candy, while Sandin had a plain cone with vanilla. I was watching him eat, and then he felt awkward because I kept staring at him, "Emillie, just say what's on your mind.", "Okay. So, do you think there is any chance we are…?", "No, we aren't. I've tested my blood to yours, we have no family acquaintance.". I let out a huge sigh of relief. "But, if Nora is…?", "She has her essence, not her blood.", "That takes so much off my mind.", I said, smiling. Sandin just looked away. "What's wrong?", "Ko-e said we aren't going to stay together.", he said, sadly. I put down my spoon. I reached across and grabbed his face, and pulled him to me, and kissed him, "Sandin, don't listen to her. I love you.", I said. But now I was also thinking. Why did she tell him that? I looked out of the window of the parlor, and Dooley was waving at us. He came inside, "Mind if I join you two?", he asked, sitting next to me. "Is this a kid from the orphanage?", Sandin asked, with a slight smile. "No. I'm Amana and Ko-e's father. Nice to meet you, Sandin Tillo.", Dooley said, holding his hand out. Sandin looked at me, lost. I laughed, and so did Dooley. We sat for a long time, Dooley eating some of my ice cream, and telling us funny stories of my mother when she was an infant, "So, you're telling me that Amana and Calypsa kept coming up with new ways to escape? How come you never helped them?", Sandin asked. Although we were having a good time, I could tell Sandin didn't trust my grandfather. "Because, I couldn't. I had to let everything run its course. It led to my wife finding herself again. Which, as cool as it was having three women, all my wife, it was better to have my Trinity back.", Dooley said, with a smile that said all too well how Trinity made him feel. "And, Trinity is like yourself? A kid?", "Well, yes. It's like I said, it's just easier. But, I have to warn you two, there are some very serious things on the horizon. I need you two to be prepared. No matter what, remember to trust each other. And, never forget what you two have.", Dooley said, smiling at us. "Are you going to leave us?", I asked sadly. "No. I'm going to stay and help. I told you, I'm here to help Calypsa.", "We've seen Nora. She is very sick.", "That is because she isn't just harboring Calypsa's essence. She is also harboring another's.". Sandin looked sick, and I couldn't believe what I was hearing, "What the hell are you talking about?", I asked. "Calypsa's essence was already tainted. It's the reason she was happy where she was. Now that Amana has placed her essence into a Plinthinian vessel, the vessel is in constant conflict. Two entities are fighting for control of Nora Mccloud. Soon, everything is going to come to a head, and when it does…", Dooley took another spoonful of ice cream, making sure to place one of the gummies in his hand, "...this, will be Plinth.", he said, squeezing the gummy, "This is why Calypsa's essence was spread around the planet. To protect it. She knew this, and that is what me and her mother made sure of.", "Why didn't you just tell this to my mother?", "Because, she won't care. Trust me, I know.", "Well, do you know where she has gone?", I asked. "Well, yes, but I'm not giving up her location. We'll just keep that to ourselves. But in the meantime, we should get back to Base.", "You're coming with us?", Sandin asked surprisedly. "Of course, I said I'd help.". Dooley, Sandin, and myself, all teleported back to Base. We arrived to a multitude of craziness. Lody came running at us, "Base is falling.", he said simply. "Really?", Dooley said with curiosity. Red looked at him, and pointed questioningly, then, Dooley rolled up his sleeves. Mileeda came out of nowhere yelling orders, "We need to make sure we can get EVERYTHING to the secondary base, so start shrinking things, and also, has anyone got anything on The General?", she said, stopping once she saw Dooley, "...you...", she said, but Dooley put his hand up, he then placed it, palm first, on the ground, and closed his eyes. Then he looked up at Mileeda, "You should have another four months before this place starts to descend again, but we really need to do something about Nora, and I mean now.", Dooley said, disappearing as he did. Then, we found ourselves in Clarise's med area. She was frantic, and looking angry, "AMANA TOOK HER!", she yelled as soon as we were in sight. I looked at Sandin and Lody, who looked at Dooley, "Well, like I said, some serious things are coming.", Dooley said, looking me hard in my face. I knew now, he was right.

CHAPTER 16

Enter Layna Lon

LAYNA: I was sitting in my office. It was late, and I was thinking of going to bed, but there were still twelve other files I needed to go through. One of major importance concerning Edge City, and the recent events. I had barely finished putting the Sicilia and Edge situations under the same category, and had listed the reasons why, and the people involved. Lyon was calling me, and I didn't want to answer, because I knew he wanted to know every detail Amana gave me about his mother, Ko-e. Ko-e has been a knife in my side ever since she made herself known to me. Tor, who was the unfortunate one who had to live with the fact she got around him, and killed a good majority of my men and women soldiers, had made it a personal quest to right this wrong. I told him not to worry so hard, and that Ko-e would get hers. But after the reports I received, I didn't know how I felt about Ko-e. She was obviously on our side, but she was so secretive, how was I supposed to know what her real role is? I wanted to just ask, but didn't know if Amana would like that. Then, I received an urgent email from P.E.D;

Dear Queen Layna Lon,

    The General(Amana Tia), is now a fugitive of P.E.D. She is guilty of the crime of Reincarnation. If discovered, you are to turn her over to P.E.D right away. TO NOT DO SO, will result in a war between Nocton and P.E.D. You've been briefed.

I knew right away that this was sent by my grandmother. She has always been short with me. My cell rang, and I looked at it, thinking it was Lyon, but it was an unmarked number, "Hello?", "Layna...help me.", "Where are you?", "Come to our spot.". I left immediately.

I rushed to the warehouse I had acquired here in the Royal City, Nocton, specifically for Amana. I turned the key mechanism with a wave of my hand, for that was the only way to get in, and I entered quickly. Amana was indeed here, with a woman she had placed in the bed. The warehouse was filled with homely goods, like a cold box, and stove, and restroom, and the whole thing, but it was also outfitted with defenses both tech, and magical, and it was the perfect place to hide, as it didn't show up on any maps. "You remember Nora Mccloud? She is sick, but if she is kept here, she will be fine.", "And that's all? What are you not telling me?". Amana looked anxious, then angry, but then decided to be honest, "I messed up, Layna. I brought back my sister. She is inside Nora, and Nora can't fully become her, because her body can't handle it. I did this to this poor woman, and I need to fix this. But, I want to do it...", "And save Calypsa at the same time.", I said. She nodded. "I received a brief from my grandmother.", "I know. I saw it. I'm hooked into the network in the dark. I can't go back, or she'll try to arrest me. So, I'm going to figure out what to do. Can you check on her for me? Please? Have Tor help you. Please, Layna.", Amana said, almost pleadingly. I looked at the woman who raised me most of my life, and saw how much she wanted this. I owed Amana everything. Looking into her eyes took me back to when it all happened. When my journey as a goddess first began.

I was just three, when I first noticed something different about me. The Royal Family is made up of three prominent names; The Dats, the

Lons, and the Tibs. My father was Arthur Lon, and he was my blood connection to Mileeda. My mother, bless her, died when I was born. My father meant the world to me when I was a child. Although we were royalty, he never let me act like it. He taught me from a young age to be generous, and considerate of everyone. My father had two siblings, Tena, and Solron. The Lon's had been the main power family of the RF for one generation, taking it from the Dat's after what happened with Tiggy. My aunt, Tena, was made Head of Family after my grandfather died. My father never really cared much, but my uncle wanted the head seat. My Uncle Solron was Sylvia's father. Sylvia and I were born three days apart, my birth being the death of my mother. The family found this suspicious. If I was the reason my mother died, there was a possibility that I had inherited the gift. My father knew this. So, he took us away for some time, then we came back. When I was young, I didn't fully understand everything that was going on. I would hear the arguments, see the angry faces made at me, and often wonder why everyone hated me so much. Sylvia, and our other cousins, were always making fun of me, and telling me that I wasn't really family. It always made me cry, and Sylvia loved it. She tortured me for such a long time when we were children. Then, one day, Amana showed up in my life. I didn't know why at first, but Amana told me that my dad was gone, and that I was going to live with her from now on.

When we first arrived at Amana's house, I thought my father was going to come and get me. I was trying my hardest to be brave and wait for him. I started to wonder how come he hadn't even called. "Layna, it's time to eat.", I heard Amana say. I slowly got out of my bed, and made my way to the dining room. Amana was sitting with me, and there were servants. They put some stone cakes in front of me, and I knew that Amana somehow knew they were my favorite. "I'm not hungry. Have you heard from my father?". Some of the servants made odd movements and hurried out of the room. Amana just stared at me, "I told you already, you're staying with me from now on.", "But...my father...". Amana stood up, and walked around the table. She waved her hand, and a t.v appeared. On the t.v, there was a funeral. Father had homeschooled me, and taught me how to read, and what I was reading couldn't be right. "No...my father...he isn't dead. No. This is a trick! WHERE IS HE?!", I yelled. Amana kneeled next to me, "I'm sorry, Layna, but this isn't a trick. Your Aunt Tena and Uncle Solron have done this. Going forward, I am your mother, and you will address me as such, until I deem it fit for it to be otherwise. I'm sorry it has to be this way, but it will be for the best. Or else, your family, who doesn't know you survived their attack, and that you are alive and well, will try and finish the job. Do you understand that, little girl?", Amana asked me and smiled. I didn't want to hear this, I just wanted my father, "Please...just tell me where he is.", I begged. Amana didn't look like she felt sorry for me, or even cared that much, but now, she placed her hand on my face, "Listen to me, child, I know how unfair this is, but now, you need to move on. I'll give you today to grieve for your father, but after that, we need to discuss why I saved you.", she said, returning to her chair, and sitting down, "Now, eat your food.".

I cried the whole day. My cousins never liked me, so I couldn't call them, and I had nobody else I could talk to about what I was feeling. Later that evening, I heard Amana yelling at somebody, "She is your damn blood! Go and talk to her!", "No.", "You are unbelievable. That girl NEEDS a family that cares about her!", "And you adopted her, so you took on that responsibility. Stop trying to force me to speak with THEM. You know how I feel, and why I hate them, so stop.". There was silence, and I chanced to look at who Amana was talking to. It was a woman with black hair, and she was looking angry. Super angry.

Angry enough to fight Amana. "Look, all I'm saying is all you have to do is talk to her.". Once again, there was silence, and I saw that she was looking in my direction. I closed the door and jumped back in the bed. The door opened, and the black-haired woman was standing in the doorway. She stepped in, and looked at me. She stared at me for long minutes, and just continued to stare. Then, she grabbed my face with her hand and moved my face side to side. She checked me over, then turned to Amana, who was also walking into the room, "I can't do this. She looks EXACTLY like that little whore. I'm leaving.", the woman said. "Mileeda, get back in that room and talk to that little girl.", Amana said, with a tone that suggested that if Mileeda didn't get back here, there was going to be a fight. "Move.", Mileeda said. "Um...excuse me... but you're really, Mileeda?", I asked. The whole family always talks about her. They always talk about how she hates us, but she is our origin. I didn't understand what that meant exactly. An origin is the beginning of something. So, what did it mean, she is OUR origin? She turned to me, looking me hard in the face, trying to instill fear into me. She knelt down before me, "Yes. I am your grandmother. Your ancestor, from many years ago. The loins that held Vicdor, your grandfather, my son. Now, I'm... sorry, for what happened to your father. He wasn't like the other ones, and I know that I shouldn't be so angry with you, but I am going to tell you that you are like me. We are different, child. We live for long years, and we are destined to fight to protect this planet. YOU, are important in a different way.", Mileeda stepped back, and walked quickly out of the room. Amana turned to me, "Listen, Layna, Mileeda has no love for her family. I tried to get her to speak with you, but you can see how that went. Look, I need you to take this part in; There is an inner struggle for the Head of Family seat for the RF. I know you're young, but you have Mileeda's blood, so you're smart. A genius even. Now, I know your father was teaching you, but I'm going to take over that now, and from now on, you will be taught how to be a goddess.", "A goddess? But, I don't know what you're talking about. That is preposterous.", I said. Amana just chuckled at me, and then gave me a bracelet, "I need you to keep this on. So I can always know where you are. We are going to get you a different identity. We will be going to outings, both political, and royal. So, in the morning, I will train you to use your ability.", Amana said, walking out of my room, and closing the door. I was angry, and confused. A goddess? What the heck was she talking about? I can't be a goddess. How could I be? That just sounds like a story. In the morning, I went to shower, then I found a sort of black uniform looking outfit. I put it on. I looked at myself in the mirror. I felt strange. I came out of my room. I noticed that there was food cooked and ready for me to eat. It was a buffet with eggs, bacon, sausage, potatoes, stone cakes, soft toast, and waffles. As I ate, I was thinking about my father and what happened to him, and how he died, when Amana came and got me, "It's time.".

I sat before Amana, waiting for her to tell me what she was going to tell me. But she didn't say anything. She just sat with her eyes closed. I chose to do the same. I felt like I was falling asleep, then, I was standing in the same room, and Amana was gearing up. She was picking a weapon out of a whole cache of weapons, "Choose one.", I looked at her like she was crazy. "What do you mean?", I asked. "I mean...choose a fucking weapon.". I looked at the different cannons. I couldn't understand. I shouldn't be allowed to play with these. These were weapons that could hurt somebody. "Are you sure?", "If you don't pick up a weapon now, you are going to die. Pick up a weapon.". I listened and picked up a cannon, and then I saw something strange coming down the lane. We were outside suddenly and I didn't know how we got here. "The things coming towards us, I want you to keep firing until they are dead. If you die, then, you die.", she said. I looked and started to scream. I felt clammy hands all over me, and then I woke up, and Amana was wiping off my forehead. "What happened?", "You died. Next time, you need to actually fire your weapon.". We tried again, this time, I did fire, but I was quickly overwhelmed by the hordes of people. We kept going, again, and again, until I screamed, "I CAN'T DO THIS!". Amana just stared at me, then suddenly, we were back in that same room, just sitting across from each other. I was dripping sweat, and Amana just looked irritated. "I suppose that will be enough of that for today. Go eat lunch, then come meet me in the library.", Amana said, getting up, dusting herself off, and walking out of the room.

I decided to watch t.v while I ate. Even though I wanted to watch cartoons, there wasn't a cartoon station. All the stations were news stations, and they were mostly all talking about my father. "Arthur Lon was most likely the victim of foul play. Many witnesses who saw him that day, claimed that he was traveling without his daughter, Layna, and had been seen arguing with his sister, Queen Tena.", one reporter was saying. There were two of them having a discussion about my father's death, "Those are big words, Saundra. You shouldn't be accusing people like that. My sources said it was a simple accident, and that Layna was with him, but there wasn't enough of her to recover.", "How horrible!", Saundra exclaimed, shaking her head sadly, "Well, Peter is with Solron right now. Peter?", Saundra said, and the scene switched to my Uncle Solron, who was sitting in a chair with Sylvia on his lap. "My brother's death...hits me the hardest. We were close as children. Sylvia will miss her cousin, Layna. They were almost inseparable.", "Is this true, Young Sylvia?", Peter asked. "Yes. I cry every night because I loved her so much.", Sylvia said, crying on impulse. I was disgusted. I knew she was lying. Sylvia knows how to make herself cry on command. It's one of the reasons she always got what she wanted. To see her lie about how much she missed me, made me want to rip her hair out with my hands. I noticed then that the fork I was holding snapped in two in my hand. I looked at it. It was a sturdy fork and shouldn't have done that. "Was Layna almost like a sister to you, Sylvia?", "Very much, sir. She and I would often stay at each other's homes, and switch clothes. Now…", Sylvia broke up and started to cry into her dad's chest. I couldn't watch anymore of this, and changed the station, but there was another news report of my father's death. This time, it was my Aunt Tena talking, "My brother was always the peaceful one out of the three of us. Always trying to handle things without violence. I admired that most about him. Now, I just have this hole.", she said, clutching her chest. My aunt was a pretty woman, but she was sort of older looking. She was in her early forties, and I was just barely noticing that her vibrant orange hair was rolled into a bun, and covered by the Royal Crown. "So, Your Highness, are you going to build a statue of your brother and niece, in remembrance?", "No, that won't be necessary. It's too extravagant. We will just move on. We've had our funeral, and I don't see why I should be brooding when I have a whole city and multiple others to worry about.", "Well, those are the words of our queen, and she, like the rest of us, will miss Arthur and Layna Lon.", "How does seeing them make you feel, Layna?", Amana asked me, as she entered the room. "Angry.", "And?", "I don't know. Just angry. Sylvia does not miss me. She always teased me.", "Exactly. They are covering up what they did. Sylvia is too young to understand, and is only saying what she is told to say. But your uncle and aunt, they are fully aware of what they did. They think that you're dead. They tried to kill you, and successfully killed your father. Now, look at Tek and Reginald.". I looked at the screen, and Tek was actually crying. I knew that Tek didn't really hate me, and was mostly just doing whatever his brother and Sylvia said. Tek was nice to me, and I knew that he was actually sad. Reginald was just acting like he had better stuff to do. They weren't really talking, it was they're parents doing the talking, but they were in the background. It was obvious they were trying to make it seem like our deaths really hit them. But, knowing what Amana has told me, only made me more angry.

After I ate, I went to the library, like Amana said. She was already in there with a pile of books set up for me. "Sit down.", Amana commanded. She handed me a book titled; Physics and Astronomy. I opened it, and all I saw were symbols and numbers. I didn't know what to think. "You're to read all of this by the end of the week.", Amana said, leaving. "But, I can't read all of this!", I said. "Yes you can.". I started to cry because I felt like Amana was being really mean to me, "STOP CRYING!", she yelled at me. I tried, but couldn't. Amana kneeled next to me, "Layna, I told you, that this was going to be difficult. I need you to study.", "But...why this much?", I asked. "Layna, your Aunt Tena is The Queen. That means she is the Head of the Family. She is a very powerful woman, who murdered your father. What does that make you want to do to her?", "Make her pay.", "So...studying all this, will help you do that. Do you trust me when I tell you that?", Amana asked, looking hard in my face. I didn't know how this would help, but I started to think about how much Amana had already done for me, and nodded.

Over the course of the next few weeks, I had finished studying the books Amana had given me, and had started to go back into the dream world to battle the zombies. The first time back, I died, again. But the second time, I started to get a better hang of what I was doing. I started to find patterns that allowed me to get through them, and even come back for others I missed. I became adept at learning their weak spots. It was literally becoming too easy. Finally, I was able to kill all the zombies. Amana was actually helping me, and I had never noticed, because I was too busy trying to survive. Amana smiled brightly at me. Soon after we were done, we were eating dinner, and there was another news report on, but this one was about Solron and Tena, "Reports are coming in that Solron is challenging his sister for the throne. If this is true, then that means that there will soon be an inner war within the RF. What do you think about that, Saundra?", "Well, I think I saw it coming after Arthur Lon's death. It's just those two now, and they are the last Lon's that are able to rule the throne. The Tib's would never make a move, considering the last time they tried. I remember when I was a little girl, and Scott Tib was embarrassed by Tena quite badly.", "Well, lets not forget the Dat's.", "Is that supposed to be a joke? It isn't funny.", Saundra said. I started to really get accustomed to her. Her reports seemed to be exactly what was happening, while her partner, Dek, mostly seemed to have false information. "What does that mean, Amana?", "So, your uncle and aunt are going to fight for the throne. Your aunt is already on it, but Solron is gonna get dirty.", Amana said, keeping her eyes on the screen. "But, what does that mean for me?", "Nothing. You're still young. Don't worry. Whoever IS on the throne when you are of age, will be removed.".

A year had passed, and I hadn't gone anywhere outside of Amana's property. She made sure that I didn't go anywhere by having the servants watch my every move. I wanted to visit my dad's grave, and leave flowers, but Amana said it's too dangerous. We began to argue about the fact that I was cooped up in here. I just wanted fresh air. Amana did something to the manor to make it more relaxing, but I wasn't really upset about being cooped up, I just wanted to go to my father's grave. I had gotten tired of being told I couldn't go. So one day, I snuck out. I realized right away that we weren't in Nocton. I didn't know where we were, but I wasn't getting to my father's grave. I was walking around the city, looking everything over. It was a nice city, but I noticed that there were people staring at me. They looked like they were seeing a ghost. As I continued walking, I saw a boy with a strange device in his hand. He was watching it, and not paying attention to where he was walking. I felt like I heard someone say my name, so I turned in that direction, and in the split second I did, the boy walked right into me. We both fell on the ground, and the boy's device fell out of his hand, and landed on the ground, and broke into three pieces. "NO! I worked forever on that!", he yelled, trying to pick up the pieces as fast as he could. I watched him with a mixture of amusement and curiosity. He looked slowly up at me, and his jaw dropped, "You're supposed to be dead…", he said, stumbling on the ground. I held my hand out for him, "I'm…", "I know who you are, and so do they!", the boy said, pointing behind me. I looked, and there were guards walking towards me. I hadn't done anything wrong, so I couldn't imagine why they would be walking up to me, or why this boy would know who I am. "Come on!", the boy yelled, standing, grabbing my hand, and leading me away. We ran down alleyways and down different streets. We finally reached a point where the boy was so exhausted, he put his back against the nearest wall, and slid down, and put his face in his knees. I watched him for a few seconds, then he looked in either direction, then said, "Okay, I have so many questions! How are you alive? I thought you died with your father! And, what the hell are you doing in Copania?", the boy asked. "Can I get your name, maybe?", I asked, kind of giggling. "My name is Tor. Tor Sove. And you are, Layna Lon.". I started to suddenly feel dread. This boy knowing who I am, those guards that were coming after me, suddenly made me realize, WHY, Amana was keeping me in the house. "I have to go.", I said, rushing to leave. "Why go now? You've already made it this far.". I turned, and Mileeda was standing there with her arms folded. I didn't know what to say, or do. I just walked up to her with my head down. Tor was suddenly nowhere to be seen. "Where did the boy go?", "I wouldn't worry about him.", Mileeda said darkly. There was a flar that suddenly appeared. It couldn't have been there before. "Get in.", Mileeda commanded. I did. She drove me back to the manor, and walked me inside. As we walked in, she quickly grabbed my hair, "YOU STUPID, LITTLE, COW! DO YOU KNOW WHAT YOU ALMOST COST US?!", "GRANDMOTHER! PLEASE?! LET GO!", I pleaded, but Mileeda just kept pulling my hair, then she released my hair, and then slapped me. "Next time, I beat you till this room runs red with your blood. You got off easy.", she said, then left. I cried into my knees. I cried for a long time. I had no idea how long it had been, but Amana finally showed up. "Amana... Mileeda...", "I know.", she said, also at the same time, removing her belt. "Amana...please...?", I pleaded, but to no avail. Amana beat me for a good five minutes. "Now, go to bed. No dinner. This is unacceptable, Layna.", she said, shaking her head as she walked out of the room.

For a long time after that, I feared Amana. I definitely never wanted to piss off my grandmother again. I felt like I did get off easy. Everything was sort of quiet. My uncle and aunt's war wasn't being publicized, so I had no idea what was happening with that. At the same time, I was worried about the boy named Tor. What had Mileeda done with him? Then, Amana arrived home one night, "Layna, we are going to a party tomorrow night. It's time I start the charade. Do you think you'll be ready?", she asked. It had been two more years, and I hadn't gotten a beating since, and I stayed inside like a good girl. I continued my training and learned that I had great depth perception. When I fought the zombies, it was too easy, so Amana changed my training to fighting more realistic foes, like Royal Army soldiers and Nocton Royal Guard. I had learned to find the perfect cover, along with weaknesses for everyone in the room. I had learned how to speak to leaders and to be considerate of their nationalism. I didn't question why Amana was teaching me these things anymore. I knew why. My Aunt Tena was true to her word about moving on from my father. In the three years that have passed, his name wasn't even mentioned anymore, nor was mine. Then I learned about the conspiracy. The conspiracy being that I was still alive, but being held captive by some weird aliens or something. I wondered where this conspiracy started. "Amana, are you sure I can go?", "It's time I start introducing my daughter I've told so many people about.", Amana said. "But, where is the party? Whose?", "It is a Year End Royal Family party.". I gulped. "But shouldn't I not be there? They're not supposed to know I'm alive.", "Layna, I'm the one who told you that.", Amana said, "Listen, do you think that I would take you without some kind of plan? You ought to know better than that, Layna. And besides, this is part of your training.", "How is going to a party, part of my training?", "Well, I told you a few years ago that you would be going to political and royal parties. These are important to your image, and also, very important for information gathering. And also...learning your enemies weakness.", she said, looking at me hard, "Layna, this will be the first mission I give you in a line of many. I want you...to find out what your Uncle Solron is hiding from your Aunt Tena. Find this information at the party.", "But how?", "Use your ability.". I tried to think about how great depth perception could help me learn something like that, but figured that if Amana thinks I can do it, then I can. I was at this time, starting to trust her completely. "And no matter what, I've let you get away with it, but from now on, you call me Mother.".

The next night came too quickly for my liking. Before I could even make a move after lunch, I was bombarded by female servants, all looking forward to playing dress up with me. They placed me in pink dresses, blue dresses, red and blue dresses, but finally settled on a pink and purple dress. They called Amana to let her know that I was ready, then a flar arrived outside. Amana stepped out of it, wearing a very highly decorated black military uniform, with a coat on and a nice cap to top it all off. "You look great, now get in.", Amana commanded, and I did. My hair was changed to purple instead of blonde, and I kept looking at myself in the mirror. I didn't think the family would recognize me because I looked older. Amana was right to wait a few years. It was starting to seem like she was always right. When we arrived, there were men outside waiting for people to arrive in their flars. Amana parked our's, and a man approached us, "Would you like me to park it for you, mam?", he asked. "No. It's fine where it is.", Amana said, grabbing my hand, and leading me inside. When I looked back, the flar had disappeared, and it didn't seem like the man remembered talking to us. Amana had been teaching me to use psychic abilities, but I was still rusty and barely getting the hang of it. We walked through the big doors that led into my Uncle Solron's manor. The last time I was here was with my father. Small memories started to come back to me. "Don't forget what you're here for, Layna.", Amana said, releasing my hand, and walking towards a group of men and women. I looked around. I wasn't lost, but I didn't know where to go. I wanted to hide in the restroom, but then thought about how mad Amana will be if I don't get that info. I walked around the party, gazing at all the people. I finally spotted my uncle and Sylvia. Sylvia looked in my direction, and started to walk towards me. I walked away and went somewhere else. I saw my other cousins, Tek and Reginald. Tek looked lost in translation, and Reginald walked right up to me, "Well, you're pretty. Who are you?", Reginald asked. "I'm...Shima.", I said, realizing Amana and I hadn't come up with a fake name to go with my identity. "Shima... Cute. Where are your parents?", Reginald asked me, looking around. "My mother is over there.". I pointed at Amana, and Reginald dropped his jaw, "Your mother is Amana Tia?!", he said, shocked. I hadn't really thought about who Amana was, or what role she had with my family. "Yes.", I answered. Tek pushed his brother out of the way, "I didn't know Amana had a daughter!", "Open your ears idiot! I've been hearing it for months!", Sylvia said, approaching us. I wanted to walk away, but Sylvia grabbed my arm, "So, what is it like having a three-thousand year old goddess as a mother?", Sylvia asked me, watching me with suspicion. "What?", I asked. Amana never told me her age, and then again, what Sylvia just asked couldn't be right. Amana is training me to be a goddess, but could she herself, really be that old? "Strange, I guess.", I answered, with some attitude in my voice. Sylvia released my arm, then looked me over, "You look familiar to me, but I don't know where I've seen you before.", she said, watching me very hard. "Well, I've only seen you on t.v.", I said. "Look, that stupid kid is actually here.", Reginald said, pointing in the direction of a boy I recognized. I quickly walked away from my cousins and approached Tor, who I was extremely surprised to see here, "Tor! What are you doing here?", I asked. He looked up, and had a puzzled look on his face, "Um, have we met?", "Tor, who is this lovely young girl you're talking to?", a woman descended upon me, placed her hand on my shoulder, and her face close to mine, "Oh my, aren't you beautiful? Why, I saw you come in with Amana. You must be her daughter. Finally. I don't see much of a resemblance. Are you adopted?", the woman asked me. She had bright brown hair, and lovely green eyes. I didn't know what to say, but Tor was suddenly looking shocked, and he grabbed me and led me away from the woman. "Layna?", he asked. "Shh, nobody can know that.", "What happened to you? A few years ago, I mean.", "I was wondering what happened to YOU.", "Well, I was with you in that alley, then I was at home. I started to tell people I saw you, and that I think aliens had you, and that they killed your dad. It was aliens, wasn't it?", Tor asked excitedly. Now I knew where the rumor started. "No. But I'm not allowed to say. Just don't tell anybody who I really am.", "You actually know this loser?", Reginald asked, approaching us, followed by Sylvia. "Hello, Reg.", Tor said, grumpily. He tried to slink away, and Sylvia took something that was in his pocket, "NO! GIVE THAT BACK!", he yelled, waving his arms frantically at whatever it was. "What the hell is this thing?", Sylvia asked, while Reginald stood over her, also examining whatever it was. Whoever Tor was, he had replaced me as Reginald and Sylvia's victim. Sylvia threw it to me, "What do you think?". Tor looked at me with big sad eyes, and I gave it back to him. "What the hell is wrong with you?", Sylvia asked, getting in my face. "It's his.", I said, standing my ground. Sylvia looked at all the adults, "Don't let me catch you alone, Shima.", she said threateningly, and then slinked off with Reginald. "Are you okay?", I asked Tor, who was making sure his device wasn't broken, "What is that thing?", I asked. "I brought it just in case, but it isn't working.", "What does it do?", I asked with a smile. "It makes me invisible.", "Really?", I asked him, looking at it, "How?", "It disrupts the molecules in the air, and makes you seem invisible. Nobody can see you, if you're within the disruption field. This is a reversed-engineered one that belonged to my uncle.", Tor said, not being able to look me in the face. "Don't worry about Sylvia and Reginald. I hate them, too. They were always mean to me.". Tor now looked a little bit better, "Yeah, they're always picking on me because of my mother.", "What about her?", I asked. "She...well... My father isn't in the picture. My uncle helps out a lot, though.", Tor said, as if this made up for his father. "Well, don't worry. I don't have a father anymore, either.", I said, with a sad tone. Tor turned on his disruptor, and I couldn't tell if we were invisible now or not. I waved my hand in front of this man sitting down nearby, but he didn't see me. "Seems like it's working just fine.", I said. But then, the man started to stare at me, "Can I help you?", he asked. I felt stupid and walked away. Tor was following me, and I didn't mind. We walked all the way around the house, which was filled with people. There was a man with vibrant-pink shaved hair. He was wearing a red suit with black stripes. He noticed me and Tor, and waved for us to come to him, "How is everything? Is the disruptor working, Tor?", "No. It did for a second. Sylvia almost took it from me.". The man knelt down, "Tor, you're going to have to stand up to them at some point.". The man looked at me, "Shima, Amana's daughter, right? I've been hearing about you.", he said, looking me over, "You're not my niece by blood, though, are you?", he asked. "Your niece?", "Amana, is my sister.", the man said with a smile. I couldn't believe this. Amana has a brother? I wondered why she hadn't told me this. "Amana is very secretive, Shima.", the man said, still smiling at me. "Yes. Is she really three-thousand?", I asked. The man told me to come closer, "If you want to know your mother, read the fairy tales.", he said. I looked at him, then looked at my mother. "Oh no, there goes my wife… This can't be good.", the man said. I looked to see who he was talking about, and saw my grandmother. "MILEEDA IS YOUR WIFE?!", I shouted, forgetting everything. The man laughed, and some people stared. "Yes. We've been married for the last one-thousand years. There may be some other numbers in there somewhere.", "Who are you?", "My name is Brixin. I'm Tor's uncle.", "And you're married to my grandmother?", I asked. Brixin raised his eyebrow, "You're related to Mileeda? How are you…?", Brixin looked at Tor, then looked back at me, "She didn't.", Brixin said, suddenly walking away. I didn't know what to think now, then I remembered I was on a mission. I decided to be more careful now. Tor was still following me, "Tor, I like you. But, there is something I have to do for my mother.", "You mean Amana? My aunt? So…you're my cousin?", Tor asked, looking disappointed. "You idiot, you know I'm not REALLY her daughter.", I said. "But, I don't get it, she is your mother now, though, right?", "In a way…I guess. But, I have to do something for her, or she will be really mad at me, okay? I need to be alone.", "I can't leave you alone! Sylvia is waiting for you to be alone. You don't know what she's like.", "I know exactly what she is like.", "NO! You haven't been around for a while. She isn't just mean, she's smart-mean. I'm telling you, let me come with you!", Tor was saying, pleadingly. I didn't know what to say. Tor was the only one who knew my real identity. "Okay, you can come with me... Actually, that's better.", I said, thinking about how he's the perfect cover. We walked around, searching for my uncle. I remembered seeing him earlier, and cursed the fact that I didn't just start following him, then. I walked past Mileeda, who was engaged in a conversation with the bright-brown haired woman from earlier, "Oh, Mileeda, look! It's Amana's daughter!", the woman said, once again descending upon me, and this time, pushing me in front of my grandmother. "Hi.", I said nervously. I still hadn't forgotten how she hit me. "Well, Shima, you look very beautiful tonight.", "That is what I told her.", the bright-brown haired lady said. "Hello, ladies.", said a man with a great wide smile and an interesting gray and purple suit on. He was followed by a woman with black and purple hair. "Mr. Mccloud, I didn't know you and Nora would be here tonight.", "Well, we decided to come and share the good news; Nora has given birth! Unfortunately, Young Adem couldn't join us tonight, so we've left him with a sitter.", "Shame, how old is he now?", "Only a year. He is the cutest thing ever.", Nora Mccloud said, looking at me, "So, who is this girl?", "She is Amana's daughter.", "NO.", Nora said, looking at me harder now. She got close to my face, "Amana is my best friend. How could she not have told me about you for so long?", Nora asked. Now I was even more lost. Amana had a brother AND a best friend? I wondered what else she hadn't told me. "Shima...that's your name, huh?", Nora said, placing her hand on my face, "Well, when Amana has time, she has got to bring you over. How would you like to meet my son?", Nora asked, smiling at me. "Um...", I said, becoming overwhelmed. I looked at my grandmother for help. "Well, Tor, how does that sound? Would you like to join them?", the brown haired woman asked. "Mom, please, can we just go?", Tor said. I looked at his mother and realized she was extremely beautiful. I wondered if she was a goddess or something. Mileeda placed her hand on my shoulder, then she turned around and looked behind her, and her husband was now standing next to her. "Uncle Brix, look at this beautiful girl.", Tor's mother said. Brixin looked at me, and motioned for me and Mileeda to come with him. He put his hand up when he saw Tor was going to follow. Tor looked disappointed, but stayed by his mother's side. "So...this girl... When were you or Amana going to tell me about her?", Brixin asked. "Last time I checked, my love, you chose not to be involved in me and Amana's affairs.", my grandmother replied. "Are you playing with me?", Brixin asked his wife, with a smile on his face. "Brixin, my love. My one love, do you trust me?", "Of course, but I don't trust my sister.". I looked for Amana and saw she was talking to my Aunt Tena. They looked like they were having a serious conversation. I looked back at my grandmother, who was lip locked with her husband, and looked like she had completely forgotten I was standing here, "Wait, for one minute.", Brixin said, pushing my grandmother off him, but keeping his hands gently wrapped around both her arms, "Mileeda, why are you here?", "To enjoy the festivities.", "I thought you wanted me to trust you?", "You don't want to know why.", Mileeda said, suddenly in a very dark tone. I didn't like it at all, and I hoped it wasn't because of me. "Talk.", Brixin said. "Fine. Tena... I must...speak with her.", "Mileeda, you and I both know, you never speak to them, you beat the shit out of them. So, is that what you're going to do to Tena?", "I...will only talk...to her.", my grandmother said, with great difficulty. "I'm not going to let you.", Brixin said, "And as for Layna here, I will discuss it further with Amana.", "YOU WILL NOT.", my grandmother hissed loudly. "This is serious. How much longer do you think you can keep up this charade? Now, we both know Amana's real daughter cannot be replaced by this girl.", "Amana has already grown to love her. Don't you feel loved, girl?", Mileeda turned to me now and asked.

"Hi!", said a small familiar voice. It was Sylvia. She was looking up at Mileeda. I saw that Reginald was too scared to even come near. "What?", "I…just wanted to…", "Don't you see me talking?", "I do…Grand…", "If you, call me grandmother, I am going to…", "What she means, Young Sylvia, is we were having a very serious discussion, so if you could please give us a moment.", Brixin said nicely. Sylvia looked at me with pure hatred, but skulked off. "Well, how do you feel, Layna?", Brixin asked me politely. I liked Brixin. I could understand his relationship with Tor. "I just… I just feel grateful.". Brixin looked at me, then looked back at Amana. "Okay…I won't say anything now, but I'm warning you, Mileeda. If this girl ends up hurt because of you and Amana's games…", "We know what we are doing. Now let her go, she is here for a reason.", Mileeda said. "I'm going to talk to Bill. Do you want to say hi to Nora? Maybe undo what you did between her and her sister?", Brixin said, still smiling at his wife. Mileeda looked angry, but before she could say something, Brixin kissed her, then he opened one eye, and winked at me. He then led her away. I looked around for my uncle, and spotted him across the way. He was surrounded by a group, but I thought that would be okay. I still didn't know what info I was looking for, and how I was going to get it, or when I'd know if I learned it. I felt a presence near me, and it was Sylvia, "You think you're special?", she said, now getting closer to me, and getting in my face again. "No. I don't even know what you're talking about.", I said. "Whatever. My grandmother, and her stupid husband were talking to you. Why? You think you're special because you're Amana's daughter. Well, I'll show you how you're not.", Sylvia said, and she got closer to me, and poked me with one of the skewer forks off one of the food trays. "OW!", I shouted, but Sylvia covered my mouth by placing her hand behind my head, and forcing my mouth onto her shoulder, and stabbed me some more. She looked like she was trying to hug me, and it didn't seem suspicious. Then she backed away, "I'm so sorry to hear that, love.", she said, walking away from me. I didn't want to feel embarrassed so I ran to the nearest restroom. I looked where she had been stabbing me, and the marks were in different places, and basically ruined my dress with the small pricks of blood soaking through. I started not to feel pain anymore, but at the same time, my feelings were hurt. I couldn't believe that she just did that. It was like Tor tried to tell me, she was more cunning. I got up, and looked at myself in the mirror. I heard someone at the door, "Layna, I saw you come in here. Are you okay?". It was Tor. I slowly opened the door, but only a crack, "I need another dress. Quick.", "I have a better idea, I got the disruptor to work. Wanna use it?", he asked, handing me his device. "Are you sure it works now, Tor?", "Aunt Amana fixed it.", he said happily. I thought about it, then I looked and saw Amana watching. Suddenly, I knew she wanted me to use the disruptor. "Give it to me.", I said, taking it, and cutting it on. I didn't feel invisible, but I looked at Tor, who smiled, "Yes.", he said. I quickly walked towards Uncle Solron, and he was talking to someone with dark blue hair that came down his back midway, and his wife was next to him, holding an infant, "Yes, I didn't really have a choice, Solron. Had to pull back off that deal quickly. Anyway, Mary is going to have to put Jane to bed soon, so we'll be leaving in a bit.", "That's a pity, Jonathan, I thought we could discuss the situation today.", "Mary, why don't you go get the flar ready, and I'll be there soon?", the man said, turning to walk away with my uncle. I followed them. They were walking away from the party. "So... have you seen it?", the man asked. "Of course I have. But it is way too dangerous. Especially with my grandmother and Amana lurking around. Did you SEE her tonight? She is actually here! And you know what that means, Jonathan.", "Of course. It means that WE will soon be taking care of the family.", Jonathan said, placing his hand on my uncle's shoulder. "Now, we both agreed that I would only give you the reins over SOME of the CONTRACTED cities. I'll still have all the power, and you'll have no power here in Nocton.", "Fine, I can live with that arrangement. But, I need to know about…him.". My Uncle Solron froze up, and then looked Jonathan hard in the face, "Listen, Raine, I told you not to even men…", a man appeared next to my uncle, and I saw nothing but fear crossing his face, "Lo… I wasn't in need of you.", Solron said, very nervously. "I didn't come because you wanted me to, I came because you are now known. Mileeda is here to remove your sister from the throne, and place you as Head, but not without a reminder.", "A reminder?", Solron asked. "Yes. A reminder of WHO, is in charge. She will punish Tena tonight for the murder of your brother. But know, BOTH your parts are known to Amana. Even now, she prepares your punishment.", "WHY?! She is the one who placed the Lons in charge! And she knows why I had to kill my brother! He would have seen that witch daughter of his grow! And after Tena's sacrifice, why should he be given differently?!", my uncle said fiercely. I didn't know what to think. My father was dead, because of me. I wanted to leave, but then something strange happened. I felt like my energy was leaving me. I thought I was imagining it for a second, but I felt rooted to the spot. "Listen, Solron, Mileeda ordered Tena not to kill Layna. They wanted another goddess in charge. I'm not surprised. After all, why do you think they chose me? Why Amana demanded that she train me, the same way…", I felt like time had stopped, "…she is training you now, Layna.", Lo said, coming up to me. I tried to move, but couldn't. "Yes, I am way more powerful than you.", he said, now taking out a knife and holding the point to my neck, "If I killed you, right now, it would end Amana's plan. She, too, doesn't know that I am alive. Just like everyone out there thinks you're dead. We are both ghosts, Layna. When Amana gets tired of you, she will do to you…what she did to me. Do you prefer to wait for that?", he asked, playing with the knife at my neck. I began to cry, then we were back in the real world, and I had done something I hadn't done before. I found myself in a different room of the manor. I recognized this room. I stayed here before. I remember Sylvia pushing me in here when I was four, and beating me up, back then. I shouldn't be surprised she is crazier than she was then. I looked around the room, and tried putting myself back in a calm state, like Amana taught me, but I couldn't focus. So much had happened at this party. The way that I was treated by Sylvia… It was horrible. And then there is Lo, who knows who I am. I had to tell this to Amana. The door opened, "Get in there, now.", my grandmother was poking my Aunt Tena's chest and forcing her inside. "Now, Mileeda, you said…", "I WILL ONLY TALK!", she shouted, and slammed the door in Brixin's face. She turned on Tena, who was trying to hold a brave composure, but it was quickly crumbling. "Now, let's discuss something, you knew that there were children there, right?", "Grandmother, Solron, he set me up. He let me…", "I asked a yes, or no question.", Mileeda said, as if speaking to a child. My aunt was brave indeed. She held her stance, and looked Mileeda in the eyes, "No.", "So, you were saying, he set you up? He PLACED those children?", "He had to have!", my aunt yelled, "You know, I would never…", "And yet… something tells me that you would. When you lose a child, it's one thing, but sacrificing a child is a whole different type of hell. I know what you lost. I know what you had to give, for this family. I know.", Mileeda said, consolingly, but then turned dark, "But if you remember what I said about not killing Layna…we may have a slight difference in our opinions of…UNDERSTANDING.", she said, now getting closer to Tena, who now moved her arms from her chest, and to her sides. "Listen to me…and listen carefully, if you lie, to me, I am going to consider it a liable excuse, to do what I really want to do right now.", "Just do it.", Tena said, breaking down, "I told you back then, I never wanted this!", "What you wanted was to die, and Amana and I had need of you, and you have disobeyed us, betrayed us even. So, now…", "Now what?! You do to me what she did to Lo? Everyone knows about that!", Tena shouted. Mileeda smiled,

"Thank you, child.", she said, as she slapped Tena, and then when Tena had fallen to the floor, Mileeda picked her up, and started to punch her, "Watch closely, Layna, this is what happens, when...you...don't...do...as...told.", Mileeda said, punching Tena with the last five words. She dropped her, then she knelt over her, "There, now you can go back among your people, and tell them how you are no longer The Queen.", Mileeda said, standing, and opening the door to an angry Brixin, who stormed in, and saw that Tena was basically fine. But, she was totally shaking. She walked out, followed by my grandmother, and then Brixin said, "Layna, cut off the disruptor.", I did. He looked at my blood soaked dress, and saw the fear and sadness in my eyes. He came to me, and knelt down, "I'm sorry, Layna. Where did this…?", he was looking at my dress, "Who did this to you?", "Sylvia. But don't tell. I'll deal with her.", I said. Brixin smiled, "You should give some of that to Tor. He needs some.", "Why don't you teach him? Like how Amana is teaching me?". Brixin's smile faded, "Layna, listen to me. You cannot trust my sister. I know her saving you LOOKS good, but she has always got an ulterior motive. Please, just tell me, that you will heed me.". I didn't know what to think. I trusted Amana. I even sort of loved her. She had been taking care of me for three years. Why shouldn't I trust her? "I don't know. She hasn't lied to me.", "Layna, you're a child. You don't know the truth about her. Why do you think she never told you about me? Or about any of her family. Or the people close to her? Mileeda is her sister-in-law, and she never mentioned that to you. And not only that, but she had a child. She recently killed her. Her daughter. She killed her own daughter.". I didn't know what to think, but what Brixin said earlier, suddenly made a lot of sense. "Layna, I know that it is going to be tough for you. I know why they saved you. They did this with Lo. It didn't turn out very well. Now he's…", "He's alive. He did this…", I lifted my neck, to show Brixin where the point of the knife was. "I know he is alive. I've always known. But, this… Amana must know about what happened to you tonight…come on. We're going to talk to her.", Brixin stood up and waved his hand, and my dress wasn't stained anymore. It was completely clean. "How did you…?", "She hasn't taught you this stuff yet? We're definitely talking to her.". Brixin marched me towards Amana, who was watching as everyone gossiped and panicked over the sudden change of rule. "Amana, we need to talk.", "No.", Amana said, not taking her eyes off the situation. "Now.", "I'm busy.", Amana said, still watching. Brixin grabbed her arm, and she yanked it, "Ohhh, you're testing me, Brother.", "Don't make me say it, Amana.", Brixin said, now folding his arms and bearing down on his sister. When she didn't say anything, and continued to glare at him, he said, "I'm ordering you to talk to me, now.", Brixin said. Amana made a strange jerk, and suddenly was up right, but angry as hell. "Now, follow me.", Brixin said, in an almost too jolly voice. We walked over to where Mileeda, Brixin, and I were standing earlier, "Now, first of all, why haven't you told me about Layna?". Amana looked like she wanted to kill Brixin, but then said, "I'll talk, if you take this stupid spell off.", "Okay.", Brixin waved his hand, and Amana was able to move again. "Because I knew what you would say.", "I would have let you do it.", Brixin said, lazily, "I don't know why you always think you have to hide things from me! I'm your brother. I'll go along with it, only because I didn't think any of those gifted needed to die in the first place. All this drama that's happening out there, is because Lo is still alive.", "So what? Alisa is dead and her essence is hidden.", "So you think it's over that easily? I told you, one-thousand years ago, you should have let ME kill her.", "It was one thousand and ten years ago, and I know that. But you know why I didn't kill her.", "Amana, I know what happened in Hell. To…", "NO! DON'T!", Amana shouted at her brother, who raised an eyebrow. I wondered what they were talking about. Sylvia was with her father, but she was still watching me. We stared at each other from across the room. She noticed my dress was clean, and had a surprised look on her face. She pointed me out to Reginald, who looked at Sylvia like he was expecting something. I ran my finger across my neck to her, and she gulped. I could tell from her movement. I turned back to Brixin and Amana, "All I'm trying to tell you, Little Sister...", "Technically, I'm older than you.", "Let's not have that discussion again. We'll talk at the family meeting? AND, just so you know, I invited Ko-e...and Scion.", Brixin said the last name carefully. "Scion? You invited that asshole?", "Tor loves him. That's his grandfather. I'm sorry, Amana. I need you to be happy about it. Please? For me? Do it because you love me?", Brixin asked. Amana smiled, "Fine. I'll tolerate him. But in the meantime, don't worry about Layna. It's on me. I'm her mother, and her name is Shima, not Layna...for now.", "Okay. Fine. Shima, do you want to know about OUR family?", Brixin asked. Amana just rolled her eyes. "Yes, I would.", "Well, then, Amana should tell you about those who are her family.", Brixin said. Amana replied, "I have to talk to Mileeda before I go, and I have to talk to Solron. Shima, did you get it?". I looked at Brixin, expecting him to tell her something, but he just stayed quiet. I shook my head. Amana looked down, "Don't worry, we're going home soon.", she said, and walked away. I looked at Brixin, "Why didn't you tell her?", "Tell her what?", "About what Lo is doing.", "Because it ruins the fun if you go straight to the source. You'll see what I mean. You need to learn how to be a goddess, because it's who you are. Some people are evil, some people are good, that's just the way it is.", Brixin said. He then placed his hand on my shoulder, nodded, then took off. I looked around for Tor, realizing I was on my own again. "I see, you're different, like your mother. That's why you act so tough.", Sylvia said. I knew she would come again. I quickly pulled her to me, and squeezed her arm until I felt something inside, "AHH...!", she screamed, and I backed away, turning on the disruptor, and disappearing. "What the hell? Reginald, where did she go? Find...her...", Sylvia started to cry.

I smiled as I made my way to the flar outside. Tor was outside with his mother, who was a different person from who I saw, "Listen to me, Tor! I don't care about your stupid toy! You said you wanted to leave, we are leaving, NOW!", she said, pushing him into their flar. I hurried and turned visible, "HEY!", I yelled. She looked up, "Shima, come say bye to Tor.", she said coldly. I walked over and handed him the disruptor. "Thank you…Shima.", he said. He then sat happily in the flar. I looked up at the woman. "Sorry, Shima, I just… My ex is here, and I wasn't expecting him…and I… I need to leave.", "But I never got your name!", "Oh, it's Clarise. I work with your mother, and I USED to be married to your cousin, Lyon. He is Tor's father. But, he is… I need to go.", she said, now getting into her flar, and starting it, and driving off. I stood there for a minute, then saw Amana walking out with Mileeda, talking closely, "So, it's settled, we wait until she is of age. But, soon we will reveal her true identity.", "Sounds right. She is waiting for you. See you later.", Mileeda said, walking to another flar, where Brixin was standing next to it. He waved at me, and then got into the flar, followed by Mileeda, then drove off. "Get in.", Amana said.

As we were driving, I chanced upon it, "Is Brixin in charge of you or something?", I asked. "He is the head of OUR family.", "Our family? Who is that?", "The Royal Family of Sebastian. Little Tor is a part of it, because his father is Sebastian's grandson, and Brixin is in charge because he is the most powerful among us, and beat me in a fight for the throne.", "He beat you?", "Well, as you can see, he is more powerful, both strength wise, and magic.", Amana said, looking down the road. "But, who is Sebastian?". I heard the name before, but only in the churches. I've never heard his name anywhere else. "Sebastian is my father. He is the one who created this planet we live on.", "How could your father CREATE a PLANET?!", I asked, unable to believe what she was saying. "Well, that's the reason we are royalty. Tig and Sebastian were best friends, so it would make sense that their descendants would rule the planet.", "Is, Sebastian's family big like mine?", "Your family isn't that big, Layna, not anymore, and we are about the same. Plus, because my brother is married to your grandmother, it's like a merging of our families.", "But, do people know Brixin is a king?", "No. Only the important people. No one outside of the royal circle knows about me, Mileeda, or my brother. There are a few others just like me, and one day, it will be you, Layna. You're going to be my age one day, and you'll have to remember to always keep yourself in check.", "What does that mean?", "It means, don't do what Lo did, and I won't have to kill you.", Amana said darkly. "What did he do?". Amana swallowed, as we were arriving in the parking lot of our manor, "He...conspired with my daughter...against me. They tried to kill me. So...I took my daughter out of the picture.", "Brixin said you killed your own daughter...", I said nervously. "I did. But she had to die. She was evil. You understand that, right?". Brixin said that some people are good, and some are just evil. I nodded. "Good. Now, lets get inside and discuss what's next.".

As we made it inside, Amana had the servants go home for the night, and me and her sat at the dining table, "So, what did you hear tonight?", Amana asked, pouring something out of a bottle, and into a wine glass. I watched the liquid, forgetting what she asked, "LAYNA!", Amana said more loudly. "Sorry, I heard Jonathan and my Uncle Solron conspiring.", "Jonathan Raine?", "I guess.", "So, did they mention what they did tonight?", Amana asked, taking a sip from her wine glass. "I don't know. They were talking about who was going to rule over what.", "I know what Solron intends to rule over, but the question is, what is it that they are trying to accomplish? You see, today, a building blew up in the middle of the city. It was found out that the property belonged to Solron, but there were people there. Children and others. They were on a tour. I believe…Solron knew his sister would attack that building, and I believe he sent those people there to make Tena look bad.", "That's what Tena said!", I said, remembering Mileeda and Tena's conversation. "Well, it doesn't matter at this point, there is nothing we can do for those people. But you can see now why I want you in charge.", Amana said, giving me a very stern look, "What happened with Sylvia?", she asked. "Nothing.", I lied. Amana smiled, "Okay. Fine. But if she goes too far… don't hesitate to tell me.", she said, getting up from the table, "Other than that, good job.", "But…I didn't get what you asked me to.", "Yeah you did. You learned about Lo, and you also learned that Raine and your uncle are conspiring. THAT is what your aunt didn't know. Having someone like Raine on his side is a dirty move. But it's okay. Solron is about to get a very hard lesson…from me.", Amana smiled, "Go to bed. We will discuss it tomorrow. And…I'm proud of you.", she said, going to her room. I got into my bed that night feeling extremely good. I had a good time at the party, other than the fact my cousin stabbed me, and my other cousin, who is supposed to be dead, is alive, and threatened to kill me. I thought about why Amana hadn't told me how she trained him, and then something strange happened.

I woke up and got out the bed, and made my way to the kitchen. As I walked in, the colors seemed off. Everything was black and white. Then, a voice I hadn't heard in a long time spoke to me, "Layna.", it said. I turned and looked in the direction of the voice, and couldn't believe my father was standing in Amana's kitchen. "Are you ready to go?", he asked, holding out his hand, then a shell went through his head. "NO!", I yelled. "Layna, get back.", Amana said, suddenly appearing in my dream. I realized it was a dream, but Amana was really here. I woke up to her holding me, "What…?", I asked, confused as to what had just happened. "The next time you have a dream like this, you ignore it. Do you understand? Don't answer any questions, and don't do anything it says. And above all, don't believe anything you hear. Do you understand?", Amana said, holding me, and kissing me on my forehead, "I do. But what happened?", "Don't worry about that, you just do as told.", she said, getting up now, and putting the blankets back on me, "I'll always protect you, Layna.", she said, kissing me again, then leaving. I turned over, smiled, and fell asleep.

CHAPTER 17

Growing Up With A Goddess

LAYNA: For the next three years, I attended parties with Amana, and paraded myself around as Shima, the hidden daughter of Amana. Everyone always asked who my father was, and Amana would always say her husband. Since I had never seen her husband, one day, I felt like I needed to ask, "Amana, do you really even HAVE a husband?", I asked one night, as we were eating dinner. "Yes, I do.", "Well, how come I never met him?", "Because he lives in a different dimension.". I spit out my water as she said this, "Another dimension?", I asked. "Layna, I told you there are other worlds.", "I thought you just meant planets! Not a different dimension. How does that even work?". Amana wiped her mouth with her napkin, then stood up, "Don't ever ask about my husband. If people are curious, tell them you've never met your father.", "But…", "Layna, don't make me repeat myself.", Amana said, now walking out of the room. I clearly had done something wrong.

Later that day, I was sitting in the living room, when the receiver rang, "Yes?", "HEY, LAYNA! What are you up to?!", Tor asked me excitedly through the receiver. "Why?", "Because, I want to show you something, come over!", he said, hanging up. In the time that had passed, I had grown closer with Tor. We were best friends for sure, and I definitely always had his back against Sylvia and Reginald. Tek was placing his attention elsewhere these days with one of the young girls from one of the other royal families. I learned that Tig's and Sebastian's aren't the only royal families that exist. There were others that didn't date back so far. One of them was the Nos'. They were very prominent three hundred years ago, but have since just been in the background. Then the other family is called the Bliks. The Bliks were still slightly famous, but not so famous that they are considered royalty around the world. The only family that's known royalty and famous is my family, the descendants of Tig. Brixin, who I had also grown close with, explained most of this to me. Amana, I had to ask, and she grudgingly explained only parts, "The Bliks betrayed us many years ago, so we took their name, and made it shit.", Amana was saying to me one day, while she was giving me new books to study. For the most part, I felt like a physics expert, but I also felt like a scientist. I studied all sorts of things that Amana wanted me to. She taught me personally when it came to using my goddess abilities, but always forced me to read stuff that, at first, seemed like I would never get it. But after careful studying, and actually putting the stuff I read in books to use, I realized that Amana was right seven years ago. I was able to read all that, and more. I started to understand that I thought on a different level from other people. I thought about only doing good, though, because I didn't want to become like my cousin, Lo. I thought about what Amana said, about killing me if I do, and I thought about how I would often catch her just watching me. Admiring me. She loved me. So I didn't understand why she hid Emillie from me.

After the events in Edge city took place, I rummaged through as much info as I could gather on it, and I discovered that Emillie was right in the middle of this. Awalli, my cousin, tried to kill her while under the influence of Corsa. Emillie, who apparently from this report that I found, died, but was brought back by Amana. Emillie should have had what Amana gave me, but she was placed in an orphanage, and forgotten. All the love that Amana showed me, she should have been giving to her own daughter. I knew that I would have to ask her about this, but didn't know if now was the time. I stared into her eyes some more, as she waited for me to tell her I'd watch Nora. "Layna?", Amana said, growing impatient, as she always does. "Amana, I love you, with all my heart. But why didn't you tell me about Nora, back then? Why didn't you just say that she was your sister? She is reincarnated, like Uncle Brixin.", I said, looking at her. "Layna, you know why! Look what's going on! I'm a fugitive from my own army!", "I didn't mean why didn't you tell everyone, just me. Why didn't you tell me? I would have never said anything.", "You would have told your husband, and you know it. And Tor has a pretty big mouth. I love him, but he does.", Amana said. "Don't try and use that excuse. Tor knew about Emillie, and never told me anything. I had to find out, after I learned that Alisa came back, and tried to kill her, and you, again.", I said. Amana glared at me, "Will you take care of her?", "Amana, tell me why you didn't tell me about my step-sister.", "Because I was protecting her. Alisa killed Septima around the second year that I had you.", "But I never noticed… Illusionment charm. That's what it was. You hid the fact that you were carrying. Then you dropped her off on Dalia, and took me in! Where is she now?", "She is with…her grandfather, and Mileeda.", "Sebastian is here? But, I thought you said he was never coming back.", "I don't know why he's here, Layna, but last time he was here, he…", Amana broke off, "Listen, I have to leave soon. So, will you please take care of her?". Once again, I was taken back.

"Layna, you won't believe what I found!", Tor said, as he led me down a strange alleyway in Copania. I was allowed to be out, now that I had an identity to hide behind. Plus, everyone knew me as Princess Shima here. Copania was a very secretive town, but most of the villagers, and people who lived in the city and further into the countryside, knew about the Royal Family of Sebastian. People were friendly and smiled at me and Tor whenever we passed. There was a kind older lady that would give us fruits when we would pass her by. I loved being here. It was so refreshing. What I hated was having to go around my real family. Sometimes, Amana would meet with Solron, and would have me wait for her to be done. I'd usually sit in the room right outside the door, and try to avoid Sylvia, who I knew was usually home with her mother. Sylvia and her mother looked slightly different, but had the same brown hair. She was almost an exact older version of her daughter. She was just as mean to me. It became clear over time that a lot of my family hated Amana. But I still loved her, after everything. Tor led me to a secret little cave that I hadn't been to before. "Look.", he said, picking something up, and handing it to me. It was a rock that seemed to glow upon mine and Tor's touch. Tor, I had learned, was a different type of god. His mother was a synthetic goddess, but his father is the son of one of Sebastian's daughters, so Sebastian's blood runs in his veins. Even though he has god blood, he is still slightly different from Amana, or Brixin, or even my grandmother. He was totally different from me, but I didn't mind that, nor did I care. "Tor, this is...amazing.", "If we go further down, there are more of them, but we don't have to go down. The rocks give off some kind of heat signature. It's strange, but I rigged up my Torter to read the signature.". The Torter was what Tor called his reverse-engineered disruptor. Tor had fixed it up to do more than just turn you invisible. "What do you mean, Tor?", "I mean, watch this.", Tor said, lifting his Torter, and keeping it in the air. I watched as it disappeared, "Where did it go?", "Come on.", Tor said, grabbing my hand, and leading me further into the cave. Tor tripped on a few rocks, but he is always clumsy like this. I thought it was cute. "Look.", he pointed, and I saw something I couldn't believe. Someone was down here. Trapped in the crystals of the cave. I tried to get closer, but then, "Well, I should have known you little adventurers would find this place. Come on, get the Torter and lets go.", Brixin said.

"Brixin, who was that?", I asked. "It was a very bad person. That's all you need to know.", "But...what if they escape out of that crystal?", Tor asked. "They won't. Well, maybe if the planet blows up.", Brixin said thinkingly, "Let's not worry about it. Are you two hungry? Lets go get ice cream.", he then said, leading us into the city. The city was very different from the village. In the village, there were little carts and outside shops and booths. But in the city, it was a lot like Nocton. It had big buildings that rose into the sky, and roads that had been paved and lined for flars, and the shops were in actual buildings. I was very excited every time I came into the city. Tor and I sat next to each other in a booth in the ice cream shop, while Brixin sat across from us. Brixin was eating vanilla ice cream with chocolate candy draped over it, while Tor and I agreed to share a sundae. "So...is Amana with my wife today?", "I don't know. I think she said she was going to Base.", "Ah...I see.", Brixin said, taking a spoonful of his ice cream. "Well, what do you two think about that cave?", "I thought it was fascinating. It's why I wanted to show Lay… Um...I mean, Shima.", Tor said, suddenly looking down and embarrassed. "It's okay, Tor, I know. But make sure to be careful around other people. Especially Reginald, Sylvia, and Tek.", Brixin said, in a friendly, non-blaming tone. Brixin was always kind towards me. But I mostly noticed he was kind towards all children. After we ate our sundae, and Brixin was done with his ice cream, we walked back to Brixin's manor. "If you guys want to hang out here for a while, go ahead, I have some things to take care of, though, so hang tight, and I'll be back.", he said, leaving the room. I thought about how he is the head of his family, and also noticed that he didn't seem to do much besides hang around. I began to wonder why Brixin was so different from Amana. I decided to ask when he came back, "Brixin, can I ask you something?". Tor was doing something to his Torter, while I was watching, and Brixin was just there if Tor needed something. "Sure.", he said, watching the Torter, "Hold on… Tor, you have to put the nug in first, then you can add the circuit. Do you see how it fits?", "Oh, yeah… Thanks, Uncle.", "Now, what was that, Layna?", "Well, I was wondering… If you are the head of your family, how come Amana works the hardest?". I remembered when I met Ko-e three years ago. It was not a good reunion in the slightest. Ko-e's son, Lyon, angered his father, and he sent Lyon away. Amana apparently hadn't seen Ko-e since Brixin first became Head of the Family five-hundred and two years ago. And, Ko-e's husband, Scion, is a nice guy, but Amana was really angry with him. They had to leave, while Brixin held Amana back from killing them both. Tor, who loves his grandparents, and couldn't understand why Amana was so angry with them, had asked his aunt what they had done. Amana yelled at him and told him to never ask her that ever again. I lived with Amana, and knew how she could get, but before then, she had been nothing but nice to Tor. Clarise was really upset with Amana. She loves her mother-in-law. Apparently, Clarise and I had some things in common. She had been raised by Ko-e, and trained as well. She admitted to me that she is more powerful than Amana, but she isn't much of a fighter, and preferred to heal, rather than kill. "That is an excellent question, Layna. It is because I am on vacation.", "Vacation? But…what do you mean?", "Well, I have a very long lifespan, so a normal vacation wouldn't suit me. So, I'm on a forty year vacation. Which barely started five years ago. So, I'm still on vacation.", he said, looking back over Tor's shoulder. "What happens when your vacation is over?", "Well…I go back to doing what my wife is doing for me now.", "And that is?", "Being in charge of the magical department of P.E.D. Mileeda has thirty-five more years, then she can take her vacation. I really wish we can take one together, but Amana would never let Ko-e fill in. She is the second best compared to me.", "But Amana knows good magic!", I said defensively. "Sure, she does. But she doesn't like to use it. She is like her nephew here, she likes to tinker and use what she makes. I like to do all those things. Never forget this, Layna...I'm a lot smarter than your stepmother.", Brixin said, smiling again, "There IS a reason I'm the head of this family, you know.", he said. I nodded and smiled as we both began helping Tor.

"Layna, we'll be attending Sylvia's birthday party.", "Why?", I asked. We never went to any of them, because when Amana would ask me, I'd say no. It was a kid's party, and the main participant was my cousin, who I hate. "I wouldn't take you if there wasn't a reason.", Amana said, watching for my angry reaction. "Have Tor do it.", I said. Amana came to me, and grabbed my arm, "Listen, I know how you feel about Sylvia, but Solron thinks that this is the perfect opportunity to best me.", "What do you mean?", I asked. "It's time to start telling you what's been going on. Ever since Solron became Head of the Family, he has been splitting his rule with Jonathan Raine. Now, Rain's Tech, Raine's company, is now being handled by Royal Family members. Meaning that Simon Tib is in charge of the Rain's Tech in Nocton. And the other ones are now trying to create tech that will only be directed for use by royal soldiers. Now, here's where you come in. They are developing something that can kill gods and goddesses easily. It's the type of technology I've forbidden him from making. He thinks I don't know, but I not only know, but I know what he is using to make it. I need you, at the birthday party, to find out what the substance is, where he is keeping it, and then, I want you to plan your own mission to destroy it.", "Okay.", I said, but at the same time, I was thinking about how the hell I was going to do that. I remembered I was successful last time when I didn't think I had been. This was the second mission Amana had given me. But she wanted me to figure out how to destroy something that I don't even know where it is, or what it is, or how I'll destroy it when I find it. I knew I shouldn't be doubting myself, especially after everything else I've proven to myself, but I wasn't sure about this mission.

Not too long after our conversation, I received another call, "Shima, we need to talk. Can you come meet me at your uncle's?", Mileeda said through the receiver. I went to meet with her. I was always afraid of being on my own with my grandmother, because I knew how she felt about those with her firstborn's blood. When I arrived, I saw her with Brixin. They were both waiting for me. "Come on in.", Brixin said happily. They both led me to the family meeting room. Clarise was waiting inside with Tor and Lyon. Lyon had black hair that glowed like his mother's, and it was cut, but he had bangs in front, and he was wearing the same black military uniform Amana always wore. "So, last time, you didn't get to meet Tor's father.". As Brixin said this, Clarise made an awkward movement. "Nice to meet you, Shima. You don't look anything like my aunt, so I'm going to assume you look like your father. Except…I knew your real parents.", Lyon said, looking at me closer, "Is this some kind of joke? This is Princess Layna! All this time, you've all been lying about her identity?!", Lyon shouted, obviously angry, but I couldn't see why. "I'm sure you see why they HAD to!", Clarise yelled. "Stay the hell out of this!", "Don't…!", "ENOUGH!", Brixin yelled, and the whole room got quiet. Even my grandmother was unnerved. I've never seen Brixin grow angry, but in this moment, his face couldn't have been more clear how he felt, "I'm not about to have you two arguing in front of these children.", "That's what you care about? What about the fact Amana is training this girl to kill? That doesn't matter to you? What about when we have another Lo situation? You want me to ignore this?", "I want you to sit down, and shut the fuck up.", Brixin said. Now he was really angry. "I didn't call you here to argue with your ex-wife, or to accuse us of anything. You're here because you are family, and need to hear what I have to say.". Lyon looked like he had a retort, but sat down, with his arms folded. "Now, to business.", Brixin said, clapping his hands together, and moving behind the desk in the room. Mileeda went and stood next to his chair, "Now, I see a growing issue with the RF. Solron is developing weapons that could potentially kill us, and some of his family. Now, of course, this wouldn't be a big deal, because WE do NEED weapons that could do something like that. But what we don't need, is these kind of weapons in the hands of Solron.", "The only reason he is able to do this, is because he found the deposit.", Mileeda said, snapping her fingers, and bringing up a map, "This area, right here…", Mileeda ran her fingers around a certain spot on the map, "…is the place we believe that the last of the gold on Plinth is placed. Solron has people mining the area now, under Amana's orders, but he is keeping some of the gold and sending it to a secret location.", Mileeda now snapped her fingers again, and the map changed, "This is where the gold is being taken.", she said, looking hard at me. "And what are we to do about it?", Lyon grunted. "Well, Amana says she will handle it, but felt that the family should know about this.", "And she couldn't make it?", Lyon asked. "If she could, she would have been here.", "My sources said, she went through the portal, Uncle.", Lyon said, now leaning forward. "Did she? Well, there is no law that says she can't.", "Actually, my law says that.", "Well, her husband lives in this other dimension, so she gets a pass.", "Why?", "Lyon…", "NO! Everyone knows you favor her! You let her get away with too much! And now…this!", Lyon yelled, pointing at me, "If Solron or Tena finds out that this girl is still alive, we will go to war! Don't you care about that?!". Brixin stood up, "So what then? Kill her? Is that what you're suggesting?", "I'm just saying…", "To kill her.", Brixin said. I looked between the both of them, "My father is dead because of me. My mom, too.", I said, glaring at Lyon. "Stay out of this, girl.", he said to me, in a very cold tone. I stood up on the chair and slapped him. He stumbled somewhat, "YOU LITTLE…!", before he could do anything, Brixin waved his hand, and Lyon couldn't move. "YOU WILL NOT TOUCH THIS CHILD!", Brixin yelled, and then, he waved his hand, and Lyon was thrown through the doors, and out of the room. The doors shattered upon impact but Brixin just waved his hands and the doors fixed like it never happened. "I told you not to call him here.", Clarise said in a pouty voice. Tor looked at me, and I just nodded that I understood. "Well, I thought he would actually be…you know… Shit…I don't know what I thought. I'd hoped he would be like he was when he was younger. I miss that. And his sister. She can't even come here, and I think that just pisses him off.", Brixin said. "Why can't she come here?", I asked. "Because she is…", "That is classified for you.", Mileeda said sternly. "Why? She's family.", Brixin said. "She is MY family. My BLOOD.", Mileeda said, standing close to her husband's face, "And my rule applies here.", she said, now in a cute tone. Brixin smiled. "Okay, it does, then.", "But…", I started to say something. "Drop it.", Mileeda said, darkly, so I did. "So, what are you going to do? You know he's just going to wait out there.", Clarise said, now getting up, and grabbing Tor's hand. "Mother, I can wait here.", "No. I'm not leaving you here.", "Now, Clarise, you are being a bit dramatic.", "Says the man that just threw him through TWO doors.", Clarise said, glaring at Brixin, who surprisingly, went to the door, and opened it. Lyon was waiting. His clothes were cleaned. Obviously, he knew magic. But he still had blood on his face. "Lyon, can you sit in here and act like a man with some sense?", Brixin asked. Lyon walked in, gave me a cold look, then sat back down in his seat. "Did I miss something?", said a voice I recognized. It was Ko-e. "I'm so, so sorry I'm late, Brother. It was that damn Rever. If only I could have caught the thing. Oh, well. How are you?", she said, kissing her brother on the cheek. "I'm fine, Ko-e.", "Mileeda, it is so good to see you. I'm sorry about…", "We are in red.", Mileeda said. This was obviously some sort of code, because Ko-e turned and looked at me. "Ah, I see. Brother, may you, me, and this girl have the room?", Ko-e asked. "Sure.", Brixin said, in a questioning sort of way. The room froze, and everyone was unable to move. Except for me, Ko-e, and Brixin. "You're, Layna. The one who was supposed to die.", Ko-e said. I didn't know how to reply. Everyone was so angry a second ago because of me, and now, Ko-e is talking to me about my identity. "It's okay, Layna, I'm your friend.", she said, now smiling. I looked at Brixin, who nodded. "But, Amana is really angry at you.", I said. "There are a lot of things my sister is mad about, but I still love her. Just like I love you. You're my step-niece. And I know how much time you spend with my grandson. I can see what will happen. As a matter of fact, Layna, what I'm about to tell you, even Amana cannot know.". Now I didn't know if I could trust her. "What?", I asked. "No. I don't think you understand. Brixin, please?", she said, now looking to Brixin for help. "Layna, Ko-e here told me some interesting things. You don't understand. Amana cannot know, because she is the reason. Just, trust me. Please?", Brixin said. I nodded. "Okay. So, I, a very long time ago, spoke with myself. It was a very interesting conversation about my future. In my future, things were different.", "Wait, what do you mean… spoke with yourself?", "I mean I had a conversation with my future-self. My husband also met his and my future versions. And he met Amana. In that future, Mileeda was killed by Amana. Because they went to war with one another.", "Why would they go to war?", "Because, Corsa got to Mileeda. You see…in that timeline, there was this difference from this one. Calypsa died, but not because she sacrificed herself. She died because Brixin killed her.", Ko-e said. I looked at Brixin, "It was in another timeline! It wasn't really me!", Brixin said in a defensive tone. "And then… Amana wanted to kill Brixin, and then things just went crazy, all the way to the point where me and Amana formed P.E.D.", "Now, in THIS timeline...", Brixin chimed in, "...I'm the one who helped Amana and Mileeda, who was dead and had nothing to do with it in that other timeline, form P.E.D.". I looked at both of them. Parts of this sounded crazy. But then other parts didn't. "So why are you telling me this?", "Well, I have to tell you this, because I ALSO know what happens in THIS timeline. And I can tell you, things are just getting started.", Ko-e said, "Layna, you will be really important. And I need you to take this message with the most urgency. You will meet a girl named Awalli Dat. She is another one of your cousins. She is five years younger than you.", "So...she is seven? So she exists? But...there are no more Dat's. Except for Lo.", I said darkly. "No. Awalli is a Dat, and not the last I might add. She is Tiggy's granddaughter, and like you, Amana has hidden her from the family. She lives a terrible life, but you must let her live this way.", "WHY?!", I asked, becoming angry now. Amana had hid things from me before, but this was something I couldn't believe. "Layna, Awalli must live this life. It is important for other events that are coming. Please, just trust me?", Ko-e pleaded. I looked at Brixin again, "Look, I prefer to live in the timeline where Amana loves me, and DOESN'T want to kill me.", Brixin said. "But I don't know what you want from me!", "Simple. At a certain point, and you will know when, you will become aware that the family knows about her. At this time, you must save her. Whatever it takes. You must.", Ko-e said. "IF, my family learns of her, and I CAN save her first, I will.", I answered. Ko-e smiled. "Perfect. That's all I needed from you. You can unpause now, Brother.", she said, and everything started to move again, and in a horrible way. "WHY THE HELL IS SHE HERE?!", Lyon said, forgetting he was supposed to be behaving now. "I invited her. Amana couldn't make it, so I wanted her here.", "She is wanted in every non-contracted city, and if I remember correctly, every contracted city as well.", Lyon said, getting to his feet. Brixin didn't even do anything this time, he just stood back. "Lyon, if you cast something at me...I am going to send you to your father, and he wants to get his hands on you, very badly.", Ko-e said, in a friendly weird way to threaten someone. "He...", Lyon began, but before anyone could make a move, "LACENDA!", Ko-e yelled, and Lyon disappeared. "Did you really send him to Scion?", "No. My husband would kill him like Amana killed Alisa. I sent him home, and put a barrier so he can't return here and dettur this meeting any further. I'm sorry for his behavior, everyone. He gets that from his Aunt Amana. Anyway, the deposits of gold. That's what this is about, right?", Ko-e said, taking Lyon's seat. Clarise smiled, and Tor jumped from his mother and ran to Ko-e, "Aw, my grandchild. I love you so much.", she said, holding him close to her. I looked at my grandmother, who gave me a cold stare for even thinking she should treat me the same. "Look, I know that you have a lot of misgivings about destroying that deposit...", Brixin was saying, but then, Ko-e interrupted. "Brother, listen to me closely. Solron, cannot have weapons that can kill us. They will use those weapons to start a war that will be fought across multiple cities. But, we also cannot just destroy the gold. We need it. We will need it. I say, we move it to a secure location, and put our own protections on it.", Ko-e said. "I agree with Ko-e.", my grandmother said. I thought about what Amana wanted me to do. She wanted me to destroy it. "Amana thinks it should be destroyed.", I said. "Of course she does.", Brixin smiled, "But she couldn't make it here, and I'll bring her up to date on what we discussed. I'll leave out the fact that this came from you.", he said, looking at his sister. Ko-e smiled, then disappeared. "Where did...?", "Home, I imagine. She was in the middle of something. Anyway, you guys can go, except you, Layna, we need to talk.".

Once Clarise and Tor were gone, my grandmother and Brixin were still waiting for me. Brixin looked at her, and she rolled her eyes and left the room. It was just me and Brixin. "So, about what Ko-e told you... I need to know you won't repeat that to your mother.", Brixin said sternly. "Brixin, I don't know if I trust her. Amana just hates her so much.", "She doesn't hate her. She is just angry. Ko-e has warned your mother multiple times on multiple occasions, and Amana chose not to listen, therefore, resulting in the aftermath that leads Amana to be angry all the time.", Brixin sat down in front of me, "When I first met Ko-e, she tried to warn me. I didn't listen to her. Then I met Amana, and I still didn't heed what Ko-e said. Because I chose not to listen to her, I lost two people I loved. So, I need you to trust me, Layna. I wouldn't just back up Ko-e against Amana's wishes if I didn't think Ko-e was honest and truthful.". I nodded my head, to show him I wouldn't say anything.

Later, I wondered if I should ask Amana about Awalli. If Awalli really was suffering, and Amana knew, then how come she was letting her suffer? What is Amana's game? I began to think about this for some time. Wondering if she was just using me in some way. For my birthday two days ago, she gave me a bracelet that she said, once I learn how to use it, I'll be grateful. But so far, it was just an ordinary bracelet. Then, I remembered she wanted me to learn info at Sylvia's party, but didn't I just gain that info? My grandmother wanted me to know where Solron is keeping the gold, because I'm supposed to get to it. When Amana and I were having dinner, she was very quiet. Not saying a word, just watching her food. Occasionally looking up at me. "Mother?", I started off, "I was wondering...is it the gold you want me to destroy?", "Good question, Layna. No. The deposits of gold is indeed Solron's source, but it isn't what I was talking about. But the place where Solron is sending the gold he thinks I don't know about, is the same place he is hiding what I'm talking about.", she said, now taking a good healthy amount of food on her fork and eating it. "So, I still have to go to Sylvia's party?",

"I'm afraid so.", "What is Lyon's problem with me?", "Lyon runs a very important part of P.E.D, and he doesn't like the idea of unorthodox methods.", Amana said, smiling at me. "Yeah, but what happened with him and Clarise?", I asked. Amana's smile faded, and then she looked down at her food again, "I happened.", she said, guiltily. "What do you mean?", "I mean that the reason Lyon won't even look at his son, or talk to his wife, is because of my hatred for my sister.", Amana said, now taking another fork full. "You hate Ko-e?", "I don't know.", Amana said, in a questioning tone, "I'm angry that she didn't try to help me save Calypsa. I'm also pissed at her, because...", Amana looked down at her food again, "Layna, go to bed.", "But...I'm not done eating.", I said. "Take it with you, then go to bed. I'll have a servant fetch your plate.", Amana now got up and walked away.

As I was laying in bed that evening, I was even more confused and angry with Amana. She was keeping way too many things from me. Maybe it was my grandmother, telling her not to tell me certain things. Maybe, she was protecting herself. That second option made more sense. Whenever I'd try talking to Amana about things I had questions about, if they were personal to her, she deflected by either yelling at me, telling me to go to bed, or just plain leaving the room to avoid the conversation. As I was laying in my room, I felt a presence. I sat up, and in the corner was a man, "Who are you?!", I yelled. He stepped into the light, and it was my father. "No. You're dead. Go away.", I said, my voice sort of cracking. "I'm here to take you away from Amana, Layna. Don't you miss me? I miss you.", my father said, coming towards me. He reached his hand out, "DON'T!", I yelled, but the warmth of his hand on my face was real. I closed my eyes and hugged him, "Father! I miss you everyday! I'm going to make Solron and Tena pay for what they did to you!", "Good. But first, I need you to kill the real person responsible.", "Who?", "Amana.",

"What? No. She didn't have anything to do with it.", "This is a lie, Layna. She is lying to you. She keeps things from you, doesn't she?", my father said. I thought about it, and realized he was right. "But...I trust her.", "MORE THAN YOUR OWN FATHER?!", my father yelled at me all of a sudden. Then, my father changed into Amana, "You're not my real daughter. You're just a pawn. Someone I can use later when I need to.", Amana said. I knew this couldn't be real. Amana would never say that to me. "You're not my mother.", I said. "That's what I'm telling you.", "That's not what I mean. Amana is my mother, and she would never say what you just said to me.". I thought about what I wanted, and saw a knife in my hand. I stabbed whatever this was, and it screamed, "YOU'LL DIE!". I woke up, with Amana standing over me. She knelt down, and I scooted away from her. "Layna, it was only a dream. You're awake.", "NO! I'm tired of you keeping things from me!", I yelled at her. I then jumped out of the bed, and stood on the opposite side. "Layna, I keep things from you, to protect you.", "No you don't. My grandmother said you can't tell me things. Admit it.", "She may have said you can't know some things. But even Tor isn't privy to everything.", Amana said, as if this made me feel better. "You don't send Tor on dangerous missions.", I retorted. "Layna, in the dream, what happened?", Amana asked, sitting on my bed. "It was you. You said...I'm not your daughter.", "But you ARE my daughter. I told you that, when I first took you in. Yes, I do have intentions for you. I'll be completely honest. You're my secret weapon, Layna. Solron thinks you're just my daughter. He has no idea that you are really his niece, and that you have learned how to infiltrate bases, or even hack terminals. You know what you are capable of because I have been training you since day two.", Amana said, standing, and walking up to me, "But, no matter what happens…", she reached for me, and I tried to fight her off, but she pulled me close, and kissed my forehead, "I will always be your mother, and I will ALWAYS, protect you. If you ever hear otherwise, it is a LIE.",

Amana said, taking my face in both her hands and smiling at me. "Try to rest. You have work to do tomorrow.", Amana said, walking out of my room. I got back in bed, almost afraid to sleep. I had more questions, but as usual, Amana avoided them.

"Layna, I need you to be ready.", Amana was saying, as I slowly moved into my bedroom to get dressed. I decided to wear the same colors, but just a different designed dress. Amana was wearing her military uniform, but this time, minus the coat and cap. She tied her hair back and it made her look very pretty, even with the scar on her face. "Amana, I never asked, but how did you get that scar?". Amana and I were already in her flar going to my Uncle's manor for Sylvia's party. "I don't like to talk about it.", "Please?", I asked in a nice way. "My... A woman named Micka did it.", "But why?", "Haven't you read those stories my brother gave you?", she asked, irritated. I only had a glimpse at them. They were interesting, but I wanted to know this stuff from the real Amana, not someone's idea of her. "Sort of.", "Well, finish them, and stop asking about my past.", she said. "Amana, you are going to have to talk to me at some point, why not just tell me?", "FINE!", she yelled, pulling off the road all of a sudden, "You want me to stop keeping things from you? Fine. Micka was a woman, who had become a queen. She was the mother of my sister, Calypsa. She was an evil, calculating woman, who everyone just assumed was mad. In reality...my mother, and her, were twin sisters. My great-grandparents hid the truth. And my brother's mother, Alex, was their younger sister. She, my mother, and Micka, are one being you have heard Brixin call, Mother. But I will never do that. Because my mother was Alisa Tia. I miss her, every fucking day. The secrets my father kept from me...", Amana was starting to grow extremely angry, "...the things he never told my mother, until it was too late, and I never saw her again.", "But I don't get it... What happened to her?", "She ascended.", Amana said simply, "Now, I don't want to talk about this. Please, Layna. I don't.", she said, now getting back on the road. I watched her for a minute before I turned away. I felt a tear coming from my right eye, and I knew it was because what Amana just said just cleared up another question that had been bothering me. Did her and Brixin have the same mother, or not? Brixin would say his mother was Trinity, when I first asked about her. He also says that is Amana's mother as well, but not to ask her about it. I didn't understand why, until right now. Somehow, Trinity took Alisa Tia. I didn't get it, even when Amana clearly explained it to me.

We pulled up at the manor, and there were people going inside just like always. Some people had paid shills just to attend the party. But others were like me, royalty, and had received an invitation. As soon as we walked in, there were a lot of children. Some were my age, others were younger. I looked towards the adults, and the first thing I thought about was how weird it would be for a child to be hanging around them. Amana had already left me, and had walked towards Brixin. Tor was standing next to him, but came to me once he saw me. Tor was taller now, and I had no idea why he was still hanging by Brixin's side at parties. "Shima, fun gig, right?", he said, looking at Sylvia, who was dressed in a very nice green dress that had big puffs on the shoulders, and the skirt was all frilly. I noticed Reginald with his brother, and both were talking to a couple of girls. "I hope everyone is enjoying themselves!", Sylvia yelled. I looked at the decor, and thought it was nice. There was pink wallpaper that had been spread with white cream in between. The drapes all matched the wallpaper, and there were ice sculptures that were carved in the image of fairy tale creatures. I was walking around with Tor, just looking at the decor. I realized that Sylvia was too busy playing a role to notice I was at her party. "So, why are you here?", "What do you mean?", "I know you're here to do something for Aunt Amana.", "Yeah, but you need to keep it down.", "I'm not going to give you away. But, I think I can help you. I brought my Tor...", "Well, well, WELL.", Reginald said, walking up, "Amana's daughter, and her stupid nephew.", Reginald said, looking back at his brother, who was approaching with two girls. I noticed that one of them was watching Tor very curiously, "Look, I don't feel like dealing with your crap, Reg, so me and Shima are...", "Hold on... what makes you think she wants to hangout with you?", Reg said, grabbing my arm. "You better let go.", I said, "Or what? You'll break my wrist like you did Sylvia's?", he asked me in a mocking tone, "You really like this loser, don't you?", "I love him. Now let me go.". Reginald released my arm, and Tor punched him. Reginald stumbled, but Tek got in Tor's face, "You've lost it, Sove.", "Maybe. But if Reginald ever touches Shima again, I'll do more than that.", Tor said, stepping closer towards Tek. The two girls were now eyeing Tor more curiously. "I think you made your point, Cousin.", I said, and we walked away, "Tor, that was amazing. I'm proud of you.", "No. I've been hearing him talking about you. I just wanted to make it clear that you're mine.", Tor said. "When did we agree to this?", "The first day that we met. My uncle told me that we met for a reason, and then, when I saw you again at the royal party four years ago, I knew. You seriously don't...?", Tor had tripped on something on the ground. I laughed a bit. "So, I'm supposed to be with somebody like you?", "Yes. I'm Sebastian's grandson and you're Tig's descendant. Just can't make it clearer than that.", Tor said, and I smiled. I saw my uncle standing with Jonathan, and a young girl who I knew must be that infant. She was standing on her own, and her hair was dark blue like her father's, but it was only to her shoulders. She was wearing a very pretty light-red dress, and was holding her father's hand. Not too far from them was Nora with her son. He was the same height as the little girl, but he had short hair on his head that was black and purple like his mother's. "So, I haven't really been feeling well.", "What do you mean, Nora?", Amana was asking. She was really worried for her. Amana was caring for Nora, almost as well as she was caring for me. "I don't know. Just really strange dreams. Do you think Clarise could help?", "Um…I'll speak with her.", "Thank you. It isn't a good time to be experiencing this. Bill is on edge because of this thing with Brookemere. And I'm just trying to hold on for dear life. Adem isn't as difficult anymore, but he does still need constant attention. Right?", Nora asked the little boy, and he nodded his head. I watched Amana, then she looked at me, and I knew I had to get to work. "Look, Tor, I need to learn something. About the gold.", "Oh, yes. The gold. I think the Torter will come in handy in this situation.", he said, taking it out, and looking at the meter he installed recently. "Yup, there is something hidden. Here, take the Torter. I'll let you handle it. Good luck. And Please bring that back when you're done.". I walked away from Tor and found my way to the back of the manor, where Solron and Jonathan had met before. The meter was reacting to something underneath me. I looked for a secret door, and I found one. Somehow, I could sense the energy that was coming from the contents behind the door. I wondered what I should do, because I still needed to find out what the other source was. As I made my way down the stairs, there was a noise, and I turned, and Sylvia was standing behind me, "So, Shima, you're here. And sneaking around. Don't think I didn't notice you the moment you came in.", she said, stepping closer to me, "I've waited a long time to see you again. I know you come here sometimes, but you stay close to Amana. I'm about to make you pay for what you did to me last time.", she said, pushing me down the stairs. I fell down hard and hit the floor. I started to get up, but I was still in pain. Then, Sylvia came upon me quickly, "This is the best birthday present. Making…you…pay!", Sylvia yelled while kicking me. I tried to grab her foot, but something was causing me to be weak. Sylvia picked me up, and started punching my face. "Now…not so tough…", she said, dropping me. I felt my nose was broken, and I couldn't understand why I was so weak. "So, now you see. You might be the daughter of a goddess, but you are NOT invincible.". I noticed that Sylvia had something on her wrist. It was a gold bracelet. "What the hell is down here anyway? I didn't even know this was here.", Sylvia said, looking around. I did too. There were barrels of something that was glowing. Sylvia got near it, and then took a piece out. She threw it at me. I looked closely at it, and saw something I couldn't believe. It was a piece of diamond. But it was some kind of combination between diamond and gold. It was draining all of my energy. I tried to get up again, but was way too weak. I activated the Torter, and turned invisible. "COME BACK!", Sylvia yelled. "SYLVIA! WHAT ARE YOU DOING IN HERE?!", my Uncle Solron yelled, coming down the stairs. "Shima was here! I followed her in here!", Sylvia replied, looking around. While they were distracted, I rolled as far away as I could from the stone, and rushed to the stairs and ran up. "There is nobody else here! How did you even open the door?", "I didn't! I just saw it open and then I saw Shima!", "I know you have issues with the girl...", "I followed her here.", Sylvia said angrily at her father. I knew that I couldn't just go back to the party, bloody, and beat up. So I rushed back into the party, still invisible, but I looked for Brixin. Brixin was talking to Bill, "...and then, I kid you not, the guy said to me, would I like to go camping with him? I told him, in a few thousand years, sure. I mean, I don't have anything against...", Brixin stopped talking, and looked down. I didn't want to make myself visible, so I whispered, "Brixin, Sylvia beat me up. I'm bloody. I need to be clean.", Brixin pointed his finger, and I felt my nose snap back in place. I then found an empty space, and turned visible. I then came back out to the party. I knew WHAT it is now, and I knew WHERE. I just needed to figure out how to destroy it. I saw Tor and gave him back the Torter, then I felt a hard hand wrap around my arm, "COME WITH ME!", my uncle said, pulling me. I saw people staring, and Brixin made his way towards Solron, "What do you think you are doing with my niece?", Brixin asked, grabbing Solron, and making him release me. "I was just about to ask your sister the same question.", he replied in a careful tone. "Meaning?", Brixin said, now pulling me to him, and pushing me behind him. "Well, Sylvia found this girl in a room she wasn't supposed to be in. Sylvia says she was sneaking around.", "And you believe this? Come on, Lon. Your daughter hates Shima. Anything to get her in trouble.", "I would believe you, but we both know, if this girl WAS sneaking around, it was on Amana's orders. You are not about to sit here and tell me that is unlikely.", Solron said, now gaining confidence and standing up to Brixin. "Well then…", Brixin said smiling, "…let's ask her.". I gulped. They both led me to the office where Solron and Amana usually meet. I sat inside looking around. There were pictures here of Sylvia and her mother, Coliapie. I looked at both of them and was sick to my stomach. Then the door opened, and Coliapie was standing in the doorway, along with Tena. "If my daughter says this girl was up to something, I believe it. She is Amana's daughter, and Amana is always herself, up to something. What the hell did you do, you stupid girl?", Coliapie asked me, descending upon me. Tena gave me a curt nod, but didn't say anything at all. Then the door opened, and my uncle stormed in, followed by Brixin and Amana. "So, we're all here. Let's hear it, Lon.", Brixin said, falling into a seat. "Well, I caught my daughter, Sylvia, in a part of the house she should not have been in. She claims she followed YOUR daughter…", Solron pointed at Amana, "…into this part of the house she should not have been in.", "And?", Amana said cockily. Solron lost his calm, "DAMN YOU, AMANA! WHAT THE HELL ARE YOU UP TO?!", "I haven't been up to anything. The question is…what are YOU up to, Solron? We've been hearing certain things.", "Well, I don't know what you've heard, but that has nothing to do with right now. Is your daughter spying for you?", Solron asked, now sitting down himself. "I wouldn't have my daughter spying on you. What kind of stupid shit is this? Is this seriously why we are here?", Amana asked, looking around. "Don't act like you've never done it before.", Solron whispered. Amana stared at him, "What have you and I been discussing?", "To make weapons capable of preventing another Lo situation.", "And why would I have my daughter spying on you, exactly?". Solron said nothing now. He moved his mouth, then he stood up, "Well, maybe this IS all a misunderstanding. We are all practically family, and shouldn't be holding grudges where our children are concerned.". Brixin stood up, "So, there is only the slight issue of disrespect to deal with, then.", he said, still smiling at my uncle. "What disrespect?", "The accusation.", Brixin said, crossing his arms. Tena now stood between them, "There doesn't need to be any punishment or agreements. We just need to walk away.", she said, placing her hands upon both their chests. "I agree.", Amana said. Brixin lowered his arms, "Don't ever grab my niece like that ever again, Solron.", he said, then walked out, pulling me with him. "Shima, you need to be careful in the future. You should have used the disruptor when you were entering the cellar.", Brixin said, leading me back to the party. "What am I supposed to do now?", "What your mother said.". Brixin walked back into the crowd. I was lost for a few seconds, but then figured that the smart thing to do would be to just blend back in. I already had what I needed. I saw Sylvia had returned, and as usual, was telling Reginald what happened. She looked up at me, and saw that all the blood and damage she caused me was gone. She made an angry face and was going to storm towards me, but then her mother came upon her, and dragged her off. I turned and went to look for Tor.

Some time passed, and I was getting bored and ready to go. Tor and I had found ourselves in the manor's garden. "So, they are combining gold and diamond somehow? Interesting.", "It really takes all your strength.

That's the only reason Sylvia was able to best me.", I said angrily. "Don't worry. You're going to be Head of the Family. She is going to be REALLY mad when that day comes.", "I don't see how. I mean, what are Amana and Mileeda going to do? Just say, hey, here's Layna, the girl who is supposed to be dead, but NOW she is going to be your queen. It doesn't make sense, Tor.", "My aunt has a plan, you just have to trust her.", Tor said. I remembered Brixin telling me not to trust her so easily. I wondered how she felt about me almost getting caught. She played it off well, but when we get home, that will be another story. "Tor, your mother is looking for you.", Mileeda said, entering the garden. He looked at me, then slowly made his way back inside. I made to follow him, but my grandmother put her hand on my shoulder, "You almost cost us everything again tonight.", "I'm sorry. It was Sylvia.", "No. It was you being sloppy.", she said, "Don't worry. You won't be punished. All in all, you still managed to get what you came here for. Now, you and I will be plotting on how best to deal with this. Come, it's time I start training you.", she said, leading me out of the garden.

As we were going to Mileeda's flar, I noticed Brixin coming towards us. "So, that was a whole thing, huh?", he asked me with a smile. "This is no time to be joking around, Husband. Shima will be at our house for some time.", "And Amana is okay with that?", "I don't care if she is, or isn't.", Mileeda said, pushing me inside of the flar. I looked around for Amana, because I hadn't seen her since we left Solron's office. As we were driving, Mileeda's cell rang, "Yes? She is with us. I'm moving the timetable up. Because tonight was almost a disaster, and we can't afford those, Amana. Okay, I'm glad you agree. So, you're fine with her staying with me for the rest of this mission?". Mileeda grew quiet, then passed me the cell, "Amana?", "You listen to EVERYTHING she tells you. DO NOT make her angry. Her blood boils just being around her son's descendants.", Amana said, then hung up. I gave the cell back. Brixin was being quiet and not saying anything. "What?", Mileeda asked after a while. "Nothing, just...I'm starting to have doubts.", "Well, don't.", "You said you guys know what you're doing, but what if she was exposed tonight? Sylvia will catch on soon, and not only her, but Coliapie as well. You're risking too much.", "Thank you for your input.", Mileeda said, not saying anything else. Brixin got the hint, "Okay, this is my last warning.", he said. I felt bad. I didn't want them to be arguing because of me.

We arrived at Brixin's manor, and Mileeda rushed me into the house. "Go find the guest room you always stay in.", she commanded. I found it, then started to remove my dress. I found night clothes ready for me, and started to put them on. "Mileeda, you told me that you don't want anything to do with them, yet, you're going to train Layna?", "It's strategic.", "It's because you love her.", "Do not, ever say that to me again.", "Why not? She is your blood.", "And you know how I feel about them.", "I know you're not being fair. You're punishing them for Vicdor's fuck up's.", "I'm not punishing them.", "They all just want some kind of attention from you. Even Little Sylvia keeps trying, and you're so cold to her.", "My love, can we NOT talk about this?", "You and my sister are so alike. It's sort of scary.", "Amana is… You know what she is to me.", "Yeah, I know. But what about that one time?", "It was just a misunderstanding. I don't want vengeance for Corsa, because I know the truth now.", Mileeda said, as I watched through the door crack, and she sat down, with a glass of ticenta in her hand. My first thought was, who is Corsa? "Well, Amana finally killed Alisa, so I guess your hate isn't too unheard of. It's just that I hate seeing you treat Layna so badly. At least Amana is motherly towards her. You're just mean.", Brixin said, leaning back in his chair. Mileeda now got up from hers, and went and sat with Brixin in his chair, "She is my blood, but that doesn't mean I have to like her. I'll train her to run the family. They need someone in charge who I know I can trust. But I'll never show ANY of them…love.", Mileeda said, shaking her head slightly, then laid it upon Brixin's chest. Brixin kissed her forehead, and I figured I should stop watching. I wanted to earn her love, but I didn't know how. Maybe it was impossible.

The next day, Mileeda wasted no time, "UP!", she yelled at me. I got out of the bed, "I don't know how you do things at Amana's house, but here when I say to move, I expect you to be in the kitchen five minutes ago!", she yelled at me now. I started trying to rush. In my haste, I put my pants on backwards. I rushed out into the kitchen where breakfast was ready, and Mileeda and Brixin were both already in the kitchen. Brixin looked at me and started to laugh out loud. Mileeda didn't look slightly amused, "What is this?", she asked, pointing at my pants. "I… didn't realize.", I said, turning to go back. "Well, just know that you're now late, and there will be punishment.", "Mileeda, really? You're being too tough.", Brixin said. "My love, this is my training session, not yours. Enjoy your vacation.". Brixin just shook his head. I went to put my pants on the right way. Brixin knocked on the door, "Hey, just wanted to wish you luck today. Mileeda is treating you like she expects you to be an expert. AND considering you've been living with my psycho sister since you were five, I'm going to guess you are. Just, try not to have too many of these situations.", he said, smiling like always. He slinked off and went about his business. My hell was just starting.

Mileeda was having me focus on moving objects with my mind. I hadn't tried this out yet with Amana. When I tried explaining that, she just gave me a look, and I knew to hurry and do what she was saying. I tried for twenty minutes, and nothing was happening. Mileeda then decided to teach me magic. She brought out a book that had no title. Just scribbles and notes. "This is a book filled with spells and the math you'll need to know to perform the spells. Some are easy, some are really complicated. We'll start with the complicated.". She had me read and study the last eighty pages. I understood some of it. It was like physics. After some time, Mileeda had me practicing to move objects with my mind again. I sort of cheated and used magic. "DON'T USE MAGIC!", she yelled, also slapping me on the back of my head. I tried again, but couldn't focus. "We'll move on.", she said irritatedly. She started trying to teach me hand to hand. I got my ass kicked, but eventually, I had outsmarted her. Fighting came easy to me. It was just like when Amana had trained me to kill soldiers and guards. This was the first time today my grandmother smiled, "Finally. Something you can do.", she said, "Now, here is what I want you to do now. Go eat lunch. I think Tor is here with my husband, so you can take a break after your lunch. Because when you come back, we will be working on your psychic abilities again.". Mileeda walked off, and I was happy to get away.

When I walked into the sitting room, Tor was indeed here, but not with his mother. Lyon was sitting next to his son, and having a conversation with Brixin, "...telling you, Uncle, you can't keep letting her do stuff like this.", "Well what do you suppose I do, Lyon? You know how she gets whenever I try to tell her stuff. She doesn't like it.", "You're her king, and her father. You need to talk to her. I've tried, but she doesn't want to hear anything I have to say, and you know she won't listen to Mileeda, either.", Lyon said, taking a sip of juice. "You have a daughter, Uncle Brixin?", I asked, walking up. Lyon turned to me and I saw hate in his eyes, "Yes, he does. My cousin, Linda. But she doesn't come here often. I work with her at Base.", Lyon said, turning back to his uncle, "So?". Brixin sighed and waved his hand. The woman that appeared looked so much like a combination of Brixin and Mileeda, there was no mistaking that she is their daughter. "Yes, Father?", she said in an irritated tone, while also looking at something in her hand, "Wait, actually. Lyon, I need you back there. There are some strange things going on in Edge and I think it has to do with your mother.". Lyon kissed his son on his forehead and left. I looked at Tor because I always assumed he hated his father, but Tor didn't say anything. "Why, Linda?", "Why what, Father?", "Why are you giving him a hard time?", "Why not? He gives everyone else a hard time. Besides, it serves him right for what he did back on that mission in Soltor. Who is this?", she asked, pointing at me. "She is your cousin.", Brixin said. Linda looked me over, "I don't feel Sebastian's blood in her. I feel Mileeda's.", Linda said, now looking hard at her father, "I'm not going to say anything.", she said. "Good.", Brixin replied, "Now, in the meantime, can you please refrain from pissing him off? I really need him to stay out of my hair.", "So he's supposed to be all up in mine?", "You work with him.", "You're his king.". Brixin put his face in his hands, "Sometimes, I wish I let Amana stay Head of the Family.". Mileeda entered into the sitting room and saw her daughter, "Why aren't you on Base?", "Father called me here.". I could tell there was some hostility. "Well, get back to work. You aren't needed here.", "What are you doing with this girl...Mother?", Linda asked. "She is none of your concern.", "Really? She is my blood, but through my brother...so, tell me why I shouldn't be concerned.", "Because I said so.", "Oh...is that why? Why didn't I realize? I'm so stupid.", Linda said, sarcastically putting her hands on her hips and shaking her head, "I'll remember next time.", she said, then she disappeared. "Why...?", "Lyon was complaining.", "I'm going to have a talk with that man he will not forget. By the time I am...", "Let's not, Amana can handle it. You don't have to do everything, Mileeda. That's why she is there.", Brixin said, placing his arm around his wife's shoulders, and kissing her head.

"Why don't you two catch up?", Brixin said, leading his wife away. "Tor, I thought you hated your father?", "I never said that. I just said he isn't in the picture.", "I thought that meant that you hate him.", "No. I don't hate him. Him and my mom just don't get along. They always fight. That's why he isn't around. Plus, he works for my uncle on the Base, so they get pretty busy up there.". Amana was always coming and going. I began to realize that is because she is busy protecting the planet. Tor and I left the sitting room. We had walked into Brixin's garden. "I didn't know Brixin had a daughter. How come he never mentioned her?". Tor stopped walking and faced me, "I thought you would have noticed by now, but we are completely dysfunctional. My Aunt Amana has a ton of hang ups, and on top of that, Linda and Mileeda do not get along at all. Then my father and my mother...", Tor said, shaking his head. "What happened between them?", "They just can't get along. They have these strong attractions to each other, but can't stand to BE around each other. It's strange. My mother still sneaks off to be with him, when she thinks I'm not paying attention.", Tor said, throwing a rock. I was thinking about what he was saying. "Why can't your aunt come here?", "I can't tell you that. Mileeda has forbidden it.", "But what about Linda and Mileeda? Why don't they get along?", "Because Linda is angry with her mother for being herself. Can't fight that.". I didn't know what to think. My family is dysfunctional, that's why I'm supposed to be dead, but everything about Sebastian's family suggests that they need as much counseling as my family. "Why is Uncle Brixin so nice, then?", I asked. I always wondered what made him so nice and kind all the time. The only time I saw him angry was with Lyon. "Because that is WHO he is. He used to think he was just a normal guy, until everything happened to him.", "And what exactly is everything?", "You got a lot of questions today.", Tor said. Tor and I never talk about the family this much. Usually, we just discuss how much we hate Sylvia and Reg. Tek was sort of not that bad. He was just protective of his brother. Amana constantly keeping things from me started to make me curious. "Well, that is something you'd have to ask him, but I wouldn't recommend it.", "What do you mean?", "It's sort of like asking my Aunt Amana why she is upset with my grandmother. It's just something we all know never to bring up.". Brixin told me he lost two people that were important to him. I wondered if this was the situation. Tor and I walked outside into the front yard, which was quite huge. Brixin was sitting here with Mileeda, who I noticed was crying, "There, there now. I'm sure that sooner or later, the two of you will be as close as you were when she was a little girl.", "I wish so, Husband.", "It would help if you stopped holding a grudge against her.", "You saw how she was. She is really angry with me.", Mileeda said, as she continued crying into her husband's chest. Brixin noticed us, and waved his hand for us to not come near, so we walked the other way. "I don't get it. She was really mean to Linda. What did she expect?", I asked. "It was before I was born, so I couldn't tell you too much, but all I know is that Cousin Linda is five-hundred and ten years old, and she works with my father at Base. That's all I know, Layna.", Tor said, before I could ask another question. When I noticed that we were standing in front of the manor, I began to wonder why we were standing here. "Tor, are we waiting for something?", "Yes.", Tor said simply. Soon, a flar pulled up, and out stepped one of the girls from Sylvia's party. She was walking towards the manor. I looked at Tor, who smiled. As she stepped past the gate, Tor went and greeted her with a handshake, but she pulled him into a hug. She looked past his arm at me, "Shima, right? It's good to see you again.", she came up to me, and shook my hand. "Who are you?", I asked coldly. "Yennipher. It's really nice to meet you. Sylvia hates you, so that makes us friends.", she said, smiling hard at me. I didn't return the smile. "What are you doing here?", "I'm here to hangout with you and Tor.", she said, happily looking back. "Tor, I want to talk to you.", I said, pulling him to the side.

"What is she doing here?", "She is here to hangout like she said.", "Yeah, but why?", "Why not?", Tor said, now walking away from me, and going to Yennipher. "It's time to get back to your training.", Mileeda said, as I watched Tor and Yennipher go deeper into the garden.

I couldn't concentrate on my training, because I kept thinking about Tor and Yennipher. What was she doing here? She was a pretty girl, with orange hair, and freckles. Her hair was placed in pigtails, and she wore a red shirt with black pants. I kept watching them out the window. I was supposed to be meditating with my grandmother, who chose to check and see if I really was doing as she was. I was too busy watching Tor to care. Yennipher and Tor were sitting close to each other and laughing about something. I could tell they were having a conversation, and I wanted to know what they were talking about. "It'll pass.", my grandmother said. "What?", "What he is feeling with that girl, will pass. He'll come back to you. Now, focus.", "What is he feeling?", I asked, still looking out the window. "Young Tor has always been shy, and I believe you were the first girl to come up to him and actually like him. But now, he is becoming more handsome and smarter, and soon, other girls will notice him as well. Yennipher Nos down there is taken with him because of his looks. That is why this will pass and he will come back to you.". Tor was just saying that I belonged to him, and now, he was talking to Yennipher Nos? This was unacceptable. I wanted to go down there, but my grandmother pulled me from the window, "I NEED YOU TO CONCENTRATE!", she yelled at me. "I CAN'T!", I yelled back. She glared at me then looked back out the window, "You know what? Go. Be with them.", she said, walking out of the room. I felt like I was in trouble, but I didn't care. I rushed to the yard. Yennipher was holding Tor's arm, as he led her through the garden. "TOR!", I yelled. He turned around and saw me, "Shima, I thought you were busy.", "I'm not now. So, what are we doing?", I asked, looking hard at Yennipher. She didn't seem phased at all, "Tor was just showing me around.", "What was so funny earlier?", "Oh, Tor was telling me something funny about his uncle.", "I want to hear it.", "Shima, you've heard it.", Tor said, looking annoyed now. "Well, tell me again.", I demanded. "Yenni, why don't you go wait by the salt bushes and I'll join you?", Tor said. Yennipher looked confused, but walked off. "What the heck are you doing, Shima?", "What are YOU doing?", "Shima, we are supposed to be cousins. I know we really aren't, but you're acting like my jealous girlfriend.", "You said, I belong to you.", "You do! But we aren't adults! We're still kids, and you're supposed to be pretending to be my cousin. Yennipher is already suspecting something because you're acting weird.", Tor said, placing his hand on my shoulder. I realized he was right. "What are your intentions with her?", "Nothing. We're just hanging out.", "And you think that is how she feels?", I asked, looking over at her. She was watching us, and getting impatient from the looks of things. "I don't know. I think she likes me. But I've never had any girl like me before, except…", Tor grew red, then turned away from me, and went back to Yennipher. I felt like my body was splitting. "So, are you done making a fool of yourself yet?", my grandmother asked, appearing next to me. I didn't say a word and just proceeded back into the manor.

Mileeda made me suffer over the next few weeks. In between all the psychic training and meditation, we were going over my uncle's compound and looking for spots I could infiltrate, "Couldn't I just teleport in?", "No. Think about who we are dealing with. Your family has been around gods and goddesses long enough to know how to set up protections from them.", she said one day, as we were looking over the map again, "Here. Do you see this spot? There isn't any magic here. I've tested it myself to make sure. This is the spot you can enter the base from.", "And then what?", "Find the diamonds. Amana has made her own device for you, so you can find them easier. Now, the other thing that is important here, DON'T get caught. IF your uncle catches you, we will all be in for it. Solron is already suspicious of you and your mother, so it's time we start doing things more covertly. It's the reason why I brought you here.", "Ayrellia is here.", Brixin said. Mileeda looked up at him, "Thank you, I'll be there shortly.". Brixin nodded, then smiled at me, then left. "Come on.", Mileeda said, grabbing me, and leading me into the sitting room. "Hello.", Ayrellia said as we entered. She was holding a little boy's hand. "Is this my godchild?", Mileeda asked, leaning over him. The boy smiled at Mileeda and she picked him up and held him close to her. "Yes. Where did your husband get to? I had a really important question.", "You know he is on vacation. He doesn't want to be bothered with work stuff.", "I know. But I feel like he could answer better than you could. No offense.", "None taken. He is your boss. Brixin?", Mileeda called, and he came into the room, with a big bowl of ice cream covered in chocolate like he likes. "Hello, Ayrellia!", Brixin said, setting down the ice cream, and hugging her. Where is Slayn?", "He's been acting very strange since we found that artifact. I haven't been feeling well, either. Is there something I should be worried about?". Brixin looked at his wife. "The ring.", "Oh! I'll need to discuss this with both of you present. If you can bring him here, that would be greatly appreciated.", "I'll try.", Ayrellia said, taking her son back from Mileeda. "Hold on, let me see my godson.", Brixin demanded. He held him, "Looks just like his old man. This is going to be a strong kid. And...we will discuss more about him in our meeting.", Brixin said, now putting the kid down. The kid looked at Mileeda again. "Sandin, it's time to go.", Ayrellia said, grabbing his hand, smiling at Mileeda and Brixin, and then leaving. "Who was that?", "You've met Nora, right, Shima? That is her older sister.", Brixin said, now sitting down, and enjoying his ice cream. "My mother said that Nora is her best friend.", "Well...there are reasons for that...", Brixin said, giving me a look that suggested that I shouldn't be bringing this up. I decided not to say anything else, "They have always been close. Me and Amana have special reasons for monitoring them.", Mileeda said, "Well, time to get back to work, Shima.", Mileeda now said, grabbing my hand, and taking me back into the room we were in.

A whole month had passed, and Mileeda and I had been running simulations for a week, "Now, it was supposed to be, left, left, then right, correct?", Mileeda asked, bearing down upon me. Because for the one-hundredth time, I had failed at the last part. I was supposed to be getting through the base without being caught. But every time I got to the place where the diamonds were hidden, I was always captured. And my uncle not only learned that Amana IS sending me on missions, but that I'm also Layna Lon, his brother's daughter, still alive. "Grandmother...I am! But there are always guards right there that I can't get passed, and I've tried EVERYTHING!", I yelled in frustration. "Watch me.", she said, then we ran the simulation again, but this time, Mileeda was getting through the base. She did all the first things quickly. She snuck around and no guards noticed her. Then, she made it to the shaft where the diamonds are hidden. There was a guard right outside the door, carrying what was known as a royal cannon. These didn't fire normal shells. They were infused with some kind of magic. Mileeda didn't even hesitate to head straight for the shaft. She took a knife from her sleeve, and threw it at the guard and hit him straight in the head. The man fell to the floor, then Mileeda quickly opened the door and went inside. I watched as she took out the bomb Amana created, planted it, and then ended the simulation. Then she looked down at me. "Now, what do you have to say?", "I have to say that...was amazing.", I said, smiling at her, "I didn't think to kill the guard. I didn't want to have to kill him.", "You don't have a choice in the matter. If you don't kill that guard, you will fail. Now, once you've planted the bomb, your next goal will be to get to a safe distance to activate it. It will destroy all of the diamonds and the whole base will be destroyed. You're worried about killing ONE guard, but you will be killing ALL of them.", Mileeda said, in her dark tone. I gulped, but realized there was no other way around this. Now I tried again. This time, I killed the guard. Once I killed him, I went into the shaft, and saw the diamonds. They were embedded in the walls, and were being mined by men in minercoats. I looked around, and realized that these men were innocent and just doing a job. I couldn't kill them, either. "GET OUT! THERE IS A BOMB!", I yelled. The men all looked around, confused, but then some of them started to move towards the door. I planted it, and waited until I saw men running out. I knew they would have to get off of the base. "Mileeda, end the simulation.", I said. She did. She wasn't happy with me. "This is taking too long. You need to stop these silly…", "I am not going to murder those men. So, me and you, need to come up with a way to get those workers out of there.", I said confidently. Mileeda raised an eyebrow, then kneeled on one knee before me, "You are an interesting child, Layna. I'm surprised that you thought of that. But, I'm very proud that you did. Amana and I wanted to see if you would save those men. But there is an easy way, and we can hurry and I can teach it to you. Because tomorrow, you will do this for real. Do you really think you can do all of those steps I showed you?". I nodded. "And do you think you can really kill that man? I know you've never really killed, but this life…it is kill or be killed, Layna. So, do you really believe yourself ready to begin?". I once again nodded. "Then I want you to relax, but also…", Mileeda grabbed my head, and I felt something popping into my mind clearly. It was the simulation. "That way, you can run it in your mind to remember.", she said, for the first time, smiling at me with glee. She turned away from me and walked out of the room.

"Admit it already.", "No.", "Please, Mileeda, just say it.", "No.". Brixin and Mileeda were talking about my success today, and how proud Mileeda was of me. But Brixin was trying to get her to say she loved me. "Look, I know how you feel and all that nonsense, but the way you looked at her when I saw you, it was so touching. I think I actually felt a tear…", Brixin said, playfully wiping his eyes. "She is going home after the mission, and then, I'll stay away from her.", I heard my grandmother say coldly. I was standing not too far from the room they were sitting in, and all I felt in that moment was heartbreak. I thought she was starting to like me. I ran to my room and fell onto my bed. I was crying profusely. Tor was hanging around with another girl, and I had to accept it because I can't reveal who I am. I thought my grandmother was starting to love me, but this was all just work for her. She still hates me like the rest. I was so sad and angry, and Amana hadn't called me. Not once since I've been here. I didn't know what else to feel except sadness. "Knock, knock.", Brixin said, entering my room, "What's wrong?", he asked, suddenly getting serious, and kneeling next to my bed. "I heard…my…grandmother.", I said, sniffling. "Oh, you don't have to believe that. Listen, she is just being fair towards you. It wouldn't be fair to Sylvia, or your other cousins.", "But they are horrible! I get why she hates them! But why me?!", "Because you look like someone she hated. And the rest of your family is horrible.", Brixin said, smiling, "Layna, you don't need your grandmother's love, you have my sister's. Trust me, that is better than Mileeda's. I mean, look at her and Linda. They don't get along because Linda is a straightforward person, and Mileeda and my sister love to hide things and not tell people things they should. It is their way. I got used to it. But now, I'm privy to everything because I'm the Head of the Family. But, sometimes, Amana keeps things from me, like something she THINKS I don't know, I most likely know. You get it?", Brixin asked, looking at me hard. I shook my head. "Okay, let me try this another way. Do you know how old your grandmother is?", "Three-thousand?", "Yes. And in all that time, she has experienced nothing but pain from even thinking about trusting your family. So, that is the reason why she is how she is. Does that make sense?", "Only somewhat. I mean...I don't understand what that has to do with how she treats me.", "Layna, she is THREE-THOUSAND. Think about it. Do you know how you feel when you think about Tor's new friend?". I thought about Yennipher, and all that came to my head was, fuck that shit. Brixin could see the look on my face, "Exactly. That feeling, but times one-thousand.", he said. Now I understood. My grandmother feels this way about all of us. Even me, who she has probably spent the most time with. "I wish I could change her mind.", "She will. One day. Maybe it will be you, or maybe it will be your cousin. Awalli.", "Awalli?", "Yeah. I saw her not too long ago. She looks exactly like the girl Alisa murdered. Salana. And that...was your aunt. Or I should say...Mileeda's daughter.", Brixin gave me a dark look as he said this. "Salana? I don't understand. Why was she special?", "Linda was once close with Mileeda. But, Linda didn't live up to Salana's example, so Mileeda kept pushing her, until she pushed her away. That's why they aren't close. Linda and I hardly see eye to eye. She thinks the same thing her cousin does. That I let my sister get away with too much. Even Ko-e. She's wanted, and I let her pass, because I know what she is facing. Lyon is the one making it DIFFICULT for her. I've tried making him understand the importance, but he doesn't get it. Neither does my daughter. And neither does my wife. Amana won't listen to me on it. She won't stand aside and just let bygones be bygones. But you. You get the seriousness. You haven't said anything to anyone about Awalli. So, I know I can trust you now. There is more to what Ko-e told you. Amana has hidden other things. Things that are pretty much all coming to a head soon. Layna, Ko-e was right. All this is just getting started. I thought that there may be some way I could control the situation. In some ways, I did. But, there is always that one thing that can mess everything up.", Brixin was pacing in my room now, "Can I trust that you're going to be complicit with me in what I'm about to plan, Layna?", Brixin suddenly stopped and asked me. I nodded. "At a certain point, there is going to be a man named Duke, that will come here to free that man in the cave. That man in the cave is your cousin, Lo. I trapped him there, after what he did to you at the Year End Party five years ago. Now, his mother is a woman named Abraxa. She is someone from my past. When she is here, there will be a very bad situation going on. So, I need you to face her down, until I arrive. As soon as she gets here, you face her down. Now, I can see that you won't be alone…", Brixin's eyes were golden and red suddenly. Not his normal pink. I was mesmerized by this. "You see, this is what you get for letting things get this far….", he muttered to himself. Then, his eyes shifted back. "So, you won't be alone, but I need you to be in charge. You will be the oldest and most experienced. It's time for you to start learning some of MY magic.", Brixin said, and he pointed at me. The same feeling I felt with Mileeda earlier, I felt now from Brixin. "Now, do you feel that?", "Yes. What did you do?", "You now have half the dictionary of magic that I have. You can practice these spells on your own time. But THIS has to be your priority, Layna. The fate of Plinth is riding on my plan. That's how big this is. It's bigger than the petty shit your grandmother, and my sister have you dealing with. But they aren't stupid. They know that the threat is on the horizon and that it's time to start really getting ready. You come in at the exact moment that Abraxa arrives.", "But, who is she?", I asked, perplexed by this name, and her son. "They are…my past. I…made a mistake. Before I died. I can't see too far into my past, Layna. I only know that I hurt Abraxa enough for her to raise my son to hate me. Then, he killed me.", Brixin looked stone serious, "These are not average people. They come from another planet. They are very powerful. Duke…is extremely powerful, and worst of all, they serve Corsa.", "Who is that? I keep hearing her name.", "She is the woman that is the cause of most of our misery. She is my father's oldest enemy, and she keeps coming back. No matter how hard we fight her off, she keeps coming back. And she will get to Awalli. There is nothing that you can do. Mileeda knows ways to expel her. But it only works for a bit. She still can take whoever she has a hold of.". I told Brixin about my dreams. "Yes, that's her. She was trying to get to you using your father, and your anger at Amana's secrets.", "So what do I do?", "Fight her. Everytime she enters your dreams, fight her. This is the only way to defeat Corsa. Layna, when I first learned I was Sebastian's son, I didn't know anything about Corsa or Abraxa. They were able to manipulate me into almost killing Amana. But know this, and understand it, Amana is on OUR side, and will always be. Anything negative you hear about her is a lie. She is the one who has fought against Corsa the hardest.", Brixin looked at his time teller on his wrist, "Well, I need to be getting back to my wife, and YOU need your rest. Don't worry, though…", Brixin took something out of his jacket pocket, "…Tor is letting you use the Torter for tomorrow.", he said, handing it to me. "There are some new additions you might like.", "When do you think Tor will stop hanging with Yennipher?", I blurted out, suddenly realizing I didn't mean to. "I don't know. Maybe once you can end the charade. But who knows? You know, I always say, if it is meant, then it will happen.", Brixin said, shrugging his shoulders, smiling, then walking out.

When I woke up in the morning, Amana was sitting over me, brushing my hair off my face, "Hello.", she said, smiling at me. I sat up and threw my arms around her, "I missed you!", I shouted. "I know. I've been busy.", she said, hugging me back and kissing my head. She grabbed my face, "Are you ready for today?", "Yes.", I said confidently. "Good.", Amana said, taking the blankets off me, and showing me the clothes she wanted me to wear. "We'll be changing your appearance again. That way, they won't think that you are related to me. But also, we are going to be keeping you invisible during the duration of the mission. That way, you won't have to worry about being seen, and if you are, they won't recognize you as Shima. Now, another important thing, you need to mask your energy. If the royal sensors pick up new god energy, then it will be a huge problem. From what I understand, the system hasn't been acting right, so you shouldn't have a problem.", Amana was saying more to herself than to me. "Amana, am I going to be in trouble if I fail?", I asked. "You won't. Because, you can't afford to. We need you to do this. That way, we have deniability. You understand that, right? This is a dark mission. You are not supposed to be seen or heard until your mission is complete. Then, when it is, you will have an escort to a secure location where you can resume your identity as Shima. From there, everything will be over.". I thought about all of this in my head, and saw myself running the simulation again. I continued to run it until I finished eating. I saw myself doing it invisible now, and saw how much easier it was going to be.

Night came fast, and I was all geared up. I had a cannon in a holster on my hip, the device I had to plant in the mines, a blade just incase of a close encounter, and a black-leather military outfit that came with a mask over the bottom half of my face. Brixin looked me over, "I'm not sure about this.", he said. "Brixin, she is a goddess. She is not just some child. Please stop acting like she isn't capable.", Amana said, putting the finishing touches on me. "There!", she said, putting a cap over my now green colored hair. "You look absolutely amazing!", she said, standing up. "Yeah, she looks like a little version of you.", Brixin said, looking at me again with distrust for the mission in his eyes. "She's my daughter, so what's wrong with that?", Amana said, smiling at me proudly. There was a part of me that loved being told I was like a little Amana. "Well, is she ready?", Linda said, walking in. "Yes. You know where to take her.", "Yeah, yeah, I know.", "Linda…", Amana said, approaching her niece, "…you had better make sure she comes back to me alive.", "Considering she IS my niece, you have nothing to worry about.", Linda said, waving for me to follow. But Amana placed her hand on my shoulder, and knelt down to face me, "I love you. Come back to me.", she said, pulling me into a hug. Brixin came and placed his hand on my other shoulder, "We both love you.", he said, giving me the best confident look he could manage. I hugged him, too. Then I followed Linda out the door.

"I can't believe they are really going through with this.", Linda was saying, as we rode in her flar. "Why not?", I asked. "Layna, no offense, but you ARE a child, despite what they say. I mean, you are a goddess, I can feel your energy, but it's weak compared to someone like me, or even Tor. They shouldn't be sending you on this mission.", "Should they send you?", I asked, sort of smiling. This was the first time I really spent time with my aunt. "Well…I get WHY they are sending you. I wouldn't be able to pull it off. That's one of the reason's my mother hates me.", "She doesn't hate you! She loves you!", "Yeah, maybe just enough. I'm almost no better than you lot, in her eyes. Nobody can ever be Salana.", Linda said, irritatedly. "Your dad said…Amana's daughter killed her.", "It was a lot worse than that. But, it isn't my place to tell you that story. It was before I was born.", Linda said, now smiling at me herself, "When I first saw you, I knew you weren't REALLY Amana's daughter. I've seen Alisa before. Even fought her. She is tough. But…her mother killed her, finally. My father wanted to kill her, but he is very respectable, and allowed Amana to handle her own child. Too bad it took her over one-thousand years to do it, though.", Linda said, starting to slow the flar down at a safety light. As we were waiting, I looked far ahead and could see a compound. "Are you going to leave after you drop me off?", "No.

I have a meeting with Solron's lead man here. So, I'll be on base. The device Amana gave you comes with a radio. Once you plant the bomb, just say that the baby is in the cradle, and I'll know to head towards the extraction.".

We arrived at the compound. "You should activate that Torter thing of yours now, before we get out. And I suggest you teleport outside of the flar, don't open the door.", Linda said, getting out of the flar and approaching the gate, where a guard was stationed. "Business?", the guard asked, as me and Linda approached. "I need to see Hasu.", Linda said. "We have a guest.", the guard said, and the gate opened to allow Linda inside. The compound looked exactly as it did in the simulation. I was masking my energy as best I could so that I wouldn't be detected. We were walking towards the end where a big man was standing outside of an office, "SOVE! You're late.", "I'm not late, Hasu, let's get this out of the way.", Linda said, looking back at me, and walking into the office. I looked around and realized I needed to begin. I didn't have to do any of the hiding stuff, because I was invisible. I made my way to the door that led into the mines and saw an issue right away. Instead of the guard I had to kill guarding the door, it was a royal bot. These were designed specifically to catch gods or goddesses by sensing their energies. I was masking mine, but the bot would still pick up on it. Now I didn't know what to do. I felt afraid because all the training me and Mileeda did seemed for nothing. I decided to try and go where Linda was. I made my way to the office where she was meeting with Hasu. I snuck in through the gap in the door. "There isn't enough.", Linda was saying as she looked over a barrel. "Sure there is. Just count those two barrels over there, and then you have enough.", "No. We needed sixty pounds, and this is only forty-five. You need to go back to the other compound and gather more.", "ARE YOU INSANE?!", "I'm just following orders.", Linda said, now turning and facing Hasu. It suddenly occurred to me that I knew how I could disable that bot. I made my way back out of the office, and made my way to the bot. Then I heard a familiar voice, "Are you sure that is what you want?", "There is no choice, Tena. I will not have Solron taking us to war.", Coliapie was here. Tena was with her. Tena looked around, as if something was off, "What?", Coliapie asked. "I don't know.", Tena said, still looking around. I watched as the two of them proceeded into the diamond mines. Damn, I thought. Mileeda had told me that I would have to use my psychic abilities to save the workers, but I didn't want Tena and Coliapie down there. They were messing the whole thing up. Nothing was as we had trained for at this point.

As I neared the mine, I saw the bot, and looked down at the Torter. Tor had labeled instructions on it. There was a button that said; (fry). I pushed it, and the whole base went dark. "What the hell is happening?! Someone go to the fuse box!", I heard someone yelling. Tena and Coliapie came back out of the mines, "Maybe we should go, sister-in-law?", Tena suggested, now looking almost directly at me. Once again, she nodded towards me, and I saw her lead Coliapie away. I went into the mines, and the men inside were already headed for the exit. I psychically placed the suggestion for them to leave the base. After that, I slipped past the crowd of men getting out, and looked around at all the diamonds. I felt stronger. Before I could do anything, though, I heard a strange moaning sound. I looked around to see what it could possibly be, and was mortified. It was a big dog, and it was able to smell me. I tried using my psychic abilities on it, but nothing seemed to be affecting the dog. I ran, and it chased me. I was running for a good minute, the dog right on my heels. I teleported out of it's way, and it hit a wall. I then tried to find a place to hide, but no matter where I tried to hide, it could still smell me. I decided I'd have to kill the poor creature. I stood and faced it. It came at me, and I took out my cannon and started to fire at it. But I missed, and it knocked me down. I couldn't focus on anything. It jumped on top of me, and I was holding his jaw, trying to keep him from biting my face off. I kept pushing and eventually ripped his jaw open. The dog made a sad squeal and then killed over. I stood. "I knew it.", I looked behind me, and couldn't believe what I was seeing. "SYLVIA?!", I shouted. I couldn't believe she was here of all places. "I came with my mom and aunt. Do you know who you just killed?", she asked me, going to the poor dog, "You just killed my father's childhood pet. Oh, he is so going to kill you, and your stupid mother.", she said with glee. I realized I dropped the Torter while I was dealing with the dog. "Otan. That was his name.", Sylvia said, almost like she didn't care at all, but instead was happy that it was going to get me in trouble. I quickly rushed at Sylvia, who put up a good fight. She punched me, and I felt it, and then I punched her, and she stumbled, allowing me to advance and knock her out. She fell to the floor. I wanted to leave her here, but then thought better of it. I teleported her back to her mother, they didn't notice me, and then disappeared again. I then placed the device. I came out of the mines, making sure to activate the Torter and make myself invisible. I made sure all the innocent workers were outside of the mines before I said, "The baby is in the cradle.". I made my way back to Linda's flar, and teleported in. Just then, Sylvia came rushing towards the flar, pulling her mother's hand, "I'm telling you, she was on the base in the mines! Look, she is in Aunt Linda's flar!". They all approached the flar, but by this time, I had replaced my green hair with my purple again. I had learned to clean myself magically and there was nothing on me that would suggest I was even on the base or in the mines. Sylvia pulled the door open, and I decided to get out. "What do you want?", "Don't act innocent! You killed Otan! And you were on the base! My father is right about you!", "I don't know what you're talking about! I've been waiting here for Linda!". At this moment, Linda walked out and looked over the scene. "Sylvia, we were in the mines. Me nor your Aunt Tena saw anyone that looked remotely like Shima. I don't like the girl, either...", Coliapie said, giving me a disgusted look, "...but this accusation is unwarranted and we don't need it.", "I couldn't agree more.", Linda said, "She was with me, because I like her. She is my favorite cousin. Simple as that. She was waiting for me in the flar, and didn't get out once. So, Sylvia, you need to drop this or I'll make it worse.", "How dare you threaten my daughter?", Coliapie snarled at Linda. "Well, she is my niece...", Linda said, "...and so is Tena here. So, you, Coliapie, had better fall in line. An order from me is almost the same as an order from my mother.", "You aren't OUR royal family! You're theirs!", Coliapie yelled at Linda. Linda was starting to get annoyed, and I could tell she was on the cusp of doing something horrible to Coliapie, "Cousin, can we go now?", I said, glaring at Sylvia, who was looking even more angrier now that Linda was here to back me, and called me her favorite. "Sure, let's leave before I make a mistake. But this accusation will be made known to my father.", "WAIT!", Tena yelled, grabbing Linda's arm. Linda raised an eyebrow and looked at her, "I mean...that isn't necessary. Coliapie is just upset that Shima is making Sylvia look like a fool, again. Let's just forget everything tonight.", Tena said, with a smile to Linda. Linda returned the smile, "Okay. I will. Come on, Shima, we're leaving.", Linda said, getting in the flar. I slowly did the same, taking the time to look back at Sylvia, who looked ready to kill me.

"Okay, do it.", Linda said to me, once we had been driving for fifteen minutes. I pressed the detonator and heard the explosion, but didn't really see anything. "Well, mission accomplished. They won't be able to make those weapons anymore, that's for sure. I really have to stop doubting Aunt Amana. She was the Head of the Family before.", Linda said to herself as we rode. I was too busy thinking now. Sooner or later, I'm going to reveal that I'm Layna Lon, not Shima Tia. When was that going to happen? And when it does, what will happen? Amana said that whoever is in the head seat at the time will be removed for me. What does that even mean? Not to mention when Amana told me that I'm her secret weapon. She was honest about that part, though. "Do you want to go get ice cream? My dad would always take me for ice cream when I was successful at something.", Linda said, smiling at me. She was starting to remind me a lot of her father. I smiled back, "Yes. I would.".

We were in the same parlor Brixin, Tor, and I usually visit. Linda was like her father, but when it came to which ice cream had chocolate, it was strawberry ice cream. "Listen, Shima, I know what my mother and Amana have planned for you. I spoke with Amana a few days ago, when she was telling me this plan. At first, I didn't agree. I didn't like the idea of you doing all this. But, I guess my aunt knows what she is doing. I can't believe we were successful. How did Sylvia see you?", Linda asked, taking a bite of her ice cream, and watching me intently. "She… I dropped the Torter when Otan was chasing me. I feel bad. I didn't want to kill the dog.", "Oh well. Solron shouldn't have had him there. He knew there was a possibility that the dog could get hurt there.", "Yeah, but what about when Sylvia tells her dad she saw me there?", "Well, checking the footage, you didn't look like Shima, and also, I did a little something to make them think you were in the flar the whole time.", Linda said with a dreamy smile. "But…", "Shima, it's okay. You did good. Nobody will suspect WE did it. Now, let's not talk about the mission anymore. How do you like living with Amana?", "It's okay.", "Do you love her?". I felt like this was a strange question, "Yes, I love her.", I said, realizing, of course I do. "She took you in when you were five, right?", "Yes. When my father died.", "He didn't die, he was murdered.", Linda said darkly, staring at me harder now, "I knew your father. He was a good man. He was always a good kid, too. When I heard his wife was pregnant, I was one of the first to see your mother, with you in the womb.", I was starting to see Linda in a different light more and more. When I first met her, I didn't know what to think. But now, I was starting to see so much of her father in her, that I was convinced that she liked me as much as I was starting to like her. She also made me do something I hadn't done in a long time. Think about my parents. I felt tears coming from my eyes as I asked, "Really?", "Yes. I knew both your mother and father when they were children. Solron and Tena were always conspiring. I see that same relationship in Sylvia and Reginald. They are plotting. Sylvia plans to be Head of the Family some day, and yet, you're being trained for it. What do you think is going to be going on when that time comes, Layna?", Linda asked, placing her spoon down, and watching me. "I think… I don't know.", "Well, I'll tell you. Your cousins will try and finish the job your uncle and aunt failed at. The moment you announce your real identity, you will have a target on your back the size of my father's manor. I don't want that for you, but at the same time…", Linda leaned in closer, "…you saw how Coliapie reminded me that I'm Sebastian's family and not Tig's. You see, I'm not a descendant of Nigel, I'm just the daughter of his wife. Not only that, but Simon and Lex, Your aunt and uncle, and the Dats, were all descendents of my half-brother, Vicdor. So, they feel entitled. But, I'm still Mileeda's daughter, and I still share part of their blood. So, they have to respect me, almost the same as my mother. But I can't tell them anything, because I don't really have the authority. All I can do is tell my father, who they are afraid of.", "Why?", "Because he is powerful. They're willing to stand up to Amana, but my father? Hell no. He'd annihilate all of them. Didn't Amana tell you why the Tib's can never be Head of the Family? If not, I have a funny story for you.", Linda said, already trying to hold in her laughter. "What happened?", "Well, Simon tried to be Head of the Family years ago, back when your grandfather was getting on in years. He figured that the Tib's could run the family better. Or at least he had a plan. Now his brother, Lex, was told that he had to convince him not to try. But Lex figured that his brother had a chance. Simon approached my father, hoping to speak to my mother and get her on his side.", I could already see how that went before Linda said anything, "My mother came out, listened to Simon for over an hour, and still said no.", Linda started to laugh. I only smiled. "So, after that, he decided to go after Tena, and prevent her from becoming the head. Only problem there was that at the time, Tena was pregnant. Her child would have been a god, so the family…", "I know what they did.", I said, darkly. "Yes. So, this was AFTER my mother AND Amana said NOT to do it, though. So, they asked whose bright idea it was to disobey, and well, Simon was the one. The Tibs were supposed to handle these situations discreetly and unless told otherwise, were to make sure that no harm came to the person carrying. But these idiots killed Tena's child. But they lied and told Tena they were supposed to do it.", Linda said. I looked at her ice cream and thought about how it was the same color as her hair, "So, that is the reason why the Tibs can never be Head. Because Simon and Lex lied to Tena. Tena used to be Amana's favorite. At some point, though, they began to disagree quite often. I'm thinking it was around the time she started plotting to kill your father. It was mostly jealousy and anger over the fact her child died.", "Then how come the Tibs aren't treated as bad as the Dats?", I asked. "Because, Simon and Lex made up for what they did. They gave most of their fortunes to Tena. And now, they are running that Rain's Tech in Nocton.", Linda passed me a file. I opened it, and it was basically stock information on Rain's Tech. "What do you want me to do with this?", "You're going to buy in.", Linda said, with a smile so like her father's, I couldn't help but giggle. "So, you want me to buy in? I don't understand.", "When you come out, in your REAL identity, you will need something that keeps you tethered to the family. THIS will be perfect. You will need to learn how to run a major company. Do you think you could do that?", "Well...I've learned a lot of other stuff...I don't see why I couldn't.", I said, looking at the sales and deals that had been made. I saw something that interested me. The gross of the income seemed off compared to the marketing and sales of the product being produced. Rain's Tech was all engineers and that was it. There were some great inventors there that came up with some interesting technologies, but it was mostly just producing equipment for other companies they did business with. Mccloud Industries was the rival of Rain's Tech. Everyone knew that Mccloud did better business. But looking at the information and the numbers, I saw a way I could manipulate things and do things better than Mccloud. I actually really WANTED to do this. "I will make this a priority.", I said, looking more and more at the file. "You're scary, Shima.", Linda said, and I looked up. "The way you just looked at that for only a few seconds, and you know what to do... Amana really did make you like her.", Linda said, finishing her ice cream. "I want to be like her.", I said proudly. "Let's get out of here.", she said, now getting up, and walking us back to her flar.

CHAPTER 18

Emillie Meets Brixin

LAYNA: Amana and I had always agreed on things. Only because I wanted to be so much like her. After living with her for three months, I began to think she was the coolest person ever. All the training she gave me, and all the stuff that had happened to me when I was a child, made me EXACTLY like her. Amana even told me that she molded me in her image. I loved her. She was my mother. Not my birth mother, but the woman who took me in, when my family wanted me dead. "Layna, I'm not going to ask again, if you don't want to...", "Mother, I will. I promise. I just...have questions.", "And I told you not to ask me questions. I hate questions.", "I know you do. And I hate asking.", I said, now stepping closer to her face. "What?", she growled at me. "Why is Sebastian here?", "I don't know. He's acting like he wants to help, but Emillie will learn the truth about him on her own. Then, she'll hate him as much as me.", "Uncle Brixin hates him, too.", I said. "I know he does. We all do. You just haven't seen the REAL him like we have. Now please, can you just say yes already?", she asked me, even more impatient than before. "I already said I will. Just, what are you going to do?", "I'm going to see my husband.", Amana said simply. "In the other dimension?", "Yes. They can't come there to get me, because they'd be breaking their own law.". I smiled at her, "Leave Nora in the bed. I'll check on her every two hours.", I said. Amana hugged me and kissed my cheek. "I'll come back, once my brother convinces Lyon, and Mileeda, that they HAVE to let me come back.", Amana said. She then opened the portal, looked at me, smiled, then walked through. This place was guarded and Lyon wouldn't know that a portal opened here. I looked at Nora, who was sleeping soundly. I was about to leave, when she awoke quite suddenly, "NO! MILEEDA!", she shouted. I went to her, "You're okay!", I said. She looked around, "Where am I?", "You're safe. You're in Nocton. Do you know who I am?", "You're...that...girl... Amana's daughter... I remember you. From a long time ago. Why am I here? Where is Amana?", "She had to leave. She left you with me.", I said, smiling at her. But she looked stone serious. "Is this another dream?", "What? No. I'm really here. And so are you. You're awake.", I said, placing both my hands on each of her shoulders. She looked around again, then pushed me off, and got up. She was looking everything over. "I want to see my son.", she said. "I don't think I can, and Amana didn't say otherwise. But I think it would be too risky. This place we're in...", "I WANT TO SEE MY SON!", she shouted at me. I didn't know what to say. I was starting to regret this. "Nora...please, I'm only doing as told...", "And what did she tell you, girl?", she asked, in a tone that suggested she was ready to attack. I quickly put a defensive shell around me, "She just said that you need to be taken care of.", "She didn't tell you the truth, then. What she meant... is I need to be HID.", she said. I didn't understand what she meant. She started to grab her head, then she fell onto the floor, "NORA!", I shouted. I rushed to her, and she grabbed my neck, "Tell me how to find Amana!", "You can't get to her!", I yelled, trying to pry her off me, but she was incredibly strong. She threw me, and I hit a desk, then the wall. I was trying to get up, but I was so hurt. She knelt down and started to punch me, "TELL ME!", she kept punching me, then she threw me down. "...Uncle...Brix...", I managed to say. A bright light filled the room, and then I was waking up. "What...? Where...?", "I'm lucky I got to you. She was going to kill you.", my husband said, sitting over me. He was wearing that stupid button again with the dog symbol, "Why...are you wearing that?", "Well, looks like you're getting better.", he said, kissing my head, "Where did Amana go?", "She left.", "And you almost died because of your blind devotion to her.", he said in a tone that told me we were about to have the same argument we've always had.

"Wow, I can't believe it.", Brixin said, looking at a report, "Says here that they have no idea how the compound exploded or what was down there in the first place. Trying to cover it up. Solron...when will you learn?", he said, now putting the report down. He looked at me, and I knew what he was going to say before he said it, "I was successful.", "And seen. You didn't hear him the other day. He knows something is strange about you. Why were you with Linda? That's his main question. Linda doesn't like children.", "I didn't know that. She never said anything.", "Yeah, well lucky for you, she actually DOES like you. She said you're more mature than you look.", Brixin smiled. "She reminds me of you.", I said brightly. "We are a lot alike in some ways. But she doesn't like kids. That's her main difference from me, I guess. Maybe she secretly does...", Brixin said thinkingly. Then he smiled evilly, "I'm going to use you to get my daughter to admit she likes kids.", he said, looking at me with a boyish smile. I started to laugh, then Tor came in. He ran to me and hugged me, "I'm glad you're alright!", he said. "Me, too.", I said, smiling brightly at him. He had been spending a lot of time with Yennipher, and I had been so busy that I had forgotten about the whole thing. It started to come back to me when she walked in. She didn't know why Tor was acting like I was dying or something. "Are you okay, Shima?", she asked me. "Fine.", I said in a short tone. "Good, because Tor was worried about you.", "Well, Uncle, I think I'll be getting home now.", I said. I went home and found that Amana had suddenly decided to do something almost unthinkable.

"In four years, you are announcing that you are indeed Layna Lon. It's time to end this charade.", "Why in four years?", "Because by that time, you'll be of age, and you can start making certain moves. The family won't be able to touch or stop you, and if they try, you're ready for them.", Amana said, personally cooking me breakfast. "But, won't they be mad? Won't this start a war?", "No. Solron has no power over us anymore now that we've destroyed his diamonds. Diamond makes us stronger, but mixed with gold, its effects are worn out. And it makes the gold's effect on us more dangerous.", she said. "I learned that the hard way.", I said, remembering Sylvia's birthday party. "Listen, from now on, I want you to study harder, and put more effort into learning the responsibilities of the Head of Family. If you have to, ask my brother for advice.", "Can't you just help me?", I asked. I really missed Amana. She had been extremely busy. Especially since she had brought me back from Brixin's manor. "I would, but I have something I have to tend to. Just do what I tell you, okay?", she asked, kissing my forehead, and putting eggs on my plate. "I have to go to work. Take care. I love you.", she said, smiling at me as she moved towards the door. "I love you, too.", I said, smiling back.

Later that day, I decided that I did want to go ask Uncle Brixin for advice. As I arrived at his manor, it was to find Yennipher, and the older girl she was with before, standing outside. One was holding a little girl's hand. Tor opened the door, and I watched Yennipher kiss his cheek. Then they walked inside. I didn't want to go now, and was turning around, when Linda came up from behind me, "Where are you going?", she asked, holding a bag that had food in it. I looked at her, and felt my demeanor crumble as I told her what was bothering me. "Well, don't worry about that. Why don't you find a boy to hangout with if he is going to hangout with that Nos girl?", "What boy? Tor is the only boy I know!", I yelled at her. I began crying in my hands, and Linda said,

"Come with me.", she grabbed my hand and led me to the back of the manor. Brixin was sitting back there and noticed me and Linda, "Well, I was waiting forever. I hope it didn't melt.", "No, it should be good. I magicked it a little.", Linda said, placing the bag down on the table in front of her father, and taking out it's contents. "What's wrong, Layna?", he asked me. "Tor…", "Oh, Yennipher is here. She said she'd be bringing her sister and niece. They must be here already. Well, let's take this in the house, then.", "WHAT?!", I yelled, "I mean…why can't we just eat out here?". Brixin looked at Linda, who had the same look in her eyes. "Layna, Yennipher is Tor's little girlfriend, and you're just going to have to deal with it. After some time, he'll get tired of her, though, because remember, Yennipher is not a goddess.", Linda said, now giving me a very confident smile. We walked inside, and Yennipher was sitting next to her sister, "So, Carla is only three, but she is a very bright little girl. She hasn't picked up on talking, but she is getting there.", Yennipher was saying, holding her niece, while her sister was just sitting there with her face glued to her cell. "AH, Yennipher and Saia. Good to have you here, welcome!", Brixin said, moving to Saia, and giving her a hug. Saia looked at Brixin in a way I'm sure Mileeda would kill her if she was here. "Hi, Brix. Where is your wife?", Saia asked, looking around fearfully. "She is at work. My daughter has brought food if you girls are hungry.", "Yes. Thank you!", yelled Yennipher, and she left her niece with her mother, grabbed Tor's hand, and went into the dining hall.

Saia was only nineteen and was working at her family's company. It was obvious they had hired her because of her child. Carla was being extremely funny, walking around, and trying to take other people's food. Brixin was kind, and handed her one of his chicken tenders. Linda made a face that suggested that her father may be right about her. I smiled at her as she watched Carla with silent amusement. I looked at Brixin, who was also amused but laughing out loud, "This girl is too much!", he said, standing, and going to her. He looked at her face, then looked at her mother, "She looks so much more like you than him, you know?", "I know.", Saia said, with a heavy smile towards Brixin. "Well, I'll be back. Gotta go check on the wife.", Brixin said, standing up, and walking out of the room. "He is so hot.", Saia said, watching him walk away. "First off, Saia, ew, because that is my dad, and her uncle, and second, just no.", Linda said, making a gag face. I laughed, and so did Yennipher. I stopped laughing. "Shima, can I talk to you?", she asked, now getting up, and walking out of the room. I looked at Tor, who shook his head no, but I got up and followed her. "Shima, I don't want to sound weird or crazy or anything like that...but...do you have a crush on your cousin?", she asked me with her arms folded, "I mean, everyone knows that you two were always together when you were younger and all, but I'm just trying to understand.", she said. We were both preteens. Not even full teenagers yet, and I felt like this whole situation was way above my age limit. "No, I just don't want to see him hurt.", I said. "Well...I really like him. He's smart, funny, and adorable. And brave.", she added, with a dreamy face. I wanted to tell her he isn't really my cousin and I want to be with him forever, but I couldn't yet. "Don't worry, I'm sure when he gets tired of you, he'll find someone else.", I said coldly. "Excuse me?", she said, now stepping to my face. I knew I could easily kick her ass, but I didn't know if that would be wise, but I felt like my blood was all hot. "Are you trying to pick a fight with me?", she asked, stepping back some, "Because if you are...I'm not trying to fight you. I just wanted to know what you have against me. I know that you don't have many friends, and I have never seen you at any other social events. So, who the hell are you, Shima? Why are you so defensive for MY boyfriend?", she asked. I didn't know how to answer this. I started to grow nervous, but then... "Oh, there you girl's are. Come on, there's ice cream.", Linda said, with an excited tone.

Yennipher walked away without looking at me. "What happened?", Linda asked. I told her. "Wow. You really are a little version of my aunt. It is super scary. Like how my mother and her are like two equal people. Man, you really shouldn't have done that, though. Because…", Linda stopped talking because her cell rang, "Sove. What? I don't get what that means. So…you're saying that a portal opened in the downtown area, and a crap load of cute creatures came out? How did a crap load of those things come out? Who opened the…? Damn it. I'm coming now. Just… don't do anything until I get there. Tell your other boss to follow suit. I don't want him charging in. He hasn't faced those things yet.", Linda hung up the cell, then looked at me, "Listen, I told you to deal with it. I get what you're feeling, seriously, I do. But you need to control that feeling. If you give yourself away, what my mother will do to you is ten times worse than watching Tor with that girl.", she said, then she went out to the other room, "I have to leave, I'm so sorry.", she said, looking over at Saia. "Oh, it's fine. I don't care. Leave. I know you have work to do.", she said. "Great. Later.", Linda said. I wondered what that was all about. "Saia, are you and my cousin, friends?", "Yeah. I've known her for a long time. My family used to be close with the Sove's. We know their secret. That you all are gods and goddesses.". Saia was trying to get her daughter to sit, and she wasn't having it. "Really? How did you know that?", "My whole family knows.", "Yennipher…?", "Knows that Tor is a god, yeah.". I looked over at her, and I could tell she was telling Tor what I said. "Saia, is Linda always leaving or something? You seemed disappointed she had to leave.", "Let's just say she introduced me to Carla's father.", "Who is her father?", "A boy I don't like to talk about. Linda still talks to him.", she said, angrily. I decided to drop the topic. I went to find Brixin. I walked to his personal study, and he was indeed in here, but there were holograms of other people as well. "Layna, good of you to join us. Come on in.", Brixin said, directing me to a chair. "What's going on?", I asked. Looking around, I realized Amana was here, along with Mileeda, and one other person I didn't know, "Wait, did you say… Layna? As in…?", "Yup.", Amana said, proudly smiling at me. "Oh, Sove, you've lost it. You can't get away with this.", "I take the responsibility.", Amana said. The mystery man looked at her, then shrugged his shoulders, "Well, I suppose if it was you, then I shouldn't be worried at all.", he said, now sitting in a chair that was nearby. He was sort of elderly, and I wondered who he was. "You are going to thank me, when she is Head of the RF.", Amana said. "Let's just continue the meeting, that's why I brought Layna in here. She will one day BE the Head of her family, and they are going to be pissed. It's time we started putting pieces together that could prevent Lon from trying anything else against us.", Brixin said, placing his hand on my shoulder. "It isn't going to be easy, my love, considering that he suspects Amana's daughter is playing a role in his destruction.", Mileeda said, looking longingly at her husband. "Mother, who is this man?", I asked, pointing at the old man. "Oh, where are my manners? My name is Tis.", "Okay. But who are you?", "Tis…", Brixin spoke up, "…is the child of Lona and Vicdor. He technically is the true ruler of your family.", "Lona?", I asked. "Althea. Ko-e's niece.", Amana said darkly. "Amana, she isn't here, so hold that anger.", Brixin said to Amana, who had already disappeared. "Ah, she is just beyond help.", "Well, I don't blame her. My mother did terrible things. It's the reason I've aged this way, Layna. My mother and her murderous rampage has cursed me. Amana saved me. Said that she had killed me, but she kept me alive, and raised me herself. Much like you, I consider Amana my mother, but you see what has become of me.", he said, sadly. "He's still pretty tough, though, for an old man.", Brixin said, smiling at him. "I'm not fragile.", he said, returning the smile. "Layna, tell us your opinion of how best to handle your uncle.", Brixin said, staring at me. "Well, I used to think he should die, but that would be too easy. I want him to suffer for what he did to my father. And for what he tried to do to me. I think we should make him suffer. I want him to feel his rule crumble. Crumble until it's nothing. I want his daughter to lose her stupid attitude, and his wife to bow before me. Because when we are done with him. When we take his money, his house, his pride, I will be sitting on the throne, and he will be lost and confused.", I said, looking at the holographic people. "Alright, you heard her. I completely agree.", Brixin said. "Yes, suffer. I like that.", Mileeda said. "Ah, alas, my nephew shall learn his place.", Tis said, then he disappeared. "What did I miss?", Amana said, reappearing, and looking fluttered. "Got it all out of your system?", Brixin asked, chuckling. "Don't act like you don't do it, too!", "Yeah, but not just because you mention a NAME!", Brixin said, now laughing at Amana. "STOP LAUGHING!", she shouted. Brixin started to calm down. "Look, I'm sorry, you know I can't help it. But look, you need to accept that when it comes to Lona, she'll be taken care of.", "Like how you took care of Abraxa?", Amana said. Brixin's smile completely faded, "Layna, leave.", "No, let her hear it. Let her hear how you failed to…". Brixin waved his finger in a strange motion and he summoned Amana here. He then grabbed her throat, "HOW DARE YOU?!", he yelled at her. I stood up immediately and tried to pry him off, "UNCLE, LET GO!", I yelled. He gently pushed me off, then threw my mother. She caught her footing and fell, grasping at her throat. "Layna, leave.", he said again, staring my mother down. I looked at her for her consent, "Go.", she said, standing up, and also, staring her brother down. Mileeda had appeared in the room as well, "Amana, why did you do that?", "It's the same thing for me. Lona is to me what Abraxa is to YOU!", she said, pushing her finger into her brother's chest. Brixin looked hurt, but then pulled his sister into a hug, "I'm sorry. Let's not do that, okay?", he said. Amana was crying into his shoulder. She then backed away from him. "I'm sorry, too.", she said under her breath. "Uncle…what did Abraxa do?", I asked. "She… She hurt me. That's all you have to know.", he said, "Meeting is adjourned. Are Saia and Yennipher still here? Maybe I'm not too late for that ice cream, that'll make me feel better. Want to join, Amana?", Brixin asked, looking at her hopefully, but she just looked at me, then disappeared. "I'm sorry you had to see me and her like that, Shima. Every once in a while, we fight.", he said, now smiling like his usual self. "But, that was horrible.", "What she said was horrible, but I guess I shouldn't have laughed at her. Let's forget about that.", he said, going back into the sitting room. "Finally.", Saia said as he came in. Then her smile turned into a sour face when Mileeda came in after us, "Well, Saia... And you've brought your child.", she said, approaching them, and kneeling in front of Carla, "Well, I see she has YOUR looks.", Mileeda said. I began to wonder more and more who Carla's father is. "Well, thank you, Mileeda, but I think we are going to be going.", "Oh, don't leave on my account. I'm not going to stay long. After all, I know you feel awkward eyeing my husband when I'm in the room.", she said, smiling at Saia. Saia now had a stone face. Yennipher and Tor weren't even in the room, and I began to wonder where they were. I left the room, not wanting to see the ensuing scene that was about to follow my grandmother's comment. I went outside, because I figured they'd be in the garden. I heard voices, and hid, "...tell her.", "I can't tell her that. Look, there is something that you don't know about her, and I can't tell you because it's a big secret.", "She's going on missions for her mother. That's what Sylvia told me. I didn't believe her because I know she doesn't like Shima, but Sylvia said she fought her.", "Yeah, well I don't know anything about that.", "Well, you don't have to tell me the secret, but just tell me this...is she really your cousin?". Tor shifted nervously, and then I came out of hiding, "Yennipher, I'm sorry about before. I've had some time to think, and now, I'm going to be nice. I'm sorry I acted like an ass to you before, I was just angry about something completely different. Do you mind if I just borrow Tor, just for a second?", I asked as nicely as I could. Yennipher looked confused, but then waved her hand, indicating it was okay. I walked away with him, "Listen, we can't give my identity away.", "I know. I just… I didn't know what to tell her.", "Well, that's my fault. I'm going to be good now, okay? I promise. I have to focus on what I have to do.", "What's that?", "Making Solron pay.".

Two years later, I had taken up a whole new identity. Shima was still in existence, but in order to take Rain's Tech, I needed to be someone who WASN'T connected to Amana or Sebastian's family. I was only two more years away from being old enough to do it, and my main focus at this point was seeing Solron suffer. He was suffering pretty hard. Secretly, I was already buying bonds for Rain's Tech, so I was already a board member, but I hadn't attended any of the meetings, and I was basically a threat to them. Simon Tib was incredibly worried about this mystery person investing so many shills and basically buying the whole company. I thought about Tor, but I didn't care at the moment what he was doing. I was highly focused on trying to make sure that this whole thing went smoothly. Amana was leaving me alone more and more. But I was older. Almost an adult. So many things were happening within those two years. Brixin and Mileeda were expecting another child. I was shocked to hear this, but excited. At the same time, Tor and Yennipher had split. Just like Mileeda said, but then he took up with another girl right after her. I stopped worrying about it. I was now focused solely on Rain's Tech, because it was my mission, and I knew it would take time. I watched as it did good for six months, then sales plummeted, and they had to make up for the parts they brought wholesale, compared to the business they actually did. I was the one putting up money for them to keep going. Eventually, one day, Linda showed up looking happy, "You're coming with me.", she said. I got dressed, then took my cannon just in case of anything. "Where are we going, Linda?", I asked. My voice had gotten much deeper since I was thirteen. "We're going to a board meeting. Are you ready?", "Yes.".

We were in her flar, and on the stereo was a song by a girl named Sha-la. Linda was drumming her fingers to the beat and moving her head with the rhythm. She noticed I was watching her, and she stopped, "I like this song.", she said embarrassingly. "It's okay. I like it, too.", I said, and started to sing the song, "If you don't like what I offer, then don't be a heart stopper!", "And if you don't like what I have to say, don't do the same stupid crap everyday!", Linda picked up. We both sang the song on the way to Nocton. Once we pulled up, Linda turned off her flar, "Look, you're going to have to put this thing on. It'll make you look different. And what was that name you came up with?", "Thasha Lu.", I said. Thasha Lu was the secret investor nobody could pinpoint. I looked at what Linda was handing me, and realized it was a disguiser. It was meant to give me a different appearance. There is technology that can see through this type of weapon, because that's what it is considered, but imagining that this was made by Brixin, it wouldn't be detectable. "Who made this?", "My father, duh.", Linda said, "Okay, so, you'll be good on your own in there, right?", "Of course. It's time to make Solron sorry he ever tried to kill me.", I said. Linda smiled, and gave me a hug, "I'm so glad we are, actually, family.", she said. I got out of the flar, and walked up to the huge building. There was a man outside. I had come up with some stuff myself. Being an investor, I already had clearance to enter the building, but what I didn't have was facial recognition. This guard had a face detector. I approached him, holding my suitcase, and wearing a business suit. It was all pink. The disguiser made me look older, with white and yellow hair. As I stood before the guard, he looked at me, "Don't know you, mam.", he said kindly. "Yes, this is my first time here. I'm here for the board meeting. Here are my credentials.", I said, holding out my board membership card that I had received in the mail. "Everything is in order, Ms. Lu. You can go on in.", he said, stepping aside, "It might be easier next time if you register your face at the desk.", he said, smiling, and waving as I walked away. I looked around the building, and all I saw were people moving back and forth. I knew what they did here, but to see it in person was quite invigorating. I watched people walking back and forth with PC's in their hands, and others on their cells, either talking to sales reps, or trying to sell something themselves. I went to the desk, and looked at the girl working the front. She was a beautiful girl, but she didn't seem to have any major importance, "Excuse me, where is the board meeting taking place?", I asked. "That would be the thirteenth floor, madam.", she said, giving me a device that was apparently a GPS, "That will take you straight to the meeting room.". I turned around, and behind me stood Simon and Solron, "Who are you? You're a board member? You haven't been in the other meetings.", Simon said, "I'm new.", I replied. "Thasha?", he asked, looking shocked, "I didn't think you'd ever come to a meeting.", "Well, things are looking ugly across the charts, so I decided to make an appearance.".

As we proceeded into the elevator, Solron continued to stare at me, "So, where are you from, Thasha?", "None of your business.", I said, not looking at him. "I think it isn't a good idea to address your king in such a manner.", "Well then, maybe I'll just take all my shills and invest in Mccloud industries.", "Let's not be hasty.", Simon said, giving Solron a certain look. Solron was, of course, suspicious. "I'm just curious. I mean...I've never even heard of the Lu's.", "Well, Solron, my king, I am a self-made woman, and I don't want to disclose my personal information, not even to YOU. Now, I'm here for business reasons, and that will be all I discuss.", I said, with so much finality, that Solron finally shut up.

We stepped out on the thirteenth floor, and we entered a big room. There were at least a good eight people in the room, sitting around a rectangular table. I sat down in one of the many seats on the long side. Solron sat at the head, and Simon sat next to him on the side at the end, "So, down to business. We are down in bonds.", "Yes, and I believe I see the reason for that.", I said, chiming in. I knew I had to make myself known to these people. Make them see I meant business. "Excuse me, but you're new here and…", Simon began, and some of the other people started to nod their heads. "EXCUSE ME, but I put my damn shills into this company! So you need to understand that I'm here to make sure we get the results we want, and make shills, so that we don't have to have these meetings about WHY we're FAILING!", I said to the whole table, and there were some nods, and admiring smiles, "Now, if I can continue, there is this little issue here with the manual labor units. They aren't hitting they're deadlines, and that is the reason sales are down. Because we aren't meeting our buyers orders on time. Now, I'm not saying we need to fire people, I'm saying we need to hire people.", "You're mad. That's going to cost us.", a random man said. He looked like he was in his early twenties, and I wondered immediately who he was. "No, I'm not. I'm right. This is the correct way to handle this. I understand that the hiring process is quite complicated, and that we aren't taking on any new employees. This needs to change. We need to take on more manual labor. We need welders, deburrers, and we definitely need assemblers. We can have a job fair. That way, we'll take on a large multitude of people, but we need to have all the managers to prepare to start training lots of people because…", "THIS IS RIDICULOUS!", Solron yelled, slamming his fist on the table, "You are just coming out of nowhere talking about doing something that will cost the whole company…", "What she is saying actually is making some sense, sir.", the young man said. Solron looked at him, then looked back at me, "I would like to talk to you privately, Ms. Lu.", he said. "Fine. We can talk. But, does everyone at this table think I'm right?", I asked, looking at all the faces. The first one to raise his hand was the mystery-young man. Then the rest of the table followed suit, except Simon and Solron. Simon looked confused, and Solron looked angry enough to flip the whole table. "Okay, fine, we do it your way.", Simon said grudgingly. As everyone started to get up, the young man came up to me, "My name is Henis. Henis Flo. I am very intrigued by you. You're the one who's been putting so many shills into the bonds of the company. You brought your way onto the board. You don't appear for years, then today you show up. What's up with that?", he asked. As he was staring at me, waiting for an answer, I saw a familiar woman walking up, "Is your meeting over? I have to leave soon.", "Yes, Saia, damn. Where is Carla?", "She is with Linda Sove, over there.", she pointed and I saw Linda playing with Carla. I smiled. "Carla!", called Henis, and she ran to him. "DADDY!", she yelled, jumping into his arms. "How is my Little Carli?", "Good!", she yelled, holding onto her father happily. I watched them both with interest. "Well, see you later, Thasha, I have to go take this one out for pasta pie.", he said, and Carla got excited. I watched them walk away, then I felt a hand on my shoulder, "Let's talk.", Solron said.

He took me into Simon's office. Simon was standing to the side, while Solron was sitting in his chair. "Are you in league with Amana Tia?", "I don't even know what that is supposed to mean. That is a fictional character.", I said. He eyed me, then asked, "Are you at all connected to the other main royal family?", "What the hell are you talking about?", I asked, standing up, and acting angry and confused, "I don't know what the hell you are talking about, Lon, and I don't know what to tell you. I don't know how to answer these ridiculous questions.", I said, sort of with a growl. Simon and Solron looked at each other, and then nodded. "Okay,

I'm sorry. There are some things going on and I had to ask you. It was just strange.", "What's strange are these questions.", I said. "Forget he asked.", Simon said. "Yes, very important we don't discuss this conversation. Let's just...as you said earlier, only discuss business.", Solron said, standing up, and straightening himself out. "Look, I understand your suspicions about me, but I'm all about business, and I believe Rain's Tech can be better than its competitors, don't you?", I asked, looking at Simon. Simon nudged Solron, and then they both moved towards the door, and Simon opened it. I walked out, then made sure to hurry and leave. As soon as I did, I got far away enough that I started to search for Linda's energy signature. I first changed back into Shima, then I appeared back inside the building. Linda was still here, and now she was just talking to Saia, who was on her way out, "Yeah, I know, Saia.", "And did I tell you he also told her that I'm the reason we aren't together?", "Yes, you did.", "So, what does he say to you?", "Nothing actually. I mean, you know it's all business between us.", "I know, but still...", Saia said, noticing me, "Oh, hi, Shima. Good to see you. Well, I have to go.", "So do we.", "WAIT!", Solron yelled, coming forward, "Hanging out with children, Linda?", "That is AUNT Linda to you, and Shima here is a bit different.", "And why is that?", "Doesn't matter. That's why I like her.", "Well what are you doing here, Shima?", he asked me, looking at me hard. I could tell he was getting more paranoid now. "I'm here with Linda.", "And why are you here, Aunty?", "Seriously? I come every so often to check and see what you guys have. Usually, I set up a meeting with Henis, but I didn't have time, so I was hoping to catch him, but he's got his daughter, so...I let it go.", Linda said. Solron kept looking between the both of us. "If I'm not needed, I'm leaving.", Saia said, and she left. "Look, we need to get going, too. I gotta get her home, and I have to get to Base, so later, Nephew.", "Bye.", Solron said gruffly, and he watched us walk away. I looked back at him, and he was still watching.

"He is really paranoid now.", "Oh yeah, he is definitely on high alert with you. He doesn't think Sylvia is making it up that you were in that mine, and he definitely knows something is off about Thasha. Might be wise not to make another appearance as her for a while.", Linda said, starting her flar. "I agree. I think this once was good enough. The rest I can do over the receiver. Now, it's time to start getting the rest of the board on my side, so they can vote for me to be the Head of Company.", I said, summoning my tablet I had fashioned, and adding something to my mission list. As Linda started to drive, I was thinking about how scared Solron was. He was sure I was working with Amana and he was sure that Thasha must be connected to the ROS(Royal Family of Sebastian).

As more time passed, I watched Rain's Tech bonds go up, and now I was certain it would be a good time to be more present. It had been two more years. Two years of me spending night and day worrying about Rain's Tech, and hardly taking breaks. Mileeda's son was now one and a half, and Brixin was trying to get me to take a break, "Come on, Shima!", "I told you that you don't have to call me that anymore.", I said, moving around my lab. I was working on something that I could present to the board as something new. I didn't know what I was doing yet, but Amana had always taught me that the best ideas just come to you. "Okay, Layna, then. Look, my son here, just wants to get to know you, right, Maxi?", Brixin asked his son, who was surprisingly able to walk, and somewhat understand his father. I always see Maxi staring at me, and I wanted to play with him, but I was so busy. If it wasn't Maxi staring at me, then it was Amana. Amana was obviously very proud of me. For some reason, though, she would never say it to me directly. She would always just let me catch her smiling at me. "I want to, Uncle, but I don't have the time.", "This project of yours is killing you, and you know what? I came here to tell you something.", "What?", I said, sort of irritated that he was disturbing me. "Tor is single.", he said simply. I stopped working, "Really?", I asked. During the time that I had become infatuated with taking over Rain's Tech, Tor had become the infatuation of women. After Yennipher, was another girl named Su. But this didn't last, because Su talked too much. Then it was another girl named Yellica. This didn't last, either. Then once again, it was Yennipher, who thought she could salvage their relationship, but this was to no avail. Tor was finally staying away from women. I knew I should talk to him, but I was still sort of mad at him for putting me through that. "Well, that's nice.", I said, going back to my work. I put on my welding mask, and started to sear down the middle of a big chunk of metal. I took the mask off to look at what I had done, and to make sure my lining was straight. "So, that's all you have to say? You've been waiting for him for a long time.", "Well, that's the point, isn't it?", "You can't stay mad at him for exploring.", "Yes I can.", "Layna, it isn't being fair.", "NO! What isn't fair is him knowing I couldn't reveal who I really am, AFTER he led me on to believe we were meant to be! So, fuck him.", I said, going back to my welding. Brixin just sat there, while his son was looking at which of my tools he should touch. He finally decided on my wrench, and I quickly snatched it before he picked it up. "Layna, listen to me...Mileeda was with Nigel over three-thousand years ago. He got old and died. Then she wasn't with anyone for a long time. When she met me, she didn't like me at all. She hated me to be honest. She wanted to help me, but I was being an ass at the time. Then, one day, she realized something about me.", "And what is that?", "I loved her. I didn't know how else to look at it. I wanted her. I told her, and she cursed me.", Brixin said, with a reminiscent smile. "Then how did you end up married to her, then?", "Because she realized that she had been trying to help me since she met me, because she loved me, too. Something about my situation just stuck out to her. Then when she learned Amana is my sister, she felt like that was a sign of our union. So, we've been married ever since. That was over one-thousand years ago. Now, you and Tor will be the same. You'll realize that you DO still love him. He is already wishing you were with him.", "Well, let him keep wishing.", I said, putting my welding mask back on. Brixin grabbed my wrist, "Layna, I'm just letting you know, before some other woman comes along. I'd rather see you two together, like when you were children.", "I know. But he messed that up the day he brought Yennipher Nos into the picture.", I said, snatching my wrist back from him. "Well, I can see there is no convincing you. Fine. But when he shows up here, what are you going to say to him then?", "Nothing. I'll let him knock until his knuckles bleed.". Brixin laughed at this, then picked up his son, and placed him on his shoulders, "I have to get going, but, Layna, please, take a break. You need it. I'm proud that you're working so hard, but you really need rest.", he said, giving me a stern look, then leaving. Maxi waved bye to me, and I waved back. He smiled, then faced forward, and leaned on his father's head.

I decided to listen to my uncle and take a break. On the television was that stupid reality show that followed the exploits of Sylvia, Reginald, and Tek. It was called Royal Nuts. I hated this show. All it was, was Sylvia showing off her expensive flars and jewelry, while Reginald and Tek have sex with hot girls. Yellica was on the show. Reginald tried his luck, after her and Tor were done, but Tor had an effect on women. They only wanted him back. It drove Tek and Reginald crazy. Tek was a few years older than his brother. When we were younger, Tek was the wise one. But now that he was older, he appreciated being rich and living a lavish lifestyle. "So, Sylvia, I've been meaning to ask you…about your cousin, Layna.", Setho said. Setho was a boy that Sylvia was always hanging with, and he had become a regular on the show. "Excuse me?", Sylvia said, looking at him cross, "I don't like to talk about her.", Sylvia started to fake cry, "I mean, it was when I was a kid that she died. I miss her so much.", she started to cry into Setho's chest. I changed the station. Me nor my father had been mentioned for years. But recently, it was the anniversary of our death, so there was something on television about it, so of course they were going to bring it up on Royal Nuts. I turned to the news, which was no better, "Solron, your brother and his daughter, died twelve years ago today. Is there anything on your mind?", "The only thing I think about on this day, is that my niece isn't here to enjoy her life.", "That is terrible, isn't it?", asked Saundra, who by this time, I had taken a very keen interest in. She was always asking the tough questions. I was sure she believed my aunt and uncle murdered me and my father, and I felt that I could trust her to help me finish my uncle. "Well, it is always terrible when a child is dead.", "I couldn't agree more.", Saundra said in a tone that suggested she didn't like my uncle at all. I knew I had to speak with her. I left my home, and made my way into Nocton. Once I arrived, I got out of my flar, and made my way into the news station. It was filled with people. Mainly television people, or people working on the cameras, and frequencies. I looked around. People knew me as royalty, because most of these people attended certain events Amana had taken me to. Saundra had never personally talked to me, because she didn't know exactly HOW I was royalty. After all, only certain families know about Sebastian's family. I saw Saundra talking to her usual co-host, and walked over to them, "Hello.", I said brightly. Saundra looked at me, then stood up, "Shima? That's your name, right?", "Yup. I was hoping I could speak to you privately, when you get a chance.", "Now is okay. See you later, Dek.", she said, picking up her purse.

We left the station and went to a bar that wasn't too far from it. "I'll have a beer.", she said, then looked at me. "A tall glass of Ticenta, please?", I said. "Ticenta? Pretty fancy. But I shouldn't be surprised. You're royalty after all.", Saundra said, watching me curiously, "I always wondered, though… I noticed that you seem to be heavily connected to the RF, and I noticed that there do seem to be some things happening in the background… Forgive me, I'm rambling.", she said, taking a sip of her beer. "It's okay. I'm curious to know more about you, Saundra. I understand you have some pretty heavy political views.", "Well, I just like to report the truth. But alas, I can only do so much.", "I understand. I'm the same way.", I said, taking a sip of my drink. Saundra was watching me out of the corner of her eye, and then she asked me, "So, what did you want to talk about?", "Your interview with Solron Lon.". She raised her eyebrow, "Why?", "Well…the why will be revealed, once I know for sure that I can trust you.", I said, now giving her a very serious look. She drank deeply from her glass, then looked at me very sternly, and whispered, "I've heard about you. On the low. Sylvia hates you. They say she is next up to be Head of the Family after her father, and she has a hard on for Shima Tia. Funny thing is, who the hell are you, though?", she asked, now ordering another beer. "There is only so much I can share with you, Saundra, but I'm willing to tell you, that I'm somebody you wouldn't expect.", I said, also finishing my drink, and ordering another one. Saundra looked around, then leaned closer to me, "Are you telling me that Shima Tia is only a cover for who you really are?", she asked excitedly. "Something like that. Tell me what you think about Sylvia.", "She is a little-bitch. I always hated her. I hated her as a child, and I hate her slutty-ass now.", Saundra said in an irritated tone, and she took another deep drink of her beer. "So that means she doesn't have your vote for Head of the Family, then?", "Fuck no.", Saundra said, chuckling as she did, "What does all this matter to you? What is Sylvia to you anyway?", "My cousin.", I said, watching for her reaction. She looked at me, then looked closer, and she dropped her beer. "Oh my god.", she said, now backing away from me, "But…where have you…?", she looked confused. Like she didn't know what to say. "Let's get out of here.", she said, paying the bartender, and leading me out.

As we arrived at what I had to assume was her home, I noticed she was still rattled. I got out of my flar, and she got out, and led us into her home. It was a nice home. The walls were decorated with Saundra's awards, and memory sheets of her friends, and I had to assume family. I sat down where she directed, and she left the room and came back with some wine, "That won't work on me.", I said, watching her pour me a glass. "Why not?", "Because I'm not normal.", I said, taking the glass anyway. "Layna… Layna Lon. That's who you are. But that doesn't make any sense. There were people on the scene of your death. I had only HEARD you weren't with your father.", "I wasn't. I was saved by the woman who raised me.", "SAVED? Like, this person knew they would kill you? Why would they want you dead? You were only a little girl!", Saundra said, standing up, and growing angry. She took a sip of her wine and started to pace back and forth, "So you weren't with your father, and all these years I was right about your aunt and uncle. But…if you're alive, and you're a Lon…YOU CAN BE HEAD!", she said, putting these pieces together. I nodded my head slowly. She looked taken aback, "But, that's what you're trying to do… They think you're dead, but all these years, you've been this…Shima Tia. Who is Amana? I've heard of her. Amana Tia. She is the woman that saved you. I never really thought about her, until now…", Saundra said, sitting back down, and looking at me longingly. "She is my mother. My stepmother, because my real mother died giving birth to me, so Amana is the only mother I've ever known.", "But, who is she?", she asked, leaning closer. "There is only so much I can tell you, remember?", "But I feel like this is important. She raised you. Saved you from your family. She is a major player and she is hiding in the background. Now call me crazy, but she is named after the princess from the fairy tale stories, and I find that a bit much. Now, is she one of these other royal families I've heard about?", "Yes. I can say that much.", "Which one?", "That I cannot say.", "Why?", "Because you aren't privy to it.", "But isn't it important to what we are talking about?", "No. What we are talking about is how best to dethrone my uncle.", I said, now leaning closer myself. Saundra swallowed. "That's why you came to me? You want me to use my media ties to make him look bad?", "I want you to report the truth, like you said you like to do. I'm willing to do an interview. About how my family tried to kill me, and how I survived, and I've studied for a long time, and now, I'm going to be running against my uncle for the Head Seat of the RF.". Saundra poured herself some more wine, then started to drink, not taking her eyes off of me. "Let me get this straight, you want me...to interview you? In other words, this is your coming out party?". I nodded. "Count me out. They'll kill me. Especially if they tried to kill you before. They'll think I was connected to your survival.", "You see? In order for me to fully trust you, I needed to know how brave you are. Thank you, Saundra.", I said, now standing up, and moving towards her door. "WAIT!", she shouted, moving to block me. "Move.", I said. "Wait, let's not be hasty. I was just confused.", "I can't trust you.", I said. "No. You can. I just… This is all so surprising.", "I know how it is. But I'm telling you, I need to do this. I need you to be the one to interview me.", "If I agree, I want to know about Amana.". Saundra gave me a very hard look. I couldn't just consent to reveal classified info like that, but I needed her to trust me, and I needed to be able to trust her back. "Okay, I'll tell you about her family. But not tonight. And only after you interview me.", "How do I know you'll keep your word?", "Because I'm not a liar.", "You've been lying for twelve years… But that was to protect yourself. I guess that doesn't count.", she said, now smiling. I could tell she was trying to lighten the mood, but secretly, I knew she was right. The family would be coming after her the moment the interview began. "When did you want to do this interview?", "Tomorrow, in the morning.", I said, now pushing her out of the way and opening her door, "Listen, you'll be protected. I won't let my family hurt you.",

"How can you protect me?", she said, looking at me with an incredulous stare. I snapped my fingers, and her glass of wine refilled. She stared at it, then looked back at me. "Like I said, I'll protect you.". I walked out of her house and made my way back to my flar. As I was about to start it, someone came and knocked on my window. I rolled it down, "What were you doing at Saundra Lome's home?", Sylvia asked me, looking around in my flar for something suspicious. "What? I can't visit a friend now?", "A friend? Where did you meet her?", "At a party. Now, get the hell off of my flar.", I said, starting it, and driving off. I saw Sylvia looking angry behind me, and knew that this was going to be perfect.

The next day when I awoke, it was to multiple calls from Saundra. I checked my messages, "I'm going to the station now. I called for an emergency interview. Nobody knows what's going on. I'll see you there.", she said. I took a shower. Truth be told, I was nervous. I was finally going to admit that I'm Layna Lon, and I'm not dead. I put on my favorite colors of pink and purple, but I took the dye out of my hair. The blonde looked so different to me now. I was getting ready to leave, and I turned on the television just to see what was happening at Saundra's station. Indeed they were getting ready for the interview, "So, Saundra, who is this mystery person that we'll be seeing you interview today? Why so secretive? Why call this emergency interview?", her partner, Dek, was asking. "Because, none of you will believe it until this mystery person is sitting across from me. I couldn't believe it. I still can't.", Saundra said, checking her watch, and looking around nervously. I didn't want to keep her waiting. I teleported, instead of driving, to the station. When I arrived, I walked inside. The security guard was about to stop me, but I psychically made him leave me alone. Once I was standing next to the interview station, Saundra looked up and smiled from ear to ear. "She's here.", she said. I stepped out of the shadows and made my way to the interview chair. Dek was watching me curiously, "Who are you?", he asked. "I am someone that is very lucky to be here today. No thanks to my family.", "And what does that mean, exactly?", Dek asked, shifting uncomfortably in his chair. I looked at the camera, smiled, and then said, "My name is...Layna Lon.". Immediately, Dek stood up, Saundra just smiled, but everyone else in the station was going crazy. "You're lying! Is this some kind of joke?! Saundra, why would you pull something like this?!", Dek asked, and half shouted. Saundra shook her head at him, and directed that he sit back down. I watched him, then he looked back at me, and slowly sat back in his seat. "Where have you been all this time, if you really are who you say you are?", Saundra asked, "I've been living a secret life. Hiding for my protection.", "Protection from whom?", "My uncle. Solron.". Now the station had grown quiet. "What do you mean...? Are you saying Solron Lon murdered his brother and his niece?", "No. I'm saying he MURDERED my father, and tried to murder me.", I said, looking at Saundra straight in the eye. "So, who have you been with this whole time?", Dek asked me. "That is classified, but what I can tell you, is that my uncle, and his sorry-ass rule over Nocton, is over. I'm going to be challenging him for the Head Seat.". Now there were murmurs and people looking at one another scared. Just then, a door banged open, and in walked my uncle. "NO, MOVE OUT MY WAY, DAMN IT!", he yelled at the security guard I had mind-controlled. He stood looking at me, then realization dawned on his face, "Shima... You... This whole time... My...", he fell to his knees, and looked up at me, "You're alive.", he said, reaching for me. I slapped his hand away. All of this was being recorded. Saundra was looking childishly happy. Dek was looking like he just got the best present in the world and he looked at Saundra with a boyish smile. "First of all, I dare you to try and kill me now. Do it. So everyone can know what you really are.", I said. He looked around at everyone, "She is mistaken. Her information is off. Whoever has raised you, has lied to you.", he said, now getting up, and showing his anger. "Really? I don't think they would lie. Not only have I watched YOU lie, and abuse your power, but now you're trying to play innocent? Fine. Be this way. But when I am the Head...", "YOU WILL NEVER BE!", he yelled, losing his cool, "I always knew it! All those things that have been going on, it was you! Working for Amana, and that son-of-a-bitch, Brixin!", he yelled, now pacing. Everyone was watching him. "So, as you can see, I'm not lying.", I said, turning to the camera now, "I will be the next Queen of the Royal City, and I will show you nothing but truth and honesty. I have trained since I was five for this. I promise you, people, I love you.", I said, then looked at Saundra, then departed. Leaving my uncle trying to answer a shit ton of questions.

Saundra caught up with me, "That...was...WAY better than I expected!", she said, reaching to hug me. I stopped her, "Keep my uncle in there busy. I have things to attend to.", I said, then disappeared. I arrived at Brixin's manor. He was sitting in the sitting room, watching the television, "So, now, you're saying that the woman who was just here is an imposter?", "She has to be. She can't be Layna Lon. She died, and I hate to bring it up, but there were only small traces of her DNA left at the scene. How could that woman be her?", "These were Solron's words earlier today here at Royal News. A woman, claiming to be the late Layna Lon, walked into the station today and did an interview with our famed, Saundra Lome. We're still trying to get the full story, but from what Solron is saying, this woman is nothing but an imposter, and if seen, please call your nearest RG precinct. It will be for the best.", said a different reporter. "Well, now you've done it.", Brixin said, standing up, and facing me. "It was time.", I said, walking towards the set, and trying to hear what else they were saying. Dek and Saundra were doing their usual talking bit, "So, do you truly believe that woman was Layna Lon?",

Dek asked. "It's hard to say. She does look like an older version. It has been twelve years, and most of her story seems to fit.", "If her story fits, then that means that our king killed his brother.", "Well, let's not forget that Tena may have had a hand in it, but unfortunately, Layna didn't stick around to point that much out.", she said disappointed. Brixin changed to another news station, and the scene was outside of my uncle's manor, and Sylvia was fake crying, "How could someone play a trick like this?", she was asking, dabbing her eyes. "So you're saying there is no chance that this woman is your cousin?", "That is exactly what I'm saying. And this person better hope the RG finds her, before I do.", Sylvia said, giving the camera a dark look. "Strong words from our future queen. But if I might ask, this girl said that she will be challenging your father for the throne, and not you. Does this worry you in any way?", the reporter asked. Sylvia replied, "Of course not, because this woman is NOT Layna Lon.", "Her name is Shima?", the reporter asked now, stepping closer. Sylvia made an angry face that was not easy to hide. She tried to cover her action, "Well, I know who that is, and WE are NOT related.", she said, now trying to get away. "But...Ms. Lon...", "LEAVE ME ALONE!", she yelled, then the reporter backed off, and Sylvia walked into the manor. "Well, you heard her, this woman is NOT our dearly departed princess.", "So, looks like they didn't buy it.", Brixin said, crossing his arms. "Yes, they did. Some might not believe at first, but they will. My uncle will give it away.", I said, sitting down. Brixin summoned a glass of ticenta and passed it to me. "Thank you. I need to ask your permission for something.", "And that would be?", "I told Ms. Lome that I would tell her who Amana's family is in exchange for her doing the interview.", I looked at Brixin, hoping he'd say what I wanted to hear. "Well...I suppose it is a good reason... AND you need her to trust you...", he said, thinking out loud, "Fine. Tell her, but be careful about it. Don't try to reveal too much. If anything, just stick to Amana and Calypsa.", he said. "She is a reporter, she'll have more questions.", "Then just tell her about me, Amana, and Calypsa. Don't mention Ko-e or Tor, or anyone else.", "Okay.", I said, smiling. "Hey, Unc, you ready for that game?", Tor walked in and saw me. He froze. "Hi, Layna.", he said in a small tone. "Well, thank you, Uncle, but I'm leaving now.", "Wait, Layna.", Tor had grabbed my arm. I snatched it and slapped him, "DON'T!", I yelled, trying to contain my tears I felt coming. I left so he wouldn't see them.

When I arrived back at home, I found Amana also watching news reports. She was wearing her military outfit with the coat, and was just standing in front of the monitor, tapping her chin with the remote, "Layna Lon died twelve years ago, but a woman walked into the Royal News station claiming to BE Layna Lon. I think there is something rotten going on.", "I agree, Lilary. And might I add that Solron called this girl, Shima. Now, Shima may be her real identity or a fake one that she had to come up with. At this point, we won't know until we see her again.", "And when do you think that will be?", the other journalist asked, while behind the two, there were pictures of me as a little girl, and pictures of me from this morning. "Well she said she will be running for the Head Seat, so I imagine that we will see a lot of her in the coming days. Now, onto other things...", Amana shut off the monitor and turned around. She looked at me, then smiled, "You were brilliant this morning.", she said, coming to me, and hugging me. "I'm glad you think so. By the way, I already told Uncle, but I have to tell Saundra Lome who you are.", "That's fine. I'm glad you did this on your own. I'm so proud of you.", she said, taking in my face as she always has. "My uncle is beside himself.", I said. Just as I said this, there was a knock on the manor door. One of the servants went to open it and returned with Tek. "Mr. Tek Tib is here to see, Ms. Shima.", "Call me, Layna from now on.", I commanded. "Ms. Layna, then.", the servant smiled and left. Tek just stood looking at me.

"Little Cousin.", he said, still just standing there. Amana looked between us, then left. "What do you want?", I asked. "I thought you were dead. All this time, you've been, Layna...all this time.", he said, stepping closer. "Yes, now what do you want?", I asked again. Before I could do anything, he was hugging me. I didn't know what to say or do. I hugged him back. When he broke away from me, he had a small tear in his eye, "They were always cruel, and I never said anything, then you were dead...", he said, hugging me again.

We eventually walked into Amana's garden and were catching up, "...so now, Reginald is on Sylvia's side. He's saying that you aren't, Layna, and that you're an imposter, and should be jailed for doing this.", Tek was saying as we walked. "Well, that won't matter. Solron will convince the people unwillingly, and I will campaign and earn the trust of Nocton.", I said. "Layna, you can't. Listen, you're already on the edge.", "I've been on the edge for twelve years already.", "Yeah, but you were pretending to be someone else! Now that you've admitted who you really are, you really think they won't try and finish the job?!", "I dared him to do it.", I said, smiling at the idea of Solron actually trying to kill me. "You've let Amana poison your mind.", Tek said, shaking his head. "No, she hasn't. And don't talk about her like that. She is my mother.", "Your mother died, Layna. Amana is NOT your mother. She has been pretending, just like you. But the game is over. Here.", Tek handed me a ticket for a falcon. "I'm not leaving.", I said, giving it back to him. "Layna, I love you, and I don't ever want to go through what I went through as a child. Please, take this and go!", he yelled, trying to shove it in my hand. I looked at him sadly, "I really appreciate this, Tek, but I have to do this. It's my destiny.", I said. Tek looked taken aback, "They will kill you, Shima. Sylvia will kill you. She is extremely angry now that she knows who you are. Sylvia is going to come after you to stop your campaign against her.", "It isn't against her. She will never sit on the throne. It's against her father. AND he will lose, Tek. He will, I promise. Nothing is going to happen to me.", I said, pulling him into another hug. "Now, I have stuff to take care of.", I said, ordering one of the servants to show him out.

I decided to go ahead and call Saundra, who I was sure was thinking I'd break my promise. I teleported to her home, and she was, of course, waiting for me as soon as I arrived. She didn't notice me appear, "Well, I almost thought you had forgotten.", "No, I had to get permission.", I said, walking into her door. She came in behind me, and once again, went and fetched some wine. "So, tell me about Amana.", she said, sitting down. "Well, she is a part of a very old family.", "Which one?". I hesitated, "Sebastian's.". As I said this, Saundra looked at me with scrutiny. I could tell she thought I just made this up. "Sebastian's? As in...Sebastian from the church? So, you're saying that the Amana that saved you, is the same Amana from the fairy tales, or a woman named after her?", Saundra was already looking angry and I could tell whatever answer I gave was going to upset her even more. "The Amana I'm talking about is over three-thousand years old.", "Get out.", Saundra said, standing up, and moving to her door, "I thought you would be serious with me. Especially after this morning, but now I think you're a nut.", she said. "I get it. I really do. When Amana first told me that I'm a goddess...", Saundra looked at me even more cross, "...I did not believe her. I thought that she was crazy. But, have you ever heard of Mileeda?". Saundra moved away from the door and went back to her chair, "Actually, I've met her. She is some big head honcho when it comes to the RF, but nobody has ever disclosed why. All the times I've seen her, she wasn't with the RF. But I heard she is in control or something like that...", Saundra said, now once again giving me the curious look she first gave me. "That is correct. You see, she is the origin. And also, married to Amana's brother, Brixin.". Saundra drank deep from her glass, then poured another one, "Brother?", "Yes. He is the son of Sebastian.", I said. Saundra spit out her wine she had started to drink, "WHAT?!", she asked. "Yes. Amana and Brixin are the direct children of Sebastian. And like I said, I am a goddess.", "How?", "How to what?", "How are you a goddess?", she asked, now setting the wine down, and waiting for me to show her something. "Mileeda is a goddess, and I'm her descendant. Her firstborn son's descendant.", "And that makes you a goddess?", "All of the RF have something that makes them unique. Even my cousin, Sylvia, but only certain family members are born with Mileeda's exact genetics.", I said, now seeing that Saundra was actually starting to believe me. "And is this the reason that your uncle tried to kill you?". I told her the story of Tena, and how the Tibs had killed her unborn child, and how Tena didn't really want the throne anymore after that. I explained that my uncle manipulated her into killing me and my father so that he could take over. I then explained how Amana trained me, and taught me, and introduced me to her family. "So, Brixin is married to your ancestor, Mileeda. That makes her and Amana in-laws…and at the same time, they are BOTH over three-thousand?". I nodded. "And Brixin is…?", "Well, technically, he is only one-thousand, seven-hundred, and twenty-nine, but really, he is over three-thousand as well. He was killed some time ago, and his parents reincarnated him.", "YOU MEAN TO TELL ME…?! Um, sorry, I mean, Sebastian is alive?", "Um, I've never met him, but I guess.", I said, now thinking about that. How come I've never met him? I've met his family, and he is obviously out there somewhere. "Brixin was killed…by whom?", "A woman named Abraxa.", "Abraxa? And where is this woman? I mean if she was able to kill the son of Sebastian, I'm assuming she is alive and of a really old age.", "I don't know. Brixin said she'd come back one day.", I said, now also thinking about that as well. "I can't believe this…but it makes sense. This is why your families are so close… Because your family is Tig's and the other is Sebastian's. This is incredible!", said Saundra, now getting excited and smiling at me even harder than before, "And you don't want anyone else to know this?", she asked. "They can't.", "Why?", "Saundra, please, there is a reason that the Royal Family of Sebastian stays hidden.", "I get it. But they're GODS! I mean, why hide from everyone, when they have the power to control everyone?", she said, looking at me with that same expectancy. "Because they don't want to be celebrities. They have a job to do, and it's easier to do when they aren't famous. Like the RF.", I pointed out. Saundra nodded, "What is their job?", "Protecting this planet.", I said. Saundra looked speechless now. She got up, and moved over to the armchair she had, she had been sitting on the couch. She sank into the armchair, and then looked up at me, "I can't believe this. First, you're alive, now you're telling me that you were raised by a fairy tale princess, and were a part of her family of gods?", I nodded slowly, "Are there other members of this family besides Mileeda, Brixin, and Amana?", "There was Calypsa.", "And she died, right? That was in the story. Amana had to kill her or something like that.", "Yes. That was the dark tales, I believe. But the dark tales were closer to the truth than the happy ending ones.", "How much of the truth have you been told?", "Enough to know what I have to do. Look, I've literally told you all I can tell you, so do you need anything else?", I asked, realizing I should get going. After all, I had other appearances to make and other people to convince. "I have so many questions... What about Trinity? What is she? Is she real?". I hesitated with the answer to this one, "She is...Amana's and Brixin's mother. But, like Sebastian, I've never met her.", I said, standing, and getting ready to depart. Saundra stood up, "But what are you going to do, Layna? I don't understand how you plan on beating your uncle. You're still so young. Is this all just revenge?", she asked. "No, it isn't. It's about taking care of Nocton the proper way.", I said, now opening the door. Saundra came and put her hand on it, "Yes, but I don't understand how you're a goddess.

What can you do? Besides refilling my glass.", she said. She obviously wanted to see me show off some of my ability. "Saundra, I'm not a show. I'm not someone who just uses her powers whenever she wants. I only use them if I really need to.". There was a knock on the door, and I opened it to find Sylvia. She was standing outside with a clutch of Royal Guards. "Like right now?", Saundra asked, looking at all the guards. "Well, you messed up now, Ms. Lome. Consorting with the imposter.", Sylvia said, shaking her head, "I had a feeling you were here, Shima. Now, I'm taking you in and ending this charade.", "The only charade was me being Shima. I'm Layna.", I said, smiling. Sylvia made that same angry face, and I saw her arm twitch, "YOU AREN'T MY COUSIN!", she yelled, pointing for the men to take me in. I raised my arm, and the men stopped. "What the hell are you doing? Bring her in!", Sylvia yelled at them. "Mam, look at what she's showing.". It was the Royal Crest of Sebastian. "So, can I leave? And also, if you arrest Ms. Lome here, you will be the one in a world of trouble.", "If you're Layna, then that crest doesn't count for you.", Sylvia said, stepping closer to me. "Actually, here's the thing, if I'm Layna, then you can't arrest me for being an imposter of Layna. And secondly, I was adopted into the family. I could just call my uncle here to settle this, or you can walk away now, without embarrassing yourself.". Sylvia was livid now. She grabbed me and I quickly retaliated by punching her. She retaliated by kicking me. Saundra ran into the house, while me and Sylvia started to go at it, "I HATE YOU!", she screamed at me. "I feel the same.", I said, as we were both holding each other, and trying to get a hit in. Saundra came back with a pad and a pen in her hand. She started to write frantically, then Sylvia noticed, and broke apart from me, and made towards her. She snatched the pad out of her hand, "I WILL NOT BE ONE OF YOUR STORIES!", she yelled and ripped the pad. She then turned and waved for the men to follow her back to their vehicles. She turned to me, and mouthed, "This isn't over, bitch.", and got into one of the guard vehicles and was gone. I looked back at Saundra, who was now getting out a handkerchief to wipe the blood off my cheek where Sylvia kicked me. But before she could wipe me, I waved my hand over my face, and healed my cut. The blood was gone, and it looked like it never happened. Saundra was in shock now. "Oh my...you really are a goddess... But Sylvia...", "I told you, she is different, too. She just isn't a goddess.", "But what is the difference?", "I don't have time to explain that. I'm sorry, Saundra, but I need to go.". I teleported on the spot, knowing that she'll be even more impressed. I arrived back at Brixin's manor. Brixin and Tor were watching an Airball game. I came in right at halftime. "Well, look who's back.", Brixin said, and Tor looked in my direction. "I only came to talk to you really quickly, Uncle. About what happened.", I said, ignoring Tor's gaze. My uncle got up and walked with me to his study. "That was awkward.", he said, sitting down. "Well, you made it awkward. You could have just spoken to me telepathically.", "Yeah, but I want you two to make up already. It's getting ri...", "I didn't come to talk about that. I came to talk about...", I stopped talking because Tor had walked in the room. "Layna, I want to talk.", "I'm having an important conversation.", I said, waving him off. He just stood there, not walking away. I looked at Brixin for support, "Look, Tor, let Lay...", "NO! Layna, please, just talk to me!", Tor was shouting, moving towards me. I turned away, because I felt tears coming. I tried to teleport, but couldn't and realized why, "Uncle, please...", "No. He's right. You two need to talk.", said Brixin, getting up, and walking out of the room. "I don't want anything from you!", I shouted at him. "I love you.", he said simply. "You're a liar.", "Layna, I never lied to you. But, I didn't know how to turn those girls away without revealing who you really were! I knew the importance of keeping your identity a secret. Pleas...", as Tor was walking forward, he tripped on a wire that was on the floor and he hit his face. He got up quickly, healed himself, and then came and knelt before me, "Layna, I'll do ANYTHING. Please, just come back to me.", he pleaded. I didn't know what to do. I grasped around for anything, and then, my cell rang. I quickly got up and answered, "Yes?", "We need to talk. Come meet me at the place your father died.", Tena said, then hung up. Tena had always known who I was, ever since she was dethroned, but she never said a word. I looked at Tor, "I have to go.", I said, walking out the door. He quickly caught up with me, and pulled me to him, and kissed me. I wanted to get away, but I felt myself melt, and after all, this was my first kiss. He pulled away from me, and then I grabbed him and kissed him again. "Finally.", we broke apart, and saw Brixin holding a smiling Maxi in his hands. I looked at Tor, then slapped him. Maxi started to cry. "Why did you do that?", Brixin asked, trying to calm his son. "I...love you.", I said to Tor, then disappeared. I arrived at the spot where my father died. I didn't like coming here. They put a bomb in his flar, and when it exploded, his body was too horrible to describe. Amana had left my hair on the scene to give the impression that I had died as well. I looked around and the area was nice and clean now. No flaming flar, no burned up grass of any kind. There were children playing, but it was getting late and parents were already taking their children home. There was no statue to commemorate me nor my father. But people who liked us had been bringing candles here for years. I looked around at the candles and they spelled; REST IN PEACE LAYNA. I was so overwhelmed, that I began to cry, "Your uncle was the one who went fully through with the plan. I hardly wanted to play a part in it. I knew Solron wanted the throne, and I wanted him to have it, but I needed Mileeda and Amana to not want me there.", Tena was saying as she approached me. She had been hiding. I saw the tears in her eyes. "So what? You regret killing my father?", "EVERYDAY!", she screamed at me, "Why do you think I never gave you away, even after Grandmother beat me nearly to death? Because I love you! I loved your father, but what he was proposing...

even I couldn't agree with. Layna, your father wanted to use you.", "Use me for what?", "Of course… Amana didn't tell you… She is always keeping these things secret, and that is why we hate her AND Grandmother.", Tena said, shaking her head, but getting closer to me all the while. "Kept what from me?", "The fact that your father wanted to take over the role of Sebastian's family. He felt WE are the power and WE should be the one giving orders. He felt Brixin should listen to us, and he was going to raise you to hate them. Make you powerful enough to challenge them.", "Why would I believe you?", "Layna, what do I have to GAIN by lying to you? Your father was a good man, but that idea of his was ridiculous.", "And Brixin knew he wanted to do this?", "He not only knew, but he also spoke with him. He spoke with your father about it. Nobody knows what was said in that conversation, but that is the reason that your father took you away when you were younger. He wanted to protect you from Sebastian's family.", "No, that can't be true. Amana loves me. She raised me!", I said, starting to think about what Tena was telling me. "I wouldn't lie, Layna. They were going to kill you.", "Go away. I never want to see you. Ever.", "Layna, please, I know this is hard to accept. But those people that you believe are your family, they are backstabbers. Even towards themselves. You see how they fight amongst themselves, I'm sure. I watched Brixin and Amana throw blows with each other as a little girl. They don't get along as well as they…", "I've seen them grow angry with each other. I know this already. You're not telling me nothing new, and I don't know WHY you're lying, but you are lying.", I said, stepping closer to her now, pulling out my cannon, and pointing it at her face, "What reason are you trying to manipulate me?", I asked. "I'm not trying to manipulate you. I'm just telling you the truth, and I came to warn you. Your uncle knows he can't kill you directly, and he knows that IF something does happen to you now, the people will know the truth, and Amana will come for him, and show him no mercy.

I know that she thinks of you as her daughter, so I know how protective she will be of you. I bet even now, she is probably watching you.", Tena said, not moving, not even looking at the cannon, but still talking to me, looking me straight in the eyes. "So if you believe Amana is watching you, you wouldn't risk meeting with me, unless you felt it was important.", "Lo. He's in Copania. And he's trapped in that cave, right?", "Yes.", I said, surprised she knew this. "Well, your uncle is going to free him, and have him kill you, so that he can say Sylvia tried to save you, but this mystery man was too powerful for us to stop.", "That is a feeble plan.", "That has much worse consequences.", Tena said, suddenly dead serious, "Lo could never be trusted. He was a god and a powerful one at that, trained by your mother. So, if Lo is freed, he will only serve HIS purposes. Killing you will fit into his agenda, but at the same time, so would resurrecting Amana's real daughter. Alisa.". I now started to think about her words, and fear spread through me. "Where is Solron now?", "He is already in Copania. He is guarded by Royal Tech that is shielding him from Brixin. They are going to break Lo free. I came to warn you, because it's the right thing, and I… I love you. Like I said.", Tena said, still staring straight at me. I didn't know what to say. I could tell now that she wasn't lying to me. I didn't know what to approach first, Lo or Brixin wanting to kill me. I decided to deal with the betrayal first.

First, I teleported to Brixin's manor, where Brixin and Tor had returned happily to watching the game, which was ending now. "Man, I can't believe Conner did that!", Brixin was saying, standing up, and stretching. Linda was here as well, and she was holding Maxi. I waited for Brixin to sense me, and he didn't. I realized he couldn't. "BRIXIN!", I shouted. He turned, "Layna? What's wrong?", he asked with a serious face. "You are what's wrong. You, and everyone…minus, Maxi, are nothing but liars.", I said, staring angrily at him. "Layna, when exactly have I lied to you?", Brixin asked with that smile he always has on his face. "Wipe that smile off your face.", I said darkly. He suddenly did. He got serious, "What have you heard?", he said, now approaching me. Tor was looking deathly. Linda had passed Maxi to Tor and stood up as well, "Niece... what is wrong with you?", she said, standing next to her father. "You wanted to kill me.", "Why would I want to kill you?", "Because of what my father wanted to use me for.", "Layna, how long have you known me for now?", "THAT DOESN'T MATTER!", I yelled, angry that he was still playing innocent, after I told him, and he confirmed he knew what I was talking about. "Layna, it does matter. I've always been kind to you. I once said, and you know I said this, that the gifted born shouldn't be killed. So WHY, would I want to KILL you?", he said, coming closer to me. I didn't know how to answer that. "What did you discuss with my father?", "I just told him how silly he was being, and that he would have to protect himself from Tena and Solron. I mean…come on…you know this already. Who told you about that conversation?", Brixin asked, with a highly serious tone now. "My uncle is trying to free Lo. And Tena said that he would resurrect Alisa.". Brixin made the same face Amana makes when she becomes highly pissed off, "And you wait till…NOW, to tell me this?", he said through gritted teeth. "Brixin, I didn't know what to think. I'm telling you, that's what matters.", I said. "Tena was right to tell you about this. And we will discuss this more later. But I will go to deal with this.", "Father, I'll come, too.", Linda said, taking out her cannon, and checking it. "NO! I'm going by myself.", "BUT, what if Lo is free?", Linda said to her father. "Then I'll deal with THAT, too.", he said. He summoned armor onto himself. It was a strange armor that wasn't bulky or anything. It fit his body perfectly and was black and red. He summoned a sword that I noticed had a cannon attachment on the hilt. He disappeared. I looked at Linda, and I, too, disappeared, barely hearing Tor call my name.

The cave was just like before. The rocks glowed upon my arrival. Brixin was already ahead of me. I caught up to him. "I told you to stay.", "No. I'm coming. I want to make Lo pay and punish my uncle.", I said. Brixin looked at me, then nodded, "Okay, just stay close to me. Remember what we're dealing with.", he said, proceeding forward. We heard voices after about ten minutes, "...time.", "I know that, but that is WHY I'm freeing you!", "Don't lie to me, Cousin. You're freeing me because Layna has ended the game of being Amana's daughter, and has come forward as who she really is.", Lo was saying, already freed. "Please, Lo...", "You didn't help me. You could have backed me against Brixin, and he wouldn't have been able to trap me here.", Lo was saying in a cool yet terrifying voice. Brixin was forcing me to stay back and not interfere, "But, I think he is going to KILL him!", I yelled silently. Brixin just nodded, "Some people are good, some people are evil, that's just how it is.", he said. "You've said that.", "What I didn't say, but should have, is evil always gets what's coming.", "We can't let him die like this.", "Yes we can. Because this is his punishment, and it isn't OUR place to interfere with that. Trust me. Ko-e taught me this.", "You trust her too much. Where is she now?", "Dealing with something WORSE than this.", Brixin said. I wanted to ask what could be worse than an evil god being freed and trying to reawaken an evil goddess, but I saw we didn't have much time. "Tell me, Solron, give me a REALLY good reason to help you.", "I'll help you bring your girlfriend back. I'll help you bring back Alisa. We know where her body is. Lona has her body contained. She stole it from Amana.", Solron said, bowing before Lo. I looked at Brixin, and he shook his head, "I'll have to deal with her.", he said. "STAND!", Lo yelled, and my uncle did, "I'll tell you what... I'll kill the little, Lon bitch, if you get Lona to actually BRING Alisa here. She may have stolen her body, but she knows it's too dangerous to come here. Sebastian's blood is at full strength right now! And not only that, but he is already here.", Lo said, pointing at me and

Brixin. Brixin charged from behind the rock and was dodging the orange energy blasts Lo was throwing at him. My uncle took out his cannon and started to fire at him. Brixin got hit by one of his shells, and then he fell and hit the wall. But this was a ploy. He teleported up to Lo and placed the sword straight to his neck, "Yield, now.", he said. "Go to Hell.", Lo said, and he teleported, too, but out of the cave. "SHIT!", Brixin yelled, and he teleported. I tried to sense their energies, but then I got shot. I looked up, as I was on the floor bleeding, "Time to properly die, Niece.", "You're working with…Corsa?!", I yelled at him, coughing blood, and trying to stand. "Yes. She keeps me safe, and helps me when I need it. More than Grandmother does. She hates us, but Corsa loves us. You're a fool for siding with Mileeda. Corsa is going to kill her, then you'll see, she is nothing.", he said, kicking my face. I was knocked on my stomach. As he was approaching me, I stood up and stabbed him, over, and over, and over again. His blood started to spill onto my hands. I continued stabbing him and started screaming. I screamed, and screamed, and screamed. "Layna…", he said, trying to grab me, but I ripped my hands out of his grasp and kept stabbing him. I finally stopped, and dropped my blade. I was breathing hard, watching him breathe his last breath, "…this…won't go…unanswered… Sylvia…", "Will bow before me.", I said, watching his eyes fade. Finally, he was dead. I went back to trying to sense Brixin and I found him. I teleported to him, and he was fighting Lo. Lo had summoned armor as well. Lo's was bulky, orange, and white. His sword had a blade that had multiple edges that could cut no matter what part of the blade touched you. But when it did slash Brixin, it didn't phase him at all. We were on a beach in Copania, not too far from Brixin's manor. I ran in and started to shoot my cannon. My cannon takes my energy and expels it. Amana's cannon does the same thing. It's why I made mine like her's. It is a powerful weapon. But Brixin's did the same, but it was also attached to the blade. He was shooting his black energy at Lo, who was dodging all the energy blast, "AMANA HAS TRAINED YOU WELL, LO!", Brixin yelled with a smile on his face. Lo replied, "Yes, she has.", and then he put his blade straight through Brixin. "NO!", I yelled, and started firing like mad, but Brixin had tricked Lo. He hadn't really been hurt, and he blasted him straight in the face with the sword. "You're an idiot, Lo. Alisa was using you. That's all Lona and her ever do. She killed Salana, damn it! You really think she gives a fuck about you, or ANY of Tig's descendants?! I cared about you, kid, and you betrayed me. ME!", Brixin yelled, and he blasted him again. Lo was down, and Brixin waved his hand, and Lo disappeared. "Where did you send him?", "Back to the cave.", "But he can…", "Layna…do you recall what I told you…about who was going to free Lo?", "Yes. You said your son. Duke.", "Then that's what's going to happen. I knew THIS was going to happen, too.", Brixin said, turning to me, "I just didn't know that Tena would tell you about your father's plan. Which I think now that this is taken care of, we should discuss that.", Brixin said, teleporting away. I went back to the cave. Inside, I found my uncle's body. Bloody, still, silent, and not moving. I kneeled over him, and looked at his blood all down my front. "FATHER!", I turned, and Sylvia was standing in the entrance to the cavern, with a cannon pointed straight at me, "YOU! YOU MURDERED HIM!", "He did this to himself.", I said, standing up, and cleaning the blood off of me. Sylvia charged at me, but I teleported out of her way, and to the wall. She began firing at me, and I ran, and took out my cannon. Just then, Brixin appeared, and waved his hand, and we both hit the wall, "SYLVIA, LISTEN TO ME!", he yelled, but Sylvia was already getting up and firing in his direction. He stopped the shells, then they exploded, causing him to be blown back. "How do you like my invention?", she said, advancing on him, and hitting him with her cannon. Then she shot at me again, and I started to try and fire back, but my energy wouldn't come out the end of my cannon. "What…?". I began to say, then I saw Brixin was holding his hand towards me, "Don't, Layna.", he said, standing up. Sylvia was about to fire again, but he grabbed her cannon out of her hands, "SYLVIA, DAMN IT! LISTEN TO ME!", he yelled, and Sylvia looked at her father's body and started trying to physically fight Brixin. She was throwing punches at him, and Brixin was knocking her hand away, "He had to die.", Brixin said, grabbing her, and wrapping both arms around her. "NO! YOU'RE ALL LIARS! YOU'LL PAY!", she was screaming, trying to break free of his grasp. "Sylvia, I'm sorry you had to find him like this, but he was working with the enemy. He would have inadvertently brought about the destruction of the planet. He was greedy, and cruel, and he murdered your Uncle Arthur to try and kill his little five year old niece that he was afraid of. Sylvia, I'm truly sorry, but your father had to die.", he said, loosening his grip on Sylvia and allowing her to fall before her father's bloody mess of a body. "But...what will I do...?", she said, crying over him. Brixin put his hand on her shoulder, "I know. It's hard. But this is what you will do. You will say he died trying to defend Layna from a terrible person.", Brixin said. Sylvia looked up, "You want me to lie? SHE MURDERED HIM!", Sylvia yelled, pointing at me. "IT WAS LESS THAN HE DESERVED!", I yelled back. "LAYNA, PLEASE, STAY OUT OF THIS!", Brixin yelled at me. I moved back against the wall, crossed my arms, and pouted. "Do you believe this woman is Layna?", Brixin now asked Sylvia, who was looking even more lost than when she kneeled. "I don't know.", "Answer honestly.", "...yes.", "Then you know that what I told you is the truth?", "Yes.", "So, can you make your father look like a hero, instead of the traitorous piece-of-shit he was?". Sylvia looked over his body, and ran her hand across his eyes. She then stood up. "So, now what? She takes the throne?", "You know it isn't that simple. Once your father's death is learned, it'll be the Royal Congress and someone from P.E.D that will oversee things until either of you come of age. Then you can run against each other. But, Sylvia, it'll be pointless for you. Layna was taught how to rule from a young age.", "AND WHAT HAVE I BEEN DOING?!", "Living like a spoiled brat.", I said. She looked at me. "I love and care about Nocton. I don't just want to rule, because Nocton is my family.", I said, stepping closer to her, "And I don't care if you like me, or not. You WILL bow before me.". Sylvia's face twitched, then she ran out of the cave. I meant to pursue her, but Brixin put his blade before me and stopped me. "But…", "She'll be okay. Besides, she has an important job later on.", "What is that?", "I can't tell you. Amana wouldn't want me to.", "Amana has plans for Sylvia?", "No. Amana doesn't KNOW that she has plans for Sylvia…yet.". I understood what he meant now. He meant in the future that he can see. "Come on, we'll go back to my house now.", he said, teleporting, but taking me with him. When we arrived back at the house, Tor rushed to me, "LAYNA!", he yelled, pulling me to him, "What happened?", "Brixin…", I began. "Lo is taken care of. So is…Solron.", Brixin said, looking at Linda as she entered the room holding her brother. "When you say, Solron is taken care of…", Linda said. "I mean, Layna killed him.", he said, looking down. Linda looked at me with a surprised look on her face, while Tor was stroking my hair, "Are you okay?", he asked me. I started to cry and fell into his chest. "Father, I'll report this to Mother.", Linda said, putting Maxi down in his chair, and teleporting away. Tor led me to the couch and I sat down, still crying. "So, now you're crying for him?", Tor asked me. "I'm not crying for him. I'm crying for Sylvia.", I said, realizing what I took from her and her mother. "Well, Solron was always making fast moves.", Tor said, standing, and hanging his head, "Uncle, what does it mean? What's going to happen now?", he asked Brixin, who was also looking sad. "Brixin, I did the right thing, right?", "Yes. Doesn't make it less sad. I knew Solron when he was only a boy. Tena and Arthur, too. This whole life is fucked up.", Brixin said, now standing, and for the first time, summoning his interdimensional firing range, and firing down it with his cannonblade.

For some time, I had seen that it was almost impossible to find privacy now that everyone knows who I am. I was so angry about everything, and at the same time, I was trying to just figure out what my next moves really were. In the days that had passed since I punished my uncle, everyone had somehow found out that I had killed him. Sylvia disobeyed Brixin and told everyone how I slew her father. Saundra did the interview, "So, now that your father is dead, who is taking the Head Seat? I mean, neither you nor Layna are of age yet.", "I wish I could say my mother, but she is too distraught over my father's murder.", "You keep saying his murder, but the way he was acting the day of his death, suggested that maybe he tried something against Layna. After all, he did try to kill her when she was five, isn't this correct?", Saundra asked, glaring at Sylvia. She knew Sylvia was trying to twist what really happened. I had already told her the truth before her interview with her. "That...isn't true. He was trying to protect her, and she turned on him. Vengeance for a crime my father NEVER commited. I don't appreciate what you're saying, Ms. Lome.", Sylvia said, with a murderous look in her eye. "Well, let me put this another way, then. I have sources that said your father was trying to kill us all. What do you say to that?", Saundra said, now giving Sylvia a cocky smile. Sylvia stood up, and started to attack Saundra. Security came and pulled her off, "FUCK YOU! MY FATHER NEVER KILLED HIS BROTHER!", she yelled, as she was dragged off the stage. Saundra looked mortified. The feed was cut, and I decided to go check on her. I drove to her home, and she was already there. She was still shaky. "I didn't think she'd break her cool like that.", "Her father just died. Don't you think she is still angry about that?", "Just tell me what you plan on doing now, Layna. You can't be Head yet, so what's going to happen?", "They are trying to find a temporary Head right now. But the temporary Head can only do so much, and he has to get the okay from the Royal Congress, which me and Sylvia are a part of.", I got my letter of invitation two days ago. Brixin convinced me to sit in the congress. He said it would be good to be close to what's going on. "I see. No idea who, huh?", "He won't be publicized. He is going to be kept hidden. To everyone else, it will seem like the throne is empty and that the congress is just waiting to fill the position, but to me and Sylvia, we'll be following the orders of the congress, and whoever they place in charge.", I explained. Saundra nodded. "Should I be worried about Sylvia?", "Yes, you should. You disrespected her terribly today, and she will come back at you for that.", I said, thinking in what form she would do this. My cell rang, and I answered, "Yes, Lon. What do you want? Okay, I'll come.", I said, hanging the cell up, and looking at Saundra. "I'd get away for awhile if I were you.", "You're not going to protect me?!", she yelled at me in shock. "Of course I will, but I told you, I don't just use my powers for nothing.", I said, waving my hand around her house. I made it to where there were two portals. One that went to her job, and the other to a safe spot where she wouldn't have to fear Sylvia. "If you need to go to work, then go, but you can take this portal to get back to your home and Sylvia can't touch you. When you want to come here via portal, just use this. All you have to do is squeeze.", I said, smiling, and walking away.

Tena was waiting for me. She was sitting at the park where my father died, just watching the children. I sat next to her. "So...now that Solron is dead, what do you think is going to happen?", "You already know what is happening.", "I'm not talking about the RF.", she said, looking at me sternly. "Then what are you talking about?", "I'm talking about Lo.", "He's trapped in a cave, for now.", "Ha!", Tena yelled. "What?", "You think that's the end of that?", "I know it isn't.", I said, "Have you heard of Awalli?", I asked her. She sat up, "How did you find out about her?", she asked. "I have my sources.", "Amana?", "No. Just know I know about her.", I said. Tena smiled now, "I think you'll be perfect, you know?

For the Head Seat. I can't wait.", "And what about Sylvia?", "No. Sylvia wouldn't be able to handle it. For her, it is more the idea of being the queen that she likes. You have the smarts and the bravery to actually take on the role.", she said, now reaching for me. I didn't want to let her touch me, but I did. I closed my eyes, "I'm so sorry.", she said, as I opened them, and she was crying again. I hugged her. We hugged for a long time. I couldn't think about what I wanted more than anything else in the world, besides my family to accept me.

"Layna, you know damn well that Amana couldn't have known what would happen!", Tor was yelling at me. I sat up on the bed I was in, "Look, I get it. She didn't know. That is why I'm not mad at her.", "But she knew Nora was dangerous!", "No, she just thought she was sick. She wasn't expecting her to wake up!", "Layna, you trust her TOO much. I can't let this happen anymore. She is going to get you killed!", Tor said, falling on the bed next to me. Brixin walked in with Maxi, who was playing a game in his hands, "Maxi, wait outside.", "WHY?!", he demanded. His father gave him a look, and he turned and walked out. "Nora is asleep. I was able to calm her mind.", "So, now what are you going to do?", Tor asked his uncle. "Amana has gone to her husband. What do you expect me to do, Tor? Layna is alive, Nora is resting, and everything else is out of our hands.", "But…", "Tor, I get it. You're angry with your aunt for being careless with your wife. But let's not forget, she is HER daughter.", "So that means she can risk her life whenever she wants?", Tor asked, now stepping up to his uncle. "Tor, listen to me, we have much bigger issues. I had a dream last night. About Abraxa. Somehow, Nora is connected to Abraxa. I believe she is doing something to her, and I don't know what.", Brixin said, already turning red. "Uncle, is now the time?", I asked. "Yes. Abraxa tried to kill you…through Nora. It's what I sensed when I calmed her down.", "So, she is finally coming?",

"No, Layna. I think if we stop whatever she is trying to use Nora for, THEN she will come in person.", "I thought only Corsa had that kind of power.", I said, getting more fearful of Abraxa. "Look, if I have to go get those two Edge City clowns again to help me gather some objects, I'm okay with it...I guess. Isn't Sandin, Adem's cousin?", "Yes, they are cousins.", Brixin said. "Well, he is also your godson, so I guess I'll go and see him now.", Tor said, walking up to me, kissing me, and then leaving. "Those objects will help, but only a bit. We will need the might of almost every city to defeat her and Duke.", Brixin whispered. I got out the bed and winced a little bit. "Uncle, should I go to Emillie, and bring her into the family now?", I asked. "My niece. My dangerous niece Amana is afraid will become another Alisa, and betray us…", Brixin said, looking at me sternly. "Uncle, will she?", "I can't see her doing it. But I know that we will somehow lose, and it has something to do with her. I don't know what. It doesn't mean we will lose, but still, this is a problem. Somehow, I can't see ANYTHING concerning Emillie. But I really want to meet her…", Brixin said, placing his fingers on his chin. "Before Amana left, she said that your father…". I didn't even finish, before Brixin looked at me with the most angriest face I've ever seen on him, "IF you tell me that motherfucker is here, we will have a bigger issue than you think.", "Why?", "Because he isn't here to help. He is here to screw us over. Where the hell is he now?".

EMILLIE: Me and Dooley were just sitting in the break area. Mileeda had gone to her office and shut herself up, after Dooley saved us and we realized my mother had taken Nora. I didn't know what to think. "Where is she?", I asked Dooley, who was drinking a soda. "Ah, I think...hold on…", he burped, "I think she went to Hell.", "Why would you say that? You think she's dead?", "No. I mean to her husband, your father.", Dooley said, now looking at the table suddenly, then becoming alert. "What did you just say? She's MARRIED?!", I asked, unable to believe this. And my father is ALIVE. And they are MARRIED. This kept running in my head. "Why…?", "WAIT!", Dooley shouted, standing up. Suddenly, a whole group of men and women came running in, all pointing their cannons at Dooley. Sandin was amongst them, "Emillie, get away from him!", "What are you…?", "Mileeda told me the truth about him!", Sandin shouted. Then a man with pink hair, that was short, and only a few inches off his head, came out of nowhere, and took him down. He had black and red armor that seemed to fit his body, and a sword even my mother would be jealous of. "WHAT THE HELL ARE YOU DOING HERE?! I TOLD YOU TO NEVER…!", the man stopped talking. Dooley just looked at him, and then he let him go. But the man was fighting hard to get to him, "This is how you thank me? Unbelievable. I bring you back, you've had this GREAT life, and still, you want to KILL ME?! I just wanted to spend time with my FAMILY!", Dooley shouted. "LET ME GO!", the man said, trying to break free. Suddenly, Queen Layna was here, grabbing me, and leading me away, "What are you…?", "He's been lying to you, Emillie. Come with me, and let your Uncle Brixin deal with his father. She led me out, away from the situation, "Listen, I'm…your step-sister. Amana is my mother. She raised me.", she said, giving me a smile. I didn't return the smile, "What?", I asked, unable to believe my mother kept THIS much from me. I have an uncle, who was even now trying to fight his own father, just like my mom, who pointed her cannon at him and tried to shoot him. Then there was this woman before me, who is now telling me we're sisters. "Okay, I see that Amana has kept A LOT from you, but if you just…", I broke away from her, and ran back to Dooley, to see him still standing there, with all the cannons still pointed at him, and my so called uncle, trying to break free of his spell. "FATHER, LET ME GO!", he shouted, and Dooley did, "You think I don't know why you took this form? You did this so I wouldn't harm you!", he yelled. "Of course. You'd never hurt a child.", Dooley said, wagging his finger at his son. "Leave. And if you come back, I WILL have you killed.", "Brixin…", "GET THE HELL OFF OF MY PLANET!", Brixin yelled, and he blasted black energy from his blade and Dooley disappeared. He let the energy off and kept firing, screaming all the while. Mileeda came, "HUSBAND, PLEASE! CALM DOWN!", she shouted, rushing to him. I couldn't believe what I was hearing. Then another woman came. She had pink and black hair, and somehow, I knew she was my cousin, "Father, he's gone, just relax.", "I never want that son-of-a-bitch here on this rock… DO ALL OF YOU UNDERSTAND?!", "YES, SIR!", everyone shouted, except Lody and Sandin, who looked completely as confused as me. The man was breathing hard, but turned to face me, "Emillie, come to my office.", he said, walking away. "He has an office?", I asked Mileeda, who just gave me a cold stare, and followed the man that is her husband. We walked to a part of Base that was somewhat close to the ruins of Alexandria. Brixin took his blade and slashed the air, and it opened a door to an office of epic proportions. It was like my mother's AND Mileeda's office combined. I looked around, and saw multiple screens. Some of them showed different news stations from around Plinth, but other ones had different Airball games on. I noticed around the office there were pictures. A lot of pictures. There was one with a girl with purple hair, a young handsome boy, the black and pink haired girl that was Brixin's daughter, and Mileeda was in the picture as well. They looked completely happy. "That was me. When I had to hide who I was.", Layna said, smiling over my shoulder. "So…you were living with MY family?", I asked, "When you came out, and said you were still alive…?", "Yes. I was this girl before then. I had to. My uncle…", "Why did my…?", "Your mother is a very stubborn woman, Emillie. She always makes things difficult and keeps secrets when she doesn't want to explain too much. Obviously, she never told you that you're a princess. But you DO understand WHY, correct?", Brixin asked, sitting in his seat, while Mileeda massaged his shoulders. I looked at Lody and Sandin, who had followed us here. The young man from the picture walked in, "Ah, there you, blokes are.", he said, coming up to Sandin and Lody. They shook his hand, "Tor, what are you doing here?", Lody asked. Layna went to him, and wrapped herself around him. "What the hell is going on?", I asked. All this was becoming too much, I had no idea what was happening. "This is your second cousin, Tor. He is the son of Lyon, who right now, is trying to catch your mother.", said Brixin. "More like his.", Layna mumbled. "I gave him strict orders to leave her. Now, here's the thing, Emillie. There is something much worse than Lona or Alisa coming, and I need to know that you can be of use to your family.", "What the fuck...has my family done for me?", "Are you serious?", Mileeda asked, stopping her massaging of her husband's shoulders, and moving towards me, "WE BROUGHT YOU IN! WE LET YOU LIVE, DESPITE OUR ORIGINAL PLAN OF KILLING YOU!", Mileeda yelled at me. "My love, you're the one that needs to relax now.", Brixin said, standing. "No, MY love. You have no idea how disrespectful this girl is.", Mileeda said, going back to her husband. "I'm sorry if finding out I have a huge family that my mother, and YOU I might add, kept from me, is too much to take.", I said. Even Sandin was nodding in agreement, "You told me this man is a friend.", he said, pointing at Brixin. "Mileeda and Amana are just old, they like keeping their secrets.", Brixin said, now smiling at Sandin, "You know, I'm your godfather.", Brixin said to him, smiling even harder. Sandin looked lost. Brixin moved from around his desk and came to Sandin and hugged him. Lody stepped up now, "Now hold on a damn minute. Who the hell are you and what the hell was that back there?", Lody asked, entirely confused at what the hell was happening. "I, sir, am your boss. But since you didn't know that, I won't hold it against you. I'm Brixin Sove, and I'm the Head of the Royal

Family of Sebastian and the OverSeer of P.E.D.", he said, shaking Lody's hand. "So, you're...Amana's brother? But...I didn't know Sebs...", "Had a son? Yeah, most didn't. That kid back there, WAS Sebastian.", "Then why did you attack him?", Lody asked. Mileeda spoke up, "Because he would have betrayed us. He isn't someone we can trust.", "Yeah...", Brixin chimed in, "...and he did something unforgivable. So HIM, and that BITCH Trinity, can never come to this planet, EVER!", Brixin was starting to grow angry again. "Husband...", Mileeda said, but he teleported away. "Amana always said his temper was as bad as her's.", Tor said, shaking his head. "It's this Abraxa situation, it has him rattled.", Layna said, holding Tor. "Father always said her and my brother were out there just waiting...", Linda said, leaning on her father's desk. "HELLO?!", I shouted, angry that everyone was forgetting my hurt and confusion. "Emillie, we need to get ready, we don't have time...", "Where is Hell?", "It's another dimension. Your mom's husband lives there. Sorry I never told you about him, but I couldn't.", Mileeda said. "What is his...?", "YOU DON'T NEED THAT INFO!", yelled a tall man who just walked in. He had a handsome face, and black hair that pressed upon his head that was cut and hung right above his ears. "Lyon...", Linda said, acting like she was excited. "Hello, Father.", Tor said, releasing Layna, and shaking the man's hand. "What the hell are you talking about? It's my FATHER!", "Yes, and your mother has been repeatedly breaking my law everytime she wants to screw him!", "DON'T YOU DARE TALK ABOUT YOUR AUNT THAT WAY!", Mileeda shouted. "ALL SHE DOES IS...!". Brixin reappeared, and Lyon grew silent right away. "Okay...I'm fine. Anyway, look, Emillie, I'm sorry. We all are. But I love your mother, and if she wants to keep something a secret, I respect her wishes. Amana is my favorite sister...", "SEE, I KNEW IT!", Lyon yelled angrily at his uncle, "I told you that you always let her get away with shit! Even now, after she has...", "Lyon, I am not in the mood.", Brixin said, going to sit back behind his desk. "Oh, so...?", "Father, please...can you not, man?", Tor asked. Lyon swallowed, but then fell back. "Listen, if we get any kind of entry into our atmosphere...", "Husband, they aren't coming right now. Please, go back to your vacation. I was wrong to try and...", "No. You were right. I shouldn't get one.", "NO. I didn't mean that.", "No. You go home to Maxi. I'll stay and deal with Amana.", Brixin said, kissing his wife. "Everyone, except Layna, Sandin, Lody, and Emillie, leave.". Tor, Linda, and Lyon grudgingly, and Mileeda, all turned and walked out. As they were, Sylvia rushed in, "Emillie, that boy you were with...", when she saw who else was here, she grew angry, "WHAT THE HELL...?!", "You will not talk to your queen in this manner.", Layna said, lording over Sylvia, who looked ready to kill her. "Girls, we don't have time for your squabbling. Everything I said is happening.", Brixin said. Sylvia turned from Layna, "So...I can now truly get vengeance for my father?", Sylvia asked, placing her palms on Brixin's desk. "I told you that I would help you. I promised you. Have I broken a promise to you yet, Sylvia?", Brixin asked her, and she shook her head. "WAIT! You know him?", I asked, grabbing her. "Emillie, I know your whole family. I just couldn't say, because it's a need to know basis. But most of the royal families know about your grandfather's family.", Sylvia said, placing her hands on my shoulders. I didn't know what to say. I looked at Sandin and Lody. "So, um, Brixin, sir...", Lody began to say. "Just Brixin. You don't have to be all formal or militant.", Brixin said, trying not to laugh. "Okay, so when is this bigger threat coming?", "It's already here, in the form of my reincarnated sister, Calypsa. Nora Mccloud is Calypsa, but she doesn't know that. She is confused, because Amana has hid who she is from her for a long time, leaving her vulnerable to our other enemies. So, you are my special squad. If Adem was here, he'd be on it, too, but he is too close to my sister, Ko-e, and it will be difficult. Her son, Lyon, doesn't want her involved in any way. So, we have to tread carefully.

Okay? It's time we get ready for the real fight. Because what I see coming, you will be the ones that stand out. I'm...counting on you. And don't worry, I'll be right by your side, all the way.", Brixin said, looking at all of us. "What about me? What about my mother?", "Well...your mother will come back, once I convince my wife to LET her come back. And Lyon, too...", Brixin trailed off. "Uncle, what is our timetable?", Layna asked, with a serious tone, summoning a chair for herself. "I told you, I don't know, Layna, I can't see that far because Emillie is somehow a mental block for me.", Brixin said, looking at me, "That's why, starting now, I'm going to be keeping you close, Emillie.", he said, looking me straight in the eye, then everything was frozen. Layna and my uncle were the only ones moving. "What is this?", "We need to talk.", Ko-e said, coming out of nowhere. "Ko-e, where is Awalli?", I asked. Layna raised her eyebrow, "Oh my... This is what you were talking about...", she said to Ko-e. "Yes. Now, it is time to get ready, like your uncle said. Your uncle is a good man, Emillie. He loves you very much.", "It's true.", Brixin said, smiling at me. "Then...why did you all hide from me?", I asked sadly. "Emillie, we didn't want to.", Layna said, "I barely learned about you, when I heard Alisa had been resurrected.", "And I was there the day you were born. As a matter of fact, I delivered you and Septima.", Brixin said, placing his hands on my shoulders. "Really?", "Yes. But your mother gave you to Dalia and wanted none of us to talk to you, so we didn't. I'm sorry, Emillie, I truly am, but I can't keep away any longer. Not with...Abraxa looming on the horizon. So, will you help me?". I looked at Ko-e, and my new uncle, and my new sister, who I'd always known about from watching the news when I was a kid, and following her rise to Queen in Nocton. I looked at the other people who were frozen and unable to move, and then I saw something else. Something that disturbed me. A vision. I was fighting a woman who had a red tinge to her skin, but she was extremely beautiful. Awalli was with me, and she was fighting like mad. I was fighting her just as hard, and I saw Brixin, bloody, and weak, and trying to still fight her, but she grabbed him, and picked him up by his neck, and then a boy came. He had pale white and red skin, and he took Brixin from the woman, and threw him into the air. He didn't come back down. I rushed at the boy, but he killed me before I could do anything to him, then I watched Awalli die at the hands of the woman. My mother, who came out of nowhere, bowed before the woman, then tried to shoot her, and was blasted by a little girl. The little girl looked vaguely familiar. Then I saw Dooley. He showed up and was standing next to the little girl. The woman watched them both with fear on her face. Then, Dooley stuck his sword in the ground, and him, and the girl disappeared, while the red woman was stuck and unable to move. The ground was shaking, and quaking, and then suddenly, I watched Awalli's body first, fall into the ground, then my mother's, then the boy fell in screaming, along with the red woman. I tried to move into the situation and help, but I felt a hand on my shoulder, "This is what I see. But Brixin can't see this yet.", Dooley said. "Why did they…?", "They all hate me.", he said, crying. "You told me that you're only a kid because…", "YES, I lied to you. My son would kill me if I came in my true form. I love him, but he can't see past the fact that I didn't help him. I don't know what to say. He's just like his sister. Ko-e is the only one who takes me seriously.", "What do you want from me?", "I want you to stop that vision from happening.", Dooley said, then he disappeared. Then it was me, and Layna, and the rest of the people in the room. "So, Emillie, will you help?", Brixin was asking me again. "Yes.", I replied, without hesitation. I wasn't going to let that vision happen, no matter what.

Milton Keynes UK
Ingram Content Group UK Ltd.
UKHW041829201024
449814UK00001B/258